THE TRIAL

CHARLOTTE M. YONGE

THE TRIAL

ALAN SUTTON PUBLISHING LIMITED

First published in 1864

First published in this edition in the United Kingdom in 1996
Alan Sutton Publishing Limited
Phoenix Mill · Far Thrupp · Stroud · Gloucestershire

British Library Cataloguing-in-Publication Data

A catalogue record for this book is available from the British Library.

ISBN 0–7509–1117–4

Cover picture: detail from John Gibson Lockhart (1794–1854), biographer and son-in-law of Sir Walter Scott and his wife Charlotte Sophia Scott (1799–1837), after 1838 *by Robert Scott Lauder (1803–69) (Scottish National Portrait Gallery, Edinburgh/Bridgeman Art Library, London)*

Typeset in 10/11 Bembo.
Typesetting and origination by
Alan Sutton Publishing Limited.
Printed in Great Britain by
The Guernsey Press Company Limited,
Guernsey, Channel Islands.

BIOGRAPHICAL INTRODUCTION

Like Jane Austen, Charlotte M. Yonge was born and spent most of her life in Hampshire; her life was even more private and uneventful than Jane Austen's. She was born in the village of Otterbourne on 1 August 1823 to Fanny and William Yonge; he was a retired Army Officer, who educated his daughter at home and exercised one of the two greatest influences on her life, the other being that of John Keble, rector of the neighbouring parish of Hursley, who trained her to be an ardent supporter and propagandist of the Tractarian Movement in the Church of England. Apart from rare visits to Devonshire, Oxford and London, and two short trips late in life to Ireland and France, she spent all her days in Hampshire (though this did not prevent her from setting scenes in her novels all over the world, from South Africa to Peru, from Syria to Indiana). She lived at home with her parents, and when they died, she still lived on in Otterbourne, close to her married brother.

In spite of her fame, she remained intensely shy and reserved with strangers, though a great talker with a small circle of devoted friends. Tory and reactionary in theory, she was notably philanthropic, full of social concern over poverty, bad housing and harsh employers; she contributed most of her considerable literary earnings to good causes, and found time in her busy life to spend many hours daily in teaching, voluntarily and with long-remembered brilliance, in the village school. Although she herself never went to school, let alone to university, she was a learned linguist, an immensely thorough and wide reader, especially of history, and was something of a theologian and philologist. She had an acute ear and memory for speech patterns, whether of teasing schoolboys, touchy governesses, pompous squires or village children. She collected and observed wild flowers, sea-shells, fossils. Hers was the tranquil self-educated life of thousands of upper middle-class spinsters in nineteenth-century England, but from this subdued background emerged a blaze of creative energy.

Her first book, a children's story in French, was published when she was fifteen. From then on, till she died in 1901, she was a hugely prolific writer of novels, histories, tales for children, biographical sketches, natural history studies, and researches into the origin of Christian names. Articles, translations, book reviews, introductions, contributions to symposia, and school primers flowed fron her pen. Her book titles amounted to several hundred; her total of published words has been estimated at fifteen million. For forty-two years she was also editor of a magazine for young women, *The Monthly Packet*. Her novels and historical studies were highly esteemed by such contemporaries as Tennyson, Gladstone, Trollope, Lewis Carroll, William Morris and Christina Rossetti; furthermore, they were extremely influential on young readers in the last half of the nineteenth century, particularly in promoting Tractarian ideals of duty and piety in a form which made these virtues seem glamorous rather than dreary. In the early twentieth century her popularity waned, though her children's books, such as *The Little Duke,* have remained favourites. Interest in her work, especially in her family chronicle novels, has always been maintained by a coterie of admirers; it has revived in recent years, attracting unfavourable attention from feminist critics because of her politically incorrect male-chauvinist conviction of woman's natural inferiority to man.

Her most famous novel was *The Heir of Redclyffe*, whose attractive, high-minded and doomed hero was a role model for a whole generation of young male readers. Her historical novels such as *The Chaplet of Pearls* and *The Dove in the Eagle's Nest* were popular successes, but her most sustained achievements were a succession of novels of contemporary life, chief among them *Heartsease*, *The Daisy Chain*, *Dynevor Terrace*, *Hopes and Fears*, *The Clever Woman of the Family*, *The Pillars of the House*, *The Three Brides* and *Magnum Bonum*, published between 1854 and 1879, the peak period of her long career of authorship. One of the chief charms of these family chronicles – apart from their vivid characterization and the verisimilitude of their dialogue and incidents of daily life – is Charlotte Yonge's habit, like Trollope, of re-introducing characters from previous novels into what were not exactly sequels, since each novel can stand and be read alone, but related pictures of a closely-knit world, mainly of professional upper middle-class families in rural or country-town settings. This effective device is used in *The Trial*. To enjoy the novel, it is not necessary to know that one of the two families whose interaction is the basis of the plot, the Mays, had appeared at length in a previous novel, *The Daisy Chain*. But those who have first read *The Daisy Chain* will gain added pleasure from the portrayal of two of the protagonists, Ethel and Tom May: Ethel, once a clumsy and impulsive girl and Tom, an unkempt, terrified child who later became a self-satisfied dandy, are both now, in *The Trial*, seen as impressive adults.

Both families, the Mays and the Wards, are headed by doctors, and medical dealings with epidemics of scarlet fever and typhus, bad sanitation and doubtful medicines in this novel are one of the sidelights on contemporary social problems which illuminate all Charlotte Yonge's fiction. The two families are contrasted: the Mays are shown, by telling details, to be at a slightly higher social level than the Wards (Dr May is a physician and Henry Ward a surgeon, then a lower grade in the medical hierarchy). Another contrast is the 'joyous ease' and tactful peace-keeping of 'experienced love' which prevails among the Mays, and the misunderstandings and resentments so fatally prevalent between the Wards. But the basic structure of the novel is the contrast between two couples. On the one side is Ethel May, already a confirmed spinster at twenty-five when the story begins; she has a brilliant mind and some peculiarities of manner which make her at once the main authority and the family butt in her widower father's household. Only occasionally does she have feelings of frustration and wasted powers; her resigned nobility of character makes her an object of silent adoration to Leonard Ward, whose unmerited sufferings are at the centre of *The Trial*. The contrasting couple, less saintly but perhaps more intensely realized, are Leonard's sister Averil and Ethel's brother Tom, an obstinate, prickly, though high-minded pair, whose initial wariness of each other and disastrous first proposal recall Mr Darcy and Elizabeth Bennet in *Pride and Prejudice*. Charlotte Yonge did not indulge in conventional happy endings; the portrayal of this intolerant pair, unpopular with most people though purified by adversity, is more interesting than that of two of Tom May's other sisters who, happily married to suitable husbands, become boringly conformist and narrow in sympathies.

Though contrasted families and couples form the basic pattern of *The Trial*'s plot, its theme, indicated in its title, is the problem of reconciling divine justice with human injustice and wrong. The story contains a murder and a trial in the literal sense, but the predominant meaning of its title is the test of human character, resolution and belief in a benignant Deity which unmerited suffering can impose, and how the test can be surmounted. The characters refer frequently to the Book of Job, and still more often to what was clearly the starting-point of this particular plot in Charlotte Yonge's mind: the story of Ralph de Wilton in Walter Scott's *Marmion*. De Wilton was unjustly disgraced by a conspiracy involving the manipulation of documents which could have proved his innocence; he suffered long years of misery and deprivation, and was too honourable to revenge himself when the real culprit was in his power. Finally he was vindicated, while the culprit died a terrible death. Charlotte Yonge does not offer the facile conclusion that vindication after such sufferings can simply put the sufferer back where he started out, to provide a happy ending. Instead she acutely analyses the psychology of a man unjustly accused: the doubts, the confusion, the dazed apathy when vindication comes at last, and the permanent scars.

Walter Scott, much quoted in Charlotte Yonge's novels, was perhaps the strongest literary influence on her work; but *The Trial* also owes much to Dickens's *Martin Chuzzlewit* and Frances Trollope's *The Domestic Manners of the Americans*, from which she clearly drew most of the scenes in *The Trial* of the American Middle West: the touchy independence of women servants, the gullibility of British emigrants beguiled into investing in imaginary cities which turn out to be fever-ridden swamps. In her turn she influenced later writers who developed the detective story. *The Trial,* published in 1864, four years before Wilkie Collins's *The Moonstone*, which is generally considered to be the prototype of the full-length English detective story, contains not only a fully reported murder trial but also much of the paraphernalia of scene-of-crime scrutiny, police and private following-up of clues, missing papers, analysis of blood-stains, interrogation of witnesses, consultations with solicitors, inquests, prison cells, and so on, which were to become the standard constituents of whodunits.

The Trial can be read simply as a gripping well-constructed narrative; it can be read for its vivid pictures of Victorian manners and social institutions; equally, it can be read as a thoughtful speculation on one of the greatest of moral puzzles – whether there is ultimately a principle of justice in the human condition.

ALETHEA HAYTER

CHAPTER I

'Quand on veut dessécher un marais, on ne fait pas voter les grenouilles.'
Mme Emile de Girardin.

'Richard? That's right! Here's a tea-cup waiting for you,' as the almost thirty-year-old Incumbent of Cocksmoor, still looking like a young deacon, entered the room with his quiet step, and silent greeting to its four inmates.

'Thank you, Ethel. Is papa gone out?'

'I have not seen him since dinner-time. You said he was gone out with Dr Spencer, Aubrey?'

'Yes, I heard Dr Spencer's voice – "I say Dick" – like three notes of consternation,' said Aubrey; 'and off they went. I fancy there's some illness about in the Lower Pond Buildings, that Dr Spencer has been raging so long to get drained.'

'The knell has been ringing for a little child there' added Mary; 'scarlatina, I believe——'

'But, Richard,' burst forth the merry voice of the youngest, 'you must see our letters from Edinburgh.'

'You have heard, then? It was the very thing I came to ask.'

'Oh, yes! there were five notes in one cover,' said Gertrude. 'Papa says they are to be laid up in the family archives, and labelled "The Infants' Honeymoon."'

'Papa is very happy with his own share,' said Ethel. 'It was signed, "Still his own White Flower," and it had two Calton Hill real daisies in it. I don't know when I have seen him more pleased.'

'And Hector's letter – I can say that by heart,' continued Gertrude. '"My dear Father. This is only to say that she is the darling, and for the pleasure of subscribing myself Your loving SON," – the son as big as all the rest put together.'

'I tell Blanche that he only took her for the pleasure of being my father's son,' said Aubrey, in his low lazy voice.

'Well,' said Mary 'even to the last, I do believe he had as soon drive papa out as walk with Blanche. Flora was quite scandalized at it.'

'I should not imagine that George had often driven my father out,' said Aubrey, again looking lazily up from balancing his spoon.

Ethel laughed; and even Richard smiled; then recovering herself, she said, 'Poor Hector, he never could call himself son to any one before.'

'He has not been much otherwise here,' said Richard.

'No,' said Ethel; 'it is the peculiar hardship of our weddings to break us up by pairs, and carry off two instead of one. Did you ever see me with so shabby a row of tea-cups? When shall I have them come in riding double again?'

The recent wedding was the third in the family; the first after a five years' respite. It ensued upon an attachment that had grown up with the young people, so that they had been entirely one with each other; and there had been little of formal demand either of the maiden's affection or her father's consent; but both had been implied from the first. The bridegroom was barely of age, the bride not seventeen, and Dr May had owned it was very shocking, and told Richard to say nothing about it! Hector had coaxed and pleaded, pathetically talked of his great empty house at Maplewood, and declared that till he might take Blanche away, he would not leave Stoneborough; he would bring down all sorts of gossip on his courtship, he would worry Ethel and take care she finished nobody's education. What did Blanche want with more education? She knew enough for him. Couldn't Ethel be satisfied with Aubrey and Gertrude? or he dared say she might have Mary too, if she was insatiable. If Dr May was so unnatural as to forbid him to hang about the house, why, he would take rooms at the Swan. In fact, as Dr May observed, he treated him to a modern redhaired Scotch version of 'Make me a willow cabin at your gate;' and as he heartily loved Hector and entirely trusted him – and Blanche's pretty head was a wise and prudent one, what was the use of keeping the poor lad unsettled?

So Mrs Rivers, the eldest sister and the member's wife, had come to arrange matters and help Ethel, and a very brilliant wedding it had been. Blanche was too entirely at home with Hector for flutterings or agitations, and was too peacefully happy for grief at the separation, which completed the destiny that she had always seen before her. She was a picture of a bride; and when she and Hector hung round the Doctor, insisting that Edinburgh should be the first place they should visit, and calling forth minute directions for their pilgrimage to the scenes of his youth, promising to come *home* and tell him all; no wonder he felt himself rather gaining a child than losing one. He was very bright and happy; and no one but Ethel understood how all the time there was a sensation that the present was but a strange dreamy parody of that marriage which had been the theme of earlier hopes.

The wedding had taken place shortly after Easter; and immediately after, the Rivers family had departed for London, and Tom May had returned to Cambridge, leaving the home party at the minimum of four, since, Cocksmoor Parsonage being complete, Richard had become only a daily visitor instead of a constant inhabitant.

There he sat, occupying his never idle hands with a net that he kept for such moments, whilst Ethel sat behind her urn, now giving out its last sighs, profiting by the leisure to read the county newspaper, while she continually filled up her cup with tea or milk as occasion served, indifferent to the increasing pallor of the liquid.

Mary, a 'fine young woman,' as George Rivers called her, of blooming face and sweet open expression, had begun, at Gertrude's entreaty, a game of French billiards. Gertrude had still her childish sunny face and bright hair, and even at the trying age of twelve was pleasing, chiefly owing to the caressing freedom of manner belonging to an unspoilable pet. Her request to Aubrey to join the sport had been answered with a half petulant shake of the head, and he flung himself into his father's chair, his long legs hanging over one arm – an attitude that those who had ever been under Mrs May's discipline thought impossible in the drawing-room; but Aubrey was a rival pet, and with the family characteristics of aquiline features, dark grey eyes, and beautiful teeth, had an air of fragility and easy languor, that showed his exercise of the immunities of ill-health. He had been Ethel's pupil till Tom's last year at Eton, when he was sent thither, and had taken a good place; but his brother's vigilant and tender care could not save him from an attack on the chest, that settled his public-school education for ever, to his severe mortification, just when Tom's shower of honours was displaying to him the sweets of emulation and success. Ethel regained her pupil, and put forth her utmost powers for his benefit, causing Tom to examine him at each vacation, with adjurations to let her know the instant he discovered that her task of tuition was getting beyond her. In truth, Tom fraternally held her cheap, and would have enjoyed a triumph over her scholarship; but to this he had not attained; and in spite of his desire to keep his brother in a salutary state of humiliation, candour wrung from him the admission that, even in verses, Aubrey did as well as other fellows of his standing.

Conceit was not Aubrey's fault. His father was more guarded than in the case of his elder sons, and the home atmosphere was not such as to give the boy a sense of superiority, especially when diligently kept down by his brother. Even the half year at Eton had not produced superciliousness, though it had given Eton polish to the home-bred manners; it had made sisters valuable, and awakened a desire for masculine companionship. He did not rebel against his sister's rule; she was nearly a mother to him, and had always been the most active president of his studies and pursuits; and he was perfectly obedient and dutiful to her, only asserting his equality, in imitation of Harry and Tom, by a little of the good-humoured raillery and teazing that treated Ethel as the family butt, while she was really the family authority.

'All gone, Ethel,' he said, with a lazy smile, as Ethel mechanically, with her eyes on the newspaper, tried all her vessels round, and found cream-jug, milk-jug, tea-pot, and urn, exhausted; 'will you have in the river next?'

'What a shame!' said Ethel, awakening and laughing. 'Those are the tea-maker's snares.'

'Do send it away then,' said Aubrey, 'the urn oppresses the atmosphere.'

'Very well; I'll make a fresh brew when papa comes home, and perhaps you'll have some then. You did not half finish to-night.'

Aubrey yawned; and after some speculation about their father's absence, Gertrude went to bed; and Aubrey, calling himself tired, stood up, stretched every limb portentously, and said he should go off too. Ethel looked at him anxiously, felt his hand, and asked if he were sure he had not a cold coming on. 'You are always thinking of colds,' was all the satisfaction she received.

'What has he been doing?' said Richard.

'That is what I was thinking. He was about all yesterday afternoon with Leonard Ward, and perhaps may have done something imprudent in the damp. I never know what to do. I can't bear him to be a coddle; yet he is always catching cold if I let him alone. The question is, whether it is worse for him to run risks, or to be thinking of himself.'

'He need not be doing that,' said Richard; 'he may be thinking of your wishes and papa's.'

'Very pretty of him and you, Ritchie; but *he* is not three parts of a boy or man who thinks of his womankind's wishes when there is anything spirited before him.'

'Well, I suppose one may do one's duty without being three parts of a boy,' said Richard gravely.

'I know it is true that some of the most saintly characters have been the more spiritual because their animal frame was less vigorous; but still it does not content me.'

'No, the higher the power, the better, of course, should the service be. I was only putting you in mind that there is compensation. But I must be off. I am sorry I cannot wait for papa. Let me know what is the matter to-morrow, and how Aubrey is.'

Richard went; and the sisters took up their employments – Ethel writing to the New Zealand sister-in-law her history of the wedding, Mary copying parts of a New Zealand letter for her brother, the lieutenant in command of a gun-boat on the Chinese coast. Those letters, whether from Norman May or his wife, were very delightful, they were so full of a cheerful tone of trustful exertion and resolution, though there had been perhaps more than the natural amount of disappointments. Norman's powers were not thought of the description calculated for regular mission work, and some of the chief aspirations of the young couple had had to be relinquished at the voice of authority without a trial. They had received the charge of persons as much in need of them as unreclaimed savages, but to whom there was less apparent glory in ministering. A wide-spread district of very colonial colonists, and the charge of a college for their uncultivated sons, was quite as troublesome as the most ardent self-devotion could desire; and the hardships and disagreeables, though severe, made no figure in history – nay, it required ingenuity to gather their existence from Meta's bright letters, although from Mrs Arnott's accounts, it was clear that the wife took a quadruple share. Mrs Rivers had been heard to say that Norman need not have gone so far, and sacrificed so much, to obtain an under-bred English congregation; and even the Doctor had sighed once or twice at having relinquished his favourite son to what was dull and distasteful; but Ethel could trust that this unmurmuring acceptance of the less striking career, might be another step in the discipline of her brother's ardent and ambitious nature. It is a great thing to sacrifice, but a greater to consent not to sacrifice in one's own way.

Ethel sat up for her father, and Mary would not go to bed and leave her, so the two sisters waited till they heard the latch-key. Ethel ran out, but her father was already on the stairs, and waved her back.

'Here is some tea. Are you not coming, Papa? – it is all here.'

'Thank you, I'll just go and take off this coat;' and he passed on to his room.

'I don't like that,' said Ethel, returning to the drawing-room, where Mary was boiling up the kettle, and kneeling down to make some toast.

'Why, what's the matter?'

'I have never known him go and change his coat but when some infectious thing has been about. Besides, he did not wait to let me help him off with it.'

In a few seconds the Doctor came down in his dressing-gown, and let himself be put into his easy chair; his two daughters waiting on him with fond assiduity, their eyes questioning his fagged weary face, but reading there fatigue and concern that made them – rather awe-struck – bide their time till it should suit him to speak. Mary was afraid he would wait till she was gone; dear old Mary, who at twenty-two never dreamt of regarding herself as on the same footing with her three years' senior, and had her toast been browner, would have relieved them of her presence at once. However, her father spoke after his first long draught of tea.

'Well! How true it is that judgments are upon us while we are marrying and giving in marriage!'

'What is it, Papa? Not the scarlatina?'

'Scarlat*ina*, indeed!' he said contemptuously. 'Scarlet fever in the most aggravated form. Two deaths in one house, and I am much mistaken if there will not be another before morning.'

'Who, Papa?' asked Mary.

'Those wretched Martins, in Lower Pond Buildings, are the worst. No wonder, living in voluntary filth; but it is all over the street – will be all over the town unless there's some special mercy on the place.'

'But how has it grown so bad,' said Ethel, 'without our having even heard of it?'

'Why – partly I take shame to myself – this business of Hector and Blanche kept Spencer and me away last dispensary day; and partly it was that young coxcomb, Henry Ward, thought it not worth while to trouble me about a simple epidemic. Simple epidemic indeed!' repeated Dr May, changing his tone from ironical mimicry to hot indignation. 'I hope he will be gratified with its simplicity! I wonder how long he would have gone on if it had not laid hold on him.'

'You don't mean that he has it?'

'I do. It will give him a practical lesson in simple epidemics.'

'And Henry Ward has it!' repeated Mary, looking so much dismayed that her father laughed, saying——

'What, Mary thinks when it comes to fevers being so audacious as to lay hold of the doctors, it *is* time that they should be put a stop to.'

'He seems to have petted it and made much of it,' said Ethel; 'so no wonder! What could have possessed him?'

'Just this, Ethel; and it is only human nature after all. This young lad comes down, as Master Tom will do some day, full of his lectures and his hospitals, and is nettled and displeased to find his father content to have Spencer or me called in the instant anything serious is the matter.'

'But you are a physician, Papa,' said Mary.

'No matter for that, to Mr Henry I'm an old fogie, and depend upon it, if it were only the giving a dose of salts, he would like to have the case to himself. These poor creatures were parish patients, and I don't mean that his treatment was amiss. Spencer is right, it was an atmosphere where there was no saving any one; but if he had not been so delighted with his own way, and I had known what was going on, I'd have got the Guardians and the Town Council and routed out the place. Seventeen cases, and most of them the worse form!'

'But what was Mr Ward about?'

"'Says I to myself, here's a lesson for me;
This man's but a picture of what I shall be"

when Master Tom gets the upper hand of me,' returned Dr May. 'Poor Ward, who has run to me in all his difficulties these thirty years, didn't like it at all; but Mr Henry was so confident with his simple epidemic, and had got him in such order, that he durst not speak.'

'And what brought it to light at last?'

'Everything at once. First the clerics go to see about the family where the infant died, and report to Spencer; he comes after me, and we start to reconnoitre. Then I am called in to see Shearman's daughter – a very ugly case that – and coming out I meet poor Ward himself, wanting me to see Henry, and there's the other boy sickening too. Then I went down and saw all those cases in the Lower Ponds, and have been running about the town ever since to try what can be done, hunting up nurses, whom I can't get, stirring dishes of skim milk, trying to get the funerals over to-morrow morning by daybreak. I declare I have hardly a leg to stand on.'

'Where was Dr Spencer?'

'I've nearly quarrelled with Spencer. Oh! he is in high feather! he will have it that the fever rose up bodily, like Kuhleborn, out of that unhappy drain he is always worrying about, when it is a regular case of scarlet fever, brought in by a girl at home from service; but he *will* have it that his theory is proved. Then I meant him to keep clear of it. He has always been liable to malaria and all that sort of thing, and has not strength for an illness. I told him to mind the ordinary practice for me; and what do I find him doing the next thing, but operating upon one of the worst throats he could find! I told him he was as bad as young Ward; I hate his irregular practice. I'll tell you what,' he said, vindictively, as if gratified to have what must obey him, 'you shall all go off to Cocksmoor to-morrow morning at seven o'clock.'

'You forget that we two have had it,' said Mary.

'Which of you?'

'All down to Blanche.'

'Never mind for that. I shall have enough to do without a sick house at home. You can perform quarantine with Richard, and then go to Flora, if she will have you. Well, what are you dawdling about? Go and pack up.'

'Papa,' said Ethel, who had been abstracted through all the latter part of the conversation, 'if you please, we had better not settle my going till to-morrow morning.'

'Come, Ethel, you have too much sense for panics. Don't take nonsense into your head. The children can't have been in the way of it.'

'Stay, papa,' said Ethel, her serious face arresting the momentary impatience of fatigue and anxiety, 'I am afraid Aubrey was a good while choosing fishing-tackle at Shearman's yesterday with Leonard Ward; and it may be nothing, but he did seem heavy and out of order to-night; I wish you would look at him as you go up.'

Dr May stood still for a few moments, then gave one long gasp, made a few inquiries, and went up to Aubrey's room. The boy was fast asleep; but there was that about him which softened the weary sharpness of his father's manner, and caused him to desire Ethel to look from the window whence she could see whether the lights were out in Dr Spencer's house. Yes, they were.

'Never mind. It will make no real odds, and he has had enough on his hands to-day. The boy will sleep quietly enough to-night, so let us all go to bed.'

'I think I can get a mattress into his room without waking him, if you will help me, Mary,' said Ethel.

'Nonsense,' said her father decidedly. 'Mary is not to go near him before she takes Gertrude to Cocksmoor; and you, go to your own bed and get a night's rest while you can.'

'You won't stay up, Papa.'

'I – why, it is all I can do not to fall asleep on my feet. Good night, children.'

'He does not trust himself to think or to fear,' said Ethel. 'Too much depends on him to let himself be unstrung.'

'But, Ethel, you will not leave dear Aubrey.'

'I shall keep his door open and mine; but papa is right, and it will not do to waste one's strength. In case I should not see you before you go——'

'Oh, but, Ethel, I shall come back! Don't, pray don't tell me to stay away. Richard will have to keep away for Daisy's sake, and you can't do all alone – nurse Aubrey and attend to papa. Say that I may come back.'

'Well, Mary, I think you *ought*,' said Ethel, after a moment's thought. 'If it were only Aubrey, I could manage for him; but I am more anxious about papa.'

'You don't think he is going to have it?'

'Oh no, no,' said Ethel, 'he is what he calls himself, a seasoned vessel; but he will be terribly overworked, and unhappy, and he must not come home and find no one to talk to or to look cheerful. So, Mary, unless he gives any fresh orders, or Richard thinks it will only make things worse, I shall be very glad of you.'

Mary had never clung to her so gratefully, nor felt so much honoured. 'Do you think he will have it badly?' she asked timidly.

'I don't think at all about it,' said Ethel, something in her father's manner. 'If we are to get through all this, Mary, it must not be by riding out on perhapses. Now let us put Daisy's things together, for she must have as little communication with home as possible.'

Ethel silently and rapidly moved about, dreading to give an interval for tremblings of heart. Five years of family prosperity had passed, and there had been that insensible feeling of peace and immunity from care which is strange to look back upon when one hour has drifted from smooth water to turbid currents. There was a sort of awe in seeing the mysterious gates of sorrow again unclosed; yet, darling of her own as Aubrey was, Ethel's first thoughts and fears were primarily for her father. Grief and alarm seemed chiefly to touch her through him, and she found herself praying above all that *he* might be shielded from suffering, and might be spared a renewal of the pangs that had before wrung his heart.

By early morning every one was astir; and Gertrude, bewildered and distressed, yet rather enjoying the fun of staying with Richard, was walking off with Mary.

Soon after, Dr Spencer was standing by the bedside of his old patient, Aubrey, who had been always left to his management.

'Ah, I see,' he said, with a certain tone of satisfaction, 'for once there will be a case properly treated. Now, Ethel, you and I will show what intelligent nursing can do.'

'I believe you are delighted,' growled Aubrey.

'So should you be, at the valuable precedent you will afford.'

'I've no notion of being experimented on to prove your theory,' said Aubrey, still ready for lazy mischief.

For be it known that the roving tempered Dr Spencer had been on fire to volunteer to the Crimean hospitals, and had unwillingly sacrificed the project, not to Dr May's conviction that it would be fatal in his present state of health, but to Ethel's private entreaty that he would not add to her father's distress in the freshness of Margaret's death, and the parting with Norman. He had never ceased to mourn over the lost opportunity, and to cast up to his friend the discoveries he might have made; while Dr May declared that if by any strange chance he had come back at all, he would have been so rabid on improved nursing and sanatory measures, that there would have been no living with him.

It must be owned that Dr May was not very sensible to what his friend called Stoneborough stinks. The place was fairly healthy, and his 'town councillor's conservatism,' and hatred of change, as well as the amusement of skirmishing, had always made him the champion of things as they were; and in the present emergency the battle whether the enemy had travelled by infection, or was the product of the Pond Buildings' miasma, was the favourite enlivenment of the disagreeing doctors, in their brief intervals of repose in the stern conflict which they were waging with the fever – a conflict in which they had soon to strive by themselves, for the disease not only seized on young Ward, but on his father; and till medical assistance was sent from London, they had the whole town on their hands, and for nearly a week lived without a night's rest.

The care of the sick was a still greater difficulty. Though Aubrey was never in danger, and Dr Spencer's promise of the effects of 'intelligent nursing' was fully realized, Ethel and Mary were so occupied by him, that it was a fearful thing to guess how it must fare with those households where the greater number were laid low, and in want of all the comforts that could do little.

The clergy worked to the utmost; and a letter of Mr Wilmot's obtained the assistance of two ladies from a nursing sisterhood, who not only worked incredible wonders with their own hands among the poor, but made efficient nurses of rough girls and stupid old women. Dr May, who had at first, in his distrust of innovation, been averse to the importation – as likely to have no effect but putting nonsense into girls' heads, and worrying the sick poor – was so entirely conquered, that he took off his hat to them across the street, importuned them to drink tea with his daughters, and never came home without dilating on their merits for the few minutes that intervened between his satisfying himself about Aubrey and dropping asleep in his chair. The only counter demonstration he reserved to himself was that he always called them 'Miss What-d'ye-call-her,' and 'Those gems of women,' instead of Sister Katherine and Sister Frances.

CHAPTER II

'Good words are silver, but good deeds are gold.'

Cecil and Mary.

'It has been a very good day, Papa; he has enjoyed all his meals, indeed was quite ravenous. He is asleep now, and looks as comfortable as possible,' said Ethel, five weeks after Aubrey's illness had begun.

'Thank God for that, and all His mercy to us, Ethel;' and the long sigh, the kiss, and dewy eyes, would have told her that there had been more to exhaust him than his twelve hours' toil, even had she not partly known what weighed him down.

'Poor things!' she said.

'Both gone, Ethel, both! both!' and as he entered the drawing-room, he threw himself back in his chair, and gasped with the long restrained feeling.

'Both!' she exclaimed. 'You don't mean that Leonard——'

'No, Ethel; his mother! Poor children, poor children!'

'Mrs Ward! I thought she had only been taken ill yesterday evening.'

'She only then gave way – but she never had any constitution – she was done up with nursing – nothing to fall back on – sudden collapse and prostration – and that poor girl, called every way at once, fancied her asleep, and took no alarm till I came in this morning and found her pulse all but gone. We have been pouring down stimulants all day, but there was no rousing her, and she was gone the first.'

'And Mr Ward – did he know it?'

'I thought so from the way he looked at me; but speech had long been lost, and that throat was dreadful suffering. Well, "In their death they were not divided."'

He shaded his eyes with his hand; and Ethel, leaning against his chair, could not hinder herself from a shudder at the longing those words seemed to convey. He felt her movement, and put his arm round her, saying, 'No, Ethel, do not think I envy them. I might have done so once – I had not then learnt the meaning of the discipline of being without her – no, nor what you could do for me, my child, my children.'

Ethel's thrill of bliss was so intense, that it gave her a sense of selfishness in indulging personal joy at such a moment; and indeed it was true that her father had overlived the first pangs of change and separation, had formed new and congenial habits, saw the future hope before him; and since poor Margaret had been at rest, had been without present anxiety, or the sight of decay and disappointment. Her only answer was a mute smoothing of his bowed shoulders, as she said, 'If I could be of any use or comfort to poor Averil Ward, I could go to-night. Mary is enough for Aubrey.'

'Not now, my dear. She can't stir from the boy, they are giving him champagne every ten minutes, she has the nurse, and Spencer is backwards and forwards; I think they will pull him through, but it is a near, a very near touch. Good, patient, unselfish boy he is too.'

'He always was a very nice boy,' said Ethel, 'I do hope he will get well. It would be a terrible grief to Aubrey.'

'Yes, I got Leonard to open his lips to-day by telling him that Aubrey had sent him the grapes. I think he will get through. I hope he will. He is a good friend for Aubrey. So touching it was this morning to hear him trying to ask pardon for all his faults, poor fellow – fits of temper, and the like.'

'That *is* his fault, I believe,' said Ethel, 'and I always think it a wholesome one, because it is so visible and unjustifiable, that people strive against it. And the rest? Was Henry able to see his father or mother?'

'No, he can scarcely sit up in bed. It was piteous to see him lying with his door open, listening. He is full of warm sound feeling, poor fellow. You would like to have heard the fervour with which he begged me to tell his father to have no fears for the younger ones, for it should be the most precious task of his life to do a parent's part by them.'

'Let me see, he is just of Harry's age,' said Ethel thoughtfully, as if she had not the strongest faith in Harry's power of supplying a parent's place.

'Well,' said her father, 'remember, a medical student is an older man than a lieutenant in the navy. One sees as much of the interior as the other does of the surface. We must take this young Ward by the hand, and mind he does not lose his father's practice. Burdon, that young prig that Spencer got down from London, met me at Gavin's, when I looked in there on my way home, and came the length of Minster Street with me, asking what I thought of an opening for a medical man – partnership with young Ward, &c. I snubbed him so short, that I fancy I left him thinking whether his nose was on or off his face.'

'He *was* rather premature.'

'I've settled him any way. I shall do my best to keep the town clear for that lad; there's not much more for him, as things are now, and it will be only looking close after him for a few years, which Spencer and I can very well manage.'

'If he will let you.'

'There! that's the spitefulness of women! Must you be casting up that little natural spirit of independence against him after the lesson he has had? I tell you, he has been promising me to look on me as a father! Poor old Ward! he was a good friend and fellow-worker. I owe a great deal to him.'

Ethel wondered if he forgot how much of the unserviceableness of his maimed arm had once been attributed to Mr Ward's dullness, or how many times he had come home boiling with annoyance at having been called in too late to remedy the respectable apothecary's half measures. She believed that the son had been much better educated than the father, and after the fearful lesson he had received, thought he might realize Dr May's hopes, and appreciate his kindness. They discussed the relations.

'Ward came as assistant to old Axworthy, and married his daughter; he had no relations that his son knows of, except the old aunt who left Averil her 2000*l*.'

'There are some Axworthys still,' said Ethel, 'but not very creditable people.'

'You *may* say that,' said Dr May emphatically. 'There was a scapegrace brother that ran away, and was heard of no more till he turned up, a wealthy man, ten or fifteen years ago, and bought what they call the Vintry Mill, some way on this side of Whitford. He has a business on a large scale; but Ward had as little intercourse with him as possible. A terrible old heathen.'

'And the boy that was expelled for bullying Tom is in the business.'

'I hate the thought of that!' said the doctor. 'If he had stayed on, who knows but he might have turned out as well as Ned Anderson.'

'Has not he?'

'I'm sure I have no right to say he has not, but he is a flashy slang style of youth, and I hope the young Wards will keep out of his way.'

'What will become of them? Is there likely to be any provision for them?'

'Not much, I should guess. Poor Ward did as we are all tempted to do when money goes through our hands, and spent more freely than I was ever allowed to do. Costly house, garden, greenhouses – he'd better have stuck to old Axworthy's place in Minster Street – daughter at that grand school, where she cost more than the whole half-dozen of you put together.'

'She was more worth it,' said Ethel; 'her music and drawing are first-rate. Harry was frantic about her singing last time he was at home – one evening when Mrs Anderson abused his good nature and got him to a tea-party – I began to be afraid of the consequences.'

'Pish!' said the doctor.

'And really they kept her there to enable her to educate her sisters,' said Ethel. 'The last time I called on poor Mrs Ward, she told me all about it, apologizing in the pretty way mothers do, saying she was looking forward to Averil's coming home, but that while she profited so much, they felt it due to her to give her every advantage; and did not I think – with my experience – that it was all so much for the little ones' benefit? I assured her, from my personal experience, that ignorance is a terrible thing in governessing one's sisters. Poor thing! And Averil had only come home this very Easter.'

'And with everything to learn, in such a scene as that! The first day, when only the boys were ill, there sat the girl, dabbling with her water-colours, and her petticoats reaching half across the room, looking like a milliner's doll, and neither she nor her poor mother dreaming of her doing a useful matter.'

'Who is spiteful now, Papa? That's all envy at not having such an accomplished daughter. When she came out in time of need so grandly, and showed all a woman's instinct——'

'Woman's nonsense! Instinct is for irrational brutes, and the more you cultivate a woman, the less she has of it, unless you work up her practical common sense too.'

'Some one said she made a wonderful nurse.'

'Wonderful? Perhaps so, considering her opportunities, and she does better with Spencer than with me; I may have called her to order impatiently, for she is nervous with me, loses her head, and knocks everything down with her petticoats. Then – not a word to any one, Ethel – but imagine her perfect blindness to her poor mother's state all yesterday, and last night, not even calling Burdon to look at her; why, those ten hours may have made all the difference!'

'Poor thing, how is she getting on now?'

'Concentrated upon Leonard, too much stunned to admit another idea –

no tears – hardly full comprehension. One can't take her away, and she can't bear not to do everything, and yet one can't trust her any more than a child.'

'As she is,' said Ethel, 'but as she won't be any longer. And the two little ones?'

'It breaks one's heart to see them, just able to sit by their nursery fire, murmuring in that weary, resigned, sick child's voice, "I wish nurse would come." "I wish sister would come." "I wish mamma would come." I went up to them the last thing, and told them how it was, and let them cry themselves to sleep. That was the worst business of all. Ethel, are they too big for Mary to dress some dolls for them?'

'I will try to find out their tastes the first thing to-morrow,' said Ethel; 'at any rate we can help them, if not poor Averil.'

Ethel, however, was detained at home to await Dr Spencer's visit, and Mary, whose dreams had all night been haunted by the thought of the two little nursery prisoners, entreated to go with her father, and see what could be done for them.

Off they set together, Mary with a basket in her hand, which was replenished at the toy shop in Minster Street with two china-faced dolls, and, a little farther on, parted with a couple of rolls, interspersed with strata of cold beef and butter, to a household of convalescents in the stage for kitchen physic.

Passing the school, still taking its enforced holiday, the father and daughter traversed the bridge and entered the growing suburb known as Bankside, where wretched cottages belonging to needy, grasping proprietors, formed an uncomfortable contrast to the villa residences interspersed among them.

One of these, with a well-kept lawn, daintily adorned with the newest pines and ornamental shrubs, and with sheets of glass glaring in the sun from the gardens at the back, was the house that poor Mr and Mrs Ward had bought and beautified; 'because it was so much better for the children to be out of the town.' The tears sprang into Mary's eyes at the veiled windows, and the unfeeling contrast of the spring glow of flowering thorn, lilac, laburnum, and, above all, the hard, flashing brightness of the glass; but tears were so unlike Ethel that Mary always was ashamed of them, and disposed of them quietly.

They rang, but in vain. Two of the servants were ill, and all in confusion; and after waiting a few moments among the azaleas in the glass porch, Dr May admitted himself, and led the way upstairs with silent footfalls, Mary following with breath held back. A voice from an open door called, 'Is that Dr May?' and he paused to look in and say, 'I'll be with you in one minute, Henry; how is Leonard?'

'No worse, they tell me; I say, Dr May——'

'One moment;' and turning back to Mary, he pointed along a dark passage. 'Up there, first door to the right. You can't mistake;' then disappeared, drawing the door after him.

Much discomfited, Mary nevertheless plunged bravely on, concluding 'there' to be up a narrow, uncarpeted stair, with a nursery wicket at the top, in undoing which, she was relieved of all doubts and scruples by a melancholy little duet from within. 'Mary, Mary, we want our breakfast! we want to get up! Mary, Mary, do come! please come!'

She was instantly in what might ordinarily have been a light, cheerful room, but which was in all the dreariness of grey cinders, exhausted night light, curtained windows, and fragments of the last meal. In each of two cane cribs was sitting up a forlorn child, with loose locks of dishevelled hair, pale thin cheeks glazed with tears, staring eyes, and mouths rounded with amaze at the apparition. One dropped down and hid under the bedclothes; the other remained transfixed, as her visitor advanced, saying, 'Well, my dear, you called Mary, and here I am.'

'Not our own Mary,' said the child, distrustfully.

'See if I can't be your own Mary.'

'You can't. You can't give us our breakfast.'

'Oh, I am so hungry!' from the other crib; and both burst into the feeble sobs of exhaustion. Recovering from fever, and still fasting at half-past nine! Mary was aghast, and promised an instant supply.

'Don't go;' and a bird-like little hand seized her on either side. 'Mary never came to bed, and nobody has been here all the morning, and we can't bear to be alone.'

'I was only looking for the bell.'

'It is of no use; Minna did jump out and ring, but nobody will come.'

Mary made an ineffectual experiment, and then persuaded the children to let her go by assurances of a speedy return. She sped down, brimming over with pity and indignation to communicate to her father this cruel neglect, and as she passed Henry Ward's door, and heard several voices, she ventured on a timid summons of 'Papa,' but, finding it unheard, she perceived that she must act for herself. Going down stairs, she tried the sitting-room doors, hoping that breakfast might be laid out there, but all were locked; and at last she found her way to the lower regions, guided by voices in eager tones of subdued gossip.

There, in the glow of the huge red fire, stood a well-covered table, surrounded by cook, charwoman, and their cavaliers, discussing a pile of hot-buttered toast, to which the little kitchen-maid was contributing large rounds, toasted at the fire.

Mary's eyes absolutely flashed, as she said, 'The children have had no breakfast.'

'I beg your pardon, Ma'am,' and the cook rose, 'but it is the nurse-maid that takes up the young ladies' meals.'

Mary did not listen to the rest; she was desperate, and pouncing on the bread with one hand, and the butter with the other, ran away with them to the nursery, set them down, and rushed off for another raid. She found that the commotion she had excited was resulting in the preparation of a tray.

'I am sure, Ma'am, I am very sorry,' said the cook, insisting on carrying the kettle, 'but we are in such confusion; and the nurse-maid, whose place it is, has been up most of the night with Mr Leonard, and must have just dropped asleep somewhere, and I was just giving their breakfast to the undertaker's young men, but I'll call her directly, Ma'am.'

'Oh, no, on no account. I am sure she ought to sleep,' said Mary. 'It was only because I found the little girls quite starving that I came down. I will take care of them now. Don't wake her, pray. Only I hope,' and Mary looked beseechingly, 'that they will have something good for their dinner, poor little things.'

Cook was entirely pacified, and talked about roast chicken, and presently the little sisters were sitting up in their beds, each in her wrapper, being fed by turns with delicately-buttered slices, Mary standing between like a mother-bird feeding her young, and pleased to find the eyes grow brighter and less hollow, the cheeks less wan, the voices less thin and pipy, and a little laugh breaking out when she mistook Minna for Ella.

While tidying the room, she was assailed with entreaties to call their Mary, and let them get up, they were so tired of bed. She undertook to be still their Mary, and made them direct her to the housemaid's stores, went down on her knees at the embers, and so dealt with matches, chips, and coal, that to her own surprise and pride a fire was evoked.

'But,' said Ella, 'I thought you were a Miss May.'

'So I am, my dear.'

'But ladies don't light fires,' said Minna, in open-eyed perplexity.

'Oh,' exclaimed the younger sister, 'you know Henry said he did not think any of the Miss Mays were first-rate, and that our Ave beat them all to nothing.'

The elder, Minna, began hushing; and it must be confessed that honest Mary was not superior to a certain crimson flush of indignation, as she held her head into the grate, and thought of Ethel, Flora, and Blanche, criticised by Mr Henry Ward. Little ungrateful chit! No, it was not a matter of laughing, but of forgiveness; and the assertion of the dignity of usefulness was speedily forgotten in the toilette of the small light skin-and-bone frames, in the course of which she received sundry compliments– 'her hands were so nice and soft,' 'she did not pull their hair like their own Mary,' 'they wished she always dressed them.'

The trying moment was when they asked if they might kneel at her lap for their prayers. To Mary, the twelve years seemed as nothing since her first prayers after the day of terror and bereavement, and her eyes swam with tears as the younger girl unthinkingly rehearsed her wonted formula, and the elder, clinging to her, whispered gravely, 'Please, what shall I say?'

With full heart, and voice almost unmanageable, Mary prompted the few simple words that had come to her in that hour of sorrow. She looked up, from stooping to the child's ear, to see her father at the door, gazing at them with face greatly moved. The children greeted him fondly, and he sat down with one on each knee, and caressed them as he looked them well over, drawing out their narration of the wonderful things '*she*' had done, the fingers pointing to designate who *she* was. His look at her over his spectacles made Mary's heart bound and feel compensated for whatever Mr Henry Ward might say of her. When the children had finished their story, he beckoned her out of the room, promising them that he would not keep her long.

'Well done, Molly,' he said smiling, 'it is well to have daughters good for something. You had better stay with them till that poor maid has had her sleep out, and can come to them.'

'I should like to stay with them all day, only that Ethel must want me.'

'You had better go home by dinner time, that Ethel may get some air. Perhaps I shall want one of you in the evening to be with them at the time of the funeral.'

'So soon!'

'Yes, it must be. Better for all, and Henry is glad it should be so. He is out on the sofa to-day, but he is terribly cut up.'

'And Leonard?'

'I see some improvement – Burdon does not – but I think with Heaven's good mercy we may drag him through, the pulse is rather better. Now I must go. You'll not wait dinner for me.'

Mary spent the next hour in amusing the children by the fabrication of the dolls' wardrobe, and had made them exceedingly fond of her, so that there was a very poor welcome when their own Mary at length appeared, much shocked at the duration of her own slumbers, and greatly obliged to Miss May. The little girls would scarcely let Mary go, though she pacified them by an assurance that she or her sister would come in the evening.

'Don't let it be your sister. You come, and finish our dolls' frocks!' and they hung about her, kissing her, and trying to extract a promise.

After sharing the burthen of depression, it was strange to return home to so different a tone of spirits when she found Aubrey installed in Ethel's room as his parlour, very white and weak, but overflowing with languid fun. There was grief and sympathy for the poor Wards, and anxious inquiries for Leonard; but it was not sorrow brought visibly before him, and after the decorous space of commiseration, the smiles were bright again, and Mary heard how her father had popped in to boast of his daughter being 'as good as a housemaid, or as Miss What's-her-name;' and her foray in the kitchen was more diverting to Aubrey than she was as yet prepared to understand. 'Running away with the buttered toast from under the nose of a charwoman! let Harry never talk of taking a Chinese battery after that!' Her incapacity of perceiving that the deed was either valiant or ludicrous, entertaining him particularly. 'It had evidently hit the medium between the sublime and ridiculous.'

When evening came, Mary thought it Ethel's privilege to go, as the most efficient friend and comforter; but Ethel saw that her sister's soul was with the Wards, and insisted that she should go on as she had begun.

'O Ethel, that was only with the little ones. Now you would be of use to poor Averil.'

'And why should not you? and of more use?'

'You know I am only good for small children; but if you tell me——'

'You provoking girl,' said Ethel. 'All I tell you is, that you are twenty-three years old, and I won't tell you anything, nor assist your unwholesome desire to be second fiddle.'

'I don't know what you mean, Ethel; of course you always tell me what to do, and how to do it.'

Ethel quite laughed now, but gave up the contest, only saying, as she fondly smoothed back a little refractory lock on Mary's smooth open brow, 'Very well then, go and do whatever comes to hand at Bankside, my dear. I do really want to stay at home, both on Aubrey's account, and because papa says Dr Spencer is done up, and that I must catch him and keep him quiet this evening.'

Mary was satisfied in her obedience, and set off with her father. Just as they reached Bankside, a gig drove up containing the fattest old man she had ever beheld; her father whispered that it was old Mr Axworthy, and sent her at once to the nursery, where she was welcomed with a little shriek of delight, each child bounding in her small arm-chair, and pulling her down between them on the floor for convenience of double hugging, after which she was required to go on with the doll-dressing.

Mary could not bear to do this, while the knell was vibrating on her ear, and the two coffins being borne across the threshold; so she gathered the orphans within her embrace as she sat on the floor, and endeavoured to find out how much they understood of what was passing, and whether they had any of the right thoughts. It was rather disappointing. The little sisters had evidently been well and religiously taught, but they were too childish to dwell on thoughts of awe or grief, and the small minds were chiefly fixed upon the dolls, as the one bright spot in the dreary day.

Mary yielded, and worked and answered their chatter till twilight came on, and the rival Mary came up to put them to bed, an operation in which she gave her assistance, almost questioning if she were not forgotten; but she learnt that her father was still in the house, the nurse believed looking at papers in Mr Henry's room with the other gentlemen.

'And you will sit by us while we go to sleep. Oh! don't go away!'

The nurse was thankful to her for so doing, and a somewhat graver mood had come over Minna as she laid her head on her pillow, for she asked the difficult question, 'Can Mamma see us now!' which Mary could only answer with a tender 'Perhaps,' and an attempt to direct the child to the thought of the Heavenly Father; and then Minna asked, 'Who will take care of us now?'

'Oh, will you?' cried Ella, sitting up; and both little maids holding out their arms, made a proffer of themselves to be her little children. They would be so good if she would let them be.

Mary could only fondle and smile it off, and put them in mind that they belonged to their brother and sister; but the answer was, 'Ave is not so nice as you. Oh, do let us——'

'But I can't, my dears. I am Dr May's child, you know. What could I say to him?'

'Oh! but Dr May wouldn't mind! I know he wouldn't mind! Mamma says there was never any one so fond of little children, and he is such a dear good old gentleman.'

Mary had not recognised him as an old gentleman at fifty-eight, and did not like it at all. She argued on the impracticability of taking them from their natural protectors, and again tried to lead them upwards, finally betaking herself to the repetition of hymns, which put them to sleep. She had spent some time in sitting between them in the summer darkness, when there was a low tap, and opening the door, she saw her father. Indicating that they slept, she followed him out, and a whispered conference took place as he stood below her on the stairs, their heads on a level.

'Tired, Mary? I have only just got rid of old Axworthy.'

'The nurse said you were busy with papers in Henry's room.'

'Ay – the Will. Henry behaves very well; and is full of right feeling, poor fellow!'

'What becomes of those dear little girls? They want to make themselves a present to me, and say they know you would like it.'

'So I should, the darlings! Well, as things are left, it all goes to Henry, except the 10,000*l.* Ward had insured his life for, which divides between the five. He undertakes, most properly, to make them a home – whether in this house or not is another thing; he and Averil will look after them;

and he made a most right answer when Mr Axworthy offered to take Leonard into his office,' proceeded the communicative doctor, unable to help pouring himself out, in spite of time and place, as soon as he had a daughter to himself. 'Settle nothing now – education not finished; but privately he tells me he believes his mother would as soon have sent Leonard to the hulks as to that old rascal, and the scamp, his grandnephew.'

Mary's answer to this, as his tones became incautiously emphatic, was a glance round all the attic doors, lest they should have ears.

'Now then, do you want to get home?' said the doctor, a little rebuked.

'Oh no, not if there is anything I can do.'

'I want to get this girl away from Leonard. He is just come to the state when it all turns on getting him off to sleep quietly and not disturbing him, and she is too excited and restless to do anything with her; she has startled him twice already, and then gets upset – tired out, poor thing! and will end in being hysterical if she does not get fed and rested, and then we shall be done for! Now I want you to take charge of her. See, here's her room, and I have ordered up some tea for her. You must get her quieted down, make her have a tolerable meal, and when she has worked off her excitement, put her to bed – undressed, mind – and you might lie down by her. If you can't manage her, call me. That's Leonard's door, and I shall be there all night; but don't if you can help it. Can you do this, or must I get Miss What-d'ye-call-her, the elder one, if she can leave the Greens in Randall's Alley?'

Well was it that Mary's heart was stout as well as tender; and instead of mentally magnifying the task, and diminishing her own capabilities, she simply felt that she had received a command, and merely asked that Ethel should be informed.

'I am going to send up to her.'

'And shall I give Averil anything to take?'

'Mutton-chops, if you can.'

'I meant sal-volatile, or anything to put her to sleep.'

'Nonsense! I hate healthy girls drugging themselves. You don't do that at home, Mary!'

Mary showed her white teeth in a silent laugh at the improbability, there being nothing Ethel more detested than what she rather rudely called nervous quackeries. Her father gave her a kiss of grateful approbation, and was gone.

There was a light on the table, and preparations for tea; and Mary looked round the pretty room, where the ornamental paper, the flowery chintz furniture, the shining brass of the bedstead, the frilled muslin toilet, and et ceteras, were more luxurious than what she ever saw, except when visiting with Flora, and so new as to tell a tale of the mother's fond preparation for the return of the daughter from school. In a few moments she heard her father saying, in a voice as if speaking to a sick child, 'Yes, I promise you, my dear. Be good, be reasonable, and you shall come back in the morning. No, you can't go there. Henry is going to bed. Here is a friend for you. Now, Mary, don't let me see her till she has slept.'

Mary took the other hand, and between them they placed her in an arm-chair, whose shining fresh white ground and gay rose-pattern contrasted with her heated, rumpled, over-watched appearance, as she sank her head on her hand, not noticing either Mary's presence or the doctor's departure. Mary stood doubtful for a few seconds, full of pity and embarrassment, trying to take in the needs of the case.

Averil Ward was naturally a plump well-looking girl of eighteen, with clearly-cut features, healthy highly-coloured complexion, and large bright hazel eyes, much darker than her profuse and glossy hair, which was always dressed in the newest and most stylish fashion, which, as well as the whole air of her dress and person, was, though perfectly lady-like always regarded by the Stoneborough world as something on the borders of presumption on the part of the entire Ward family.

To Mary's surprise, the five weeks' terrible visitation, and these last fearful five days of sleepless exertion and bereavement, had not faded the bright red of the cheek, nor were there signs of tears, though the eyes looked bloodshot. Indeed, there was a purple tint about the eyelids and lips, a dried-up appearance, and a heated oppressed air, as if the faculties were deadened and burnt up, though her hand was cold and trembling. Her hair, still in its elaborate arrangement, hung loose, untidy, untouched; her collar and sleeves were soiled and tumbled; her dress, with its inconvenient machinery of inflation, looked wretched from its incongruity, and the stains on the huge hanging sleeves. Not a moment could have been given to the care of her own person, since the sole burden of nursing had so grievously and suddenly descended on her.

Mary's first instinct was to pour out some warm water, and bringing it with a sponge to say, 'Would not this refresh you?'

Averil moved petulantly; but the soft warm stream was so grateful to her burning brow, that she could not resist; she put her head back, and submitted like a child to have her face bathed, saying, 'Thank you.'

Mary then begged to remove her tight heavy dress, and make her comfortable in her dressing-gown.

'Oh, I can't! Then I could not go back.'

'Yes, you could; this is quite a dress; besides, one can move so much more quietly without crinoline.'

'I didn't think of that;' and she stood up, and unfastened her hooks. 'Perhaps Dr May would let me go back now?' as a mountain of mohair and scarlet petticoat remained on the floor, upborne by an over-grown steel mouse-trap.

'Perhaps he will by-and-by; but he said you must sleep first.'

'Sleep – I can't sleep. There's no one but me. I couldn't sleep.'

'Then at least let me try to freshen you up. There. You don't know what good it used to do my sister Blanche, for me to brush her hair. I like it.'

And Mary obtained a dreamy soothed submission, so that she almost thought she was brushing her victim to sleep in her chair, before the maid came up with the viands that Dr May had ordered.

'I can't eat that,' said Averil, with almost disgust. 'Take it away.'

'Please don't,' said Mary. 'Is that the way you use me, Miss Ward, when I come to drink tea with you?'

'Oh, I beg your pardon,' was the mechanical answer.

Mary having made the long hair, glossy once more, into a huge braid, and knotted it up, came forth, and insisted that they were to be comfortable over their grilled chickens' legs. She was obliged to make her own welcome, and entertain her hostess; and strenuously she worked, letting the dry lips imbibe a cup of tea, before she attempted the solids; then coaxing and commanding, she gained her point, and succeeded in causing a fair amount of provisions to be swallowed; after which Averil seemed more inclined to linger in enjoyment of the liquids, as though the feverish restlessness were giving place to a sense of fatigue and need of repose.

'This is all wrong,' said she, with a faint bewildered smile, as Mary filled up her cup for her. 'I ought to be treating you as guest, Miss May.'

'Oh, don't call me Miss May! Call me Mary. Think me a sister. You know I have known something of like trouble, only I was younger, and I had my sisters.'

'I do not seem to have felt anything yet,' said Averil, passing her hands over her face. 'I seem to be made of stone.'

'You have *done*: and that is better than feeling.'

'Done! and how miserably! Oh, the difference it might have made, if I had been a better nurse!'

'Papa and Dr Spencer both say you have been a wonderful nurse, considering——' the last word came out before Mary was aware.

'Oh, Dr May has been so kind and so patient with me, I shall never forget it. Even when I scalded his fingers with bringing him that boiling water – but I always do wrong when he is there – and now he won't let me go back to Leonard.'

'But, Averil, the best nurse in the world can't hold out for ever. People must sleep, and make themselves fit to go on.'

'Not when there is only one:' and she gasped.

'All the more reason, when there is but one. Perhaps it is because you are tired out that you get nervous and agitated. You will be quite different after a rest.'

'Are you sure?' whispered Averil, with her eyes rounded, 'are you sure that is all the reason?'

'What do you mean?' said Mary.

Averil drew in her breath, and squeezed both hands tight on her chest, as she spoke very low: 'They sent me away from mamma – they told me papa wanted me: then they sent me from him; they said I was better with Leonard; and – and I said to myself, nothing should make me leave Leonard.'

'It was not papa – *my* father – that sent you without telling you,' said Mary confidently.

'No,' said Averil.

'No; I have heard him say that he would take all risks, rather than deceive anybody,' said Mary eagerly. 'I have heard him and Dr Spencer argue about what they called pious frauds, and he always said they were want of faith. You may trust him. He told me Leonard was in the state when calm sleep was chiefly wanted. I know he would think it cruel not to call you if there were need; and I do not believe there will be need.'

Something like this was reiterated in different forms; and though Averil never regularly yielded, yet as they sat on, there came pauses in the conversation, when Mary saw her nodding, and after one or two vibrations in her chair, she looked up with lustreless glassy eyes. Mary took one of these semi-wakened moments, and in the tone of caressing authority, that had been already found effectual, said she must sleep in bed; took no notice of the murmur of refusal, but completed the undressing, and fairly deposited her in her bed.

Mary's scrupulous conscience was distressed at having thus led to the omission of all evening orisons; but if her own simple-hearted loving supplications at the orphan's beside could compensate for their absence, she did her utmost. Then, as both the room-door and that of the sick-chamber had been left open, she stole into the passage, where she could see her father, seated at the table, and telegraphed to him a sign of her success. He durst not move, but he smiled and nodded satisfaction; and Mary, after tidying the room, and considering with herself, took off her more cumbrous garments, wrapped herself in a cloak, and lay down beside Averil, not expecting to sleep, but passing to thoughts of Harry, and of that 23rd Psalm, which they had agreed to say at the same hour every night. By how many hours was Harry beforehand with her? That was a calculation that to Mary was always like the beads of the chaplain of Norham Castle. Certain it is, that after she had seen Harry lighting a fire to broil chickens' legs in a Chinese temple, under the willow-pattern cannon-ball tree, and heard Henry Ward saying it was not like a lieutenant in the navy, she found herself replying, 'Use before gentility;' and in the enunciation of this – her first moral sentiment – discovered that it was broad daylight.

What o'clock it was she could not guess. Averil was sound asleep, breathing deeply and regularly, so that it was a pleasure to listen to her; and Mary did not fear wakening her by a shoeless voyage of discovery to the place whence Dr May was visible.

He turned at once, and with his noiseless tread came to her. 'Asleep still? So is he. All right. Here, waken me the moment he stirs.'

And rather by sign than word, he took Mary into the sick room, indicated a chair, and laid himself on a sofa, where he was instantaneously sound asleep, before his startled daughter had quite taken everything in; but she had only to glance at his haggard wearied face, to be glad to be there, so as to afford him even a few moments of vigorous slumber with all his might.

In some awe, she looked round, not venturing to stir hand or foot. Her chair was in the full draught of the dewy morning breeze, so chilly, that she drew her shawl tightly about her; but she knew that this had been an instance of her father's care, and if she wished to make the slightest move, it was only to secure a fuller view of the patient, from whom she was half cut off by a curtain at the foot of the bed. A sort of dread, however, made Mary gaze at everything around her before she brought her eyes upon him – her father's watch on the table, indicating ten minutes to four, the Minster Tower in the rising sun-light – nay, the very furniture of the room, and Dr May's position, before she durst familiarize herself with Leonard's appearance – he whom she had last seen as a sturdy, ruddy, healthful boy, looking able to outweigh two of his friend Aubrey.

The original disease had long since passed into typhus, and the scarlet eruption was gone, so that she only saw a yellow whiteness, that, marked by the blue veins of the bared temples, was to her mind death-like. Mary had not been sheltered from taking part in scenes of suffering; she had seen sickness and death in cottages, as well as in her own home, and she had none of the fanciful alarms, either of novelty or imagination, to startle her in the strange watch that had so suddenly been thrust on her; but what did fill her with a certain apprehension, was the new and lofty beauty of expression that sat on that sleeping countenance. 'A nice boy,' 'rather a handsome lad,' 'a boy of ingenuous face,' they had always called Leonard Ward, when animated with health and spirits; and the friendship between him and Aubrey had been encouraged, but without thinking of him as more than an ordinary lad of good style. Now, however, to Mary's mind, the broad brow and wasted features in their rest, had assumed a calm nobility that was like those of Ethel's favourite champions – those who conquered by 'suffering and being strong.' She looked and listened for the low regular breath, almost doubting at one moment whether it still were drawn, then only reassured by its freedom and absence from effort, that it was not soon to pass away. There was something in that look as if death must set his seal on it, rather than as if it could return to the flush of health, and the struggle and strife of school-boy life and of manhood.

More than an hour had passed, and all within the house was as still as ever; and through the window there only came such sounds as seem like audible silence – the twittering of birds, the humming of bees, the calls of boys in distant fields, the far-away sound of waggon wheels – when there was a slight move, and Mary, in the tension of all her faculties, had well-nigh started, but restrained herself; and as she saw the half-closed fingers stretch, and the head turn, she leant forward, and touched her father's hand.

Dr May was on his feet even before those brown eyes of Leonard's had had time to unclose; and as Mary was silently moving to the door, he made a sign to her to wait.

She stood behind the curtain: 'You are better for your sleep.'

'Yes, thank you – much better.'

The doctor signed towards a tray, which stood by a spirit-lamp, on a table in the further corner. Mary silently brought it, and as quietly obeyed the finger that directed her to cordial and spoon – well knowing the need – since that unserviceable right arm always made these operations troublesome to her father.

'Have you been here all night, Dr May?'

'Yes; and very glad to see you sleeping so well.'

'Thank you.' And there was something that made Mary's eyes dazzle with tears in the tone of that 'Thank you.' The doctor held out his hand for the spoon she had prepared, and there was another 'Thank you;' then, 'Is Ave there?'

'No, I made her go to bed. She is quite well; but she wanted sleep sorely.'

'Thank you,' again said the boy; then with a moment's pause, 'Dr May, tell me *now*.'

Mary would have fled at breaking treacherously in upon such tidings; but a constraining gesture of her father obliged her to remain, and keep the cordial ready for immediate administration.

'My dear, I believe you know,' said Dr May, bending over him – and Mary well knew what the face must be saying.

'Both?' the faint tones asked.

'Recollect the sorrow that they have been spared,' said Dr May in his lowest tenderest tones, putting his hand out behind him, and signing to Mary for the cordial.

'*She* could not have borne it;' and the feebleness of those words made Mary eager to put the spoon once more into her father's hands.

'That is right, my boy. Think of their being together;' and Mary heard tears in her father's voice.

'Thank you,' again showed that the cordial was swallowed; then a pause, and in a quiet, sad, low tone, 'Poor Ave!'

'Your mending is the best thing for her.'

Then came a long sigh; and then, after a pause, the doctor knelt down, and said the Lord's Prayer – the orphan's prayer, as so many have felt it in the hour of bereavement.

All was quite still, and both he and Mary knelt on for some short space; then he arose in guarded stillness, hastily wiped away the tears that were streaming over his face, and holding back the curtain, showed Mary the boy, again sunk into that sweet refreshing sleep. 'That is well over,' he said, with a deep sigh of relief, when they had moved to a safe distance. 'Poor fellow! he had better become used to the idea while he is too weak to think.'

'He is better?' asked Mary, repressing her agitation with difficulty.

'I believe the danger is over; and you may tell his sister so when she wakes.'

CHAPTER III

'And a heart at leisure from itself
To soothe and sympathise.'

Miss Waring.

Recovery had fairly set in, and 'better' was the universal bulletin, eating and drinking the prevailing remedy.

Henry Ward had quickly thrown off his illness. The sense that all depended on him, acted as a stimulus to his energies; he was anxious to be up and doing, and in a few days was downstairs, looking over his father's papers, and making arrangements. He was eager and confident, declaring that his sisters should never want a home while he lived; and, when he first entered his brother's room, his effusion of affection overwhelmed Leonard in his exceeding weakness, and the thought of which during the rest of the day often brought tears to his eyes.

Very grateful to Dr May, Henry declared himself anxious to abide by his advice; and discussed with him all his plans. There had been no will, but the house and land of course were Henry's. The other property gave about 2,000*l.* to each of the family; and Averil had about as much again from the old aunt, from whom she had taken her peculiar name. The home of all should, of course, still be their present one; Averil would teach her sisters, and superintend the house; and Leonard continue at the school, where he had a fair chance of obtaining the Randall scholarship in the course of a year or two. 'And if not,' said Henry, 'he may still not lose his University education. My father was proud of Leonard; and if he would have sent him there, why should not I?'

And when Dr May thought how his own elder sons had insisted on greater advantages of education for their juniors than they had themselves enjoyed, he felt especially fatherly towards the young surgeon. On only one point was he dissatisfied, and that he could not press. He thought the establishment at Bankside too expensive, and counselled Henry to remove into the town, and let the house; but this was rejected on the argument of the uncertainty of finding a tenant, and the inexpediency of appearing less prosperous; and considering that Mr and Mrs Ward had themselves made the place, Dr May thought his proposal hard-hearted. He went about impressing every one with his confidence in Henry Ward, and fought successfully at the Board of Guardians to have him considered as a continuation of his father, instead of appointing a new union doctor; and he watched with paternal solicitude that the young man's first return to his practice should be neither too soon for his own health or his patients' fears; giving him no exhortation more earnest, nor more thankfully accepted, than that he was to let no scruple prevent his applying to himself in the slightest difficulty; calling him in to pauper patients, and privately consulting in cases which could not be visited gratis. The patronage of Henry Ward was one of the hobbies that Dr May specially loved, and he cantered off upon it with vehemence such as he had hardly displayed for years.

Aubrey recovered with the tardiness of a weakly constitution, and was long in even arriving at a drive in the brougham: for Dr May had set up a brougham. As long as Hector Ernescliffe's home was at Stoneborough, driving the doctor had been his privilege, and the old gig had been held together by diligent repairs; but when Maplewood claimed him, and Adams was laid aside by rheumatism, Flora would no longer be silenced, and preached respectability and necessity. Dr May did not admit the plea, unless Adams were to sit inside and drive out of window; but then he was told of the impropriety of his daughters going out to dinner in gigs, and the expense of flies. When Flora talked of propriety in that voice, the family might protest and grumble, but were always reduced to obedience; and thus Blanche's wedding had been the occasion of Ethel being put into a hoop, and the doctor into a brougham. He was better off under the tyranny than she was, in spite of the solitude he had bewailed. Young Adams was not the companion his father had been, and was no loss; and he owned that he now got through a great deal of reading, and at times a great deal of sleep; and mourned for nothing but his moon and stars – so romantic a regret, that Dr Spencer advised him not to mention it.

After Aubrey's first drives, Dr Spencer declared that the best way of invigorating him would be to send him for a month to the sea-side, while the house could be thoroughly purified before Gertrude's return. Dr Spencer and Mary would take care of Dr May; and Ethel had begun to look forward to a *tête-à-tête* with Aubrey by the sea, which they had neither of them ever seen, when her anticipations were somewhat dashed by her father's exclaiming, that it would be the best thing for Leonard Ward to go with them. She said something about his not being well enough to travel so soon.

'Oh, yes, he will!' said Dr May; 'he only wants stimulus to get on fast enough. I declare I'll ask Henry about it; I'm just going to meet him at the hospital.'

And before another word could be said, he let himself out at the back door of the garden, in which they had been meeting Richard, who was now allowed to come thus far, though both for Daisy's sake and his flock's, he had hitherto submitted to a rigorous quarantine; and the entire immunity of Cocksmoor from the malady was constantly adduced by each doctor as a convincing proof of his own theory.

'Well, I do hope that will go off!' exclaimed Ethel, as soon as her father was out of hearing. 'It will be a terrible upset to all one's peace and comfort with Aubrey!'

'Indeed – what harm will the poor boy do?' asked Richard.

'Make Aubrey into the mere shame-faced, sister-hating, common-place creature, that the collective boy thinks it due to himself to be in society,' said Ethel; 'and me from an enjoying sister, into an elderly, care-taking, despised spinster – a burden to myself and the boys.'

'But why, Ethel, can't you enjoy yourself?'

'My dear Richard, just imagine turning loose a lot of boys and girls, with no keeper, to enjoy themselves in some wild sea place! No, no: the only way to give the arrangement any shade of propriety, will be to be elderly, infuse as much vinegar as possible into my countenance, wear my spectacles, and walk at a staid pace up and down the parade, while my two sons disport themselves on the rocks.'

'If you really think it would not be proper,' said Richard, rather alarmed, 'I could run after my father.'

'Stuff, Richard; papa must have his way; and if it is to do the boy good, I can sacrifice a crab – I mean myself – not a crustacean. I am not going to be such a selfish wretch as to make objections.'

'But if it would not be the correct thing? Or could not you get some one to stay with you?'

'I can make it the correct thing. It is only to abstain from the fun I had hoped for. I meant to have been a girl, and now I must be a woman, that's all; and I dare say Aubrey will be the happier for it – boys always are.'

'If you don't like it, I wish you would let me speak to papa.'

'Richard, have you these five years been the safety-valve for my murmurs without knowing what they amount to?'

'I thought no one complained unless to get a thing remedied.'

'Exactly so. That is man! And experience never shows man that woman's growls relieve her soul, and that she dreads nothing more than their being acted on! All I wish is, that this scheme may die a natural death; but I should be miserable, and deserved to be so, if I raised a finger to hinder it. What, must you go? Rule Daisy's lines if she writes to Meta, please.'

'I did so. I have been trying to make her write straighter.'

'Of course you have. I expect I shall find her organ of order grown to a huge bump when she comes home. Oh! when will our poor remnants be once more a united family? and when shall I get into Cocksmoor school again?'

When Dr May came home, his plan was in full bloom. Henry had gratefully accepted it, and answered for his brother being able to travel by the next Monday; and Dr May wanted Ethel to walk with him to Bankside, and propose it there – talking it over with the sister, and making it her own invitation. Ethel saw her fate, and complied, her father talking eagerly all the way.

'You see, Ethel, it is quite as much for his spirits as his health that I wish it. He is just the age that our Norman was.'

That was the key to a great deal. Ethel knew that her father had never admitted any of the many excuses for the neglect of Norman's suffering for the three months after his mother's death; but though it thrilled her all over, she was not prepared to believe that any one, far less any Ward, could be of the same sensitive material as Norman. To avoid answering, she went more than half way, by saying, 'Don't you think I might ask those poor girls to come with him?'

'By no manner of means,' said the doctor, stopping short. 'It is just what I want, to get him away from his sister. She minds nothing else; and if it were not for Mary, I don't know what the little ones would do; and as to Henry, he is very good and patient; but it is the way to prevent him from forming domestic tastes to have no mistress to his house. He will get into mischief, or marry, if she does not mind what she is about.'

'That must come to an end when Leonard is well, and goes back to school.'

'And that won't be till after the holidays. No, some break there must be. When he is gone, Mary can put her into the way of doing things; she is anxious to do right; and we shall see them do very well. But this poor boy – you know he has been always living at home, while the others were away; he was very fond of his mother, and the first coming out of his room was more than he could bear. I must have him taken from home till he is well again, and able to turn to other things.'

And before Ethel's eyes came a vision of poor Mrs Ward leaning on her son's arm, on Saturday afternoon walks, each looking fond and proud of the other. She felt her own hardness of heart, and warmed to the desire of giving comfort.

Bankside was basking in summer sunshine, with small patches of shade round its young shrubs and trees, and a baking heat on the little porch.

The maid believed Miss Ward was in the garden. Mr Leonard had been taken out to-day; and the doctor moving on, they found themselves in the cool pretty drawing-room rather over-crowded with furniture and decoration, fresh and tasteful, but too much of it, and a contrast to the Mays' mixture of the shabby and the curious, in the room that was so decidedly for use, and not for show.

What arrested the attention was, however, the very sweetest singing Ethel had ever heard. The song was low and sad, but so intensely sweet, that Dr May held up his hand to silence all sound, and stood with restrained breath and moistened eyes. Ethel, far less sensitive to music, was nevertheless touched as she had never before been by sound; and the more, as she looked through the window and saw in the shade of a walnut-tree, a sofa, at the foot of which sat Averil Ward in her deep mourning, her back to the window, so that only her young figure and the braids of her fair hair were to be seen; and beyond, something prostrate, covered with wrappers. The sweet notes ended, Dr May drew a deep sigh, wiped his spectacles, and went on; Ethel hung back, not to startle the invalid by the sight of a stranger; but as Averil rose, she saw him raising himself, with a brightening smile on his pale face, to hold out his hand to the doctor. In another minute Averil had come to her, shaken hands, and seated herself where she could best command a view of her brother.

'I am glad to see him out of doors,' said Ethel.

'Henry was bent on it; but I think the air and the glare of everything is too much for him; he is so tired and oppressed.'

'I am sure he must like your singing,' said Ethel.

'It is almost the only thing that answers,' said Averil, her eyes wistfully turning to the sofa; 'he can't read, and doesn't like being read to.'

'It is very difficult to manage a boy's recovery,' said Ethel. 'They don't know *how* to be ill.'

'It is not that,' replied the sister, as if she fancied censure implied, 'but his spirits. Every new room he goes into seems to beat him down; and he lies and broods. If he could only talk!'

'I know that so well!' said Ethel. But to Averil the May troubles were of old date, involved in the mists of childhood. And Ethel, seeing that her words were not taken as sympathy, continued, 'Do not the little girls amuse him?'

'Oh no! they are too much for him; and I am obliged to keep them in the nursery. Poor little things! I don't know what we should do if your sister Mary were not so kind.'

'Mary is very glad,' began Ethel confusedly. Then rushing into her subject: 'Next week, I am to take Aubrey to the sea-side; and we thought if Leonard would join us, the change might be good for him.'

'Thank you,' Averil answered, playing with her heavy jet watch-guard. 'You are very good; but I am sure he could not move so soon.'

'Ave,' called Leonard at that moment; and Ethel, perceiving that she likewise was to advance, came forth in time to hear, 'O Ave! I am to go to the sea next week, with Aubrey May and his sister. Won't it——'

Then becoming aware of the visitor, he stopped short, threw his feet off the sofa, and stood up to receive her.

'I can't let you come if you do like that,' she said, shaking his long thin hand; and he let himself down again, not, however, resuming his recumbent posture, and giving a slight but effective frown to silence his sister's entreaties that he would do so. He sat, leaning back as though exceedingly feeble, scarcely speaking, but his eyes eloquent with eagerness. And very fine eyes they were! Ethel remembered her own weariness, some twelve or fourteen years back, of the raptures of her baby-loving sisters about those eyes; and now in the absence of the florid colouring of health, she was the more struck by the beauty of the deep liquid brown, of the blue tinge of the white, and of the lustrous light that resided in them, but far more by their power of expression, sometimes so soft and melancholy, at other moments earnest, pleading, and almost flashing with eagerness. It was a good mouth too, perhaps a little inclined to sternness of mould about the jaw and chin; but that might have been partly from the absence of all softening roundness, ageing the countenance for the time, just as illness had shrunk the usually sturdy figure.

'Has Ethel told you of our plan?' asked Dr May of the sister.

'Yes,' she hesitated, in evident confusion and distress. 'You are all very kind; but we must see what Henry says.'

'I have spoken to Henry! He answers for our patching Leonard up for next week; and I have great faith in Dr Neptune.'

Leonard's looks were as bright as Averil's were disturbed.

'Thank you, thank you very much! but can he possibly be well enough for the journey?'

Leonard's eyes said 'I shall.'

'A week will do great things,' said Dr May: 'and it is a very easy journey – only four hours' railway, and a ten miles' drive.'

Averil's face was full of consternation; and Leonard leant forward with hope dancing in his eyes.

'You know the place,' continued Dr May; 'Coombe Hole. Quite fresh, and unhackneyed. It is just where Devon and Dorset meet. I am not sure in which county; but there's a fine beach, and beautiful country. The Riverses found it out, and have been there every autumn; besides sending their poor little girl and her governess down when London gets too hot. Flora has written to the woman of the lodgings she always has, and will lend them the maid she sends with little Margaret; so they will be in clover.'

'Is it not a very long way?' said Averil, thinking how long those ten yards of lawn had seemed.

'Not as things go,' said Dr May. 'You want Dr Spencer to reproach you with being a Stoneborough fungus. There are places in Wales nearer by the map, but without railway privilege; and as to a great gay place, they would all be sick of it.'

'Do you feel equal to it? as if you should like it, Leonard?' asked his sister, in a trembling would-be grateful voice.

'Of all things,' was the answer.

Ethel thought the poor girl had suffered constraint enough, and that it was time to release the boy from his polite durance; so she rose to take leave, and again Leonard pulled himself upright to shake hands.

'Indeed,' said Ethel, when Averil had followed them into the drawing-room, 'I am sorry for you. It would go very hard with me to make Aubrey over to any one! but if you do trust him with me, I must come and hear all you wish me to do for him.'

'I cannot think that he will be able or glad to go when it comes to the point,' said Averil with a shaken tone.

Dr May was nearer than she thought, and spoke peremptorily. 'Take care what you are about! You are *not* to worry him with discussions. If he can go, he will; if not, he will stay at home; but pros and cons are prohibited. Do you hear, Averil?'

'Yes; very well.'

'Papa you really are very cruel to that poor girl,' were Ethel's first words outside.

'Am I? I wouldn't be for worlds, Ethel. But some how she always puts me in a rage. I wish I knew she was not worrying her brother at this moment!'

No, Averil was on the stair-case, struggling, choking, with the first tears she had shed. All this fortnight of unceasing vigilance and exertion, her eyes had been dry, for want of time to realize, for want of time to weep; and now she was ashamed that hurt feeling rather than grief had opened the fountain. She could not believe that it was not a cruel act of kindness, to carry one so weak as Leonard away from home to the care of a stranger. She apprehended all manner of ill consequences; and then nursing him and regarding his progress as her own work, had been the sedative to her grief, which would come on her, 'like an armed man,' in the dreariness of his absence. Above all, she felt herself ill requited by his manifest eagerness to leave her who had nursed him so devotedly – her, his own sister, for the stiff, plain Miss May whom he hardly knew. The blow from the favourite companion brother, so passionately watched and tended, seemed to knock her down; and Dr May, with medical harshness, forbidding her the one last hope of persuading him out of the wild fancy, filled up the measure.

Oh, those tears! How they would swell up at each throb of the wounded heart, at each dismal foreboding of the desponding spirit. But she had no time for them! Leonard must not be left alone, with no one to cover him up with his wrappers.

The tears were strangled, the eyes indignantly dried. She ran out at the garden door. The sofa was empty! Had Henry come home and helped him in? She hurried on to the window; Leonard was alone in the drawing-room, resting breathlessly on an ottoman within the window.

'Dear Leonard! Why didn't you wait for me?'

'I thought I'd try what I could do. You see I am much stronger than we thought.' And he smiled cheerfully, as he helped himself by the furniture to another sofa. 'I say, Ave, do just give me the map – the one in Bradshaw will do. I want to find this place.'

'I don't think there is a Bradshaw,' said Averil, reluctantly.

'Oh yes, there is – behind the candlestick, on the study chimney-piece.'

'Very well.' There were more tears to be gulped down – and perhaps they kept her from finding the book.

'Where's the Bradshaw?'

'I didn't see it.'

'I tell you I know it was there. The left-hand candlestick, close to the letter-weight. I'll get it myself.'

He was heaving himself up, when Averil prevented him by hastening to a more real search, which speedily produced the book.

Eagerly Leonard unfolded the map, making her steady it for his shaking hand, and tracing the black toothed lines.

'There's Bridport – ten miles from there. Can you see the name, Ave?'

'No, it is not marked.'

'Never mind. I see where it is; and I can see it is a capital place; just in that little jag, with famous bathing. I wonder if they will stay long enough for me to learn to swim?'

'You are a good way from that as yet,' said poor Averil, her heart sinking lower and lower.

'Oh, I shall be well at once when I get away from here!'

'I hope so.'

'Why, Ave!' he cried, now first struck with her tone, 'don't you know I shall?'

'I don't know,' she said, from the soreness of her heart; 'but I can't tell how to trust you with strangers.'

'Strangers! You ungrateful child!' exclaimed Leonard, indignantly. 'Why, what have they been doing for you all this time?'

'I am sure Miss May, at least, never came near us till to-day.'

'I'm very glad of it! I'm sick of everything and everybody I have seen!'

Everybody! That was the climax! Averil just held her tongue; but she rushed to her own room, and wept bitterly and angrily. Sick of her after all her devotion! Leonard, the being she loved best in the world!

And Leonard, distressed and hurt at the reception of his natural expression of the weariness of seven weeks' sickness and sorrow, felt above all the want of his mother's ever-ready sympathy and soothing, and as if the whole world, here, there, and everywhere, would be an equally dreary waste. His moment of bright anticipation passed into heavy despondency, and turning his head from the light, he dropped asleep with a tear on his cheek.

When he awoke it was at the sound of movements in the room, slow and cautious, out of regard to his slumbers – and voices, likewise low – at least one was low, the other that whisper of the inaudibility of which Averil could not be disabused. He lay, looking for a few moments through his eyelashes, before exerting himself to move. Averil, her face still showing signs of recent tears, sat in a low chair, a book in her lap, talking to her brother Henry.

Henry was of less robust frame than Leonard promised to be, and though on a smaller scale, was more symmetrically made, and had more regular features than either his brother or sister, but his eyes were merely quick lively black beads, without anything of the clear depths possessed by the others. His hair too was jet black, whereas theirs was a pale nut brown; and his whiskers, long and curling, so nearly met under his chin, as to betray a strong desire that the hirsute movement should extend to the medical profession. Always point-device in apparel, the dust on his boot did not prevent its perfect make from being apparent; and the entire sit of his black suit would have enabled a cursory glance to decide that it never came out of the same shop as Dr May's.

'O Henry!' were the words that he first heard distinctly.

'It will be much better for every one – himself and you included.'

'Yes, if——'

'If – nonsense. I tell you he will be quite well enough. See how well I am now; how fast I got on as soon as I took to tonics. – Ha, Leonard, old fellow! what, awake? What do you say to this plan of old May's?'

'It is very kind of him; and I should be very glad if I am well enough, but next week is very soon,' said Leonard, waking in the depression in which he had gone to sleep.

'Oh, next week! That is as good as next year in a matter like this, as May agreed with me; here, let us have your pulse. You have let him get low, Averil. A basin of good soup will put more heart into you, and you will feel ready for anything.'

'I have got on to-day,' said Leonard, briskly raising himself, as though the cheerful voice had been cordial in itself.

'Of course you have, now that you have something to look forward to; and you will be in excellent hands; the very thing I wanted for you, though I could not see how to manage it. I am going to dress. I shall tell them to send in dinner; and if I am not down, I shall be in the nursery – You won't come in to dinner, Leonard?'

'No,' said Leonard, with a shudder.

'I shall send you in some gravy soup, that you may thank me for. Ave never would order anything but boiled chickens for *you*, and forgets that other people ever want to eat. There will be a chance of making a housekeeper of her now.'

How selfish, thought Averil, to want to get rid of poor Leonard, that I may attend to *his* dinners. Yet Henry had spoken in perfect good humour.

Henry came down with a little sister in each hand. They were his especial darlings; and with a touch of fatherly fondness, he tried to compensate to them for their sequestration from the drawing-room, the consequence of Averil not having established her authority enough to keep their spirits from growing too riotous for Leonard's weakness. Indeed, their chatter was Henry's sole enlivenment, for Averil was constantly making excursions to ask what her patient would eat, and watch its success; and but for his pleasure in the little girls popping about him, he would have had a meal as dull as it was unsettled. As soon as the strawberries were eaten, he walked out through the window with them clinging to him, and Averil returned to her post.

'Some music, Ave,' said Leonard, with an instinctive dread of her conversation.

She knew her voice was past singing, and began one of her most renowned instrumental pieces, which she could play as mechanically as a musical-box.

'Not that jingling airified thing!' cried Leonard, 'I want something quiet and refreshing. There's an evening hymn that the Mays have.'

'The Mays know nothing of music,' said Averil.

'Stay, this is it:' and he whistled a few bars.

'That old thing! Of course I know that. We had it every Sunday at Brighton.'

She began it, but her eyes were full of tears, partly because she hated herself for the irritation she had betrayed. She was a sound, good, honest-hearted girl; but among all the good things she had learned at Brighton, had not been numbered the art of ruling her own spirit.

CHAPTER IV

'Griefs hidden in the mind like treasures,
Will turn with time to solemn pleasures.'

On the Monday morning, the two convalescents shook hands in the waiting-room at the station, surveying each other rather curiously; while Ethel, trying to conquer her trepidation, gave manifold promises to Averil of care and correspondence.

Dr Spencer acted escort, being far more serviceable on the railway than his untravelled friend, whose lame arm, heedless head, and aptitude for missing trains and mistaking luggage, made him a charge rather than an assistant. He was always happiest among his patients at home; and the world was still ill enough to employ him so fully, that Ethel hoped to be less missed than usual. Indeed, she believed that her absence would be good in teaching him Mary's full-grown worth, and Mary would be in the full glory of notability in the purification of the house.

The change was likewise for Dr Spencer's good. He had almost broken down in the height of the labour, and still looked older and thinner for it; and after one night at Coombe, he was going to refresh himself by one of his discursive tours.

He was in high spirits, and the pink of courtesy; extremely flattered by the charge of Ethel, and making her the ostensible object of his attention, to the relief of the boys, who were glad to be spared the sense of prominent invalidism. The change was delightful to them. Aubrey was full of life and talk, and sat gazing from the window, as if the line from Stoneborough to Whitford presented a succession of novelties.

'What's that old place on the river there, with crow-stepped gables and steep roofs, like a Flemish picture?'

'Don't you know?' said Leonard, 'it is the Vintry mill, where my relative lives, that wants to make a dusty miller of me.'

'No fear of that, old fellow,' said Aubrey, regarding him in some dismay, 'you've got better things to grind at.'

'Ay; even if I don't get the Randall next time, I shall be sure of it another.'

'You'll have it next.'

'I don't know; here is a quarter clean gone, and the other fellows will have got before me.'

'Oh, but most of them have had a spell of fever!'

'Yes, but they have not had it so thoroughly,' said Leonard. 'My memory is not properly come back yet; and your father says I must not try it too soon.'

'That's always his way,' said Aubrey. 'He would not let Ethel so much as pack up my little Homer.'

Leonard's quick, furtive glance at Ethel was as if he suspected her of having been barely prevented from torturing him.

'Oh, it was not her doing,' said Aubrey, 'it was I! I thought Tom would find me gone back; and, you know, we must keep up together, Leonard, and be entered at St John's at the same time.'

For Aubrey devoutly believed in Tom's college at Cambridge, which had recovered all Dr May's allegiance.

The extra brightness was not of long duration. It was a very hot day, such as exactly suited the salamander nature of Dr Spencer; but the carriage became like an oven. Aubrey curled himself up in a corner and went to sleep; but Leonard's look of oppressed resignation grieved Ethel, and the blue blinds made him look so livid, that she was always fancying him fainting; and then his shyness was dreadful – it was impossible to elicit from him anything but 'No thank you.'

He did nearly faint when they left the train; and while Aubrey was eagerly devouring the produce of the refreshment room, had to lie on a bench under Dr Spencer's charge, for Ethel's approach only brought on a dangerous spasm of politeness. How she should get on with him for a month, passed her imagination.

There was a fresher breeze when they drove out of the station, up a Dorset ridge of hill, steep, high, terraced and bleak; but it was slow climbing up, and everyone was baked and wearied before the summit was gained, and the descent commenced. Even then, Ethel, sitting backwards, could only see height develop above height, all green, and scattered with sheep, or here and there an unfenced turnip-field, the road stretching behind like a long white ribbon, and now and then descending between steep chalk cuttings in slopes, down which the carriage slowly scrooped on its drag, leaving a broad blue-flecked trail. Dr Spencer was asleep, hat off, and the wind lifting his snowy locks; and she wished the others were, but Aubrey lamented on the heat and the length, and Leonard leant back in his corner, past lamentation.

Down, down! The cuttings were becoming precipitous cliffs, the drag made dismal groans; Aubrey, after a great slip forward, looking injured, anchored himself, with his feet against the seat, by Ethel; and Dr Spencer was effectually wakened by an involuntary forward plunge of his opposite neighbour. 'Can this be safe?' quoth Ethel, 'should not some of us get out?'

'Much you know of hills, you level landers!' was the answer; and just then they were met and passed by four horses dragging up a stage coach, after the fashion of a fly on a window-pane – a stage coach! delightful to the old-world eyes of Dr Spencer, recalling a faint memory to Ethel, and presenting a perfect novelty to Aubrey.

Then came a sudden turn upon flat ground, and a short cry of wonder broke from Aubrey. Ethel was sensible of a strange salt weedy smell, new to her nostrils, but only saw the white-plastered, grey-roofed houses through which they were driving; but, with another turn, the buildings were only on one side – on the other there was a wondrous sense of openness, vastness, freshness – something level, grey, but dazzling; and before she could look again, the horses stopped, and close to her, under the beetling, weather-stained white cliff, was a low fence, and within it a verandah and a door, where stood Flora's maid, Barbara, in all her respectability.

Much wit had been expended by Aubrey on being left to the tender mercy of cruel Barbara Allen, in whom Ethel herself anticipated a tyrant; but at the moment she was invaluable. Every room was ready and inviting, and nothing but the low staircase between Leonard and the white bed, which was the only place fit for him; while for the rest, the table was speedily covered with tea and chickens; Abbotstoke eggs, inscribed with yesterday's date; and red mail-clad prawns, to prove to touch and taste that this was truly sea-side. The other senses knew it well: the open window let in the indescribable salt, fresh odour, and the entire view from it was shore and sea; there seemed nothing to hinder the tide from coming up the ridge of shingle, and rushing straight into the cottage; and the ear was constantly struck by the regular roll and dash of the waves. Aubrey, though with the appetite of recovery and sea air combined, could not help pausing to listen; and, when his meal was over, leant back in his chair, listened again, and gave a sigh of content. 'It is one constant hush, hushaby,' he said; 'it would make one sleep pleasantly.'

His companions combined their advice to him so to use it; and in less than half an hour Ethel went to bid him good-night, in the whitest of beds and cleanest of tiny chambers, where he looked the picture of sleepy satisfaction, when she opened his window, and admitted the swell and dash that fascinated his weary senses.

'My child is all right,' said Ethel, returning to Dr Spencer; 'can you say the same of yours?'

'He must rest himself into the power of sleeping. I must say it was a bold experiment; but it will do very well, when he has got over the journey. He was doing no good at home.'

'I hope he will here.'

'Depend on it he will. And now what are you intending?'

'I am thirsting to see those waves near. Would it be against the manners and customs of sea-places for me to run down to them so late?'

'Sea-places have no manners and customs.'

Ethel tossed on her hat with a feeling of delight and freedom. 'Oh, are you coming, Dr Spencer? I did not mean to drag you out. You had rather rest, and smoke.'

'This is rest,' he answered.

The next moment, the ridge of the shingle was passed, and Ethel's feet were sinking in the depth of pebbles, her cheeks freshened by the breeze, her lips salted by the spray tossed in by the wind from the wave crests. At the edge of the water she stood – as all others stand there – watching the heaving from far away come nearer, nearer, curl over in its pride of green glassy beauty, fall into foam, and draw back, making the pebbles crash their accompanying 'frsch.' The repetition, the peaceful majesty, the blue expanse, the straight horizon, so impressed her spirit as to rivet her eyes and chain her lips; and she receded step by step before the tide, unheeding anything else, not even perceiving her companion's eyes fixed on her, half curiously, half sadly.

'Well, Ethel,' at last he said.

'I never guessed it!' she said, with a gasp. 'No wonder Harry cannot bear to be away from it. Must we leave it?' as he moved back.

'Only to smooth ground,' said Dr Spencer; 'it is too dark to stay here among the stones and crab-pots.'

The summer twilight was closing in; lights shining in the village under the cliffs, and looking mysterious on distant points of the coast; stars were shining forth in the pale blue sky, and the young moon shedding a silver rippled beam on the water.

'If papa were but here!' said Ethel, wakening from another gaze, and recollecting that she was not making herself agreeable.

'So you like the expedition?'

'The fit answer to that would be, "It is very pretty," as the Cockney said to Coleridge at Lodore.'

'So I have converted a Stoneborough fungus!'

'What! to say the sea is glorious? A grand conversion!'

'To find anything superior to Minster Street.'

'Ah, you are but half reclaimed! You are a living instance that there is no content unless one has begun life as a fungus.'

She was startled by his change of tone. 'True, Ethel. Content might have been won, if there had been resolution to begin without it.'

'I beg your pardon,' she faltered, 'I ought not to have said it. I forgot there was such a cause.'

'Cause – you know nothing about it.'

She was silent, distressed, dismayed, fearing that she had spoken wrongly, and had either mistaken or been misunderstood.

'Tell me, Ethel,' he presently said, 'what can you know of what made me a wanderer?'

'Only what papa told me.'

'He – he was the last person to know.'

'He told me,' said Ethel, hurrying it out in a fright, 'that you went away – out of generosity – not to interfere with his happiness.'

Then she felt as if she had done a shocking thing, and waited anxiously, while Dr Spencer deliberately made a deep hole in the shingle with his stick. 'Well,' at last he said, 'I thought that matter was unknown to all men – above all to Dick!'

'It was only after you were gone, that he put things together and made it out.'

'Did – she – know?' said Dr Spencer, with a long breath.

'I cannot tell,' said Ethel.

'And how or why did he tell you?' (rather hurt).

'It was when first you came. I am sure no one else knows it. But he told me because he could not help it; he was so sorry for you.'

They walked the whole length of the parade, and had turned before Dr Spencer spoke again; and then he said, 'It is strange! My one vision was of walking on the seashore with her; and that just doing so with you, should have brought up the whole as fresh as five-and-thirty years ago!'

'I wish I was more like her,' said Ethel.

No more was wanting to make him launch into the descriptions, dear to a daughter's heart, of her mother in her sweet serious bloom of young womanhood, giving new embellishments to the character already so closely enshrined in his hearer's heart, the more valuable that the stream of treasured recollection flowed on in partial oblivion of the person to whom it was addressed, or, at least, that she was the child of his rival; for, from the portrait of the quiet bright maiden, he passed to the sufferings that his own reserved nature had undergone from his friend's out-spoken enthusiasm. The professor's visible preference for the youth of secure prospects, had not so much discouraged as stung him; and in a moment of irritation at the professor's treatment, and the exulting hopes of his unconscious friend, he had sworn to himself, that the first involuntary token of regard from the young lady towards one or the other, should decide him whether to win name and position for her sake, or to carry his slighted passion to the utmost parts of the earth, and never again see her face.

'Ethel,' he said, stopping short, 'never threaten Providence – above all, never keep the threat.'

Ethel scarcely durst speak, in her anxiety to know what cast the die; though with all Dr Spencer's charms, she could not but pity the delusion that could have made him hope to be preferred to her father – above all, by her mother. Nor could she clearly understand from him *what* had dispelled his hopes. Something it was that took place at the pic-nic on Arthur's Seat, of which she had previously heard as a period of untold bliss. That something, still left in vague mystery, had sealed the fate of the two friends.

'And so,' said Dr Spencer, 'I took the first foreign appointment that offered. And my poor father, who had spent his utmost on me, and had been disappointed in all his sons, was most of all disappointed in me. I held myself bound to abide by my rash vow; loathed tame English life without her, and I left him to neglect in his age.'

'You could not have known or expected!' exclaimed Ethel.

'What right had I to expect anything else? It was only myself that I thought of. I pacified him by talk of travelling, and extending my experience, and silenced my conscience by intending to return when ordinary life should have become tolerable to me – a time that never has come. At last, in the height of that pestilential season in India, came a letter, warning me that my brother's widow had got the mastery over my poor father, and was cruelly abusing it, so that only my return could deliver him. It was when hundreds were perishing, and I the only medical man near; when to have left my post would have been both disgraceful and murderous. Then I was laid low myself; and while I was conquering the effects of cholera, came tidings that made it nothing to me whether they or I conquered. This,' and he touched one of his white curling locks, 'was not done by mere bodily exertion or ailment.'

'You would have been too late any way,' said Ethel.

'No, not if I had gone immediately. I might have got him out of that woman's hands, and made his life happy for years. There was the sting, but the crime had been long before. You know the rest. I had no health to remain, no heart to come home; and then came vagrancy indeed. I drifted wherever restlessness or impulse took me, till all my working years were over, and till the day when the sight of your father's wedding-ring showed me that I should not break my mad word by accepting the only welcome that any creature gave me.'

'And, oh! surely you have been comforted by him?'

'Comforted! Cut to the heart would be truer. One moment, I could only look at him as having borne off my treasure to destroy it; but then there rose on me his loving, patient, heart-broken humility and cheerfulness; and I saw such a character, such a course, as showed me how much better he had deserved her, and filled me with shame at having ever less esteemed him. And through all, there was the same dear Dick May, that never, since the day we first met at the pump in the school court, had I been able to help loving with all my heart – the only being that was glad to see me again. When he begged me to stay and watch over your sister, what could I do but remain while she lived?'

'So he bound you down! Oh, you know how we thank you! no, you can't, nor what you have been to him, and to all of us, through the worst of our sad days. And though it was a sacrifice, I do not think it was bad for you.'

'No, Ethel. When you implored me to give up my Crimean notion, to spare your father pain, I did feel for once that you at least thought me of value to some one.'

'I cannot bear you to speak so,' cried Ethel. 'You to talk of having been of no use!'

'No honest man of principle and education can be utterly useless; but when, three days ago, I recollected that it was my sixtieth birthday, I looked back, and saw nothing but desultory broken efforts, and restless changes. Your father told me, when I thought him unaware of the meaning of his words, that if I had missed many joys, I had missed many sorrows; but I had taken the way to make my one sorrow a greater burden than his many.'

'But you do not grieve for my mother still?' said Ethel anxiously. 'Even his grief is a grave joy to him now; and one is always told that such things, as it was with you, are but a very small part of a man's life.'

'I am not one of the five hundred men, whom any one of five hundred women might have equally pleased,' said Dr Spencer; 'but it is so far true, that the positive pain and envy wore out, and would not have interfered with my after life, but for my own folly. No, Ethel; it was not the loss of her that embittered and threw away my existence; it was my own rash vow, and its headstrong fulfilment, which has left me no right to your father's peaceful spirit.'

'How little we guessed!' said Ethel. 'So cheerful and ready as you always are.'

'I never trouble others,' he said abruptly. 'Neither man nor woman ever heard a word of all this; and you would not have heard it now, but for that sea; and you have got your mother's voice, and some of her ways, since you have grown older and more sedate.'

'Oh, I am so glad!' said Ethel, who had been led to view her likeness to her father as natural, that to her mother as acquired.

Those were the last words of the conversation; but Ethel leaning from her window to listen to the splash of the waves, suspected that the slowly moving meteor she beheld, denoted that a cigar was soothing the emotions excited by their dialogue. She mused long over that revelation of the motives of the life that had always been noble and generous, in the midst of much that was eccentric and wayward; and constantly the beat of the waves repeated to her the half-comprehended words, 'Never threaten Providence.'

After superintending Aubrey's first bath, and duly installing the vice-M.D. and her charges, Dr Spencer departed; and Ethel was launched on an unknown ocean, as pilot to an untried crew. She had been told to regard Leonard's bashfulness as a rare grace; but it was very inconvenient to have the boy wretchedly drooping, and owning nothing amiss, apparently unacquainted with any English words, except 'Thank you' and 'No, thank you.' Indeed, she doubted whether the shyness were genuine, for stories were afloat of behaviour at Stoneborough parties, which savoured of audacity; and she vainly consulted Aubrey whether the cause of his discomfiture were her age or her youth, her tutorship or her plain face. Even Aubrey could not elicit any like or dislike, wish or complaint; and shrugging up his shoulders, decided that it was of no use to bother about it; Leonard would come to his senses in time. He was passive when taken out walking, submissive when planted on a three-cornered camp-stool that expanded from a gouty walking-stick, but seemed so inadequately perched, and made so forlorn a spectacle, that they were forced to put him in-doors out of the glare of sea and sky, and hoping that he would condescend to the sofa when Ethel was out of sight.

Punctilio broke down the next morning; and in the midst of breakfast, he was forced to lie down, and allow Ethel to bathe his face with vinegar and water; while she repented of the 'make-the-best-of-it' letter of the yesterday, and sent Aubrey out on a secret commission of inquiry about medical men, in case of need. Aubrey was perfectly well, and in such a state of desultory enjoyment and sea-side active idleness, that he was quite off her mind, only enlivening her morning of nursing by his exits and entrances, to tell of fresh discoveries, or incidents wonderful to the inland mind.

After dinner, which had driven Leonard to lie on his bed, Aubrey persuaded his sister to come to see his greatest prize; a quaint old local naturalist, a seafaring man, with a cottage crammed with pans of live wonders of the deep in water, and shelves of extinct ones, 'done up in stane pies,' not a creature, by sea or land, that had haunted Coombe for a few million of ages, seemed to have escaped him. Such sea-side sojourns as the present, are the prime moments for coquetries with the lighter branches of natural science; and the brother and sister had agreed to avail themselves of the geological facilities of their position, the fascinations of Hugh Miller's autobiography having entirely gained them during Aubrey's convalescence. Ethel tore herself away from the discussion of localities with the old man, who was guide as well as philosopher, boatman as well as naturalist, and returned to her patient, whom she found less feverish, though sadly low and languid.

'I wish I knew what to do for you,' she said, sitting down by him. 'What would your sister do for you?'

'Nothing,' he wearily said; 'I mean, a great deal too much.'

The tone so recalled Norman's dejected hopelessness, that she could not help tenderly laying her cool hands on the hot brow, and saying, 'Yes, I know how little one can do as a sister – and the mockery it is to think *that one place* can ever be taken!'

The brown eyes looked at her with moist earnestness that she could hardly bear, but closed with a look of relief and soothing, as she held her hand on his forehead. Presently, however, he said, 'Don't let me keep you in.'

'I have been out, thank you. I am so glad to try to do anything for you.'

'Thank you. What o'clock is it, please? Ah, then I ought to take that draught! I forgot it in the morning.'

He permitted her to fetch it and pour it out; but as she recognised a powerful tonic, she exclaimed, 'Is this what you are taking? May it not make you feverish?'

'No doubt it does,' he said, lying down again; 'it was only Henry——'

'What! did not my father know of it?'

'Of course he does not; as it seems to be poison.'

'Not exactly that,' said Ethel; 'but I was surprised for it was talked of for Aubrey; but they said it wanted watching.'

'Just like Henry,' observed Leonard.

'Well,' said Ethel, repressing her indignation, 'I am glad, at least, to find a possible cause for your bad night. We shall see you refreshed to-morrow, and not wishing yourself at home.'

'Don't think that I wish that. Home is gone for ever.'

'Home may be gone higher – up to the real Home,' said Ethel, blushing with the effort at the hint, and coming down to earthlier consolations; 'but even the fragments will grow into home again here, and you will feel very differently.'

Leonard did not answer; but after a pause said, 'Miss May, is not it a horrid pity girls should go to school?'

'I am no judge, Leonard.'

'You see,' said the boy, 'after the little girls were born, my mother had no time for Ave, and sent her to Brighton, and there she begged to stay on one half after another, learning all sorts of things; but only coming home for short holidays, like company, for us to wonder at her and show her about, thinking herself ever so much in advance of my poor mother; and now she knows just nothing at all of her!'

'You cannot tell, Leonard, and I am sure she has been devoted to you.'

'If she had stayed at home like you, she might have known how to let one alone. Oh, you can't think what peace it was yesterday!'

'Was it peace? I feared it was desertion.'

'It is much better to be by oneself, than always worried. To have them always at me to get up my spirits, when the house is miserable——'

'Ah,' said Ethel, 'I remember your mother rejoicing that she had not to send you from home, and saying you were always so kind and gentle to her.'

'Did she?' cried the boy eagerly. 'Oh, but she forgot——' and he hid his face, the features working with anguish.

'So pleased and proud she used to look, walking with you on Saturday afternoons.'

'Those Saturdays! They were the only walks she ever would take; but she would always come with me.'

More followed in the same strain; and Ethel began to gather more distinct impressions of the Ward family. She saw that her present charge was warm and sound-hearted, and that the strength of his affections had been chiefly absorbed by the homely housewifely mother, comparatively little esteemed by the modernized brother and sister. Of the loss of his father he seemed to think less; it seemed, indeed, rather to reconcile him to that of his mother, by the grief it spared her; and it confirmed Ethel's notion, that Mr Ward, a busy and dull man, paid no great attention to his children between the plaything period and that of full development. The mother was the home; and Averil, though Leonard showed both love for and pride in her, had hitherto been a poor substitute; while as to Henry, there was something in each mention of him which gave Ethel an undefined dread of the future of the young household, and a doubt of the result of her father's kind schemes of patronage.

At any rate, this conversation had the happy effect of banishing constraint, and satisfying Ethel that the let-alone system was kindness, not neglect. She was at ease in discussing fossils, though he contributed no word, and she let him sleep or wake as he best liked; whilst Aubrey read to her the 'Cruise of the Betsey.'

Henry's prescription was sent to invigorate the fishes, when its cessation was found to be followed by the recovery of sleep and appetite; and in the cool of the evening, by a disposition to stroll on the beach, and lie under the lee of a rock upon a railway rug, which Ethel had substituted for the 'three-legged delusion.'

There he was left, while his companions went fossil-hunting, and stayed so long as to excite their compunction, and quicken their steps when they at length detached themselves from the enticing blue lias.

'What has he got there?' cried Aubrey. 'Hello, old fellow! have you fallen a prey to a black cat?'

'Cat!' returned Leonard indignantly; 'don't you see it is the jolliest little dog in the world?'

'You call that a dog?' said the other boy with redoubled contempt; 'it is just big enough for little Margaret's Noah's Ark!'

'It really is a beauty!' said Ethel. 'I have known one of Flora's guests bring a bigger one in her muff.'

'It is the most sensible little brute,' added Leonard. 'See; beg, my man, beg!'

And the beauteous little black-coated King Charles erected itself on its hind legs, displaying its rich ruddy tan waistcoat and sleeves, and beseeching with its black diamond eyes for the biscuit, dropped and caught in mid-air. It was the first time Leonard had looked bright.

'So you expect us to sanction your private dog stealing?' said Aubrey.

'I have been watching for his mistress to come back,' said Leonard; 'but she must have passed an hour ago; and she does not deserve to have him, for she never looked back for him; and he had run up to me, frisking and making much of me, as if he had found an old friend.'

'Perhaps it will run home when we move.'

No such thing; it trotted close at Leonard's heels, and entered the house with them. Barbara was consulted, and on Leonard's deposition that the dog's mistress was in deep mourning, opined that she could be no other than the widow of an officer, who during his lingering illness had been often laid upon the beach, and had there played with his little dogs. This one, evidently very young, had probably, in the confusion of its puppy memory, taken the invalid for its lost master.

'Stupid little thing,' said Aubrey; 'just like an under-sized lady's toy.'

'It knows its friends. These little things have twice the sense of overgrown dogs as big and as stupid as jackasses.'

A retort from Leonard was welcome in Ethel's ears, and she quite developed his conversational powers, in an argument on the sagacity of all canine varieties. It was too late to send the little animal home; and he fondled and played with it till bedtime, when he lodged it in his own room; and the attachment was so strong, that it was with a deep sigh, that at breakfast he accepted Aubrey's offer of conveying it home.

'There she is!' he exclaimed in the midst, gazing from the window.

'And see the perfection of the animal!' added Aubrey, pointing to a broad-backed waddling caricature of the little black fairy.

'Restitution must be made, little as she deserves you, you little jewel,' said Leonard, picking up the object of his admiration. 'I'll take you out.'

'No, no; I am not so infectious,' said Ethel, tying on her hat; 'I had better do it.'

And after Leonard's parting embrace to his favourite, she received it;

and quickly overtaking the pensive steps of the lady, arrested her progress with, 'I beg your pardon, but I think this is your dog.'

'Poor little Mab!' as the dog struggled to get to her, and danced gladly round her. 'I missed her last night, and was coming to look for her.'

'She joined one of our party,' said Ethel; 'and he was not strong enough to follow you. Indeed, he has had scarlet fever, so perhaps it was better not. But he has taken great care of the little dog, and hopes it is not the worse.'

'Thank you. I wish poor Mab may always meet such kind friends,' said the lady sadly.

'She secured her welcome,' said Ethel. 'We were very grateful to her, for it was the first thing that has seemed to interest him since his illness; and he has just lost both his parents.'

'Ah! Thank you.'

Ethel wondered at herself for having been so communicative; but the sweet sad face and look of interest had drawn her words out; and on her return she made such a touching history of the adventure, that Leonard listened earnestly, and Aubrey looked subdued.

When they went out Leonard refused to spread his rug in that only bed of pulverized shingle; and Ethel respected his avoidance of it as delicacy to her whose husband had no doubt often occupied that spot.

'He is a thorough gentleman,' said she, as she walked away with Aubrey.

'He might be an Eton fellow,' was the significant reply.

'I wonder what made him so?' said Ethel musingly.

'Looking at Tom,' returned Aubrey, not in jest.

'Even with that advantage, I don't quite see where he learnt that refined consideration.'

'Pshaw, Ethel! The light of nature would show that to any one but a stupex.'

Ethel was not sorry that such were Aubrey's views of courtesy; but all thought of that subject was soon lost in the pursuit of ammonites.

'I wonder what Leonard will have picked up now?' they speculated, as they turned homewards with their weighty baskets; but what was their amazement, when Leonard waved his hand, pointing to the little black dog again at his feet?

'She is mine!' he exclaimed, 'my own! Mrs Gisborne has given her to me; and she is to be the happiest little mite going!'

'Given!'

'Yes. She came as soon as you were gone, and sat by me, and talked for an hour, but she goes to-morrow to live with an old hag of an aunt.'

'Really, you seem to have been on confidential terms.'

'I mean that she must be a nuisance, because she doesn't like dogs; so that Mrs Gisborne can only take the old one, which she could never part with. So she wanted to give Mab to some one who would be kind to her; and she has come to the right shop; hasn't she, my queen?'

'I thought she almost wished it this morning,' said Ethel, 'when she heard how you and Mab had taken to each other: but it is a very choice present; the creature looks to me to be of a very fine sort.'

'Now Miss May, how could you know that?'

'Why, by her own deportment! Don't you know the aristocratic look that all high bred animals have – even bantams?'

Leonard looked as if this were the most convincing proof of Ethel's wisdom, and proceeded. 'Well, she is descended from a real King Charles, that Charles II brought from France, and gave to Mrs Jane Lane; and they have kept up the breed ever since.'

'So that Mab will have the longest pedigree in Stoneborough; and we must all respect her!' said Ethel, stroking the black head.

'I am only surprised at Leonard's forgetting his place,' said Aubrey. 'Walking before her majesty, indeed!'

'Oh, attendants do come first sometimes.'

'Then it should be backwards! I have a mind to try lying on the beach to-morrow, looking interesting, to see what will descend upon me!'

'A great yellow mongrel,' said Ethel, 'As always befalls imitators in the path of the hero.'

'What? You mean that it was all the work of Leonard's *beaux yeux?*'

Leonard gave a sort of growl, intimating that Aubrey was exciting his displeasure; and Ethel was glad to be at home, and break off the conversation; but in a few minutes Aubrey knocked at her door, and edging himself in, mysteriously said, 'Such fun! So it was your *beaux yeux*, not Leonard's, that made the conquest!'

'I suppose she was touched with what I said of poor Leonard's circumstances, and the pleasure the creature gave him.'

'That is as prosy as Mary, Ethel. At any rate, the woman told Leonard yours was the most irresistibly attractive countenance she ever saw, short of beauty; and that's not the best of it, for he is absolutely angry.'

'No wonder,' laughed Ethel.

'No, but it's about the beauty! He can't conceive a face more beautiful than yours.'

'Except the gargoyle on the church tower,' said Ethel, gaping into as complete a model of that worthy as flesh and blood could perpetrate.

'But he means it,' persisted Aubrey, fixing his eyes critically on his sister's features, but disturbed by the contortions into which she threw them. 'Now don't, don't. I never saw any fellow with a hundredth part of your gift for making faces,' he added, between the unwilling paroxysms of mirth at each fresh grimace; 'but I want to judge of you; and – oh!

that solemn one is worse than all; it is like Julius Caesar, if he had ever been photographed! – but really, when one comes to think about it, you are not so *very* ugly after all; and are much better looking than Flora, whom we were taught to believe in.'

'Poor Flora! You were no judge in her blooming days, before wear and tear came.'

'And made her like our Scotch grandfather.'

'But Blanche! your own Blanche, Aubrey! She might have extended Leonard's ideas of beauty.'

'Blanche has a pretty little visage of her own; but it's not so well worth looking at as yours,' said Aubrey. 'One has seen to the end of it at once; and it won't light up. Hers is just the May blossom; and yours the – the – I know – the orchis! I have read of a woman with an orchidaceous face!'

Teeth, tongue, lips, eyes, and nose, were at once made to serve in hitting off an indescribable likeness to an orchis blossom, which was rapturously applauded, till Ethel, relaxing the strain and permitting herself to laugh triumphantly at her own achievement, said 'There! I do pride myself on being of a high order of the grotesque.'

'It is not the grotesque that he means,' said Aubrey, 'he is very cracked indeed. He declares that when you came and sat by him the day before yesterday, you were perfectly lovely.'

'Oh then, I understand and it is no matter,' said Ethel.

CHAPTER V

'They stwons, they stwons, they stwons, they stwons.'

Scouring of the White Horse.

'So (wrote Ethel in her daily letter to her father), mine is at present a maternal mission to Leonard, and it is highly gratifying. I subscribe to all your praise of him, and repent of my ungracious murmurs at his society. You had the virtue, and I have the reward (the usual course of this world), for his revival is a very fresh and pleasant spectacle, burning hot with enthusiasm. Whatever we do, he overdoes, till I recollect how Wilkes said he had never been a Wilkite. Three days ago, a portentous looking ammonite attracted his attention; and whereas he started from the notion that earth was dirt, and stones were stones, the same all over the world, he has since so far outstripped his instructors, that as I write this he is drawing a plan of the strata, with the inhabitants dramatically arranged, Aubrey suggesting tragic scenes and uncomplimentary likenesses. His talent for drawing shows that Averil's was worth culture. If our geology alarm Richard, tell him that I think it safer to get it over young, and to face apparent discrepancies with revelation, rather than leave them to be discovered afterwards as if they had been timidly kept out of sight. And whether Hugh Miller's theory be right or wrong, his grand fervid language leaves the conviction that undoubting confidence in revelation consists with the clearest and most scientific mind.'

'*June 30th.* – I consider my boys as returned to their normal relations. I descended on them as they were sparring like lion clubs at play; Leonard desisted in confusion at my beholding such savage doings, but cool and easy, not having turned a hair; Aubrey, panting, done up, railing at him as first cousin to Hercules, all as a delicate boast to me of his friend's recovered strength. Aubrey's forte is certainly veneration. His first class of human beings is a large one, though quizzing is his ordinary form of adoration. For instance, he teazes Mab and her devoted slave some degrees more than the victim can bear, and then relieves his feelings in my room by asseverations that the friendship with Leonard will be on the May and Spencer pattern. The sea is the elixir of life to both; Leonard looks quite himself again, "*only more so*," and Aubrey has a glow never seen since his full moon visage waned, and not all tan, though we are on the high road to be coffee berries. Aubrey daily entertains me with heroic tales of diving and floating, till I tell them they will become enamoured of some 'lady of honour who lives in the sea,' grow fishes' tails and come home no more. And really, as the time wanes, I feel that such a coast is Elysium – above all, the boating. The lazy charm, the fresh purity of air, the sights and sounds, the soft summer wave when one holds one's hand over the side, the excitement of sea-weed catching, and the nonsense we all talk, are so delicious and such new sensations, (except the nonsense, which loses by your absence, O learned doctor!) that I fully perceive how pleasures untried cannot even be conceived. But ere the lotos food has entirely depraved my memory, I give you warning to come and fetch us home, now that the boys are in full repair. Come yourself, and be feasted on shrimps and mackerel, and take one sail to the mouth of the bay. I won't say who shall bring you; it would be fun to have Daisy, and Mary ought to have a holiday, but then Richard would take better care of you, and Tom would keep you in the best order. Could you not all come? only if you don't yourself, I won't promise not to take up with a merman.'

* * *

'*July 4th.* – Very well. If this is to make a strong man of Aubrey, *tant mieux*, and even home and Cocksmoor yearnings concern me little in this Castle of Indolence, so don't flatter yourself that I shall grumble at having had to take our house on again. Let us keep Leonard; we should both miss him extremely, and Aubrey would lose half the good without some one to swim, scramble, and fight with. Indeed, for the poor fellow's own sake, he should stay, for though he is physically as strong as a young megalosaur, and in the water or on the rocks all day, I don't think his head is come to application, nor his health to bearing depression; and I see he dreads the return, so that he had better stay away till school begins again.'

⋆ ⋆ ⋆

'*July 7th.* – Oh! you weak-minded folks! Now I know why you wanted to keep me away – that you might yield yourselves a prey to Flora. Paper and chintz forsooth! All I have to say is this, Miss Mary – as to my room, touch it if you dare! I leave papa to protect his own study, but for the rest, think, Mary, what your feelings would be if Harry were to come home, and not know what room he was in! If I am to choose between the patterns of chintz, I prefer the sea-weed variety, as in character with things in general, and with the present occasion; and as to the carpet, I hope that Flora, touched with our submission, will not send us anything distressing.'

⋆ ⋆ ⋆

'*July 17th.* – Can you send me any more of the New Zealand letters? I have copied out the whole provision I brought with me for the blank book, and by the way have inoculated Leonard with such a missionary fever as frightens me. To be sure, he is cut out for such work. He is intended for a clergyman (on grounds of gentility, I fear), and is too full of physical energy and enterprise to take readily to sober parochial life. His ardour is a gallant thing, and his home ties not binding; but it is not fair to take advantage of his present inflammable state of enthusiasm, and the little we have said has been taken up so fervently, that I have resolved on caution for the future. It is foolish to make so much of a boy's eagerness, especially when circumstances have brought him into an unnatural dreamy mood; and probably these aspirations will pass away with the sound of the waves, but they are pretty and endearing while they last in their force and sincerity.

"Just at the age 'twixt boy and youth,
When thought is speech, and speech is truth;"

and one's heart beats at the thought of what is possible to creatures of that age.'

* * *

'*July 21st.* – You, who taught us to love our Walter Scott next to our Christian Year, and who gave us half-crowns for rehearsing him when other children were learning the Robin's Petition, what think you of this poor boy Leonard knowing few of the novels and none of the poems? No wonder the taste of the day is grovelling lower and lower, when people do not begin with the pure high air of his world! To take up one of his works after any of our present school of fiction is like getting up a mountain side after a feverish drawing-room or an offensive street. If it were possible to know the right moment for a book to be really tasted – not thrust aside because crammed down – no, it would not be desirable, as I was going to say, we should only do double mischief. We are not sent into the world to mould people, but to let them mould themselves; and the internal elasticity will soon unmake all the shapes that just now seem to form under my fingers like clay.

'At any rate, the introduction of such a congenial spirit to Sir Walter was a real treat; Leonard has the very nature to be fired by him, and Aubrey being excessively scandalized at his ignorance, routed a cheap "Marmion" out of the little book-shop, and we beguiled a wet afternoon with it; Aubrey snatching it from me at all the critical passages, for fear I should not do them justice, and thundering out the battle, which stirred the other boy like a trumpet sound. Indeed, Leonard got Mab into a corner, and had a very bad cold in the head when De Wilton was re-knighted; and when "the hand of Douglas was his own," he jumped up and shouted out, "Well done, old fellow!" Then he took it to himself and read it all over again, introductions and all, and has raved ever since. I wish you could see Aubrey singing out some profane couplet of "midnight and not a nose," or some more horrible original parody, and then dodging apparently in the extremity of terror, just as Leonard furiously charges him.

'But you would have been struck with their discussions over it. Last night, at tea, they began upon the woeful result of the Wager of Battle, which seemed to oppress them as if it had really happened. Did I believe in it? Was I of the Lady Abbess's opinion, that

"Perchance some form was unobserved,
Perchance in prayer or faith he swerved?"

This from Aubrey, while Leonard rejoined that even if De Wilton had so done, it was still injustice that he should be so cruelly ruined, and Marmion's baseness succeed. It would be like a king wilfully giving wrong judgment because the right side failed in some respectful observance. He was sure such a thing could never be. Did I ever know of a real case where Heaven did not show the right? It was confusing and alarming, for both those boys sat staring at me as if I could answer them; and those wonderful searching eyes of Leonard's were fixed, as if his whole acquiescence in the dealings of Providence were going to depend on the reply, that could but be unsatisfactory. I could only try plunging deep. I said it was Job's difficulty, and it was a new light to Leonard that Job was about anything but patience. He has been reading the Book all this Sunday evening; and is not De Wilton a curious introduction to it? But Aubrey knew that I meant the bewilderment of having yet to discover that Divine Justice is longer sighted than human justice, and he cited the perplexities of high-minded heathen. Thence we came to the Christian certainty that "to do well and suffer for it is thank-worthy;" and that though no mortal man can be so innocent as to feel any infliction wholly unmerited and disproportioned, yet human injustice at its worst may be working for the sufferer an exceeding weight of glory, or preparing him for some high commission below. Was not Ralph de Wilton far nobler and purer as the poor palmer, than as Henry the Eighth's courtier? And if you could but have heard our sequel, arranging his orthodoxy, his Scripture reading, and his guardianship of distressed monks and nuns, you would have thought he had travelled to some purpose; only he would certainly have been burnt by one party, and beheaded by the other. On the whole, I think Leonard was a little comforted, and I cannot help hoping that the first apparently cruel wrong that comes before him may be the less terrible shock to his faith from his having been set to think out the question by "but half a robber and but half a knight."'

* * *

'*August 1st.* – Yesterday afternoon we three were in our private geological treasury. Leonard making a spread-eagle of himself in an impossible place on the cliff side, trying to disinter what hope, springing eternal in the human breast, pronounced to be the paddle of a saurian; Aubrey, climbing as high as he durst, directing operations and making discoveries; I, upon a ledge half way up, guarding Mab and poking in the *débris*, when one of the bridal pairs, with whom the place is infested, was seen questing about as if disposed to invade our premises. Aubrey, reconnoitring in high dudgeon, sarcastically observed that all red-haired men are so much alike, that he should have said yonder was Hec——. The rest ended in a view halloo from above and below, and three bounds to the beach, whereon I levelled my glass, and perceived that in very deed it was Mr and Mrs Ernescliffe who were hopping over the shingle. Descending, I was swung off the last rock in a huge embrace, and Hector's fiery moustache was scrubbing both my cheeks before my feet touched the ground, and Blanche with both arms round my waist. They were ready to devour us alive in their famine for a Stoneborough face; and as Flora and Mary are keeping home uninhabitable, found themselves obliged to rush away from Maplewood in the middle of their county welcomes for a little snatch of us, and to join us in vituperating the new furniture. If Mary could only hear Hector talk of a new sofa that he can't put his boots upon – he says it is bad enough at Maplewood, but that he *did* hope to be still comfortable at home. They have to get back to dine out to-morrow, but meantime the fun is more fast and furious than ever, and as soon as the tide serves, we are to fulfil our long-cherished desire of boating round to Lyme. I won't answer for the quantity of discretion added to our freight, but at least there is six feet more of valour, and Mrs Blanche for my chaperon. Bonnie Blanche is little changed by her four months' matrimony, and only looks prettier and more stylish, but she is painfully meek and younger-sisterish, asking my leave instead of her husband's, and distressed at her smartness in her pretty shady hat and undyed silk, because I was in trim for lias-grubbing. Her appearance ought to be an example to all the brides in the place with skirts in the water, and nothing on to keep off eyes, sun, or wind from their faces. I give Flora infinite credit for it. Blanche and Aubrey walk arm in arm in unceasing talk, and that good fellow, Hector, has included Leonard in the general fraternity. They are highly complimentary, saying they should have taken Aubrey for Harry, he is so much stouter and rosier, and that Leonard is hugely grown. Here come these three boys shouting that the boat is ready; I really think Hector is more boyish and noisy than ever.

"Five precious souls and all agog,
To dash through thick or thin."

I'll take the best care of them in my power. Good-bye.'

* * *

'*August 2nd*. – Safe back, without adventure, only a great deal of enjoyment, for which I am doubly thankful, as I almost fancied we were fey, one of the many presentiments that come to nothing, but perhaps do us rather good than harm for all that. I hope I did not show it in my letter, and communicate it to you. Even when safe landed, I could not but think of the Cobb and Louisa Musgrove, as I suppose every one does. We slept at the inn; drove with the Ernescliffes to the station this morning, and came back to this place an hour ago, after having been steeped in pleasure. I shall send the description of Lyme to Daisy to-morrow, having no time for it now, as I want an answer from you about our going to Maplewood. The 'married babies' are bent upon it, and Hector tries to demonstrate that it is the shortest way home, to which I can't agree; but as it may save another journey, and it will be nice to see them in their glory, I told them that if you could spare us, we would go from the 29th to the 4th of September. This will bring Leonard home four days before the end of the holidays, for he was been most warmly invited, Hector adopting him into the brotherhood of papa's pets. I am glad he is not left out; and Mary had better prove to Averil that he will be much happier for having no time at home before the half year begins. He still shrinks from the very name being brought before him. Let me know, if you please, whether this arrangement will suit, as I am to write to Blanche. Dear little woman, I hope Hector won't make a spoilt child of her, they are so very young, and their means seem so unlimited to them both, Hector wanting to make her and us presents of whatever we admired, and when she civilly praised Mab, vehemently declaring that she should have just such another if money could purchase, or if not, he would find a way. "Thank you, Hector dear, I had rather not," placidly responds Blanche, making his vehemence fall so flat, and Leonard's almost exulting alarm glide into such semi-mortification, that I could have laughed, though I remain in hopes that her "rather not" may always be as prudent, for I believe it is the only limit to Hector's gifts.

★ ★ ★

'*29th*, 8 A.M. – Farewell to the Coombe of Coombes. I write while waiting for the fly, and shall post this at Weymouth, where we are to be met. We have been so happy here, that I could be sentimental, if Leonard were not *tête-à-tête* with me, and on the verge of that predicament. "Never so happy in his life," quotha, "and never will be again – wonders when he shall see this white cliff again." But, happily, in tumbles Aubrey with the big claw of a crab, which he insists on Leonard's wearing next his heart as a souvenir of Mrs Gisborne; he is requited with an attempt to pinch his nose therewith, and——

'2.30 P.M. Weymouth. – The result was the upset of my ink, whereof you see the remains; and our last moments were spent in reparations and apologies. My two squires are in different plight from what they were ten weeks ago, racing up hills that if then half killed them to come down, and lingering wistfully on the top for last glimpses of our bay. I am overwhelmed with their courtesies, and though each is lugging about twenty pounds weight of stones, and Mab besides in Leonard's pocket, I am seldom allowed to carry my own travelling bag. Hector has been walking us about while his horses are resting after their twenty miles, but we think the parade and pier soon seen, and are tantalized by having no time for Portland Island, only contenting ourselves with an inspection of shop fossils, which in company with Hector, is a sort of land of the "Three Wishes," or worse; for on my chancing to praise a beautiful lump of Purbeck stone, stuck as full of *paludinoe* as a pudding with plums, but as big as my head and much heavier, he brought out his purse at once; and when I told him he must either enchant it on to my nose, or give me a negro slave as a means of transport, Leonard so earnestly volunteered to be the bearer, that I was thankful for my old rule against collecting curiosities that I do not find and carry myself.

* * *

'*August 30th*, Maplewood. – I wonder whether these good children *can* be happier, unless it may be when they receive you! How much they do make of us! and what a goodly sight at their own table they are! They are capable in themselves of making any place charming, though the man must have been enterprising who sat down five-and-twenty years ago to reclaim this park from irreclaimable down. I asked where were the maples? and where was the wood? and was shown five stunted ones in a cage to defend them from the sheep, the only things that thrive here, except little white snails, with purple lines round their shells. "There now, isn't it awfully bleak?" says Hector, with a certain comical exultation. "How was a man ever to live here without her?" And the best of it is, that Blanche thinks it beautiful – delicious free air, open space, view over five counties, &c. Inside, one traces Flora's presiding genius, Hector would never have made the concern so perfect without her help; and Blanche is no child in her own house, but is older and more at home than Hector, so that one would take her for the heiress, making him welcome and at ease. Not that it is like the Grange, Blanche is furious if I remark any little unconscious imitation or similarity – "As if we could be like Flora and George indeed!" Nor will they. If Blanche rules, it will be unawares to herself. And where Hector is, there will always be a genial house, overflowing with good humour and good nature. He has actually kept the 1st of September clear of shooting parties that he may take these two boys out, and give them a thorough day's sport in his turnip fields. "License? Nonsense, he thought of that before, and now Aubrey may get some shooting out of George Rivers." After such good nature my mouth is shut, though, *ay di me*, all the world and his wife are coming here on Monday evening, and unless I borrow of Blanche, Mrs Ernescliffe's sister will "look like ane scrub."'

* * *

'*September 2nd.* – Train at Stoneborough, 6.30. That's the best news I have to give. Oh, it has been a weary while to be out of sight of you all, though it has been pleasant enough, and the finale is perfectly brilliant. Blanche, as lady of the house, is a sight to make a sister proud; she looks as if she were born to nothing else, and is a model of prettiness and elegance. Hector kept coming up to me at every opportunity to admire her. "Now, old Ethel, look at her! Doesn't she look like a picture? *I* chose that gown, you know;" then again after dinner, "Well, old Ethel, didn't it go off well? Did you ever see anything like her? There, just watch her among the old ladies. I can't think where she learnt it all, can you?" And it certainly was too perfect to have been learnt. It was not the oppression that poor dear Flora gives one by doing everything so well, as if she had perfectly balanced what was due to herself and everybody else; it was just Blanche, simple and ready, pleasing herself by doing what people liked, and seeing what they did like. It was particularly pretty to see how careful both she and Hector were not to put Leonard aside – indeed, they make more of him than of Aubrey, who is quite able to find his own level. Even his tender feelings as to Mab are respected, and Blanche always takes care to invite her to a safe seat on a fat scarlet cushion on the sofa (Mrs Ledwich's wedding present), when the footmen with the tea might be in danger of demolishing her. Leonard, and his fine eyes, and his dog, were rather in fashion yesterday evening. Blanche put out his Coombe sketches for a company trap, and people talked to him about them, and he was set to sing with Blanche, and then with some of the young ladies. He seemed to enjoy it, and his nice modest gentlemanlike manner told. The party was not at all amiss in itself. I had a very nice clerical neighbour, and it is a very different thing to see and hear Hector at the bottom of the table from having poor dear George there. But oh! only one dinner more before we see our own table again, and Tom at the bottom of it. Hurrah! I trust this is the last letter you will have for many a day, from

'Your loving and dutiful daughter,

'ETHELDRED MAY.'

CHAPTER VI

'The XII statute remember to observe
For all the paine thou hast for love and wo
All is too lite her mercie to deserve
Thou musten then thinke wher er thou ride or go
And mortale wounds suffre thou also
All for her sake, and thinke it well besette
Upon thy love, for it maie not be bette.'

Chaucer's Court of Love.

'Good-bye, Leonard,' said Ethel, as the two families, after mustering strong at the station, parted at the head of Minster Street; and as she felt the quivering lingering pressure of his hand, she added with a smile, 'Remember, any Saturday afternoon. And you will come for the books.'

Glad as she was to be anchored on her father's arm, and clustered round with rejoicing brothers and sisters, she could not be devoid of a shade of regret for the cessation of the intimate intercourse of the last nine weeks, and a certain desire for the continuance of the confidential terms that had arisen. The moment's pang was lost in the eager interchange of tidings too minute for correspondence, and in approval of the renovation of the drawing-room, which was so skilful that her first glance would have detected no alteration in the subdued tones of paper, carpet, and chintz, so complete was their loyalty to the spirit of perpetuity. Flora told no one of the pains that, among her many cares, she had spent upon those tints, not so much to gratify Ethel, as because her own wearied spirit craved the repose of home sameness, nor how she had finally sent to Paris for the paper that looked so quiet, but was so exquisitely finished, that the whole room had a new air of refinement.

The most notable novelty was a water-coloured sketch, a labour of love from the busy hands in New Zealand, which had stolen a few hours from their many tasks to send Dr May the presentment of his namesake grandson. Little Dickie stood before them, a true son of the humming-bird sprite, delicately limbed and featured, and with elastic springiness, visible even in the pencilled outline. The dancing dark eyes were all Meta's, though the sturdy clasp of the hands, and the curl that hung over the brow, brought back the reflection of Harry's baby days.

It would have been a charming picture, even if it had not been by Meta's pencil, and of Norman's child, and it chained Ethel for more than one interval of longing loving study.

Tom interrupted her in one of these contemplations. 'Poor Flora,' he said, with more feeling than he usually allowed to affect his voice, 'that picture is a hard trial to her. I caught her looking at it for full ten minutes, and at last she turned away with her eyes full of tears.'

'I do not wonder,' said Ethel. 'There is a certain likeness to that poor little Leonora, and I think Flora misses her more every year.'

'Such a child as Margaret is just the thing to cause the other to be missed.'

'What do you think of Margaret this time?' said Ethel, for Tom alone ever durst seriously touch on the undefined impression that all entertained of Flora's only child.

'If Flora were only silly about her,' said Tom, 'one might have some hope; but unluckily she is as judicious there as in everything else, and the child gets more deplorable every year. She has got the look of deformity, and yet she is not deformed; and the queer sullen ways of deficiency, but she has more wit than her father already, and more cunning.'

'As long as there is a mind to work on, one hopes,' said Ethel.

'I could stand her better if she were foolish!' exclaimed Tom, 'but I can't endure to see her come into the room to be courted by every one, and be as cross as she dares before her mother. Behind Flora's back, I don't know which she uses worst, her father or her grandfather. I came down upon little Miss at last for her treatment of the doctor, and neither he nor Rivers have forgiven me.'

'Poor child! I don't believe she has ever known a moment's thorough health or comfort! I always hope that with Flora's patience and management she may improve.'

'Pshaw, Ethel! she will always be a misfortune to herself and everybody else.'

'I have faith in good coming out of misfortunes.'

'Illustrated, I suppose, by ravings about *your* young Ward. Mary is crazy about his sister, and the doctor lunatic as to the brother, who will soon kick at him for his pains.'

'I own to thinking Leonard capable of great things.'

Tom made a grimace equal to what Ethel could do in that way, thrust his hands deep into his pockets, and philosophically observed, 'Behold the effects of patronage! Blind Cupid is nothing to him.'

Ethel let it pass, caring too much for Leonard to set him up as a mark for Tom's satire, which was as different from Aubrey's as quinine from orange peel, though properly used, it was a bracing tonic, such as she often found wholesome. A cynical younger brother is a most valuable possession to a woman who has taken a certain position in her own world.

Tom was a sterling character, highly and deeply principled, though not demonstrative, and showing his Scots descent. None of the brothers had been extravagant, but Tom, with the income of his lately achieved fellowship, performed feats of economy, such as attaining to the purchase of an ultra perfect microscope, and he was consistently industrious, so exactly measuring his own powers that to undertake was with him to succeed, and no one suffered anxiety on his account. As Dr Spencer said, he was as sure to fall on his legs as a sandy cat, and so nobody cared for him. At home he was sufficient to himself, properly behaved to his father, civil to Richard, unmerciful in ridicule, but merciful in dominion over the rest, except Ethel, whom he treated as an equal, able to retort in kind, reserving for her his most highly flavoured sallies, and his few and distant approaches to such confidence as showed her how little she knew him. His father esteemed but did not 'get on with' him, and his chief and devoted adherent was Aubrey, to whom he was always kind and helpful. In person Tom was tall and well-made, of intelligent face, of which his spectacles seemed a natural feature, well-moulded fine-grained hands, and dress the perfection of correctness, though the precision and dandyism had been pruned away.

Ethel would have preferred that Leonard and Averil should not have walked in on the Saturday after her return, just when Tom had spread his microscope apparatus over the table, and claimed Mary's assistance in setting up objects; and she avoided his eye when Mary and Averil did what he poetically called rushing into each other's arms, whilst she bestowed her greetings on Leonard and Mab.

'Then she may come in?' said Leonard. 'Henry has banished her from the drawing-room, and we had much ado to get her allowed even in the school-room.'

'It is so tiresome,' said his sister, 'just one of Henry's fancies.'

Ethel, thinking this disloyal, remarked that those who disliked dogs in the house could not bear them, and did not wonder that Tom muttered 'Original.'

'But such a little darling as this!' cried Averil, 'and after Mrs Ernescliffe had been so kind. Mary, you must see how clever she is. Leonard is teaching her to play on the piano.'

'I congratulate you,' quietly said Tom; and somehow Ethel felt that those three words were a satire on her 'capable of great things;' while Leonard drew up, and Averil coloured, deferring the exhibition of Mab's accomplishments till "another time," evidently meaning out of Tom's presence.

'Aubrey is gone to the Grange with papa,' Ethel said, glad to lead away from Mab.

'He told me he was going,' said Leonard, 'but he said *you* would be at home.'

Ethel knew that the intonation of that *you* had curled Tom's lip with mischief, and dreading that Leonard should discover and resent his mood, she said, 'We think one of your sea eggs has got among ours; will you come to the school-room and see?'

And leaving Tom to tease and be bored by the young ladies, she led the way to the school-room, where Aubrey's fossils, each in its private twist of paper, lay in confusion on the floor, whence they were in course of being transferred to the shelf of a cupboard.

Leonard looked at the disorder with astonished admiration.

'Yes,' said Ethel, 'it is a great mess, but they are to have a regular cabinet, when Richard has time, or Aubrey has money, too equally unlikely chances.'

'How much does a cabinet cost?'

'Jones would make a plain deal one for about five-and-twenty shillings.'

'I can't unpack mine properly,' said Leonard disconsolately. 'Ave is going to make a place for them, but Henry votes them rubbish.'

'They are dreadful rubbish,' said Ethel. 'It goes against my conscience to guard them from the housemaid, and if my sister Flora came in here, I should be annihilated.'

'Of course one expects that in *women*.'

'Oh, Richard would be as much distracted! It is a provision of Nature that there should be some tidy ones, or what would the world come to?'

'It would be a great deal less of a bore.'

'Not at all; we should stifle ourselves at last if we had our own way. Never mind, Leonard, we make them go through quite as much as they make us.'

'I am sure I hope so.'

'No, no, Leonard,' she said, becoming less playful, 'we must not do it on purpose. Even unconsciously, we plague the spirits of order quite enough, and they have the right on their side after all.'

'I think a lady is the person to say what one may do or not in the drawing-room; don't you?' said Leonard.

'That depends.'

'And you let your brother spread his things all over yours?'

'So I do; but I would not if papa minded it, or even if this were Richard's house, and he did not like it. Don't begin with worries about trifles, pray, Leonard.'

'It is not *I* that care about trifles,' returned the boy. 'How was one to reckon on a man setting up a monomania about dogs' paws in the hall?'

'I have feared we were rather foolish; I ought to have reminded you to ask whether Mab would be welcome.'

'I was not going to ask leave, I have no one whose leave to ask,' said Leonard, in tones at first proud, then sad.

'That's a bad beginning,' returned Ethel. 'As master of the house, your brother has a right to your compliance, and if you do not all give way to each other, you will have nothing but dissension and misery.'

'*All to each other*; yes, that is fair.'

'He must have given way to you in letting you keep the dog at all in the house,' said Ethel. 'It is a real instance of kindness, and you are bound to let her be as little in his way as possible.'

'He does mean well, I suppose,' said Leonard; 'but he is an awful bother, and poor Ave gets the worst of it. One has no patience with finikin ways in a man.'

'There's no telling how much I owe to my finikin brother Richard,' said Ethel; 'and if you teach Ave to be loyal to the head of your family, you will do her as much good as you will do harm by chafing against his ordinances.'

'Don't you hate such nonsense, Miss May?'

'I can't love order as much as I honour it. Set tastes aside. The point is, that if you are to hold together Leonard, it must be my bearing and forbearing, and above all, to your elder brother.'

'Well, it is a blessing that I shall be in school on Monday.'

'So it is,' said Ethel; 'but, barring these fidgets, Leonard, tell me,' and she looked kindly at him, 'how is it at home? Better than you expected, I hope.'

'Blank enough,' said Leonard; 'I didn't think I should have minded the sound of the surgery door so much.'

'You will have Sunday to help you.'

'Yes, Ave and I have been down to the churchyard; Ave *does* care, poor girl. She knows better what it is now, and she was glad to have me to talk to again, though Miss Mary has been so kind to her.'

'Oh, nobody can be so much to her as you.'

'Poor Ave!' said Leonard tenderly. 'And look here, this is my father's watch, and she made me this chain of my mother's hair. And they have given me a photograph of my mother's picture; Henry had it done long ago, but thought it would upset me to give it before I went away. If he could but have guessed how I lay and wished for one!'

'Those are the things one never can guess, even when one would give worlds to do so.'

'You – O Miss May, you always know the thing that is comfortable.'

'Well,' said Ethel, 'what will be comfortable now is that you should be the man above being affronted by other people's nonsense – the only way to show we did not all spoil each other at Coombe. Now, here is Woodstock for you, and tell me if this be not your *Cidaris*. Oh, and we have found out the name of your funny spiked shell.'

Ten minutes of palaeontology ensued; and she was leading the way back to the drawing-room, when he exclaimed, 'Have you heard about the match, Miss May?'

'Match? Oh, the cricket match?'

'Stoneborough against All England, on St Matthew's Day, so I shall have got my hand in.'

'All England, meaning every one that can be scraped up that is not Stoneborough,' returned Ethel. 'George Larkins has been over here canvassing Tom and Aubrey. But you can't be going to play, Leonard; papa does not half like it for Aubrey.'

'Perhaps not for Aubrey,' said Leonard; 'but I am as well as ever, and luckily they can't make up a decent eleven without me. You will come and see us, Miss May? I'll find you the jolliest place between the old lime and the cloister door.'

'As if I had not known the meads ages before your time!' said Ethel.

'I thought you never came to the matches?'

'Ah! you don't remember my brothers' Stoneborough days, when Norman was cricket mad, and Harry after him, and my father was the best cricketer in Stoneborough till his accident.'

'Yes, Dr May always comes to see the matches,' said Leonard. 'You will, won't you now, Miss May? I didn't think you knew anything about cricket, but it will be all the better now.'

Ethel laughed, and half promised.

Cocksmoor existed without Ethel on that holiday; and indeed she was self-reproachful, though pleased, at finding her presence so great a treat to her father. Leonard might do the honours of the lime-tree nook, but she spent but little time there, for Dr May made her walk about with him as he exchanged greetings with each and all, while Gertrude led Richard about at her will, and Mary consorted with the Ward girls. With no one on her mind, Ethel could give free attention to the smoothly shaven battle field, where within the grey walls shaded by the overhanging elms, the young champions were throwing all the ardour and even the chivalry of their nature into the contest.

The annual game had been delayed by the illness in the spring, and the school had lost several good players at the end of the half year; but on the other hand, the holidays being over, George Larkins had been unable to collect an eleven either in full practice or with public school training; and the veteran spectators were mourning the decay of cricket, and talking of past triumphs. The school had the first innings, which resulted in the discomfiture of Fielder, one of their crack champions, and with no great honour to any one except Folliot, the dux, and Leonard Ward, who both acquitted themselves so creditably, that it was allowed that if others had done as well, Stoneborough might have had a chance.

But when 'All England' went in, the game seemed to be more equally balanced. Aubrey May, in spite of devoted practice under Tom's instructions, was, from nervous eagerness, out almost as soon as in, and in his misery of shame and despair felt like the betrayer of his cause. But in due time, with the sun declining, and the score still low, Tom May came forward, as the last hope of 'All England,' lissom, active, and skilled, walking up to his wicket with the easy confidence of one not greatly caring, but willing to show the natives what play might be.

And his play *was* admirable; the fortunes of the day began to tremble in the balance; every one, spectators and all, were in a state of eager excitement; and Aubrey, out of tone and unable to watch for the crisis, fairly fled from the sight, rushed through the cloister door, and threw himself with his face down upon the grass, shivering with suspense. There he lay till a sudden burst of voices and cheers showed that the battle was over.

The result? He could not believe eyes or ears as he opened the door, to behold the triumphant gestures of Stoneborough, and the crest-fallen air of his own side, and heard the words, 'Folliot missed two chances of longleg – Ward – tremendous rush – caught him out – with only one run to tie.'

Dr May was shaking hands with Leonard in congratulation, not solely generous, for let his sons be where they would, Stoneborough triumphs were always the doctor's, and he was not devoid of gratitude to any one who *would* defeat Tom. Noting, however, the flitting colour, fluttering breath, and trembling limbs, that showed the effect of the day's fatigue and of the final exertion, he signed back the boys, and thrust Leonard within the cloister door, bidding Aubrey fetch his coat, and Ethel keep guard over him, and when he was rested and cooled, to take him home to the High Street, where his sisters would meet him.

'But – Sir – the – supper!' gasped Leonard, leaning against the door-post, unable to stand alone.

'I dare say. Keep him safe, Ethel.'

And the doctor shut the door, and offered himself to appease the lads who were clamouring for the hero of their cause; while Leonard sank back on the bench, past words or looks for some moments.

'You have redeemed your pennon with your last gasp,' said Ethel, half reproachfully.

'I was determined,' panted the boy. 'I don't know how I did it. I couldn't fail with you looking on. You did it by coming.'

Reply was spared by Aubrey's return, with the coat in one hand, and a glass of ale in the other. 'You are go to home with Ethel at once,' he pronounced with the utmost zest, 'that is, as soon as you are rested. My father says you must not think of the supper, unless you particularly wish to be in bed for a week; but we'll all drink your health, and I'll return thanks – the worst player for the best.'

This was the first time Aubrey had been considered in condition for such festivities, and the gratification of being superior to somebody might account for his glee in invaliding his friend.

Cricket suppers were no novelties to Leonard; and either this or his exhaustion must have made him resign himself to his fate, and walk back with Ethel as happily as at Coombe.

The sisters soon followed, and were detained to drink tea. The cricketers' mirth must have been fast and furious if it exceeded that at home, for the doctor thought himself bound to make up for the loss to Leonard, put forth all his powers of entertainment, and was comically confidential about 'these Etonians that think so much of themselves.'

Averil was lively and at ease, showing herself the pleasant well-informed girl whom Ethel had hitherto only taken on trust, and acting in a pretty motherly way towards the little sisters. She was more visibly triumphant than was Leonard, and had been much gratified by a request from the Bankside curate that she would entirely undertake the harmonium at the chapel. She had been playing on it during the absence of the schoolmaster, and with so much better effect than he could produce, that it had been agreed that he would be best in his place among the boys.

'Ah!' said the doctor, 'two things in one are apt to be like Aubrey's compromise between walking-stick and camp-stool – a little of neither.'

'I don't mean it to be a little of neither with me, Dr May,' said Averil. 'I shall have nothing to do with my choir on week-days, till I have sent these pupils of mine to bed.'

'Are you going to train the choir too?' asked Leonard.

'I must practise with them, or we shall not understand one another; besides, they have such a horrid set of tunes, Mr Scudamour gave me leave to change them. He is going to have hymnals, and get rid of Tate and Brady at once.'

'Ah! poor Nahum!' sighed the doctor with such a genuine sigh, that Averil turned round on him in amazement.

'Yes,' said Ethel, 'I'm the only one conservative enough to sympathize with you, papa.'

'But *does* any one approve of the New Version?' cried Averil, recovering from her speechless wonder.

'Don't come down on me,' said the doctor, holding up his hands. 'I know it all; but the singing psalms are the singing psalms to me – and I can't help my bad taste – I'm too old to change.'

'Oh! but, papa, you *do* like those beautiful hymns that we have now?' cried Gertrude.

'Oh! yes, yes, Gertrude, I acquiesce. They are a great improvement; but then, wasn't it a treat when I got over to Woodside Church the other day, and found them singing, "No change of times shall ever shock?"' and he began to hum it.

'That is the Sicilian Mariners' hymn,' said Averil. 'I can sing you that whenever you please.'

'Thank you; on condition you sing the old Tate and Brady, not your "O Sanctissima, O Purissima,"' said the doctor a little mischievously.

'Which is eldest, I wonder?' asked Ave, smiling, pleased to comply with any whim of his; though too young to understand the associations that entwine closely around all that has assisted or embodied devotion.

The music went from the sacred to the secular; and Ethel owned that the perfectly pronounced words and admirable taste made her singing very different from that which adorned most dinner parties. Dr May intensely enjoyed, and was between tears and bravos at the charge of the Six Hundred, when the two brothers entered, and stood silently listening.

That return brought a change. Aubrey was indeed open and bright, bursting out with eager communications the moment the song ceased, then turning round with winning apologies, and hopes that he was not interrupting; but Tom looked so stiff and polite as to chill every one, and Averil began to talk of the children's bed time.

The doctor and Aubrey pressed for another song so earnestly that she consented; but the spirit and animation were gone, and she had no sooner finished than she made a decided move to depart, and Dr May accompanied the party home.

'Is my father going to put that fellow to bed?' said Tom, yawning, as if injured by the delay of bedtime thus occasioned.

'Your courtesy does not equal his,' said Ethel.

'Nor ever will,' said Tom.

'Never,' said Ethel, so emphatically that she nettled him into adding:

'He is a standing warning against spoiling one's patients. I wouldn't have them and their whole tag-rag and bobtail about my house for something!'

'O Tom, for shame!' cried Mary, bursting out in the wrath he had intended to excite.

'Ask him which is tag, which rag, and which bobtail,' suggested Ethel.

'Mab, I suppose,' said Gertrude, happily closing the discussion, but it was re-animated by her father's arrival.

'That's a nice girl,' he said, 'very nice; but we must not have her too often in the evening, Mary, without Henry. It is not fair to break up people's home party.'

'Bobber than bobtail,' murmured Tom, with a gesture only meant for Ethel.

'Ave said he would be out till quite late, papa,' said Mary in self-defence.

'She ought to have been back before him,' said Dr May. 'He didn't seem best pleased to have found her away; and let me tell you, young woman, it is hard on a man who has been at work all day to come home and find a dark house and nobody to speak to.'

Mary looked melancholy at this approach to reproof, and Tom observed in an undertone,

'Never mind, Mary, it is only to give papa the opportunity of improving his pupil, while you exchange confidence with your bosom friend. I shall be gone in another month, and there will be nothing to prevent the perfect fusion of families.'

No one was sorry that the evening here came to an end.

'I hope,' said Dr May at the Sunday's dinner, 'that the cricket match has not done for that boy; I did not see him among the boys.'

'No,' said Mary, 'but he has met with some accident, and has the most terrible bruised face. Ave can't make out how he did it. Do you know, Aubrey?'

The doctor and his two sons burst out laughing.

'I thought,' said Ethel rather grieved, 'that those things had gone out of fashion.'

'So Ethel's protégé, or prodigy, which is it?' said Tom, 'is turning out a muscular Christian on her hands.'

'Is a muscular Christian one who has muscles, or one who trusts in muscles?' asked Ethel.

'Or a better cricketer than an Etonian?' added the doctor.

Tom and Aubrey returned demonstrations that Eton's glory was untarnished, and the defeat solely owing to 'such a set of sticks.'

'Aubrey,' said Ethel, in their first private moment, 'was this a fight in a good cause? for if so, I will come down with you and see him.'

Aubrey made a face of dissuasion, ending in a whistle.

'Do at least tell me it is nothing I should be sorry for,' she said anxiously.

He screwed his face into an intended likeness of Ethel's imitation of an orchis, winked one eye, and looked comical.

'I see it can't be really bad,' said Ethel, 'so I will rest on your assurance, and ask no indiscreet questions.'

'You didn't see, then?' said Aubrey, aggrieved at the failure of his imitation. 'You don't remember the beauty he met at Coombe?'

'Beauty! None but Mab.'

'Well, they found it out and chaffed him. Fielder said he would cut out as good a face out of an old knob of apple wood, and the doctor in petticoats came up again, he got into one of his rages, and they had no end of a shindy, better than any, they say, since Lake and Benson fifteen years ago; but Ward was in too great a passion, or he would have done for Fielder long before old Hoxton was seen mooning that way. So you see, if any of the fellows should be about, it would never do for you to be seen going to bind up his wounds, but I can tell him you are much obliged, and all that.'

'Obliged, indeed!' said Ethel. 'What, for making me the laughing-stock of the school?'

'No, indeed,' cried Aubrey, distressed. 'He said not a word – they only found it out – because he found that seat for you, and papa sent him away with you. They only meant to poke fun, and it was his caring that made it come home to him. I wonder you don't like to find that such a fellow stood up for you.'

'I don't like to be made ridiculous.'

'Tom does not know it, and shall not,' eagerly interposed Aubrey.

'Thank you,' said she, with all her heart.

'Then don't be savage. You know he can't help it if he does think you so handsome, and it is very hard that you should be affronted with him, just when he can't see out of one of his eyes.'

'For that matter,' said Ethel, her voice trembling, 'one likes generosity in any sort of a cause; but as to this, the only way is to laugh at it.'

Aubrey thought this 'only way' hardly taken by the cachinnation with which she left him, for he was sure that her eyes were full of tears; and after mature consideration he decided that he should only get into a fresh scrape by letting Leonard know that she was aware of the combat and its motive.

'If I were ten years younger, this might be serious,' meditated Ethel. 'Happily, it is only a droll adventure for me in my old age, and I have heard say that a little raving for a grown-up woman is a wholesome sort of delusion at his time of life. So I need not worry about it, and it is pretty and touching while it lasts, good fellow!'

Ethel had, in fact, little occasion to worry herself; for all special manifestations of Leonard's devotion ceased. Whether it were that Tom with his grave satirical manner contrived to render the house disagreeable to both brother and sister, or whether Leonard's boyish bashfulness had taken alarm, and his admiration expended itself in the battle for her charms, there was no knowing. All that was certain was, that the Wards seldom appeared at Dr May's, although elsewhere Mary and Aubrey saw a great deal of their respective friends, and through both, Ethel heard from time to time of Leonard, chiefly as working hard at school, but finding that his illness had cost him not only the last half year's learning, but some memory and power of application. He was merging into the ordinary schoolboy – a very good thing for him no doubt – though less beautiful than those Coombe fancies. And what were they worth?

CHAPTER VII

'Little specks of daily trouble –
Petty grievance, petty strife –
Filling up with drops incessant
To the brim the cup of life.

Deeper import have these trifles
Than we think or care to know:
In the air a feather floating,
Tells from whence the breezes blow.'

Rev G. Monsell.

The first brightening of the orphaned house of Bankside had been in Leonard's return. The weeks of his absence had been very sore ones to Averil, while she commenced the round of duties that were a heavy burthen for one so young, and became, instead of the petted favourite, the responsible head of the house.

She was willing and glad to accept the care of her little sisters – docile bright children – who were pleased to return to the orderly habits so long interrupted, and were so intelligent, that her task of teaching was a pleasant one; and almost motherly love towards them grew up as she felt their dependence on her, and enjoyed their caresses.

With Henry she had less in common. He expected of her what she had not learnt, and was not willing to acquire. A man interfering in the woman's province meets little toleration; and Henry was extremely precise in his requirements of exact order, punctuality, and excellence, in all the arrangements of his house. While breaking her in to housekeeping, he made himself appear almost in the light of a task-master – and what was worse, of a despised task-master. Averil thought she could not respect a brother whose displeasure was manifested by petulance, not sternness, and who cared not only about his dinner, but about the tidy appearance of the drawing-room – nay, who called that tasty which she thought vulgar, made things stiff where she meant them to be easy and elegant, and prepared the place to be the butt of Tom May's satire.

Henry was not a companion to her. His intellect was lower, his education had not been of the same order, and he had not the manly force of character that makes up for everything in a woman's eyes. Where she had talents, he had pretensions – just enough to make his judgments both conceited and irritating; and where her deeper thoughts and higher aspirations were concerned, she met either a blank or a growing jealousy of the influence of the clergy and of the May family.

Yet Henry Ward was really a good brother, sacrificing much to his orphan sisters, and living a moral and religious life – such as gained for him much credit, and made Mrs Ledwich congratulate Averil on the great excellence and kindness of her incomparable brother.

Averil assented, and felt it a dreary thing to have an incomparable brother.

But when Leonard came home, the face of the house was changed. Now she had something to look forward to. Now there was something to hear that stirred her deeper feelings – some one who would understand and respond – some one to make common cause with. Little as she saw of the schoolboy, there was life in her day, for sympathy and comprehension had come home with him.

After all, there were recesses in Leonard's confidence to which Ave did not penetrate; but there was quite enough to be very happy upon, especially those visions that had been built on the Melanesian letters. They were not near enough to terrify her with the thought of separation, and she was sufficiently imbued with Mary May's sentiments to regard mission-work as the highest ambition. Leonard's strong will and manly disposition would have obtained her homage and affection, even without the lofty sentiments and the lesser graces that made the brother and sister thoroughly suited to one another; and the bond of union was unfortunately cemented by equal annoyance at Henry's peculiarities.

It certainly was rather hard on a young head of a family to have a younger brother his superior in every respect, and with an inseparable sister. That Henry had not found out Leonard's superiority was no reason that it should not gall him; and his self-assertions were apt to be extremely irritating. Even in the first flush of welcome, he had made it plain that he meant to be felt as master of the house, and to enforce those petty regulations of exact order that might be easily borne from a mother, or played with in a sister – would be obeyed grudgingly from a father, but could be intolerable in a brother.

The reception of Mab and the ammonites was but an earnest of similar ungracious acts on the one hand, and aggressions on the other, often unintentional. Averil did, indeed, smooth matters, but she shared Leonard's resentment; and outward submission was compensated by murmur and mockery in private.

Still the household worked on fairly; and Mrs Ledwich was heard to declare, with tears in her eyes, that it was beautiful to see such a happy family of love as those dear young Wards!

'The happy family in Trafalgar Square!' muttered Dr Spencer.

The confidence of the happy family was on this wise. When Leonard came home with his unpresentable face, he baffled all Ave's anxious questions; and she was only enlightened by Henry's lamentations, in his absence, over the hopelessness of a brother who was so low and vulgar as to box! Her defence being met by a sneer, she flew to tell Leonard of the calumny, and was laughed at for her innocence; but extorted that he had fought with a fellow that talked impudently of some of the Mays – cause fully sufficient in her eyes; nor did Henry utter any open reproof, though he contrived to exasperate his brother into fierce retort and angry gesture by an unnecessary injunction not to show that ungentlemanly face.

Full consciousness of the difficulties presented by the characters of the two brothers would have been far too oppressive; and perhaps it was better for Averil that she had it not, but had her own engrossing interests and employments drawing off her attention and enlivening her spirits. Her church music was her object in life – the dedication of the talent that had been cultivated at so much time and cost, and the greatest honour and enjoyment she could imagine; and she had full participation from Leonard, who had a hearty love for sacred music, readily threw himself into her plans, and offered voice and taste to assist her experiments. Nor had her elder brother any objection to her being thus brought forward: he was proud of her performance, and gratified with the compliments it elicited; and all went well till the new hymnals arrived, and books upon books, full of new tunes, anthems, and chants, were accumulating on the music-stand.

'What are you about there all the evening, not opening your lips?'

'Leonard is writing out his verses, and I am copying music.'

'I wonder you neither of you will remember that that table was never meant to be littered over with all sorts of rubbish!'

'I thought tables were to put things on,' returned Leonard coolly.

'Drawing-room tables were not made to be inked! That cover will be ruined in a day or two!'

'Very well – then we'll pay for it!' said Leonard, in the same aggravating tone.

'Here are newspapers spread between it and the ink,' said Averil, displaying them with an air of injured innocence that made Henry subside; but he presently exclaimed:

'Is that copying to go on all night? Can't you speak, nor play anything, to send one off to sleep?'

With a martyr look, yet a satirical glance, Averil opened the piano; and Henry settled himself in the master's armchair, as one about to enjoy well-earned rest and entertainment after a hard day's work.

'I say, what doleful drone have you there?'

'I am trying a new chant for the *Nunc Dimittis*.'

'Nothing but that day and night! Give us something worth hearing.'

'I thought you only wanted to go to sleep.'

'I don't want to dream myself into church, listening to Scudamour's proses: I've quite enough of that on Sunday.'

Ave began to play one of her school waltzes; and the touch of her fingers on the keys had so sharp-edged and petulant a tone, that Leonard smiled to himself as he ran his fingers through his hair over his books. Nor was it soothing to Henry, who, instead of going to sleep, began to survey the room, and get food for annoyance.

'I say,' said he, looking across at a little brass-barred book-case of ornamental volumes on the opposite cheffoniere, 'what book is out there?'

'Scott's Lay,' said Leonard; 'it is up in my room.'

'I told you, Ave, not to let the drawing-room books be carried about the house to be spoilt!' said Henry, who seldom reproved his brother direct, but generally through Ave.

'You'd better get some made of wood then,' said Leonard.

'Remember then, Ave, I say I will not have my books taken out, and left about over the house.'

Leonard dashed out of the room passionately, and presently came thundering down again, every step audible the whole way, and threw the book on the table, bringing in a whirlwind, and a flaring sloping candle dropping upon the precious cloth. Henry started up and pointed.

'I'm glad of it!' exclaimed Leonard; 'it will be a little amusement for you. Good night, Ave! I'm going to finish upstairs, since one can't read, write, or touch a book without your being rowed!'

He was gone, and Averil, though rather frightened, gave him infinite credit for keeping his temper; and perhaps he deserved it, considering the annoyance and the nature of the provocation; but she did not reflect how much might have been prevented by more forethought and less pre-occupation. She said not a word, but quietly returned to her copying, and when Henry came with paper and poker to remove the damage, she only shoved back her chair, and sat waiting, pen in hand, resigned and ironical.

'I declare,' grumbled Henry, as he examined the remaining amount of damage, 'these day-schools are a great inconvenience; there's no keeping a place fit to be seen with a great uncivilized lad always hanging about!'

'Leonard is considered particularly gentlemanlike,' said Ave, with lips compressed, to keep back something about old bachelors.

'Now, I should have thought a lady would have some regard to her own drawing-room, and object to slovenliness – elbows on table, feet everywhere!'

'Nothing is in worse taste than constraint,' said Ave from the corners of her mouth – 'at least for those that can trust their manners without it.'

'I tell you, Ave, you are spoiling the boy. He is more conceited than ever since the Mays noticed him.'

'Leonard conceited!'

'Yes; he is getting as stuck up as Tom May himself – your model, I believe!'

'I thought he was yours!'

'Mine?'

'Yes; you always seem to aim at a poor imitation of him.'

There was a blushing angry stammer in reply; and she suppressed her smile, but felt triumphant in having hit the mark. Unready at retort, he gathered himself up, and said: 'Well, Ave, I have only this to say, that if you choose to support that boy in his impertinences, there will be no bearing it; and I shall see what I shall do.'

Seeing what shall be done is a threat stimulating to some, but appalling to others; and Averil was of the latter class, with no desire for such a spectacle, be it what it might. She did not apologize for the trifle – possible ink, a spot of wax, a borrowed book, were far beneath an apology; but she made up her mind to humour Henry's follies magnanimously, and avoid collisions, like an admirable peace-maker. As soon as bed-time came, she repaired to Leonard's room; and Henry, as he went along the passage, heard the two young voices ringing with laughter! Her retort had been particularly delightful to Leonard. 'That's right, Ave! I'm glad you set him down, for I thought afterwards whether I ought not to have stood by you, only his way of pitching into me through you puts me into such a rage: I shall do something desperate some day!'

'Never mind it, Leonard; it does not hurt me; and if it did, I should like to bear a great deal for you.'

'That's all the wrong way,' said Leonard, smiling affectionately.

'No; men do and women suffer.'

'That's trite!' said Leonard, patting her fondly. 'I like you to *do* – as you call it – Miss May *does*, and every one that is worth anything. I say, Ave, when I go out to the islands, you are coming too?'

'Oh yes! I know I could do a great deal. If nothing else, I could sing; and they have a great aptitude for singing, Mary was telling me. But that reminds me I must finish copying the hymn for next Sunday; Henry hindered me, and I have six copies more to do.'

'I'll do some of them,' said Leonard. 'Let us go down now the coast is clear, if the fire is not out.'

They went down softly, Mab and all, nursed up the fire that Henry had raked out; and if Saturnalia could be held over the writing out of a hymn tune, they did it! At any rate, it had the charm of an assertion of independence; and to Averil it was something like a midnight meeting of persecuted Christians – to Leonard it was 'great fun.'

That evening was not a solitary specimen.

Averil and Leonard intended to obviate causes of offence; but they were young and heedless, and did not feel bound to obedience. A very little temptation made them forget or defy Henry's fancies; and Leonard was easily lashed into answers really unbecoming and violent, for which he could not bring himself to be sorry, when he thought over the petty interference and annoyance that had caused them.

These small tyrannies and frets made Averil the more devoted to the music, which was her rest, her delight, and not only exalted her above cares, but sanctioned her oblivion of them. The occupation grew upon her, never ending, still beginning, with fresh occasions for practice and new lessons, but though Bankside boys were willing to be taught, yet it was chiefly in hope of preferment as choristers at the Minster; and she soon found that a scholar no sooner proved his voice good for anything, than he went off to be trained for the choir on the foundation, which fed, clothed, and apprenticed its young singers. She found she must betake herself to an elder race if she wanted a reliable staff of voices; and some young men and women showing themselves willing, a practice, with Mr Scudamour to keep order, was organized for late evenings, twice in the week. This was rather much! Henry opposed at first, on the ground that the evening would be broken up; to which she answered that for such a purpose they ought to be willing to sacrifice a little domestic comfort; and when he muttered a petulant 'Pshaw,' looked at him in reproof for sacrilege. She was not going to be one of the womankind sitting up in a row till their lords and masters should be pleased to want them!

Next, he insisted that he would not have her going about the place after dark; but she was fortified by the curate's promise to escort her safely, and reduced him to a semi-imprecation which she again viewed as extremely wicked. The existence of that meek little helpless Mrs Scudamour, always shut up in a warm room with her delicate baby, cut off Henry from any other possible objection, and he was obliged to submit.

Leonard would gladly have been his sister's companion on her expeditions, but he must remain at home and prepare for the morrow's school-work, and endure the first hour of dreariness unenlivened by her smile and greeting, and, what was worse, without the scanty infusion of peace produced by her presence. Her rapid departure after dinner always discomposed Henry; and the usual vent for his ill-humour was either a murmur against the clergy and all their measures, or the discovery of some of Leonard's transgressions of his code. Fretted and irritable at the destruction of evening comfort, he in his turn teazed the fiery temper of his brother. If there were nothing worse, his grumbling remarks interrupted, and too often they were that sort of censure that is expressively called knagging. Leonard would reply angrily, and the flashes of his passion generally produced silence. Neither brother spoke to Averil of these evening interludes, which were becoming almost habitual; but they kept Leonard in a constant sore sense of injury, yet of uneasy conscience. He looked to the Randall scholarship as his best hope of leaving home and its torments, but his illness had thrown him back: he had not only lost the last quarter, but the acquirements of the one before it were obscured; and the vexations themselves so harassed and interrupted his evening studies, that he knew it was unreasonable to hope for it at the next examination, which, from various causes, was to come after the Christmas holidays; and it would be well if he could even succeed in the summer.

Innocent as the Mays were of the harmonium business, Henry included them in the annoyance it gave. It was the work of the curate – and was not Dr May one in everything with the clergy? had he not been instrumental in building the chapel? was it not the Mays and the clergy who had made Ave inconveniently religious and opinionative, to say nothing of Leonard? The whole town was priest-led and bigoted; and Dr May was the despot to whom all bowed down.

This was an opinion Henry would hardly have originated: it was the shaft of an abler man than he – no other than Harvey Anderson, who had lately become known to the world by a book proving King John to have been the most enlightened and patriotic of English sovereigns, enduring the Interdict on a pure principle of national independence, and devising Magna Charta from his own generous brain – in fact, presenting a magnificent and misunderstood anticipation of the most advanced theories of the nineteenth century. The book had made so much noise in the world, that the author had been induced to quit his college tutorship, and become editor of a popular magazine. He lived in London, but often came down to spend Sunday with his mother, and had begun to be looked on as rather the lion of the place. Henry took in his magazine, and courted his notice, often bringing him into Averil's way that she might hear her heroes treated with irony more effectual than home-made satire; but Ave was staunch. She hated the sight of Mr Anderson; never cut the leaves of his magazine; and if driven to sing to him, took as little pains as her musical nature would let her do. But the very strength of her dislike gave it an air of prejudice, and it was set down less to principle than to party spirit and May influence.

There was another cause for Henry's being soured. He was not of the nature to be filial with Dr May; and therefore gratitude oppressed, and patronage embittered him. The first months of warm feeling at an end, the old spirit of independence revived, and he avoided consulting the physician as much as possible. More than once his management of a case was not approved by Dr May; and the strong and hasty language, and the sharp reproofs that ensued, were not taken as the signs of the warm heart and friendly interest, but as the greatest offences – sullenly, but not the less bitterly endured.

Moreover, one of the Whitford surgeons had been called in by a few of the out-lying families who had hitherto been patients of the Wards; and worse than all, Mrs Rivers took her child up to London for three days in November, and it became known – through a chain of tongues – that it was for the enlargement of tonsils, on which Mr Ward had operated a year before.

'Old May was playing him false!' was Henry's cry. 'His professions were humbug! He would endure no one who did not submit to his dictation; and he would bring in a stranger to ruin them all!'

Little did Henry know of Dr May's near approach to untruth in denying that he had a house to let to the opposition surgeon – of his attestations to his daughter that young Ward was a skilful operator – or of his vexation when she professed herself ready to undergo anything for his pleasure, but said that little Margaret's health was another thing.

Yet even this might have been forgiven, but for that worst rub of all – Tom May's manners. His politeness was intense – most punctilious and condescending in form – and yet provoking beyond measure to persons who, like Henry and Averil, had not playfulness enough to detect with certainty whether they were being made game of or not, nor whether his smoothly-uttered compliments were not inuendos. Henry was certain of being despised, and naturally chafed against the prospect of the future connexion between the two medical men of the town; and though Tom was gone back to Cambridge, it was the rankling remembrance of his supercilious looks that, more than any present offence or independence of spirit, made the young surgeon kick against direction from the physician. Here, too, Averil was of the same mind. She had heard Tom May observe that his sister Gertrude would play quite well enough for a lady; for the mission of a lady's music was to put one to sleep at home, and cover conversation at a party; as to the rest – unprofessionals were a mistake!

After that, the civil speeches with which Tom would approach the piano only added insult to injury.

CHAPTER VIII

'Ne'er readier at alarm-bell's call,
Thy burghers rose to man thy wall,
Than now in danger shall be thine,
Thy dauntless voluntary line.'

Marmion.

'Drive fast, Will,' said Dr May, hastily stepping into his carriage in the early darkness of a December evening. 'Five already, and he is to be there by 5.25.'

'He' was no other than Harry May, and 'there' was the station. With the tidings of the terrible fight of Peiho had come a letter from a messmate of Harry's with an account of his serious wound in the chest, describing it as just short of immediately dangerous. Another letter had notified his amendment, and that he was invalided home, a few cheery words from Harry himself scrawled at the end showing that his power was far less than his good will: and after two months' waiting and suspense, a telegram had come from Plymouth, with the words, 'Stoneborough, 5.25.'

In ignorance as to the state of the traveller, and expecting to find him in a condition requiring great care and watching, Dr May had laid his injunctions on the eager family not to rush up to the station *en masse* to excite and overwhelm, but to leave the meeting there entirely to himself and his brougham. He had, therefore, been exceedingly annoyed that one of Henry Ward's pieces of self-assertion had delayed him unnecessarily at a consultation; and when at last he had escaped, he spent most of his journey with his body half out of window, hurrying Will Adams, and making noises of encouragement to the horse; or else in a strange tumult of sensation between hope and fear, pain and pleasure, suspense and thankfulness, the predominant feeling being vexation at not having provided against this contingency by sending Richard to the station.

After all the best efforts of the stout old chestnut, he and the train were simultaneously at the station, and the passengers were getting out on the opposite platform. The Doctor made a dash to cross in the rear of the train but was caught and held fast by a porter with the angry exclamation, 'She's backing, Sir:' and there he stood in an agony, feeling all Harry's blank disappointment, and the guilt of it besides, and straining his eyes through the narrow gaps between the blocks of carriages.

The train rushed on, and he was across the line the same instant, but the blank was his. Up and down the gas-lighted platform he looked in vain among the crowd, only his eye suddenly lit on a black case close to his feet, with the three letters M A Y; and the next moment a huge chest appeared out of the darkness, bearing the same letters, and lifted on a truck by the joint strength of a green porter, and a pair of broad blue shoulders. Too ill to come on – telegraph, mail train – rushed through the poor doctor's brain as he stepped forward as if to interrogate the chest. The blue shoulders turned, a ruddy sun-burnt face lighted up, and the inarticulate exclamation on either side was of the most intense relief and satisfaction.

'Where are the rest?' said Harry, holding his father's hand in no sick man's grasp.

'At home; I told them not to come up; I thought——'

'Well, we'll walk down together! I've got you all to myself. I thought you had missed my telegram. Hello, Will, how d'ye do? what, this thing to drive down in?'

'I thought you were an invalid, Harry,' said Dr May, with a laughing yet tearful ring in his agitated tone, as he packed himself and his son in.

'Ay! I wished I could have let you know sooner how well I had got over it,' said Harry, in the deep full voice of strong healthy manhood. 'I am afraid you have been very anxious.'

'We are used to it, my boy,' said the doctor huskily, stroking the great firm fingers that were lying lovingly on his knee; 'and if it always ends in this way, it ought to do us more good than harm.'

'It has not done harm, I hope,' said Harry, catching him up quick. 'Not to old Mary?'

'No, Mary works things off, good girl. I flatter myself you will find us all in high preservation.'

'All – all at home! That's right.'

'Yes, those infants from Maplewood and all. You are sure you are all right, Harry?'

'As sure as my own feelings can make me, and the surgeon of the *Dexter* to back them,' said Harry. 'I don't believe my lungs were touched after all, but you shall all sit upon me when you like – Tom and all. It was a greater escape than I looked for,' he added, in a lower voice. 'I did not think to have had another Christmas here.'

The silence lasted for the few moments till the carriage drew up behind the limes; the doors were thrown open, and the doctor shouted to the timid anxious figure that alone was allowed to appear in the hall, 'Come and lift him out, Mary.'

The drawing-room was a goodly sight that evening; and the doctor, as he sat leaning back in weary happiness, might be well satisfied with the bright garland that still clustered round his hearth, though the age of almost all forbade their old title of Daisies. The only one who still asserted her right to that name was perched on the sailor's knee, insisting on establishing that there was as much room for her there as there had been three years ago; though, as he had seated himself on a low foot-stool, her feet were sometimes on the ground, and moreover her throne was subject to sudden earthquakes, which made her, nothing loth, cling to his neck, draw his arm closer round her, and lean on his broad breast, proud that universal consent declared her his likeness in the family; and the two presenting a pleasant contrasting similarity – the open honest features, blue eyes, and smile, expressive of hearty good-will and simple happiness, were so entirely of the same mould in the plump, white-skinned, rosy-cheeked, golden-haired, girl, and in the large powerful bronzed ruddy sailor, with the thick mass of curls, at which Tom looked with hostility as fixed, though less declared, than that of his Eton days.

Those were the idle members upon the hearth-rug. On the sofa, with a small table to herself, and a tall embroidery frame before her, nearly hiding her slight person, sat Mrs Ernescliffe, her pretty head occasionally looking out over the top of her work to smile an answer, and her artistically arranged hair and the crispness of her white dress and broad blue ribbons marking that there was a step in life between her and her sisters; her husband sat beside her on the sofa, with a red volume in his hand, with 'Orders,' the only word visible above the fingers, one of which was keeping his place. Hector looked very happy and spirited, though his visage was not greatly ornamented by a moustache, sandier even than his hair, giving effect to every freckle on his honest face. A little behind was Mary, winding one of Blanche's silks over the back of a chair, and so often looking up to revel in the contemplation of Harry's face, that her skein was in a wild tangle, which she studiously concealed lest the sight should compel Richard to come and unravel it with those wonderful fingers of his.

Richard and Ethel were arranging the 'sick albums,' which they had constructed – one of cheap religious prints, with texts and hymns, to be lent in cases of lingering illness; the other, commonly called the 'profane,' of such scraps as might please a sick child, pictures from worn-out books or advertisements, which Ethel was colouring – Aubrey volunteering aid that was received rather distrustfully, as his love of effect caused him to array the model school children in colours gaudy enough, as Gertrude complained, 'to corrupt a saint.' Nor was his dilettante help more appreciated at a small stand, well provided with tiny drawers, and holding a shaded lamp, according to Gertrude, 'burning something horrible ending in gen, that would kill anybody but Tom, who managed it,' but which threw a beautiful light upon the various glass dishes, tubes, and slides, and the tall brass microscope that Tom was said to love better than all his kith and kin, and which afforded him occupation for his leisure moments.

'I say, Harry,' he asked, 'did you get my letter?'

'Your letter – of what date? I got none since Mary's of the second of May, when every one was down in the fever. Poor old Ward, I never was more shocked; what is become of the young ones?'

'Oh! you must ask Mary, Miss Ward is a bosom friend of hers.'

'What! the girl that sang like the lark? I must hear her again. But she won't be in tune for singing now, poor thing! What are they doing? Henry Ward taken to the practice? He used to be the dirtiest little sneak going, but I hope he is mended now.'

'Ask my father,' said mischievous Tom; and Dr May answered not, nor revealed his day's annoyance with Henry.

'He is doing his best to make a home for his brother and sisters,' said Richard.

'My letter,' said Tom, 'was written in Whitsun week; I wish you had had it.'

'Ay, it would have been precious from its rarity,' said Harry. 'What commission did it contain, may I ask?'

'You have not by good luck brought me home a Chinese flea?'

'He has all the fleas in creation,' said Daisy confidentially; 'cats', and dogs', and hedgehogs', and human; and you would have been twice as welcome if you had brought one.'

'I've brought no present to nobody. I'd got my eye on a splendid ivory junk, for Blanche's wedding present, at Canton, but I couldn't even speak to send any one after it. You have uncommon bad luck for a sailor's relatives.'

'As long as you bring yourself home we don't care,' said Blanche, treating the loss of the junk with far more resignation than did Tom that of the flea.

'If you only had a morsel of river mud sticking anywhere,' added Tom, 'you don't know the value the infusoria might be.'

'I had a good deal more than a morsel sticking to me once,' said Harry; 'it was owing to my boat's crew that I am not ever so many feet deep in it now, like many better men. They never lost sight of me, and somehow hauled me out.'

Gertrude gave him a hug, and Mary's eyes got so misty, that her skein fell into worse entanglements than ever.

'Were you conscious?' asked Ethel.

'I can't say. I'm clear of nothing but choking and gasping then, and a good while after. It was a treacherous unlucky affair, and I'm afraid I shall miss the licking of rascally John Chinaman. If all I heard at Plymouth is true, we may have work handy to home.'

'At home you may say,' said his father, '*Dulce et, &c.* is our motto. Didn't you know what a nest of heroes we have here to receive you? Let me introduce you to Captain Ernescliffe, of the Dorset Volunteer Rifle Corps; Private Thomas May, of the Cambridge University Corps; and Mr Aubrey Spencer May, for whom I have found a rifle, and am expected to find a uniform as soon as the wise heads have settled what colour will be most becoming.'

'Becoming! No, papa!' indignantly shouted Aubrey: 'it is the colour that will be most invisible in skirmishing.'

'Grey, faced with scarlet,' said Hector, decidedly.

'Yes, that is the colour of the invincible Dorsets,' said Dr May. 'There you see our great authority with his military instructions in his hand.'

'No, sir,' replied Hector, 'it's not military instructions, it is Crauford's General Orders.'

'And,' added the doctor, 'there's his bride working the colours, and Mary wanting to emulate her.'

'I don't think George will ever permit us to have colours,' said Ethel; 'he says that Rifles have no business with them, for that they are of no use to skirmishers.'

'The matter has been taken out of George's hands,' said Aubrey; 'there would not have been a volunteer in the country if he had his way.'

'Yes,' explained Ethel, 'the real soldier can't believe in volunteers, nor cavalry in infantry; but he is thoroughly in for it now.'

'Owing to his Roman matron,' quoth Tom. 'It was a wonderful opening for public spirit when Lady Walkingham insisted on Sir Henry refusing the use of the park for practice for fear we should make targets of the children. So the Spartan mother at Abbotstoke, gallantly setting Margaret aside, sent for the committee at once to choose the very best place in the park.'

'Papa is chairman of the committee,' added Aubrey, 'he is mayor this year, so we must encourage it.'

'And Aubrey hit four times at a hundred yards,' triumphantly declared Gertrude, 'when Edward Anderson and Henry Ward only got a ball in by accident.'

'Henry Ward ought to be shot at himself,' was Aubrey's sentiment, 'for not letting Leonard be in the corps.'

'The fellow that you brought to Maplewood?' asked Hector. 'I thought he was at school.'

'Didn't you know that old Hoxton has given leave to any of the sixth form to drill and practise? and that trumpery fellow, Henry, says he can't afford the outfit, though his sister would have given the uniform.'

'Let me tell you, young folks,' said the doctor, 'that you are not to suppose it always hails crack rifles on all sorts of improved systems, as it does when Captain Hector is in the house.'

'They are only on trial, sir,' apologized Hector.

'Very odd then that they all have an eagle and H.E. on them,' observed the doctor drily.

'Oh! they'll take them again, or I shall find a use for them,' said Hector.

'Well, if Henry can't afford two,' said Aubrey, holding to his point, 'he ought to give up to his brother; he knows no more how to handle a rifle——'

'That's the very reason,' muttered Tom.

'And Flora is going to give a great party,' proceeded Gertrude, 'as soon as the uniform is settled, and they are enrolled. Blanche and Hector are to stay for it, and you'll have to wear your lieutenant's uniform, Harry.'

'I can't be going to balls till I've been up to report myself fit for service,' said Harry.

'It is not to be a ball,' said Blanche's soft serious voice over her green silk banner; 'it is to be a breakfast and concert, ending in a dance, such as we had at Maplewood.'

'Hollo!' said Harry, starting, 'now I begin to believe in Mrs Ernescliffe, when I hear her drawing down herself as an example to Flora.'

'Only a precedent,' said Blanche, blushing a little, but still grave. 'We have had some experience, you know. Our corps was one of the earliest enrolled, and Hector managed it almost entirely. It was the reason we have not been able to come here sooner, but we thought it right to be foremost, as the enemy are sure to attempt our coast first.'

'I believe the enemy are expected on every coast at first,' was Ethel's aside, but it was not heard; for Harry was declaring,

'Your coast! they will never get the length of that. I was talking to an old messmate of mine in the train, who was telling me how we could burn their whole fleet before it could get out of Cherbourg.'

'If they should slip by,' began Hector.

'Slip by!' and Harry had well nigh dislodged Daisy by his vehemence in demonstrating that they were welcome to volunteer, but that the Channel Fleet would prevent the rifles from being seriously put to the proof – a declaration highly satisfactory to the ladies, and heartily backed up by the doctor, though Blanche looked rather discomfited, and Hector argued loud for the probability of active service.

'I say, Aubrey,' said Tom, rather tired of the land and sea debate, 'do just reach me a card, to take up some of this sand upon.'

Aubrey obeyed, and reading the black-edged card as he handed it, said, 'Mrs Pug. What? Pug ought to have been calling upon Mab.'

'Maybe she will, in good earnest,' observed Tom again in Ethel's ear; while the whole room rang with the laughter that always befalls the unlucky wight guilty of a blunder in a name.

'You don't mean that you don't know who she is, Aubrey?' was the cry.

'I – how should I?'

'What, not Mrs Pugh?' exclaimed Daisy.

'Pew or Pug – I know nothing of either. Is this edge as mourning for all the old pews that have been demolished in the church?'

'For shame, Aubrey,' said Mary seriously. 'You must know it is for her husband.'

Aubrey set up his eyebrows in utter ignorance.

'How true it is that one half the world knows nothing of the other!' exclaimed Ethel. 'Do you really mean you have never found out the great Mrs Pugh, Mrs Ledwich's dear suffering Matilda?'

'I've seen a black lady sitting with Mrs Ledwich in church.'

'Such is life,' said Ethel. 'How little she thought herself living in such an unimpressible world!'

'She is a pretty woman enough,' observed Tom.

'And very desirous of being useful,' added Richard. 'She and Mrs Ledwich came over to Cocksmoor this morning, and offered any kind of assistance.'

'At Cocksmoor!' cried Ethel, much as if it had been the French.

'Every district is filled up here, you know,' said Richard, 'and Mrs Ledwich begged me as a personal favour to give her some occupation that would interest her and cheer her spirits, so I asked her to look after those new cottages at Gould's End, quite out of your beat, Ethel, and she seemed to be going about energetically.'

Tom looked unutterable things at Ethel, who replied with a glance between diversion and dismay.

'Who is the lady?' said Blanche. 'She assaulted me in the street with inquiries and congratulations about Harry, declaring she had known me as a child, a thing I particularly dislike:' and Mrs Ernescliffe looked like a ruffled goldfinch.

'Forgetting her has not been easy to the payers of duty calls,' said Ethel. 'She was the daughter of Mrs Ledwich's brother, the Colonel of Marines, and used in old times to be with her aunt; there used to be urgent invitations to Flora and me to drink tea there because she was of our age. She married quite young, something very prosperous and rather aged, and the glories of dear Matilda's villa at Bristol have been our staple subject; but Mr Pugh died in the spring, leaving his lady five hundred a year absolutely her own, and she is come to stay with her aunt, and look for a house.'

'Et cetera,' added Tom.

'What, in the buxom widow line?' asked Harry.

'No, no!' said Richard, rather indignantly.

'No, in the pathetic line,' said Ethel; 'but that requires some self-denial.'

'Our tongues don't lose their venom, you see, Harry,' put in the doctor.

'No indeed, papa,' said Ethel, really anxious to guard her brothers. 'I was very sorry for her at first, and perhaps I pity her more now than even then. I was taken with her pale face and dark eyes, and I believe she was a good wife, and really concerned for her husband; but I can't help seeing that she knows her grief is an attraction.'

'To simple persons,' muttered Tom along the tube of his microscope.

'The sound of her voice showed her to be full of pretension,' said Blanche. 'Besides, Mrs Ledwich's trumpeting would fix my opinion in a moment.'

'Just so,' observed the doctor.

'No, papa,' said Ethel, 'I was really pleased and touched in spite of Mrs Ledwich's devotion to her, till I found out a certain manoeuvring to put herself in the foreground, and not let her sorrow hinder her from any enjoyment or display.'

'She can't bear any one to do what she does not.'

'What! Mary's mouth open against her too?' cried Dr May.

'Well, papa,' insisted Mary, 'nobody wanted her to insist on taking the harmonium at Bankside last Sunday, just because Averil had a cold in her head; and she played so fast, that every one was put out, and then said she would come to the practice that they might understand one another. She is not even in the Bankside district, so it is no business of hers.'

'There, Richard, her favours are equally distributed,' said Aubrey; 'but if she would take that harmonium altogether, one would not mind – it makes Henry Ward as sulky as a bear to have his sister going out all the evening, and he visits it on Leonard. I dare say if she stayed at home he would not have been such a brute about the rifle.'

'I should not wonder,' said Dr May. 'I sometimes doubt if home is sweetened to my friend Henry.'

'O papa!' cried Mary, bristling up, 'Ave is very hard worked, and she gives up everything in the world but her church music, and that is her great duty and delight.'

'Miss Ward's music must be a sore trial to the Pug,' said Tom; 'will it be at this affair at Abbotstoke?'

'That's the question,' said Ethel. 'It never goes out, yet is to be met everywhere, just over-persuaded at the last moment. Now Flora, you will see, will think it absolutely improper to ask her; and she will be greatly disappointed not to have the chance of refusing, and then yielding at the last minute.'

'Flora must have her,' said Harry.

'I trust not,' said Blanche, shrinking.

'Flora will not ask her,' said Tom, 'but she will be there.'

'And will dance with me,' said Harry.

'No, with Richard,' said Tom.

'What!' said Richard, looking up at the sound of his name.

All laughed, but were ashamed to explain, and were relieved that their father rang the bell.

'At that unhappy skein still, Mary?' said Mrs Ernescliffe, as the good-nights were passing. 'What a horrid state it is in!'

'I shall do it in time,' said Mary, 'when there is nothing to distract my attention. I only hope I shall not hurt it for you.'

'Chuck it into the fire at once; it is not worth the trouble,' said Hector.

Each had a word of advice, but Mary held her purpose, and persevered till all had left the room except Richard, who quietly took the crimson tangle on his wrists, turned and twisted, opened passages for the winder, and by the magic of his dexterous hands, had found the clue to the maze, so that all was proceeding well, though slowly, when the study door opened, and Harry's voice was heard in a last good-night to his father. Mary's eyes looked wistful, and one misdirection of her winder tightened an obdurate loop once more.

'Run after Harry,' said Richard, taking possession of the ivory. 'Good night; I can always do these things best alone. I had rather – yes, really – good night:' and his kiss had the elder brother's authority of dismissal.

His Maimouna was too glad and grateful for more than a summary 'thank you,' and flew up stairs in time to find Harry turning, baffled, from her empty room. 'What, only just done that interminable yarn?' he said.

'Richard is doing it. I could not help letting him, this first evening of you.'

'Good old Richard! he is not a bit altered since I first went to sea, when I was so proud of that,' said Harry, taking up his midshipman's dirk, which formed a trophy on Mary's mantel-shelf.

'Are we altered since you went last?' said Mary.

'The younger ones, of course. I was in hopes that Aubrey would have been more like old June, but he'll never be so much of a fellow.'

'He is a very dear good boy,' said Mary, warmly.

'Of course he is,' said Harry, 'but, somehow, he will always have a woman-bred way about him. Can't be helped, of course; but what a pair of swells Tom and Blanche are come out!' and he laughed good-naturedly.

'Is not Blanche a beautiful dear darling?' cried Mary, eagerly. 'It is so nice to have her. They could not come at first because of the infection, and then because of the rifle corps, and now it is delicious to have all at home.'

'Well, Molly, I'm glad it wasn't you that have married. Mind, you mustn't marry till I do.'

And Harry was really glad that Mary's laugh was perfectly 'fancy free,' as she answered, 'I'm sure I hope not, but I won't promise, because that might be unreasonable, you know.'

'Oh, you prudent, provident Polly? But,' added Harry, recalled to a sense of time by a clock striking eleven, 'I came to bring you something, Mary. You shall have it, if you will give me another.'

Mary recognised, with some difficulty, a Prayer-Book with limp covers that Margaret had given him after his first voyage. Not only was it worn by seven years' use, but it was soiled and stained with dark brownish red, and a straight round hole perforated it from cover to cover.

'Is it too bad to keep?' said Harry. 'Let me just cut out my name in Margaret's hand, and the verse of the 107th Psalm; luckily the ball missed that.'

'The ball?' said Mary, beginning to understand.

'Yes. Every one of those circles that you see cut out there, was in here,' said Harry, laying his hand over his chest, 'before the ball, which I have given to my father.'

'O Harry!' was all Mary could say, pointing to her own name in a pencil scrawl on the fly leaf.

'Yes, I set that down because I could not speak to tell what was to be done with it, when we didn't know that that book had really been the saving of my life. That hair's-breadth deviation of the bullet made all the difference.'

Mary was kissing the blood-stained book, and sobbing.

'Why, Mary, what is there to cry for? It is all over now, I tell you. I am as well as man would wish, and there's no more about it but to thank God, and try to deserve His goodness.'

'Yes, yes, I know, Harry; but to think how little we knew, or thought, or felt – going on in our own way when you were in such danger and suffering!'

'Wasn't I very glad you were going on in your own way?' said Harry. 'Why, Mary, it was that which did it – it has been always that thought of you at the Minster every day, that kept me to reading the Psalms, and so having the book about me. And did not it do one good to lie and think of the snug room, and my father's spectacles, and all as usual? When they used to lay me on the deck of the *Dexter* at night, because I could not breathe below, I used to watch old Orion, who was my great friend in the Loyalty Isles, and wish the heathen name had not stuck to the old fellow, he always seemed so like the Christian warrior, climbing up with his shield before him and his. A home like this is a shield to a man in more ways than one, Mary. Hollo, was that the street door?'

'Yes; Ritchie going home. Fancy his being at the silk all this time! I am so sorry!'

Maugre her sorrow, there were few happier maidens in England than Mary May, even though her service was distracted by the claims of three slave-owners at once, bound as she was, to Ethel, by habitual fidelity, to Harry, by eager adoration, to Blanche, by willing submission. Luckily, their requisitions (for the most part unconscious) seldom clashed, or, if they did, the two elders gave way, and the bride asserted her supremacy in the plenitude of her youthful importance and prosperity.

Thus she carried off Mary in her barouche to support her in the return of bridal calls, while the others were organizing a walk to visit Flora and the rifle target. Gertrude's enthusiasm was not equal to walking with a weapon that *might* be loaded, nor to being ordered out to admire the practice, so she accompanied the sisters; Tom was reading hard; and Ethel found herself, Aubrey, and the sailor, the only ones ready to start.

This was a decided treat, for Aubrey and she were so nearly one, that it was almost a tête-à-tête with Harry, though it was not his way to enter by daylight, and without strong impulse, on what regarded himself, and there were no such confidences as those to Mary on the previous night; but in talking over home details, it was easier to speak without Tom's ironical ears and caustic tongue.

Among other details, the story of the summer that Ethel and Aubrey had spent at Coombe was narrated, and Aubrey indulged himself by describing what he called Ethel's conquest.

'It is more a conquest of Norman's, and of Melanesia,' said Ethel. 'If it were not nonsense to build upon people's generous visions at seventeen, I should sometimes hope a spark had been lit that would shine some day in your islands, Harry.'

Going up that hill was not the place for Etheldred May to talk of the futility of youthful aspirations; but it did not so strike either of the brothers, to whom Cocksmoor had long been a familiar fact. Harry laughed to hear the old Ethel so like herself; and Aubrey said, 'By the bye, what did you do, the day you walked him to Cocksmoor? he was fuller of those islands than ever after it.'

'I did not mean it,' said Ethel; 'but the first day of the holidays I came on him disconsolate in the street, with nothing to do, and very sore about Henry's refusal to let him volunteer; he walked on with me till we found ourselves close to Cocksmoor, and I found he had never seen the church, and would like to stay for evening service, so I put him into the parsonage while I was busy, and told him to take a book.'

'I know,' said Aubrey; 'the liveliest literature you can get in Richard's parlour are the Missionary Reports.'

'Exactly so; and he got quite saturated with them; and when we walked home, I was so thankful that the rifle grievance should be a little displaced, that I led him on to talk and build castles rather more than according to my resolutions.'

'Hello, Ethel!' said Harry.

'Yes, I think spontaneous castles are admirable, but I mistrust all timber from other people's woods.'

'But isn't this a horrid shame of Henry?' said Aubrey, 'Such a little prig as he is, to take the place of such a fellow as Leonard, a capital shot already.'

'I wish Henry had been magnanimous,' said Ethel.

'I'd as soon talk of a magnanimous weasel from what I recollect,' said Harry.

'And he is worse now, Harry,' continued Aubrey. 'So spruce and silky out of doors, and such a regular old tyrannical bachelor in-doors. He is jealous of Leonard, any one can see, and that's the reason he won't give him his due.'

'You observe,' said Ethel, 'that this boy thinks the youngest brother's due is always to come first.'

'So it is, in this family,' said Harry. 'No one comes *so* last as old Ritchie.'

'But of course,' said Aubrey, rather taken aback, 'if I were not youngest, I should have to knock under to some one.'

Ethel and Harry both laughed heartily; one congratulating him on not having carried the principle into the cock-pit, the other adding, 'Don't indoctrinate Leonard with it; there is enough already to breed bitterness between those brothers! Leonard ought to be kept in mind that Henry has so much to harass him, that his temper should be borne patiently with.'

'He!'

'I don't think papa's best endeavours have kept all his father's practice for him, and I am sure their rate of living must make him feel pinched this Christmas.'

'Whew! He will be in a sweeter humour than ever!'

'I have been trying to show Leonard that there's room for magnanimity on his side at least; and don't you go and upset it all by common place abuse of tutors and governors.'

'I upset it!' cried Aubrey: 'I might as well try to upset the Minster as a word from you to Leonard.'

'Nonsense! What's that?' For they were hailed from behind, and looking round saw two tall figures – weapon in hand, in pursuit. They proved to be Hector Ernescliffe and Leonard Ward, each bearing one of what Dr May called the H.E. rifles; but Leonard looked half shy, half grim, and so decidedly growled off all Aubrey's attempts at inquiry or congratulation, that Ethel hazarded none, and Aubrey looked discomfited, wearing an expression which Harry took to mean that the weight of his rifle fatigued him, and insisted on carrying it for him, in spite of his rather insulted protests and declarations that the sailor was an invalid. Ethel had walked forwards, and found Leonard at her side, with a darkening brow as he glanced back at the friendly contest.

'Harry spoils Aubrey as much as all the others do,' said Ethel lightly, deeming it best to draw out the sting of the rankling thought.

'Ay! None of them would leave him to be pitied and offered favours by some chance person,' said Leonard.

'You don't call my brother Hector a chance person?'

'Did you say anything to him, Miss May?' said Leonard, turning on her a flushed face, as if he could almost have been angered with her.

'I said not one word.'

'Nor Aubrey?'

'The volunteer politics were discussed last night, and Henry got abused among us; but papa defended him, and said it did not rain rifles. That's all – whatever Hector may have done was without a word to either of us – very likely on the moment's impulse. Did he go to Bankside after you?'

'No. I was looking in at Shearman's window,' said Leonard, rather sheepishly, 'at the locks of the new lot he has got in, and he came and asked if I were going to choose one, for he had got a couple down from London, and the man had stupidly put his cypher on both, so he would be glad if I would take one off his hands. I didn't accept – I made that clear – but then he begged, as if it was to oblige him, that I would come out to Abbotstoke and help him try the two, for he didn't know which he should keep.'

'Very ingenious of him,' said Ethel, laughing.

'Now, Miss May, do tell me what I ought to do. It is *such* a beauty, better than any Shearman ever dreamt of; just look at the finish of the lock.'

'By the time you have shot with it——'

'Now don't, pray,' said Leonard, 'I haven't any one to trust for advice but you.'

'Indeed, Leonard, I can see no objection. It is a great boon to you, and no loss to Hector, and he is quite enough my father's son for you to look on him as a friend. I can't but be very glad; for the removal of this vexation ought to make you get on all the better with your brother.'

'Ave would be delighted,' said Leonard; 'but somehow——'

'Somehow' was silenced by a coalescing of the party at a gate; and Hector and Harry were found deep in an argument in which the lieutenant's Indian reminiscences of the Naval Brigade was at issue with the captain's Southdown practice, and the experiences of the one meeting the technicalities of the other were so diverting, that Leonard forgot his scruples till at the entrance of the park he turned off towards the target with Hector and Aubrey, while the other two walked up to the house.

The Grange atmosphere always had a strange weight of tedium in it, such as was specially perceptible after the joyous ease of the house in the High Street. No one was in the drawing-room, and Harry gazed round at the stiff, almost petrified, aspect of the correct and tasteful arrangement of the tables and furniture, put his hands in his pockets, and yawned twice, asking Ethel why she did not go in search of Flora. Ethel shook her head; and in another moment Flora appeared in eager welcome; she had been dressing for a drive to Stoneborough to see her brother, little expecting him to be in a state for walking to her. With her came her little girl, a child whose aspect was always a shock to those who connected her with the two Margarets whose name she bore. She had inherited her father's heavy mould of feature and dark complexion, and the black eyes had neither sparkle in themselves nor relief from the colour of the sallow cheek; the pouting lips were fretful, the whole appearance unhealthy, and the dark bullet-shaped head seemed too large for the thin bony little figure. Worn, fagged, and aged as Flora looked, she had still so much beauty, and far more of refinement and elegance, as to be a painful foil and contrast to the child that clung to her, waywardly refusing all response to her uncle's advances.

Flora made a sign to him to discontinue them, and talked of her husband, who was hunting, and heard the history of Harry's return and recovery. In the midst, little Margaret took heart of grace, crossed the room, and stood by the sailor, and holding up a great India-rubber ball as large as her own head, asked, 'Uncle Harry, were you shot with a cannon-ball as big as this?'

Thereupon she was on his knee, and as he had all his father's fascination for children, he absolutely beguiled her into ten minutes of genuine childish mirth, a sight so rare and precious to her mother, that she could not keep up her feint of talking to Ethel. The elderly dame, part nurse, part nursery governess, presently came to take Miss Rivers out; but Miss Rivers, with a whine in her voice, insisted on going nowhere but to see the shooting, and Uncle Harry must come with her; and come he did, the little bony fingers clasping tight hold of one of his large ones.

'Dear Harry!' said Flora, 'he wins every one! It is like a cool refreshing wind from the sea when he comes in.'

In Flora's whole air, voice, and manner, there was apparent a relaxation and absence of constraint such as she never allowed herself except when alone with Ethel. Then only did she relieve the constant strain, then only did the veritable woman show herself, and the effort, the toil, the weariness, the heart-ache, of her life become visible; but close together as the sisters lived, such tête-à-têtes were rare, and perhaps were rather shunned than sought, as perilous and doubtful indulgences. Even now, Flora at once fixed a limit by ordering the carriage to meet her in a quarter of an hour at the nearest point to the rifle ground, saying she would walk there, and then take home Ethel and any brother who might be tired.

'And see that Margaret does not come to harm,' said Ethel.

'I am not afraid of that,' said Flora, something in her eye belying her; 'but she might be troublesome to Harry, and I had rather he did not see one of her fights with Miss Morton.'

'How has she been? I thought her looking clearer and better to-day,' said Ethel, kindly.

'Yes, she is pretty well just now,' said Flora, allowing herself in one of her long deep sighs, before descending into the particulars of the child's anxiously-watched health. If she had been describing them to her father, there would have been the same minuteness, but the tone would have implied cheerful hope; whereas to Ethel she took no pains to mask her dejection. One of the points of anxiety was whether one shoulder were not outgrowing the other, but it was not easy to discover whether the appearance were not merely owing to the child's feeble and ungainly carriage. 'I cannot torment her about that,' said Flora. 'There are enough miseries for her already without making more, and as long as it does not affect her health, it matters little.'

'No, certainly not,' said Ethel, who had hardly expected this from Flora.

Perhaps her sister guessed her thought, for she said, 'Things are best as they are, Ethel; I am not fit to have a beautiful admired daughter. All the past would too easily come over again, and my poor Margaret's troubles may be the best balance for her.'

'Yes,' said Ethel, 'it is bad enough to be an heiress, but a beautiful heiress is in a worse predicament.'

'Health would improve her looks,' began the maternal instinct of defence, but then breaking off. 'We met Lord H—— yesterday, and the uniform is to be like the northern division. Papa will hear it officially to-morrow.'

'The northern has grey, and green facings.'

'You are more up in it than I. All we begged for was, that it might be inexpensive, for the sake of the townspeople.'

'I hear of little else,' said Ethel, laughing; 'Dr Spencer is as hot on it as all the boys. Now, I suppose, your party is to come off?'

'Yes, it ought,' said Flora, languidly; 'I waited to see how Harry was, he is a great element towards making it go off well. I will talk it over with Blanche; it will give somebody pleasure if she thinks she manages it.'

'Will it give George no pleasure?'

'I don't know; he calls it a great nuisance, but he would not like not to come forward, and it is quite right that he should.'

'Quite right,' said Ethel; 'it is every one's duty to try to keep it up.'

With these words the sisters came within sight of the targets, and found Margaret under Harry's charge, much interested, and considerably in the way. The tidings of the colour of the uniform were highly appreciated; Aubrey observed that it would choke off the snobs who only wanted to be like the rifle brigade, and Leonard treated its inexpensiveness as a personal matter, having apparently cast off his doubts, under Hector's complimentary tuition. Indeed, before it grew too dark for taking aim, he and the weapon were so thoroughly united, that no further difficulty remained but of getting out his thanks to Mr Ernescliffe.

Averil was sitting alone over the fire in the twilight, in a somewhat forlorn mood, when the door was pushed ajar, and the muzzle of a gun entered, causing her to start up in alarm, scarcely diminished by the sight of an exultant visage, though the words were, 'Your money or your life.'

'Leonard, don't play with it, pray!'

'It's not loaded.'

'Oh! but one never can tell:' then, half ashamed of her terror, 'pray put it back, or we shall have an uproar with Henry.'

'This is none of Henry's. He will never own such a beauty as this.'

'Whose is it? Not your's? Is it really a rifle? H.E.? What's that?'

'Hector Ernescliffe! Didn't I tell you he was a princely fellow?'

'Given it to you? Leonard, dear, I am so happy! Now I don't care for anything! What a gallant volunteer you will make!' and she kissed him fondly. 'We will order the uniform as soon as ever it is settled, and I hope it will be a very handsome one.'

'It will be a cheap one, which is more to the purpose. I could get part myself, only there's the tax for Mab, and the subscription to the cricket club.'

'I would not have you get any of it! You are *my* volunteer, and I'll not give up my right to any one, except that Minna and Ella want to give your belt.'

'Where are those children?' he asked.

'Henry has taken them to Laburnum Grove, where I am afraid they are being crammed with cake and all sorts of nonsense.'

'What could have made him take them there?'

'Oh! some wish of Mrs Pugh's to see the poor little dears,' said Averil, the cloud returning that had been for a moment dispelled.

'What's the row?' asked Leonard, kindly. 'Has he been bothering you?'

'He wants me to sound Mary May about an invitation for Mrs Pugh to Mrs Rivers's volunteer entertainment. I am glad I did not say no one in mourning ought to go, for I must go now you are a volunteer.'

'But you didn't consent to mention her?'

'No, indeed! I knew very well you would say it was a most improper use to make of the Mays' kindness, and I can't see what business she has there! Then he said, no, she was certain not to go, but the attention would be gratifying and proper.'

'That is Mrs Rivers's look-out.'

'So I said, but Henry never will hear reason. I did not tell you of our scene yesterday over the accounts; he says that we must contract our expenses, or he shall be ruined; so I told him I was ready to give up the hot-house, or the footman, or the other horse, or anything he would specify; but he would not hear of it – he says it would be fatal to alter our style of living, and that it is all my fault for not being economical! O Leonard, it is very hard to give up all one cared for to this housekeeping, and then never to please!'

Leonard felt his brother a tyrant. 'Never mind, Ave dear,' said he, 'go on doing right, and then you need not care for his unreasonableness. You are a dear good girl, and I can't think how he can have the heart to vex you.'

'I *don't* care while I have you, Leonard,' she said, clinging to him.

At that moment the others were heard returning, and an ironical look passed between the brother and sister at certain injunctions that were heard passing about the little India-rubber goloshes; but Henry had returned in high good humour, was pleased to hear of his brother's good fortune, pronounced it very handsome in Mr Ernescliffe, and even offered to provide the rest of the equipment; but this was proudly rejected by Averil, with some of the manifestations of exclusive partiality that naturally wounded the elder brother. He then announced an engagement that he had made with Mrs Ledwich for a musical evening the next week. Averil had her harmonium at her tongue's end, but the evening was a free one, chosen on purpose to accommodate her; she had no excuse, and must submit.

'And practise some of your best pieces, Ave,' said Henry. 'Mrs Pugh was kind enough to offer to come and get up some duets with you.'

'I am greatly obliged,' said Averil, drily, 'but I do not play duets.'

'You would do wisely to accept her kindness,' argued Henry. 'It would be a great advantage to you to be intimate with a lady of her opportunities.'

'I do not like patronage,' said Averil.

'Ave! Ave!' cried the children, who had been trying to attract her attention, 'if you will let us go to Laburnum Grove by twelve o'clock to-morrow, Mrs Pugh will show us her book of the pretty devices of letters, and teach us to make one.'

'You will have not finished lessons by twelve.'

'But if we have?'

'No, certainly not; I can't have you bothering every one about that nonsensical fashion.'

'You shall go, my dears,' said Henry. 'I can't think why your sister should be so ill-natured.'

Averil felt that this was the way to destroy her authority, and though she kept silence, the tears were in her eyes, and her champion broke forth, 'How can you be such a brute, Henry?'

'Come away, my dears,' said Averil, rising, and holding out her hands to her sisters, as she recollected how bad the scene was for them; but it was only Minna who obeyed the call, Ella hung about Henry, declaring that Leonard was naughty, and Ave was cross.

'Well,' shouted Leonard, 'I shan't stay to see that child set against her sister! I wonder what you mean her to come to, Henry?'

It was no wonder that Minna and Ella squabbled together as to which was cross, Henry or Averil, and the spirit of party took up its fatal abode in the house of Bankside.

CHAPTER IX

'Too oft my anxious eye has spied
That secret grief thou fain wouldst hide –
The passing pang of humbled pride.'

Scott.

The winter was gay, between musical evenings, children's parties, clerical feastings of district visitors, *soirées* for Sunday-school teachers, and Christmas-trees for their scholars. Such a universal favourite as Harry, with so keen a relish for amusement, was sure to fall an easy prey to invitations; but the rest of the family stood amazed to see him accompanied everywhere by Tom, to whom the secular and the religious dissipations of Stoneborough had always hitherto been equally distasteful. Yet he submitted to a Christmas course of music, carpet-dances, and *jeux de société* on the one hand, and on the other conferred inestimable obligations on the ecclesiastical staff by exhibitions of his microscope and of some of the ornamental sports of chemistry.

'The truth is,' was the explanation privately dropped out to Ethel, 'that some one really must see that those two don't make fools of themselves.'

Ethel stared; then, coming to the perception who 'those two' meant, burst out laughing, and said, 'My dear Tom, I beg your pardon, but, on the whole, I think that is more likely to befall some one else.'

Tom held his head loftily, and would not condescend to understand anything so foolish.

He considered Bankside as the most dangerous quarter, for Harry was enraptured with Miss Ward's music, extolled her dark eyes, and openly avowed her attraction; but there were far more subtle perils at Laburnum Grove. The fair widow was really pretty, almost elegant, her weeds becoming; and her disposition so good, so religious, so charitable, that, with her activity, intelligence, and curate-worship, she was a dangerous snare to such of mankind as were not sensible of her touch of pretension. As to womankind, it needed a great deal of submissiveness to endure her at all; and this was not Averil Ward's leading characteristic.

In fact, the ubiquity of Mrs Pugh was a sore trial to that young lady, just so superior herself as to detect the flimsiness of the widow's attainments. It was vexatious to find that by means of age, assumption, and position, these shallow accomplishments made a prodigious show in the world, while her own were entirely overlooked. She thought she despised the admiration of the second-rate world of Stoneborough, but it nettled her to see it thus misplaced; and there was something provoking in the species of semi-homage paid in that quarter by the youths of the May family.

As to the sailor, Averil frankly liked him very much; he was the pleasantest young man, of the most open and agreeable manners, who had ever fallen in her way. He was worthy to be Mary's brother, for he was friendly to Leonard, and to herself had a truthfully flattering way that was delightful. Without any sentiment in the case, she always felt disappointed and defrauded if she were prevented from having a conversation with him; and when this happened it was generally either from his being seized upon by Mrs Pugh, or from her being baited by his brother Tom.

Averil was hard to please, for she was as much annoyed by seeing Tom May sitting courteous and deferential by the side of Mrs Pugh, as by his attentions to herself. She knew that he was playing the widow off, and that, when most smooth and bland in look and tone, he was inwardly chuckling; and to find the identical politeness transferred to herself made her feel not only affronted but insulted by being placed on the same level. Thus, when at a '*réunion*' at Laburnum Grove, she had been looking on with intense disgust while Tom was admiring Mrs Pugh's famous book of devices from letters, translating the mottoes, and promising contributions, the offence was greatly increased by his coming up to her (and that too just as Harry was released by the button-holding Mr Grey) and saying,

'Of course you are a collector too, Miss Ward; I can secure some duplicates for you.'

She hoard such fooleries? She have Mrs Pugh's duplicates? No wonder she coldly answered, 'My little sister has been slightly infected, thank you, but I do not care for such things.'

'Indeed! Well, I always preserve as many as I can, as passports to a lady's favour.'

'That depends on how much sense the lady has,' said Averil, trusting that this *was* a spirited set down.

'You do not consider. Philosophically treated, they become a perfect school in historical heraldry, nay in languages, in mathematical drawing, in illumination,' said Tom, looking across to the album in which Mrs Pugh's collection was enshrined, each device appropriately framed in bright colours. His gravity was intolerable. Was this mockery or not? However, as answer she must, she said,

'A very poor purpose for which to learn such things, and a poor way of learning them.'

'True,' said Tom, 'one pastime is as good as another; and the less it pretends to, the better. On the whole, it may be a beneficial outlet for the revival of illumination.'

Did this intolerable person know that there was an 'illuminator's guide' at home, and a great deal of red, blue, and gold paint, with grand designs for the ornamentation of Bankside chapel? Whether he knew it or not, she could not help answering, 'Illumination is desecrated by being used on such subjects.'

'And is not that better than the subjects being desecrated by the illumination?'

Mrs Pugh came to insist on that 'sweet thing of Mendelssohn's' from her dear Miss Ward; and Averil obeyed, not so glad to escape as inflamed by vexation at being prevented from fighting it out and learning what he really meant; though she was so far used to the slippery nature of his arguments as to know that it was highly improbable that she should get at anything in earnest.

'If his sisters were silly, I should not mind,' said she to Leonard; 'then he might hold all women cheap from knowing no better; but when they like sensible things, why is every one else to be treated like an ape?'

'Never mind,' said Leonard, 'he sneers at everybody all alike! I can't think how Dr May came to have such a son, or how Aubrey can run after him so.'

'I should like to know whether they really think it irreverent to do illuminations.'

'Nonsense, Ave; why should you trouble yourself about what he says to teaze you? bad luck to him!'

Nevertheless Averil was not at ease till she had asked Mary's opinion of illumination, and Mary had referred to Ethel, and brought back word that all depended on the spirit of the work; that it was a dangerous thing, for mere fashion, to make playthings of texts of Scripture; but that no one could tell the blessing there might be in dwelling on them with loving decoration, or having them placed where the eye and thought might be won by them. In fact, Ethel always hated fashion, but feared prejudice.

The crown of the whole carnival was to be the Abbotstoke entertainment on the enrolment of the volunteers. Preparations went on with great spirit, and the drill sergeant had unremitting work, the target little peace, and Aubrey and Leonard were justly accused of making fetishes of their rifles. The town was frantic, no clothes but uniforms could be had, and the tradesmen forgot their customers in the excitement of electing officers.

Averil thought it very officious of Mrs Pugh to collect a romantic party of banner-working young ladies before the member's wife or the mayor's family had authorized it; and she refused to join, both on the plea of want of time, and because she heard that Mr Rivers, a real dragoon, declared colours to be inappropriate to riflemen. And so he did; but his wife said the point was not martial correctness, but popular feeling; so Mary gratified the party by bringing her needle, Dr Spencer took care the blazonry of the arms of the old abbey was correct, and Flora asked the great lady of the county to present the banner, and gave the invitation to Mrs Pugh, who sighed, shook her head, dried her eyes, and said something about goodness and spirits; and Mrs Rivers professed to understand, and hope Mrs Pugh would do exactly as best suited her.

Was this manoeuvring, or only living in the present?

Mary accompanied Harry for a long day of shopping in London when he went to report himself, starting and returning in the clouds of night, and transacting a prodigious amount of business with intense delight and no fatigue; and she was considered to have fitted out the mayor's daughters suitably with his municipal dignity, of which Ethel piqued herself on being proud.

The entertainment was not easy to arrange at such a season, and Blanche's 'experience,' being of early autumn, was at fault; but Flora sent for all that could embellish her conservatories, and by one of the charities by which she loved to kill two birds with one stone, imported a young lady who gained her livelihood by singing at private concerts, and with her for a star, supported by the Minster and Cathedral choirs, hoped to get up sufficient music to occupy people till it should be late enough to dance. She still had some diplomacy to exercise, for Mrs Ledwich suggested asking dear Ave Ward to sing, her own dearest Matilda would not object on such an occasion to assist the sweet girl; and Mrs Rivers, after her usual prudent fashion, giving neither denial nor assent, Mrs Ledwich trotted off, and put Averil into an agony that raised a needless storm in the Bankside house; Leonard declaring the request an insult, and Henry insisting that Ave ought to have no scruples in doing anything Mrs Pugh thought proper to be done. And finally, when Ave rushed with her despair to Mary May, it was to be relieved at finding that Mrs Rivers had never dreamt of exposing her to such an ordeal.

Though it was the year 1860, the sun shone on the great day, and there were exhilarating tokens of spring, singing birds, opening buds, sparkling drops, and a general sense of festivity; as the grey and green began to flit about the streets, and while Mr Mayor repaired to the Town Hall to administer the oaths to the corps, his unmartial sons and his daughters started for the Grange to assist Flora in the reception of her guests.

The Lord Lieutenant's wife and daughters, as well as the Ernescliffes, had slept there, and Ethel found them all with Flora in the great hall, which looked like a winter garden, interspersed with tables covered with plate and glass, where eating and drinking might go on all day long. But Ethel's heart sank within her at the sight of Flora's haggard face and sunken eyes. 'What is the matter?' she asked Blanche, an image of contented beauty.

'Matter? Oh, they have been stupid in marking the ground, and Hector is gone to see about it. That's all. He is not at all tired.'

'I never supposed he was,' said Ethel; 'but what makes Flora look so ill?'

'Oh, that tiresome child has got another cold, and fretted half the night. It is all their fault for giving way to her; and she has done nothing but whine this whole morning because she is not well enough to go out and see the practice! I am sure it is no misfortune that she is not to come down and be looked at.'

Ethel crossed over to Flora, and asked whether she should go up and see little Margaret.

'I should be so thankful,' said poor Flora; 'but don't excite her. She is not at all well, and has had very little sleep.'

Ethel ran up-stairs, and found herself in the midst of a fight between the governess and Margaret, who wanted to go to the draughty passage window, which she fancied had a better view than that of her nursery. Luckily, Aunt Ethel was almost the only person whom Margaret did not like to see her naughty; and she subsided into a much less objectionable lamentation after Uncle Harry and his anchor buttons. Ethel promised to try whether he could be found, and confident in his good nature, ran down, and boldly captured him as he was setting out to see Hector's operations. He came with a ready smile, and the child was happy throughout his stay. Flora presently stole a moment's visit, intending her sister's release as well as his; but Ethel, in pity to governess as well as pupil, declared the nursery window to be a prime post of observation, and begged to be there left.

Margaret began to believe that they were very snug there, and by the time the bugles were heard, had forgotten her troubles in watching the arrivals.

Up came the grey files, and Ethel's heart throbbed and her eye glistened at their regular tread and military bearing. Quickly Margaret made out papa; but he was too real a soldier to evince consciousness of being at his own door, before the eyes of his wife and daughter; and Aubrey's young face was made up in imitation of his impassiveness. Other eyes were less under control, and of these were a brown pair that wandered restlessly, till they were raised to the nursery window, and there found satisfaction.

The aunt and niece were too immediately above the terrace to see what passed upon it, nor could they hear the words; so they only beheld the approach of the Ensign, and after a brief interval, his return with the tall green silk colours, with the arms of the old abbey embroidered in the corner and heard the enthusiastic cheer that rang out from all the corps.

Then the colours led the way to the ground for practice, for manoeuvres were as yet not ready for exhibition. Almost all the gentlemen followed; and such ladies as did not object to gunpowder or damp grass, thither betook themselves, guided by the ardent Mrs Ernescliffe. Having disposed of the others in the drawing-rooms and gardens, Flora and her father came to the nursery, and Ethel was set at liberty to witness the prowess of her young champions, being assured by Flora, that she would be of more use there in keeping the youthful population out of danger than in entertaining the more timid in the house.

She slipped out and hurried down a narrow path towards the scene of action, presently becoming aware of four figures before her, which her glass resolved into Harry and Tom, a lady in black, and a child. Evidently the devoted Tom was keeping guard over one of the enchantresses, for the figure was that of Averil Ward, though, as Ethel said, shaking hands, she was hardly to be known with only *one* sister.

'We have been delayed,' said Averil; 'poor little Ella was in an agony about the firing, and we could not leave her till your brother' – indicating Harry – 'was so kind as to take her to Gertrude.'

'True to the Englishwoman's boast of never having seen the smoke of an engagement,' said Tom.

'A practising is not an engagement,' said Ethel.

'There may be quite as many casualties,' quoth Tom, indulging in some of the current ready-made wit on the dangers of volunteering, for the pure purpose of teazing; but he was vigorously fallen upon by Harry and Ethel, and Averil brightened as she heard him put to the rout. The shots were already heard, when two more black figures were seen in the distance, going towards the gate.

'Is that Richard?' exclaimed Tom.

'Aye, and I do believe, the widow!' rejoined Harry.

'Oh, yes,' said Averil. 'I heard her talking about Abbotstoke Church, and saying how much she wished to see it. She must have got Mr May to show it to her.'

Ethel, who had no real fears for Richard herself, looked on amused to watch how the guardian spirit was going to act. He exclaimed, 'By the by, Miss Ward, would you not like to see it? They have a very nice brass to old Mr Rivers, and have been doing up the chancel.'

'Thank you,' said Ave, 'I should prefer going to see how Leonard is getting on.'

'Right, Miss Ward,' said Harry; 'the church won't run away.'

'Well, then,' said Tom, after a moment's hesitation, 'I think I shall just run down, as the church is open, and see what sort of work they have made of the chancel.'

Ethel had the strongest fancy to try what he would do if she were to be seized with a desire to inspect the chancel; but she did not wish to let Harry and Averil appear on the ground under no escort but Minna's, and so permitted Tom to leave them to her keeping, and watched him hasten to break up the *tête-à-tête*.

Coming among the spectators, who, chiefly drawn up on the carriage drive, were watching from a safe distance the grey figures in turn take aim and emit from their rifles the flash and cotton-wool-like tuft of smoke, Ethel's interest was somewhat diminished by hearing that all the other marksmen had been distanced by the head keepers of Abbotstoke and Drydale, between whom the contest really lay.

'The rest is a study of character,' said Dr Spencer, taking a turn up and down the road with her. 'I have been watching the various pairs of brothers; and I doubt if any stand the test as well as the house of May.'

'There's only one in the field to-day.'

'Yes, but I've seen them together before now, and I will say for even Tom that he has no black looks when his junior shoots better than he does.'

'Oh, yes! But then it is Aubrey!'

Dr Spencer laughed. 'Lucky household where that "*it is*" accounts for all favours to the youngest, instead of for the countenance falling at his successes.'

'I am afraid I know whom you mean. But he has no generosity in him.'

'And his sister helps to make him jealous.'

'I am afraid she does; but though it is very sad, one can't wonder at her preference of the great to the small.'

'Poor girl, I wonder how she will get on when there is a new inmate in the happy family.'

'Ha! you shocking old gossip, what have you found out now?'

'Negotiation for the introduction of a Pug dog from the best circles – eh?'

'Well, if he were alone in the world, it would be a capital match.'

'So she thinks, I fancy; but 500*l.* a year might do better than purchase so many incumbrances. Depend upon it, the late lamented will remain in the ascendant till there are no breakers ahead.'

In process of time, ladies, volunteers, and all, were assembled in the great music-room for the concert; and Ethel, having worked hard in the service of the company, thought her present duty lay with the sick child, and quietly crept away, taking, however, one full view of the entire scene, partly for her own satisfaction, partly in case Margaret should be inclined to question her on what every one was doing.

There was the orchestra, whose erection Richard had superintended; there was the conductor in his station, and the broad back of the Cathedral organist at the piano, the jolly red visages of the singing men in their ranks, the fresh faces of the choristers full of elation; the star from London, looking quiet and lady-like, courteously led to her place by George Rivers himself. But, for all his civility, how bored and sullen he looked! and how weary were poor Flora's smiles, though her manner was so engaging, and her universal attention so unremitting! What a contrast to the serene, self-enfolded look of happiness and prosperity on the pretty youthful face of Blanche, her rich delicate silk spreading far beyond the sofa where she sat among the great ladies; and her tall yellow-haired husband leaning against the wall behind her, in wondering contemplation of his Blanche taking her place in her own county.

Further back, among the more ordinary herd, Ethel perceived Mrs Pugh, bridling demurely, with Tom on guard over her on one side, and Henry Ward looking sulky on the other, with his youngest sister in his charge. The other was looking very happy upon Leonard's knee, close to Averil and Mary, who were evidently highly satisfied to have coalesced. Averil was looking strikingly pretty – the light fell favourably on her profuse glossy hair, straight features, and brilliant colouring; her dark eyes were full of animation, and her lips were apart with a smile as she listened to Leonard's eager narration; and Ethel glanced towards Harry to see whether he were admiring. No; Harry was bringing in a hall arm-chair in the background, for a very large, heavy, vulgar-looking old man, who seemed too ponderous and infirm for a place on the benches. Richard made one of a black mass of clergy, and Aubrey and Gertrude had asserted their independence by perching themselves on a window-seat, as far as possible from all relations, whence they nodded a merry saucy greeting to Ethel, and she smiled back again, thinking her tall boy in his grey tunic and black belt, and her plump girl in white with green ribbons, were as goodly a pair as the room contained.

But where was the Doctor?

Ethel had a shrewd suspicion where she should find him; and in the nursery he was, playing at spillekens with his left hand.

It was not easy to persuade him that the music would be wasted on her, and that he ought to go down that it might receive justice; but Margaret settled the question. 'You may go, grandpapa, Aunt Ethel is best to play at spillekens, for she has not got a left hand.'

'There's honour for me, who used to have two!' and therewith Ethel turned him out in time for the overture.

Margaret respected her aunt sufficiently not to be extra wayward with her, and between the spillekens, and a long story about cousin Dickie in New Zealand, all went well till bed-time. There was something in the child's nervous temperament that made the first hours of the night peculiarly painful to her, and the sounds of the distant festivity added to her excitability. She fretted and tossed, moaned and wailed, sat up in bed and cried, snapped off attempts at hymns, would not listen to stories, and received Ethel's attempts at calm grave commands with bursts of crying, and calls for mamma and papa. The music had ceased, tuning of violins was heard, and Ethel dreaded the cries being heard down stairs. She was at her wits' end, and was thinking who would most avail, and could be fetched with least sensation, when there was a soft knock at the door, and Harry's voice said, 'Hollo, what's the matter here?' In he came with his white glove half on, and perceiving the state of the case said, 'Can't go to sleep?'

'Oh Uncle Harry, take me;' and the arms were stretched out, and the tear-stained face raised up.

'We'll put you to sleep as sound as if you were in a hammock just off middle watch,' said Harry; and the next moment he had her rolled up in her little blue dressing-gown, nestling on his broad shoulder, while he walked up and down the room, crooning out a nautical song, not in first-rate style, but the effect was perfect; the struggles and sobs were over, and when at the end of a quarter of an hour Harry paused and looked at the little thin sharp face, it was softened by peaceful sleep.

Ethel pointed to the door. There stood Flora, her eyes full of tears.

Harry laid the little sleeper on her bed, and covered her up. Flora laid her arm on his shoulder and gave him such a kiss as she had not given even when he had come back as from the dead. Then she signed to them to come, but sped away before them, not trusting herself to speak. Ethel tarried with Harry, who was in difficulties with gloves too small for his broad hand, and was pshawing at himself at having let Tom get them for him at Whitford.

'Oh Harry,' said Ethel, 'you are the most really like papa of us all! How did you come to think of it?'

'I'd have given a good deal if any one would have walked quarter deck with me some nights last summer,' said Harry, still intent on the glove. 'What is to be done, Ethel? that rogue Tom always snaps up all the beauty. I dare say he has engaged Miss Ward and the widow both.'

It was no time for sentiment; so Ethel suggested getting half into one glove, and carrying the other. 'You'll be quite irresistible enough, Harry! And if all the beauty is engaged, I'll dance with you myself.'

'Will you?' cried the Lieutenant with sparkling eyes, 'then you are a jolly old Ethel! Come along, then;' and he took her on his arm, ran down stairs with her, and before she well knew where she was, or what was going on, she found herself in his great grasp passive as a doll, dragged off into the midst of a vehement polka that took her breath away.

She trusted to him, and remained in a passive, half-frightened state, glad he was so happy; but in the first pause heartily wishing he would let her go, instead of which she only heard, 'Well done, old Ethel, you'll be a prime dancer yet! you're as light as a feather;' and before she had recovered her breath, off he led her with 'Go it again!'

When at length, panting and bewildered, she was safely placed on a seat, with 'You've had enough, have you? mind, I sha'n't let you off another time,' she found that her aberration had excited a good deal of sensation in her own family. Blanche and Gertrude could not repress their amusement; and Dr May, with merry eyes, declared that she was coming out in a new light. She had only time to confide to him the reason that she had let Harry do what he pleased with her, before two volunteers were at her side.

'Miss May, I did not think you ever danced!'

'Nor I,' said Ethel; 'but you see what sailors can do with one.'

'Now, Ethel,' said the other over his shoulder, 'now you have danced with Harry, you *must* have this waltz with me.'

'A dangerous precedent, Ethel,' said the Doctor, laughing.

'I couldn't waltz to save my life, Aubrey,' said Ethel; 'but if you can bear me through a polka as well as Harry did, you may try the next.'

'And won't you – will you – for once dance with me?' said his companion imploringly.

'Very well, Leonard, if I can get through a quadrille;' and therewith Ethel was seized upon by both boys to hear the story of every hit and miss, and of each of the difficulties that their unpractised corps had encountered in getting round the corners between Stoneborough and the Grange. Then came Leonard's quadrille, which it might be hoped was gratifying to him; but which he executed with as much solemn deference as if he had been treading a minuet with a princess, plainly regarding it as the great event of the day. In due time, he resigned her to Aubrey; but poor Aubrey had been deluded by the facility with which the strong and practised sailor had swept his victim along; and Ethel grew terrified at the danger of collisions, and released herself and pulled him aside by force, just in time to avoid being borne down by the ponderous weight of Miss Boulder and her partner.

'You did not come to grief with Harry!' muttered the discomfited boy.

'No more did the lamb damage the eagle; but remember the fate of the jackdaw, Mr Grey-coat! I deserve some ice for my exertions, so come into the hall and get some, and tell me if you have had better luck elsewhere.'

'I have had no partner but Minna Ward, and she trips as if one was a dancing master.'

'And how has Tom been managing?'

'Stunningly civil! He began with Ave Ward, in the Lancers, and it was such fun – he chaffed her in his solemn way, about music I believe it was, and her harmonium. I could not quite hear, but I could see she was in a tremendous taking, and she won't recover it all the evening.'

'What a shame it is of Tom!'

'Oh! but it is such fun! And since that he has been parading with Pug.'

'She has not danced!'

'Oh no! She got an audience into Meta's little sitting-room – Henry Ward, Harvey Anderson, and some of the curates; they shut the door, and had some music on their own hook.'

'Was Richard there?'

'At first; but either he could not bear to see Meta's piano profaned, or he thought it too strong when they got to the sacred line, for he bolted, and is gone home.'

'There's Harry dancing with Fanny Anderson. He has not got Miss Ward all this time.'

'Nor will,' said Aubrey. 'Tom had put her in such a rage that she did not choose to dance with that cousin of hers, Sam Axworthy, so she was obliged to refuse every one else; and I had to put up with that child!'

'Sam Axworthy! He does not belong to our corps. How does he come here?'

'Oh! the old man has some houses in the borough, and an omnium gatherum like this was a good time to do the civil thing to him. There he is; peep into the card-room, and you'll see his great porpoise back, the same old man that Harry in his benevolence assisted to a chair. He shook hands with Leonard, and told him there was a snug desk at the Vintry Mill for him.'

'I dare say!'

'And when Leonard thanked him, and said he hoped to get off to Cambridge, he laughed that horrid fat laugh, and told him learning would never put him in good case. Where shall I find you a place to sit down? Pug and her tail have taken up all the room,' whispered Aubrey, as by the chief of the glittering tables in the hall, he saw Mrs Pugh, drinking tea, surrounded by her attendant gentlemen, and with her aunt and Ella Ward, like satellites, a little way from her.

'Here is a coign of vantage,' said Ethel, seating herself on a step a little way up the staircase. 'How those people have taken possession of that child all day!'

'I fancy Leonard is come to reclaim her,' said Aubrey, 'don't you see him trying to work through and get at her? and Miss Ward told me she was going home early, to put the children to bed. Ha! what's the row? There's Leonard flaring up in a regular rage! Only look at his eyes – and Henry just like Gertrude's Java sparrow in a taking——'

'It must not be,' cried Ethel, starting up to attempt she knew not what, as she heard Leonard's words, 'Say it was a mistake, Henry! You cannot be so base as to persist!'

There it became evident that Ethel and Aubrey were seen over the balusters; Leonard's colour deepened, but his eye did not flinch; though Henry quailed and backed, and the widow gave a disconcerted laugh; then Leonard pounced on his little sister and carried her off to the cloak-room. 'What treason could it have been?' muttered Aubrey; 'we shall get it all from Ward;' but when Leonard re-appeared it was with his sister cloaked and bonneted on his arm, each leading a little one; he took them to the entrance and was seen no more.

Nor was the true history of that explosion ever revealed in the May family, though it had grave consequences at Bankside.

Rumour had long declared at Stoneborough that the member's little daughter was carefully secluded on account of some deformity, and Mrs Pugh had been one of many ladies who had hoped to satisfy their curiosity on this head upon the present occasion. She had asked Henry Ward whether it were so, and he had replied with pique that he had no means of judging, he had never been called in at the Grange. By way of salve to his feelings, the sympathizing lady had suggested that the preference for London advice might be from the desire of secrecy, and improbable as he knew this to be, his vanity had forbidden him to argue against it. When no little Miss Rivers appeared, the notion of her affliction gained ground, and Leonard, whose grey back was undistinguishable from other grey backs, heard Mrs Pugh citing his brother as an authority for the misfortune which Mr and Mrs Rivers so carefully concealed as to employ no surgeon from their own neighbourhood.

Falsehood, slander, cruelty, ingratitude, breach of hospitality, were the imputations that fired the hot brain of Leonard, and writhed his lips, as he started round, confronted the lady, and assured her it was a – a – a gross mistake. His father had always attended the child, and she must have misunderstood his brother. Then, seeing Henry at a little distance, Leonard summoned him to contradict the allegation, but at that moment the sudden appearance of the two Mays put the whole conclave to silence.

Not aware that Mrs Pugh had confounded together his intelligence and her surmise, and made him responsible for both, Henry was shocked and grieved at his brother's insulting and violent demeanour, and exhausted himself in apologies and denunciations; while the kind-hearted lady interceded for the boy, declaring that she doted on his generous spirit, but not confessing the piece of female embroidery which had embroiled the matter, probably not even aware of it, though sincerely and kindly desirous to avert the brother's anger. Her amiability therefore only strengthened Henry's sense of his brother's outrage, and his resolve to call him to account.

It was impossible that night, for Leonard had gone home with the sisters, and was in bed long before his brother returned. But at breakfast Henry found the forces drawn up against him, and his first attempt to remonstrate was retorted by the demand what he could mean by spreading such an abominable report – cruel – unfounded – ungrateful – spiteful–

Averil indeed divined that it was Mrs Pugh's invention; but Henry was not inclined to give up Mrs Pugh, and continued in the belief that Leonard's fiery imagination had fabricated the sentence, and then most improperly charged it on the lady, and on himself. Had it been as Leonard stated, said Henry, his conduct was shameful and required an apology; whereupon Leonard burst out in passion at being disbelieved, and Averil was no less indignant. The storm raged till the business of the day interrupted it; and in Henry's absence, Averil and her brother worked up their wrath again, at the atrocity of the assertion regarding the child of their entertainers, the grand-daughter of their truest, kindest friend.

Averil would have rushed to Mary with the whole story, but for Leonard's solemn asseveration that if ever it came to the ears of any one of the Mays, he should send back his rifle to Mr Ernescliffe, and work his way out to one of the colonies rather than again look any of the family in the face.

Henry divided his opponents next time, asking Leonard, in his sister's absence, whether he had come to his senses and would apologize? Leonard hoped Henry had come to his! On the whole, the dispute had lost some asperity by the absence of Averil, and though Leonard held his ground, and maintained that he had every right to deny the statement, and that it was Henry's duty to make Mrs Pugh contradict it everywhere, yet the two approached nearer together, and there was less misunderstanding, fewer personalities.

But Averil could not forget or forgive. She persisted in manifesting her displeasure, and recurred to the subject till her pertinacity wore out Leonard himself.

'Nonsense, Ave,' he said at last, 'it was a foolish woman's gossip that Henry ought to have quashed; but that is no reason you should treat them like toads.'

'Would you have me sanction vile slander?'

'As if you were sanctioning slander by being decently civil! Is not it an intolerable thing that we three should never sit down to a meal in peace together?'

'O Leonard, don't you think I feel the misery?'

'Put an end to it then, and don't pit those poor children one against the other. Just fancy Minna's saying to me, "I love you and sister, but Ella loves Mrs Pugh and Henry."'

'Yes, they have set Ella against me. She always appeals to Henry, and I can do nothing with her.'

Leonard looked out of the window and whistled, then said as if he had made a discovery, 'I'll tell you what, Ave, something must be done to set things to rights between us, and I believe the best thing will be to call on Mrs Pugh.'

'Not to apologize! O Leonard!'

'Stuff and nonsense! Only to show we don't bear malice. Henry had been at you to call ever so long before this, had he not?'

'I can't see any reason for intimacy.'

'I declare, Ave, you are too bad! I only want you just to keep the peace with your own brother. You have led him the life of a dog these three days, and now when I want you to be a little obliging, you talk of intimacy!'

'Only because I know how it will be. If I give that woman an inch, she will take an ell.'

'Let her then. It would be much better than always living at daggers-drawn with one's brother.' Then, after waiting for her to say something, he added, 'If you won't go with me, I shall go alone.'

Averil rose, subdued but not convinced, reverencing her brother, but afraid of his concessions.

However, the call turned out well. Mrs Pugh had a talent for making herself agreeable, and probably had liked the boy for his outburst. She would not let Mab be excluded, loaded her with admiration, and was extremely interested in the volunteer practice, so that both the young people were subjugated for the time by her pleasant manners, and went away ashamed of their own rancour against one so friendly and good natured, and considerably relieved of their burden of animosity.

Their greeting to their brother was so cordial that he perceived their good will, and was sorry that the dread of an evening of warfare had induced him to accept an invitation to dine at the Swan with Sam Axworthy and a party of his friends.

CHAPTER X

'This night is my departing night,
    For here nae longer must I stay;
There's neither friend nor foe of mine
    But wishes me away.
What I have done through lack of wit,
    I never never can recall:
I hope ye're all my friends as yet.
    Good-night, and joy be with you all.'

Armstrong's Good-night.

The storm had blown over, but heavy flakes of cloud still cumbered the air, and gusts of wind portended that it might gather again.

Henry Ward took this opportunity of giving his first dinner-party. He said it was a necessary return for the civilities they had received; and to Averil's representation that it transgressed the system of rigid economy that so much tormented her, he replied by referring her to Mrs Pugh for lessons in the combination of style and inexpensiveness.

Averil had almost refused, but the lady herself proffered her instructions, and reluctance was of no avail; nothing but demonstrations from which her conscience shrank, could have served to defend her from the officious interference so eagerly and thankfully encouraged by the master of the house. Vainly did she protest against pretension, and quote the example of the Grange; she found herself compelled to sacrifice the children's lessons to learn of Mrs Pugh to make the paper flowers that, with bonbons and sweetmeats, were to save the expense of good food on the dinner table, and which she feared would be despised by Miss May, nay, perhaps laughed over with 'Mr Tom!'

She hated the whole concern, even the invitation to Dr and Miss May, knowing that it was sent in formal vanity, accepted in pure good nature, would bring them into society they did not like, and expose her brother's bad taste. Only one thing could have added to her dislike, namely – that which all Stoneborough perceived excepting herself and Leonard – that this dinner was intended as a step in Henry's courtship, and possibly as an encouragement of Harvey Anderson's liking for herself. Averil held her head so high, and was so little popular, that no one of less assurance than Mrs Ledwich herself would have dared approach her with personal gossip; and even Mrs Ledwich was silent here; so that Averil, too young and innocent to connect second marriages with recent widowhood, drew no conclusions from Henry's restless eagerness that his household should present the most imposing appearance.

While the bill of fare was worrying Averil, Leonard was told by

Aubrey, that this father had brought home a fossil Tower of Babel, dug up with some earth out of a new well, three miles off, with tidings of other unheard-of-treasures; and a walk was projected in quest of them, in which Leonard was invited to join. He gladly came to the early dinner, where he met reduced numbers – the Ernescliffes being at Maplewood, Tom at Cambridge, and Harry in the Channel fleet; and as usual, he felt the difference between the perfect understanding and friendship in the one home, and the dread of dangerous subjects in the other. The expedition had all the charms of the Coombe times; and the geological discoveries were so numerous and precious, that the load became sufficient to break down the finders, and Ethel engaged a market-woman to bring the baskets in her cart the next morning.

That morning a note from Richard begged Ethel to come early to Cocksmoor to see Granny Hall, who was dying. Thus left to their own devices, Aubrey and Gertrude conscientiously went through some of their studies; then proceeded to unpack their treasury of fossils, and endeavour to sort out Leonard's share, as to which doubts arose. Daisy proposed to carry the specimens at once to Bankside, where she wanted to see Leonard's prime echinus; and Aubrey readily agreed, neither of the young heads having learnt the undesirableness of a morning visit in a house preparing for a dinner-party too big for it.

However, Leonard made them extremely welcome. It was too foggy a day for rifle practice, and all the best plate and china were in the school-room, his only place of refuge; Ave was fluttering about in hopes of getting everything done before Mrs Pugh could take it out of her hands, and the energies of the household were spent on laying out the dining table. It was clearly impossible to take Gertrude anywhere but into the drawing-room, which was in demi-toilette state, the lustres released from their veils, the gayer cushions taken out of their hiding-places, and the brown holland covers half off. This was the only tranquil spot, and so poor little Mab thought, forbidden ground though it was. Even in her own home, the school-room, a strange man had twice trod upon her toes; so no wonder, when she saw her own master and his friends in the drawing-room, that she ventured in, and leaping on a velvet cushion she had never seen before, and had never been ordered off, she there curled herself up and went to sleep, unseen by Leonard, who was in eager controversy upon the specimens, which Gertrude, as she unpacked, set down on floor, chair, or ottoman, unaware of the offence she was committing. So, unmolested, the young geologists talked, named, and sorted the specimens, till the clock striking the half hour, warned the Mays that they must return; and Leonard let them out at the window, and crossed the lawn to the side gate with them to save the distance.

He had just returned, and was kneeling on the floor hastily collecting the fossils, when the door opened, and Henry Ward, coming home to inspect the preparations, beheld the drawing-room bestrewn with the rough stones that he had proscribed, and Mab, not only in the room, but reposing in the centre of the most magnificent cushion in the house!

His first movement of indignation was to seize the dog with no gentle hand. She whined loudly; and Leonard, whom he had not seen, shouted angrily 'Let her alone;' then, at another cry from her, finding his advance to her rescue impeded by a barricade of the crowded and disarranged furniture, he grew mad with passion, and launched the stone in his hand, a long sharp-pointed belemnite. It did not strike Henry, but a sound proclaimed the mischief, as it fell back from the surface of the mirror, making a huge star of cracks, unmarked by Leonard, who, pushing sofa and ottoman to the right and left, thundered up to his brother, and with uplifted hand demanded what he meant by his cruelty.

'Is – is this defiance?' stammered Henry, pointing to the disordered room. 'Look here, Averil,' as she appeared at the sounds, 'do you defend this boy now he has very nearly killed me?'

'Killed you!' and Leonard laughed angrily; but when Henry held up the elf-bolt, and he saw its sharp point, he was shocked, and he saw horror in Averil's face.

'I see,' he said gravely. 'It was a mercy I did not!' and he paused. 'I did not know what I was about when you were mis-using my dog, Henry. Shake hands; I am sorry for it.'

But Henry had been very much frightened as well as angered, and thought, perhaps, it was a moment to pursue his advantage.

'You treat things lightly,' he said, not accepting the hand. 'See what you have done.'

'I am glad it was not your head,' said Leonard. 'What does it cost? I'll pay.'

'More than your keep for a year,' moaned Henry, as he sighed over the long limbs of the starfish-like fracture.

'Well, I will give up anything you like, if you will only not be sulky about it, Henry. It was unlucky, and I'm sorry for it; I can't say more!'

'But I can,' said Henry with angry dignity, re-inforced by the sight of the seamed reflection of his visage in the shivered glass. 'I tell you, Leonard, there's no having you in the house; you defy my authority, you insult my friends, you waste and destroy more than you are worth, and you are absolutely dangerous. I would as soon have a wild beast about the place. If you don't get the Randall next week, and get off to the University, to old Axworthy's office you go at once.'

'Very well, I will,' said Leonard, turning to collect the fossils, as if he had done with the subject.

'Henry, Henry, what are you saying?' cried the sister.

'Not a word, Ave,' said Leonard. 'I had rather break stones on the road than live were my keep is grudged, and there's not spirit enough to get over a moment's fright.'

'It is not any one individual thing,' began Henry, in a tone of annoyance, 'but your whole course——'

There he paused, perceiving that Leonard paid no attention to his words, continuing quietly to replace the furniture and collect the fossils, as if no one else were in the room, after which he carried the basket upstairs.

Averil hurried after him. 'Leonard! oh why don't you explain? Why don't you tell him how the stones came there?'

Leonard shook his head sternly.

'Don't you mean to do anything?'

'Nothing.'

'But you wanted another year before trying for the scholarship.'

'Yes; I have no chance there.'

'He will not do it! He cannot mean it!'

'I do then. I will get my own living, and not be a burthen, where my brother cannot forgive a broken glass or a moment's fright,' said Leonard; and she felt that his calm resentment was worse than his violence.

'He will be cooler, and then——'

'I will have no more said to him. It is plain that we cannot live together, and there's an end of it. Don't cry, or you won't be fit to be seen.'

'I won't come down to dinner.'

'Yes, you will. Let us have no more about it. Someone wants you.'

'Please, Ma'am, the fish is come.'

'Sister, Sister, come and see how I have done up the macaroons in green leaves.'

'Sister, Sister, do come and reach me down some calycanthus out of the greenhouse!'

'I will,' said Leonard, descending; and for the rest of the day he was an efficient assistant in the decorations, and the past adventure was only apparent in the shattered glass, and the stern ceremonious courtesy of the younger brother towards the elder.

Averil hurried about, devoid of all her former interest in so doing things for herself as to save interference; and when Mrs Ledwich and Mrs Pugh walked in, overflowing with suggestions, she let them have their way, and toiled under them with the sensation of being like 'dumb driven cattle.' If Leonard were to be an exile, what mattered it to her who ruled, or what appearance things made?

Only when she went to her own room to dress, had she a moment to realize the catastrophe, its consequences, and the means of averting them.

So appalled was she, that she sat with her hair on her shoulders as if spell-bound, till the first ring at the door aroused her to speed and consternation, perhaps a little lessened by one of her sisters rushing in to say that it was Mrs Ledwich and Mrs Pugh, and that Henry was still in the cellar, decanting the wine.

Long before the hosts were ready, Dr May and Ethel had likewise arrived, and became cognizant of the fracture of the mirror, for, though the nucleus was concealed by a large photograph stuck into the frame, one long crack extended even to the opposite corner. The two ladies were not slow to relate all that they knew; and while the aunt dismayed Ethel by her story, the niece, with much anxiety, asked Dr May how it was that these dear nice superior young people should have such unfortunate tempers – was it from any error in management? So earnest was her manner, so inquiring her look, that Dr May suspected that she was feeling for his opinion on personal grounds, and tried to avert the danger by talking of the excellence of the parents, but he was recalled from his eulogium on poor Mrs Ward.

'Oh yes! one felt for them so very much, and they are so religious, so well principled, and all that one could wish; but family dissension is so dreadful. I am very little used to young men or boys, and I never knew anything like this.'

'The lads are too nearly of an age,' said the Doctor.

'And would such things be likely to happen among any brothers?'

'I should trust not!' said the Doctor emphatically.

'I should so like to know in confidence which you think likely to be most to blame.'

Never was the Doctor more glad that Averil made her appearance! He carefully avoided getting near Mrs Pugh for the rest of the evening, but he could not help observing that she was less gracious than usual to the master of the house; while she summoned Leonard to her side to ask about the volunteer proceedings, and formed her immediate court of Harvey Anderson and Mr Scudamore.

The dinner went off fairly, though heavily. Averil, in her one great trouble, lost the sense of the minor offences that would have distressed her pride and her taste had she been able to attend to them, and forgot the dullness of the scene in her anxiety to seek sympathy and counsel in the only quarter where she cared for it. She went mechanically through her duties as lady of the house, talking common-place subjects dreamily to Dr May, and scarcely even giving herself the trouble to be brief with Mr Anderson, who was on her other side at dinner.

In the drawing-room, she left the other ladies to their own devices in her eagerness to secure a few minutes with Ethel May, and disabuse her of whatever Mrs Ledwich or Mrs Pugh might have said. Ethel had been more hopeful before she heard the true version; she had hitherto allowed much for Mrs Ledwich's embellishments; and she was shocked and took shame to her own guiltless head for Gertrude's thoughtlessness.

'Oh no!' said Averil, 'there was nothing that any one need have minded, if Henry had waited for explanation! And now, will you get Dr May to speak to him? If he only knew how people would think of his treating Leonard so, I am sure he would not do it.'

'He cannot!' said Ethel. 'Don't you know what he thinks of it himself? He said to papa last year that your father would as soon have sent Leonard to the hulks as to the Vintry Mill.'

'Oh, I am so glad some one heard him. He would care about having that cast up against him, if he cared for nothing else.'

'It must have been a mere threat. Leonard surely has only to ask his pardon.'

'No, indeed, not again, Miss May!' said Averil. Leonard asked once, and was refused, and cannot ask again. No, the only difficulty is whether he ought not to keep to his word, and go to the mill if he does not get the Randall.'

'Did he say he would?'

'Of course he did, when Henry threatened him with it, and talked of the burden of his maintenance! He said, "Very well, I will," and he means it!'

'He will not mean it when the spirit of repentance has had time to waken.'

'He will take nothing that is grudged him,' said Averil. 'Oh! is it not hard that I cannot get at my own money, and send him at once to Cambridge, and never ask Henry for another farthing?'

'Nay, Averil; I think you can do a better part by trying to make them forgive one another.'

Averil had no notion of Leonard's again abasing himself, and though she might try to bring Henry to reason by reproaches, she would not persuade. She wished her guest had been the sympathizing Mary rather than Miss May, who was sure to take the part of the elder and the authority. Repentance! Forgiveness! If Miss May should work on Leonard to sue for pardon and toleration, and Mrs Pugh should intercede with Henry to take him into favour, she had rather he were at the Vintry Mill at once in his dignity, and Henry be left to his disgrace.

Ethel thought of Dr Spencer's words on the beach at Coombe, 'Never threaten Providence!' She longed to repeat them to Leonard, as she watched his stern determined face, and the elaborately quiet motions that spoke of a fixed resentful purpose; but to her disappointment and misgiving, he gave her no opportunity, and for the first time since their sea-side intercourse, held aloof from her.

Nor did she see him again during the week that intervened before the decision of the scholarship, though three days of it were holidays. Aubrey, whom she desired to bring him in after the rifle drill, reported that he pronounced himself sorry to refuse, but too busy to come in, and he seemed to be cramming with fiery vehemence for the mere chance of success.

The chance was small. The only hope lay in the possibility of some hindrance preventing the return of either Forder or Folliot; and in the meantime the Mays anxiously thought over Leonard's prospects. His remaining at home was evidently too great a trial for both brothers, and without a scholarship he could not go to the University. The evils of the alternative offered by his brother were duly weighed by the Doctor and Ethel with an attempt to be impartial.

Mr Axworthy, though the mill was the centre of his business, was in fact a corn merchant of considerable wealth, and with opportunities of extending his connexion much further. Had his personal character been otherwise, Dr May thought a young man could not have a better opening than a seat in his office, and the future power of taking shares in his trade; there need be no loss of position, and there was great likelihood both of prosperity and the means of extensive usefulness.

Ethel sighed at the thought of the higher aspirations that she had fostered till her own mind was set on them.

'Nay,' said the Doctor, 'depend upon it, the desk is admirable training for good soldiers of the Church. See the fearful evil that befalls great schemes entrusted to people who cannot deal with money matters; and see, on the other hand, what our merchants and men of business have done for the Church; and do not scorn "the receipt of custom."'

'But the man, papa!'

'Yes, there lies the hitch! If Leonard fails, I can lay things before Henry, such as perhaps he may be too young to know, and which must change his purpose.'

Mr Axworthy's career during his youth and early manhood was guessed at rather than known, but even since his return and occupation of the Vintry Mill, his vicious habits had scandalized the neighbourhood; and though the more flagrant of these had been discontinued as he advanced in age, there was no reason to hope that he had so much 'left off his sins, as that his sins had left him off.' His great nephew, who lived with him and assisted in his business, was a dashing sporting young man of no good character, known to be often intoxicated, and concerned in much low dissipation, and as dangerous an associate as could be conceived for a high-spirited lad like Leonard. Dr May could not believe that any provocation of temper, any motive of economy, any desire to be rid of encumbrances to his courtship, could induce a man with so much good in him, as there certainly was in Henry Ward, to expose his orphan brother to such temptations; and he only reserved his remonstrance in the truth that it would not be needed, and the desire to offer some better alternative of present relief.

One of the examiners was Norman's old school and college friend, Charles Cheviot, now a clergyman and an under-master at one of the great schools recently opened for the middle classes, where he was meeting with great success, and was considered a capital judge of boy's characters. He was the guest of the Mays during the examination; and though his shy formal manner, and convulsive efforts at young lady talk greatly affronted Gertrude, the brothers liked him.

He was in consternation at the decline of Stoneborough school since Mr Wilmot had ceased to be an under-master; the whole tone of the school had degenerated, and it was no wonder that the Government inquiries were ominously directed in that quarter. Scholarship was at a low ebb, Dr Hoxton seemed to have lost what power of teaching he had ever possessed, and as Dr May observed, the poor old school was going to the dogs. But even in the present state of things Leonard had no chance of excelling his competitors. His study, like theirs, had been mere task-work, and though he showed more native power than the rest, yet perhaps this had made the mere learning by rote even more difficult to an active mind full of inquiry. He was a whole year younger than any other who touched the foremost ranks, two years younger than several; and though he now and then showed a feverish spark of genius, reminding Mr Cheviot of Norman in his famous examination, it was not sustained – there were will and force, but not scholarship – and besides, there was a wide blurred spot in his memory, as though all the brain-work of the quarter before his illness had been confused, and had not yet become clear. There was every likelihood that a few years would make him superior to the chosen Randall scholar, but at present his utmost efforts did not even place him among the seven whose names appeared honourably in the newspaper. It was a failure; but Mr Cheviot had become much interested in the boy for his own sake, as well as from what he heard from the Mays, and he strongly advised that Leonard should at Easter obtain employment for a couple of years at the school in which he himself was concerned. He would thus be maintaining himself, and pursuing his own studies under good direction, so as to have every probability of success in getting an open scholarship at one of the Universities.

Nothing could be better, and there was a perfect jubilee among the Mays at the proposal. Aubrey was despatched as soon as breakfast was over to bring Leonard to talk it over, and Dr May undertook to propound it to Henry on meeting him at the hospital; but Aubrey came back looking very blank, Leonard had started of his own accord that morning to announce to his uncle his acceptance of a clerk's desk at the Vintry Mill!

Averil followed upon Aubrey's footsteps, and arrived while the schoolroom was ringing with notes of vexation and consternation. She was all upon the defensive. She said that not a word had passed on the subject since the dinner-party, and there had not been a shadow of a dispute between the brothers; in fact, she evidently was delighted with Leonard's dignified position and strength of determination, and thought this expedition to the Vintry Mill a signal victory.

When she heard what the Mays had to propose, she was enchanted; she had no doubt of Henry's willing consent, and felt that Leonard's triumph and independence were secured without the sacrifice of prospects, which she had begun to regard as a considerable price for his dignity.

But Dr May was not so successful with Henry Ward. He did not want to disoblige his uncle, who had taken a fancy to Leonard, and might do much for the family; he thought his father would have changed his views of the uncle and nephew had he known them better, he would not accept the opinion of a stranger against people of his own family, and he had always understood the position of an usher to be most wretched; nor would he perceive the vast difference between the staff of the middle school and of the private commercial academy. He evidently was pleased to stand upon his rights, to disappoint Dr May, and perhaps to gratify his jealousy by denying his brother a superior education.

Yet in spite of this ebullition, which had greatly exasperated Dr May, there was every probability that Henry's consent might be wrung out or dispensed with, and plans of attack were being arranged at the tea-table, when a new obstacle arose, in the shape of a note from Leonard himself.

'My dear Aubrey,

'I am very much obliged to Dr May and Mr Cheviot for their kind intentions; but I have quite settled with Mr Axworthy, and I enter on my new duties next week. I am sorry to leave our corps, but it is too far off, and I must enter the Whitford one.

'Yours,

'L.A. WARD.'

'The boy is mad with pride and temper,' said the Doctor.

'And his sister has made him so,' added Ethel.

'Shall I run down to Bankside and tell him it is all bosh?' said Aubrey, jumping up.

'I don't think that is quite possible under Henry's very nose,' said Ethel. 'Perhaps they will all be tamer by tomorrow, now they have blown their trumpets; but I am very much vexed.'

'And really,' added Mr Cheviot, 'if he is so wrong headed, I begin to doubt if I could recommend him.'

'You do not know how he has been galled and irritated,' said the general voice.

'I wonder what Mrs Pugh thinks of it,' presently observed the Doctor.

'Ah!' said Ethel, 'Mrs Pugh is reading "John of Anjou."'

'Indeed!' said the Doctor; 'I suspected the wind was getting into that quarter. Master Henry does not know his own interest; she was sure to take part with a handsome lad.'

'Why have you never got Mrs Pugh to speak for him?' said Mary. 'I am sure she would.'

'O Mary! simple Mary, you to be Ave's friend, and not know that her interposition is the only thing wanting to complete the frenzy of the other two!'

Ethel said little more that evening, she was too much grieved and too anxious. She was extremely disappointed in Leonard, and almost hopeless as to his future. She saw but one chance of preventing his seeking this place of temptation, and that was in the exertion of her personal influence. His avoidance of her showed that he dreaded it, but one attempt must be made. All night was spent in broken dreams of just failing to meet him, or of being unable to utter what was on her tongue; and in her waking moments she almost reproached herself for the discovery how near her heart he was, and how much pleasure his devotion had given her.

Nothing but resolution on her own part could bring about a meeting, and she *was* resolute. She stormed the castle in person, and told Averil she *must* speak to Leonard. Ave was on her side now, and answered with tears in her eyes that she should be most grateful to have Leonard persuaded out of this dreadful plan, and put in the way of excelling as he ought to do; she never thought it would come to this.

'No,' thought Ethel; 'people blow sparks without thinking they may burn a house down.'

Ave conducted her to the summer-house, where Leonard was packing up his fossils. He met them with a face resolutely bent on brightness. 'I am to take all my household goods,' he said, as he shook hands with Ethel.

'I see,' said Ethel gravely; and as Averil was already falling out of hearing, she added, 'I thought you were entirely breaking with your old life.'

'No, indeed,' said Leonard, turning to walk with her in the paths; 'I am leaving the place where it is most impossible to live in.'

'This has been a place of great, over-great trial, I know,' said Ethel, 'but I do not ask you to stay in it.'

'My word is my word,' said Leonard, snapping little boughs off the laurels as he walked.

'A hasty word ought not to be kept.'

His face looked rigid, and he answered not.

'Leonard,' she said, 'I have been very unhappy about you, for I see you doing wilfully wrong, and entering a place of temptation in a dangerous spirit.'

'I have given my word,' repeated Leonard.

'O Leonard, it is pride that is speaking, not the love of truth and constancy.'

'I never defend myself,' said Leonard.

Ethel felt deeply the obduracy and pride of these answers; her eyes filled with tears, and her hopes failed.

Perhaps Leonard saw the pain he was giving, for he softened, and said, 'Miss May, I have thought it over, and I cannot go back. I know I was carried away by passion at the first moment, and I was willing to make amends. I was rejected, as you know. Was it fit that we should go on living together?'

'I do not ask you to live together.'

'When he reproached me with the cost of my maintenance, and threatened me with the mill if I lost the scholarship, which he knew I could not get, I said I would abide by those words. I do abide by them.'

'There is no reason that you should. Why should you give up all your best and highest hopes, because you cannot forgive your brother?'

'Miss May, if I lived with you and the Doctor, I could have such aims. Henry has taken care to make them sacrilege for me. I shall never be fit now, and there's an end of it.'

'You might——'

'No, no, no! A school, indeed! I should be dismissed for licking the boys before a week was out! Besides, I want the readiest way to get on in the world; I must take care of my sisters; I don't trust one moment to Henry's affection for any of them. This is no home for me, and it soon may be no home for them!' and the boy's eyes were full of tears, though his voice struggled for firmness and indifference.

'I am very sorry for you, Leonard,' said Ethel, much more affectionately, as she felt herself nearer her friend of Coombe. 'I am glad you have some better motives, but I do not see how you will be more able to help them in this way.'

'I shall be near them,' said Leonard; 'I can watch over them. And if – if – it is true what they say about Henry and Mrs Pugh – then they could have a cottage near the mill, and I could live with them. Don't you see, Miss May?'

'Yes; but I question whether, on further acquaintance, you will wish for your sisters to be with their relations there. The other course would put you in the way of a better atmosphere for them.'

'But not for six years,' said Leonard. 'No, Miss May; to show you it is not what you think in me, I will tell you that I had resolved the last thing to ask Henry's pardon for my share in this unhappy half-year; but this is the only resource for me or my sisters, and my mind is made up.'

'O Leonard, are you not deceiving yourself? Are the grapes ever so sour, or the nightshade below so sweet, as when the fox has leapt too short, and is too proud to climb?'

'Nightshade! Why, pray?'

'My father would tell you; I know he thinks your cousin no safe companion.'

'I know that already, but I can keep out of his way.'

'Then this is the end of it,' said Ethel, feeling only half justified in going so far, 'the end of all we thought and talked of at Coombe!'

There was a struggle in the boy's face, and she did not know whether she had touched or angered him. 'I can't help it,' he said, as if he would have recalled his former hardness; but then softening, 'No, Miss May; why should it be? A man can do his duty in any state of life.'

'In any state of life where God has placed him; but how when it is his own self-will?'

'There are times when one must judge for one's self.'

'Very well, then, I have done, Leonard. If you can conscientiously feel that you are acting for the best, and not to gratify your pride, then I can only say I hope you will be helped through the course you have chosen. Good-bye.'

'But – Miss May – though I cannot take your advice——' he hesitated, 'this is not giving me up?'

'Never, while you let me esteem you.'

'Thank you,' he said, brightening; 'that is something to keep my head above water, even if this place were all you think it.'

'My father thinks,' said Ethel.

'I am engaged now; I cannot go back,' said Leonard. 'Thank you, Miss May.'

'Thank you for listening patiently,' said Ethel. 'Good-bye.'

'And – and,' he added earnestly, following her back to the house, 'you do not think the Coombe days cancelled?'

'If you mean my hopes of you,' said Ethel, with a swelling heart, 'as long as you do your duty – for – for the highest reason, they will only take another course, and I will try to think it the right one.'

Ethel had mentally made this interview the test of her regard for Leonard. She had failed, and so had her test; her influence had not succeeded, but it had not snapped; the boy, in all his wilfulness, had been too much for her, and she could no longer condemn and throw him off!

Oh! why will not the rights and wrongs of this world be more clearly divided?

CHAPTER XI

'The stream was deeper than I thought
When first I ventured here,
I stood upon its sloping edge
Without a rising fear.'

H. Bonar.

It was a comfort to find that the brothers parted on good terms. The elder was beholden to the younger for the acquiescence that removed the odium of tyranny from the expulsion; and when the one great disturbance had silenced the ephemeral dissensions that had kept both minds in a constant state of irritation, Henry wanted, by kindness and consideration, to prove to himself and the world that Leonard's real interests were his sole object; and Leonard rejoiced in being at peace, so long as his pride and resolution were not sacrificed. He went off as though his employment had been the unanimous choice of the family, carrying with him his dog, his rifle, his fishing-rod, his fossils, and all his other possessions, but with the understanding that his Sundays were to be passed at home, by way of safeguard to his religion and morals, bespeaking the care and consideration of his senior, as Henry assured himself and Mrs Pugh, and tried to persuade his sister and Dr May.

But Dr May was more implacable than all the rest. He called Henry's action the deed of Joseph's brethren, and viewed the matter as the responsible head of a family; he had a more vivid contemporaneous knowledge of the Axworthy antecedents, and he had been a witness to Henry's original indignant repudiation of such a destiny for his brother. He was in the mood of a man whose charity had endured long, and refused to condemn, but whose condemnation, when forced from him, was therefore doubly strong. The displeasure of a loving charitable man is indeed a grave misfortune.

Never had he known a more selfish and unprincipled measure, deliberately flying in the face of his parents' known wishes before they had been a year in their graves, exposing his brother to ruinous temptation with his eyes open. The lad was destroyed body and soul, as much as if he had been set down in Satan's own clutches; and if they did not mind what they were about, he could drag Aubrey after him! As sure as his name was Dick May, he would sooner have cut his hand off than have sent the boys to Coombe together, could he have guessed that this was to be the result!

Such discourses did not tend to make Ethel comfortable. If she had been silly enough to indulge in a dream of her influence availing to strengthen Leonard against temptation, she must still have refrained from exerting it through her wonted medium, since it was her father's express desire that Aubrey, for his own sake, should be detached from his friend as much as possible.

Aubrey was the greatest present difficulty. Long before their illness the boys had been the resource of each other's leisure, and Coombe had made their intimacy a friendship of the warmest nature. Aubrey was at an age peculiarly dependent on equal companionship, and in the absence of his brothers, the loss of his daily intercourse with Leonard took away all the zest of life. Even the volunteer practice lost its charm without the rival with whom he chiefly contended, yet whose success against others was better to him than his own; his other occupations all wanted partnership, and for the first time in his life he showed weariness and contempt of his sisters' society and pursuits. He rushed off on Sunday evenings for a walk with Leonard; and though Dr May did not interfere, the daughters saw that the abstinence was an effort of prudence, and were proportionately disturbed when one day at dinner, in his father's absence, Aubrey, who had been overlooking his fishing-flies with some reviving interest, refused all his sisters' proposals for the afternoon, and when they represented that it was not a good fishing-day, owned that it was not, but that he was going over to consult Leonard Ward about some grey hackles.

'But you mustn't, Aubrey,' cried Gertrude, aghast.

Aubrey made her a low mocking bow.

'I am sure papa would be very much vexed,' added she, conclusively.

'I believe it was luckless Hal that the mill-wheel tore in your nursery rhymes, eh, Daisy,' said Aubrey.

'Nursery rhymes, indeed!' returned the offended young lady; 'you know it is a very wicked place, and papa would be very angry at your going there.' She looked at Ethel, extremely shocked at her not having interfered, and disregarding all signs to keep silence.

'Axworthy – worthy of the axe,' said Aubrey, well pleased to retort a little teasing by the way; 'young Axworthy baiting the trap, and old Axworthy sitting up in his den to grind the unwary limb from limb!'

'Ethel, why don't you tell him not?' exclaimed Gertrude.

'Because he knows papa's wishes as well as I do,' said Ethel; 'and it is to them that he must attend, not to you or me.'

Aubrey muttered something about his father having said nothing to him; and Ethel succeeded in preventing Daisy from resenting this answer. She herself hoped to catch him in private, but he easily contrived to baffle this attempt, and was soon marching out of Stoneborough in a state of rampant independence, manhood, and resolute friendship, which nevertheless chose the way where he was least likely to encounter a little brown brougham.

Otherwise he might have reckoned three and a half miles of ploughed field, soppy lane, and water meadow, as more than equivalent to five miles of good turnpike road.

Be that as it might, he was extremely glad when, after forcing his way through a sticky clayey path through a hazel copse, his eye fell on a wide reach of meadow land, the railroad making a hard line across it at one end, and in the midst, about half a mile off, the river meandering like a blue ribbon lying loosely across the green flat, the handsome buildings of the Vintry Mill lying in its embrace.

Aubrey knew the outward aspect of the place, for the foreman at the mill was a frequent patient of his father's, and he had often waited in the old gig at the cottage door at no great distance; but he looked with more critical eyes at the home of his friend.

It was a place with much capacity, built, like the Grange, by the monks of the convent, which had been the germ of the cathedral, and showing the grand old monastic style in the solidity of its stone barns and storehouses, all arranged around a court, whereof the dwelling-house occupied one side, the lawn behind it with fine old trees, and sloping down to the water, which was full of bright ripples after its agitation around the great mill-wheel. The house was of more recent date, having been built by a wealthy yeoman of Queen Anne's time, and had long ranges of square-headed sash windows, surmounted by a pediment, carved with emblems of Ceres and Bacchus, and a very tall front door, also with a pediment, and with stone steps leading up to it. Of the same era appeared to be the great gateway, and the turret above it, containing a clock, the hands of which pointed to 3.40.

Aubrey had rather it had been four, at which time the office closed. He looked round the court, which seemed very clean and rather empty – stables, barns, buildings, and dwelling-house not showing much sign of life, excepting the ceaseless hum and clack of the mill, and the dash of the water which propelled it. The windows nearest to him were so large and low, that he could look in and see that the first two or three belonged to living rooms, and the next two showed him business fittings, and a back that he took to be Leonard's; but he paused in doubt how to present himself, and whether this were a welcome moment; and he was very glad to see in a doorway of the upper story of the mill buildings, the honest floury face of his father's old patient – the foreman.

Greeting him in the open cordial way common to all Dr May's children, Aubrey was at once recognised, and the old man came down a step-ladder in the interior to welcome him, and answer his question where he should find Mr Ward.

'He is in the office, sir, there, to the left hand as you go in at the front door, but——' and he looked up at the clock, 'maybe, you would not mind waiting a bit till it strikes four. I don't know whether master might be best pleased at young gentlemen coming to see him in office hours.'

'Thank you,' said Aubrey. 'I did not mean to be too soon, Hardy, but I did not know how long the walk would be.'

Perhaps it would have been more true had he said that he had wanted to elude his sisters, but he was glad to accept a seat on a bundle of sacks tremulous with the motion of the mill, and to enter into a conversation with the old foreman, one of those good old peasants whose integrity and skill render them privileged persons, worth their weight in gold long after their bodily strength has given way.

'Well, Hardy, do you mean to make a thorough good miller of Mr Ward?'

'Bless you, Master May, he'll never stay here long enough.'

'Why not?'

'No, nor his friends didn't ought to let him stay!' added Hardy.

'Why?' said Aubrey. 'Do you think so badly of your own trade, Hardy?'

But he could not get an answer from the oracle on this head. Hardy continued, 'He's a nice young gentleman, but he'll never put up with it.'

'Put up with what?' asked Aubrey, anxiously; but at that instant a carter appeared at the door with a question for Master Hardy, and Aubrey was left to his own devices, and the hum and clatter of the mill, till the clock had struck four; and beginning to think that Hardy had forgotten him, he was about to set out and reconnoitre, when to his great joy Leonard himself came hurrying up, and heartily shook him by the hand.

'Hardy told me you were here,' he said. 'Well done, old fellow, I didn't think they would have let you come and see me.'

'The girls did make a great row about it,' said Aubrey, triumphantly, 'but I was not going to stand any nonsense.'

Leonard looked a little doubtful; then said, 'Well, will you see the place, or come and sit in my room? There is the parlour, but we shall not be so quiet there.'

Aubrey decided for Leonard's room, and was taken through the front door into a vestibule paved with white stone, with black lozenges at the intersections. 'There,' said Leonard, 'the office is here, you see, and my uncle's rooms beyond, all on the ground-floor, he is too infirm to go up stairs. This way is the dining-room, and Sam has got a sitting-room beyond then there are the servants' rooms. It is a great place, and horridly empty.'

Aubrey thought so, as his footsteps echoed up the handsome but ill-kept stone staircase, with its fanciful balusters half choked with dust, and followed Leonard along a corridor, with deep windows overlooking the garden and river, and great panelled doors opposite, neither looking as if they were often either cleaned or opened, and the passage smelling very fusty.

'Pah!' said Aubrey; 'it puts me in mind of the wings of houses in books that get shut up because somebody has been murdered! Are you sure it is not haunted, Leonard?'

'Only by the rats,' he answered, laughing; 'they make such an intolerable row, that poor little Mab is frightened out of her wits, and I don't know whether they would not eat her up if she did not creep up close to me. I'm tired of going at them with the poker, and would poison every man Jack of them if it were not for the fear of her getting the dose by mistake.'

'Is that what Hardy says you will never put up with?' asked Aubrey; but instead of answering, Leonard turned to one of the great windows, saying,

'There now, would not this be a charming place if it were properly kept?' and Aubrey looked out at the great cedar, spreading out its straight limbs and flakes of dark foliage over the sloping lawn, one branch so near the window as to invite adventurous exits, and a little boat lying moored in the dancing water below.

'Perfect!' said Aubrey. 'What fish there must lie in the mill tail!'

'Ay, I mean to have a try at them some of these days, I should like you to come and help, but perhaps – Ha, little Mab, do you wonder what I'm after so long? Here's a friend for you:' as the little dog danced delighted round him, and paid Aubrey her affectionate respects. Her delicate drawing-room beauty did not match with the spacious but neglected-looking room whence she issued. It had three great uncurtained windows looking into the court, with deep window-seats, olive-coloured painted walls, the worse for damp and wear, a small amount of old-fashioned solid furniture, and all Leonard's individual goods, chiefly disposed of in a cupboard in the wall, but Averil's beautiful water-coloured drawings hung over the chimney. To Aubrey's petted home-bred notions it was very bare and dreary, and he could not help exclaiming, 'Well, they don't lodge you sumptuously!'

'I don't fancy many clerks in her Majesty's dominions have so big and airy an apartment to boast of,' said Leonard, 'Let's see these flies of yours.'

Their mysteries occupied the boys for some space; but Aubrey returned to the charge. 'What is it that Hardy says you'll never put up with, Leonard?'

'What did the old fellow say?' asked Leonard, laughing; and as Aubrey repeated the conversation, ending with the oracular prediction, he laughed again, but said proudly, 'He'll see himself wrong then. I'll put up with whatever I've undertaken.'

'But what does he mean?'

'Serving one's apprenticeship, I suppose,' said Leonard; 'they all think me a fine gentleman, and above the work, I know, though I've never stuck at anything yet. If I take to the business, I suppose it is capable of being raised up to me – it need not pull me down to it, eh?'

'There need be no down in the case,' said Aubrey. 'My father always says there is no *down* except in meanness and wrong. But,' as if that mention brought a recollection to his mind, 'what o'clock is it? I must not stay much longer.'

'I'll walk a bit of the way home with you,' said Leonard, 'but I must be back by five for dinner. I go to rifle practice two days in the week, and I don't like to miss the others, for Sam's often out, and the poor old man does not like being left alone at meals.'

The two boys were at the room door, when Aubrey heard a step, felt the fustiness enlivened by the odour of a cigar, and saw a figure at the top of the stairs.

'I say, Ward,' observed Mr Sam, in a rude domineering voice, 'Spelman's account must be all looked over to-night; he says that there is a blunder. D'ye hear?'

'Very well.'

'Who have you got there?'

'It is Aubrey May.'

'Oh! good morning to you,' making a kind of salutation, 'have you been looking at the water? We've got some fine fish there, if you like to throw a line any day. – Well, that account must be done to-night, and if you can't find the error, you'll only have to do it over again.'

Leonard's colour had risen a good deal, but he said nothing, and his cousin ran down stairs and drove off in his dog-cart.

'Is it much of a business?' said Aubrey, feeling extremely indignant.

'Look here,' said Leonard, leading the way down stairs and into the office, where he pointed to two huge account books. 'Every page in that one must I turn over this blessed night; and if he had only told me three hours ago, I could have done the chief of it, instead of kicking my heels all the afternoon.'

'Has he any right to order you about, out of office hours, and without a civil word either? Why do you stand it?'

'Because I can stand anything better than being returned on Henry's hands,' said Leonard, 'and he has spite enough for that. The thing must be done, and if he won't do it, I must, that's all. Come along.'

As they went out the unwieldy figure of the elder Mr Axworthy was seen, leaning out of his open window, smoking a clay pipe. He spoke in a much more friendly tone, as he said, 'Going out, eh? Mind the dinner-time.'

'Yes, Sir,' said Leonard, coming nearer, 'I'm not going far.'

'Who have you got there?' was again asked.

'One of the young Mays, sir. I was going to walk part of the way back.'

Aubrey thought the grunt not very civil; and as the boys and Mab passed under the gateway, Leonard continued, 'There's not much love lost between him and your father; he hates the very name.'

'I should expect he would,' said Aubrey, as if his hatred were an honour.

'I fancy there's some old grievance,' said Leonard, 'where he was wrong of course. Not that that need hinder your coming over, Aubrey; I've a right to my own friends, but——'

'And so have I to mine,' said Aubrey eagerly.

'But you see,' added Leonard, 'I wouldn't have you do it – if – if it vexes your sister. I can see you every Sunday, you know, and we can have some fun together on Saturdays when the evenings get longer.'

Aubrey's face fell; he had a strong inclination for Leonard's company, and likewise for the trout in the mill tail, and he did not like his independence to be unappreciated.

'You see,' said Leonard, laying his hand kindly on his shoulder, 'it is very jolly of you, but I know they would hate it in the High Street if you were often here, and it is not worth that. Besides, Aubrey, to tell the plain truth, Sam's not fit company for any decent fellow.'

'I can't think how he came to ask me to fish.'

'Just to show he is master, because he knew the poor old man would not like it! It is one reason he is so savage with me, because his uncle took me without his consent.'

'But, Leonard, it must be worse than the living at home ever was.'

Leonard laughed. 'Its different being jawed in the way of business and at one's own home. I'd go through a good deal more than I do here in the week to have home what it is now on Sunday. Why, Henry really seems glad to see me, and we have not had the shadow of a row since I came over here. Don't you tell Ave all this, mind, and you may just as well not talk about it at home, you know, or they will think I'm going to cry off.'

Aubrey was going to ask what he looked to; but Leonard saw, or thought he saw, a weasel in the hedge, and the consequent charge and pursuit finished the dialogue, the boys parted, and Aubrey walked home, his satisfaction in his expedition oozing away at every step, though his resolve to assert his liberty grew in proportion.

Of course it had not been possible to conceal from Dr May where Aubrey was gone, and his annoyance had burst out vehemently, the whole round of objurgations against the Wards, the Vintry Mill, and his own folly in fostering the friendship, were gone through, and Ethel had come in for more than she could easily bear, for not having prevented the escapade. Gertrude had hardly ever seen her father so angry, and sat quaking for her brother; and Ethel meekly avoided answering again, with the happy trustfulness of experienced love.

At last, as the tea was nearly over, Aubrey walked in, quite ready for self-defence. Nobody spoke for a little while, except to supply him with food; but presently Dr May said, not at all in the tone in which he had talked *of* his son's journey, 'You might as well have told me of your intentions, Aubrey.'

'I didn't think they mattered to anybody,' said Aubrey; 'we generally go our own way in the afternoon.'

'Oh!' said Dr May. 'Interference with the liberty of the subject?'

Aubrey coloured, and felt he had not quite spoken truth. 'I could not give him up, father,' he said, less defiantly.

'No, certainly not; but I had rather you only saw him at home. It will be more for our peace of mind.'

'Well father,' said Aubrey, 'I am not going there any more. He told me not himself:' and then with laughing eyes he added, 'He said you would not like it, Ethel.'

'Poor boy!' said Ethel, greatly touched.

'Very right of him,' said Dr May, well pleased. 'He is a fine lad, and full of proper feeling. What sort of a berth has the old rogue given him, Aubrey?'

Much relieved that matters had taken this course, Aubrey tried to tell only as much as his friend would approve, but the medium was not easily found, and pretty nearly the whole came out. Dr May was really delighted to hear how Sam treated him.

'If that fellow takes the oppressive line, there may be some hope,' he said. 'His friendship is the worse danger than his enmity.'

When the sisters had bidden good night, the doctor detained Aubrey to say very kindly, 'My boy I do not like to hear of your running counter to your sister.'

'I'm not going there again,' said Aubrey, willing to escape.

'Wait a minute, Aubrey,' said Dr May; 'I want to tell you that I feel for you in this matter more than my way of talking may have made it seem to you. I have a great regard for your friend Leonard, and think he has been scandalously used, and I don't want to lessen your attachment to him. Far be it from me to think lightly of a friendship, especially of one formed at your age. Your very name, my boy, shows that I am not likely to do that!'

Aubrey smiled frankly, his offended self-assertion entirely melted.

'I know it is very hard on you, but you can understand that the very reasons that made me so averse to Leonard's taking this situation, would make me anxious to keep you away from his relations there, not necessarily from him. As long as he is what he is now, I would not lift a finger to keep you from him. Have I ever done so, Aubrey?'

'No, papa.'

'Nor will I, as long as he is what I see him now. After this, Aubrey, is it too much to ask of you to keep out of the way of the persons with whom he is thrown?'

'I will do so, papa. He wishes it himself.' Then with an effort, he added, 'I am sorry I went to-day; I ought not, but——' and he looked a little foolish.

'You did not like taking orders from the girls? No wonder, Aubrey; I have been very thankful to you for bearing it as you have done. It is the worst of home education that these spirits of manliness generally have no vent but mischief. But you are old enough now to be thankful for such a friend and adviser as Ethel, and I don't imagine that she orders you.'

'No,' said Aubrey, smiling and mumbling; 'but Daisy——'

'Oh, I can quite understand the aggravation of Daisy happening to be right; but you must really be man enough to mind your own conscience, even if Daisy is imprudent enough to enforce it.'

'It was not only that,' said Aubrey, 'but I could not have Ward thinking I turned up my nose at his having got into business.'

'No, Aubrey, he need never fancy it is the business that I object to, but the men. Make that clear to him, and ask him to this house as much as you please. The more "thorough" he is in his business, the more I shall respect him.'

Aubrey smiled, and thanked his father with a cleared brow, wondering at himself for having gone without consulting him.

'Good night, my boy. May this friendship of yours be a life-long stay and blessing to you both, even though it may cost you some pain and self-command, as all good things must, Aubrey.'

That evening Ethel had been writing to Cambridge. Tom had passed his examination with great credit, and taken an excellent degree, after which he projected a tour in Germany, for which he had for some time been economizing, as a well-earned holiday before commencing his course of hospitals and lectures. Tom was no great correspondent, and had drilled his sisters into putting nothing but the essential into their letters, instead, as he said, of concealing it in flummery. This is a specimen of the way Tom liked to be written to.

Stoneborough, Feb. 20th.

'My dear Tom,

'Dr Spencer says nothing answers so well as a knapsack. Get one at——. The price is £ *s. d.* Order extra fittings as required, including a knife and fork. Letters from N.Z. of the 1st of November; all well. I wish Aubrey was going with you; he misses Leonard Ward so sorely, as to be tempted to follow him to the Vintry Mill. I suspect your words are coming true, and the days of petticoat government ending. However, even if he would not be in your way, he could not afford to lose six months' study before going into residence.

'Your affectionate sister,

'ETHELDRED MAY.'

Tom wrote that he should spend a night in London and come home. When he came, the family exclaimed that his microscope, whose handsome case he carried in his hand, was much grown. 'And improved too, I hope,' said Tom, proceeding to show off various new acquisitions and exchanges in the way of eye-pieces, lenses, and other appliances of the most expensive order, till his father exclaimed,

'Really, Tom, I wish I had the secret of your purse.'

'The fact is,' said Tom, 'that I thought more would be gained by staying at home, so I turned my travels into a binocular tube,' &c.

Aubrey and Gertrude shouted that Tom certainly *did* love the microscope better than any earthly thing; and he coolly accepted the inference.

Somewhat later, he announced that he had decided that he should be better able to profit by the London lectures and hospitals, if he first studied for half a year at the one at Stoneborough, under the direction of his father and Dr Spencer.

Dr May was extremely gratified, and really esteemed this one of the greatest compliments his science had ever received; Dr Spencer could not help observing, 'I did not think it was in him to do such a wise thing. I never can fathom the rogue. I hope he was not bitten during his benevolent exertions last winter.'

Meantime, Tom had observed that he had time to see that Aubrey was decently prepared for Cambridge, and further promoted the boy to be his out-of-door companion, removing all the tedium and perplexity of the last few weeks, though apparently merely indulging his own inclinations. Ethel recognised the fruit of her letter, and could well forgive the extra care in housekeeping required for Tom's critical tastes, nay, the cool expulsion of herself and Gertrude from her twenty years' home, the school-room, and her final severance from Aubrey's studies, though at the cost of a pang that reminded her of her girlhood's sorrow at letting Norman shoot ahead of her. She gave no hint; she knew that implicit reserve was the condition of his strange silent confidence in her, and that it would be utterly forfeited unless she allowed his fraternal sacrifice to pass for mere long-headed prudence.

Aubrey's Saturday and Sunday meetings with his friend were not yielded, even to Tom, who endeavoured to interfere with them, and would fain have cut the connexion with the entire family, treating Miss Ward with the most distant and supercilious bows on the unpleasantly numerous occasions of meeting her in the street, and contriving to be markedly scornful in his punctilious civility to Henry Ward when they met at the hospital. His very look appeared a sarcasm, to the fancy of the Wards; and he had a fashion of kindly inquiring after Leonard, that seemed to both a deliberate reproach and insult.

Disputes had become less frequent at Bankside since Leonard's departure, and few occasions of actual dissension arose; but the spirit of party was not extinguished, and the brother and sister had adopted lines that perhaps clashed less because they diverged more.

Averil had, in reply to the constant exhortations to economize, resolved to decline all invitations, and this kept her constantly at home, or with her harmonium; whereas Henry made such constant engagements, that their dining together was the exception, not the rule. After conscientiously teaching her sisters in the morning, she devoted the rest of her day to their walk, and to usefulness in the parish. She liked her tasks, and would have been very happy in them, but for the constant anxiety that hung over her lest her home should soon cease to be her home.

Henry's devotion to Mrs Pugh could no longer be mistaken. The conviction of his intentions grew upon his sister, first from a mere absurd notion, banished from her mind with derision, then from a misgiving angrily silenced, to a fixed expectation, confirmed by the evident opinion of all around her, and calling for decision and self-command on her own part.

Perhaps her feelings were unnecessarily strong, and in some degree unjust to Mrs Pugh; but she had the misfortune to be naturally proud and sensitive, as well as by breeding too refined in tone for most of those who surrounded her. She had taken a personal dislike to Mrs Pugh from the first; she regarded pretension as insincerity, and officiousness as deliberate insult, and she took the recoil of her taste for the judgment of principle. To see such a woman ruling in her mother's, her own, home would be bad enough; but to be ruled by her, and resign to her the management of the children, would be intolerable beyond measure. Too unhappy to speak of her anticipations even to Leonard or to Mary May, she merely endeavoured to throw them off from day to day; till one evening, when the days had grown so long that she could linger in the twilight in the garden before her singing practice, she was joined by Henry, with the long apprehended 'I want to speak to you, Ave.'

Was it coming? Her heart beat so fast, that she could hardly hear his kind commencement about her excellent endeavours, and the house's unhappy want of a mistress, the children's advantage, and so on. She knew it could only tend to one point, and longed to have it reached and passed. Of course she would be prepared to hear who was the object of his choice, and she could not but murmur 'Yes,' and 'Well.'

'And, Ave, you will, I hope, be gratified to hear that I am not entirely rejected. The fact is, that I spoke too soon.' Averil could have jumped for joy, and was glad it was too dusk for her face to be seen. 'I do not believe that her late husband could have had any strong hold on her affections; but she has not recovered the shock of his loss, and entreated, as a favour granted to her sentiments of respect for his memory, not to hear the subject mentioned for at least another year. I am permitted to visit at the house as usual, and no difference is to be made in the terms on which we stand. Now, Ave, will you – may I ask of you, to do what you can to remove any impression that she might not be welcome in the family?'

'I never meant——' faltered Averil, checked by sincerity.

'You have always been – so – so cold and backward in cultivating her acquaintance, that I cannot wonder if she should think it disagreeable to you; but, Ave, when you consider my happiness, and the immense advantage to all of you, I am sure you will do what is in your power on my behalf.' He spoke more affectionately and earnestly than he had done for months; and Averil was touched, and felt that to hang back would be unkind.

'I will try,' she said. 'I do hope it may turn out for your happiness, Henry.'

'For all our happiness,' said Henry, walking down to the gate and along the road with her, proving all the way that he was acting solely for the good of the others, and that Averil and the children would find their home infinitely happier.

A whole year – a year's reprieve – was the one thought in Averil's head, that made her listen so graciously, and answer so amiably, that Henry parted with her full of kind, warm feeling.

As the sage said, who was to be beheaded if he could not in a year teach the king's ass to speak – what might not happen in a year; the king might die, the ass might die, or he might die – any way there was so much gained: and Averil, for the time, felt as light-hearted as if Mrs Pugh had vanished into empty air. To be sure, her own life had, of late, been far from happy; but this extension of it was hailed with suppressed ecstasy – almost as an answer to her prayers. Ah, Ave, little did you know what you wished in hoping for *anything* to prevent the marriage!

She did obey her brother so far as to call upon Mrs Pugh, whom she found in ordinary mourning, and capless – a sign that dismayed her; but, on the other hand, the lady, though very good-natured and patronizing, entertained her with the praises of King John, and showed her a copy of Magna Charta in process of illumination. Also, during her call, Tom May walked in with a little book on drops of water; and Averil found the lady had become inspired with a microscopic *furore*, and was thinking of setting up a lens, and preparing objects for herself, under good tuition.

Though Averil was very desirous that Mrs Pugh should refuse her brother, yet this was the last service she wished the May family to render her. She was sure Tom May must dislike and despise the widow as much as she did; and since the whole town was unluckily aware of Henry's intentions, any interference with them was base and malicious, if in the way of mere amusement and flirtation. She was resolved to see what the game was, but only did see that her presence greatly disconcerted 'Mr Thomas May.'

Henry was wretched and irritable in the velvet paws of the widow, who encouraged him enough to give him hope, and then held him aloof, or was equally amiable to some one else. Perhaps the real interpretation was, that she loved attention. She was in all sincerity resolved to observe a proper period of widowhood, and not determined whether, when, or how, it should terminate: courtship amused her, and though attracted by Henry and his good house, the evidences of temper and harshness had made her unwilling to commit herself; besides that, she was afraid of Averil, and she was more flattered by the civilities of a lioncel like Harvey Anderson; or if she could be sure of what Mr Thomas May's intentions were, she would have preferred an embryo physician to a full-grown surgeon – at any rate, it was right by her poor dear Mr Pugh to wait.

She need not have feared having Averil as an inmate. Averil talked it over with Leonard, and determined that no power on earth should make her live with Mrs Pugh. If that were necessary to forward his suit, she would make it plain that she was ready to depart.

'Oh, Leonard, if my uncle were but a nice sort of person, how pleasant it would be for me and the children to live there, and keep his house; and I could make him so comfortable, and nurse him!'

'Never, Ave!' cried Leonard; 'don't let the thing be talked of.'

'Oh no, I know it would not do with Samuel there; but should we be too young for your old scheme of having a cottage together near?'

'I did not know what the Axworthys were like,' returned Leonard.

'But need we see them much?'

'I'll tell you what, Ave, I've heard them both – yes, the old man the worst of the two – say things about women that made my blood boil.' Leonard was quite red as he spoke. 'My father never let my mother see any of the concern, and now I know why, I'll never let you do so.'

'Then there is only one other thing to be done,' said Averil; 'and that is for me to go back to school as a parlour boarder, and take the children with me. It would be very good for them, and dear Mrs Wood would be very glad to have me.'

'Yes,' said Leonard, 'that is the only right thing, Ave; and the Mays will say so, too. Have you talked it over with them?'

'No; I hate talking of this thing.'

'Well, you had better get their advice. It is the best thing going!' said Leonard, with a sigh that sounded as if he wished he had taken it.

But it was not to Averil that he said so. To her he spoke brightly of serving the time for which he was bound to his uncle; then of making a fresh engagement, that would open a home to her; or, better still, suppose Sam did not wish to go on with the business, he might take it, and make the mill the lovely place it might be. It was to Aubrey May that the boy's real feelings came out, as, on the Sunday evening, they slowly wandered along the bank of the river. Aubrey had *seen* a specimen of his life at the mill, and been kept up to the knowledge of its events; and he well knew that Leonard was heartily sick of it. That the occupation was uncongenial and tedious in the extreme to a boy of good ability and superior education – nay, that the drudgery was made unnecessarily oppressive, was not the point he complained of, though it was more trying than he had expected. That was the bed that he had made, and that he must lie upon. It was the suspicion of frauds and tricks of the trade, and, still worse, the company that he lived in. Sam Axworthy hated and tyrannized over him too much to make dissipation alluring; and he was only disgusted by the foul language, coarse manners, and the remains of intemperance worked off in violent temper.

The old man, though helpless and past active vice, was even more coarse in mind and conversation than his nephew; and yet his feebleness, and Sam's almost savage treatment of him, enlisted Leonard's pity on his side. In general, the old man was kind to Leonard, but would abuse him roundly when the evidences of his better principles and training, or his allegiance to Dr May, came forward; and Leonard, though greatly compassionating him, could not always bear his reproaches with patience, and was held back from more attention to him than common humanity required, by an unlucky suggestion that he was currying favour in the hope of supplanting Sam.

'Old Hardy is the only honest man in the place, I do believe,' said Leonard. 'I'll tell you what, Aubrey, I have made up my mind, there is one thing I will not do. If ever they want to make me a party to any of their cheatings, I'll be off. That window and the cedar-tree stand very handy. I've been out there to bathe in the early summer mornings, plenty of times already, so never you be surprised if some fine day you hear – *non est inventus*.'

'And where would you go?'

'Get up to London, and see if my quarter's salary would take me out in the steerage to some diggings or other. What would your brother say to me if I turned up at the Grange – New Zealand?'

'Say! Mention Ethel, and see what he would not say.'

And the two boys proceeded to arrange the details of the evasion in such vivid colouring, that they had nearly forgotten all present troubles, above all when Leonard proceeded to declare that New Zealand was too tame and too settled for him, he should certainly find something to do in the Feejee Isles, where the high spirit of the natives, their painted visages, and marvellous head-dresses, as depicted in Captain Erskine's voyage, had greatly fired his fancy, and they even settled how the gold fields should rebuild the Market Cross.

'And when I'm gone, Aubrey, mind you see to Mab,' he said, laughing.

'Oh! I thought Mab was to act Whittington's Cat.'

'I'm afraid they would eat her up; besides, there's the voyage. No, you must keep her till I come home, even if she is to end like Argus. Would you die of joy at seeing me, eh, little black neb?'

CHAPTER XII

'Let us meet,
And question this most bloody piece of work,
To know it farther.'

Macbeth.

'If you please, sir, Master Hardy from the Vintry Mill wants to see you,' said a voice at Dr May's door early in the morning; and the doctor completed his dressing in haste, muttering to himself exclamations of concern that the old man's malady should have returned.

On entering the study, Hardy's appearance, whiter than even the proverbial hue of his trade, his agitation of feature, confused eye, and trembling lip, inspired fears that the case was more alarming than had been apprehended; but to cheer him, the doctor began, 'Frightened about yourself, Master Hardy, eh? You've come out without breakfast, and that's enough to put any man out of heart.'

'No, sir,' said the old man, 'it is nothing about myself; I wish it were no worse; but I've not got the heart to go to tell the poor young gentleman, and I thought——'

'What – what has happened to the boy?' exclaimed Dr May, sharply, standing as if ready to receive the rifle shot which he already believed had destroyed Leonard.

'That's what we can't say, sir,' returned Hardy; 'but he is gone, no one knows where. And, sir, my poor master was found at five o'clock this morning, in his chair in his sitting-room, stone dead from a blow on the head.'

'Mind what you are saying!' shouted the doctor passionately. 'You old scoundrel, you don't mean to tell me that you are accusing the lad!'

'I accuse nobody, sir,' said the old man, standing his ground, and speaking steadily, but respectfully, 'I wouldn't say nothing to bring any one into trouble if I could help it; and I came to ask you what was to be done.'

'Yes, yes; I beg your pardon, Hardy, but it sounded enough to overset one. Your poor master murdered, you say!'

Hardy nodded assent.

'And young Ward missing? Why, the burglars must have hurt the poor fellow in defending his uncle. Have you searched the place?'

'I never thought of that, sir,' said Hardy, his countenance much relieved; 'it would be more like such a young gentleman as Mr Ward.'

'Then we'll get over to the mill as fast as we can, and see what can be done,' said Dr May, snatching up his hat and gloves. 'You come and walk with me to Bankside, and tell me by the way about this terrible business. Good heavens! they'll have thrown the boy into the river!'

And calling out that his carriage should follow to Bankside, the doctor dashed up stairs, and knocked at Ethel's door. 'My dear,' he said, 'there has been a robbery or something at the Vintry Mill. I must go and see Henry Ward about it. Poor old Axworthy is murdered, and I'm terribly afraid Leonard has met with some foul play. You or Mary had better go and see about Ave presently, but don't believe a word of anything till you see me again.'

And shutting the door, while Ethel felt as if the room were reeling round with her, Dr May was in a few seconds more hastening along by Hardy's side, extracting from him the little he had to tell. The old man had been unlocking the door of the mill at five o'clock, when he was summoned by loud shrieks from the window of Mr Axworthy's sitting-room, and found that the little maid had been appalled by the sight of her master sunk forward from his gouty chair upon the table, his hair covered with blood. Hardy had been the first to touch him, and to perceive that he had long been dead. The housekeeper, the only other servant who slept in the house, had rushed in half-dressed; but neither nephew appeared. Young Axworthy had gone the previous day to the county races, leaving the time of his return doubtful; and Leonard Ward did not answer when called. It was then found that his room was empty, his bed untouched, and the passage window outside his door left open. The terrified servants held confused consultation, and while the groom had hurried off to give the alarm at Whitford, and ride on in search of Sam Axworthy, Hardy had taken another horse and started to inform Henry Ward, but his heart failing him, he had come to beg the doctor to break the intelligence to the family.

Dr May had few doubts that the robbers must have entered by the passage window, and meeting resistance from Leonard, must have dragged him out, and perhaps thrown him from it, then having gone on to their murderous work in the old man's sitting-room. In that great rambling house, where the maids slept afar off, and the rats held nightly gambols, strange noises were not likely to be observed; and the thought of Leonard lying stunned and insensible on the grass, made the doctor's pace almost a run, as if he were hastening to the rescue.

When Mr Ward sent down word that he was not up, Dr May replied that he must see him in bed, and followed upon the very heels of the messenger, encountering no amiable face, for Henry had armed himself for defence against any possible reproaches for his treatment of any patient. Even when Dr May began, 'Henry, my poor fellow, I have frightful news for you,' his mouth was opening to reply, 'I knew we should lose that case,' let the patient be who he might, when the few simple words put to flight all petulant jealousy, and restored Henry Ward to what he had been when in his hour of sickness and affliction he had leant in full confidence on Dr May's unfailing kindness.

He was dressed by the time the brougham was at the door, and would have hurried off without telling his sister of the alarm; but Dr May, knowing that the town must soon be ringing with the news, was sending him to Averil's room, when both rejoiced to see Mary enter the house. Charging her to keep Averil quiet, and believe nothing but what came from themselves, they thrust on her the terrible commission and hastened away, dwelling on the hope that every moment might be important.

Old Hardy had already mounted his cart-horse, and for him farm roads so shortened the distance, that he received them at the entrance of the courtyard, which was crowded with excited gazers and important policemen.

'Found him?' was the instantaneous question of both; but Hardy shook his head so sadly, that the Doctor hastily exclaimed, 'What then?'

'Sir,' said Hardy very low, and with a deprecating look, 'he *did* go up by the mail train to London last night – got in at Blewer Station at 12.15. They have telegraphed up, sir.'

'I'll lay my life it is all a mistake,' said Dr May, grasping Henry's arm as if to give him support, and looking him in the face as though resolved that neither should be cast down.

'That's not all, sir,' added Hardy, still addressing himself to the elder gentleman. 'There's his rifle, sir.'

'Why, he was not shot!' sharply cried Dr May. 'You told me so yourself.'

'No, sir; but – you'll see for yourself presently! There's the blood and grey hairs on the stock, sir.'

'Never fear, Henry; we shall see,' said Dr May, pressing on, and adding as soon as they were out of hearing, 'Nothing those folks, even the best of them, like so well as laying on horrors thick enough.'

A policeman stood at the house door to keep off idlers; but Dr May's character and profession, as well as his municipal rank, caused way to be instantly made for them. They found a superintendent within, and he at once began, 'Most unfortunate business, Mr Mayor – very mysterious;' then, as a sign from the doctor made him aware of Henry Ward's near concern, he added, 'Shall I inform young Mr Axworthy that you are here?'

'Is he come?'

'Yes, sir. He had only slept at the Three Goblets, not half a mile across the fields, you know, Mr Mayor – came home too late to disturb the house here, slept there, and was on the spot at the first intelligence – before I was myself,' added the superintendent a little jealously.

'Where is he?'

'In his room, sir. He was extremely overcome, and retired to his room as soon as the necessary steps had been taken. Would you wish to see the room, sir? We are keeping it locked till the inquest takes place; but——'

Henry asked, 'When?' his first word since his arrival, and almost inarticulate.

He was answered that it would probably be at two that afternoon; the Whitford coroner had intimated that he was ready, and the down train would be in by one. A telegram had just arrived, reporting that the electric message had anticipated the mail train, and that young Mr Ward would be brought down in time.

'Never mind, never heed, Henry,' persisted Dr May, pressing the young man's arm as they proceeded to the door of the sitting-room; 'he must be intensely shocked, but he will explain the whole. Nay, I've no doubt we shall clear him. His rifle, indeed! I could swear to his rifle anywhere.'

The superintendent had by this time opened the door of the sitting-room, communicating on one side with the office, on the other with the old man's bed-room.

Except that the body had been carried to the bed in the inner chamber, all remained as it had been found. There were no signs of robbery – not even of a struggle. The cushions of the easy chair still bore the impress of the sitter's weight; the footstool was hardly pushed aside; the massive library table was undisturbed; the silver spoons and sugar-tongs beside the tumbler and plate on the supper tray; the yellow light of the lamp still burnt; not a paper was ruffled, not a drawer pulled out. Only a rifle stood leaning against the window shutter, and towards it both friend and brother went at once, hoping and trusting that it would be a stranger to their eyes.

Alas! alas! only too familiar were the rich brown mottlings of the stock, the steel mountings, the eagle crest, and twisted H.E. cypher! and in sickness of heart the doctor could not hide from himself the dark clot of gore and the few white hairs adhering to the wood, and answering to the stain that dyed the leather of the desk.

Henry could not repress an agonized groan, and averted his face; but his companion undaunted met the superintendent's eye and query, 'You know it, sir?'

'I do. It was my son-in-law's present to him. I wonder where he kept it, for the ruffians to get hold of it.'

The superintendent remained civil and impassive, and no one spoke to break the deathly hush of the silent room, filled with the appliances of ordinary business life, but tainted with the awful unexplained mark that there had been the foot of the shedder of blood in silence and at unawares.

The man in authority at length continued his piteous exhibition. Dr Rankin of Whitford had arrived on the first alarm; but would not the gentlemen see the body? And he led them on, Dr May's eyes on the alert to seize on anything exculpatory, but detecting nothing; seeing only the unwieldy helpless form and aged feeble countenance of the deceased, and receiving fresh impressions of the brutality and cowardice of the hand that could have struck the blow. He looked, examined, defined the injury, and explained that it must have caused instant death, thus hoping to divert attention from his pale horror-stricken companion, whose too apparent despondency almost provoked him.

At the doctor's request they were taken up the staircase into the corridor, and shown the window, which had been found nearly closed but not fastened, as though it had been partially shut down from the outside. The cedar bough almost brushed the glass, and the slope of turf came so high up the wall, that an active youth could easily swing himself down to it; and the superintendent significantly remarked that the punt was on the farther side of the stream, whereas the evening before it had been on the nearer. Dr May leant out over the window sill, still in the lingering hope of seeing – he knew not what; but he only became oppressed by the bright still summer beauty of the trees and grass and sparkling water, insensible of the horror that brooded over all. He drew back his head; and as the door hard by was opened, Leonard's little dog sprang from her basket kennel, wagging her tail in hopes of her master, but in her disappointment greeting one whom dogs always hailed as a friend.

'Poor little doggie! good little Mab! If only you could tell us!' and the creature fondly responded to his gentle hand, though keeping aloof from Henry, in mindfulness of past passages between them, while Henry could evidently not bear to look at her.

They gazed round the room, but it conveyed no elucidation of the mystery. There were Leonard's books in their range on the drawers, his fossils in his cupboard, his mother's photograph on his mantel-piece, his sister's drawings on the wall. His grey uniform lay on the bed as if recently taken off, his ordinary office coat was folded on a chair, and he seemed to have dressed and gone in his best clothes. While anxiously seeking some note of explanation, they heard a step, and Sam Axworthy entered, speaking fast and low in apology for not having sooner appeared, but he had been thoroughly upset; as indeed he looked, his whole appearance betraying the disorder of the evening's dissipation, followed by the morning's shock.

Most unfortunate, he said, that he had not returned earlier. His friend Black – Tom Black, of Edsall Green – had driven him home in his dog-cart, set him down at the turn to cross the fields – moon as light as day – no notion of the lateness till he got in sight of the great clock, and saw it was half-past twelve; so knowing the early habits of the place, he had thought it best to turn back, and get a bed at the Three Goblets. If he had only come home, he might have prevented mischief! There ensued a few common-place words on the old man's infirm state, yet his independent habits, and reluctance to let any servant assist him, or even sleep near him. Sam spoke as if in a dream, and was evidently so unwell, that Dr May thought it charitable to follow the dictates of his own disgust at breaking bread in that house of horrors, and refuse offers of breakfast. He said he must go home, but would return for the inquest, and asked whether Henry would remain to meet his brother.

'No, no, thank you,' said Henry huskily, as with the driest of throats, and a perceptible shudder, he turned to go away; the doctor pausing to caress little Mab, and say, 'I had better take home this poor little thing. She may come to harm here, and may be a comfort to the sister.'

No objection came from Sam, but Mab herself ran back to her house, and even snarled at the attempt to detach her from it. 'You are a faithful little beast,' he said, 'and your master will soon be here to set all straight, so I will leave you for the present;' and therewith he signed farewell, and breathed more freely as he gained the outer air.

'I'll tell you what, Henry,' he said, as they drove out of the courtyard, 'we'll bring out Bramshaw to watch the case. He will see through this horrible mystery, and throw the suspicion in the right quarter, whatever that may be, depend upon it.'

Henry had thrown himself back in the carriage with averted face, and only answered by a groan.

'Come, don't be so downcast,' said Dr May; 'it is a frightful affair, no doubt, and Leonard has chosen a most unlucky moment for this escapade; but he will have a thorough warning against frolics.'

'Frolics indeed!' said Henry, bitterly.

'Well, I'll be bound that's all he has attempted, and it has got him into a horrid scrape; and ten to one but the police have got the real ruffians in their hands by this time.'

'I have no hope,' said Henry.

'More shame for you not to feel a certain confidence that He who sees all will show the right.'

'If!' said Henry, breaking off with a sound and look of such intense misery as almost to stagger the doctor himself, by reminding him of Leonard's violent temper, and the cause Henry had to remember his promptness of hand; but that Ethel's pupil, Aubrey's friend, the boy of ingenuous face, could under any provocation strike helpless old age, or having struck, could abscond without calling aid, actuated by terror, not by pity or repentance, was more than Dr May could believe; and after brief musing, he broke out in indignant refutation.

'I should have thought so. I wish, I still could believe so,' sighed Henry; 'but——' and there they lapsed into silence, till, as they came near the town, Dr May offered to set him down at Bankside.

'No! no, thank you,' he cried in entreaty. 'I cannot see her – Ave.'

'Then come home with me. You shall see no one, and you will look up when you are not faint and fasting. You young men don't stand up against these things like us old stagers.'

As the carriage stopped, several anxious faces were seen on the watch, but the doctor signed them back till he had deposited Henry in his study, and then came among them.

Gertrude was the first to speak. 'O papa, papa, what is it? Mrs Pugh has been here to ask, and Ethel won't let me hear, though Tom and Aubrey know.'

'I took refuge in your order to believe nothing till you came,' said Ethel, with hands tightly clasped together.

'It is true, then?' asked Tom.

'True that it looks as bad as bad can be,' said the doctor, sighing heavily, and proceeding to state the aspect of the case.

'It is a trick – a plot,' cried Aubrey passionately; 'I know it is! He always said he would run away if they tried to teach him dishonesty; and now they have done this and driven him away, and laid the blame on him. Ethel, why don't you say you are sure of it?'

'Leonard would be changed indeed if this were so,' said Ethel, trembling as she stood, and hardly able to speak articulately.

Aubrey broke out with a furious 'If,' very different from Henry Ward's.

'It would not be the Leonard we knew at Coombe,' said Ethel. 'He might be blind with rage, but he would never be cowardly. No. Unless he own it, nothing shall ever make me believe it.'

'Own it! For shame, Ethel,' cried Aubrey.

And even the doctor exclaimed, 'You are as bad as poor Henry himself, who has not got soul enough to be capable of trusting his brother.'

'I do trust,' said Ethel, looking up. 'I shall trust his own word;' and she sat down without speaking, and knitted fast, but her needles clattered.

'And how about that poor girl at Bankside?' said the doctor.

'I went down there,' said Tom, 'just to caution the servants against bringing in stories. She found out I was there, and I had to go in and make the best of it.'

'And what sort of a best?' said the doctor.

'Why, she knew he used to get out in the morning to bathe, and was persuaded he had been drowned; so I told her I knew he was alive and well, and she would hear all about it when you came back. I brought the youngest child away with me, and Gertrude has got her up-stairs; the other would not come. Poor thing! Mary says she is very good and patient; and I must say she was wonderfully reasonable when I talked to her.'

'Thank you, Tom,' said his father with warmth; 'it was very kind of you. I wonder if Ave knew anything of this runaway business; it might be the saving of him!'

'I did,' said Aubrey eagerly; 'at least, I know he said he would not stay if they wanted to put him up to their dishonest tricks; and he talked of that very window!'

'Yes, you impudent fellow; and you were telling Mrs Pugh so, if I hadn't stopped you,' said Tom. 'You'll be taken up for an accomplice next, if you don't hold your tongue.'

'What did he say?' asked the doctor, impatiently; and then declared that he must instantly go to Bankside, as soon as both he and Henry had taken some food; 'for,' he added, 'we are both too much shaken to deal rationally with her.'

Ethel started up in shame and dismay at having neglected to order anything. The doctor was served in the study alone with Henry, and after the briefest meal, was on his way to Bankside.

He found Averil with the crimson cheek and beseeching eye that he knew so well, as she laid her trembling hand on his, and mutely looked up like a dumb creature awaiting a blow.

'Yes, my dear,' he said, tenderly, 'your brother needs prayer such as when we watched him last year; he is in peril of grave suspicion.' And as she stood waiting and watching for further explanation, he continued, 'My dear, he told you everything. You do not know of any notion of his of going away, or going out without leave?'

'Why is Leonard to be always suspected of such things?' cried Averil. 'He never did them!'

'Do you know?' persisted Dr May.

'But you are mayor!' cried Averil, indignantly, withdrawing her hand. 'You want me to accuse him!'

'My dear, if I were ten times mayor, it would make no difference. My jurisdiction does not even cross the river here; and if it did, this is a graver case than I deal with. I am come, as his friend, to beg you to help me to account for his unhappy absence in any harmless way. Were it ever so foolish or wrong, it would be the best news that ever I heard.'

'But – but I can't,' said Averil. 'I never knew he was going out! I know he used to get out at the passage window to bathe and fish before the house was astir – and – you *know* he is safe, Dr May?'

Dr May would almost sooner have known that he was at the bottom of the deepest pool in the river, than where he was. 'He is safe, my poor child. He is well, and I trust he will be able to prove his innocence; but he must so account for his absence as to clear himself. Averil, there is a charge against him – of being concerned in your uncle's death.'

Averil's eyes dilated, and she breathed short and fast, standing like a statue. Little Minna, whom the doctor had scarcely perceived, standing in a dark corner, sprang forward, exclaiming, 'O Ave, don't be afraid! Nobody can hurt him for what he did not do!'

The words roused Averil, and starting forward, she cried, 'Dr May, Dr May, you will save him! He is fatherless and motherless, and his brother has always been harsh to him; but you will not forsake him; you said you would be a father to us! Oh, save Leonard!'

'My dear, as I would try to save my own son, I will do my utmost for him; but little or nothing depends on me or on any man. By truth and justice he must stand or fall, and you must depend on the Father of the fatherless, who seeth the truth! as this dear child tells you,' with his hand on Minna's head, 'he cannot be *really* injured while he is innocent.'

Awed into calm Averil let him seat her beside him, and put her in possession of the main facts of the case, Minna standing by him, her hand in his, evidently understanding and feeling all that passed.

Neither could throw light on anything. Leonard had been less communicative to them than to Aubrey, and had kept his resolution of uncomplainingly drinking the brewst he had brewed for himself. All Averil could tell was, that her uncle had once spoken to Henry in commendation of his steadiness and trustworthiness, though at the same time abusing him for airs and puppyism.

'Henry would tell you. Where is Henry?' she added.

'In my study. He could not bear to bring you these tidings. You must be ready to comfort him, Ave.'

'Don't let him come,' she cried. 'He never was kind to Leonard. He drove him there. I shall always feel that it was his doing.'

'Averil,' said Dr May gravely, 'do you forget how much that increases his suffering? Nothing but mutual charity can help you through this fiery trial. Do not let anger and recrimination take from you the last shreds of comfort, and poison your prayers. Promise me to be kind to Henry, for indeed he needs it.'

'O, Dr May,' said Minna, looking up with her eyes full of tears, 'indeed I will. I was cross to Henry because he was cross to Leonard, but I won't be so any more.'

Ave dropped her head, as if it were almost impossible to her to speak.

Dr May patted Minna's dark head caressingly, and said to the elder sister, 'I will not urge you more. Perhaps you may have Leonard back, and then joy will open your hearts; or if not, my poor Ave, the sight of Henry will do more than my words.'

Mary looked greatly grieved, but said nothing, only following her father to take his last words and directions. 'Keep her as quiet as you can. Do not worry her, but get out this root of bitterness if you can. Poor, poor things!'

'That little Minna is a dear child!' said Mary. 'She is grown so much older than Ella, or than she was last year. She seems to understand and feel like a grown-up person. I do think she may soften poor Ave more than I can; but, papa, there is excuse. Mr Ward must have made them more miserable than we guessed.'

'The more reason she must forgive him. O, Mary, I fear a grievous lesson is coming to them! but I must do all I can. Good-bye, my dear; do the best you can for them;' and he set forth again with a bleeding heart.

At the attorney's office, he found the principal from home, but the partner, Edward Anderson, on the *qui vive* for a summons to attend on behalf of his fellow townsman, and confident that however bad were the present aspect of affairs, his professional eye would instantly find a clue.

Aubrey was in an agony of excitement, but unable to endure the notion of approaching the scene of action; and his half-choked surly 'Don't' was sufficient to deter his brother Thomas, who had never shown himself so kind, considerate, and free from sneer or assumption. In 'hours of ease' he might seem selfish and exacting, but a crisis evoked the latent good in him, and drew him out of himself.

Nor would Henry return to Bankside. After many vacillations, the moment for starting found him in a fit of despair about the family disgrace, only able to beg that 'the unhappy boy' should be assured that no expense should be spared in his defence; or else, that if he were cleared and returned home, his welcome should be most joyful. But there Henry broke off, groaned, said they should never look up again, and must leave the place.

Except for Averil's own sake, Dr May would almost have regretted his exhortations in favour of her eldest brother.

In due time the doctor arrived at the mill, where the inquest was to take place, as the public-house was small, and inconveniently distant; and there was ample accommodation in the large rambling building. So crowded was the court-yard, that the doctor did not easily make his way to the steps of the hall door; but there, after one brief question to the policeman in charge, he waited, though several times invited in.

Before long, all eyes turned one way, as a closed fly, with a policeman on the box, drove in at the gateway, stopped, and between the two men on guard appeared a tall young figure.

The doctor's first glance showed him a flushed and weary set of features, shocked and appalled; but the eyes, looking straight up in their anxiety, encountered his with an earnest grateful appeal for sympathy, answered at once by a step forward with outstretched hand. The grip of the fingers was heated, agitated, convulsive, but not tremulous; and there was feeling, not fear, in the low husky voice that said, 'Thank you. Is Henry here?'

'No, he is too – too much overcome; but he hopes to see you at home to-night; and here is Edward Anderson, whom he has sent to watch the proceedings for you.'

'Thank you,' said Leonard, acknowledging Edward's greeting. 'As far as I am concerned, I can explain all in a minute; but my poor uncle – I little thought——'

There was no opportunity for further speech in private, for the coroner had already arrived, and the inquiry had been only deferred until Leonard should have come. The jury had been viewing the body, and the proceedings were to take place in the large low dining-room, where the southern windows poured in a flood of light on the faces of the persons crowded together, and the reflections from the rippling water danced on the ceiling. Dr May had a chair given him near the coroner, and keenly watched the two nephews – one seated next to him, the other at some distance, nearly opposite. Both young men looked haggard, shocked, and oppressed: the eye of Axworthy was unceasingly fixed on an inkstand upon the table, and never lifted, his expression never varied; and Leonard's glance flashed inquiringly from one speaker to another, and his countenance altered with every phase of the evidence.

The first witness was Anne Ellis, the young maid-servant, who told of her coming down at ten minutes after five that morning, the 6th of July, and on going in to clean the rooms, finding her master sunk forward on the table. Supposing him to have had a fit, she had run to the window and screamed for help, when Master Hardy, the foreman, and Mrs Giles, the housekeeper, had come in.

James Hardy deposed to having heard the girl's cry while he was unlocking the mill door. Coming in by the low sash window, which stood open, he had gone up to his master, and had seen the wound on the head, and found the body quite cold. Mrs Giles coming in, they had carried it to the bed in the next room; and he had gone to call the young gentlemen, but neither was in his room. He knew that it had been left uncertain whether Mr Samuel would return to sleep at home between the two days of the county races, but he did not expect Mr Ward to be out; and had then observed that his bed had not been slept in, and that the passage window outside his room was partly open. He had then thought it best to go into Stoneborough to inform the family.

Rebecca Giles, the housekeeper, an elderly woman, crying violently, repeated the evidence as to the discovery of the body. The last time she had seen her master alive, was when she had carried in his supper at nine o'clock, when he had desired her to send Mr Ward to him; and had seemed much vexed to hear that the young man had not returned from rifle practice, little thinking, poor old gentleman! – but here the housekeeper was recalled to her subject. The window was then open, as it was a sultry night, but the blind down. Her master was a good deal crippled by gout, and could not at that time move actively nor write, but could dress himself, and close a window. He disliked being assisted; and the servants were not in the habit of seeing him from the time his supper was brought in till breakfast next morning. She had seen Mr Ward come home at twenty minutes or half after nine, in uniform, carrying his rifle; she had given the message, and he had gone into the sitting-room without putting down the rifle. She believed it to be the one on the table, but could not say so on oath; he never let any one touch it; and she never looked at such horrid murderous things. And some remarks highly adverse to the volunteer movement were cut short.

William Andrews, groom, had been called by Anne Ellis, had seen the wound, and the blood on the desk, and had gone to fetch a surgeon and the police from Whitford. On his return, saw the rifle leaning against the shutter; believed it to be Mr Ward's rifle.

Charles Rankin, surgeon, had been called in to see Mr Axworthy, and arrived at seven o'clock A.M. Found him dead, from a fracture of the skull over the left temple, he should imagine, from a blow from a heavy blunt instrument, such as the stock of a gun. Death must have been instantaneous, and had probably taken place seven or eight hours before he was called in. The marks upon the rifle before him were probably blood; but he could not say so upon oath, till he had subjected them to microscopic examination. The hair was human, and corresponded with that of the deceased.

Samuel Axworthy had slept at the Three Goblets, in consequence of finding himself too late for admission at home. He had been wakened at half-past five, and found all as had been stated by the previous witnesses; and he corroborated the housekeeper's account of his uncle's habits. The rifle he believed to belong to his cousin, Leonard Ward. He could not account for Leonard Ward's absence on that morning. No permission, as far as he was aware, had been given him to leave home; and he had never known his uncle give him any commission at that hour.

The different policemen gave their narrations of the state of things – the open window, the position of the boat, &c. And the ticket-clerk at the small Blewer Station stated that at about 12.15 at night, Mr Ward had walked in without baggage, and asked for a second-class ticket to London.

Leonard here interposed an inquiry whether he had not said a day ticket; and the clerk recollected that he had done so, and had spoken of returning by four o'clock; but the train, being reckoned as belonging to the previous day, no return tickets were issued for it, and he had therefore taken an ordinary one, and started by the mail train.

The London policeman, who had come down with Leonard, stated that, in consequence of a telegraphic message, he had been at the Paddington Station at 6.30 that morning; had seen a young gentleman answering to the description sent to him, asked if his name were Leonard Ward, and receiving a reply in the affirmative, had informed him of the charge, and taken him into custody. The bag that he placed on the table he had found on the young man's person.

Every one was startled at this unexpected corroboration of the suspicion. It was a heavy looking bag, of reddish canvas, marked with a black circle, containing the letters F.A. Gold; the neck tied with a string; the contents were sovereigns, and a note or two.

Dr May looked piteously, despairingly, at Leonard; but the brow was still open and unclouded, the eye glanced back re-assurance and confidence.

The policeman added that he had cautioned the young man to take care what he said, but that he had declared at once that his uncle had sent him to lodge the sum in Drummond's Bank, and that he would show a receipt for it on his return.

The coroner then proceeded to examine Leonard, but still as a witness. Edward Anderson spoke to him in an under tone, advising him to be cautious, and not commit himself; but Leonard, rather impatiently thanking him, shook him off, and spoke with freedom and openness.

'I have nothing to keep back,' he said. 'Of course I know nothing of this frightful murder, nor what villain could have got hold of the rifle, which, I am sorry to say, is really mine. Last evening I used it at drill and practice on Blewer Heath, and came home when it grew dusk, getting in at about half-past nine. I was then told by Mrs Giles that my uncle wished to speak to me, and was displeased at my staying out so late. I went into his room as I was, and put my rifle down in a corner by the window, when he desired me to sit down and listen to him. He then told me that he wished to send me to town by the mail train, to take some cash to Drummond's Bank, and to return by to-day's four o'clock train. He said he had reasons for wishing no one to be aware of his opening an account there, and he undertook to explain my absence. He took the sum from the private drawer of his desk, and made me count it before him, 124*l.* 12*s.* in sovereigns and bank notes. The odd money he gave me for my expenses, the rest I put in the bag that I fetched out of the office. He could not hold a pen, and could therefore give me no letter to Messrs Drummond, but he made me write a receipt for the amount in his memorandum book. I wished him good-night, and left him still sitting in his easy chair, with the window open and the blind down. I found that I had forgotten my rifle, but I did not go back for it, because he disliked the disturbance of opening and shutting doors. While I was changing my dress, I saw from the window that some one was still about in the court, and knowing that my uncle wished me to avoid notice, I thought it best to let myself out by the passage window, as I had sometimes done in early mornings to bathe or fish, and go across the fields to Blewer Station. I got down into the garden, crossed in the punt, and went slowly by Barnard's hatch; I believe I stopped a good many times, as it was too soon, and a beautiful moonlight night, but I came to Blewer soon after twelve, and took my ticket. At Paddington I met this terrible news.'

As the boy spoke, his bright eyes turned from one listener to another, as though expecting to read satisfaction on their faces; but as doubt and disbelief clouded all, his looks became almost constantly directed to Dr May, and his voice unconsciously passed from a sound of justification to one of pleading. When he ceased, he glanced round as if feeling his innocence established.

'You gave a receipt, Mr Ward,' said the coroner. 'Will you tell us where it is likely to be?'

'It must be either on or in my uncle's desk, or in his pocket. Will some one look for it? I wrote it in his memorandum book – a curious old black shagreen book, with a silver clasp. I left it open on the desk to dry.'

A policeman went to search for it; and the coroner asked what the entry had been.

'July 5th, 1860. Received, 120*l.* L.A. Ward,' – was the answer. 'You will find it about the middle of the book, or rather past it.'

'At what time did this take place?'

'It must have been towards ten. I cannot tell exactly, but it was later than half-past nine when I came in, and he was a good while bringing out the money.'

The policeman returned, saying he could not find the book; and Leonard begging to show where he had left it, the coroner and jury accompanied him to the room. At the sight of the red stain on the desk, a shuddering came over the boy, and a whiteness on his heated brow; nor could he at once recover himself so as to proceed with the search, which was still in vain; though with a voice lowered by the sickness of horror, he pointed out the place where he had laid it, and the pen he had used; and desk, table, drawer, and the dead man's dress were carefully examined.

'You must know it, Sam,' said Leonard. 'Don't you remember his putting in the cheque – old Bilson's cheque for his year's rent – twenty-five pounds? I brought it in and he put it away one day last week. You were sitting there.'

Sam stammered something of 'Yes; he did recollect something of it.'

Inquiries were made of the other persons concerned with Mr Axworthy. Hardy thought his master used such a book, but had never seen it near; Mrs Giles altogether disbelieved its existence; and Sam could not be positive – his uncle never allowed any one to touch his private memorandums.

As, with deepened anxiety, Dr May returned to the dining-room, he caught a glimpse of Henry Ward's desponding face, but received a sign not to disclose his presence. Edward Anderson wrote, and considered; and the coroner, looking at his notes again, recurred to Leonard's statement that he had seen some one in the yard.

'I thought it was one of the men waiting to take my cousin Axworthy's horse. I did not know whether he had ridden or gone by train; and I supposed that some one would be looking out for him.'

Questions were asked whether any of the servants had been in the yard, but it was denied by all; and on a more particular description of the person being demanded, Leonard replied that the figure had been in the dark shade of the stables, and that he only knew that it was a young man – whether a stranger or not he did not know; he supposed now that it must have been the – the murderer, but at the time he had thought it one of the stable men; and as his uncle had particularly wished that his journey should be a secret, the sight had only made him hasten to put out his light, and depart unseen. It was most unfortunate that he had done so.

Others ironically whispered, 'Most unfortunate.'

The coroner asked Mr Anderson whether he had anything to ask or observe; and on his reply in the negative, proceeded to sum up the evidence for the consideration of the jury.

It seemed as if it were only here that Leonard perceived the real gist of the evidence. His brow grew hotter, his eyes indignant, his hands clenched, as if he with difficulty restrained himself from breaking in on the coroner's speech; and when at length the question was put to the jury, he stood, the colour fading from his cheek, his eyes set and glassy, his lip fallen, the dew breaking out on his brow, every limb as it were petrified by the shock of what was thus first fully revealed to him.

So he stood, while the jury deliberated in low gruff sorrowful murmurs; and after a few minutes, turned round to announce with much sadness that they could do no otherwise than return a verdict of wilful murder against Leonard Ward.

'Mr Leonard Ward,' said the coroner, a gentleman who had well known his father, and who spoke with scarcely concealed emotion, 'it becomes my painful duty to commit you to Whitford Gaol for trial at the next assizes.'

Dr May eagerly offered bail, rather as the readiest form of kindness than in the hope of its acceptance, and it was of course refused; but he made his way to the prisoner, and wrung his chill hand with all his might. The pressure seemed to waken the poor lad from his frozen rigidity; the warmth came flowing back into his fingers as his friend held them; he raised his head, shut and re-opened his eyes, and pushed back his hair, as though trying to shake himself loose from a too horrible dream. His face softened and quivered as he met the doctor's kind eyes; but bracing himself again, he looked up, answered the coroner's question – that his Christian name was Leonard Axworthy, his age within a few weeks of eighteen; and asked permission to fetch what he should want from his room.

The policeman, in whose charge he was, consented both to this, and to Dr May being there alone with him for a short time.

Then it was that the boy relaxed the strain on his features, and said in a low and strangled voice, 'O Dr May, if you had only let me die with them last year!'

'It was not I who saved you. He who sent that ordeal, will bring you through – this,' said Dr May, with a great sob in his throat that belied his words of cheer.

'I thank Him at least for having taken her,' said Leonard, resting his head on the mantel-shelf beneath his mother's picture, while his little dog sat at his foot, looking up at him, cowed and wistful.

Dr May strove for words of comfort, but broke utterly down; and could only cover his face with his hands, and struggle with his emotion, unable to utter a word.

Yet perhaps none would have been so comforting as his genuine sympathy, although it was in a voice of extreme distress that Leonard exclaimed, 'Dr May, Dr May, pray don't! you ought not to grieve for me!'

'I'm a fool,' said Dr May, after some space, fighting hard with himself. 'Nonsense! we shall see you out of this! We have only to keep up a good heart, and we shall see it explained.'

'I don't know; I can't understand,' said Leonard, passing his hand over his weary forehead. 'Why could they not believe when I told them just how it was?'

At that moment the policeman opened the door, saying 'Here, Sir;'

and Henry hurried in, pale and breathless, not looking in his brother's face, as he spoke fast and low.

'Ned Anderson says there's nothing at all to be made of this defence of yours; it is of no use to try it. The only thing is to own that he found fault with you, and in one of your rages – you know——'

'You too, Henry!' said Leonard, in dejected reproach.

'Why – why, it is impossible it could have been otherwise – open window, absconding, and all. We all know you never meant it; but your story won't stand; and the only chance, Anderson says, is to go in for manslaughter. If you could only tell anything that would give him a clue to pick up evidence while the people are on the spot.'

Leonard's face was convulsed for a moment while his brother was speaking; but he recovered calmness of voice, as he mournfully answered, 'I have no right to wonder at your suspicion of me.'

Henry for the first time really looked at him, and instinctively faltered, 'I beg your pardon.'

'Indeed,' said Leonard with the same subdued manner, 'I cannot believe that any provocation could make me strike a person like that old man; and here there was none at all. Except that he was vexed at first at my being late, he had never been so near kindness.'

'Then is this extraordinary story the truth?'

'Why should I not tell the truth?' was the answer, too mournful for indignation.

Henry again cast down his eyes, Leonard moved about making preparations, Dr May leant against the wall – all too much oppressed for speech; till, as Leonard stooped, poor little Mab, thrusting her black head into his hand, drew from him the words, 'My doggie, what is to become of you?'

A sort of hoarse explosion of 'Ave' from Henry was simultaneous with the doctor's 'I tried to get her home with me in the morning, but she waited your orders.'

'Miss May would not have her *now*. After all, prussic acid would be the truest mercy,' said Leonard, holding the little creature up to his face, and laying his cheek against her silken coat with almost passionate affection.

'Not while there are those who trust your word, Leonard; as Ethel said this morning.'

He raised the face which he had hidden against the dog, and looked earnestly at the doctor as if hardly venturing to understand him; then a ray of real gladness and comfort darted into his eyes, which so enlivened Dr May, that he was able to say cheerfully, 'We will take good care of her till you come for her.'

'Then, Henry,' said Leonard, 'it is not unkindness, nor that I remember things, but indeed I think it will be better for you all, since Dr May is so –

so——' The word kind was so inadequate, that it stuck in his throat. 'Take this to Ave,' putting his mother's likeness in his hand, 'and tell her I will write.'

'Poor Ave!'

Leonard imploringly shook his head; the mention of his sister shook him more than he could bear; and he asked the time.

'Nearly six.'

'Only six! What an endless day! There, I am ready. There is no use in delaying. I suppose I must show what I am taking with me.'

'Wait,' said his brother. 'Cannot you say anything to put us on the track of the man in the yard?'

'I did not see him plain.'

'You've no notion?' said Henry, with a movement of annoyance.

'No. I only looked for a moment; for I was much more anxious to get off quietly, than to make any one out. If I had only waited ten minutes, it might have been the saving of his life; but my commission was so like fun, and so important too, that I thought of nothing else. Can it be not twenty-four hours ago?'

'And why don't you explain why he sent you?'

'I cannot say it so certainly as to be of the slightest use,' said Leonard. 'He never expressed it either; and I have no right to talk of my suspicions.'

'Eh! was it to put it out of Sam's way?'

'So I suppose. Sam used to get all he chose out of the poor old man; and I believe he thought this the only chance of keeping anything for himself; but he never told me so. Stay! Bilson's cheque might be tracked. I took it myself, and gave the receipt; you will find it entered in the books – paid on either the twenty-third or fourth.'

'Then there's something to do, at any rate,' cried Henry, invigorated. 'Anderson shall hunt out the balance and Sam's draughts on it. I'll spare no expense, Leonard, if it is to my last farthing; and you shall have the best counsel that can be retained.'

Leonard signed thanks with some heartiness, and was going to the door, when Henry detained him. 'Tell me, Leonard, have you no suspicion?'

'It must have been the person I saw in the court, and, like a fool, did not watch. The window was open, and he could have easily got in and come out. Can't they see that if it had been me, I should have made off at once that way?'

'If you could only tell what the fellow was like!'

'I told you he was in the dark,' said Leonard; and without giving time for more, he called in the man outside, showed the clothes and books he had selected, put them into his bag, and declared himself ready, giving his hand to the doctor, who drew him near and kissed his brow, as if he had been Harry setting forth on a voyage.

'Good-bye, my dear fellow; God bless you; I'll soon come to see you.'

'And I,' said Henry, 'will bring Bramshaw to see what is to be done.'

Leonard wrung his brother's hand, murmuring something of love to his sisters; then put Mab into Dr May's arms, with injunctions that the little creature understood and obeyed, for though trembling and whining under her breath, she was not resisting.

It might be to shorten her distress as well as his own that Leonard passed quickly down-stairs, and entered the carriage that was to take him to the county gaol.

CHAPTER XIII

'Tears are not always fruitful; their hot drops
    Sometimes but scorch the cheek and dim the eye
Despairing murmurs over blackened hopes,
    Not the meek spirit's calm and chastened cry.
Oh, better not to weep, than weep amiss!
    For hard it is to learn to weep aright;
To weep wise tears, the tears that heal and bless,
    The tears which their own bitterness requite.'

H. Bonar.

To one of the most tender-hearted of human beings had the office of conveying ill tidings been most often committed, and again Dr May found himself compelled to precede Henry Ward into the sister's presence, and to break to her the result of the inquest.

He was no believer in the efficacy of broken news, but he could not refuse when Henry in his wretchedness entreated not to be the first in the infliction of such agony; so he left the carriage outside, and walked up to the door; and there stood Averil, with Ethel a few steps behind her. His presence was enough revelation. Had things gone well, he would not have been the forerunner; and Averil, meaning perhaps to speak, gave a hoarse hysterical shriek, so frightful as to drive away other anxieties, and summon Henry in from his watch outside.

All day the poor girl had kept up an unnatural strain on her powers, vehemently talking of other things, and, with burning cheeks and shining eyes, moving incessantly from one employment to another; now her needle, now her pencil – roaming round the garden gathering flowers, or playing rattling polkas that half stunned Ethel in her intense listening for tidings. Ethel, who had relieved guard and sent Mary home in the afternoon, had vainly striven to make Ave rest or take food; the attempt had brought on such choking, that she could only desist, and wait for the crisis. The attack was worse than any ordinary hysterics, almost amounting to convulsions; and all that could be done was to prevent her from hurting herself, and try to believe Dr May's assurance that there was no real cause for alarm, and that the paroxysms would exhaust themselves.

In time they were spent, and Ave lay on her bed half torpid, feebly moaning, but with an instinctive dread of being disturbed. Henry anxiously watched over her, and Dr May thought it best to leave the brother and sister to one another. Absolute quiet was best for her, and he had skill and tenderness enough to deal with her, and was evidently somewhat relieved by the necessity of waiting on her. It was the best means, perhaps, of uniting them, that they should be thus left together; and Dr May would have taken home little pale frightened Minna, who had been very helpful all the time.

'Oh, please not, Dr May,' she said, earnestly. 'Indeed I will not be troublesome, and I can give Henry his tea, and carry Ave's cup. Please, Henry, don't send me:' and she took hold of his hand, and laid it against her cheek. He bent down over her, and fondled her; and there were tears that he could not hide as he tried both to thank Dr May, and tell her that she need not leave him.

'No,' said Dr May; 'it would be cruel to both of you. – Good-bye, little Minna; I never wanted to carry away a little comforter.'

'I believe you are right, papa,' said Ethel, as she went out with him to the carriage; 'but I long to stay, it is like doing something for that boy.'

'The *best* you did for him, poor dear boy! was the saying you trusted his word. The moment I told him that, he took comfort and energy.'

Ethel's lips moved into a strange half smile, and she took Mab on her lap, and fondled her. 'Yes,' she said, 'I believe I stand for a good deal in his imagination. I was afraid he would have been wrecked upon that horrid place; but after all, this may be the saving of him.'

'Ah! if that story of his would only be more *vraisemblable*.'

There was only time briefly to narrate it before coming home, where the first person they met was Aubrey, exceeding pale, and in great distress. 'Papa, I must tell you,' he said, drawing him into the study. 'I have done terrible harm, I am afraid.' And he explained, that in the morning, when Mrs Pugh had come down full of inquiries and conjectures, and had spoken of the possibility of Leonard's having been drowned while bathing, he had unguardedly answered that it could be no such thing; Leonard had always meant to run away, and by that very window, if the Axworthys grew too bad.

Prudent Tom had silenced him at the time, but had since found that it had got abroad that the evasion had long been meditated with Aubrey's privity, and had been asked by one of the constabulary force if his brother would not be an important witness. Tom had replied that he knew nothing about it; but Aubrey was in great misery, furious with Mrs Pugh, and only wanting his father to set off at once to assure *them* it was all nonsense.

'No, Aubrey, they neither would, nor ought to, take my word.'

'Just hear, papa, and you would know the chaff it was.'

'I cannot hear, Aubrey. If we were to discuss it, we might give it an unconscious colouring. You must calm your mind, and exactly recall what passed; but do not talk about it to me or to any one else. You must do nothing to impair the power of perfect truth and accuracy, which is a thing to be prayed for. If any one – even the lawyer who may have to get up the case against him – asks you about it, you must refuse to answer till the trial; and then – why, the issue is in the hands of Him that judgeth righteously.'

'I shall never remember nor speak with his eyes on me, seeing me betray him!'

'You will be no worse off than I, my boy, for I see I am in for identifying Hector's rifle; the Mill people can't swear to it, and my doing it will save his brother something.'

'No, it is not like me. Oh! I wish I had stayed at Eton, even if I had died of it! Tom says it all comes of living with women that I can't keep my mouth shut; and Leonard will be so hurt that I——'

'Nay, any tolerable counsel will make a capital defence out of the mere fact of his rhodomontading. What, is that no comfort to you?'

'What! to be the means of making a fool of him before all the court – seeing him hear our talk by the river-side sifted by those horrid lawyers?'

The doctor looked even graver, and his eye fixed as on a thought far-away, as the boy's grief brought to his mind the Great Assize, when all that is spoken in the ear shall indeed be proclaimed on the house-tops.

There was something almost childish in the despair of Aubrey, for he had not become alarmed for the result of this trial. His misery was chiefly shame at his supposed treason to friendship, and failure in manly reserve; and he could not hold up his head all the evening, but silently devoted himself to Mab, endeavouring to make her at home, and meeting with tolerable success.

Tom was no less devoted to Ella Ward. It was he who had brought her home, and he considered her therefore as his charge. It was curious to see the difference that a year had made between her and Minna. They had the last summer been like one child, and had taken the stroke that had orphaned them in the same childish manner; but whether the year from eight to nine had been of especial growth to Minna, or whether there had been a stimulus in her constant association with Averil, the present sorrow fell on her as on one able to enter into it, think and feel, and assume her sweet mission of comfort; whilst Ella, though neither hard nor insensible, was still child enough to close her mind to what she dreaded, and flee willingly from the pain and tedium of affliction. She had willingly accepted 'Mr Tom's' invitation, and as willingly responded to his attentions. Gertrude did not like people in the 'little girl' stage, and the elder sisters had their hands and hearts full, and could only care for her in essentials; but Tom undertook her amusement, treated her to an exhibition of his microscope, and played at French billiards with her the rest of the evening, till she was carried off to bed in Mary's room, when he pronounced her a very intelligent child.

'I think her a very unfeeling little thing,' said Gertrude. 'Very unbecoming behaviour under the circumstances.'

'What would you think becoming behaviour?' asked Tom.

'I won't encourage it,' returned Daisy, with dignified decision, that gave her father his first approach to a laugh on that day; but nobody was in spirits to desire Miss Daisy to define from what her important sanction was withdrawn.

Mary gave up her Sunday-school class to see how Averil was, and found Henry much perturbed. He had seen her fast asleep at night, and in the morning Minna had carried up her breakfast, and he was about to follow it, as soon as his own was finished, when he found that she had slipped out of the house, leaving a message that she was gone to practise on the harmonium.

He was of the mind that none of the family could or ought to be seen at church; and though Mary could not agree with him, she willingly consented to go to the chapel and try what she could do with his sister. She met Mrs Ledwich on the way, coming to inquire and see whether she or dear Matilda could do anything for the 'sweet sufferer.' Even Mary could not help thinking that this was not the epithet most befitting poor Ave; and perhaps Mrs Ledwich's companionship made her the less regret that Ave had locked herself in, so that there was no making her hear, though the solemn chants, played with great fervour, reached them as they waited in the porch. They had their own seats in the Minster, and therefore could not wait till the sexton should come to open the church.

There was no time for another visit till after the second service, and then Dr May and Mary, going to Bankside, found that instead of returning home, Ave had again locked herself up between the services, and that Minna, who had ventured on a mission of recall, had come home crying heartily both at the dreary disappointment of knocking in vain, and at the grand mournful sounds of funeral marches that had fallen on her ear. Every one who had been at the chapel that day was speaking of the wonderful music, the force and the melody of the voluntary at the dismissal of the congregation; no one had believed that such power resided in the harmonium. Mr Scudamore had spoken to Miss Ward most kindly both before and after evening service, but his attempt to take her home had been unavailing; she had answered that she was going presently, and he was obliged to leave her.

Evening was coming on, and she had not come; so the other keys were fetched from the sexton's, and Dr May and his daughter set off to storm her fortress. Like Minna, the doctor was almost overpowered by the wonderful plaintive sweetness of the notes that were floating through the atmosphere, like a wailing voice of supplication. They had almost unnerved him, as he waited while Mary unlocked the door.

The sound of its opening hushed the music; Averil turned her head, and recognising them, came to them, very pale, and with sunken eyes. 'You are coming home, dear Ave,' said Mary; and she made no resistance or objection, only saying, 'Yes. It has been so nice here!'

'You must come now, though,' said the doctor. 'Your brother is very much grieved at your leaving him.'

'I did not mean to be unkind to him,' said Averil, in a low subdued voice; 'he was very good to me last night. Only – this is peace – this,' pointing to her instrument, 'is such a soothing friend. And surely this is the place to wait in!'

'The place to wait in indeed, my poor child, if you are not increasing the distress of others by staying here. Besides, you must not exhaust yourself, or how are you to go and cheer Leonard?'

'Oh! there is no fear but that I shall go to-morrow,' said Averil; 'I mean to do it!' the last words being spoken in a resolute tone, unlike the weariness of her former replies.

And with this purpose before her, she consented to be taken back by Mary to rest on the sofa, and even to try to eat and drink. Her brother and sister hung over her, and waited on her with a tender assiduous attention that showed how they had missed her all day; and she received their kindness gratefully, as far as her broken wearied state permitted.

Several inquiries had come throughout the day from the neighbours; and while Mary was still with Ave, a message was brought in to ask whether Miss Ward would like to see Mrs Pugh.

'Oh no, no, thank her, but indeed I cannot,' said Averil, shivering uncontrollably as she lay.

Mary felt herself blushing, in the wonder what would be kindest to do, and her dread of seeing Henry's face. She was sure that he too shrank, and she ventured to ask, 'Shall I go and speak to her?'

'Oh, do, do,' said Averil, shuddering with eagerness.

'Thank you, Miss Mary,' said Henry slowly. 'She is most kind – but – under the circumstances——'

Mary went, finding that he only hesitated. She had little opportunity for saying anything; Mrs Pugh was full of interest and eagerness, and poured out her sympathy and perfect understanding of dear Averil's feelings; and in the midst Henry came out of the room, with a stronger version of their gratitude, but in terrible confusion. Mary would fain have retreated, but could not, and was witness to the lady's urgent entreaties to take Minna home, and Henry's thankfulness; but he feared – and retreated to ask the opinion of his sisters, while Mrs Pugh told Mary that it was so very bad for the poor child to remain, and begged to have Ella if she were a moment's inconvenience to the May family.

Henry came back with repeated thanks, but Minna could not bear to leave home; and in fact, he owned, with a half smile that gave sweetness to his face, she was too great a comfort to be parted with. So Mrs Pugh departed, with doubled and trebled offers of service, and entreaties to be sent for at any hour of the day or night when she could be of use to Averil.

Mary could not but be pleased with her, officious as she was. It looked as if she had more genuine feeling for Henry than had been suspected, and the kindness was certain, though some of it might be the busy activity of a not very delicate nature, eager for the importance conferred by intimacy with the subjects of a great calamity. Probably she would have been gratified by the *éclat* of being the beloved of the brother of the youth whose name was in every mouth, and her real goodness and benevolent heart would have committed her affections and interest beyond recall to the Ward family, had Averil leant upon her, or had Henry exerted himself to take advantage of her advances.

But Henry's attachment had probably not been love, for it seemed utterly crushed out of him by his shame and despair. Everything connected with his past life was hateful to him; he declared that he could never show his face at Stoneborough again, let the result be what it might – that he could never visit another patient, and that he should change his name and leave the country, beginning on that very Sunday afternoon to write a letter to his principal rival to negotiate the sale of his practice.

In fact, his first impression had returned on him, and though he never disclaimed belief in Leonard's statement, the entire failure of all confirmation convinced him that the blow had been struck by his brother in sudden anger, and that, defend him as he might and would, the stain was on his house, and the guilt would be brought home.

Resolved, however, to do his utmost, he went with Mr Bramshaw for a consultation with Leonard on the Monday. Averil could not go. She rose and dressed, and remained resolute till nearly the last minute, when her feverish faint giddiness overpowered her, and she was forced to submit to lie on the sofa, under Minna's care; and there she lay, restless and wretched, till wise little Minna sent a message up to the High-street, which brought down Mary and Dr Spencer. They found her in a state of nervous fever, that sentenced her to her bed, where Mary deposited her and watched over her, till her brother's return, more desponding than ever.

Dr May, with all Henry's patients on his hands as well as his own, had been forced to devote this entire day to his profession; but on the next, leaving Henry to watch over Averil, who continued very feeble and feverish, he went to Whitford, almost infected by Henry's forebodings and Mr Bramshaw's misgivings. 'It is a bad case,' the attorney had said to him, confidentially. 'But that there is always a great reluctance to convict upon circumstantial evidence, I should have very little hope, that story of his is so utterly impracticable; and yet he looks so innocent and earnest all the time, and sticks to it so consistently, that I don't know what to make of it. I can't do anything with him, nor can his brother either; but perhaps you might make him understand that we could bring him clear off for manslaughter – youth, and character and all. I should not doubt of a verdict for a moment! It is awkward about the money, but the alarm would be considered in the sentence.'

'You don't attend to his account of the person he saw in the court-yard?'

'The less said about that the better,' returned Mr Bramshaw. 'It would only go for an awkward attempt to shift off the suspicion, unless he would give any description; and that he can't, or won't do. Or even if he did, the case would be all the stronger against his story – setting off, and leaving a stranger to maraud about the place. No, Dr May; the only thing for it is to persuade the lad to own to having struck the old man in a passion: every one knows old Axworthy could be intolerably abusive, and the boy always was passionate. Don't you remember his flying out at Mr Rivers's, the night of the party, and that affair which was the means of his going to the mill at all? I don't mind saying so to you in confidence, because I know you won't repeat it, and I see his brother thinks so too; but nothing is likely to turn out so well for him as that line of defence; as things stand now, the present one is good for nothing.'

Dr May was almost as much grieved at the notion of the youth's persistence in denying such a crime, as at the danger in which it involved him, and felt that if he were to be brought to confession, it should be from repentance, not expediency.

In this mood he drove to Whitford Gaol, made application at the gates, and was conducted up the stairs to the cell.

The three days of nearly entire solitude and of awful expectation had told like double the number of years; and there was a stamp of grave earnest collectedness on the young brow, and a calm resolution of aspect and movement, free from all excitement or embarrassment, as Leonard Ward stood up with a warm grateful greeting, so full of ingenuous reliance, that every doubt vanished at the same moment.

His first question was for Averil; and Dr May made the best of her state. 'She slept a little more last night, and her pulse is lower this morning; but we keep her in bed, half to hinder her from trying to come here before she is fit. I believe this ailment is the best thing for her and Henry both,' added the doctor, seeing how much pain his words were giving. 'Henry is a very good nurse; it occupies him, and it is good for her to feel his kindness! Then Minna has come out in the prettiest way: she never fails in some sweet little tender word or caress just when it is wanted.'

Leonard tried to smile, but only succeeded in keeping back a sob; and the doctor discharged his memory of the messages of love of which he had been the depository. Leonard recovered his composure during these, and was able to return a smile on hearing of Ella's conquest of Tom, of their Bible prints on Sunday, and their unwearied French billiards in the week. Then he asked after little Mab.

'She is all a dog should be,' said Dr May. 'Aubrey is her chief friend, except when she is lying at her ease on Ethel's dress.'

The old test of dog-love perhaps occurred to Leonard, for his lips trembled, and his eyes were dewy, even while they beamed with gladness.

'She is a great comfort to Aubrey,' the doctor added. 'I must beg you to send that poor fellow your forgiveness, for he is exceedingly unhappy about something he repeated in the first unguarded moment.'

'Mr Bramshaw told me,' said Leonard, with brow contracted.

'I cannot believe,' said Dr May, 'that it can do you any real harm. I do not think the prosecution ought to take notice of it; but if they do, it will be easy to sift it, and make it tell rather in your favour.'

'Maybe so,' said Leonard, still coldly.

'Then you will cheer him with some kind message?'

'To be sure. It is the time for me to be forgiving every one,' he answered, with a long tightly-drawn breath.

Much distressed, the doctor paused, in uncertainty whether Leonard were actuated by dread of the disclosure or resentment at the breach of confidence; but ere he spoke, the struggle had been fought out, and a sweet sad face was turned round to him, with the words, 'Poor old Aubrey! Tell him not to mind. There will be worse to be told out than our romancings together, and he will feel it more than I shall! Don't let him vex himself.'

'Thank you,' said the father, warmly. 'I call that pardon.'

'Not that there is anything to forgive,' said Leonard, 'only it is odd that one cares for it more than—— No, no, don't tell him that, but that I know it does not signify. It must not come between us, if this is to be the end; and it will make no difference. Nothing can do that but the finding my receipt. I see that book night and day before my eyes, with the very blot that I made in the top of my L.'

'You know they are searching the garden and fields, and advertising a reward, in case of its having been thrown away when rifled, or found to contain no valuables.'

'Yes!' and he rested on the word as though much lay behind.

'Do you think it contained anything worth keeping?'

'Only by one person.'

'Ha!' said the doctor, with a start.

Instead of answering, Leonard leant down on the narrow bed on which he was seated, and shut in his face between his hands.

The doctor waited, guessed, and grew impatient. 'You don't mean that fellow, Sam? Do you think he has it? I should like to throttle him, as sure as my name's Dick May!' (this in soliloquy between his teeth.) 'Speak up, Leonard, if you have any suspicion.'

The lad lifted himself with grave resolution that gave him dignity. 'Dr May,' he said, 'I know that what I say is safe with you, and it seems disrespectful to ask your word and honour beforehand, but I think it will be better for us both if you will give them not to make use of what I tell you. It weighs on me so, that I shall be saying it to the wrong person, unless I have it out with you. You promise me?'

'To make no use of it without your consent,' repeated the doctor, with rising hope; 'but this is no case for scruples – too much is at stake.'

'You need not tell me that,' Leonard replied, with a shudder; 'but I have no proof. I have thought again and again and again, but can find no possible witness. He was always cautious, and drink made him savage, but not noisy.'

'Then you believe——' The silence told the rest.

'If I did not see how easy people find it to believe the same of me on the mere evidence of circumstances, I should have no doubt,' said Leonard, deliberately.

'Then it was he that you saw in the yard?'

'Remember, all I saw was that a man was there. I concluded it was Andrews, waiting to take the horse; and as he is a great hanger-on of Sam, I wished to avoid him, and not keep my candle alight to attract his attention. That was the whole reason of my getting out of the window, and starting so soon; as unlucky a thing as I could have done.'

'You are sure it was not Andrews?'

'*Now* I am. You see Sam had sent home his horse from the station, though I did not know it; and, if you remember, Andrews was shown to have been at his father's long before. If he had been the man, he could speak to the time my light was put out.'

'The putting out of your light must have been the signal for the deed to be done.'

'My poor uncle! Well might he stare round as if he thought the walls would betray him, and start at every chinking of that unhappy gold in his helpless hands! If we had only known who was near – perhaps behind the blinds——' and Leonard gasped.

'But this secrecy, Leonard, I cannot understand it. Do you mean that the poor old man durst not do what he would with his own?'

'Just so. Whenever Sam knew that he had a sum of money, he laid hands on it. Nothing was safe from him that Mr Axworthy had in the Whitford Bank.'

'That can be proved from the accounts?'

'You recollect the little parlour between the office and my uncle's sitting-room? There I used to sit in the evening, and to feel, rather than hear, the way Sam used to bully the poor old man. Once – a fortnight ago, just after that talk with Aubrey – I knew he had been drinking, and watched, and came in upon them when there was no bearing it any longer. I was sworn at for my pains, and almost kicked out again; but after that Mr Axworthy made me sit in the room, as if I were a protection; and I made up my mind to bear it as long as he lived.'

'Surely the servants would bear witness to this state of things?'

'I think not. Their rooms are too far off for overhearing, and my uncle saw as little of them as possible. Mrs Giles was Sam's nurse, and cares for him more than any other creature; she would not say a word against him even if she knew anything; and my uncle would never have complained. He was fond of Sam to the last, proud of his steeple chases and his cleverness, and desperately afraid of him; in a sort of bondage, entirely past daring to speak.'

'I know,' said Dr May, remembering how his own Tom had been fettered and tongue-tied by that same tyrant in boyhood. 'But he spoke to you?'

'No,' said Leonard. 'After that scene much was implied between us, but nothing mentioned. I cannot even tell whether he trusted me, or only made me serve as a protector. I believe that row was about this money, which he had got together in secret, and that Sam suspected, and wanted to extort; but it was exactly as I said at the inquest, he gave no reason for sending me up to town with it. He knew that I knew why, and so said no more than that it was to be private. It was pitiful to see that man, so fierce and bold as they say he once was, trembling as if doing something by stealth, and the great hard knotty hands so crumpled and shaky, that he had to leave all to me. And that they should fancy *I* could go and hurt him!' said Leonard, stretching his broad chest and shoulders in conscious strength.

'Yes, considering who it was, I do not wonder that you feel the passion-theory as insulting as the accusation.'

'I ought not,' said Leonard, reddening. 'Every one knows what my temper can do. I do not think that a poor old feeble man like that could have provoked me to be so cowardly, but I see it is no wonder they think so. Only they might suppose I would not have been a robber, and go on lying now, when they take good care to tell me that it is ruinous!'

'It is an intolerable shame that they can look you in the face and imagine it for a moment,' said the doctor, with all his native warmth.

'After all,' said Leonard, recalled by his sympathy, 'it *is* my own fault from beginning to end that I am in this case. I see now that it was only God's mercy that prevented my brother's blood being on me, and it was my unrepenting obstinacy that brought me to the mill; so there will be no real injustice in my dying, and I expect nothing else.'

'Hush, Leonard; depend upon it, while there is Justice in Heaven, the true criminal cannot go free,' cried the doctor much agitated.

Leonard shook his head.

'Boyish hastiness is not murder,' added the doctor.

'So I thought. But it might have been, and I never repented. I brought all this on myself; and while I cannot feel guiltless in God's sight, I cannot expect it to turn out well.'

'Turn out well,' repeated the doctor. 'We want Ethel to tell us that this very repentance and owning of the sin, *is* turning out well – better than going on in it.'

'I can see that,' said Leonard. 'I do hope that if – if I can take this patiently, it may show I am sorry for the real thing – and I may be forgiven. Oh! I am glad prisoners are not cut off from church.'

Dr May pressed his hand in much emotion; and there was a silence before another question – whether there were nothing that could be of service.

'One chance there is, that Sam might relent enough to put that receipt where it could be found without implicating him. He must know what it would do for me.'

'You are convinced that he has it?'

'There must be papers in the book valuable to him; perhaps some that he had rather were not seen. Most likely he secured it in the morning. You remember he was there before the police.'

'Ay! ay! ay! the scoundrel! But, Leonard, what possessed you not to speak out at the inquest, when we might have searched every soul on the premises?'

'I did not see it then. I was stunned by the horror of the thing – the room where I had been so lately, and that blood on my own rifle too. It was all I could do at one time not to faint, and I had no notion they would not take my explanation; then, when I found it rejected, and everything closing in on me, I was in a complete maze. It was not till yesterday, when I was alone again, after having gone over my defence with Mr Bramshaw, and shown what I could prove, that I saw exactly how it must have been, as clear as a somnambulist. I sometimes could fancy I had seen Sam listening at the window, and have to struggle not to think I knew him under the stable wall.'

'And you are not such a – such a – so absurd as to sacrifice yourself to any scruple, and let the earth be cumbered with a rascal who, if he be withholding the receipt, is committing a second murder! It is not generosity, it is suicide.'

'It is not generosity,' said the boy, 'for if there were any hope, that would not stop me; but no one heard nor saw but myself, and I neither recognised him – no, I did not – nor heard anything definite from my uncle. Even if I had, no one – no one but you, believes a word I speak; nay, even my own case shows what probabilities are worth, and that I may be doing him the same wrong that I am suffering. I should only bring on myself the shame and disgrace of accusing another.'

The steady low voice and unboyish language showed him to be speaking from reflection, not impulse. The only tremulous moment was when he spoke of the one friend who trusted him, and whom his words were filling with a tumult of hope and alarm, admiration, indignation, and perplexity.

'Well, well,' the doctor said, almost stammering, 'I am glad you have been open with me. It may be a clue. Can there be any excuse for overhauling his papers? Or can't we pick a hole in that *alibi* of his? Now I recollect, he had it very pat, and unnecessarily prominent. I'll find some way of going to work without compromising you. Yes, you may trust me! I'll watch, but say not a word without your leave.'

'Thank you,' said Leonard. 'I am glad it is you – you who would never think a vague hope of saving me better than disgrace and dishonour.'

'We will save you,' said the doctor, becoming eager to escape to that favourite counsellor, the lining of his brougham, which had inspired him with the right theory of many a perplexing symptom, and he trusted would show him how to defend without betraying Leonard. 'I must go and see about it. Is there anything I can do for you – books, or anything?'

'No, thank you – except – I suppose there would be no objection to my having a few finer steel pens.' And to explain his wants, he took up his Prayer-book, which his sister had decorated with several small devotional prints. Copying these minutely line by line in pen and ink, was the solace of his prison hours; and though the work was hardly after drawing-masters' rules, the hand was not untaught, and there was talent and soul enough in the work to strike the doctor.

'It suits me best,' said Leonard. 'I should go distracted with nothing to do; and I can't read much – at least, not common books. And my sisters may like to have them. Will you let me do one for you?'

The speaking expression of those hazel eyes almost overcame the doctor, and his answer was by bending head and grasping hand. Leonard turned to the Collects, and mutely opened at the print of the Sun of Consolation, which he had already outlined, looked up at his friend, and turned away, only saying, 'Two or three of the sort with elastic nibs; they have them at the post-office.'

'Yes, I'll take care,' said Dr May, afraid to trust his self-command any longer. 'Good-bye, Leonard. Tom says I adopt every one who gets through a bad enough fever; so what will you be to me after this second attack?'

The result of the doctor's consultation with his brougham was his stopping it at Mr Bramshaw's door, to ascertain whether the search for the receipt had extended to young Axworthy's papers; but he found that they had been thoroughly examined, every facility having been given by their owner, who was his uncle's executor, and residuary legatee, by a will dated five years back, leaving a thousand pounds to the late Mrs Ward, and a few other legacies, but the mass of the property to the nephew.

Sam's 'facilities' not satisfying the doctor, it was further explained that every endeavour was being made to discover what other documents were likely to have been kept in the missing memorandum-book, so as to lead to the detection of any person who might present any such at a bank; and it was made evident that everything was being done, short of the impracticability of searching an unaccused man, but he could not but perceive that Mr Bramshaw's 'ifs' indicated great doubt of the existence of receipt and of pocket-book. Throwing out a hint that the time of Sam's return should be investigated, he learnt that this had been Edward Anderson's first measure, and that it was clear, from the independent testimony of the ostler at Whitford, the friend who had driven Sam, and the landlord of the Three Goblets, that there was not more than time for the return exactly as described at the inquest; and though the horse was swift and powerful, and might probably have been driven at drunken speed, this was too entirely conjectural for anything to be founded on it. Nor had the cheque by Bilson on the Whitford Bank come in.

'Something must assuredly happen to exonerate the guiltless, it would be profane to doubt,' said Dr May, continually to himself and to the Wards; but Leonard's secret was a painful burthen that he could scarcely have borne without sharing it with that daughter who was his other self, and well proved to be a safe repository.

'That's *my* Leonard,' said Ethel. 'I know him much better now than any time since the elf-bolt affair! They have not managed to ruin him among them.'

'What do you call this?' said Dr May, understanding her, indeed, but willing to hear her thought expressed.

'Thankworthy,' she answered, with a twitching of the corners of her mouth.

'You will suffer for this *exaltation*,' he said, sadly; 'you know you *have* a tender heart, for all your flights.'

'And *you* know you have a soul as well as a heart,' said Ethel, as well as the swelling in her throat would allow.

'To be sure, this world would be a poor place to live in, if admiration did not make pity bearable,' said the doctor; 'but – but don't ask me, Ethel: you have not had that fine fellow in his manly patience before your eyes. Talk of your knowing him! You knew a boy! I tell you, this has made him a man, and one of a thousand – so high-minded and so simple, so clear-headed and well-balanced, so entirely resigned and free from bitterness! What could he not be? It would be grievous to see him cut off by a direct dispensation – sickness, accident, battle; but for him to come to such an end, for the sake of a double murderer – Ethel – it would almost stagger one's faith!'

'Almost!' repeated Ethel, with the smile of a conqueror.

'I know, I know,' said the doctor. 'If it be so, it will be right; one will try to believe it good for him. Nay, there's proof enough in what it has done for him already. If you could only see him!'

'I mean to see him, if it should go against him,' said Ethel, 'if you will let me. I would go to him as I would if he were in a decline, and with more reverence.'

'Don't talk of it,' cried her father. 'For truth's sake, for justice's sake, for the country's sake, I *can* not, *will* not, believe it will go wrong. There is a Providence, after all, Ethel!'

And the doctor went away, afraid alike of hope and despondency; and Ethel thought of the bright young face, of De Wilton, of Job, and of the martyrs; and when she was not encouraging Aubrey, or soothing Averil, her heart *would* sink, and the tears that would not come would have been very comfortable.

It was well for all that the assizes were so near that the suspense was not long protracted; for it told upon all concerned. Leonard, when the doctor saw him again, was of the same way of thinking, but his manner was more agitated; he could not sleep, or if he slept, the anticipations chased away in the day-time revenged themselves in his dreams; and he was very unhappy, also, about his sister, whose illness continued day after day. She was not acutely ill, but in a constant state of low fever; every faculty in the most painful state of tension, convinced that she was quite able to get up and go to Leonard, and that her detention was mere cruelty; and then, on trying to rise, refused by fainting. Her searching questions and ardent eyes made it impossible to keep any feature in the case from her knowledge. Sleep was impossible to her; and once when Henry tried the effect of an anodyne, it produced a semi-delirium, which made him heartily repent of his independent measure. At all times she was talking – nothing but the being left with a very stolid maid-servant ever closed her lips; and she so greatly resented being thus treated, that the measure was seldom possible. Henry seldom left her. He was convinced that Leonard's sentence would be hers likewise, and he watched over her with the utmost tenderness and patience with her fretfulness and waywardness, never quitting her except on their brother's behalf, when Ethel or Mary would take his place. Little Minna was always to be found on her small chair by the bed-side, or moving about like a mouse, sometimes whispering her one note, 'They can't hurt him, if he has not done it,' and still quietly working at the pair of slippers that had been begun for his birthday present. Mary used to bring Ella, and take them out walking in the least-frequented path; but though the little sisters kissed eagerly, and went fondly hand in hand, they never were sorry to part: Ella's spirits oppressed Minna, and Minna's depression vexed the more volatile sister; moreover, Minna always dreaded Mary's desire to carry her away – as, poor child, she looked paler, and her eyes heavier and darker, every day.

No one else, except, of course, Dr May, was admitted. Henry would not let his sister see Mr Scudamore or Mr Wilmot, lest she should be excited; and Averil's 'No one' was vehement as a defence against Mrs Pugh or Mrs Ledwich, whom she suspected of wanting to see her, though she never heard of more than their daily inquiries.

Mrs Pugh was, in spite of her exclusion, the great authority with the neighbourhood for all the tidings of 'the poor Wards,' of whom she talked with the warmest commiseration, relating every touching detail of their previous and present history, and continually enduring the great shock of meeting people in shops or in the streets, whom she knew to be reporters or photographers. In fact, the catastrophe had taken a strong hold on the public mind; and 'Murder of an Uncle by his Nephew,' 'The Blewer Tragedy,' figured everywhere in the largest type; newsboys on the railway shouted, 'To-day's paper – account of inquest;' and the illustrated press sent down artists, whose three-legged cameras stared in all directions, from the Vintry Mill to Bankside, and who aimed at the school, the Minster, the volunteers, and Dr Hoxton himself. Tom advised Ethel to guard Mab carefully from appearing stuffed in the chamber of horrors at Madame Tussaud's; and the furniture at the mill would have commanded any price. Nay, Mrs Pugh was almost certain she had seen one of the 'horrid men' bargaining with the local photographer for her own portrait, in her weeds, and was resolved the interesting injury should never be forgiven!

She really had the 'trying scenes' of two interviews with both Mr Bramshaw and the attorney from Whitford who was getting up the prosecution, each having been told that she was in possession of important intelligence. Mr Bramshaw was not sanguine as to what he might obtain from her, but flattered her with the attempt, and ended by assuring her, like his opponent, that there was no need to expose her to the unpleasantness of appearing in court.

Aubrey was not to have the same relief, but was, like his father, subpoenaed as a witness for the prosecution. He had followed his father's advice, and took care not to disclose his evidence to the enemy, as he regarded the Whitford lawyer. He was very miserable, and it was as much for his sake as that of the immediate family, that Ethel rejoiced that the suspense was to be short.

Counsel of high reputation had been retained; but as the day came nearer, without bringing any of the disclosures on which the doctor had so securely reckoned, more and more stress was laid on the dislike to convict on circumstantial evidence, and on the saying that the English law had rather acquit ten criminals than condemn one innocent man.

CHAPTER XIV

'Ah! I mind me now of thronging faces,
  Mocking eyed, and eager, as for sport;
Hundreds looking up, and in high places
  Men arrayed for judgment and a court.

'And I heard, or seemed to hear, one seeking
  Answer back from one he doomed to die,
Pitifully, sadly, sternly speaking
  Unto one – and oh! that one, 'twas I.'

Rev G.E. Monsell.

The 'Blewer Murder' was *the* case of the Assize week; and the court was so crowded that, but for the favour of the sheriff, Mr and Mrs Rivers, with Tom and Gertrude, could hardly have obtained seats. No others of the family could endure to behold the scene, except from necessity; and indeed Ethel and Mary had taken charge of the sisters at home, for

Henry could not remain at a distance from his brother, though unable to bear the sight of the proceedings; he remained in a house at hand.

Nearly the whole population of Stoneborough, Whitford, and Blewer, was striving to press into court; but before the day's work began, Edward Anderson had piloted Mrs Pugh to a commodious place, under the escort of his brother Harvey, who was collecting materials for an article on criminal jurisprudence.

Some of those who, like the widow and little Gertrude, had been wild to be present, felt their hearts fail them when the last previous case had been disposed of; and there was a brief pause of grave and solemn suspense and silent breathless expectation within the court, unbroken, except by increased sounds of crowding in all the avenues without.

Every one, except the mere loungers, who craved nothing but excitement, looking awed and anxious; and the impression was deepened by the perception that the same feeling, though restrained, affected the judge himself, and was visible in the anxious attention with which he looked at the papers before him, and the stern sadness that had come over the features naturally full of kindness and benevolence.

The prisoner appeared in the dock. He had become paler, and perhaps thinner, for his square determined jaw, and the resolute mould of his lips, were more than usually remarkable, and were noted in the physiognomical brain of Harvey Anderson; as well as the keen light of his full dark hazel eye, the breadth of his brow, with his shining light brown hair brushed back from it; the strong build of his frame, and the determined force, apparent even in the perfect quiescence of his attitude.

Leonard Axworthy Ward was arraigned for the wilful murder of Francis Axworthy, and asked whether he pleaded Guilty or Not guilty.

His voice was earnest, distinct and firm; and his eyes were raised upwards, as though he were making the plea of 'Not guilty,' not to man alone, but to the Judge of all the earth.

The officer of the court informed him of his right to challenge any of the jury, as they were called over by name; and as each came to be sworn, he looked full and steadily at each face, more than one of which was known to him by sight, as if he were committing his cause into their hands. He declined to challenge; and then crossing his arms on his breast, cast down his eyes, and thus retained them through the greater part of the trial.

The jurymen were then sworn in, and charged with the issue; and the counsel for the prosecution opened the case, speaking more as if in pity than in indignation, as he sketched the history, which it was his painful duty to establish. He described how Mr Axworthy, having spent the more active years of his life in foreign trade, had finally returned to pass his old age among his relatives; and had taken to assist him in his business a great-nephew, and latterly another youth in the same degree of relation, the son of his late niece – the prisoner, who on leaving school had been taken into his uncle's office, lodged in the house, and became one of the family. It would, however, be shown by witnesses that the situation had been extremely irksome to the young man; and that he had not been in it many months, before he had expressed his intention of absconding, provided he could obtain the means of making his way in one of the colonies. Then followed a summary of the deductions resulting from the evidence about to be adduced, and which carried upon its face the inference that the absence of the cousin, the remoteness of the room, the sight of a large sum of money, and the helplessness of the old man, had proved temptations too strong for a fiery and impatient youth, long fretted by the restraints of his situation, and had conducted him to violence, robbery, and flight. It was a case that could not be regarded without great regret and compassion; but the gentlemen of the jury must bear in mind in their investigation, that pity must not be permitted to distort the facts, which he feared were only too obvious.

The speech was infinitely more telling from its fair and commiserating tone towards the prisoner; and the impression that it carried, not that he was to be persecuted by having the crime fastened on him, but that truth must be sought out at all hazards.

'Even he is sorry for Leonard! I don't hate him as I thought I should,' whispered Gertrude May, to her elder sister.

The first witness was, as before, the young maid-servant, Anne Ellis, who described her first discovery of the body; and on further interrogation, the situation of the room, distant from those of the servants, and out of hearing – also her master's ordinary condition of feebleness. She had observed nothing in the room, or on the table, but knew the window was open, since she had run to it, and screamed for help, upon which Master Hardy had come to her aid.

Leonard's counsel then elicited from her how low the window was, and how easily it could be entered from without.

James Hardy corroborated all this, giving a more minute account of the state of the room; and telling of his going to call the young gentlemen, and finding the open passage window and empty bed-room. The passage window would naturally be closed at night; and there was no reason to suppose that Mr Ward would be absent. The bag shown to him was one that had originally been made for the keeping of cash, but latterly had been used for samples of grain, and he had last seen it in the office.

The counsel for the prisoner inquired what had been on the table at Hardy's first entrance; but to this the witness could not swear, except that the lamp was burning, and that there were no signs of disorder, nor was the dress of the deceased disarranged. He had seen his master put receipts, and make memorandums, in a large, black, silver-clasped pocket-book, but had never handled it, and could not swear to it; he had seen nothing like it since his master's death. He was further asked how long the prisoner had been at the Mill, his duties there, and the amount of trust reposed in him; to which last the answer was, that about a month since, Mr Axworthy had exclaimed that if ever he wanted a thing to be done, he must set Ward about it. Saving this speech, made in irritation at some omission on Sam's part, nothing was adduced to show that Leonard was likely to have been employed without his cousin's knowledge; though Hardy volunteered the addition that Mr Ward was always respectful and attentive, and that his uncle had lately thought much more of him than at first.

Rebekah Giles gave her account of the scene in the sitting-room. She had been in the service of the deceased for the last four years, and before in that of his sister-in-law, Mr Samuel's mother. She had herself closed the passage window at seven o'clock in the evening, as usual. She had several times previously found it partly open in the morning, after having thus shut it over-night, but never before, Mr Ward's bed unslept in. Her last interview with Mr Axworthy was then narrated, with his words – an imprecation against rifle practice, as an excuse for idle young rascals to be always out of the way. Then followed her communication to the prisoner at half-past nine, when she saw him go into the parlour, in his volunteer uniform, rifle in hand, heard him turn the lock of the sitting-room door, and then herself retired to bed.

Cross examination did not do much with her, only showing that, when she brought in the supper, one window had been open, and the blinds, common calico ones, drawn down, thus rendering it possible for a person to lurk unseen in the court, and enter by the window. Her master had assigned no reason for sending for Mr Ward. She did not know whether Mr Axworthy had any memorandum book; she had seen none on the table, nor found any when she undressed the body, though his purse, watch, and seals were on his person.

Mr Rankin's medical evidence came next, both as to the cause of death, the probable instrument, and the nature of the stains on the desk and rifle.

When cross examined, he declared that he had looked at the volunteer uniform without finding any mark of blood, but from the nature of the injury it was not likely that there would be any. He had attended Mr Axworthy for several years, and had been visiting him professionally during a fit of the gout in the last fortnight of June, when he had observed that the prisoner was very attentive to his uncle. Mr Axworthy was always unwilling to be waited on, but was unusually tolerant of this nephew's exertions on his behalf, and had seemed of late to place much reliance on him.

Doctor Richard May was the next witness called. The sound of that name caused the first visible change in the prisoner's demeanour, if that could be called change, which was only a slight relaxation of the firm closing of the lips, and one sparkle of the dark eyes, ere they were again bent down as before, though not without a quiver of the lids.

Dr May had brought tone, look, and manner to the grave impartiality, which even the most sensitive man is drilled into assuming in public; but he durst not case one glance in the direction of the prisoner.

In answer to the counsel for the prosecution, he stated that he was at the Vintry Mill at seven o'clock on the morning of the 6th of July, not professionally, but as taking interest in the Ward family. He had seen the body of the deceased, and considered death to have been occasioned by fracture of the skull, from a blow with a blunt heavy instrument. The superintendent had shown him a rifle, which he considered, from the marks on it, as well as from the appearance of the body, to have produced the injury. The rifle was the one shown to him; it was the property of Leonard Ward. He recognised it by the crest and cypher H.E. It had belonged to his son-in-law, Hector Ernescliffe, by whom it had been given to Leonard Ward.

Poor Doctor! That was a cruel piece of evidence; and his son and daughters opposite wondered how he could utter it in that steady matter-of-fact way; but they knew him to be sustained by hopes of the cross-examination; and he soon had the opportunity of declaring that he had known Leonard Ward from infancy, without being aware of any imputation against him; but had always seen him highly principled and trustworthy, truthful and honourable, kind-hearted and humane – the last person to injure the infirm or aged.

Perhaps the good doctor, less afraid of the sound of his own voice, and not so much in awe as some of the other witnesses, here in his eagerness overstepped the bounds of prudence. His words indeed brought a tremulous flicker of grateful emotion over the prisoner's face; but by carrying the inquiry into the region of character and opinion, he opened the door to a dangerous re-examination by the Crown lawyer, who required the exact meaning of his unqualified commendation, especially in the matter of humanity, demanding whether he had never known of any act of violence on the prisoner's part. The colour flushed suddenly into Leonard's face, though he moved neither eye nor lip; but his counsel appealed to the judge, and the pursuit of this branch of the subject was quashed as irrelevant; but the doctor went down in very low spirits, feeling that his evidence had been damaging, and his hopes of any ray of light becoming fainter.

After this, the village policeman repeated the former statements, as to the state of the various rooms, the desk, locked and untouched, the rifle, boat, &c. further explaining that the distance from the Mill to Blewer Station, by the road, was an hour and half's walk, by the fields, not more than half an hour's.

The station-master proved the prisoner's arrival at midnight, his demand of a day-ticket, his being without luggage, and in a black suit; and the London policeman proved the finding of the money on his person, and repeated his own explanation of it.

The money was all in sovereigns, except one five and one ten-pound note; and Edward Hazlitt, the clerk of the Whitford Bank, was called to prove the having given the latter in change to Mr Axworthy for a fifty-pound cheque, on the 10th of May last.

This same clerk had been at the volunteer drill on the evening of the 5th of July, had there seen the prisoner, had parted with him at dusk, towards nine o'clock, making an engagement with him to meet on Blewer Heath for some private practice at seven o'clock on Monday evening. Thought Mr Axworthy did sometimes employ young Ward on his commissions; Mr Axworthy had once sent him into Whitford to pay in a large sum, and another time with an order to be cashed. The dates of these transactions were shown in the books; and Hazlitt added, on further interrogation, that Samuel Axworthy could not have been aware of the sum being sent to the bank, since he had shortly after come and desired to see the account, which had been laid before him as confidential manager, when he had shown surprise and annoyance at the recent deposit, asking through whom it had been made. Not ten days subsequently, an order for nearly the entire amount had been cashed, signed by the deceased, but filled up in Samuel's handwriting.

This had taken place in April; and another witness, a baker, proved the having paid the five-pound note to old Mr Axworthy himself on the 2nd of May.

Samuel Axworthy himself was next called. His florid face wore something of the puffed, stupefied look it had had at the inquest, but his words were ready, and always to the point. He identified the bag in which the money had been found, giving an account of it similar to Hardy's and adding that he had last seen it lying by his cousin's desk. His uncle had no account with any London bank, all transactions had of late passed through his own hands, and he had never known the prisoner employed in any business of importance – he could not have been kept in ignorance of it if it had previously been the case. The deceased had a black shagreen pocket-book, with a silver clasp, which he occasionally used, but the witness had never known him give it out of his own hand, nor take a receipt in it. Had not seen it on the morning of the 6th, nor subsequently. Could not account for the sum found on the person of the prisoner, whose salary was 50*l.* per annum, and who had no private resources, except the interest of 2,000*l.*, which, he being a minor, was not in his own hands. Deceased was fond of amassing sovereigns, and would often keep them for a long time in the drawer of his desk, as much as from 50*l.* to 100*l.* There was none there when the desk was opened on the 6th of July, though there had certainly been gold there two days previously. It was kept locked. It had a small Bramah key, which his uncle wore on his watch-chain, in his waist-coat pocket. The drawer was locked when he saw it on the morning of the 6th.

The doctor, who had joined his children, gave a deep respiration, and relaxed the clenching of his hand, as this witness went down.

Then it came to the turn of Aubrey Spencer May. The long waiting, after his nerves had been wound up, had been a severe ordeal, and his delicacy of constitution and home breeding had rendered him peculiarly susceptible. With his resemblance to his father in form and expression, it was like seeing the doctor denuded of that shell of endurance with which he had contrived to conceal his feelings. The boy was indeed braced to resolution, but the resolution was equally visible with the agitation in the awe-stricken brow, varying colour, tightened breath, and involuntary shiver, as he took the oath. Again Leonard looked up with one of his clear bright glances, and perhaps a shade of anxiety; but Aubrey, for his own comfort, was too short-sighted for meeting of eyes from that distance.

Seeing his agitation, and reckoning on his evidence, the counsel gave him time, by minutely asking if his double Christian name were correctly given, his age, and if he were not the son of Dr May.

'You were the prisoner's school-fellow, I believe?'

'No,' faltered Aubrey.

'But you live near him?'

'We are friends,' said Aubrey with sudden firmness and precision; and from the utterance of that emphatic *are*, his spirit returned.

'Did you often see him?'

'On most Sundays, after church.'

'Did you ever hear him say he had any thoughts of the means of leaving the Mill privately?'

'Something like it,' said Aubrey, turning very red.

'Can you tell me the words?'

'He said if things went on, that I was not to be surprised if I heard "*non est inventus*."' said Aubrey, speaking as if rapidity would conceal the meaning of the words, but taken aback by being made to repeat and translate them to the jury.

'And did he mention any way of escaping?'

'He said the window and cedar-tree were made for it, and that he often went out that way to bathe,' said Aubrey.

'When did this conversation take place?'

'On Sunday, the 22nd of June,' said Aubrey, in despair, as the Crown lawyer thanked him, and sat down.

He felt himself betrayed into having made their talk wear the air of deliberate purpose, and having said not one word of what Mr Bramshaw had hailed as hopeful. However, the defending barrister rose up to ask him what he meant by having answered 'Something like it.'

'Because,' said Aubrey, promptly, 'though we did make the scheme, we were neither of us in earnest.'

'How do you know the prisoner was not in earnest?'

'We often made plans of what we should like to do.'

'And had you any reason for thinking this one of such plans?'

'Yes,' said Aubrey; 'for he talked of getting gold enough to build up the market-cross, or else of going to see the Feejee Islands.'

'Then you understood the prisoner not to express a deliberate purpose, so much as a vague design.'

'Just so,' said Aubrey. 'A design that depended on how things went on at the Mill.' And being desired to explain his words, he added, that Leonard had said he could not bear the sight of Sam Axworthy's tyranny over the old man, and was resolved not to stay, if he were made a party to any of the dishonest tricks of the trade.

'In that case, did he say where he would gave gone?'

'First to New Zealand, to my brother, the Reverend Norman May.'

Leonard's counsel was satisfied with the colour the conversation had now assumed; but the perils of re-examination were not over yet, for the adverse lawyer requested to know whence the funds were to have come for this adventurous voyage.

'We laughed a little about that; and he said he should have to try how far his quarter's salary would go towards a passage in the steerage.'

'If your friend expressed so strong a distaste to his employers and their business, what induced him to enter it?'

Leonard's counsel again objected to this inquiry, and it was not permitted. Aubrey was dismissed, and, flushed and giddy, was met by his brother Tom, who almost took him in his arms as he emerged from the passage.

'O Tom! what have I done?'

'Famously, provided there's no miller in the jury. Come,' as he felt the weight on his arm, 'Flora says I am to take you down and make you take something.'

'No, no, no, I can't! I must go back.'

'I tell you there's nothing going on. Every one is breathing and baiting.' And he got him safe to a pastrycook's, and administered brandy cherries, which Aubrey bolted whole like pills, only entreating to return, and wanting to know how he thought the case going.

'Excellently. Hazlitt's evidence and yours ought to carry him through. And Anderson says they have made so much out of the witnesses for the prosecution, that they need call none for the defence; and so the enemy will be baulked of their reply, and we shall have the last word. I vow I have missed my vocation. I know I was born for a barrister.'

'Now may we come back?' said the boy, overwhelmed by his brother's cheeriness; and they squeezed into court again, Tom inserting Aubrey into his own former seat, and standing behind him on half a foot at the angle of the passage. They were in time for the opening of the defence, and to hear Leonard described as a youth of spirit and promise, of a disposition that had won him general affection and esteem, and recommended to universal sympathy by the bereavement which was recent in the memory of his fellow-townsmen; and there was a glance at the mourning which the boy still wore.

'They had heard indeed that he was quick-tempered and impulsive; but the gentlemen of the jury were some of them fathers, and he put it to them whether a ready and generous spirit of indignation in a lad were compatible with cowardly designs against helpless old age; whether one whose recreations were natural science and manly exercise, showed tokens of vicious tendencies; above all, whether a youth, whose friendship they had seen so touchingly claimed by a son of one of the most highly respected gentlemen in the county, were evincing the propensities that lead to the perpetration of deeds of darkness.'

Tom patted Aubrey on the shoulder; and Aubrey, though muttering 'humbug,' was by some degrees less wretched.

'Men did not change their nature on a sudden,' the counsel continued; 'and where was the probability that a youth of character entirely unblemished, and of a disposition particularly humane and generous, should at once rush into a crime of the deep and deadly description, to which a long course of dissipation, leading to perplexity, distress, and despair, would be the only inducement?'

He then went on to speak of Leonard's position at the Mill, as junior clerk. He had been there for six months, without a flaw being detected, either in his integrity, his diligence, or his regularity; indeed, it was evident that he had been gradually acquiring a greater degree of esteem and confidence than he had at first enjoyed, and had been latterly more employed by his uncle. That a young man of superior education should find the daily drudgery tedious and distasteful, and that one of sensitive honour should be startled at the ordinary, he might almost say proverbial, customs of the miller's trade – was surprising to no one; and that he should unbosom himself to a friend of his own age, and indulge together with him in romantic visions of adventure, was, to all who remembered their own boyhood, an illustration of the freshness and ingenuousness of the character that thus unfolded itself. Where there were day-dreams, there was no room for plots of crime.

Then ensued a species of apology for the necessity of entering into particulars that did not redound to the credit of a gentleman, who had appeared before the court under such distressing circumstances as Mr Samuel Axworthy; but it was needful that the condition of the family should be well understood, in order to comprehend the unhappy train of events which had conducted the prisoner into his present situation. He then went through what had been traceable through the evidence – that Samuel Axworthy was a man of expensive habits, and accustomed to drain his uncle's resources to supply his own needs; showing how the sum, which had been entrusted to the prisoner, to be paid into the local bank, had been drawn out by the elder nephew as soon as he became aware of the deposit; and how, shortly after, the prisoner had expressed to Aubrey May his indignation at the tyranny exercised on his uncle.

'By-and-by, another sum is amassed,' continued Leonard's advocate. 'How dispose of it? The local bank is evidently no security from the rapacity of the elder nephew. Once aware of its existence, he knows how to use means for compelling its surrender; and the feeble old man can no longer call his hard-earned gains his own except on sufferance. The only means of guarding it is to lodge it secretly in a distant bank, without the suspicion of his nephew Samuel; but the invalid is too infirm to leave his apartment; his fingers, crippled by gout, refuse even to guide the pen. He can only watch for an opportunity, and this is at length afforded by the absence of the elder nephew for two days at the county races. This will afford time for a trustworthy and intelligent messenger to convey the sum to town, deposit it in Messrs Drummond's bank, and return unobserved. When, therefore, supper is brought in, Mr Axworthy sends for the lad on whom he has learnt to depend, and shows much disappointment at his absence. Where is he? Is he engaged with low companions in the haunts of vice, that are the declivity towards crime? Is he gaming, or betting, or drinking? No. He has obeyed the summons of his country; he is a zealous volunteer, and is eagerly using a weapon, presented to him by a highly respected gentleman of large fortune in a neighbouring county; nay, so far is he from any sinister purpose, that he is making an appointment with a fellow-rifleman for the ensuing Monday. On his return at dark, he receives a pressing summons to his uncle's room, and hastens to obey it without pausing to lay aside his rifle. The commission is explained, and well understanding the painfulness of the cause, he discreetly asks no questions, but prepares to execute it. The sum of 124*l.* 12*s.* is taken from the drawer of the desk, the odd money assigned to travelling expenses, the 120*l.* placed in a bag brought in from the office for the purpose, bearing the initials of the owner, and a receipt in a private pocket-book was signed by him for the amount, and left open on the table for the ink to dry.

'Who that has ever been young, can doubt the zest and elevation of receiving for the first time a confidential mission? Who can doubt that even the favourite weapon would be forgotten where it stood, and that it would only be accordant to accredited rules that the window should be preferable to the door? Had it not already figured in the visions of adventure in the Sunday evening's walk? was it not a favourite mode of exit in the mornings, when bathing and fishing were more attractive than the pillow? Moreover, the moonlight disclosed what appeared like a figure in the court-yard, and there was reason at the time to suppose it a person likely to observe and report upon the expedition. The opening of the front door might likewise attract notice; and if the cousin should, as was possible, return that night, the direct road was the way to meet him. The hour was too early for the train which was to be met, but a lighted candle would reveal the vigil, and moonlight on the meadows was attractive at eighteen. Gentlemen of soberer and maturer years might be incredulous, but surely it was not so strange or unusual for a lad, who indulged in visions of adventure, to find a moonlight walk by the riverside more inviting than a bedroom.

'Shortly after, perhaps as soon as the light was extinguished, the murder must have been committed. The very presence of that light had been guardianship to the helpless old man below. When it was quenched, nothing remained astir, the way from without was open, the weapon stood only too ready to hand, the memorandum-book gave promise of booty and was secured, though nothing else was apparently touched. It was this very book that contained the signature that would have exonerated the prisoner, and to which he fearlessly appealed upon his arrest at the Paddington Station, before, for his additional misfortune, he had time to discharge himself of his commission, and establish his innocence by the deposit of the money at the bank. He has thus for a while become the victim of a web of suspicious circumstances. But look at these very circumstances more closely, and they will be found perfectly consistent with the prisoner's statement, never varying, be it remembered, from the explanation given to the policeman in first surprise and horror of the tidings of the crime.

'It might have been perhaps thought that there was another alternative between entire innocence and a deliberate purpose of robbery and murder – namely, that reproof from the old man had provoked a blow, and that the means of flight had been hastily seized upon in the moment of confusion and alarm. This might have been a plausible line of defence, and secure of a favourable hearing; but I beg to state that the prisoner has distinctly refused any such defence, and my instructions are to contend for his perfect innocence. A nature, such as we have already traced, is, as we cannot but perceive, revolted by the bare idea of violence to the aged and infirm, and recoils as strongly from the one accusation as from the other.

'The prisoner made his statement at the first moment, and has adhered to it in every detail, without confusion or self-contradiction. It does not attempt to explain all the circumstances, but they all tally exactly with his story; he is unable to show by whom the crime could have been committed, nor is he bound in law or justice so to do; nay, his own story shows the absolute impossibility of his being able to explain what took place in his absence. But mark how completely the established facts corroborate his narrative. Observe first the position in which the body was found, the head on the desk, the stain of blood corresponding with the wound, the dress undisturbed, all manifestly untouched since the fatal stroke was dealt. Could this have been the case, had the key of the drawer of gold been taken from the waistcoat pocket, the chain from about the neck of the deceased, and both replaced after the removal of the money and relocking the drawer? Can any one doubt that the drawer was opened, the money taken out, and the lock secured, while Mr Axworthy was alive and consenting? Again, what robber would convey away the spoil in a bag bearing the initials of the owner, and that not caught up in haste, but fetched in for the purpose from the office? Or would so tell-tale a weapon as the rifle have been left conspicuously close at hand? There was no guilty precipitation, for the uniform had been taken off and folded up, and with a whole night before him, it would have been easy to reach a more distant station, where his person would not have been recognised. Why, too, if this were the beginning of a flight and exile, should no preparation have been made for passing a single night from home? why should a day-ticket have been asked for? No, the prisoner's own straightforward, unvarnished statement is the only consistent interpretation of the facts, otherwise conflicting and incomprehensible.

'That a murder has been committed is unhappily too certain. I make no attempt to unravel the mystery. I confine myself to the far more grateful task of demonstrating, that to fasten the imputation on the accused, would be to overlook a complication of inconsistencies, all explained by his own account of himself, but utterly inexplicable on the hypothesis of his guilt.

'Circumstantial evidence is universally acknowledged to be perilous ground for a conviction; and I never saw a case in which it was more manifestly delusive than in the present, bearing at first an imposing and formidable aspect, but on examination, confuted in every detail. Most assuredly,' continued the counsel, his voice becoming doubly earnest, 'while there is even the possibility of innocence, it becomes incumbent on you, gentlemen of the jury, to consider well the fearful consequences of a decision in a matter of life or death – a decision for which there can be no reversal. The facts that have come to light are manifestly incomplete. Another link in the chain has yet to be added; and when it shall come forth, how will it be if it should establish the guiltlessness of the prisoner too late? Too late, when a young life of high promise, and linked by close family ties, and by bonds of ardent friendship with so many, has been quenched in shame and disgrace, for a crime to which he may be an utter stranger.

'The extinction of the light in that upper window was the sign for darkness and horror to descend on the Mill! Here is the light of life still burning, but a breath of yours can extinguish it in utter gloom, and then who may rekindle it? Nay, the revelation of events that would make the transactions of that fatal night clear as the noonday, would never avail to rekindle the lamp, that may yet, I trust, shine forth to the world – the clearer it may be, from the unmerited imputations, which it has been my part to combat, and of which his entire life is a confutation.'

Mrs Pugh was sobbing under her veil; Gertrude felt the cause won. Tom noiselessly clapped the orator behind his brother's back, and nodded his approval to his father. Even Leonard lifted up his face, and shot across a look, as if he felt deliverance near after the weary day, that seemed to have been a lifetime already, though the sunbeams were only beginning to fall high and yellow on the ceiling, through the heated stifling atmosphere, heavy with anxiety and suspense. Doctor May was thinking of the meeting after the acquittal, of the telegram to Stoneborough, of the sister's revival, and of Ethel's greeting.

Still the judge had to sum up; and all eyes turned on him, knowing that the fate of the accused would probably depend on the colouring that the facts adduced would assume in his hands. Flora, who met him in society, was struck by the grave and melancholy bracing, as it were, of the countenance, that she had seen as kindly and bright as her father's; and the deep, full voice, sad rather than stern, the very tone of which conveyed to every mind how heavy was the responsibility of justice and impartiality. In effect, the very force of the persuasions made for the defence, unanswered by the prosecution, rendered it needful for him to give full weight to the evidence for the other side; namely, the prisoner's evident impatience of his position, and premeditated flight, the coincidence of the times, the being the last person seen to enter the room, and with the very weapon that had been the instrument of the crime; the probability that the deceased had himself opened the drawer, the open window, the flight, and the missing sum being found on his person, the allegation that the receipt would be found in the pocket-book, unsupported by any testimony as to the practice of the deceased; the strangeness of leaving the premises so much too early for the train, and, by his own account, leaving a person prowling in the court, close to his uncle's window. No opinion was given; but there was something that gave a sense that the judge felt it a crushing weight of evidence. Yet so minutely was every point examined, so carefully was every indication weighed which could tend to establish the prisoner's innocence, that to those among his audience who believed that innocence indubitable, it seemed as if his arguments proved it, even more triumphantly than the pleading of the counsel, as, vibrating between hope and fear, anxiety and gratitude, they followed him from point to point of the unhappy incident, hanging upon every word, as though each were decisive.

When at length he ceased, and the jury retired, the breathless stillness continued. With some, indeed, there was the relaxation of long-strained attention, eyes unbent, and heads turned; but Flora had to pass her arm round her little sister, to steady the child's nervous trembling; Aubrey sat rigid and upright, the throbs of his heart well-nigh audible; and Dr May leant forward, and covered his eyes with his hand; Tom, who alone dared glance to the dock, saw that Leonard too had retired. Those were the most terrible minutes they had ever spent in their lives; but they were minutes of hope – of hope of relief from a burthen, becoming more intolerable with every second's delay ere the rebound.

Long as it seemed to them, it was not in reality more than a quarter of an hour before the jury returned, and with slow grave movements, and serious countenances, resumed their places. Leonard was already in his; his cheek paler, his fingers locked together, and his eyes scanning each as they came forward, and one by one their names were called over. His head was erect, and his bearing had something undaunted, though intensely anxious.

The question was put by the clerk of the court, 'How find you? guilty or not guilty?'

Firmly, though sadly, the foreman rose, and his answer was, 'We find the prisoner guilty; but we earnestly recommend him to mercy.'

Whether Tom felt or not that Aubrey was in a dead faint, and rested against him as a senseless weight, he paid no visible attention to aught but one face, on which his eyes were riveted as though nothing would ever detach them – and that face was not the prisoner's.

Others saw Leonard's face raised upwards, and a deep red flush spread over brow and cheek, though neither lip nor eye wavered.

Then came the question whether the prisoner had anything to say, wherefore judgment should not be passed upon him.

Leonard made a step forward, and his clear steady tone did not shake for a moment as he spoke. 'No. I see that appearances are so much against me, that man can hardly decide otherwise. I have known from the first that nothing could show my innocence but the finding of the receipt. In the absence of that one testimony, I feel that I have had a fair trial, and that all has been done for me that could be done; and I thank you for it, my Lord, and you, Gentlemen,' as he bent his head; then added, 'I should like to say one thing more. My Lord, you would not let the question be asked, how I brought all this upon myself. I wish to say it myself, for it is that which makes my sentence just in the sight of God. It is true that, though I never lifted my hand against my poor uncle, I did in a moment of passion fling a stone at my brother, which, but for God's mercy, might indeed have made me a murderer. It was for this, and other like outbreaks, that I was sent to the Mill; and it may be just that for it I should die – though *indeed* I never hurt my uncle.'

Perhaps there was something in the tone of that one word, *indeed*, which by recalling his extreme youth, touched all hearts more than even the manly tone of his answer, and his confession. There was a universal weeping and sobbing throughout the court; Mrs Pugh was on the verge of hysterics, and obliged to be supported away; and Gertrude was choking between the agony of contagious feeling and dread of Flora's displeasure; and all the time Leonard stood calm, with his brave head and lofty bearing, wound up for the awful moment of the sentence.

The weeping was hushed, when the crier of the court made proclamation, commanding all persons on pain of imprisonment to be silent. Then the judge placed on his head the black cap, and it was with trembling hands that he did so; the blood had entirely left his face, and his lips were purple with the struggle to contend with and suppress his emotion. He paused, as though he were girding himself up to the most terrible of duties, and when he spoke his voice was hollow, as he began:

'Leonard Axworthy Ward, you have been found guilty of a crime, that would have appeared impossible in one removed from temptation by birth and education such as yours have been. What the steps may have been that led to such guilt, must lie between your own conscience and that God whose justice you have acknowledged. To Him you have evidently been taught to look; and may you use the short time that still remains to you, in seeking His forgiveness by sincere repentance. I will forward the recommendation to mercy, but it is my duty to warn you that there are no such palliating circumstances in the evidence, as to warrant any expectation of a remission of the sentence.'

And therewith followed the customary form of sentence, ending with the solemn 'And may God Almighty have mercy on your soul!'

Full and open, and never quailing, had the dark eyes been fixed upon the judge all the time; and at those last words, the head bent low, and the lips moved for 'Amen.'

Then Tom, relieved to find instant occupation for his father, drew his attention to Aubrey's state; and the boy between Tom and George Rivers was, as best they could, carried through the narrow outlets, and laid down in a room, opened to them by the sheriff, where his father and Flora attended him, while Tom flew for remedies; and Gertrude sobbed and wept as she had never done in her life.

It was some time before the swoon yielded, or Dr May could leave his son, and then he was bent on at once going to the prisoner; but he was so shaken and tremulous, that Tom insisted on giving him his arm, and held an umbrella over him in the driving rain.

'Father,' he said, as soon as they were in the street, 'I can swear who did it.'

Dr May just hindered himself from uttering the name; but Tom answered as if it had been spoken.

'Yes. I saw the face of fiendish barbarity that once was over me, when I was a miserable little school-boy! He did it; and he has the receipt.'

Dr May squeezed his arm. 'I have not betrayed the secret, have I?'

'You knew that he knew it!'

'Not knew – suspected – generosity.'

'I saw him! I saw him cast those imploring earnest eyes of his on the scoundrel as he spoke of the receipt – and the villain try to make himself of stone. Well, if I have one wish in life, it is to see that fellow come to the fate he deserves. I'll never lose sight of him; I'll dog him like a blood-hound!'

'And what good will that do, when – Tom, Tom, we must move Heaven and earth for petitions. I'll take them up myself, and get George Rivers to take me to the Home Secretary. Never fear, while there's justice in Heaven.'

'Here's Henry!' exclaimed Tom, withholding his father, who had almost run against the brother, as they encountered round a corner.

He was pale and bewildered, and hardly seemed to hear the doctor's hasty asseverations that he would get a reprieve.

'He sent me to meet you,' said Henry. 'He wants you to go home – to Ave I mean. He says that is what he wants most – for you to go to her now, and to come to him to-morrow, or when you can; and he wants to hear how Aubrey is,' continued Henry, as if dreamily repeating a lesson.

'He saw then——?'

'Yes; and that seems to trouble him most.'

Dr May was past speaking, and Tom was obliged to answer for him – that Aubrey was pretty well again, and had desired his dearest, dearest love; then asked how Leonard was.

'Calm and firm as ever,' said Henry, half choked. 'Nothing seems to upset him, but speaking of – of you and Aubrey, Dr May – and poor Ave. But – but they'll be together before long.'

'No such thing,' said Dr May. 'You will see that certainty cures, when suspense kills; and for him, I'll never believe but that all will be right yet. Are you going home?'

'I shall try to be with – with the dear unhappy boy as long as I can, and then I'll come home.'

Dr May grasped Henry's hand, gave a promise of coming, and a message of love to the prisoner; tried to say something more, but broke down, and let Tom lead him away.

CHAPTER XV

'Under the shroud
Of His thunder-cloud
Lie we still when His voice is loud,
And our hearts shall feel
The love notes steal,
As a bird sings after the thunder peal.'

C.F.A.

Not till dusk could Dr May get back to Stoneborough, and then, in an evening gleam of that stormy day, he was met at the gate of Bankside by Richard and Ethel.

'You need not come in, papa,' said Ethel. 'She is asleep. She knows.'

Dr May sighed with unspeakable relief.

'Mr Bramshaw telegraphed, and his clerk came down. It was not so very bad! She saw it in our faces, and she was so worn out with talking and watching, that – that the very turning of her face to the wall with hope over, became asleep almost directly.'

'That is well,' murmured the doctor. 'And can you be spared, my dear? If you could come I should be glad, for poor Aubrey is quite done up.'

'I can come. Mary is with her, and Richard will stay to meet Henry, if he is coming home, or to send up if they want you; but I think she will not wake for many hours; and then – oh! what can any one do?'

So Richard turned back to the sorrowful house; and Dr May, tenderly drawing Ethel's arm into his own, told her, as they walked back, the few incidents that she most wanted to hear, as best he could narrate them. 'You have had a heart-rending day, my dear,' he said; 'you and Mary, as well as the rest of us.'

'There was one comfort!' said Ethel, 'and that was his own notes. Ave has all that he has written to her from Whitford under her pillow, and she kept spreading them out, and making us read them, and – oh! their braveness and cheeriness – they did quite seem to hold one up! And then poor little Minna's constant little robin-chirp of faith, "God will not let them hurt him." One could not bear to tell the child, that though indeed they cannot hurt him, it may not be in her sense! Look here! These are her slippers. She has worked on all day to finish them, that they might be done and out of sight when he came home this evening. The last stitch was done as Richard came in; and now I thought I could only take them out of every one's sight.'

'Poor things! poor things! And how was it with the child when she heard?'

'The old sweet note,' said Ethel, less steadily than she had yet spoken, '"nothing could hurt him for what he had not done." I don't know whether she knows what – what is in store. At least she is not shaken yet, dear child.'

'And Ave – how did you manage with her through all the day?'

'Oh! we did as we could. We tried reading the things Mr Wilmot had marked, but she was too restless; her hands would wander off to the letters, caressing them, and she would go back to talk of him – all his ways from a baby upwards. I hope there was no harm in letting her do it, for if there is anything to do one good, it is his noble spirit.'

'If you had only seen his face to-day,' exclaimed the doctor, half angrily, 'you would not feel much comfort in the cutting off such a fellow. No, no, it won't be. We'll petition – petition – petition – and save him, we will! Minna will be right yet! They *shall* not hurt him!'

'Is there really hope in that way?' said Ethel, and a quiver of relief agitated her whole frame.

'Every hope! Every one I have seen, or Tom either, says so. We have only to draw up a strong enough representation of the facts, his character, and all that; and there's his whole conduct before and since to speak for itself. Why, when it was all over, George heard every one saying, either he was a consummate hypocrite, or he must be innocent. Harvey Anderson declares the press will take it up. We shall certainly get him off.'

'You don't mean pardoned!'

'Commutation of the penalty. Come on,' said the doctor, hurrying at his headlong pace, 'there's no time to be lost in getting it drawn up.'

Ethel was dragged on so fast, that she could not speak; but it was with willing haste, for this was the sort of suspense in which motion and purpose were a great relief after the day's weary waiting. Gertrude, quite spent with excitement and tears, had wisely betaken herself to bed; and it would have been well had Aubrey followed her example, instead of wandering up and down the room in his misery, flushed though wan, impetuously talking treason against trial by Jury, and abusing dignitaries. They let him have it out, in all its fury and violence, till he had tired out his first vehemence, and could be persuaded to lie on the sofa while the rough draught of the petition was drawn up, Tom writing, and every one suggesting or discussing, till the doctor, getting thorough mastery over the subject, dictated so fluently and admirably, that even Tom had not a word to gainsay, but observed to Ethel, when his father had gone up to bed, and carried Aubrey off, 'What an exceedingly able man my father is!'

'Is this the first time you have found that out?' said Ethel.

'Why, you know it is not his nature to make the most of himself! But studying under him brings it out more; and there's a readiness about him that I wish was catching. But I say, Ethel, what's this? I no more doubt who did the deed, than I do who killed Abel; but I had once seen Cain's face, and I knew it again. It is true that the boy was aware, and told my father?'

'Did he tell you so?'

'Only asked if he had betrayed the secret. If they both know it – why, if it be Leonard's taste, I suppose I must say nothing to the contrary, but he might as well consider his sister.'

'What do you know, Tom?' said she, perplexed.

'Only that there's some secret; and if it be as I am given to understand, then it is a frenzy that no lucid person should permit.'

'No, Tom,' said Ethel, feeling that the whole must be told, 'it is no certainty – only unsupported suspicion, which he could not help telling papa after binding him on honour to make no use of it. Putting things together, he was sure who the man in the yard was; but it was not recognition, and he could not have proved it.'

'What Quixotry moved my father not to put the lawyers on the scent?'

Ethel explained; and for her pains Tom fell upon her for her folly in not having told him all, when he could have gone to Blewer and gathered information as no professional person could do; then lamented that he had let Aubrey keep him from the inquest, when the fellow's hang-dog look would have been sure to suggest to him to set Anderson to get him searched. Even now he would go to the Mill, and try to hunt up something.

'Tom, remember papa's promise!'

'Do you think a man can do nothing without committing himself, like poor Aubrey? No, Ethel; the doctor may be clever, but that's no use if a man is soft, and he is uncommonly soft; and you should not encourage him in it.'

Ethel was prevented from expressing useless indignation by the arrival of Mary, asking where papa was.

'Gone to bed. He says he must go off at six to-morrow, there are so many patients to see. Ave does not want him, I hope?'

'No, she is still asleep; I was only waiting for Richard, and he had dreadful work with that poor Henry.'

'What kind of work?'

'Oh, I believe it has all come on him now that it was his fault – driving Leonard to that place; and he was in such misery, that Richard could not leave him.'

'I am glad he has the grace to feel it at last,' said Tom.

'It must be very terrible!' said Mary. 'He says he cannot stay in that house, for every room reproaches him; and he groaned as if he was in tremendous bodily pain.'

'What, you assisted at this scene?' said Tom, looking at her rather sharply.

'No; but Richard told me; and I heard the groans as I sat on the stairs.'

'Sat on the stairs?'

'Yes. I could not go back to Ave's room for fear of waking her.'

'And how long?'

'Towards an hour, I believe. I did all that piece,' said Mary, displaying a couple of inches of a stocking leg, 'and I think it was pretty well in the dark.'

'Sitting on the stairs for an hour in the dark,' said Tom, as he gave Mary the candle he had been lighting for her. 'That may be called unappreciated devotion.'

'I never can tell what Tom means,' said Mary, as she went up stairs with Ethel. 'It was a very comfortable rest. I wish you had had the same, dear Ethel, you look so tired and worn out. Let me stay and help you. It has been such a sad long day; and oh! how terrible this is! And you know him better than any of us, except Aubrey.'

Mary stopped almost in dismay, for her sister, usually so firm, broke down entirely, and sitting down on a low chair, threw an arm round her, and resting her weary brow against her, gave way to long tearless sobs, or rather catches of breath. 'Oh! Mary! Mary!' she said, between her gasps, 'to think of last year – and Coombe – and the two bright boys – and the visions – and the light in those glorious eyes – and that this should be the end!'

'Dear, dear Ethel,' said Mary, with fast flowing tears and tender caresses, 'you have kept us all up; you have always shown us it was for the best.'

'It is! it is!' cried Ethel. 'I do, I *will* believe it! If I had only seen his face as papa tells of it, I could keep hold of the glory of it and the martyr spirit. Now I only see his earnest, shy, confiding look – and – and I don't know how to bear it.' And Ethel's grasp of Mary in both arms was tightened, as if to support herself under her deep labouring sobs of anguish.

'Ah! he was very fond of you.'

'There never was any one beyond our own selves that loved me so well. I always knew it would not last – that it ought not; but oh! it was endearing; and I did think to have seen him a shining light!'

'And don't you tell us he is a shining light now?' said Mary, among the tears that really almost seemed to be a relief, as if her sister herself had shed them; and as she knelt down, Ethel laid her head on her shoulder, and spoke more calmly.

'He is,' she said, 'and I ought to be thankful for it! I think I am generally – but now – it makes it the more piteous – the hopes – the spirit – the determination – all to be quenched, and *so* quenched – and to have nothing – nothing to do for him.'

'But, Ethel, papa says your messages do him more good than anything; and papa will let you go and see him, and that will comfort him.'

Ethel's lips gave a strange sort of smile; she thought it was at simple Mary's trust in her power, but it would hardly have been there but for the species of hope thus excited, and the sense of sympathy. Mary was not one to place any misconstruction on what had passed; she well knew that Leonard had almost taken a brother's place in Ethel's heart, and she prized him at the rate of her sister's esteem. Perhaps her prominent thought was how cruel were those who fancied that Ethel's lofty faith was unfeeling, and how very good Leonard must be to be thus mourned. At any rate, she was an excellent comforter, in the sympathy that was neither too acute nor too obtuse; and purely to oblige her, Ethel for the first time submitted to her favourite panacea of hair brushing, and found that in very truth those soft and steady manipulations were almost mesmeric in soothing away the hard oppressive excitement, and bringing on a gentle and slumberous resignation.

The sisters were early astir next morning, to inflict on their father a cup of cocoa, which he rebelled against, but swallowed, and to receive his last orders, chiefly consisting of messages to Tom about taking the petition to be approved of by Dr Spencer and others, and then having it properly drawn out. Mary asked if women might sign it, and was answered with an impatient 'Pshaw!'

'But ladies do have petitions of their own,' said Mary, with some diffidence. 'Could not we have one?'

His lips were compressed for another 'Pshaw,' when he bethought himself. 'Well, I don't know – the more the better. Only it won't do for you to set it going. Flora must be the woman for that.'

'Oh, then,' cried Mary, eagerly, 'might not I walk over to breakfast at the Grange, and talk to Flora? Ethel, you would not mind going to Ave instead? Or will you go to Flora?'

'You had better,' said Ethel. 'I must stay on Aubrey's account; and this is your doing, Mary,' she added, looking at her warmly.

'Then put on your hat, Mary, and take a biscuit,' said the doctor, 'and you shall have a lift as far as the cross roads.'

Thus the morning began with action and with hope. Mary found herself very welcome at the Grange, where there was much anxiety to hear of Aubrey, as well as the more immediate sufferers. The Riverses had dined at Drydale, and had met the judges, as well as a good many of the county gentlemen who had been on the grand jury and attended on the trial. They had found every one most deeply touched by the conduct of the prisoner. The judge had talked to Flora about her young brother, and the friendship so bravely avouched; had asked the particulars of the action to which Leonard had alluded, and shown himself much interested in all that she related.

She said that the universal impression was that the evidence was dead against Leonard, and taken apart, led to such conviction of his guilt, that no one could wonder at the verdict; but that his appearance and manner were such, that it was almost impossible, under their influence, not to credit his innocence. She had reason to believe that petitions were already in hand both from the county and the assize town, and she eagerly caught at Mary's proposal of one from the ladies of Stoneborough.

'I'll drive in at once before luncheon, and take you home, Mary,' she said. 'And, first of all, we will begin with the two widows, and half the battle will be won.'

Nay, more than half the battle proved to be already gained in that quarter. The writing table was covered with sheets of foolscap, and Mrs Pugh was hard at work copying the petition which Mr Harvey Anderson had kindly assisted in composing, and which the aunt and niece had intended to have brought to the Grange for Mrs Rivers's approval that very day. Harvey Anderson had spent the evening at Mrs Ledwich's in drawing it up, and giving his advice; and Flora, going over it word for word with Mrs Pugh, felt that it could hardly have been better worded.

'He is a very clever, a very rising young man, and so feeling,' said Mrs Ledwich to Mary while this was going on. 'In fact, he is a perfect knight-errant on this subject. He is gone to London this morning to see what can be done by means of the press. I tell Matilda it is quite a romance of modern life; and indeed, the sweet girl is very romantic still – very young, even after all she has gone through.'

Not understanding this, Mary let it pass in calculations on the number of possible signatures, which the two ladies undertook to collect.

'That is well,' said Flora, as they went away. 'It could not be in better hands. It will thrive the better for our doing nothing but writing our names.'

They met Tom on the like errand, but not very sanguine, for he said there had of late been an outcry against the number of reprieves granted, and the public had begun to think itself not sufficiently protected. He thought the best chance was the discovery of some additional fact that might tell in favour of Leonard, and confident in his own sagacity, was going to make perquisitions at the Mill. Every one had been visiting of late, and now that he knew more, if he and his microscope could detect one drop of human blood in an unexpected place, they would do better service to the prisoner than all the petitions that could be signed.

Averil was somewhat better; the feverishness had been removed by her long sleep of despair, and her energy revived under the bodily relief, and the fixed purpose of recovering in time to see her brother again; but the improvement was not yet trusted by Henry, who feared her doing too much unless he was himself watching over her, and therefore only paid Leonard a short visit in the forenoon, going and returning by early trains.

He reported that Leonard was very pale, and owned to want of sleep, adding, however, 'It does not matter. Why should I wish to lose any time?' Calm and brave as ever, he had conversed as cheerfully as Henry's misery would permit, inquiring into the plans of the family, which he knew were to depend on his fate, and acquiescing in his brother's intention of quitting the country; nay, even suggesting that it might be better for his sisters to be taken away before all was over, though he, as well as Henry, knew that to this Averil would never have consented. He had always been a great reader of travels, and he became absolutely eager in planning their life in the wild, as if where they were he must be, till the casual mention of the word 'rifle' brought him to sudden silence, and the consciousness of the condemned cell; but even then it was only to be urgent in consoling his brother, and crowding message on message for his sisters; begging Henry not to stay, not to consider him for a moment, but only whatever might be best for Ave.

In this frame Henry had left him; and late in the afternoon, Dr May had contrived to despatch his work and make his way to the jail, where, as he entered, he encountered the chaplain, Mr Reeve, a very worthy, but not a very acute man. Pausing to inquire for the prisoner, he was met by a look of oppression and perplexity. The chaplain had been with young Ward yesterday evening, and was only just leaving him; but then, instead of the admiring words the doctor expected, there only came a complaint of the difficulty of dealing with him; so well instructed, so respectful in manner, and yet there was a coldness, a hardness about him, amounting to sullenness, rejecting all attempts to gain his confidence, or bring him to confession.

Dr May had almost been angry, but he bethought himself in time that the chaplain was bound to believe the verdict of the court; and besides, the good man looked so grieved and pitiful, that it was impossible to be displeased with him, especially when he began to hope that the poor youth might be less reserved with a person who knew him better, and to consult Dr May which of the Stoneborough clergy had better be written to as likely to be influential with him. Dr May recommend Mr Wilmot, as having visited the boy in his illness, as well as prepared him for Confirmation; and then, with a heavier load of sadness on his heart, followed the turnkey on his melancholy way.

When the door was opened, he saw Leonard sitting listlessly on the side of his bed, resting his head on his hand, entirely unoccupied; but at the first perception who his visitor was, he sprang to his feet, and coming within the arms held out to him, rested his head on the kind shoulder.

'My dear boy – my brave fellow,' said Dr May, 'you got through yesterday nobly.'

There was none either of the calmness or the reserve of which Dr May had been told, in the hot hands that were wringing his own, nor in the choking struggling voice that tried to make the words clear – 'Thank you for what you said – and dear Aubrey – how is he?'

'I came away at six, before he was awake,' said the doctor; 'but he will not be the worse for it, never fear! I hope his evidence was less trying than you and he expected.'

Leonard half smiled. 'I had forgotten that,' he said, 'it was so long ago! No, indeed – the dear fellow was – like a bright spot in that day – only – only it brought back all we were – all that is gone for ever.'

The tenderness of one whom he did not feel bound to uphold like his brother had produced the outbreak that could not fail to come to so warm, open, and sensitive a nature, and at such an age. He was bold and full of fortitude in the front of the ordeal, and solitude pent up his feelings; but the fatherly sympathy and perfect confidence drew forth expression, and a vent once opened, the rush of emotion and anguish long repressed was utterly overpowering. His youthful manhood struggled hard, but the strangled sobs only shook his frame the more convulsively, and the tears burnt like drops of fire, as they fell among the fingers that he spread over his face in the agony of weeping for his young vigorous life, his blasted hopes, the wretchedness he caused, the disgrace of his name.

'Don't, don't fight against it,' said Dr May, affectionately drawing him to his seat on the bed, as, indeed, the violence of the paroxysm made him scarcely able to stand. 'Let it have its way; you will be all the better for it. It ought to be so – it must.'

And in tears himself, the doctor turned his back, and went as far away as the cell would permit, turning towards the books that lay on a narrow ledge that served for a table. 'How long, O Lord, how long?' were the words that caught his eye in the open Psalms; and, startled as if at unauthorized prying, he looked up at the dull screened and spiked window above his head, till he knew by the sounds that the worst of the uncontrollable passion had spent itself, and then he came back with the towel dipped in water, and cooled the flushed heated face as a sister might have done.

'Oh – thank you – I am ashamed,' gasped the still sobbing boy.

'Ashamed! No; I like you the better for it,' said the doctor, earnestly. 'There is no need that we should not grieve together in this great affliction, and say out all that is in our hearts.'

'All!' exclaimed Leonard. 'No – no words can say that! Oh! was it for such as this that my poor mother made so much of me – and I got through the fever – and I hoped – and I strove – Why – why should I be cut off – for a disgrace and a misery to all?' and again came the heart-broken sobs, though less violently.

'Not to those who look within, and honour you, Leonard.'

'Within! Why, how bad I have been, since *this* is the reckoning! I deserve it, I know – but——' and his voice again sank in tears.

'Ethel says that your so feeling comforts her the most; to know that you have not the terrible struggle of faith disturbed by injustice.'

'If – I have not,' said Leonard, 'it is her doing. In those happy days when we read Marmion, and could not believe that God would not always show the right, she showed me how we only see bits and scraps of His Justice here, and it works round in the end! Nay, if I had not done that thing to Henry, I should not be here now! It is right! It is right!' he exclaimed between the heaving sobs that still recurred. 'I do try to keep before me what she said about Job – when it comes burning before me, why should that man be at large, and I here? or when I think how his serpent-eye fell under mine when I tried that one word about the receipt, that would save my life. Oh! that receipt!'

'Better to be here than in his place, after all!'

'I'd rather be a street-sweeper!' bitterly began Leonard. – 'Oh, Dr May, do let me have that!' he cried, suddenly changing his tone, and holding out his hand, as he perceived in the doctor's button-hole a clove-pink, presented at a cottage door by a grateful patient. For a space he was entirely occupied with gazing into its crimson depths, inhaling the fragrance, and caressingly spreading the cool damask petals against his hot cheeks and eyelids. 'It is so long since I saw anything but walls!' he said.

'Three weeks,' sadly replied the doctor.

'There was a gleam of sunshine when I got out of the van yesterday. I never knew before what sunshine was. I hope it will be a sunny day when I go out for the last time!'

'My dear boy, I have good hopes of saving you. There's not a creature in Stoneborough, or round it, that is not going to petition for you – and at your age——'

Leonard shook his head in dejection. 'It has all gone against me,' he said. 'They all say there's no chance. The chaplain says it is of no use unsettling my mind.'

'The chaplain is an old——' began Dr May, catching himself up only just in time, and asking, 'How do you get on with him?'

'I can hear him read,' said Leonard, with the look that had been thought sullen.

'But you cannot talk to him?'

'Not while he thinks me guilty.' Then, at a sound of warm sympathy from his friend, he added, 'I suppose it is his duty; but I wish he would keep away. I can't stand his aiming at making me confess, and I don't want to be disrespectful.'

'I see, I see. It cannot be otherwise. But how would it be if Wilmot came to you?'

'Would Mr May?' said Leonard, with a beseeching look.

'Richard? He would with all his heart; but I think you would find more support and comfort in a man of Mr Wilmot's age and experience, and that Mr Reeve would have more trust in him; but it shall be exactly as will be most comforting to you.'

'If Mr Wilmot would be so good, then,' said Leonard, meekly. 'Indeed, I want help to bear it patiently! I don't know how to die; and yet it seemed not near so hard a year ago, when they thought I did not notice, and I heard Ave go away crying, and my mother murmuring, again and again, "Thy will be done!" – the last time I heard her voice. Oh, well that she has not to say it now!'

'Well that her son can say it!'

'I want to be able to say it,' said the boy, fervently; 'but this seems so hard – life is so sweet.' Then, after a minute's thought: 'Dr May, that morning, when I awoke, and asked you for *them* – papa and mamma – you knelt down and said the Lord's Prayer. Won't you now?'

And when those words had been said, and they both stood up again, Leonard added: 'It always seems to mean more and more! But oh, Dr May! that forgiving – I can't ask any one but you if——' and he paused.

'If you forgive, my poor boy! Nay, are not your very silence and forbearance signs of practical forgiveness? Besides, I have always observed that you have never used one of the epithets that I can't think of him without.'

'Some feelings are too strong for common words of abuse,' said Leonard, almost smiling; 'but I hope I may be helped to put away what is wrong. – Oh, must you go?'

'I fear I must, my dear; I have a patient to see again, on my way back, and one that will be the worse for waiting.'

'Henry has not been able to practise. I want to ask one thing, Dr May, before you go. Could not you persuade them, since home is poisoned to them, at any rate to go at once? It would be better for my sisters than being here – when – and they would only remember that last Sunday at home.'

'Do you shrink from another meeting with Averil?'

His face was forced into calmness. 'I will do without it, if it would hurt her.'

'It may for the time; but to be withheld would give her a worse heart-ache through life.'

'Oh, thank you!' cried Leonard, his face lighting up; 'it is something still to hope for.'

'Nay, I've not given you up yet,' said the doctor, trying for a cheerful smile. 'I've got a prescription that will bring you through yet – London advice, you know. I've great faith in the consulting surgeon at the Home Office.'

By the help of that smile and augury, the doctor got away, terribly beaten down, but living on his fragment of hope; though obliged to perceive that every one who merely saw the newspaper report in black and white, without coming into personal contact with the prisoner, could not understand how the slightest question of the justice of the verdict could arise. Even Mr Wilmot was so convinced by the papers, that the doctor almost repented of the mission to which he had invited him, and would, if he could, have revoked what had been said. But the vicar of Stoneborough, painful as was the duty, felt his post to be by the side of his unhappy young parishioner, equally whether the gaol chaplain or Dr May were right, and if he had to bring him to confession, or to strengthen him to 'endure grief, suffering wrongfully.'

And after the first interview, no more doubts on that score were expressed; but the vicar's tone of pitying reverence in speaking of the prisoner was like that of his friends in the High Street.

Tom May spared neither time nor pains in beating up for signatures for the petition; but he had a more defined hope, namely, that of detecting something that might throw the suspicion into the right quarter. The least contradiction of the evidence might raise a doubt that would save Leonard's life, and bring the true criminal in peril of the fate he so richly deserved. The Vintry Mill was the lion of the neighbourhood, and the crowds of visitors had been a reason for its new master's vacating it, and going into lodgings in Whitford; so that Tom, when he found it convenient to forget his contempt of the gazers and curiosity hunters who thronged there, and to march off on a secret expedition of investigation, found no obstacle in his way, and at the cost of a fee to Mrs Giles, who was making a fortune, was free to roam and search wherever he pleased. Even his careful examination of the cotton blind, and his scraping of the window-sill with a knife, were not remarked; for had not the great chair been hacked into fragmentary relics, and the loose paper of the walls of Leonard's room been made mincemeat of, as memorials of 'the murderer, Ward?'

One long white hair picked out of a mat below the window, and these scrapings of the window-sill, Tom carried off, and also the scrapings of the top bar of a stile between the Mill and the Three Goblets. That evening, all were submitted to the microscope. Dr May was waked from a doze by a very deferential 'I beg your pardon, sir,' and a sudden tweak, which abstracted a silver thread from his head; and Mab showed somewhat greater displeasure at a similar act of plunder upon her white chemisette. But the spying was followed by a sigh; and, in dumb show, Ethel was made to perceive that the Vintry hair had more affinity with the canine than the human. As to the scrapings of the window, nothing but vegetable fibre could there be detected; but on the stile, there was undoubtedly a mark containing human blood-disks; Tom proved that both by comparison with his books, and by pricking his own finger, and kept Ethel to see it after every one else was gone up to bed. But as one person's blood was like another's, who could tell whether some one with a cut finger had not been through the stile? Tom shook his head; there was not yet enough on which to commit himself. 'But I'll have him! – I'll have him yet!' said he. 'I'll never rest while that villain walks the earth unpunished!'

Meantime, Harvey Anderson did yeoman's service by a really powerful article in a leading paper, written from the very heart of an able man, who had been strongly affected himself, and was well practised in feeling in pen and ink. Every word rang home to the soul, and all the more because there was no defence nor declamation against the justice of the verdict, which was acknowledged to be unavoidable; it was merely a pathetic delineation of a terrible mystery, with a little meditative philosophy upon it, the moral of which was, that nothing is more delusive than fact, more untrue than truth. However, it was copied everywhere, and had the great effect of making it the cue of more than half the press to mourn over, rather than condemn, 'the unfortunate young gentleman.'

Mrs Pugh showed every one the article, and confided to most that she had absolutely ventured to suggest two or three of the sentences. But a great deal might be borne from Mrs Pugh, in consideration of her indefatigable exertions with the ladies' petition; and it was a decided success. The last census had rated Market Stoneborough at 7,561 inhabitants, and Mrs Pugh's petition bore no less than 3,024 female names, in which she fairly beat that of the mayor, but then she had been less scrupulous as to the age at which people should be asked to sign; as long as the name could be written at all, she was not particular whose it was.

Dr May made his patients agree to accept as his substitute Dr Spencer or Mr Wright, to whom Henry Ward intended to resign practice and house. He himself was to go to London for a couple of nights with George Rivers, who was exceedingly gratified at having the charge of him all to himself, and considered that the united influence of member and mayor must prevail. Dr Spencer, on the contrary, probably by way of warning, represented Mr Mayor as ruining everything by his headlong way of setting about it, declaring that he would abuse everybody all round, and assure the Home Secretary, that, as sure as his name was Dick May, it was quite impossible the boy could have hurt a fly; though a strict sense of truth would lead him to add the next moment, that he was terribly passionate, and had nearly demolished his brother.

Dr May talked of his caution and good behaviour, which, maybe, were somewhat increased by this caricature, but he ended by very hearty wishes that these were the times of Jeanie Deans; if the pardon depended on our own good Queen, he should not doubt of it a moment. Why, was not the boy just the age of her own son?

And verily there was no one in the whole world whom poor Averil envied like Jeanie Deans.

So member and mayor went to London together, and intense were the prayers that speeded them and followed them. The case was laid before the Home Secretary, the petitions presented, and Dr May said all that man might say on ground where he felt as if overpartizanship might be perilous. The matter was to have due consideration: nothing more definite or hopeful could be obtained; but there could be no doubt that this meant a real and calm re-weighing of the evidence, with a consideration of all the circumstances. It was something for the doctor that a second dispassionate study should be given to the case; but his heart sank as he thought of that cold, hard statement of evidence, without the counter testimony of the honest, tearless eyes and simple good faith of the voice and tone.

And when he entered the railway carriage on his road home, the newspaper that George Rivers attentively pressed upon him bore the information that Wednesday, the 21st, would be the day, according to usage, for the execution of the condemned criminal, Leonard Axworthy Ward. If it had been for the execution of Richard May, the doctor could hardly have given a deeper groan.

He left the train at the county town. He had so arranged, that he might see the prisoner on his way home; but he had hardly the heart to go, except that he knew he was expected, and no disappointment that he could help must add to the pangs of these last days.

Leonard was alone, but was not, as before, sitting unemployed; he carefully laid down his etching work ere he came forward to meet his friend; and there was not the bowed and broken look about him, but a fixed calmness and resolution, as he claimed the fatherly embrace and blessing with which the doctor now always met him.

'I bring you no certainty, Leonard. It is under consideration.'

'Thank you. You have done everything,' returned Leonard, quietly; 'and——' then pausing, he added, 'I know the day now – the day after my birthday.'

'Let us – let us hope,' said the doctor, greatly agitated.

'Thank you,' again said Leonard; and there was a pause, during which Dr May anxiously studied the face, which had become as pale and almost as thin as when the lad had been sent off to Coombe, and infinitely older in the calm steadfastness of every feature.

'You do not look well, Leonard.'

'No; I am not quite well; but it matters very little,' he said, with a smile. 'I am well enough to make it hard to believe how soon all sense and motion will be gone out of these fingers!' and he held up his hand, and studied the minutiae of its movement with a strange grave sort of curiosity.

'Don't – don't, Leonard!' exclaimed the doctor. 'You may be able to bear it, but I cannot.'

'I thought you would not mind, you have so often watched death.'

'Yes; but——' and he covered his face with his hands.

'I wish it did not pain you all so much,' said Leonard, quietly. 'But for that, I can feel it to be better than if I had gone in the fever, when I had no sense to think or repent; or if I had – I hardly knew my own faults.'

'You seem much happier now, my boy.'

'Yes,' said Leonard; 'I am more used to the notion, and Mr Wilmot has been so kind. Then I am to see Ave to-morrow, if she is well enough. Henry has promised to bring her, and leave her alone with me; and I do hope – that I shall be able to convince her that it is not so very bad for me – and then she may be able to take comfort. You know she would, if she were nursing me now in my bed at Bankside; so why should she not when she sees that I don't think this any worse, but rather better?'

The doctor was in no mood to think any comfort possible in thus losing one like Leonard, and he did not commit himself to an untruth. There was a silence again, and Leonard opened his book, and took out his etchings, one which he had already promised the doctor, another for Aubrey, and at the third the doctor exclaimed inarticulately with surprise and admiration.

It was a copy of the well-known Cross-bearing Form in the Magdalen College Chapel Altar-piece, drawn in pen and ink on a half-sheet of thick note-paper; but somehow, into the entire Face and Figure there was infused such an expression as now and then comes direct from the soul of the draughtsman – an inspiration entirely independent of manual dexterity, and that copies, however exact, fail to render; nay, which the artist himself fails to renew. The beauty, the meekness, the hidden Majesty of the Countenance, were conveyed in a marvellous manner, and were such as would bring a tear to the eye of the gazer, even had the drawing been there alone to speak for itself.

'This is your doing, Leonard?'

'I have just finished it. It has been one of my greatest comforts——'

'Ah!'

'Doing those lines;' and he pointed to the thorny Crown. 'I seem to get ashamed of thinking this hardness. Only think, Dr May, from the very first moment the policeman took me in charge, nobody has said a rough word to me. I have never felt otherwise than that they meant justice to have its way as far as they knew, but they were all consideration for me. To think of that, and then go over the scoffs and scourgings!' – there was a bright glistening tear in Leonard's eye now – 'it seems like child's play to go through such a trial as mine.'

'Yes! you have found the secret of willingness.'

'And,' added the boy, hesitating between the words, but feeling that he must speak them, as the best balm for the sorrow he was causing, 'even my little touch of the shame and scorn of this does make me know better what it must have been, and yet – so thankful when I remember why it was – that I think I could gladly bear a great deal more than this is likely to be.'

'Oh! my boy, I have no fears for you now.'

'Yes, yes – have fears,' cried Leonard, hastily. 'Pray for me! You don't know what it is to wake up at night, and know something is coming nearer and nearer – and then *this* – before one can remember all that blesses it – or the Night of that Agony – and that He knows what it is——'

'Do we not pray for you?' said Dr May, fervently, 'in church and at home? and is not this an answer? Am I to take this drawing, Leonard, that speaks so much?'

'If – if you think Miss May – would let me send it to her? Thank you; it will be very kind of her. And please tell her, if it had not been for that time at Coombe, I don't know how I could ever have felt the ground under my feet. If I have one wish that never can be——'

'What wish, my dear dear boy? Don't be afraid to say. Is it to see her?'

'It was,' said Leonard, 'but I did not mean to say it. I know it cannot be.'

'But, Leonard, she has said that if you wished it, she would come as if you were lying on your bed at home, and with more reverence.'

Large tears of gratitude were swelling in Leonard's eyes, and he pressed the doctor's hand, but still said, almost inarticulately, 'Ought she?'

'I will bring her, my boy. It will do her good to see how – how her pupil, as they have always called you in joke, Leonard, can be willing to bear the Cross after his Master. She has never let go for a moment the trust that it was well with you.'

'Oh! Dr May, it was the *one* thing – and when I had gone against all her wishes. It is so good of her! It is the *one* thing;' and there was no doubt from his face that he was indeed happy.

And Dr May went home that day softened and almost cheered, well-nigh as though he had had a promise of Leonard's life, and convinced that in the region to which the spirits of Ethel and her pupil could mount, resignation would silence the wailings of grief and sorrow; the things invisible were more than a remedy for the things visible.

That Ethel should see Leonard before the last, he was quite resolved; and Ethel, finding that so it was, left the *when* in his hands, knowing the concession to be so great, that it must be met by grateful patience on her own side, treasuring the drawing meanwhile with feelings beyond speech. Dr May did not wish the meeting to take place till he was really sure that all hope was at an end; he knew it would be a strong measure, and though he did not greatly care for the world in general, he did not want to offend Flora unnecessarily: in matters of propriety she was a little bit of a conscience to him, and though he would brave her or any one else when a thing was right, especially if it were to give one last moment of joy to Leonard, she was not to be set at naught till the utmost extremity.

And for one day, the sight of Averil would be enough. She had struggled into something sufficiently like recovery to be able to maintain her fitness for the exertion; and Henry had recognised that the unsatisfied pining was so preying on her as to hurt her more than the meeting and parting could do, since, little as he could understand how it was, he perceived that Leonard could be depended on for support and comfort. With him, indeed, Leonard had ever shown himself cheerful and resolute, speaking of anything rather than of himself, and never grieving him with the sight of those failings of flesh and heart that would break forth where there was more congenial sympathy, yet where they were not a reproach.

So Averil, with many a promise to be 'good,' and strongly impressed with warnings that the chance of another meeting depended on the effects of this one, was laid back in the carriage, leaving poor little Minna to Mary's consolation. Minna was longing to go too, but Henry had forbidden it, and not even an appeal to Dr May had prevailed; so she was taken home by Mary, and with a child's touching patience, was helped through the weary hours, giving wandering though gentle attention to Ella's eager display of the curiosities of the place, and explanations of the curious games and puzzles taught by 'Mr Tom.' Ethel, watching the sweet wistful face, and hearing the subdued voice, felt a reverence towards the child, as though somewhat of the shadow of her brother's cross had fallen on her.

The elder brother and sister meanwhile arrived at the building now only too familiar to one of them; and, under her thick veil, unconscious of the pitying looks of the officials, Averil was led, leaning on Henry's arm, along the whitewashed passages, with their slate floors, and up the iron stairs, the clear, hard, light coldness chilling her heart with a sense of the stern, relentless, inevitable grasp in which the victim was held. The narrow iron door flew open at the touch of the turnkey; a hand was on her arm, but all swam round with her, and she only knew it was the well-known voice; she did not follow the words between her brothers and the turnkey about the time she was to be left there, but she gave a start and shudder when the door sprung fast again behind her, and at the same instant she felt herself upheld by an arm round her waist.

'Take off your bonnet, Ave; let me see you,' he said, himself undoing the strings, and removing it, then bending his face to hers for a long, almost insatiable kiss, as they stood strained in one intense embrace, all in perfect silence on the sister's part.

'I have been making ready for you,' he said at length, partly releasing her; 'you are to sit here;' and he deposited her, still perfectly passive in his hands, upon his bed, her back against the wall. 'Put up your feet! There!' And having settled her to his satisfaction, he knelt down on the floor, one arm round her waist, one hand in hers, looking earnestly up into her face, with his soul in his eyes, her other hand resting on his shoulder.

'How are the little ones, Ave?'

'Very well. Minna so longed to come.'

'Better not,' said Leonard; 'she is so little, and these white walls might distress her fancy. They will remember our singing on the last Sunday evening instead. Do you remember, Ave, how they begged to stay on and on till it grew so dark that we could not see a word or a note, and went on from memory?' and he very softly hummed the restful cadence, dying away into

'Till in the ocean of Thy love
We lose ourselves in Heaven above.'

'How can you bear to think of those dear happy days?'

'Because you will be glad of them by-and-by,' said Leonard; 'and I am very glad of them now, though they might have been so much better, if only we had known.'

'They were the only happy days of all my life!'

'I hope not – I trust not, dearest. You may and ought to have much better and happier days to come.'

She shook her head, with a look of inexpressible anguish, almost of reproach.

'Indeed I mean it, Ave,' he said; 'I have thought it over many times, and I see that the discomfort and evil of our home was in the spirit of pride and rebellion that I helped you to nurse. It was like a wedge, driving us farther and farther apart; and now that it is gone, and you will close up again, when you are kind and yielding to Henry – what a happy peaceful home you may make out in the prairie land!'

'As if we could ever——'

'Nay, Averil, could not you recover it if I were dying now of sickness? I know you would, though you might not think so at the time. Believe me, then, when I say that I am quite willing to have it as it is – to be my own man to the last – to meet with such precious inestimable kindness from so many. Of course I should like to live longer, and do something worth doing; but if I am to die young, there is so much blessing even in this way, that nothing really grieves me but the thought of you and Henry; and if it makes you one together, even that is made up.'

Awe struck, and as if dreaming, she did not answer, only smoothing caressingly the long waves of bright brown hair on his forehead. She was surprised by his next question.

'Ave! how has Mrs Pugh behaved?'

'Oh! the woman! I have hardly thought of her! She has been very active about the petition, somebody said; but I don't believe Henry can bear to hear of her any more than I can. What made you think of her?'

'Because I wanted to know how it was with Henry, and I could not ask him. Poor fellow! Well, Ave, you see he will depend on you entirely for comfort, and you must promise me that shall be your great business and care.'

'How you do think of Henry!' she said, half jealously.

'Of course, Ave. You and I have no past to grieve over together, but poor Henry will never feel free of having left me to my self-willed obstinacy, and let me go to that place. Besides, the disgrace in the sight of the world touches him more, and you can tread that down more easily than he.' Then, in answer to a wondering look, 'Yes, you can, when you recollect that it is crime, not the appearance of it, that is shame. I do not mean that I do not deserve all this – but – but——' and his eye glistened, 'Ave, dear, if I could only bring out the words to tell you how much peace and joy there is in knowing that – with that vast difference – it is like in some degree what was borne to save us, I really don't think you could go on grieving over me any more; at least not more than for the loss,' he added, tenderly; 'and you'll not miss me so much in a new country, you know, with Henry and the children to take care of. Only promise me to be kind to Henry.'

And having drawn forth a faint promise, that he knew would have more force by-and-by, Leonard went on, in his low quiet voice, into reminiscences that sounded like random, of the happy days of childhood and early youth, sometimes almost laughing over them, sometimes linking his memory as it were to tune or flower, sport or study, but almost for joy, and never for pain; and thus passed the time, with long intervals of silent thought and recollection on his part, and of a sort of dreamy stupor on his sister's, during which the strange peaceful hush seemed to have taken away her power of recalling the bitter complaints of cruel injustice, and the broken-hearted lamentations she had imagined herself pouring out in sympathy with her victim brother. Instead of being wrung with anguish, her heart was lulled and quelled by wondering reverence; and she seemed to herself scarcely awake, and only dimly conscious of the pale-cheeked bright-eyed face upturned to her, so calm and undaunted, yet so full of awe and love, the low steady tender voice, and the warm upholding arm.

A great clock struck, and Leonard said, 'There! they were to come at four, and then the chaplain is coming. He is grown so very kind now! Ave, if they would let you be with me at my last Communion! Will you? Could you bear it? I think then you would know all the peace of it!'

'Oh, yes! make them let me come.'

'Then it is not good-bye,' he said, as he fetched her bonnet and cloak, and put them on with tender hands, as if she were a child, in readiness as steps approached, and her escort reappeared.

'Here she is, Henry,' he said, with a smile. 'She has been very good; she may come again.' And then, holding her in his arms once more, he resigned her to Henry, saying, 'Not good-bye, Ave; we will keep my birth-day together.'

CHAPTER XVI

'The captives went
To their own places, to their separate glooms,
Uncheered by glance, or hand, or hope, to brood
On those impossible glories of the past,
When they might touch the grass, and see the sky,
And do the works of men. But manly work
Is sometimes in a prison.'

S.M. Queen Isabel.

'Commutation of punishment, to penal servitude for life.'

Such were the tidings that ran through Stoneborough on Sunday morning, making all feel as if a heavy oppression had been taken from the air. In gratitude to the merciful authorities, and thankfulness for the exemption from death, the first impressions were that Justice was at last speaking, that innocence could not suffer, and that right was re-asserting itself. Even when the more sober and sad remembered that leniency was not pardon, nor life liberty, they were hastily answered that life was everything – life was hope, life was time, and time would show truth.

Averil's first tears dropped freely, as she laid her head on Mary's shoulder, and with her hand in Dr May's, essayed to utter the words, 'It is your doing – you have twice saved him for me;' and Minna stood calmly glad, but without surprise. 'I knew they could not hurt him; God would not let them.'

The joy and relief were so great as to absorb all thought or realization of what this mercy was to the prisoner himself, until Dr May was able to pay him a visit on Monday afternoon. It was at a moment when the first effects of the tidings of life had subsided, and there had been time to look forth on the future with a spirit more steadfast than buoyant. The strain of the previous weeks was reacting on the bodily frame, and indisposition unhinged the spirits; so that, when Dr May entered, beaming with congratulations, he was met with the same patient glance of endurance, endeavouring at resignation, that he knew so well, but without the victorious peace that had of late gained the ascendant expression. There was instead an almost painful endeavour to manifest gratitude by cheerfulness, and the smile was far less natural than those of the last interview, as fervently returning the pressure of the hand, he said, 'You were right, Dr May, you have brought me past the crisis.'

'A sure sign of ultimate recovery, my boy. Remember, *dum spiro spero*.'

Leonard attempted a responsive smile, but it was a hopeless business. From the moment when at the inquest he found himself entangled in the meshes of circumstance, his mind had braced itself to endure rather than hope; and his present depressed state, both mental and bodily, rendered even that endurance almost beyond his powers. He could only say, 'You have been very good to me.'

'My dear fellow, you are sadly knocked down; I wish——' and the doctor looked at him anxiously.

'I wish you had been here yesterday,' said Leonard, 'then you would not have found me so. No, not thankless, indeed!'

'No, indeed; but – yes, I see it was folly – nay, harshness, to expect you to be glad of what lies before you, my poor boy.'

'I am – am thankful,' said Leonard, struggling to make the words truth. 'Wednesday is off my mind – yes, it is more than I deserve – I knew I was not fit to die, and those at home are spared. But I am as much cut off from them – perhaps more – than by death. And it is the same disgrace to them, the same exile. I suppose Henry still goes——'

'Yes, he does.'

'Ah! then one thing, Dr May – if you had a knife or scissors – I do not know how soon they may cut my hair, and I want to secure a bit for poor Ave.'

Dr May was too handless to have implements of the first order, but a knife he had, and was rather dismayed at Leonard's reckless hacking at his bright shining wavy hair, pulling out more than he cut, with perfect indifference to the pain. The doctor stroked the chestnut head as tenderly as if it had been Gertrude's sunny curls, but Leonard started aside, and dashing away the tears that were overflowing his eyes under the influence of the gentle action, asked vigorously, 'Have you heard what they will do with me?'

'I do not know thoroughly. A year or six months may be at one of the great model establishments, then probably you will be sent to some of the public works,' said the doctor, sadly. 'Yes, it is a small boon to give you life, and take away all that makes life happy.'

'If it were only transportation!'

'Yes. In a new world you could live it down, and begin afresh. And even here, Leonard, I look to finding you like Joseph in his prison.'

'The iron entering into his soul?' said Leonard, with a mournful smile.

'No; in the trustworthiness that made him honoured and blessed even there. Leonard, Leonard, conduct *will* tell. Even there, you can live this down, and will!'

'Eighteen to-morrow,' replied the boy. 'Fifty years of it, perhaps! I know God can help me through with it, but it is a long time to be patient!'

By way of answer, the doctor launched into brilliant auguries of the impression the prisoner's conduct would produce, uttering assurances, highly extravagant in his Worship the Mayor, of the charms of the modern system of prison discipline, but they fell flat; there could be no disguising that penal servitude for life *was* penal servitude for life, and might well be bitterer than death itself. Sympathy might indeed be balm to the captive, but the good doctor pierced his own breast to afford it, so that his heart sank even more than when he had left the young man under sentence of death. His least unavailing consolations were his own promises of frequent visits, and Aubrey's of correspondence, but they produced more of dejected gratitude than of exhilaration. Yet it was not in the way of murmur or repining, but rather of 'suffering and being strong,' and only to this one friend was the suffering permitted to be apparent. To all the officials he was simply submissive and gravely resolute; impassive if he encountered sharpness or sternness, but alert and grateful towards kindliness, of which he met more and more as the difference between dealing with him and the ordinary prisoners made itself felt.

To Dr May alone was the depth of pain betrayed; but another comforter proved more efficient in cheering the prisoner, namely, Mr Wilmot, who, learning from the doctor the depression of their young friend, hastened to endeavour at imparting a new spring of life on this melancholy birthday. Physically, the boy was better, and perhaps the new day had worn off somewhat of the burthen of anticipation, for Mr Wilmot found him already less downcast, and open to consolation. It might be, too, that the sense that the present was to have been his last day upon earth, had made him more conscious of the relief from the immediate shadow of death, for he expressed his thankfulness far more freely and without the effort of the previous day.

'And, depend on it,' said Mr Wilmot, 'you are spared because there is something for you to do.'

'To bear,' said Leonard.

'No, to *do*. Perhaps not immediately; but try to look on whatever you have to bear, not only as carrying the cross, as I think you already feel it——'

'Or there would be no standing it at all.'

'True,' said Mr Wilmot; 'and your so feeling it convinces me the more that whatever may follow is likewise to be looked upon as discipline to train you for something beyond. Who knows what work may be in store, for which this fiery trial may be meant to prepare you?'

The head was raised, and the eyes brightened with something like hope in their fixed interrogative glance.

'Even as things are now, who knows what good may be done by the presence of a man educated, religious, unstained by crime, yet in the same case as those around him? I do not mean by quitting your natural place, but by merely living as you *must* live. You were willing to have followed your Master in His death. You now have to follow Him by living as one under punishment; and be sure it is for some purpose for others as well as yourself.'

'If there is any work to be done for Him, it is all right,' said Leonard, cheerily; and as Mr Wilmot paused, he added, 'It would be like working for a friend – if I may dare say so – after the hours when this place has been made happy to me. I should not mind anything if I might only feel it working for Him.'

'Feel it. Be certain of it. As you have realized the support of that Friend in a way that is hardly granted, save in great troubles, so now realize that every task is for Him. Do not look on the labour as hardship inflicted by mistaken authority——'

'Oh, I only want to get to that! I have been so long with nothing to do!'

'And your hearty doing of it, be it what it may, as unto the Lord, can be as acceptable as Dr May's labours of love among the poor – as entirely a note in the great concord in heaven and earth as the work of the ministry itself – as completely in unison. Nay, further, such obedient and hearty work will form you for whatever may yet be awaiting you, and what that may be will show itself in good time, when you are ready for it.'

The right chord was touched, the spirit of energy was roused, and Leonard was content to be a prisoner of hope, not the restless hope of liberation, but the restful hope that he might yet render faithful service even in his present circumstances.

Not much passed his lips in this interview, but its effect was apparent when Dr May again saw him, and this time in company with Aubrey. Most urgent had been the boy's entreaties to be taken to see his friend, and Dr May had only hesitated because Leonard's depression had made himself so unhappy that he feared its effect on his susceptible son, whose health had already suffered from the long course of grief and suspense. But it was plain that if Aubrey were to go at all, it must be at once, since the day was fixed for the prisoner's removal, and the still nearer and dearer claims must not clash with those of the friend. Flora shook her head, and reminded her father that Leonard would not be out of reach in future, and that the meeting now might seriously damage Aubrey's already uncertain health.

'I cannot help it, Flora,' said the doctor; 'it may do him some temporary harm, but I had rather see him knocked down for a day or two, than breed him up to be such a poor creature as to sacrifice his friendship to his health.'

And Mrs Rivers, who knew what the neighbourhood thought of the good doctor's infatuation, felt that there was not much use in suggesting how shocked the world would be at his encouragement of the intimacy between the convict and his young son.

People did look surprised when the doctor asked admission to the cell for his son as well as himself; and truly Aubrey, who in silence had worked himself into an agony of nervous agitation, looked far from fit for anything trying. Dr May saw that he must not ask to leave the young friends alone together; but in his reverence for the rights of their friendship, he withdrew himself as far as the limits of the cell would allow, turned his back, and endeavoured to read the Thirty-nine Articles in Leonard's Prayer-book; but in spite of all his abstraction, he could not avoid a complete consciousness that the two lads sat on the bed, clinging with arms round one another like young children, and that it was Leonard's that was the upright sustaining figure, his own Aubrey's the prone and leaning one. And of the low whispering murmurs that reached his would-be deafened ear, the gasping almost sobbing tones were

Aubrey's. The first distinct words that he could not help hearing were, 'No such thing! There can't be slavery where one works with a will!' and again, in reply to something unheard, 'Yes, one can! Why, how did one do one's Greek?' – 'Very different!' – 'How?' – 'Oh!' – 'Yes; but you are a clever chap, and had her to teach you, but I only liked it because I'd got it to do. Just the same with the desk-work down at the Mill; so it may be the same now.'

Then came fragments of what poor Aubrey had expressed more than once at home – that his interest in life, in study, in sport, was all gone with his friend.

'Come, Aubrey, that's stuff. You'd have had to go to Cambridge, you know, without me, after I doggedly put myself at that place. There's just as much for you to do as ever there was.'

'How you keep on with your *do*!' cried Ethel's spoilt child, with a touch of petulance.

'Why, what are we come here for – into this world, I mean – but to *do*?' returned Leonard; 'and I take it, if we do it right, it does not much matter what or where it is.'

'I shan't have any heart for it!' sighed Aubrey.

'Nonsense! Not with all your people at home?' and though the voice fell again, the doctor's ears distinguished the murmur, 'Why, just the little things she let drop are the greatest help to me here, and you always have her——'

Then ensued much that was quite inaudible; and at last Leonard said, 'No, old fellow; as long as you don't get ashamed of me, thinking about you, and knowing what you are about, will be one of the best pleasures I shall have. And look here, Aubrey, if we only consider it right, you and I will be just as really working together, when you are at your books, and I am making mats, as if we were both at Cambridge side by side! It is quite true, is it not, Dr May?' he added, since the doctor, finding it time to depart, had turned round to close the interview.

'Quite true, my boy,' said the doctor; 'and I hope Aubrey will try to take comfort and spirit from it.'

'As if I could!' said Aubrey impatiently, 'when it only makes me more mad to see what a fellow they have shut up in here!'

'Not mad, I hope,' said Dr May; 'but I'll tell you what it should do for both of us, Aubrey. It should make us very careful to be worthy to remain his friends.'

'O Dr May!' broke in Leonard, distressed.

'Yes,' returned Dr May, 'I mean what I say, however you break in, Master Leonard. As long as this boy of mine is doing his best for the right motives, he will care for you as he does now – not quite in the same despairing way, of course, for holes in one's daily life *do* close themselves up with time – but if he slacks off in his respect or affection for you, then I shall begin to have fears of him. Now come away, Aubrey, and remember for your comfort it is not the good-bye it might have been,' he added, as he watched the mute intensity of the boys' farewell clasp of the hands; but even then had some difficulty in getting Aubrey away from the friend so much stronger as the consoler than as the consoled, and, unconsciously showing how in the last twenty-four hours his mind had acted on the topics presented to him by Mr Wilmot.

Changed as he was from the impetuous boyish lad of a few weeks since, a change even more noticeable when with his contemporary than in intercourse with elder men, yet the nature was the same. Obstinacy had softened into constancy, pride into resolution, generosity made pardon less difficult, and elevation of temper bore him through many a humiliation that, through him, bitterly galled his brother.

Whatever he might feel, prison regulations were accepted by him as matters of course, not worth being treated as separate grievances. He never showed any shrinking from the assumption of the convict dress, whilst Henry was fretting and wincing over the very notion of his wearing it and trying to arrange that the farewell interview should precede its adoption.

CHAPTER XVII

'Scorn of *me* recoils on you.'

E.B. Browning.

After the first relief, the relaxation of his brother's sentence had by no means mitigated Henry Ward's sense of disgrace, but had rather deepened it by keeping poor Leonard a living, not a dead, sorrow.

He was determined to leave England as soon as possible, that his sisters might never feel that they were the relatives of a convict; and bringing Ella home, he promulgated a decree that Leonard was never to be mentioned; hoping that his existence might be forgotten by the little ones.

To hurry from old scenes, and sever former connexions, was his sole thought, as if he could thus break the tie of brotherhood. There was a half-formed link that had more easily snapped. His courtship had been one of prudence and convenience, and in the overwhelming period of horror and suspense had been almost forgotten. The lady's attempts at sympathy had been rejected by Averil without obstruction from him, for he had no such love as could have prevented her good offices from becoming oppressive to his wounded spirit, and he had not sufficient energy or inclination to rouse himself to a response.

And when the grant of life enabled him to raise his head and look around him, he felt the failure of his plans an aggravation of his calamity, though he did not perceive that his impatience to rid himself of an encumbrance, and clear the way for his marriage, had been the real origin of the misfortune. Still he was glad that matters had gone no further, and that there was no involvement beyond what could be handsomely disposed of by a letter, resigning his pretensions, and rejoicing that innate delicacy and prudence had prevented what might have involved the lady's feeling more deeply in the misfortune of his family: representing himself in all good faith as having retreated from her proffered sympathy out of devoted consideration for her, and closing with elaborate thanks for her exertions on behalf of 'his unhappy brother.'

The letter had the honour of being infinitely lauded by Mrs Ledwich, who dwelt on its nobleness and tenderness in many a *tête-à-tête*, and declared her surprise and thankfulness at the immunity of her dear Matilda's heart. In strict confidence, too, Dr Spencer (among others) learnt that – though it was not to be breathed till the year was out, *above all* till the poor Wards were gone – the dear romantic girl had made her hand the guerdon for obtaining Leonard's life.

'So there's your fate, Dick,' concluded his friend.

'You forget the influence of the press,' returned Dr May. 'People don't propose such guerdons without knowing who is to earn them.'

'Yes, she has long believed in King John,' said Ethel.

Meantime Averil Ward was acquiescing in all Henry's projects with calm desperate passiveness. She told Mary that she had resolved that she would never again contend with Henry, but would let him do what he would with herself and her sisters. Nor had his tenderness during her illness been in vain; it had inspired reliance and affection, such as to give her the instinct of adherence to him as the one stay left to her. With Leonard shut up, all places were the same to her, except that she was in haste to escape from the scenes connected with her lost brother; and she looked forward with dull despairing acquiescence to the new life with which Henry hoped to shake off the past.

A colony was not change enough for Henry's wishes; even there he made sure of being recognised as the convict's brother, and was resolved to seek his new home in the wide field of America, disguising his very name, as Warden, and keeping up no communication with the prisoner except under cover to Dr May.

To this unfailing friend was committed the charge of the brother. He undertook to watch over the boy, visit him from time to time, take care of his health, and obtain for him any alleviations permitted by the prison rules; and as Henry reiterated to Averil, it was absolutely certain that everything possible from external kindness was thus secured. What more could they themselves have done, but show him their faces at the permitted intervals? which would be mere wear and tear of feeling, very bad for both parties.

Averil drooped, and disputed not – guessing, though not yet understanding, the heart hunger she should feel even for such a dreary glimpse.

Every hour seemed to be another turn of the wheel that hurried on the departure. The successor wished to take house and furniture as they stood, and to enter into possession as soon as possible, as he already had taken the practice. This coincided with Henry's burning impatience to be quit of everything, and to try to drown the sense of his own identity in the crowds of London. He was his sisters' only guardian, their property was entirely in his hands, and no one had the power of offering any obstacle, so that no delay could be interposed; and the vague design passed with startling suddenness to a fixed decision, to be carried into execution immediately. It came in one burst upon the May household that Averil and her sisters were coming to spend a last evening before their absolute packing to go on the Saturday to London, where they would provide their outfit, and start in a month for America.

The tidings were brought by Mary, who had, as usual, been spending part of the morning with Averil. No one seemed to be so much taken by surprise as Tom, whose first movement was to fall on his sisters for not having made him aware of such a preposterous scheme. They thought he knew. He knew that all the five quarters of the world had been talked of in a wild sort of a way; but how could he suppose that any man could be crazed enough to prefer to be an American citizen, when he might remain a British subject?

Repugnance to America was naturally strong in Tom, and had of late been enhanced by conversations with an Eton friend, who, while quartered in Canada, had made excursions into the States, and acquired such impressions as high-bred young officers were apt to bring home from a superficial view of them. Thus fortified, he demanded whether any reasonable person had tried to bring Henry Ward to his senses.

Ethel believed that papa had advised otherwise.

'Advised! It should have been enforced! If he is fool enough to alter his name, and throw up all his certificates, what is to become of him? He will get no practice in any civilized place, and will have to betake himself to some pestilential swamp, will slave his sisters to death, spend their money, and destroy them with ague. How can you sit still and look on, Ethel?'

'But what could I do?'

'Stir up my father to interfere.'

'I thought you always warned us against interfering with Henry Ward.'

He treated this speech as maliciously designed to enrage him. 'Ethel!' he stammered, 'in a case like this – where the welfare – the very life – of one – of your dearest friend – of Mary's, I mean – I did think you would have been above——'

'But, Tom, I would do my utmost, and so would papa, if it were possible to do anything; but it is quite in vain. Henry is resolved against remaining under British rule, and America seems to be the only field for him.'

'Much you know or care!' cried Tom. 'Well, if no one else will, I must!'

With which words he departed, leaving his sister surprised at his solicitude, and dubious of the efficacy of his remonstrance, though she knew by experience that Tom was very different in a great matter from what he was in a small one.

Tom betook himself to Bankside, and the first person he encountered there was his little friend, Ella, who ran up to him at once.

'Oh, Mr Tom, we are going to America! Shall you be sorry?'

'Very sorry,' said Tom, as the little hand was confidingly thrust into his.

'I should not mind it, if you were coming too, Mr Tom!'

'What, to play at French billiards?'

'No, indeed! To find objects for the microscope. I shall save all the objects I meet, and send them home in a letter.'

'An alligator or two, or a branch of the Mississippi,' said Tom, in a young man's absent way of half-answering a pet child; but the reply so struck Ella's fancy, that, springing through the open French window, she cried, 'Oh, Ave, Ave, here is Mr Tom saying I am to send him a branch of the Mississippi in a letter, as an object for his microscope!'

'I beg your pardon,' said Tom, shocked at Averil's nervous start, and still more shocked at her appearance. She looked like one shattered by long and severe illness; her eyes were restless and distressed, her hair thrust back as if it oppressed her temples, her manner startled and overwrought, her hand hot and unsteady – her whole air that of one totally unequal to the task before her. He apologized for having taken her by surprise, and asked for her brother. She answered, that he was busy at Mr Bramshaw's, and she did not know when he would come in. But still Tom lingered; he could not bear to leave her to exertions beyond her strength. 'You are tiring yourself,' he said; 'can I do nothing to help you?'

'No, no, thank you; I am only looking over things. Minna is helping me, and I am making an inventory.'

'Then you must let me be of use to you. You must be as quiet as possible. You need rest.'

'I can't rest; I'm better busy!' she said hastily, with quick, aimless, bustling movements.

But Tom had his father's tone, as he gently arrested the trembling hand that was pulling open a drawer, and with his father's sweet, convincing smile, said, 'What's that for?' then drew up a large arm-chair, placed her in it, and, taking pen and list, began to write – sometimes at her suggestion, sometimes at his own – giving business-like and efficient aid.

The work was so grave and regular, that Ella soon found the room tedious, and crept out, calling Minna to aid in some of their own personal matters.

Slowly enumerating the articles they came to the piano. Averil went up to it, leant fondly against it, and softly touched the keys. 'My own,' she said, 'bought for a surprise to me when I came home from school! And oh, how he loved it!'

'Every one had reason to love it,' said Tom, in a low voice; but she did not heed or hear.

'I cannot – cannot part with it! When I sit here, I can almost feel him leaning over me! You must go – I will pay your expenses myself! I wonder if we should have such rough roads as would hurt you,' she added, caressingly toying with the notes, and bringing soft replies from them, as if she were conversing with a living thing.

'Ah!' said Tom, coming nearer, 'you will, I hope, take care to what your brother's impetuosity might expose either *this*, or yourself.'

'We shall all fare alike,' she said, carelessly.

'But how?' said Tom.

'Henry will take care of that.'

'Do you know, Miss Ward, I came down here with the purpose of setting some matters before your brother that might dissuade him from making the United States his home. You have justly more influence than I. Will you object to hear them from me?'

Ave could not imagine why Tom May, of all people in the world, should thrust himself into the discussion of her plans; but she could only submit to listen, or more truly to lean back with wandering thoughts and mechanical signs of assent, as he urged his numerous objections. Finally, she uttered a meek 'Thank you,' in the trust that it was over.

'And will you try to make your brother consider these things?'

Poor Ave could not have stood an examination on 'these things,' and feeling inadequate to undertake the subject, merely said something of 'very kind, but she feared it would be of no use.'

'I assure you, if you would persuade him to talk it over with me, that I could show him that he would involve you all in what would be most distasteful.'

'Thank you; but his mind is made up. No other course is open.'

'Could he not, at least, go and see what he thinks of it, before taking you and your sisters?'

'Impossible!' said Averil. 'We must all keep together; we have no one else.'

'No, indeed, you must not say that,' cried Tom, with a fire that startled Averil in the midst of her languid, dreary indifference.

'I did not mean,' she said, 'to be ungrateful for the kindness of your family – the doctor and dear Mary, above all; but you must know——'

'I know,' he interrupted, 'that I cannot see you exiling yourself with your brother, because you think you have no one else to turn to – you, who are so infinitely dear——'

'This is no time for satire,' she said, drawing aside with offence, but still wearily, and as if she had not given attention enough to understand him.

'You mistake me,' he exclaimed; 'I mean that no words can tell how strong the feeling is that – that – No, I never knew its force till now; but, Averil, I cannot part with you – you who are all the world to me.'

Lifting her heavy eyelids for a moment, she looked bewildered, and then, moving towards the door, said, 'I don't know whether this is jest or earnest – any way, it is equally unsuitable.'

'What do you see in me,' cried Tom, throwing himself before her, 'that you should suppose me capable of jesting on such a subject, at such a moment?'

'I never saw anything but supercilious irony,' she answered, in the same dreamy, indifferent way, as if hardly aware what she was saying, and still moving on.

'I cannot let you go thus. You must hear me,' he cried, and he wheeled round an easy chair, with a gesture of entreaty; which she obeyed, partly because she was hardly alive to understand his drift, partly because she could scarcely stand; and there she sat, in the same drowsy resignation with which she had listened to his former expostulation.

Calm collected Tom was almost beside himself. 'Averil! Averil!' he cried, as he sat down opposite and bent as close to her as possible, 'if I could only make you listen or believe me! What shall I say? It is only the honest truth that you are the dearest thing in the whole world to me! The very things that have given you most offence arose from my struggles with my own feelings. I tried to crush what would have its way in spite of me, and now you see its force.' He saw greater life and comprehension in her eye as he spoke, but the look was not encouraging; and he continued: 'How can I make you understand! Oh! if I had but more time! – but – but it was only the misery of those moments that showed me why it was that I was always irresistibly drawn to you, and yet made instinctive efforts to break the spell; and now you will not understand.'

'I do understand,' said Averil, at length entirely roused, but chiefly by resentment. 'I understand how much a country surgeon's daughter is beneath an M.D.'s attention, and how needful it was to preserve the distance by marks of contempt. As a convict's sister, the distance is so much widened, that it is well for both that we shall never meet again.'

Therewith she had risen, and moved to the door.

'Nay, nay,' he cried; 'it is for that very reason that all my past absurdity is trampled on! I should glory in a connexion with such as Leonard! Yes, Averil,' as he fancied he saw her touched, 'you have never known me yet; but trust yourself and him to me, and you will give him a true brother, proud of his nobleness. You shall see him constantly – you shall keep your sisters with you. Only put yourself in my hands, and you shall know what devotion is.'

He would have said more, but Averil recalled herself, and said: 'This is mere folly; you would be very sorry, were I to take you at your word. It would be unworthy in me towards your father, towards Henry, towards you, for me to listen to you, even if I liked you, and that you have taken good care to prevent me from doing.' And she opened the door, and made her way into the hall.

'But, Averil! – Miss Ward!' he continued, pursuing her, 'If, as I swear I will, I track out the real offender, bring him to justice, proclaim Leonard's innocence? Then——'

She was half-way up the stairs. He had no alternative but to take his hat and stride off in a tumult of dismay, first of all at the rejection, and next at his own betrayal of himself. Had he guessed what it would come to, would he ever have trusted himself in that drawing-room? This was the meaning of it all, was it? He, the sensible man of the family, not only to be such an egregious ass, but to have made such a fool of himself! For he was as furious at having committed himself to *himself*, as he was at his avowal to Averil – he, who had always been certain of loving so wisely and so well, choosing an example of the true feminine balance of excellence, well born, but not too grand for the May pretensions; soundly religious, but not philanthropically pious; of good sense and ability enough for his comfort, but not of overgrown genius for his discomfort; of good looks enough for satisfaction, but not for dangerous admiration; of useful, but not overwhelming wealth; of creditable and not troublesome kindred – that he should find himself plunged headlong into love by those brown eyes and straight features, by the musical genius, talents anything but domestic, ill-regulated enthusiasm, nay, dislike to himself, in the very girl whose station and family he condemned at the best, and at the very time when her brother was a convict, and her sisters dependent! Was he crazed? Was he transformed? What frenzy had come over him to endear her the more for being the reverse of his ideal? And, through all, his very heart was bursting at the thought of the wounds he had given her in his struggles against the net of fascination. He had never imagined the extent of the provocation he gave; and, in truth, his habitual manner was such, that it was hard to distinguish between irony and genuine interest. And now it was too late! What should he be henceforth to her? What would Stoneborough and his future be to him? He would, he believed, have taught himself to acquiesce, had he seen any chance of happiness before her; but the picture he drew of her prospects justified his misery, at being only able to goad her on, instead of drawing her back. He was absolutely amazed at himself. He had spoken only the literal truth, when he said that he had been unconscious of the true nature of the feelings that always drew him towards her, though only to assert his independence, and make experiments by teazing in his ironically courteous way. Not until the desolate indifference of her tone had incited him to show her that Henry was not *all* that remained to her, had he arrived at the perception that, in the late weeks of anxiety, she had grown into his heart, and that it was of no use to argue the point with himself, or think what he would do, the fact was accomplished – his first love was a direct contradiction to his fixed opinions, he had offended her irrevocably and made a fool of himself, and she was going away to dreariness!

At first he had rushed off into the melancholy meadows, among the sodden hay-cocks still standing among the green growth of grass; but a shower, increasing the damp forlornness of the ungenial day, made him turn homewards. When, late in the afternoon, Ethel came into the school-room for some Cocksmoor stores, she found him leaning over his books on the table. This was his usual place for study; and she did not at once perceive that the attitude was only assumed on her entrance, so kneeling in front of her cupboard, she asked, 'What success?'

'I have not seen him.'

'Oh! I thought I saw you going——'

'Never mind! I mean,' he added with some confusion, 'I wish for a little peace. I have a horrid headache.'

'You!' exclaimed Ethel; and turning round, she saw him leaning back in his chair, a defenceless animal without his spectacles, his eyes small and purple ringed, his hair tossed about, his spruceness gone. 'I am sure you are not well,' she said.

'Quite well. Nonsense, I only want quiet.'

'Let me give you some of Aubrey's camphor liniment.'

'Thank you,' submitting to a burning application to his brow; but as she lingered in anxiety, 'I really want nothing but quiet.'

How like Norman he looks! thought Ethel, as she cast her last glance and departed. Can he be going to be ill? If he would only tell when anything is the matter! I know papa says that some of us feel with our bodies, and some with our minds; but then I never knew Tom much affected any way, and what is all this to him? And a sigh betrayed the suppressed heartache that underlaid all her sensations. I am afraid it must be illness; but any way, he will neither tell nor bear to have it noticed, so I can only watch.

Enter the two little Wards, with a message that Ave was sorry, but that she was too much tired to come that evening; and when Mary regretted not having been able to come and help her, Ella answered that 'Mr Tom had come and helped her for a long time.'

'Yes,' said Minna; 'but I think he must have done it all wrong, for do you know, I found the list he had made torn up into little bits.'

Ethel almost visibly started, almost audibly exclaimed.

At tea-time Tom appeared, his trimness restored, but not his usual colouring; and Ella hailed him with reproaches for having gone away without telling her. The soft attention of which the child had a monopoly did not fail, though he bent down, trying to keep her to himself, and prevent their colloquy from attracting notice; but they were so close behind Ethel's chair, that she could not help hearing: 'We were only gone to dig up the violets that you are to have, and if you had only stayed you would have seen Henry, for he came in by the little gate, and when I went to tell you, you were gone.'

Ethel wondered whether the blushes she felt burning all over her face and neck would be remarked by those before her, or would reveal to Tom, behind her, that the child was giving her the key to his mystery. Marvelling at the exemplary gentleness and patience of his replies to his little coquettish tormentor, she next set herself to relieve him by a summons to Ella to tea and cherries. Fortunately the fruit suggested Dr May's reminiscences of old raids on cherry orchards now a mere name, and he thus engrossed all the younger audience not entirely pre-occupied. He set himself to make the little guests forget all their sorrows, as if he could not help warming them for the last time in the magic of his own sunshine; but Ethel heard and saw little but one figure in the quietest corner of the room, a figure at which she scarcely dared to look.

'And there you are!' so went her thoughts. 'It is true then! Fairly caught! Your lofty crest vailed at last – and at such a time! O Tom, generous and true-hearted, in spite of all your nonsense! How could she help being touched? In the net and against his will! Oh, triumph of womanhood! I am so glad! No, I'm not, it is best this way, for what an awkward mess it would have been! She is dear Leonard's sister to be sure, and there is stuff in her, but papa does not take to her, and I don't know whether she would fit in with Tom himself! But oh! the fun it would have been to see Flora's horror at finding her one prudent brother no better than the rest of us! Dear old Tom! The May heart has been too strong for the old Professor nature! What a retribution for his high mightiness! Harry and Richard to be guarded from making fools of themselves! What a nice cloak for jealousy! But it is no laughing matter! How miserable, how thoroughly upset, he is! Poor dear Tom! If I could only go and kiss you, and tell you that I never loved you half so well; but you would rather die than let out one word, I know! Why, any one of the others would have had it all out long ago! And I don't know whether it is quite safe to screen the lamp from those aching eyes that are bearing it like a martyr! There! Well, may be, he will just stand the knowing that I know, provided I don't say a word; but I wish people would not be so "self-contained!"'

Self-contained Tom still continued in the morning, though looking sallow and wan; but, in a political argument with his father, he was snappish and overbearing, and in the course of the day gave another indication of being thrown off his balance, which was even harder for Ethel to endure.

Throughout the suspense on Leonard's account, Aubrey had been a source of anxiety to all, especially to Tom. The boy's sensitive frame had been so much affected, that tender dealings with him were needful, and all compulsion had been avoided. His father had caused him to be put on the sick list of the volunteers; and as for his studies, though the books were daily brought out, it was only to prevent the vacuum of idleness; and Tom had made it his business to nurse his brother's powers, avoid all strain on the attention, and occupy without exciting, bearing with his fitful moods of despondence or of hope, whether they took the form of talking or of dreaming.

But now that all was over, every one knew that it was time to turn over a new leaf; and Tom, with his sore heart, did it with a vengeance, and on the first instance of carelessness, fell on the poor family pet, as a younger brother and legitimate *souffre douleur*, with vehemence proportioned to his own annoyance. It was a fierce lecture upon general listlessness, want of manliness, spirit, and perseverance, indifference to duties he had assumed. Nonsense about feelings – a fellow was not worth the snap of a finger who could not subdue his feelings – trash.

The sisters heard the storm from the drawing-room, and Gertrude grew hotly indignant, and wanted Ethel to rush in to the rescue; but Ethel, though greatly moved, knew that female interposition only aggravated such matters, and restrained herself and her sister till she heard Tom stride off. Then creeping in on tiptoe, she found the boy sitting stunned and confounded by the novelty of the thing.

'What can it be all about, Ethel? I never had such a slanging in my life!'

'I don't think Tom is quite well. He had a bad headache last night.'

'Then I hope – I mean, I think – he must have made it worse! I know mine aches, as if I had been next door to the great bell;' and he leant against his sister.

'I am afraid you really were inattentive.'

'No worse than since the heart has gone out of everything. But that was not all! Ethel, can it really be a disgrace, and desertion, and all that, if I don't go on with those volunteers, when it makes me sick to think of touching my rifle?' and his eyes filled with tears.

'It would be a great effort, I know,' said Ethel, smoothing his hair; 'but after all, you volunteered not for pleasure, but because your country wanted defence.'

'The country? I don't care for it, since it condemned him, when he was serving it.'

'He would not say that, Aubrey! He would only be vexed to hear that you gave in, and were fickle to your undertaking. Indeed, if I were the volunteer, I should think it due to him, not to shrink as if I were ashamed of what he was connected with.'

Aubrey tried to answer her sweet high-spirited smile, but he had been greatly hurt and distressed, and the late reproach to his manhood embittered his tears without making it easier to repress them; and pushing away his chair, he darted up-stairs.

'Poor dear fellow! I've been very hard on him, and only blamed instead of comforting,' thought Ethel sadly, as she slowly entered the passage; 'what shall I think of, to make a break for both of those two?'

'So you have been cockering your infant,' said Tom, meeting her. 'You mean to keep him a baby all his life.'

'Tom, I want to talk to you,' said she.

In expectation of her displeasure, he met it half way, setting his back against the passage wall, and dogmatically declaring, 'You'll be the ruin of him if you go on in this way! How is he ever to go through the world if you are to be always wiping his tears with an embroidered pocket-handkerchief, and cossetting him up like a blessed little sucking lamb?'

'Of course he must rough it,' said Ethel, setting her back against the opposite wall; 'I only want him to be hardened; but after a shock like this, one cannot go on as if one was a stock or stake. Even a machine would have its wheels out of order——'

'Well, well, but it is time that should be over.'

'So it is;' and as the sudden thought flashed on her, 'Tom, I want you to reconsider your journey, that you gave up in the spring, and take him——'

'I don't want to go anywhere,' he wearily said.

'Only it would be so good for him,' said Ethel earnestly; 'he really ought to see something taller than the Minster tower, and you are the only right person to take him, you are so kind to him.'

'For instance?' he said, smiling.

'Accidents will happen in the best regulated families; besides, he did want shaking up. I dare say he will be the better for it. There's the dinner bell.'

To her surprise, she found his arm round her waist, and a kiss on her brow. 'I thought I should have caught it,' he said; 'you are not half a fool of a sister after all.'

Aubrey was not in the dining-room; and after having carved, Tom, in some compunction, was going to look for him, when he made his appearance in his uniform.

'Oho!' said the doctor, surprised.

'There's to be a grand parade with the Whitford division,' he answered; and no more was said.

Not till the eight o'clock twilight of the dripping August evening did the family re-assemble. Ethel had been preparing for a journey that Mary and Gertrude were to make to Maplewood; and she did not come down till her father had returned, when following him into the drawing-room, she heard his exclamation, 'Winter again!'

For the fire was burning, Tom was sitting crumpled over it, with his feet on the fender, and his elbows on his knees, and Aubrey in his father's arm-chair, his feet over the side, so fast asleep, that neither entrance nor exclamation roused him; the room was pervaded with an odour of nutmeg and port wine, and a kettle, a decanter, and empty tumblers told tales. Now the doctor was a hardy and abstemious man, of a water-drinking generation; and his wife's influence had further tended to make him – indulgent as he was – scornful of whatever savoured of effeminacy or dissipation, so his look and tone were sharp, and disregardful of Aubrey's slumbers.

'We got wet through,' said Tom; 'he was done up, had a shivering fit, and I tried to prevent mischief.'

'Hm!' said the doctor, not mollified. 'Cold is always the excuse. But another time don't teach your brother to make this place like a fast man's rooms.'

Ethel was amazed at Tom's bearing this so well. With the slightest possible wrinkle of the skin of his forehead, he took up the decanter and carried it off to the cellaret.

'How that boy sleeps!' said his father, looking at him.

'He has had such bad nights!' said Ethel. 'Don't be hard on Tom, he is very good about such things, and would not have done it without need. He is so careful of Aubrey!'

'Too careful by half,' said the doctor, smiling placably as his son returned. 'You are all in a league to spoil that youngster. He would be better if you would not try your hand on his ailments, but would knock him about.'

'I never do that without repenting it,' said Tom; then, after a pause, 'It is not spirit that is wanting, but you would have been frightened yourself at his state of exhaustion.'

'Of collapse, don't you mean?' said the doctor, with a little lurking smile. 'However, it is vexatious enough; he had been gaining ground all the year, and now he is regularly beaten down again.'

'Suppose I was to take him for a run on the Continent!'

'What, tired of the hospital?'

'A run now and then is duty, not pleasure,' replied Tom quietly; while Ethel burnt to avert from him these consequences of his peculiar preference for appearing selfish.

'So much for railway days! That will be a new doctrine at Stoneborough. Well, where do you want to go?'

'I don't want to go anywhere.'

Ethel would not have wondered to see him more sullen than he looked at that moment. It was lamentable that those two never could understand each other, and that either from Tom's childish faults, his resemblance to his grandfather, or his habitual reserve, Dr May was never free from a certain suspicion of ulterior motives on his part. She was relieved at the influx of the rest of the party, including Richard; and Aubrey wakening, was hailed with congratulations on the soundness of his sleep, whilst she looked at Tom with a meaning smile as she saw her father quietly feel the boy's hand and brow. The whole family were always nursing the lad, and scolding one another for it.

Tom had put himself beside Ethel, under the shade of her urn, and she perceived that he was ill at ease, probably uncertain whether any confidences had been bestowed on her or Mary from the other side. There was no hope that the topic would be avoided, for Richard began with inquiries for Averil.

'She is working herself to death,' said Mary sadly; 'but she says it suits her.'

'And it does,' said the doctor; 'she is stronger every day. There is nothing really the matter with her.'

'Contrary blasts keep a ship upright,' said Gertrude, 'and she has them in abundance. We found her in the midst of six people, all giving diametrically opposite advice.'

'Dr Spencer was really helping, and Mr Wright was there about his own affairs,' said Ethel in a tone of repression.

'And Mrs Ledwich wanted her to settle on the Ohio to assist the runaway slaves,' continued Gertrude.

'It does not teaze her as if she heard it,' said Mary.

'No,' said the doctor, 'she moves about like one in a dream, and has no instinct but to obey her brother.'

'Well, I am glad to be going,' said Daisy; 'it will be flat when all the excitement is over, and we have not the fun of seeing Tom getting rises out of Ave Ward.'

This time Tom could not repress a sudden jerk, and Ethel silenced her sister by a hint that such references were not nice when people were in trouble.

'By-the-bye,' said Aubrey, 'speaking of going away, what were you saying while I was asleep? or was it a dream that I was looking through Tom's microscope at a rifle bullet in the Tyrol?'

'An inspiration from Tom's brew,' said the doctor.

'Weren't you saying anything?' said Aubrey eagerly. 'I'm sure there was something about duty and pleasure. Were you really talking of it?'

'Tom was; and if it is to put some substance into those long useless legs, I don't care if you do start off.'

Aubrey flashed into a fresh being. He had just been reading a book about the Tyrol, and Tom not caring at all where they were to go, this gave the direction. Aubrey rushed to borrow a continental Bradshaw from Dr Spencer, and the plan rapidly took form; with eager suggestions thrown in by every one, ending with the determination to start on the next Monday morning.

'That's settled,' said Tom wearily, when he and Ethel, as often happened, had lingered behind the rest; 'only, Ethel, there's one thing. You must keep your eye on the Vintry Mill, and fire off a letter to me if the fellow shows any disposition to bolt.'

'If I can possibly find out——'

'Keep your eyes open; and then Hazlitt has promised to let me know if that cheque of Bilson's is cashed. If I am away, telegraph, and meantime set my father on the scent. It may not hang that dog himself, but it may save Leonard.'

'Oh, if it would come!'

'And meantime – silence, you know——'

'Very well;' then lingering, 'Tom, I am sure you did the right thing by Aubrey, and so was papa afterwards.'

His brow darkened for a moment, but shaking it off he said, 'I'll do my best for your cosset lamb, and bring him back in condition.'

'Thank you; I had rather trust him with you than any one.'

'And how is it that no one proposes a lark for you, old Ethel?' said Tom, holding her so as to study her face. 'You look awfully elderly and fagged.'

'Oh, I'm going to be left alone with the doctor, and that will be the greatest holiday I ever had.'

'I suppose it is to you,' said Tom, with a deep heavy sigh perhaps glad to have some ostensible cause for sighing.

'Dear Tom, when you are living here, and working with him——'

'Ah – h!' he said almost with disgust, 'don't talk of slavery to me before my time. How I hate it, and everything else! Good-night!'

'Poor Tom!' thought Ethel. 'I wish papa knew him better and would not goad him. Will Averil ever wake to see what she has done, and feel for him? Though I don't know why I should wish two people to be unhappy instead of one, and there is weight enough already. O Leonard, I wonder if your one bitter affliction will shield you from the others that may be as trying, and more tempting!'

CHAPTER XVIII

'All bright hopes and hues of day
Have faded into twilight grey.'

Christian Year.

'No fear of Aubrey's failing,' said Tom; 'he has a better foundation than nine-tenths of the lads that go up, and he is working like a man.'

'He always did work heartily,' said Ethel, 'and with pleasure in his work.'

'Ay, like a woman.'

'Like a scholar.'

'A scholar is a kind of woman. A man, when he's a boy, only works because he can't help it, and afterwards for what he can get by it.'

'For what he can do with it would have a worthier sound.'

'Sound or sense, it is all the same.'

'Scaffolding granted, what is the building?'

Tom apparently thought it would be working like a woman to give himself the trouble of answering; and Ethel went on in her own mind, 'For the work's own sake – for what can be got by it – for what can be done with it – because it can't be helped – Are these all the springs of labour here? Then how is work done in that solitary cell? Is it because it can't be helped, or is it "as the Lord's freeman?" And when he can hear of Aubrey's change, will he take it as out of his love, or grieve for having been the cause?'

For the change had been working in Aubrey ever since Leonard had altered his career. The boy was at a sentimental age, and had the susceptibility inseparable from home breeding; his desire to become a clergyman had been closely connected with the bright visions of the happy days at Coombe, and had begun to wane with the first thwarting of Leonard's plans; and when the terrible catastrophe of the one friend's life occurred, the other became alienated from all that they had hoped to share together. Nor could even Dr May's household be so wholly exempt from the spirit of the age, that Aubrey was not aware of the strivings and trials of faith at the University. He saw what Harvey Anderson was, and knew what was passing in the world; and while free from all doubts, shrank boyishly from the investigations that he fancied might excite them. Or perhaps these fears of possible scruples were merely his self-justification for gratifying his reluctance.

At any rate, he came home from his two months' tour, brown, robust, with revived spirits; but bent on standing an examination for the academy at Woolwich. He had written about it several times before his return, and his letters were, as his father said, 'so appallingly sensible that perhaps he would change his mind.' But it was not changed when he came home; and Ethel, though sorely disappointed, was convinced by her own sense as well as by Richard's prudence, that interference was dangerous. No one in Israel was to go forth to the wars of the Lord save those who 'willingly offered themselves;' and though grieved that her own young knight should be one of the many champions unwilling to come forth in the Church's cause she remembered the ordeal to Norman's faith, and felt that the exertion of her influence was too great a responsibility.

'You don't like this,' said Tom, after a pause. 'It is not my doing, you know.'

'No, I did not suppose it was,' said Ethel. 'You would not withhold any one in these days of exceeding want of able clergymen.'

'I told him it would be a grief at home,' added Tom; 'but when a lad gets into that desperate mood, he always may be a worse grief if you thwart him; and I give you credit, Ethel, you have not pulled the curb.'

'Richard told me not.'

'Richard represents the common sense of the family when I am not at home.'

Tom was going the next day to his course of study at the London hospitals, and this – the late afternoon – was the first time that he and his sister had been alone together. He had been for some little time having these short jerks of conversation, beginning and breaking off rather absently. At last he said, 'Do those people ever write?'

'Prisoners, do you mean? Not for three months.'

'No – exiles.'

'Mary has heard twice.'

He held out Mary's little leathern writing case to her.

'O Tom!'

'It is only Mary.'

Ethel accepted the plea, aware that there could be no treason between herself and Mary, and moreover that the letters had been read by all the family. She turned the key, looked them out, and standing by the window to catch the light, began to read –

'You need not be afraid, kind Mary,' wrote Averil, on the first days of her voyage; 'I am quite well, as well as a thing can be whose heart is dried up. I am hardened past all feeling, and seem to be made of India rubber. Even my colour has returned – how I hate to see it, and to hear people say my roses will surprise the delicate Americans. Fancy, in a shop in London I met an old school-fellow, who was delighted to see me, talked like old times, and insisted on knowing where we were staying. I used to be very fond of her, but it was as if I had been dead and was afraid she would find out I was a ghost, yet I talked quite indifferently, and never faltered in my excuses. When we embarked, it was no use to know it was the last of England, where *he* and you and home and life were left. How I envied the poor girl, who was crying as if her heart would break!'

On those very words, broke the announcement of Mr Cheviot. Tom coolly held out his hand for the letters, so much as a matter of course, that Ethel complied with his gesture, and he composedly pocketed them, while she felt desperately guilty. Mary's own entrance would have excited no compunction, Ethel would have said that Tom wanted to hear of the voyage; but in the present case, she could only blush, conscious that the guest recognised her sister's property, and was wondering what business she had with it, and she was unwilling to explain, not only on Tom's account, but because she knew that Mr Cheviot greatly disapproved of petitioning against the remission of capital sentences, and thought her father under a delusion.

After Tom's departure the next day, she found the letters in her work-basket, and restored them to Mary, laughing over Mr Cheviot's evident resentment at the detection of her doings.

'I think it looked rather funny,' said Mary.

'I beg your pardon,' said Ethel, much astonished; 'but I thought, as every one else had seen them——'

'Tom always laughed at poor Ave.'

'He is very different now; but indeed, Mary, I am sorry, since you did not like it.'

'Oh!' cried Mary, discomfited by Ethel's apology, 'indeed I did not mean that, I wish I had not said anything. You know you are welcome to do what you please with all I have. Only,' she recurred, 'you can't wonder that Mr Cheviot thought it funny.'

'If he had any call to think at all,' said Ethel, who was one of those who thought that Charles Cheviot had put a liberal interpretation on Dr May's welcome to Stoneborough. He had arrived after the summer holidays as second master of the school, and at Christmas was to succeed

Dr Hoxton, who had been absolutely frightened from his chair by the commissions of inquiry that had beset the Wichcote foundation; and in compensation was at present perched on the highest niche sacred to conservative martyrdom in Dr May's loyal heart.

Charles Cheviot was a very superior man, who had great influence with young boys, and was admirably fitted to bring about the much required reformation in the school. He came frequently to discuss his intentions with Dr May, and his conversation was well worth being listened to; but even the doctor found three evenings in a week a large allowance for good sense and good behaviour – the evenings treated as inviolable even by old friends like Dr Spencer and Mr Wilmot, the fast waning evenings of Aubrey's home life.

The rest were reduced to silence, chess, books, and mischief, except when a treat of facetious small talk was got up for their benefit. Any attempt of the ladies to join in the conversation was replied to with a condescending levity that reduced Ethel to her girlhood's awkward sense of forwardness and presumption; Mary was less disconcerted, because her remarks were never so aspiring, and Harry's wristbands sufficed her; but the never daunted Daisy rebelled openly, related the day's events to her papa, fearless of any presence, and when she had grown tired of the guest's regular formula of expecting to meet Richard, she told him that the adult school always kept Richard away in the winter evenings; 'But if you want to see him, he is always to be found at Cocksmoor, and he would be very glad of help.'

'Did he express any such wish?' said Mr Cheviot, looking rather puzzled.

'Oh dear, no; only I thought you had so much time on your hands.'

'Oh no – oh no!' exclaimed Mary, in great confusion, 'Gertrude did not mean – I am sure I don't know what she was thinking of.'

And at the first opportunity, Mary, for once in her life, administered to Gertrude a richly deserved reproof for sauciness and contempt of improving conversation; but the consequence was a fancy of the idle younglings to make Mary accountable for the 'infesting of their evenings,' and as she was always ready to afford sport to the household, they thus obtained a happy outlet for their drollery and discontent, and the imputation was the more comical from his apparent indifference and her serene composure; until one evening when, as the bell rung, and mutterings passed between Aubrey and Gertrude, of 'Day set,' and 'Cheviot's mountains lone,' the head of the family, for the first time, showed cognizance of the joke, and wearily taking down his slippered feet from their repose said, 'Lone! yes, there's the rub! I shall have to fix days of reception if Mary will insist on being so attractive.'

Mary, with an instinct that she was blamed, began to be very sorry, but broke off amid peals of merriment, and blushes that were less easily extinguished; and which caused Ethel to tell each of the young ones privately, that their sport was becoming boy and frog work, and she would have no more of it. Daisy was inclined to be restive; but Ethel told her that many people thought this kind of fun could never be safe or delicate. 'I have always said that it might be quite harmless, if people knew where to stop – now show me that I am right.'

And to Aubrey she put the question, whether he would like to encourage Daisy in being a nineteenth-century young lady without reticence?

However, as Mary heard no more of their mischievous wit, Ethel was quite willing to let them impute to herself a delusion that the schoolmaster was smitten with Mary, and to laugh with them in private over all the ridiculous things they chose to say.

At last Flora insisted on Ethel's coming with her to make a distant call, and, as soon as they were in the carriage, said, 'It was not only for the sake of Mrs Copeland, though it is highly necessary you should go, but it is the only way of ever speaking to you, and I want to know what all this is about Mary?'

'The children have not been talking their nonsense to you!'

'No one ever talks nonsense to me – intentionally, I mean – not even you, Ethel; I wish you did. But I hear it is all over the town. George has been congratulated, and so have I, and one does not like contradicting only to eat it up again.'

'You always did hear everything before it was true, Flora.'

'Then is it going to be true?'

'O Flora, can it be possible?' said Ethel, with a startled, astonished look.

'Possible! Highly obvious and proper, as it seems to me. The only doubt in my mind was whether it were not too obvious to happen.'

'He is always coming in,' said Ethel, 'but I never thought it was really for that mischief! The children only laugh about it as the most preposterous thing they can think of, for he never speaks to a woman if he can help it.'

'That may not prevent him from wanting a good wife.'

'Wanting a wife – ay, as he would want a housekeeper, just because he has got to the proper position for it; but is he to go and get our bonny Mary in that way, just for an appendage to the mastership?'

'Well done, old Ethel! I'm glad to see you so like yourself. I remember when we thought Mrs Hoxton's position very sublime.'

'I never thought of positions!'

'Never! I know that very well; and I am not thinking of it now, except as an adjunct to a very worthy man, whom Mary will admire to the depths of her honest heart, and who will make her very happy.'

'Yes, I suppose if she once begins to like him, that he will,' said Ethel, slowly: 'but I can't bring myself to swallow it yet. She has never given in to his being a bore, but I thought that was her universal benevolence; and he says less to her than to any one.'

'Depend upon it, he thinks he is proceeding *selon les régles*.'

'Then he ought to be flogged! Has he any business to think of my Mary, without falling red hot in love with her? Why, Hector was regularly crazy that last half-year; and dear old Polly is worth ever so much more than Blanche.'

'I must say you have fulfilled my desire of hearing you talk nonsense, Ethel. Mary would never think of those transports.'

'She deserves them all the more.'

'Well, she is the party most concerned, though she will be a cruel loss to all of us.'

'She will not go far, if——'

'Yes, but she will be the worse loss. You simple Ethel, you don't think that Charles Cheviot will let her be the dear family fag we have always made of her?'

'Oh no – that always was wrong.'

'And living close by, she will not come on a visit, all festal, to resume home habits. No, you must make up your mind, Ethel – *if*, as you say, *if* – he will be a man for monopolies, and he will resent anything that he thinks management from you. I suspect it is a real sign of the love that you deny, that he has ventured on the sister of a clever woman, living close by, and a good deal looked up to.'

'Flora, Flora, you should not make one wicked. If she is to be happy, why can't you let me rejoice freely, and only have her drawn off from me bit by bit, in the right way of nature?'

'I did not tell you to make you dislike it – of course not. Only I thought that a little tact, a little dexterity, might prevent Charles Cheviot from being so much afraid of you, as if he saw at once how really the head of the family you are.'

'Nonsense, Flora, I am no such thing. If I am domineering, the sooner any one sees it and takes me down the better. If this does come, I will try to behave as I ought, and not to mind so Mary is happy; but I can't act, except just as the moment leads me. I hope it will soon be over, now you have made me begin to believe in it. I am afraid it will spoil Harry's pleasure at home! Poor dear Harry, what will he do?'

'When does he come?'

'Any day now; he could not quite tell when he could get away.'

When they came back, and Dr May ran out to say, 'Can you come in, Flora? we want you,' the sisters doubted whether his excitement were due to the crisis, or to the arrival. He hurried them into the study, and shut the door, exulting and perplexed. 'You girls leave one no rest,' he said. 'Here I have had this young Cheviot telling me that the object of his attentions has been apparent. I'm sure I did not know if it were Mab or one of you. I thought he avoided all alike; and poor Mary was so taken by surprise that she will do nothing but cry, and say, "No, never;" and when I tell her she shall do as she pleases, she cries the more; or if I ask her if I am to say Yes, she goes into ecstasies of crying! I wish one of you would go up, and see if you can do anything with her.'

'Is he about the house?' asked Flora, preparing to obey.

'No – I was obliged to tell him that she must have time, and he is gone home. I am glad he should have a little suspense – he seemed to make so certain of her. Did he think he was making love all the time he was boring me with his gas in the dormitories? I hope she will serve him out!'

'He will not be the worse for not being a lady's man,' said Flora, at the door.

But in ten minutes, Flora returned with the same report of nothing but tears; and she was obliged to leave the party to their perplexity, and drive home; while Ethel went in her turn to use all manner of pleas to her sister to cheer up, know her own mind, and be sure that they only wished to guess what would make her happiest. To console or to scold were equally unsuccessful; and after attempting all varieties of treatment, bracing or tender, Ethel found that the only approach to calm was produced by the promise that she should be teazed no more that evening, but be left quite alone to recover, and cool her burning eyes and aching head. So, lighting her fire, shaking up a much-neglected easy chair, bathing her eyes, desiring her not to come down to tea, and engaging both that Gertrude should not behold her, and that papa would not be angry, provided that she tried to know what she really wished, and be wiser on the morrow, Ethel left her. The present concern was absolutely more to persuade her to give an answer of some sort, than what that answer should be. Ethel would not wish; Dr May had very little doubt; and Gertrude, from whom there was no concealing the state of affairs, observed, 'If she cries so much the first time she has to know her own mind, it shows she can't do without some one to know it for her.'

The evening passed in expeditions of Ethel's to look after her patient, and in desultory talk on all that was probable and improbable between Dr May and the younger ones, until just as Ethel was coming down at nine o'clock with the report that she had persuaded Mary to go to bed, she was startled by the street door being opened as far as the chain would allow, and a voice calling, 'I say, is any one there to let me in?'

'Harry! O Harry! I'm coming;' and she had scarcely had time to shut the door previous to taking down the chain, before the three others were in the hall, the tumult of greetings breaking forth.

'But where's Polly?' he asked as soon as he was free to look round them all.

'Going to bed with a bad headache,' was the answer, with which Daisy had sense enough not to interfere; and the sailor had been brought into the drawing-room, examined on his journey, and offered supper, before he returned to the charge.

'Nothing really the matter with Mary, I hope?'

'Oh! no – nothing.'

'Can't I go up and see her?'

'Not just at present,' said Ethel. 'I will see how she is when she is in bed, but if she is going to sleep, we had better not disturb her.'

'Harry thinks she must sleep better for the sight of him,' said the doctor; 'but it is a melancholy business. – Harry, your nose is out of joint.'

'Who is it?' said Harry, gravely.

'Ah! you have chosen a bad time to come home. We shall know no comfort till it is over.'

'Who?' cried Harry; 'no nonsense, Gertrude, I can't stand guessing.'

This was directed to Gertrude, who was only offending by pursed lips and twinkling eyes, because he could not fall foul of his father. Dr May took pity, and answered at once.

'Cheviot!' cried Harry. 'Excellent! He always did know how to get the best of everything. Polly turning into a Mrs Hoxton. Ha! ha! Well, that is a relief to my mind.'

'You did look rather dismayed, certainly. What were you afraid of?'

'Why, when that poor young Leonard Ward's business was in the papers, a messmate of mine was asked if we were not all very much interested, because of some attachment between some of us. I thought he must mean me or Tom, for I was tremendously smitten with that sweet pretty girl, and I used to be awfully jealous of Tom; but when I heard of Mary going to bed with a headache, and that style of thing, I began to doubt, and I couldn't stand her taking up with such a dirty little nigger as Henry Ward was at school.'

'I think you might have known Mary better!' exclaimed Gertrude.

'And it's not Tom either?' he asked.

'Exactly the reverse,' laughed his father.

'Well, Tom is a sly fellow, and he had a knack of turning up whenever one wanted to do a civil thing by that poor girl. Where is she now?'

'At New York.'

'They'd better take care how they send me to watch the Yankees, then.'

'Your passion does not alarm me greatly,' laughed the doctor. 'I don't think it ever equalled that for the reigning ship. I hope there's a vacancy in that department for the present, and that we may have you at home a little.'

'Indeed, sir, I'm afraid not,' said Harry. 'I saw Captain Gordon at Portsmouth this morning, and he tells me he is to go out in the *Clio* to the Pacific station, and would apply for me as his first lieutenant, if I liked to look up the islands again. So, if you have any commissions for Norman, I'm your man.'

'And how soon?'

'Uncertain – but Cheviot and Mary must settle their affairs in good time; I've missed all the weddings in the family hitherto, and won't be baulked of Polly's. I say, Ethel, you can't mean me not to go and wish her joy.'

'We are by no means come to joy yet,' said Ethel; 'poor Mary is overset by the suddenness of the thing.'

'Why, I thought it was all fixed.'

'Nothing less so,' said the doctor. 'One would think it was a naiad that had had an offer from the mountains next, for she has been shedding a perfect river of tears ever since; and all that the united discernment of the family has yet gathered is, that she cries rather more when we tell her she is right to say No, than when we tell her she is right to say Yes.'

'I declare, Ethel, you must let me go up to her.'

'But, Harry, I promised she should hear no more about it to-night. You must say nothing unless she begins.'

And thinking a quiet night's rest, free from further excitement, the best chance of a rational day, Ethel was glad that her mission resulted in the report, 'Far too nearly asleep to be disturbed;' but on the way up to bed, soft as Harry's foot-falls always were, a voice came down the stairs, 'That's Harry! Oh, come!' and with a face of triumph turned back to meet Ethel's glance of discomfited warning, he bounded up, to be met by Mary in her dressing-gown. 'O Harry, why didn't you come?' as she threw her arms round his neck.

'They wouldn't let me.'

'I did think I heard you; but when no one came I thought it was only Richard, till I heard the dear old step, and then I knew. O Harry!' and still she gasped, with her head on his shoulder.

'They said you must be quiet.'

'O Harry! did you hear?'

'Yes, indeed,' holding her closer, 'and heartily glad I am; I know him as well as if I had sailed with him, and I could not wish you in better hands.'

'But – O Harry dear –' and there was a struggle with a sob between each word, 'indeed – I won't – mind if you had rather not.'

'Do you mean that you don't like him?'

'I should see him, you know, and perhaps he would not mind – he could always come and talk to papa in the evenings.'

'And is that what you want to put a poor man off with, Mary?'

'Only – only – if you don't want me to——'

'I not want you to – ? Why, Mary, isn't it the very best thing I could want for you? What are you thinking about?'

'Don't you remember, when you came home after your wound, you said I – I mustn't——' and she fell into such a paroxysm of crying that he had quite to hold her up in his arms, and though his voice was merry, there was a moisture on his eye-lashes. 'Oh, you Polly! You're a caution against deluding the infant mind! Was that all? Was that what made you distract them all? Why not have said so?'

'Oh, never! They would have said you were foolish.'

'As I was for not knowing that you wouldn't understand that I only meant you were to wait till the right one turned up. Why, if I had been at Auckland, would you have cried till I came home?'

'Oh, I'm sorry I was silly! But I'm glad you didn't mean it, dear Harry!' squeezing him convulsively.

'There! And now you'll sleep sound, and meet them as fresh as a fair wind to-morrow. Eh?'

'Only please tell papa I'm sorry I worried him.'

'And how about somebody else, Mary, whom you've kept on tenter-hooks ever so long? Are you sure he is not walking up and down under the limes on the brink of despair?'

'Oh, do you think – ? But he would not be so foolish!'

'There now, go to sleep. I'll settle it all for you, and I shan't let any one say you are a goose but myself. Only sleep, and get those horrid red spots away from under your eyes, or perhaps he'll repent his bargain,' said Harry, kissing each red spot. 'Promise you'll go to bed the instant I'm gone.'

'Well,' said Dr May, looking out of his room, 'I augur that the spirit of the flood *has* something to say to the spirit of the fell.'

'I should think so! Genuine article – no mistake.'

'Then what was all this about?'

'All my fault. Some rhodomontade of mine about not letting her marry had cast anchor in her dear little ridiculous heart, and it is well I turned up before she had quite dissolved herself away.'

'Is that really all?'

'The sum total of the whole, as sure as——' said Harry, pausing for an asseveration, and ending with 'as sure as your name is Dick May;' whereat they both fell a-laughing, though they were hardly drops of laughter that Harry brushed from the weather-marked pucker in the corner of his eyes; and Dr May gave a sigh of relief, and said, 'Well, that's right!'

'Where's the latch-key? I must run down and put Cheviot out of his misery.'

'It is eleven o'clock, he'll be gone to bed.'

'Then I would forbid the banns. Where does he hang out? Has he got into old Hoxton's?'

'No, it is being revivified. He is at Davis's lodgings. But I advise you not, a little suspense will do him good.'

'One would think you had never been in love,' said Harry, indignantly. 'At least, I can't sleep till I've shaken hands with the old fellow. Good-night, father. I'll not be long.'

He kept his word, and the same voice greeted him out of the dressing-room, 'How was the spirit of the fell? Sleep'st thou, brother?'

'Brother, nay,' answered Harry, 'he was only looking over Latin verses! He always was a cool hand.'

'The spirit of the Fell – Dr Fell, with a vengeance,' said Dr May. 'I say, Harry, is this going to be a mere business transaction on his part? Young folks have not a bit of romance in these days, and one does not know where to have them; but if I thought——'

'You may be sure of him, sir,' said Harry, speaking the more eagerly because he suspected the impression his own manner had made; 'he is thoroughly worthy, and feels Mary's merits pretty nearly as much as I do. More, perhaps, I ought to say. There's more warmth in him than shows. I don't know that Norman ever could have gone through that terrible time after the accident, but for the care he took of him. And that little brother of his that sailed with me in the *Eurydice*, and died at Singapore – I know how he looked to his brother Charles, and I do assure you, father, you could not put the dear Mary into safer, sounder hands, or where she could be more prized or happier. He is coming up to-morrow morning, and you'll see he is in earnest in spite of all his set speeches. Good-night, father; I am glad to be in time for the last of my Polly.'

This was almost the only moment at which Harry betrayed a consciousness that his Polly was less completely his own. And yet it seemed as if it must have been borne in on him again and again, for Mary awoke the next morning as thoroughly, foolishly, deeply in love as a woman could be, and went about comporting herself in the most comically common-place style, forgetting and neglecting everything, not hearing nor seeing, making absurd mistakes, restless whenever Mr Cheviot was not present, and then perfectly content if he came to sit by her, as he always did; for his courtship – now it had fairly begun – was equally exclusive and determined. Every day they walked or rode together, almost every evening he came and sat by her, and on each holiday they engrossed the drawing-room, Mary looking prettier than she had ever been seen before; Aubrey and Gertrude both bored and critical; Harry treating the whole as a pantomime got up for his special delectation, and never betokening any sense that Mary was neglecting him. It was the greatest help to Ethel in keeping up the like spirit, under the same innocent unconscious neglect from the hitherto devoted Mary, who was only helpful in an occasional revival of mechanical instinct in lucid intervals, and then could not be depended on. To laugh good-naturedly and not bitterly, to think the love-making pretty and not foolish, to repress Gertrude's saucy scorn, instead of encouraging it, would have been far harder without the bright face of the brother who generously surrendered instead of repining.

She never told herself that there was no proportion between the trials, not only because her spirits still suffered from the ever-present load of pity at her heart, nor because the loss would be hourly to her, but also because Charles Cheviot drew Harry towards him, but kept her at a distance, or more truly laughed her down. She was used to be laughed at; her ways had always been a matter of amusement to her brothers, and perhaps it was the natural assumption of brotherhood to reply to any suggestion or remark of hers with something intended for drollery, and followed with a laugh, which, instead of as usual stirring her up to good-humoured repartee, suppressed her, and made her feel foolish and awkward. As to Flora's advice, to behave with tact, she could not if she would, she would not if she could; in principle she tried to acquiesce in a man's desire to show that he meant to have his wife to himself, and in practice, she accepted his extinguisher because she could not help it.

Mr Cheviot was uneasy about the chances of Aubrey's success in the examination at Woolwich, and offered assistance in the final preparation; but though Aubrey willingly accepted the proposal, two or three violent headaches from overstudy and anxiety made Dr May insist on his old regimen of entire holiday and absence of work for the last week; to secure which repose, Aubrey was sent to London with Harry for a week's idleness and the society of Tom, who professed to be too busy to come home even for Christmas. Mr Cheviot's opinion transpired through Mary, that it was throwing away Aubrey's only chance.

In due time came the tidings that Aubrey had the second largest number of marks, and had been highly commended for the thoroughness of his knowledge, so different from what had been only crammed for the occasion. He had been asked who had been his tutor, and had answered, 'His brother,' fully meaning to spare Ethel publicity; and she was genuinely thankful for having been shielded under Tom's six months of teaching. She heartily wished the same shield would have availed at home, when Charles Cheviot gave that horrible laugh, and asked her if she meant to stand for a professor's chair. She faltered something about Tom and mathematics. 'Ay, ay,' said Charles; 'and these military examinations are in nothing but foreign languages and trash;' and again he laughed his laugh, and Mary followed his example. Ethel would fain have seen the fun.

'Eh, Cheviot, what two of a trade never agree?' asked Dr May, in high glory and glee.

'Not my trade, papa,' said Ethel, restored by his face and voice, 'only the peculiarity of examiners, so long ago remarked by Norman, of only setting questions that one can answer.'

'Not your trade, but your amateur work?' said Mr Cheviot, again exploding, and leaving Ethel to feel demolished. Why, she wondered presently, had she not held up her knitting, and merrily owned it for her trade – why, but because those laughs took away all merriment, all presence of mind, all but the endeavour not to be as cross as she felt. Was this systematic, or was it only bad taste?

The wedding was fixed for Whitsuntide; the repairs and drainage necessitating early and long holidays; and the arrangements gave full occupation. Mary was the first daughter who had needed a portion, since Mr Cheviot was one of a large family, and had little of his own. Dr May had inherited a fair private competence, chiefly in land in and about the town, and his professional gains, under his wife's prudent management, had been for the most part invested in the like property. The chief of his accumulation of ready money had been made over to establish Richard at Cocksmoor; and though living in an inexpensive style, such as that none of the family knew what it was to find means lacking for aught that was right or reasonable, there was no large amount of capital available. The May custom had always been that the physician should inherit the landed estate; and though this was disproportionately increased by the doctor's own acquisitions, yet the hold it gave over the town was so important, that he was unwilling it should be broken up at his death, and wished to provide for his other children by charges on the rents, instead of by sale and division. All this he caused Richard to write to Tom, for though there was no absolute need of the young man's concurrence in arranging Mary's settlements, it was a good opportunity for distinctly stating his prospects, and a compliment to consult him.

Feeling that Tom had thus been handsomely dealt with, his letter to his father was the greater shock, when, after saying that he doubted whether he could come home for the wedding, he expressed gratitude for the opening held out to him, but begged that precedents applicable to very different circumstances might not be regarded as binding. He was distressed at supplanting Richard, and would greatly prefer the property taking its natural course. It would be so many years, he trusted, before there would be room for his services, even as an assistant, at Stoneborough, that he thought it would be far more advisable to seek some other field; and his own desire would be at once to receive a younger son's share, if it were but a few hundreds, and be free to cut out his own line.

'What is he driving at, Ethel?' asked the doctor, much vexed. 'I offer him what any lad should jump at; and he only says, "Give me the portion of goods that falleth to me." What does that mean?'

'Not prodigality,' said Ethel. 'Remember what Sir Matthew Fleet said to Dr Spencer – "Dick's ability and common sense besides."'

'Exactly what makes me suspicious of his coming the disinterested over me. There's something behind! He is running into debt and destruction among that precious crew about the hospitals.'

'Harry saw nothing wrong, and thought his friends in good style.'

'Every one is in good style with Harry, happy fellow! He is no more a judge than a child of six years old – carries too much sunshine to see shades.'

'A lieutenant in the navy can hardly be the capital officer that our Harry is without some knowledge of men and discipline.'

'I grant you, on his own element; but on shore he goes about in his holiday spectacles, and sees a bird of paradise in every cock-sparrow.'

'Isn't *there* a glass house that can sometimes make a swan?' said Ethel, slyly touching her father's spectacles; 'but with you both, there's always a something to attract the embellishing process; and between Harry and Aubrey, Dr Spencer and Sir Matthew, we could hardly fail to have heard of anything amiss.'

'I don't like it.'

'Then it is hard,' said Ethel, with spirit. 'So steady as he has always been, he ought to have the benefit of a little trust.'

'He was never like the others; I don't know what to be at with him! I should not have minded but for that palaver about elder brothers.'

Defend as Ethel might, it was still with a misgiving lest disappointment should have taken a wrong course. It was hard to trust where correspondence was the merest business scrap, and neither Christmas nor the sister's marriage availed to call Tom home; and though she had few fears as to dissipation, she did dread hardening and ambition, all the more since she had learnt that Sir Matthew Fleet was affording to him a patronage unprecedented from that quarter.

No year of Etheldred May's life had been so trying as this last. It seemed like her first step away from the aspirations of youth, into the graver fears of womanhood. With all the self-restraint that she had striven to exercise at Coombe, it had been a time of glorious dreams over the two young spirits who seemed to be growing up by her side to be faithful workers, destined to carry out her highest visions; and the boyish devotion of the one, the fraternal reverence of the other, had made her very happy. And now? The first disappointment in Leonard had led – not indeed to less esteem for him, but to that pitying veneration that could only be yielded by a sharing in spirit of the like martyrdom; a continued thankfulness and admiration, but a continual wringing of the heart. And her own child and pupil, Aubrey, had turned aside from the highest path; and in the unavowed consciousness that he was failing in the course he had so often traced out with her, and that all her aid and ready participation in his present interests were but from her outward not her inward heart, he had never argued the point with her, never consulted her on his destination. He had talked only to his father of his alteration of purpose, and had at least paid her the compliment of not trying to make her profess that she was gratified by the change. In minor matters, he depended on her as much as ever; but Harry was naturally his chief companion, and the prime of his full and perfect confidence had departed, partly in the step from boy to man, but more from the sense that he was not fulfilling the soldiership he had dreamt of with her, and that he had once led her to think his talents otherwise dedicated. She had few fears for his steadiness, but she had some for his health, and he was something taken away from her – a brightness had faded from his image.

And this marriage – with every effort at rejoicing and certainty of Mary's present bliss and probability of future happiness, it was the loss of a sister, and not the gain of a brother, and Mr Cheviot did his utmost to render the absence of repining a great effort of unselfishness. And even with her father, her possession of Tom's half-revealed secret seemed an impairing of absolute confidence; she could not but hope that her father did her brother injustice, and in her tenderness towards them both this was a new and painful sensation. Her manner was bright and quaint as ever, her sayings perhaps less edged than usual, because the pain at her heart made her guard her tongue; but she had begun to feel middle-aged, and strangely lonely. Richard, though always a comfort, would not have entered into her troubles; Harry, in his atmosphere of sailor on shore, had nothing of the confidant, and engrossed his father; Mary and Aubrey were both gone from her, and Gertrude was still a child. She had never so longed after Margaret or Norman. But at least her corner in the Minster, her table at home with her Bible and Prayer-Book, were still the same, and witnessed many an outpouring of her anxiety, many a confession of the words or gestures that she had felt to have been petulant, whether others had so viewed them or not.

CHAPTER XIX

'Long among them was seen a maiden, who waited and wondered,
Lowly and meek in spirit, and patiently suffering all things;
Fair was she, and young, but alas! before her extended
Dreary and vast and silent, the desert of life.'

'Evangeline'. *Longfellow.*

'Sister, sister! who is it? Going to be married! Oh, do tell us!' cried Ella Warden – as she now was called – capering round her elder sister, who stood beneath a gas-burner, in a well-furnished bed-room, reading a letter, its enclosure clasped within a very trembling hand.

'Mary May, dear Mary,' answered Averil, still half absently.

'And who?'

'Mr Cheviot,' said Averil, thoroughly rousing herself, and, with a quick movement, concealing the enclosure in her bosom. 'I remember him; he was very good, when——'

And there she paused; while Ella chattered on: 'Oh, sister, if you were but at home, you would be a bridesmaid now, and perhaps we should. Little Miss Rivers was Mrs Ernescliffe's bridesmaid. Don't you remember, Minna, how we saw her in her little cashmere cloak?'

'Oh, don't, Ella!' escaped from Minna, like a cry of pain, as she leant back in a rocking-chair, and recollected who had held her up in his arms to watch Blanche May's wedding procession.

'And how soon will she be married, sister, and where will she live?' asked the much-excited Ella.

'She will be married in Whitsun week, and as he is headmaster, they will live in Dr Hoxton's house. Dear, good Mary, how glad I am that she is so full of happiness – her letter quite brims over with it! I wonder if I may work anything to send to her.'

'I should like to send her some very beautiful thing indeed,' cried Ella, with emphasis, and eyes dilating at some visionary magnificence.

'Ah, I have nothing to send her but my love! And I may send *her* that still,' said Minna, looking up wistfully at Averil, who bent down and kissed her.

'And Ave won't let me send mine to Mr Tom, though I'm sure I do love him the best of them all,' said Ella.

'That wasn't——' half whispered Minna, but turned her head away, with a sigh of oppression and look of resignation, sad in so young a child, though, indeed, the infantine form was fast shooting into tall, lank girlhood. Ella went on: 'I *shall* send him the objects for his microscope, when I get into the country; for I promised, so sister *can't* prevent me.'

'Oh, the country! – when shall we go there?' sighed Minna.

'Your head aches to-night, my dear,' said Averil, looking anxiously at her listless attitude, half-opened eyes, and the deep hollows above her collar-bones.

'It always does after the gas is lighted,' said the child, patiently; 'it is always so hot here.'

'It is just like being always in the conservatory at the Grange,' added Ella. 'I do hate this boarding-house. It is very unkind of Henry to keep us here – fifteen weeks now.'

'Oh, Ella,' remonstrated Minna, 'you mustn't say that!'

'But I shall say it,' retorted Ella. 'Rosa Willis says what she pleases, and so shall I. I don't see the sense of being made a baby of, when every one else of our age eats all they like, and is consulted about arrangements, and attends classes. And sister owns she does not know half so much as Cora!'

This regular declaration of American independence confounded the two sisters, and made Averil recall the thoughts that had been wandering: 'No, Ella, in some things I have not learnt so much as Cora; but I believe I know enough to teach you, and it has been a comfort to me to keep my two little sisters with me, and not send them to be mixed up among strange girls. Besides, I have constantly hoped that our present way of life would soon be over, and that we should have a home of our own again.'

'And why can't we?' asked Ella, in a much more humble and subdued voice.

'Because Henry cannot hear of anything to do. He thought he should soon find an opening in this new country; but there seem to be so many medical men everywhere that no one will employ or take into partnership a man that nothing is known about; and he cannot produce any of his testimonials, because they are all made out in his old name, except one letter that Dr May gave him. It is worse for Henry than for us, Ella; and all we can do for him is not to vex him with our grievances.'

Poor Averil! her dejected, patient voice, sad soft eyes, and gentle, persuasive manner, were greatly changed from those of the handsome, accomplished girl, who had come home to be the family pride and pet; still more, perhaps, from the wilful mistress of the house and the wayward sufferer of last summer.

'And shan't we go to live in the dear beautiful forest, as Cora Muller wishes?'

There was a tap at the door, and the children's faces brightened, though a shade passed over Averil's face, as if everything at that moment were oppressive; but she recovered a smile of greeting for the pretty creature who flew up to her with a fervent embrace – a girl a few years her junior, with a fair, delicate face and figure, in a hothouse rose style of beauty.

'Father's come!' she cried.

'How glad you must be!'

'And now,' whispered the children, 'we shall know about going to Indiana.'

'He says Mordaunt is as tall as he is, and that the house is quite fixed for me; but I told him I must have one more term, and then I will take you with me. Ah! I am glad to see the children in white. If you would only change that plain black silk, you would receive so much more consideration.'

'I don't want it, Cora, thank you,' said Averil, indifferently; and, indeed, the simple mourning she still wore was a contrast to her friend's delicate, expensive silk.

'But I want it for you,' pleaded Cora. 'I don't want to hear my Averil censured for English *hauteur*, and offend my country's feelings, so that she keeps herself from seeing the best side.'

'I see a very good, very dear side of one,' said Averil, pressing the eager hand that was held out to her, 'and that is enough for me. I was not a favourite in my own town, and I have not spirits to make friends here.'

'Ah! you will have spirits in our woods,' she said. 'You shall show me how you go gipsying in England.'

'The dear, dear woods! Oh, we must go!' cried the little girls.

'But it is going to be a town,' said Minna, gravely.

Cora laughed. 'Ah, there will be plenty of bush this many a day, Minna! No lack of butternuts and hickories, I promise you, nor of maples to paint the woods gloriously.'

'You have never been there?' said Averil, anxiously.

'No; I have been boarding here these two years, since father and brothers located there; but we had such a good time when we lived at my grandfather's farm, in Ohio, while father was off on the railway business.'

A gong resounded through the house, and Averil, suppressing a disappointed sigh, allowed Cora to take possession of her arm, and, followed by the two children, became parts of a cataract of people who descended the great staircase, and flowed into a saloon, where the dinner was prepared.

Henry, with a tall, thin, wiry-looking gentleman, was entering at the same time, and Averil found herself shaking hands with her brother's companion, and hearing him say, 'Good evening, Miss Warden; I'm glad to meet my daughter's friend. I hope you feel at home in our great country.'

It was so exactly the ordinary second-rate American style, that Averil, who had expected something more in accordance with the refinement of everything about Cora, except a few of her tones, was a little disappointed, and responded with difficulty; then, while Mr Muller greeted her sisters, she hastily laid her hand on Henry's arm, and said, under her breath, 'I've a letter from him.'

'Hush!' Henry looked about with a startled eye and repressing gesture. Averil drew back, and, one hand on her bosom, pressing the letter, and almost holding down a sob, she took her accustomed seat at the meal. Minna, too languid for the rapidity of the movements, hardly made the exertion of tasting food. Ella, alert and brisk, took care of herself as effectually as did Rosa Willis, on the opposite side of the table. Averil, all one throb of agitation, with the unread letter lying at her heart, directed all her efforts to look, eat, and drink, as usual; happily, talking was the last thing that was needed.

Averil had been greatly indebted to Miss Muller, who had taken pity on the helpless strangers – interested, partly by her own romance about England, partly by their mourning dresses, dark melancholy eyes, and retiring, bewildered manner. A beautiful motherless girl, under seventeen – left, to all intents and purposes, alone in New York – attending a great educational establishment, far more independent and irresponsible than a young man at an English University, yet perfectly trustworthy – never subject to the *bevues* of the 'unprotected female,' but self-reliant, modest, and graceful, in the heterogeneous society of the boarding-house – she was a constant marvel to Averil, and a warm friendship soon sprang up. The advances were, indeed, all on one side; for Ave was too sad, and oppressed with too heavy a secret, to be readily accessible; but there was an attraction to the younger, fresher, freer nature, even in the mystery of her mournful reserve; and the two drew nearer together from gratitude, and many congenial feelings, that rendered Cora the one element of comfort in the boarding-house life; while Henry in vain sought for occupation.

Cora had been left under the charge of the lady of the boarding-house, a distant connexion, while her father, who had been engaged in more various professions than Averil could ever conceive of or remember, had been founding a new city in Indiana, at once as farmer and land-agent, and he had stolen a little time, in the dead season, to hurry up to New York, partly on business, and partly to see his daughter, who had communicated to him her earnest desire that her new friends might be induced to settle near their future abode.

American meals were too serious affairs for conversation; but such as there was, was political, in all the fervid heat of the first commencements of disunion and threatenings of civil war. After the ladies had repaired to their saloon, with its grand ottomans, sofas, rocking-chairs, and piano, the discussion continued among them; Cora talking with the utmost eagerness of the tariff and of slavery, and the other topics of the day, intensely interesting, and of terrible moment, to her country; but that country, Averil had not yet learnt to feel her own, and to her all was one dreary whirl of words, in which she longed to escape to her room, and read her letter. Ella had joined Rosa Willis, and the other children; but Minna, as usual, kept under her sister's wing, and Averil could not bear to shake herself free of the gentle child. The ladies of the boarding-house – some resident in order to avoid the arduous duties of housekeeping, others temporarily brought thither in an interregnum of servants, others spending a winter in the city – had grown tired of asking questions that met with the scantiest response, took melancholy for disdain, and were all neglectful, some uncivil, to the grave, silent English girl; and she was sitting alone, with Minna's hand in hers, as she had sat for many a weary evening, when her brother and Mr Muller came up together, and, sitting down on either side of her, began to talk of the rising city of Massissauga – admirably situated – excellent water privilege, communicating with Lake Michigan – glorious primeval forest – healthy situation – fertile land – where a colossal fortune might be realized in maize, eighties, sections, speculations. It was all addressed to her, and it was a hard task to give attention, so as to return a rational answer, while her soul would fain have been clairvoyante, to read the letter in her breast. She did perceive, at last, though not till long after the children had gone to bed, what the project was, that the family should become the purchasers of shares, which would give them a right to a portion of the soil, excellent at present for growing corn, and certain hereafter to be multiplied in value for building; that Henry might, in the meantime, find an opening for practice, but might speedily be independent of it. It sounded promising, and it was escape – escape from forced inaction, from an uncongenial life, from injury to the children, and it would be with Cora, her one friend. What was the demur, and why were they consulting her, who, as Henry knew, was ready to follow him wherever he chose to carry her? At last came a gleam of understanding: 'Then, Doctor, you will talk it over with your sister, and give me your ultimatum;' and therewith Mr Muller walked away to mingle in other conversation, and Henry coming closer to his sister, she again eagerly said, 'I have it here; you shall see it to-morrow, when I have read it.'

'It——'

'The letter.'

'How can you be so unguarded? You have not let the children know? Take care then, I will not have the subject revived with them.'

'But Minna——'

'It is this heated stove atmosphere. She will soon forget if you don't keep it up, and she will be herself when we leave this place, and it depends on you when we do that, Ave.'

'On me!' she said, with bewildered face.

And Henry, marvelling at her slowness of comprehension, made her understand that the advance of money, for the purchase at Massissauga, must come from her means. His own had been heavily drained by the removal, the long period of inaction, and moreover what remained had been embarked in shares in a company, absolutely certain to succeed, but where they were not at once available for sale. Averil was now of age, her property was in her own power, and could not, her brother assured her, be better invested, than on ground certain to increase in value. She looked at him, confused and distressed, aware that it was too important a step to be taken without consideration, yet unable to compose her thoughts, or recollect objections.

'Must I answer to-night?' she said.

'No, there is no need for that. But we must close to-morrow with Muller, for it is not a chance that will long go begging.'

'Then let me go, please, Henry,' she said, imploringly. 'I will tell you to-morrow, but I can't now. I don't seem to understand anything.'

It was late, and he released her, with a kind good-night, though still with a sign of caution. Cora, however, hastened to join her, and walk up the stairs with her, eagerly inquiring into the success of the negotiation, and detailing what she had gathered from her father as to the improvements he had been making. She would fain have made Averil come into her bedroom to build castles there; but this was more than could be borne, and breaking from her at last, Averil reached her own room, not to think of Mr Muller's project, but to cast an anxious glance at each of the little beds, to judge whether the moment had come when that famishing hunger might be appeased by the crumb which for these mortal hours had lain upon her craving heart – the very first since the one on the arrival at Milbank.

Each brown head was shrouded in the coverings, the long dark fringes rested safely on the cheeks, and Averil at length drew out the treasure, and laid it on her hand to dwell on its very sight. The address needed to be looked at with lingering earnestness, as if it had indeed been a missive from another world; she looked, and was tardy to unfold it, as though, now the moment was come, the sense of being in communication with her brother must be tasted to the utmost, ere entering on the utterances that must give pain; and when she did open the envelope, perhaps the first sensation was disappointment – the lines were not near enough together, the writing not small enough, to satisfy even the first glance of the yearning eye. It was cheerful, it spoke of good health, and full occupation, with the use of books, daily exercise, the chaplain's visits, schooling and attendance at chapel, and of the great pleasure of having heard from her. 'And that good Dr May inclosed your letter in one written to me with his own hand, a kindness I never dared to think of as possible, but which he promises to repeat. Your letter and his are the continual food of my thoughts, and are valued beyond all power of words. I only hope you knew that I have not been allowed to write sooner, and have not expected letters.' Then came a few brief comments on her last inquiries, and entreaties that she would give him full information of all details of their present life; 'It will carry me along with you, and I shall live with you, both as I read, and as I dwell on it afterwards. Do not indulge in a moment's uneasiness about me, for I am well, and busy; every one is as kind to me as duty permits, and Dr May is always ready to do all in his power for me.' There were a few affectionate words for Henry, and 'I long to send a message to the children, but I know it is better for them to let me drop from their minds, only you must tell me all about them; I want to know that the dear little Minna is bright and happy again.'

No confidences, only generalities; not even any reference to the one unbroken bond of union, the one support, except in the three scanty final words, the simplest of blessings. It was not satisfying; but Averil recalled, with a start, that no wonder the letter was meagre, since it was necessarily subject to inspection; and how could the inner soul be expressed when all must pass under strangers' eyes, who would think such feelings plausible hypocrisy in a convicted felon. Again she took it up, to suck to the utmost all that might be conveyed in the short common-place sentences, and to gaze at them as if intensity of study could reveal whether the cheerfulness were real or only assumed. Be they what they might, the words had only three weeks back been formed by Leonard's hand, and she pressed her lips upon them in a fervent agony of affection.

When she roused herself and turned her head, she perceived on Minna's pillow two eyes above the bed-clothes, intently fixed on her. Should she see, or should she not see? She believed that the loving heart was suffering a cruel wrong, she yearned to share all with the child, but she was chained by the command of one brother, and by that acquiescence of the other which to her was more than a command. She would not see, she turned away, and made her preparations for the night without betraying that she knew that the little one was awake, resuming the tedious guard on the expression of her face. But when her long kneeling had ended, and with it that which was scarcely so much conscious intercession as the resting an intolerable load on One who alone knew its weight, just as she darkened the room for the night, the low voice whispered, 'Ave, is it——?'

And Averil crept up to the little bed, 'Yes, Minna; he is well! He hopes you are bright and happy, but he says it is best you should forget him.' The brow was cold and clammy, the little frame chill and trembling, the arms clasped her neck convulsively. She lifted the child into her own bed, pressed tight to her own bosom, and though no other word passed between the sisters, that contact seemed to soothe away the worst bitterness; and Averil slept from the stillness enforced on her by the heed of not disturbing Minna's sleep.

Little that night had she reckoned of the plan needing so much deliberation! When she awoke it was to the consciousness that besides the arrival of Leonard's letter, something had happened – there was some perplexity – what was it? And when it came back she was bewildered. Her own fortune had always appeared to her something to fall back on in case of want of success, and to expend it thus was binding the whole family down at a perilous moment, to judge by the rumours of battle and resistance. And all she had ever heard at home, much that she daily heard at New York, inclined her to distrust and dislike of American speculations. It was Cora's father! Her heart smote her for including him in English prejudice, when Henry liked and trusted him! And she had disobeyed and struggled against Henry too long. She had promised to be submissive and yielding. But was this the time? And the boarding-house life – proverbially the worst for children – was fast Americanizing Ella, while Minna drooped like a snowdrop in a hothouse, and idleness might be mischievous to Henry.

Oh, for some one to consult! for some one to tell her whether the risk was a foolish venture, or if the terms were safe! But not a creature did she know well enough to seek advice from! Even the clergyman, whose church she attended, was personally unknown to her; Cora Muller was her sole intimate, there was a mutual repulsion between her and the other ladies, and still more with the gentlemen. A boarding-house was not the scene in which to find such as would inspire confidence, and they had no introductions. There was no one to turn to; and in the dreary indifference that had grown over her, she did not even feel capable of exerting her own judgment to the utmost, even if she had been able to gather certain facts, or to know prudent caution from blind prejudice – often woman's grievous difficulty. What could a helpless girl of one-and-twenty, in a land of strangers, do, but try to think that by laying aside the use of her own judgment she was trusting all to Providence, and that by leaving all to her brother she was proving her repentance for her former conduct.

There, too, were her sisters, clamorous with hopes of the forest life; and there was Cora, urging the scheme with all the fervour of girlish friendship, and in herself no small element in its favour, engaging for everything, adducing precedents for every king of comfort and success, and making Ave's consent a test of her love. One question Averil asked of her – whether they should be utterly out of reach of their Church? Cora herself had been bred up to liberal religious ways, and was ready to attend whatever denomination of public worship came first to hand, though that which had descended from the Pilgrim Fathers came most naturally. She had been at various Sunday schools, and was a good conscientious girl, but had never gone through the process of conversion, so that Rosa Willis had horrified Ella by pronouncing her 'not a Christian.' She had no objection to show her English friends the way to the favourite Episcopal Church, especially as it was esteemed fashionable; and her passion for Averil had retained her there, with growing interest, drawn on by Averil's greater precision of religious knowledge, and the beauty of the Church system, displayed to her as the one joy and relief left to one evidently crushed with suffering. The use of Averil's books, conversations with her, and the teaching she heard, disposed her more and more to profess herself a member of the Episcopal Church, and she was unable to enter into Averil's scruples at leading her to so decided a step without her father's sanction. 'Father would be satisfied whatever profession she made. Did people in England try to force their children's consciences?' Cora, at Averil's desire, ascertained that Massissauga had as yet no place of worship of its own; but there was a choice of chapels within a circuit of five miles, and an Episcopal Church seven miles off, at the chief town of the county. Moreover, her father declared that the city of Massissauga would soon be considerable enough to invite every variety of minister to please every denomination of inhabitant. Averil felt that the seven miles off church was all she could reasonably hope for, and her mind was clear on that score, when Henry came to take her out walking for the sake of being able to talk more freely.

No longer afraid of being overheard, he gave kind attention to Leonard's letter; and though he turned away from the subject sooner than she wished, she was not exacting. Again he laid before her the advantages of their migration, and assured her that if there were the slightest risk he would be the last to make the proposal. She asked if it were safe to invest money in a country apparently on the eve of civil war?

He laughed the idea to scorn. How could the rebel states make war, with a population of negroes sure to rise against their masters? Where should their forces come from? Faction would soon be put down, and the union be stronger than ever. It was what Averil had been hearing morning, noon, and night, so no wonder she believed it, and was ashamed of a futile girlish fear.

And was Henry sure that it was a healthy place? Had she not heard of feverish swamps in Indiana?

Oh yes, in new unsettled places; but there had hardly been an ailment in the Muller family since they had settled at Massissauga.

And Averil's last murmur was – Could he find out anything about other people's opinion of the speculation? did they know enough about Mr Muller to trust themselves entirely in his hands?

Henry was almost angry – Could not his sister trust him to take all reasonable precaution? It was the old story of prejudice against whatever he took up.

Poor Averil was disarmed directly. The combats of will and their consequences rose up before her, and with them Leonard's charges to devote herself to Henry. She could but avow herself willing to do whatever he pleased. She only hoped he would be careful.

All thenceforth was pleasant anticipation and hope. Averil's property had to be transferred to America, and invested in shares of the land at Massissauga; but this was to cause no delay in arranging for the removal, they were only to wait until the winter had broken up, and the roads become passable after the melting of the snows; and meantime Mr Muller was to have their house prepared. Cora would remain and accompany them, and in the intervening time promised to assist Averil with her judgment in making the necessary purchases for 'stepping westward.'

When Averil wrote their plans to her English friends, she felt the difficulty of pleading for them. She was sensible that at Stoneborough the risking of her property would be regarded as folly on her part, and something worse on that of her brother; and she therefore wrote with every effort to make the whole appear her own voluntary act – though the very effort made her doubly conscious that the sole cause for her passive acquiescence was, that her past self-will in trifles had left her no power to contend for her own opinion in greater matters – the common retribution on an opinionative woman of principle.

Moreover, it was always with an effort that she wrote to Mary May. A rejected offer from a brother is a rock in a correspondence with a sister, and Averil had begun to feel greatly ashamed of the manner of her own response. Acceptance would have been impossible; but irritating as had been Tom May's behaviour, insulting as had been his explanation, and provoking his pertinacity, she had begun to feel that the impulse had been too generous and disinterested to deserve such treatment, and that bitterness and ill-temper had made her lose all softness and dignity, so that he must think that his pitying affection had been bestowed on an ungrateful vixen, and be as much disgusted with the interview as she was herself. She did not wish him to love her; but she regretted the form of the antidote, above all, since he was of the few who appreciated Leonard; and the more she heard of Ella's narrations of his kindness, the more ashamed she grew. Every letter to or from Mary renewed the uncomfortable sense, and she would have dropped the correspondence had it not been her sole medium of communication with her imprisoned brother, since Henry would not permit letters to be posted with the Milbank address.

CHAPTER XX

'A little hint to solace woe,
A hint, a whisper breathing low,
"I may not speak of what I know."'

Tennyson.

At the pace at which rapid people walk alone, when they wish to devour both the way and their own sensations, Ethel May was mounting the hill out of the town in the premature heat assumed by May in compliment to Whitsun week, when a prolonged shout made her turn. At first she thought it was her father, but her glass showed her that it was the brother so like him in figure that the London-made coat, and the hair partaking of the sand instead of the salt, were often said to be the chief distinction. Moreover, the dainty steps over the puddles were little like the strides of the doctor, and left no doubt that it was the one wedding guest who had been despaired of.

'O Tom, I am glad you are come!'

'What a rate you were running away at! I thought you had done with your hurricane pace.'

'Hurricane because of desperate hurry. I'm afraid I can't turn back with you.'

'Where is all the world?'

'Blanche is helping Mary arrange the Hoxton – I mean her own drawing-room; Hector has brought a dog-cart to drive papa about in; Daisy is gone with Harry and Aubrey to the Grange for some camellias.'

'And Ethel rushing to Cocksmoor!'

'I can't help it, Tom,' she said, humbly; 'I wish I could.'

'What's this immense pannier you are carrying?'

'It is quite light. It is twelve of the hats for the children to-morrow. Mary was bent on trimming them all as usual, and I was deluded enough to believe she would, till last evening I found just one and a half done! I did as many as I could at night, till papa heard me rustling about and thumped. Those went early this morning; and these are the rest, which I have just finished.'

'Was there no one to send?'

'My dear Tom, is your experience of weddings so slight as to suppose there is an available being in the family the day before?'

'I'm sure I don't desire such experience. Why could not they be content without ferreting me down?'

'I am very glad you have come. It would have been a great mortification if you had stayed away. I never quite believed you would.'

'I had much rather see the operation I shall miss to-morrow morning. I shall go back by the two o'clock train.'

'To study their happiness all the way up to town?'

'Then by the mail——'

'I won't torment you to stay; but I think papa will want a talk with you.'

'The very thing I don't want. Why can't he dispose of his property like other people, and give Richard his rights?'

'You know Richard would only be encumbered.'

'No such thing; Richard is a reasonable being – he will marry some of these days – get the living after Wilmot, and——'

'But you know how papa would be grieved to separate the practice from the house.'

'Because he and his fathers were content to bury themselves in a hole, he expects me to do the same. Why, what should I do? The place is over-doctored already. Every third person is a pet patient sending for him for a gnat-bite, gratis, taking the bread out of Wright's mouth. No wonder Henry Ward kicked! If I came here, I must practise on the lap-dogs! Here's my father, stronger than any of us, with fifteen good years' work in him at the least! He would be wretched at giving up to me a tenth part of his lambs, and that tenth would keep us always in hot water. His old-world practice would not go down with me, and he would think everything murder that was fresher than the year 1830.'

'I thought he was remarkable for having gone on with the world,' said Ethel, repressing some indignation.

'So he has in a way, but always against the grain. He has a tough lot of prejudices; and you may depend upon it, they would be more obstinate against me than any one else, and I should be looked on as an undutiful dog for questioning them, besides getting the whole credit of every case that went wrong.'

'I think you are unjust,' said Ethel, flushing with displeasure.

'I wish I were not, Ethel; but when there is one son in a family who can do nothing that is not taken amiss, it is hard that he should be the one picked out to be pinned down, and, maybe, goaded into doing something to be really sorry for.'

There was truth enough in this to seal Ethel's lips from replying that it was Tom's own fault, since his whole nature and constitution were far more the cause than his conduct, and she answered, 'You might get some appointment for the present, till he really wants you.'

'To be ordered home just as I am making something of it, and see as many cases in ten years as I could in a month in town. Things are altered since his time, if he could only see it. What was the use of giving me a first-rate education, if he meant to stick me down here?'

'At least I hope you will think long before you inflict the cruel disappointment of knowing that not one of his five sons will succeed to the old practice.'

'The throne, you mean, Ethel. Pish!'

The 'Pish' was as injurious to her hereditary love for 'the old practice,' and for the old town, as to her reverence for her father. One angry 'Tom!' burst from her lips, and only the experience that scolding made him worse, restrained her from desiring him to turn back if this was the best he had to say. Indeed she wondered to find him still by her side, holding the gate of the plantation open for her. He peered under her hat as she went through –

'How hot you look!' he said, laying hold of the handles of the basket.

'Thank you; but it is more cumbrous than heavy,' she said, not letting go; 'it is not *that*——'

An elision which answered better than words, to show that his speech, rather than hill or load, had made her cheeks flame; but he only drew the great basket more decisively from her hand, put his stick into the handle, and threw it over his shoulder; and no doubt it was a much greater act of good nature from him than it would have been from Richard or Harry.

'This path always reminds me of this very matter,' he said; 'I talked it over with Meta here, on the way to lay the foundation-stone at Cocksmoor, till Norman overtook us and monopolized her for good, poor little thing. She was all in the high romantic strain, making a sort of knight hospitalier of my father. I wonder what she is like by this time, and how much of *that* she has left.'

'Of the high romantic strain? I should think it was as much as ever the salt of life to her. Her last letter described her contrivances to make a knapsack for Norman on his visitation tour. Oh, fancy old June a venerable archdeacon!'

'You don't think a colonial archdeacon is like one of your great portly swells in a shovel hat.'

'It must be something remarkable that made Norman portly. But as for the shovel hat, Mrs Meta has insisted on having it sent out. I was going to tell you that she says, "I do like such a good tough bit of stitchery, to fit my knight out for the cause."'

'Marriage and distance have not frozen up her effusions.'

'No; when people carry souls in their pens, they are worth a great deal more, if they are to go to a distance.'

'Ah! by-the-bye, I suppose Cheviot has put a fresh lock on Mary's writing-case.'

'I suspect some of Mary's correspondence will devolve on me. Harry has asked me already.'

'I wished you had mentioned more about the letters of late. Leonard wanted to know more than I could tell him.'

'You don't mean that you have seen him? O Tom, how kind of you! Papa has been trying hard to get a day now that these first six months are up; but there are two or three cases that wanted so much watching that he has not been able to stir.'

'I know how he lets himself be made a prisoner, and that it was a chance whether any one saw the poor fellow at all.'

'I am so glad' – and Ethel turned on him a face still flushed, but now with gratitude. 'How was he looking?'

'The costume is not becoming, and he has lost colour and grown hollow-eyed; but I saw no reason for being uneasy about him; he looked clear and in health, and has not got to slouch yet. It is shocking to see such a grand face and head behind a grating.'

'Could he talk?'

'Why, the presence of a warder is against conversation, and six months of shoe-making in a cell does not give much range of ideas. There was nothing to be done but to talk on right a-head, and judge by his eyes if he liked it.'

'I suppose you could find out nothing about himself?'

'He said he got on very well; but one does not know what that means. I asked if he got books; and he said there was a very good library, and he could get what gave him something to think of; and he says they give interesting lectures in school.'

'You could not gather what is thought of him?'

'No; I saw but a couple of officers of the place, and could only get out of them "good health and good conduct." I do not expect even his conduct makes much impression as to his innocence, for I saw it stated the other day that the worst prisoners are those that are always getting convicted for petty offences; those that have committed one great crime are not so depraved, and are much more amenable. However, he has only three months more at Pentonville, and then he will go to Portland, Chatham, or Gibraltar.'

'Oh, I hope it will not be Gibraltar! But at least that terrible solitude will be over.'

'At any rate, his spirit is not broken. I could see his eye light up after I had talked a little while, and he fell into his natural tone again. He would not try to put out his hand to me when he came down; but when I went away, he put it through and we had a good hearty shake. Somehow it made one feel quite small.'

Ethel could have pledged herself for the soundness of Tom's nature after those words; but all she did was in an unwonted tone to utter the unwonted exclamation – 'Dear Tom.'

'If my father does not come up, I shall see him once more before he leaves Pentonville,' added Tom; 'and so you must mind and let me know all about his people in America. I found he had no notion of the row that is beginning there, so I said not a word of it. But what is all this about going to Indiana?'

'They are going at the end of April to settle in a place called Massissauga, where Henry is to farm till practice comes to him. It is towards the north of the State, in the county of Pulaski.'

'Ay, in one of the pestilential swamps that run up out of Lake Michigan. All the fertile ground there breeds as many fevers and agues as it does stalks of corn.'

'Indeed! how did you hear that?'

'I looked up the place after Leonard told me of it. It is as unlucky a location as the ill luck of that fellow Henry could have pitched on. Some friend Leonard spoke of – a Yankee, I suppose, meaning to make a prey of them.'

'The father of their young lady friend at the boarding-house.'

'Oh! a Yankee edition of Mrs Pugh!'

'And the worst of it is that this is to be done with poor Averil's fortune. She has written to Mr Bramshaw to sell out for her, and send her the amount, and he is terribly vexed; but she is of age, and there are no trustees nor any one to stop it.'

'All of a piece,' muttered Tom; then presently he swung the basket round on the ground with a vehement exclamation – 'If any man on this earth deserved to be among the robbers and murderers, I know who it is.' Then he shouldered his load again, and walked on in silence by his sister's side to the school door.

Richard had been obliged to go to a benefit club entertainment; and Ethel, knowing the limited literary resources of the parsonage, was surprised to find Tom still waiting for her, when the distribution and fitting of the blue-ribboned hats was over, and matters arranged for the march of the children to see the wedding, and to dine afterwards at the grammar-school hall.

'O Tom, I did not expect to find you here.'

'It is not fit for you to be walking about alone on a Whit Monday.'

'I am very glad to have you, but I am past that.'

'Don't talk nonsense; girls are girls till long past your age,' said Tom.

'It is not so much age, as living past things,' said Ethel.

'It was not only that,' added Tom; 'but I've more to say to you, while one can be sure of a quiet moment. Have you heard anything about that place?' and he pointed in the direction of the Vintry Mill.

'I heard something of an intention to part with it, and have been watching for an advertisement; but I can see none in the *Courant*, or on the walls.'

'Mind he does not slip off unawares.'

'I don't know what to do now that old Hardy is cut off from us. I tried to stir up Dr Spencer to go and investigate, but I could not tell him why, and he has not the same interest in going questing about as he used to have. People never will do the one thing one wants particularly!'

Tom's look and gesture made her ask if he knew of anything wrong with their old friend; and in return, she was told that Dr Spencer's recent visit to London had been to consult Sir Matthew Fleet. The foundations of mortal disease had been laid in India; and though it might long remain in abeyance, there were from time to time symptoms of activity; and tedious lingering infirmity was likely to commence long before the end.

'And what do you think the strange old fellow charged me as we walked away from dining at Fleet's?'

'Secrecy, of course,' returned the much-shocked Ethel.

'One does keep a secret by telling you. It was to have my eye on some lodging with a decent landlady, where, when it is coming to that, he can go up to be alone, out of the way of troubling Dick, and of all of you.'

'Tom, how dreadful!'

'I fancy it is something of the animal instinct of creeping away alone, and partly his law to himself not to trouble Dick.'

'An odd idea of what would trouble Dick!'

'So I told him; but he said, after seeing what it cost my father to watch dear Margaret's long decay, he would never entail the like on him. It is queer, and it is beautiful, the tender way he has about my father, treating him like a pet to be shielded and guarded – a man that has five times the force and vigour of body and mind that he has now, whatever they may have been.'

'Very beautiful, and I cannot help telling you how beautiful,' said Ethel, greatly moved; 'only remember, it is not to be mentioned.'

'Ha! did he ever make you an offer? I have sometimes suspected it.'

'No indeed! It was much – much more beautiful than that!'

'Our mother then? I had thought of that too, and it accounts for his having always taken to you the most of us.'

'Why, I'm the least like her of us all!'

'So they say, I know, and I can't recollect enough to judge, except that' – and Tom's voice was less clear for a moment – 'there was something in being with her that I've never found again, except now and then with you, Ethel. Well, he never got over it, I suppose.'

And Ethel briefly told of the rash resolution, the unsettled life, the neglect of the father's wishes, the grievous remorse, the broken health, and restless aimless wanderings, ending at last in loving tendance of the bereaved rival. It had been a life never wanting in generosity or benevolence, yet falling far short of what it might have been – a gallant voyage made by a wreck – and yet the injury had been less from the disappointment than from the manner of bearing it. Suddenly it struck her that Tom might suspect her of intending a personal application of the history, and she faltered; but he kept her to it by his warm interest and many questions.

'And, O Tom, he must not be allowed to go away in this manner! Nothing would so cut papa to the heart!'

'I don't believe he ever will, Ethel. He may go on for years as he is; and he said in the midst that he meant to live to carry out the drainage. Besides, if it comes gradually on him, he may feel dependent and lose the energy to move.'

'Oh! what a sorrow for papa! But I know that not to watch over him would make it all the worse.'

They walked on gravely till, on the top of the hill, Tom exclaimed, 'They've mounted the flag on the Minster steeple already.'

'It went up yesterday for Harvey Anderson and Mrs Pugh. There was a proposal to join forces, and have a double wedding – so interesting, the two schoolfellows and two young friends. The Cheviot girls much regretted it was not to be.'

'Cheviot girls! Heavens and earth! At home?'

'Not sleeping; but we shall have them all day to-morrow, for they cannot get home the same day by setting off after the wedding. There will be no one else, for even our own people are going, for Harry is to go to Maplewood with Blanche, and Aubrey has to be at Woolwich; but we shall all be at home to-night.'

'Last time was in the volunteer days, two or three centuries ago.'

It was strange how, with this naturally least congenial of all the family, Ethel had a certain understanding and fellow-feeling that gave her a sense of rest and relief in his company, only impaired by the dread of rubs between him and his father. None, however, happened; Dr May had been too much hurt to press the question of the inheritance, and took little notice of Tom, being much occupied with the final business about the wedding, and engrossed by Hector and Harry, who always absorbed him in their short intervals of his company. Tom went to see Dr Spencer, and brought him in, so cheerful and full of life, that what Ethel had been hearing seemed like a dream, excepting when she recognised Tom's unobtrusive gentleness and attention towards him.

She was surprised and touched through all the harass and hurry of that evening and morning, to find the 'must be dones' that had of late devolved on her alone, now lightened and aided by Tom, who appeared to have come for the sole purpose of being always ready to give a helping hand where she wanted it, with all Richard's manual dexterity, and more resource and quickness. The refreshment of spirits was the more valuable as this was a very unexciting wedding. Even Gertrude, not yet fourteen, had been surfeited with weddings, and replied to Harry's old wit of 'three times a bridesmaid and never a bride,' that she hoped so, her experience of married life was extremely flat; and a glance at Blanche's monotonous dignity, and Flora's worn face, showed what that experience was.

Harry was the only one to whom there was the freshness of novelty, and he was the great element of animation; but as the time came near, honest Harry had been seized with a mortal dread of the tears he imagined an indispensable adjunct of the ceremony, and went about privately consulting every one how much weeping was inevitable. Flora told him she saw no reason for any tears, and Ethel that when people felt very much they couldn't cry; but on the other hand, Blanche said she felt extremely nervous, and knew she should be overcome; Gertrude assured him that on all former occasions Mary did all the crying herself; and Aubrey told him that each bridesmaid carried six handkerchiefs, half for herself and half for the bride.

The result was, that the last speech made by Harry to his favourite sister in her maiden days was thus: – 'Well, Mary, you do look uncommonly nice and pretty; but now' – most persuasively – 'you'll be a good girl and not cry, will you?' and as Mary fluttered, tried to smile, and looked out through very moist eyes, he continued, 'I feel horribly soft-hearted to-day, and if you howl I must, you know; so mind, if I see you beginning, I shall come out with my father's old story of the spirit of the flood and the spirit of the fell, and that will stop it, if anything can.'

The comicality of Harry's alarm was nearly enough to 'stop it,' coupled with the great desire of Daisy that he should be betrayed into tears; and Mary did behave extremely well, and looked all that a bride should look. Admirable daughter and sister, she would be still more in her place as wife; hers was the truly feminine nature that, happily for mankind, is the most common-place, and that she was a thoroughly generic bride is perhaps a testimony to her perfection in the part, as in all others where quiet unselfish womanhood was the essential. Never had she been so sweet in every tone, word, and caress; never had Ethel so fully felt how much she loved her, or how entirely they had been one, from a time almost too far back for memory. There had not been intellectual equality; but perhaps it was better, fuller, affection, than if there had been; for Mary had filled up a part that had been in some measure wanting in Ethel. She had been a sort of wife to her sister, and thus was the better prepared for her new life, but was all the sorer loss at home.

The bridegroom! How many times had Ethel to remind herself of her esteem, and security of Mary's happiness, besides frowning down Gertrude's saucy comments, and trying to laugh away Tom's low growl that good things always fell to the share of poor hearts and narrow minds. Mr Cheviot did in fact cut a worse figure than George Rivers of old, having a great fund of natural bashfulness and self-consciousness, which did not much damage his dignity, but made his attempts at gaiety and ease extremely awkward, not to say sheepish. Perhaps the most trying moment was the last, when hearing a few words between Ethel and Mary about posting a mere scrap, if only an empty envelope, from the first resting-place, he turned round, with his laugh, to object to rash promises, and remind his dear sister Ethel that post offices were not always near at hand! After that, when Mary in her bright tenderness hung round her sister, it was as if that was the last fond grasp from the substance – as if only the shadow would come back and live in Minster Street.

Perhaps it was because Ethel had tried to rule it overwise, Mr Cheviot had insisted that the Cocksmoor children's share in the festivity should be a dinner in the Wichcote Hall, early in the day, after which they had to be sent home, since no one chose to have the responsibility of turning them loose to play in the grammar-school precincts, even in the absence of the boys. Richard was much afraid of their getting into mischief, and was off immediately after church to superintend the dinner, and marshal them home; and the rest of the world lost the resource that entertaining them generally afforded the survivors after a marriage, and which was specially needed with the two Cheviot sisters to be disposed of. By the time the Riverses were gone home, and the Ernescliffes and Harry off by the train, there were still four mortal hours of daylight, and oh! for Mary's power of making every one happy!

Caroline and Annie Cheviot were ladylike, nice-looking girls; but when they found no croquet mallets in the garden, they seemed at a loss what life had to offer at Stoneborough! Gertrude pronounced that 'she played at it sometimes at Maplewood, where she had nothing better to do,' and then retreated to her own devices. Ethel's heart sank both with dread of the afternoon, and with self-reproach at her spoilt child's discourtesy, whence she knew there would be no rousing her without an incapacitating discussion; and on she wandered in the garden with the guests, receiving instruction where the hoops might be planted, and hearing how nice it would be for her sister to have such an object, such a pleasant opportunity of meeting one's friends – an interest for every day. 'No wonder they think I want an object in life,' thought Ethel; 'how awfully tiresome I must be! Poor things, what can I say to make it pleasanter? – Do you know this Dielytra? I think it is the prettiest of modern flowers; but I wish we might call it Japan fumitory, or by some English name.'

'I used to garden once, but we have no flower-beds now, they spoilt the lawn for croquet.'

'And here comes Tom,' thought Ethel; 'poor Tom, he will certainly be off to London this evening.'

Tom, however, joined the listless promenade; and the first time croquet was again mentioned, observed that he had seen the Andersons knocking about the balls in the new gardens by the river; and proposed to go down and try to get up a match. There was an instant brightening, and Tom stepped into the drawing-room, and told Daisy to come with them.

'To play at croquet with the Andersons in the tea-gardens!' she exclaimed. 'No, I thank you, Thomas!'

He laid his hand on her shoulder – 'Gertrude,' he said, 'it is time to have done being a spoilt baby. If you let Ethel fag herself ill, you will rue it all your life.'

Frightened, but without clear comprehension, she turned two scared eyes on him, and replaced the hat that she had thrown on the table, just as Ethel and the others came in.

'Not you, Ethel,' said Tom; 'you don't know the game.'

'I can learn,' said Ethel, desperately bent on her duty.

'We would teach you,' volunteered the Cheviots.

'You would not undertake it if you knew better,' said Tom, smiling. 'Ethel's hands are not her strong point.'

'Ethel would just have to be croqued all through by her partner,' said Gertrude.

'Besides, my father will be coming in and wanting you,' added Tom; 'he is only at the hospital or somewhere about the town. I'll look after this child.'

And the two sisters, delighted that poor little Gertrude should have such a holiday treat as croquet in the public gardens, away from her governess elder sister, walked off glorious; while Ethel, breathing forth a heavy sigh, let herself sink into a chair, feeling as if the silence were in itself invaluable, and as if Tom could not be enough thanked for having gained it for her.

She was first roused by the inquiry, 'Shall I take in this letter, ma'am? it is charged four shillings over weight. And it is for Mr Thomas, ma'am,' impressively concluded the parlour-maid, as one penetrated by Mr Thomas's regard to small economies.

Ethel beheld a letter bloated beyond the capacities of the two bewigged Washingtons that kept guard in its corner, and addressed in a cramped hand unknown to her; but while she hesitated, her eye fell on another American letter directed to Miss Mary May, in Averil Ward's well-known writing, and turning both round, she found they had the same post-mark, and thereupon paid the extra charge, and placed the letter where Tom was most likely to light naturally on it without public comment. The other letter renewed the pang at common property being at an end. 'No, Mab,' she said, taking the little dog into her lap, 'we shall none of us hear a bit of it! But at least it is a comfort that this business is over! You needn't creep under sofas now, there's nobody to tread upon your dainty little paws. What is to be done, Mab, to get out of a savage humour – except thinking how good-natured poor Tom is!'

There was not much sign of savage humour in the face that was lifted up as Dr May came in from the hospital, and sitting down by his daughter, put his arm round her. 'So there's another bird flown,' he said. 'We shall soon have the old nest to ourselves, Ethel.'

'The Daisy is not going just yet,' said Ethel, stroking back the thin flying flakes over his temples. 'If we may believe her, never!'

'Ah! she will be off before we can look round,' said the doctor; 'when once the trick of marrying gets among one's girls, there's no end to it, as long as they last out.'

'Nor to one's boys going out into the world,' said Ethel: both of them talking as if she had been his wife, rather than one of these flyaway younglings herself.

'Ah! well,' he said, 'it's very pretty while it lasts, and one keeps the creatures; but after all, one doesn't rear them for one's own pleasure. That only comes by the way of their chance good-will to one.'

'For shame, doctor!' said Ethel, pretending to shake him by the collar.

'I was thinking,' he added, 'that we must not require too much. People must have their day, and in their own fashion; and I wish you would tell Tom – I've no patience to do it myself – that I don't mean to hamper him. As long as it is a right line, he may take whichever he pleases, and I'll do my best to set him forward in it; but it is a pity——'

'Perhaps a few years of travelling, or of a professorship, might give him time to think differently,' said Ethel.

'Not he,' said the doctor; 'the more a man lives in the world, the more he depends on it. Where is the boy? is he gone without vouchsafing a good-bye?'

'Oh no, he has taken pity on Annie and Caroline Cheviot's famine of croquet, and gone with them to the gardens.'

'A spice of flirtation never comes amiss to him.'

'There, that's the way!' said Ethel, half-saucily, half-caressingly; 'that poor fellow never can do right! Isn't it the very thing to keep him away from home, that we all may steal a horse, and he can't look over the wall, no, not with a telescope?'

'I can't help it, Ethel. It may be very wrong and unkind of me – Heaven forgive me if it is, and prevent me from doing the boy any harm! but I never can rid myself of a feeling of there being something behind when he seems the most straightforward. If he had only not got his grandfather's mouth and nose! And,' smiling after all – 'I don't know what I said to be so scolded; all lads flirt, and you can't deny that Master Tom divided his attentions pretty freely last year between Mrs Pugh and poor Ave Ward.'

'This time, I believe, it was out of pure kindness to me,' said Ethel, 'so I am bound to his defence. He dragged off poor Daisy to chaperon them, that I might have a little peace.'

'Ah! he came down on us this morning,' said the doctor, 'on Richard and Flora and me, and gave us a lecture on letting you grow old, Ethel – said you were getting over-tasked, and no one heeding it; and looking – let's look' – and he took off his spectacles, put his hand on her shoulder, and studied her face.

'Old enough to be a respectable lady of the house, I hope,' said Ethel.

'Wiry enough for most things,' said the Doctor, patting her shoulder, reassured; 'but we must take care, Ethel; if you don't fatten yourself up, we shall have Flora coming and carrying you off to London for a change, and for Tom to practise on.'

'That is a threat! I expected he had been prescribing for me already, never to go near Cocksmoor, for that's what people always begin by——'

'Nothing worse than pale ale.' At which Ethel made one of her faces. 'And to make a Mary of that chit of a Daisy. Well, you may do as you please – only take care, or Flora will be down upon us.'

'Tom has been very helpful and kind to me,' said Ethel. 'And papa, he has seen Leonard; and he says he looked so noble that to shake hands with him made him feel quite small.'

'I never heard anything so much to Tom's credit! Well, and what did he say of the dear lad?'

The next step was to mention Averil's letter to Mary, which could not be sent on till tidings had been permitted by Mr Cheviot.

'Let us see it,' said the doctor.

'Do you think Charles Cheviot would like it?'

'Cheviot is a man of sense,' said the open-hearted doctor, 'and there may be something to authorize preventing this unlucky transfer of her fortune.'

Nothing could be further from it; but it was a long and interesting letter, written in evidently exhilarated spirits, and with a hopeful description of the new scenes. Ethel read it to her father, and he told every one about it when they came in. Tom manifested no particular interest; but he did not go by the mail train that night, and was not visible all the morning. He caught Ethel alone however at noon, and said, 'Ethel, I owe you this,' offering the amount she had paid for the letter.

'Thank you,' she said, wondering if this was to be all she should hear about it.

'I am going by the afternoon train,' he added; 'I have been over to Blewer. It is true, Ethel, the fellow can't stand it; he has sent down a manager, and is always in London! Most likely to dispose of it by private contract there, they say.'

'And what has become of old Hardy?'

'Poor old fellow, he has struck work, looks terribly shaky. He took me for my father at first sight, and began to apologise most plaintively – said no one else had ever done him any good. I advised him to come in and see my father, though he is too far gone to do much for him.'

'Poor old man, can he afford to come in now?'

'Why, I helped him with the cart hire. It is no use any way, he knows no more than we do, and his case is confirmed; but he thinks he has offended my father, and he'll die more in peace for having had him again. Look here, what a place they have got to.'

And without further explanation of the 'they,' Tom placed a letter in Ethel's hands.

'My dear Mr Thomas,

'I send you the objects I promised for your microscope; I could not get any before because we were in the city; but if you like these I can get plenty more at Massissauga, where we are now. We came here last week, and the journey was very nice, only we went bump bump so often, and once we stuck in a marsh, and were splashed all over. We are staying with Mr Muller and Cora till our own house is quite ready; and it was only begun a fortnight ago, and we are to get in next week. I thought this would have been a town, it looked so big and so square in the plan; but it is all trees still, and there are only thirteen houses built yet. Ours is all by itself in River Street, and all the trees near it have been killed, and stand up all dead and white, because nobody has time to cut them down. It looks very dismal, but Ave says it will be very nice by-and-by, and Rufus Muller says it has mammoth privileges. I send you a bit of rattlesnake skin. They found fifteen of them asleep under a stone, just where our house is built, and sometimes they come into the kitchen. I do not know the names of the other things I send; and I could not ask Ave, for she said you would not want to be bothered with a little girl's letter, and I was not to ask for an answer. Rosa Willis says no young lady of my age would ask her sister's permission, and not even her mother's, unless her mamma was very intellectual and highly educated, and always saw the justice of her arguments; but Minna and I do not mean to be like that. I would tell Ave if you did write to me, but she need not read it unless she liked.

'I am, your affectionate little friend,

'ELLA'

'Well!' said Tom, holding out his hand for more when she had restored this epistle.

'You have heard all there was in it, except——'

'Except what I want to see.'

And Ethel, as she had more or less intended all along, let him have Averil's letter, since the exception was merely a few tender words of congratulation to Mary. The worst had been done already by her father; and it may here be mentioned that though nothing was said in answer to her explanation of the opening of the letter, the head-master never recovered the fact, and always attributed it to his dear sister Ethel.

'For the future,' said Tom, as he gave back the thin sheets, 'they will all be for the Cheviots' private delectation.'

'I shall begin on my own score,' said Ethel. 'You know if you answer this letter, you must not mention that visit of yours, or you will be prohibited, and one would not wish to excite a domestic secession.'

'It would serve the unnatural scoundrel right,' said Tom. 'Well, I must go and put up my things. You'll keep me up to what goes on at home, and if there's anything out there to tell Leonard——'

'Wait a moment, Tom!' – and she told him what the doctor had said about his plans.

'Highly educated and intellectual,' was all the answer that Tom vouchsafed; and whether he were touched or not she could not gather.

Yet her spirit felt less weary and burdened, and more full of hope than it had been for a long time past. Averil's letter showed the exhilaration of the change, and of increasing confidence and comfort in her friend Cora Muller. Cora's Confirmation had brought the girls into contact with the New York clergy, and had procured them an introduction to the clergyman of Winiamac, the nearest church, so that there was much less sense of loneliness; moreover, the fuller and more systematic doctrine, and the development of the beauty and daily guidance of the Church, had softened the bright American girl, so as to render her infinitely dearer to her English friend, and they were as much united as they could be, where the great leading event of the life of one remained a mystery to the other. Yet perhaps it helped to begin a fresh life, that the intimate companion of that new course should be entirely disconnected with the past.

Averil threw herself into the present with as resolute a will as she could muster. With much spirit she described the arrival at the Winiamac station, and the unconcealed contempt with which the mass of luggage was regarded by the Western world, who 'reckoned it would be fittest to make kindlings with.' Heavy country wagons were to bring the furniture; the party themselves were provided for by a light wagon and a large cart, driven by Cora's brother, Mordaunt, and by the farming-man, Philetus, a gentleman who took every occasion of asserting his equality, if not his superiority to the new comers; demanded all the Christian names, and used them without prefix; and when Henry impressively mentioned his eldest sister as Miss Warden, stared and said, 'Why, doctor, I thought she was not your old woman!' – the Western epithet of a wife. But as Cora was quite content to leave Miss behind her in civilized society, and as they were assured that to stand upon ceremony would leave them without domestic assistance, the sisters had implored Henry to waive all preference for a polite address.

The loveliness of the way was enchanting – the roads running straight as an arrow through glorious forest lands of pine, beech, maple, and oak, in the full glory of spring, and the perspective before and behind making a long narrowing green bower of meeting branches; the whole of the borders of the road covered with lovely flowers – May-wings, a butterfly-like milkwort, pitcher-plant, convolvulus; new insects danced in the shade – golden orioles, blue birds, the great American robin, the field officer, with his orange epaulettes, glanced before them. Cora was in ecstasy at the return to forest scenery, the Wards at its novelty, and the escape from town. Too happy were they at first to care for the shaking and bumping of the road, and the first mud-hole into which they plunged was almost a joke, under Mordaunt Muller's assurances that it was easy fording, though the splashes flew far and wide. Then there was what Philetus called 'a mash with a real handsome bridge over it,' *i.e.* a succession of tree trunks laid side by side for about a quarter of a mile. Here the female passengers insisted on walking – even Cora, though her brother and Philetus both laughed her to scorn; and more especially for her foot-gear, delicate kid boots, without which no city damsel stirred. Averil and her sisters, in the English boots scorned at New York, had their share in the laugh, while picking their way from log to log, hand in hand, and exciting Philetus's further disdain by their rapture with the glorious flowers of the bog.

But where was Massissauga? Several settlements had been passed, the houses looking clean and white in forest openings, with fields where the lovely spring green of young maize charmed the eye.

At last the road grew desolate. There were a few patches of corn, a few squalid-looking log or frame houses, a tract of horrible dreary blackness; and still more horrible, beyond it was a region of spectres – trees white and stripped bare, lifting their dead arms like things blasted. Averil cried out in indignant horror, 'Who has done this?'

'We have,' answered Mordaunt. 'This is Maclellan Square, Miss Warden, and there's River Street,' pointing down an avenue of skeletons. 'If you could go to sleep for a couple of years, you would wake up to find yourself in a city such as I would not fear to compare with any in Europe. Your exhausted civilization is not as energetic as ours, I calculate.'

The energetic young colonist turned his horse's head up a slight rising ground, where something rather more like habitation appeared; a great brick-built hotel, and some log houses, with windows displaying the wares needed for daily consumption, and a few farm buildings. It was backed by cornfields; and this was the great Maclellan Street, the chief ornament of Massissauga. Not one house had the semblance of a garden; the wilderness came up to the very door, except where cattle rendered some sort of enclosure necessary.

Cora exclaimed, 'Oh Mordaunt, I thought you would have had a garden for me!'

'I can fix it any time you like,' said he; 'but you'll be the laughing-stock of the place, and never keep a flower.'

The Mullers' abode was a sound substantial log house, neatly whitened, and with green shutters, bearing a festal appearance, full of welcome, as Mr Muller, his tall bearded son Rufus, and a thin but motherly-looking elderly woman, came forth to meet the travellers; and in the front, full stare, stood a trollopy-looking girl, every bar of her enormous hoop plainly visible through her washed-out flimsy muslin. This was Miss Ianthe, who condescended to favour the family with her assistance till she should have made up dollars enough to buy a new dress! The elder woman, who went by the name of Cousin Deborah, would have been a housekeeper in England – here she was one of the family – welcomed Cora with an exchange of kisses, and received the strangers with very substantial hospitality, though with pity at their unfitness for their new home, and utter incredulity as to their success.

Here the Wards had been since their arrival. Their frame-house, near the verdant bank of the river, was being finished for them; and a great brass plate, with Henry's new name and his profession, had already adorned the door. The furniture was coming; Cousin Deborah had hunted up a Cleopatra Betsy, who might perhaps stay with them if she were treated on terms of equality; a field was to be brought into cultivation as soon as any labour could be had. Minna was looking infinitely better already, and Averil and Cora were full of designs for rival housewifery; Averil taking lessons meantime in ironing, dusting, and the arts of the kitchen, and trusting that in the two years' time, the skeletons would have given place – if not indeed to houses, to well-kept fields.

Such was her account.

How much was reserved for fear of causing anxiety? Who could guess?

CHAPTER XXI

'Quanto si fende
La rocca per dar via a chi va suso
N'andai 'nfino ove'l cerchiar sì prende
Com'io nel quinto giro fui dischiuso
Vidi gente per esso che piangea
Giacendo a terra tutta volta in giuso
Adhoesit pavimento anima mia
Sentia dir loro con sì alti sospiri
Che la parola appena s'intendea.
"O eletti di Deo, i cui soffriri
E giustizia e speranza fan men duri——"'

'Purgatorio'. *Dante.*

'Ah, sir, we have learnt the way to get your company,' said Hector Ernescliffe, as he welcomed his father-in-law at Maplewood; 'we have only to get under sentence.'

'Sick or sorry, Hector; that's the attraction to an old doctor.'

'And,' added Hector, with the importance of his youthful magisterial dignity, 'I hope I have arranged matters for you to see him. I wrote about it; but I am afraid you will not be able to see him alone.'

Great was the satisfaction with which Hector took the conduct of the expedition to Portland Island; though he was inclined to encumber it with more lionizing than the good doctor's full heart was ready for. Few words could he obtain, as in the bright August sunshine they steamed out from the pier at Weymouth, and beheld the grey sides of the island, scarred with stone quarries, stretching its lengthening breakwater out on one side, and on the other connected with the land by the pale dim outline of the Chisell Bank. The water was dancing in golden light; white sailed or red sailed craft plied across it; a ship of the line lay under the lee of the island, practising gunnery, the three bounds of her balls marked by white columns of spray each time of touching the water; pleasure parties crowded the steamer; but to Dr May the cheerfulness of the scene made a depressing contrast to the purpose of his visit, as he fixed his eyes on the squared outline of the crest of the island, and the precipitous slope from thence to the breakwater, where trains of loaded trucks rushed forth to the end, discharged themselves, and hurried back.

Landing at the quay, in the midst of confusion, Hector smiled at the doctor's innocent proposal of walking, and bestowed him in a little carriage, with a horse whose hardworked patience was soon called out, as up and up they went, through the narrow, but lively street, past the old-fashioned inn, made memorable by a dinner of George III; past the fossil tree, clamped against a house like a vine; past heaps of slabs ready for transport; a church perched up high on the slope, and a parsonage in a place that looked only accessible to goats. Lines of fortification began to reveal themselves, and the doctor thought himself arrived; but he was to wind further on, and be more struck with the dreariness and inhospitality of the rugged rock, almost bare of vegetation; the very trees of stone, and older than our creation; the melancholy late ripening harvest within stone walls, the whole surface furrowed by stern rents and crevices riven by nature, or cut into greater harshness by the quarries hewn by man. The grave strangeness of the region almost marked it out for a place of expiation, like the mountain rising desolate from the sea, where Dante placed his prisoners of hope.

The walls of a vast enclosure became visible; and over them might be seen the tops of great cranes, looking like the denuded ribs of umbrellas. Buildings rose beyond, with deep arched gateways; and a small town was to be seen further off. Mr Ernescliffe sent in his card at the governor's house, and found that the facilities he had asked for had been granted. They were told that the prisoner they wished to see was at work at some distance; and while he was summoned, they were to see the buildings. Dr May had little heart for making a sight of them, except so far as to judge of Leonard's situation; and he was passively conducted across a gravelled court, turfed in the centre, and containing a few flower-beds, fenced in by Portland's most natural productions, zamias and ammonites, together with a few stone coffins, which had once inclosed corpses of soldiers of the Roman garrison. Large piles of building inclosed the quadrangle; and passing into the first of these, the doctor began to realize something of Leonard's present existence. There lay before him the broad airy passage, and either side the empty cells of this strange hive, as closely packed, and as chary of space, as the compartments of the workers of the honeycomb.

'Just twice as wide as a coffin,' said Hector, doing the honours of one, where there was exactly width to stand up between the bed and the wall of corrugated iron; 'though, happily, there is more liberality of height.'

There was a ground glass window opposite to the door, and a shelf, holding a Bible, Prayer and hymn book, and two others, one religious, and one secular, from the library. A rust-coloured jacket, with a black patch marked with white numbers, and a tarpaulin hat, crossed with two lines of red paint on the crown, hung on the wall. The doctor asked for Leonard's cell, but it was in a distant gallery; and he was told that when he had seen one, he had seen all. He asked if these were like those that Leonard had previously inhabited at Milbank and Pentonville; and hearing that they were on the same model, he almost gasped at the thought of the young enterprising spirit thus caged for nine weary months, and to whom this bare confined space was still the only resting-place. He *could* not look by any means delighted with the excellence of the arrangements, grant it though he might; and he was hurried on to the vast kitchens, their ranges of coppers full of savoury steaming contents, and their racks of loaves looking all that was substantial and wholesome; but his eyes were wandering after the figures engaged in cooking, to whom he was told such work was a reward; he was trying to judge how far they could still enjoy life; but he turned from their stolid low stamp of face with a sigh, thinking how little their condition could tell him of that of a cultivated nature.

He was shown the chapel, unfortunately serving likewise for a schoolroom; the centre space fitted for the officials and their families, the rest with plain wooden benches. But it was not an hour for schooling; and he went restlessly on to the library, to gather all the consolation he could from seeing that the privation did not extend to that of sound and interesting literature. He had yet to see the court, where the prisoners were mustered at half-past five in the morning, thence to be marched off in their various companies to work. He stood on the terrace from which the officials marshalled them, and he was called on to look at the wide and magnificent view of sea and land; but all he would observe to Hector was, 'That boy's throat has always been tender since the fever.' He was next conducted to the great court, the quarry of the stones of the present St Paul's, and where the depression of the surface since work began there, was marked by the present height of what had become a steep conical edifice, surmounted by a sort of watch-tower. There he grew quite restive, and hearing a proposal of taking him to the Verne Hill works half a mile off, he declared that Hector was welcome to go; he should wait for his boy.

Just then the guide pointed out at some distance a convict approaching under charge of a warder; and in a few seconds more, the doctor had stepped back to a small room, where, by special favour, he was allowed to be with the prisoner, instead of seeing him through a grating, but only in the presence of a warder, who was within hearing, though not obtrusively so. Looking, to recognise, not to examine, he drew the young man into his fatherly embrace.

'You have hurt your hands,' was his first word, at the touch of the bruised fingers and broken skin.

'They are getting hardened,' was the answer, in an alert tone, that gave the doctor courage to look up and meet an unquenched glance; though there was the hollow look round the eyes that Tom had noticed, the face had grown older, the expression more concentrated; the shoulders had rounded; the coarse blue shirt and heavy boots were dusty with the morning's toil, and the heat and labour of the day had left their tokens; but the brow was as open, the mouth as ingenuous as ever, the complexion had regained a hue of health, and the air of alacrity and exhilaration surprised as much as it gratified the visitor.

'What is your work?' he asked.

'Filling barrows with stones, and wheeling them to the trucks for the breakwater,' answered Leonard, in a tone like satisfaction. 'But pray, if you are so kind, tell me,' he continued, with anxiety that he could not suppress, 'what is this about war in America?'

'Not near Indiana; no fear of that, I trust. But how did you know, Leonard?'

'I saw, for one moment at a time, in great letters on a placard of the contents of newspapers, at the stations as we came down here, the words, "Civil War in America;" and it has seemed to be in the air here ever since. But Averil has said nothing in her letters. Will it affect them?'

The doctor gave a brief sketch of what was passing, up to the Battle of Bull Run; and his words were listened to with such exceeding avidity, that he was obliged to spend more minutes than he desired on the chances of the war, and the Massissauga tidings, which he wished to make sound more favourable than he could in conscience feel that they were; but when at last he had detailed all he knew from Averil's letters, and it had been drunk in with glistening eyes, and manner growing constantly less constrained, he led back to Leonard himself: 'Ethel will write at once to your sister when I get home; and I think I may tell her the work agrees with you.'

'Yes; and this is man's work; and it is for the defences,' he added, with a sparkle of the eye.

'Very hard and rough,' returned the doctor, looking again at the wounded hands and hard-worked air.

'Oh, but to put out one's strength again, and have room!' cried the boy, eagerly.

'Was it not rather a trying change at first?'

'To be sure I *was* stiff, and didn't know how to move in the morning, but that went off fast enough; and I fill as many barrows a day as any one in our gang.'

'Then I may tell your sister you rejoice in the change?'

'Why, it's work one does not get deadly sick of, as if there was no making one's self do it,' said Leonard eagerly; 'it *is* work! and besides, here is sunshine and sea. I can get a sight of that every day; and now and then I can get a look into the bay, and Weymouth – looking like the old time.' That was his first sorrowful intonation; but the next had the freshness of his age, 'And there are thistles!'

'Thistles?'

'I thought you cared for thistles; for Miss May showed me one at Coombe; but it was not like what they are here – the spikes pointing out and pointing in along the edges of the leaves, and the scales lapping over so wonderfully in the bud.'

'Picciola!' said the doctor to himself; and aloud, 'Then you have time to enjoy them?'

'When we are at work at a distance, dinner is brought out, and there is an hour and a half of rest; and on Sunday we may walk about the yards. You should have seen one of our gang, when I got him to look at the chevaux de frise round a bud, how he owned it was a regular patent invention; it just answered to Paley's illustration.'

'What, the watch?' said the doctor, seeing that the argument had been far from trite to his young friend. 'So you read Paley?'

'I read all such books as I could get up there,' he answered; 'they gave one something to think about.'

'Have you no time for reading here?'

'Oh, no! I am too sleepy to read except on school days and Sundays,' he said, as if this were a great achievement.

'And your acquaintance – is he a reader of Paley too?'

'I believe the chaplain set him on it. He is a clerk, like me, and not much older. He is a regular Londoner, and can hardly stand the work; but he won't give in if he can help it, or we might not be together.'

Much the doctor longed to ask what sort of a friend this might be, but the warder's presence forbade him; and he could only ask what they saw of each other.

'We were near one another in school at Pentonville, and knew each other's faces quite well, so that we were right glad to be put into the same gang. We may walk about the yard together on Sunday evening too.'

The doctor had other questions on his lips that he again restrained, and only asked whether the Sundays were comfortable days.

'Oh, yes,' said Leonard, eagerly; but then he too recollected the official, and merely said something common-place about excellent sermons, adding, 'And the singing is admirable. Poor Averil would envy such a choir as we have! We sing so many of the old Bankside hymns.'

'To make your resemblance to Dante's hill of penitence complete, as Ethel says,' returned the doctor.

'I should like it to be a hill of purification!' said Leonard, understanding him better than he had expected.

'It will, I think,' said the doctor, 'to one at least. I am comforted to see you so brave. I longed to come sooner, but——'

'I am glad you did not.'

'How!' But he did not pursue the question, catching from look and gesture, that Leonard could hardly have then met him with self-possession; and as the first bulletin of recovery is often the first disclosure of the severity of an illness, so the doctor was more impressed by the prisoner's evident satisfaction in his change of circumstances, than he would have been by mere patient resignation; and he let the conversation be led away to Aubrey's prospects, in which Leonard took full and eager interest.

'Tell Aubrey I am working at fortifications too,' he said, smiling.

'He could not go to Cambridge without you.'

'I don't like to believe that,' said Leonard, gravely; 'it is carrying the damage I have done further: but it can't be. He always was fond of mathematics, and of soldiering. How is it at the old Mill?' he added, suddenly.

'It is sold.'

'Sold?' and his eyes were intently fixed on the doctor.

'Yes, *he* is said to have been much in debt long before; but it was managed quietly – not advertised in the county papers. He went to London, and arranged it all. I saw great renovations going on at the Mill, when I went to see old Hardy.'

'Good old Hardy! how is he?'

'Much broken. He never got over the shock; and as long as that fellow stayed at the Mill, he would not let me attend him.'

'Ha!' exclaimed Leonard, but caught himself up.

A message came that Mr Ernescliffe feared to miss the boat; and the doctor could only give one tender grasp and murmured blessing, and hurry away, so much agitated that he could hardly join in Hector's civilities to the officials, and all the evening seemed quite struck down and overwhelmed by the sight of the bright brave boy, and his patience in his dreary lot.

After this, at all the three months' intervals at which Leonard might be seen, a visit was contrived to him, either by Dr May or Mr Wilmot; and Aubrey devoted his first leave of absence to staying at Maplewood, that Hector might take him to his friend; but he came home expatiating so much on the red hair of the infant hope of Maplewood, and the fuss that Blanche made about this new possession, that Ethel detected an unavowed shade of disappointment. Light and whitewash, abundant fare, garments sufficient, but eminently unbecoming, were less impressive than dungeons, rags, and bread and water; when, moreover, the prisoner claimed no pity, but rather congratulation on his badge of merit, improved Sunday dinner, and promotion to the carpenter's shop, so as absolutely to excite a sense of wasted commiseration and uninteresting prosperity. Conversation constrained both by the grating and the presence of the warder, and Aubrey, more tenderly sensitive than his brother, and devoid of his father's experienced tact, was too much embarrassed to take the initiative, was afraid of giving pain by dwelling on his present occupations and future hopes, and confused Leonard by his embarrassment. Hector Ernescliffe discoursed about Charleston Harbour and New Orleans; and Aubrey stood with downcast eyes, afraid to seem to be scanning the convict garb, and thus rendering Leonard unusually conscious of wearing it. Then when in parting, Aubrey, a little less embarrassed, began eagerly and in much emotion to beg Leonard to say if there was anything he could get for him, anything he could do for him, anything he would like to have sent him, and began to promise a photograph of his father, Leonard checked him, by answering that it would be an irregularity – nothing of personal property was allowed to be retained by a prisoner.

Aubrey forgot all but the hardship, and began an outburst about the tyranny.

'It is quite right,' said Leonard, gravely; 'there is nothing that might not be used for mischief if one chose.'

And the warder here interfered, and said he was quite right, and it always turned out best in the end for a prisoner to conform himself, and his friends did him no good by any other attempt, as Mr Ernescliffe could tell the young gentleman. The man's tone, though neither insolent nor tyrannical, but rather commendatory of his charge, contrasting with his natural deference to the two gentlemen, irritated poor Aubrey beyond measure, so that Hector was really glad to have him safe away, without his having said anything treasonable to the authorities. The meeting, so constrained and uncomfortable, had but made the friends more vividly conscious of the interval between the cadet and the convict, and, moreover, tended to remove the aureole of romance with which the unseen captive had been invested by youthful fancy.

To make the best of a prolonged misfortune does absolutely lessen sympathy, by diminishing the interest of the situation; and even the good doctor himself was the less concerned at any hindrance to his visits to Portland, as he uniformly found his prisoner cheerful, approved by officials, and always making some small advance in the scale of his own world, and not, as his friends without expected of him, showing that he felt himself injured instead of elated by such rewards as improved diet, or increased gratuities to be set to his account against the time when, after eight years, he might hope for exportation with a ticket of leave to Western Australia.

The halo of approaching death no longer lighted him up; and after the effusion of the first meeting, his inner self had closed up, he was more ready to talk of American news than of his own feelings, and seemed to look little beyond the petty encouragements devised to suit the animal natures of ordinary prisoners; and his visitors sometimes feared lest his character were not resisting the deadening, hardening influence of the unvaried round of manual labour among such associates. He had been soon advanced from the quarry to the carpenter's shop, and was in favour there from his activity and skill; but his very promotions were sad – and it was more sad, as some thought, for him to be gratified by them. But, as Dr May always ended, what did they know about him?

CHAPTER XXII

'Oh, Bessie Bell and Mary Gray,
They were twa bonnie lasses;
They bigged a bower on yon burn side,
And theekt it ower wi' rashes.'

The early glory of autumn was painting the woods of Indiana – crimson, orange, purple, as though a rainbow of intensified tints had been broken into fragments, and then scattered broadcast upon the forest. But though ripe nuts hung on many a bough, the gipsyings had not yet taken place, except at home – when Minna, in her desperate attempts at making the best of things, observed, 'Now we have to make the fire ourselves, let us think it is all play, and such fun.'

But 'such fun' was hard when one or other of the inmates of the house was lying on the bed shaking with ague, and the others creeping wearily about, even on their intermediate days. They had been deluded into imprudent exposure in the lovely evenings of summer, and had never shaken off the results.

'Come, Ella,' said Minna one afternoon, as she descended the bare rickety stairs; 'Ave is getting better; and if we can get the fire up, and make some coffee and boil some eggs, it will be comfortable for her when she comes down and Henry comes in.'

Ella, with a book in her hand, was curled up in a corner of a sofa standing awry among various other articles of furniture that seemed to have tumbled together by chance within the barn-like room. Minna began moving first one and then the other, daintily wiping off the dust, and restoring an air of comfort.

'Oh dear!' said Ella, unfolding herself; 'I am so tired. Where's Hetta Mary!'

'Oh, don't you know, Hetta Mary went home this morning because Henry asked her where his boots were, and she thought he wanted her to clean them.'

'Can't Mrs Shillabeer come in?'

'Mrs Shillabeer said she would never come in again, because Averil asked her not to hold the ham by the bone and cut it with her own knife when Henry was there! Come, Ella, it is of no use. We had better do things ourselves, like Cora and Ave, and then we shall not hear people say disagreeable things.'

The once soft, round, kitten-like Minna, whom Leonard used to roll about on the floor, had become a lank, sallow girl, much too tall for her ten years, and with a care-stricken, thoughtful expression on her face, even more in advance of her age than was her height. She moved into the kitchen, a room with an iron stove, a rough table, and a few shelves, looking very desolate. The hands of both little girls had become expert in filling the stove with wood, and they had not far to seek before both it and the hearth in the sitting-room were replenished, and the flame beginning to glow.

'Where's the coffee-mill?' said Minna, presently looking round in blank despair.

'Oh dear!' said Ella, 'I remember now; that dirty little Polly Mason came to borrow it this morning. I said we wanted it every day: but she guessed we could do without it, for they had got a tea-party, and her little brother had put in a stone and spoilt Cora Muller's; and she snatched it up and carried it off.'

'He will serve ours the same, I suppose,' said Minna. 'It is too far off to go for it; let us make some tea.'

'There's no tea,' said Ella; 'a week ago or more that great Irene Brown walked in and reckoned we could lend her 'ma some tea and sugar, 'cause we had plenty. And we have used up our own since; and if we did ask her to return the loan, hers is such nasty stuff that nobody could drink it. What shall we do, Minna?' and she began to cry.

'We must take some coffee up to the hotel,' said Minna, after a moment's reflection; 'Black Joe is very good-natured, and he'll grind it.'

'But I don't like to go all by myself,' said Ella; 'into the kitchen too, and hear them say things about Britishers.'

'I'll go, dear,' said Minna, gently, 'if you will just keep the fire up, and boil the eggs, and make the toast, and listen if Ave calls.'

Poor Minna, her sensitive little heart trembled within her at the rough contemptuous words that the exclusive, refined tone of the family always provoked, and bodily languor and weariness made the walk trying; but she was thinking of Ave's need, and resolutely took down her cloak and hat. But at that moment the latch was raised, and the bright graceful figure of Cora stood among them, her feathered hat and delicate muslin looking as fresh as at New York.

'What, all alone!' she said; 'I know it is poor Ave's sick day. Is she better?'

'Yes, going to get up and come down; but——' and all the troubles were poured out.

'True enough, the little wretch did spoil our mill, but Rufus mended it; and as I thought Polly had been marauding on you, I brought some down.'

'Ah! I thought I smelt it most deliciously as you came in, but I was afraid I only fancied it because I was thinking about it. Dear Cora, how good you are!'

'And have you anything for her to eat?'

'I was going to make some toast.'

'Of that dry stuff! Come, we'll manage something better:' and off came the dainty embroidered cambric sleeves, up went the coloured ones, a white apron came out of a pocket, and the pretty hands were busy among the flour; the children assisting, learning, laughing a childlike laugh.

'Ave!' cried Cora, turning round, and making a comic threatening gesture with her floury fingers; 'you ought not to have come till we were fixed. Go and sit in your chair by the fire.'

'Dear Cora!'

But Cora ran at her; and the wan trembling creature put on smile, and was very glad to comply; being totally unequal to resist or even to stand long enough to own her dread of Henry's finding all desolate and nothing to eat.

Presently Cora tripped in, all besleeved and smartened, to set cushions behind the tired back and head, and caress the long thin fingers. 'I've left Minna, like King Alfred, to watch the cakes,' she said; 'and Ella is getting the cups. So your fifth girl is gone.'

'The fifth in five months! And we let her sit at table, and poor dear Minna has almost worn out her life in trying to hinder her from getting affronted.'

'I've thought what to do for you, Ave. There's the Irish woman, Katty Blake – her husband has been killed. She is rough enough, but tender in her way; and she must do something for herself and her child.'

'Her husband killed!'

'Yes, at Summerville. I thought you had heard it. Mordaunt wrote to me to tell her; and I shall never forget her wailing at his dying away from his country. It was not lamentation for herself, but that he should have died far away from his own people.'

'She is not long from the old country; I should like to have her if – if we can afford it. For if the dividends don't come soon from that building company, Cora, I don't know where to turn——'

'Oh, they must come. Father has been writing to Rufus about the arrangements. Besides, those Irish expect less, and understand old country manners better, if you can put up with their breakages.'

'I could put up with anything to please Henry, and save Minna's little hard-worked bones.'

'I will send her to-morrow. Is it not Minna's day of ague?'

'Yes, poor dear. That is always the day we get into trouble.'

'I never saw a child with such an instinct for preventing variance, or so full of tact and pretty ways; yet I have seen her tremble under her coaxing smile, that even Mis' Shillabeer can't resist.'

'See, see!' cried Ella, hurrying in, 'surely our contingent is not coming home!'

'No,' said Cora, hastening to the door, 'these must be a reinforcement marching to take the train at Winiamac.'

'Marching?' said Ella, looking up archly at her. 'We didn't let our volunteers march in that way.'

They were sturdy bearded backwoodsmen, rifle on shoulder, and with grave earnest faces; but walking rather than marching, irregularly keeping together, or straggling, as they chose.

'Your volunteers!' cried Cora, her eyes flashing; 'theirs was toy work! These are bound for real patriotic war!' and she clasped her hands together, then waved her handkerchief.

'It is sad,' said Averil, who had moved to the window, 'to see so many elderly faces – men who must be the prop of their families.'

'It is because ours is a fight of men, not of children; not one of your European wars of paltry ambition, but a war of principle!' cried Cora, with that intensity of enthusiasm that has shed so much blood in the break-up of the Great Republic.

'They do look as Cromwell's Ironsides may have done,' said Averil; 'as full of stern purpose.'

And verily Averil noted the difference. Had a number of European soldiers been passing so near in an equally undisciplined manner, young women could not have stood forth as Cora was doing, unprotected, yet perfectly safe from rudeness or remark; making ready answer to the inquiry for the nearest inn – nay, only wishing she were in her own house, to evince her patriotism by setting refreshment before the defenders of her cause. Her ardour had dragged Averil up with her a little way, so as to feel personally every vicissitude that befell the North, and to be utterly unaware of any argument in favour of the Confederates; but still Averil was, in Cora's words, 'too English;' she could not, for the life of her, feel as she did when equipping her brother against possible French invasions; and when Mordaunt Muller had been enrolled in the Federal army, she had almost offended the exultant sister by condolence instead of congratulation.

Five months had elapsed since the arrival of Averil in Massissauga – months of anxiety and disappointment, which had sickened Henry of plans of farming, and lessened his hopes of practice. The same causes that affected him at New York told in Indiana; and even if he had been employed, the fees would have been too small to support the expense of horses. As to farming, labour was scarce, and could only be obtained at the cost of a considerable outlay, and, moreover, of enduring rude self-assertions that were more intolerable to Henry than even to his sisters. The chief hope of the family lay in the speculation in which Averil's means had been embarked, which gave them a right to their present domicile, and to a part of the uncleared waste around them; and would, when Massissauga should begin to flourish, place them in affluence. The interest of the portions of the two younger girls was all that was secure, since these were fortunately still invested at home. Inhabitants did not come, lots of land were not taken; and the Mullers evidently profited more by the magnificent harvest produced by their land than by the adventure of city founding. Still, plenty and comfort reigned in their house, and Cora had imported a good deal of refinement and elegance, which she could make respected where Averil's attempts were only sneered down. Nor had sickness tried her household. Owing partly to situation – considerably above the level of River Street – partly to the freer, more cleared and cultivated surroundings – partly likewise to experience, and Cousin Deborah's motherly watchfulness – the summer had passed without a visitation of ague, though it seemed to be regarded as an adjunct of spring, as inevitable as winter frost. Averil trembled at the thought, but there was no escape; there were absolutely no means of leaving the spot, or of finding maintenance elsewhere. Indeed, Cora's constant kindness and sympathy were too precious to be parted with, even had it been possible to move. And the boarding-house, Massissauga was a kind of home; and the more spirits and energy failed, the more she clung to it.

Mr Muller had lately left home to arrange for the sale of his corn, and had announced that he might perhaps pay a visit to his son Mordaunt in the camp at Lexington. Cora was expecting a letter from him, and the hope that 'Dr Warden' might bring one from the post-office at Winiamac had been one cause of her visit on this afternoon; for the mammoth privileges of Massissauga did not include a post-office, nor the sight of letters more than once a week.

The table had just been covered with preparations for a meal, and the glow of the fire was beginning to brighten the twilight, when the sound of a horse's feet came near, and Henry rode past the window, but did not appear for a considerable space, having of late been reduced to become his own groom. But even in the noise of the hoofs, even in the wave of the hand, the girls had detected gratified excitement.

'Charleston has surrendered! The rebels have submitted!' cried Cora.

And Averil's heart throbbed with its one desperate hope. No! *That* would have brought him in at once.

After all, both were in a state to feel it a little flat when he came in presenting a letter to Miss Muller, and announcing, 'I have had a proposal, ladies; what would you say to seeing me a surgeon to the Federal forces? – Do you bid me go, Miss Muller?'

'I bid every one go who can be useful to my country,' said Cora.

'Don't look alarmed, Averil,' said Henry, affectionately, as he met her startled eyes; 'there is no danger. A surgeon need never expose himself.'

'But how – what has made you think of it?' asked Averil, faintly.

'A letter from Mr Muller – a very kind letter. He tells me that medical men are much wanted, and that an examination by a Board is all that is required, the remuneration is good, and it will be an introduction that will avail me after the termination of the war, which will end with the winter, at latest.'

'And father has accepted an office in the commissariat department!' exclaimed Cora, from her letter.

'Yes,' answered Henry; 'he tells me that, pending more progression here, it is wiser for us both to launch into the current of public events, and be floated upwards by the stream.'

'Does he want you to come to him, Cora?' was all that Averil contrived to say.

'Oh no, he will be in constant locomotion,' said Cora. 'I shall stay to keep house for Rufus. And here are some directions for him that I must carry home. Don't come, Dr Warden; I shall never cure you of thinking we cannot stir without an escort. You will want to put a little public spirit into this dear Ave. That's her one defect: and when you are one of us, she will be forced to give us her heart.'

And away ran the bright girl, giving her caresses to each sister as she went.

The little ones broke out, 'Oh Henry, Henry, you must not go away to the wars!' and Averil's pleading eyes spoke the same.

Then Henry sat down and betook himself to argument. It would be folly to lose the first opening to employment that had presented itself. He grieved indeed to leave his sisters in this desolate, unhealthy place; but they were as essentially safe as at Stoneborough; their living alone for a few weeks, or at most months, would be far less remarkable here than there; and he would be likely to be able to improve or to alter their present situation, whereas they were now sinking deeper and more hopelessly into poverty every day. Then, too, he read aloud piteous accounts of the want of medical attendance, showing that it was absolutely a cruelty to detain such assistance from the sick and wounded. This argument was the one most appreciated by Averil and Minna. The rest were but questions of prudence; this touched their hearts. Men lying in close tents, or in crowded holds of ships, with festering wounds and fevered lips, without a hand to help them – some, too, whom they had seen at New York, and whose exulting departure they had witnessed – sufferers among whom their own Cora's favourite brother might at any moment be numbered – the thought brought a glow of indignation against themselves for having wished to withhold him.

'Yes, go, Henry; it is right, and you shall hear not another word of objection,' said Averil.

'You can write or telegraph the instant you want me. And it will be for a short time,' said Henry, half repenting when the opposition had given way.

'Oh, we shall get on very well,' said Minna, cheerfully; 'better, perhaps, for you know we don't mind far-West manners; and I'll have learnt to do all sorts of things as well as Cora when you come home!'

And Henry, after a year's famine of practice, was in better spirits than since that fatal summer morning. Averil felt how different a man is in his vocation, and deprived of it.

'Oh yes,' she said to herself, 'if I had let ourselves be a drag on him when he is so much needed, I could never have had the face to write to our dear sufferer at home in his noble patience. It is better that we should be desolate than that he should be a wreck, or than that mass of sickness should be left untended! And the more desolate, the more sure of One Protector.'

There was true heroism in the spirit in which this young girl braced herself to uncomplaining acceptance of desertion in this unwholesome swamp, with her two little ailing sisters, beside the sluggish stream, amid the skeleton trees – heroism the greater because there was no enthusiastic patriotism to uphold her – it was only the land of her captivity, whence she looked towards home like Judah to Jerusalem.

CHAPTER XXIII

'Prisoner of hope thou art; look up and sing,
In hope of promised spring.'

Christian Year.

In the summer of 1862, Tom May was to go up for his examination at the College of Physicians; but only a day or two before it he made his appearance at home, in as much excitement as it was in him to betray. Hazlitt, the banker's clerk, at Whitford, had written to him tidings of the presentation of the missing cheque for £25, which Bilson had paid to old Axworthy shortly before the murder, and which Leonard had mentioned as in the pocket-book containing his receipt for the sum that had been found upon him. Tom had made a halt at Whitford, and seen the cheque, which had been backed by the word Axworthy, with an initial that, like all such signatures of the nephew, might stand either for S. or F., and the stiff office hand of both the elder and younger Axworthy was so much alike, that no one could feel certain whose writing it was. The long concealment, after the prisoner's pointed reference to it, was, however, so remarkable, that the home conclave regarded the cause as won; and the father and son hastened triumphantly to the attorneys' office.

Messrs Bramshaw and Anderson were greatly struck, and owned that their own minds were satisfied as to the truth of their client's assertion; but they demurred as to the possibility of further steps. An action for forgery, Tom's first hope, he saw to be clearly impossible; Samuel Axworthy appeared to have signed the cheque in his own name, and he had every right to it as his uncle's heir; and though the long withholding of it, as well as his own departure, were both suspicious circumstances, they were not evidence. Where was there any certainty that the cheque had ever been in the pocket-book? or even if it had, how did it prove the existence of young Ward's acknowledgment? Might it not have been in some receptacle of papers hitherto not opened? There was no sufficient case to carry to the police, after a conviction like Leonard's, to set them on tracing the cheque either to an unknown robber, or to Sam Axworthy, its rightful owner.

Mr Bramshaw likewise dissuaded Dr May from laying the case before the Secretary of State, as importunity without due grounds would only tell against him if any really important discovery should be made: and the Doctor walked away, with blood boiling at people's coolness to other folk's tribulations, and greatly annoyed with Tom for having acceded to the representations of the men of law, and declining all co-operation in drawing up a representation for the Home Office, on the plea that he had no time to lose in preparing for his own examination, and must return to town by the next train, which he did without a syllable of real converse with any one at home.

The Doctor set to work with his home helpers, assisted by Dr Spencer; but the work of composition seemed to make the ground give way under their feet, and a few adroit remarks from Dr Spencer finally showed him and Ethel that they had not yet attained the prop for the lever that was to move the world. He gave it up; but still he did not quite forgive Tom for having been so easily convinced, and ready to be dismissed to his own affairs.

However, Dr May was gratified by the great credit with which his son passed his examination, and took his degree; and Sir Matthew Fleet himself wrote in high terms of his talent, diligence, and steadiness, volunteering hopes of being able to put him forward in town in his own line, for which Tom had always had a preference; and adding, that it was in concurrence with his own recommendation that the young man wished to pursue his studies at Paris – he had given him introductions that would enable him to do so to the greatest advantage, and he hoped his father would consent. The letter was followed up by one from Tom himself, as usual too reasonable and authoritative to be gainsaid, with the same representation of advantages to be derived from a course of the Parisian hospitals.

'Ah, well! he is after old Fleet's own heart,' said Dr May, between pride and mortification. 'I should not grudge poor Fleet some one to take interest in his old age, and I did not look to see him so warm about anything. He has not forgotten Calton Hill! But the boy must have done very well! I say, shall we see him Sir Thomas some of these days, Ethel, and laugh at ourselves for having wanted to make him go round in a mill after our old fashion?'

'You were contented to run round in your mill,' said Ethel, fondly, 'and maybe he will too.'

'No, no, Ethel, I'll not have him persuaded. Easy going folk, too lazy for ambition, have no right to prescribe for others. Ambition turned sour is a very dangerous dose! Much better let it fly off! I mean to look out of my mill yet, and see Sir Thomas win the stakes. Only I wish he would come and see us; tell him he shall not hear a word to bother him about the old practice. People *have* lived and died at Stoneborough without a May to help them, and so they will again, I suppose.'

Ethel was very glad to see how her father had made up his mind to what was perhaps the most real disappointment of his life, but she was grieved that Tom did not respond to the invitation, and next wrote from Paris. It was one of his hurried notes, great contrasts to such elaborate performances as his recent letter. 'Thanks, many thanks to my father,' he said; 'I knew you would make him see reason, and he always yields generously. I was too much hurried to come home; could not afford to miss the trail. I had not time to say before that the Bank that sent the cheque to Whitford had it from a lodging-house in town. Landlord had a writ served on S.A.; as he was embarking at Folkestone, he took out the draft and paid. He knew its import, if Bramshaw did not. I hope my father was not vexed at my not staying. There are things I cannot stand, namely, discussions and Gertrude.'

Gertrude was one of the chief cares upon Ethel's mind. She spent many thoughts upon the child, and even talked her over with Flora.

'What is it, Flora? is it my bad management? She is a good girl, and a dear girl; but there is such a want of softness about her.'

'There is a want of softness about all the young ladies of the day,' returned Flora.

'I have heard you say so, but——'

'We have made girls sensible and clear-headed, till they have grown hard. They have been taught to despise little fears and illusions, and it is certainly not becoming.'

'We had not fears, we were taught to be sensible.'

'Yes, but it is in the influence of the time! It all tends to make girls independent.'

'That's very well for the fine folks you meet in your visits, but it does not account for my Daisy – always at home, under papa's eye – having turned nineteenth century – What is it, Flora? She is reverent in great things, but not respectful except to papa, and *that* would not have been respect in one of us – only he likes her sauciness.'

'That is it, partly.'

'No, I won't have that said,' exclaimed Ethel. 'Papa is the only softening influence in the house – the only one that is tender. You see it is unlucky that Gertrude has so few that she really does love, with anything either reverend or softening about them. She is always at war with Charles Cheviot, and he has not fun enough, is too lumbering altogether, to understand her, or set her down in the right way; and she domineers over Hector like the rest of us. I did hope the babies might have found out her heart, but, unluckily, she does not take to them. She is only bored by the fuss that Mary and Blanche make about them.'

'You know we are all jealous of both Charles Cheviots, elder and younger.'

'I often question whether I should not have taken her down and made her ashamed of all the quizzing and teazing at the time of Mary's marriage. But one cannot be always spoiling bright merry mischief, and I am only elder sister after all. It is a wonder she is as good to me as she is.'

'She never remembered our mother, poor dear.'

'Ah! that is the real mischief,' said Ethel. 'Mamma would have given the atmosphere of gentleness and discretion, and so would Margaret. How often I have been made, by the merest pained look, to know when what I said was saucy or in bad taste, and I – I can only look forbidding, or else blurt out a reproof that *will* not come softly.'

'The youngest *must* be spoilt,' said Flora, 'that's an ordinance of nature. It ends when a boy goes to school, and when a girl——'

'When?'

'When she marries – or when she finds out what trouble is,' said Flora.

'Is that all you can hold out to my poor Daisy!'

'Well, it is the way of the world. There is just now a reaction from sentiment, and it is the less feminine variety. The softness will come when there is a call for it. Never mind when the foundation is safe.'

'If I could only see that child heartily admiring and looking up! I don't mean love – there used to be a higher, nobler reverence!'

'Such as you and Norman used to bestow on Shakspeare and Scott, and – the vision of Cocksmoor.'

'Not only *used*,' said Ethel.

'Yes, it is your soft side,' said Flora; 'it is what answers the purpose of sentiment in people like you. It is what I should have thought living with you would have put into any girl; but Gertrude has a satirical side, and she follows the age.'

'I wish you would tell her so – it is what she especially wants not to do! But the spirit of opposition is not the thing to cause tenderness.'

'No, you must wait for something to bring it out. She is very kind to my poor little Margaret, and I won't ask how she talks *of* her.'

'Tenderly; oh yes, that she always would do.'

'There, then, Ethel, if she can talk tenderly of Margaret, there can't be much amiss at the root.'

'No; and you don't overwhelm the naughty girl with baby talk.'

'Like our happy, proud young mothers,' sighed Flora; and then letting herself out – 'but indeed, Ethel, Margaret is very much improved. She has really begun to wish to be good. I think she is struggling with herself.'

'Something to love tenderly, something to reverence highly.' So meditated Ethel, as she watched her sunny-haired, open-faced Daisy, so unconquerably gay and joyous that she gave the impression of sunshine without shade. There are stages of youth that are in themselves unpleasing, and yet that are nobody's fault, nay, which may have within them seeds of strength. Tom's satire had fostered Daisy's too congenial spirit, and he reaped the consequence in the want of repose and sympathy that were driving him from home, and shutting him up within himself. Would he ever forgive that flippant saying, which Ethel had recollected with shame ever since – shame more for herself than for the child, who probably had forgotten, long ago, her 'shaft at random sent'?

Then Ethel would wonder whether, after all, her discontent with Gertrude's speeches was only from feeling older and graver, and perhaps from a certain resentment at finding how the course of time was wearing down the sharp edge of compassion towards Leonard.

A little more about Leonard was gathered when the time came of release for his friend the clerk Brown. This young man had an uncle at Paris, engaged in one of the many departments connected with steam that carry Englishmen all over the world; and Leonard obtained permission to write to Dr Thomas May, begging him to call upon the uncle, and try if he could be induced to employ the penitent and reformed nephew under his own eye. It had been wise in Leonard to write direct, for if the request had been made through any one at home, Tom would have considered it as impossible; but he could not resist the entreaty, and his mission was successful. The uncle was ready to be merciful, and undertook all the necessary arrangements for, and even the responsibility of, bringing the ticket-of-leave-man to Paris, where he found him a desk in his office. One of Tom's few detailed epistles was sent to Ethel after this arrival, when the uncle had told him how the nephew had spoken of his fellow-prisoner. It was to Leonard Ward that the young man had owed the inclination to open his heart to religious instruction, hitherto merely endured as a portion of the general infliction of the penalty, a supposed engine for dealing with the superstitious, but entirely beneath his attention.

The sight of the educated face had at first attracted him, but when he observed the reverential manner in chapel, he thought it mere acting the ''umble prisoner,' till he observed how unobtrusive, unconscious, and retiring was every token of devotion, and watched the eyes, brightened or softened in praise or in prayer, till he owned the genuineness and guessed the depth of both, then perceived in school how far removed his unknown comrade was from the mere superstitious boor. This was the beginning. The rest had been worked out by the instruction and discipline of the place, enforced by the example, and latterly by the conversation, of his fellow-prisoner, until he had come forth sincerely repenting, and with the better hope for the future that his sins had not been against full light.

He declared himself convinced that Ward far better merited to be at large than he did, and told of the regard that uniform good conduct was obtaining at last, though not till after considerable persecution, almost amounting to personal danger from the worse sort of convicts, who regarded him as a spy, because he would not connive at the introduction of forbidden indulgences, and always stood by the authorities. Once his fearless interposition had saved the life of a warder, and this had procured him trust, and promotion to a class where his companions were better conducted, and more susceptible to good influences, and among them Brown was sure that his ready submission and constant resolution to do his work were producing an effect. As to his spirits, Brown had never known him break down but once, and that was when he had come upon a curious fossil in the stone. Otherwise he was grave and contented, but never laughed or joked as even some gentlemen prisoners of more rank and age had been known to do. The music in the chapel was his greatest pleasure, and he had come to be regarded as an important element in the singing.

Very grateful was Dr May to Tom for having learnt, and still more for having transmitted, all these details; and Ethel was not the less touched, because she knew they were to travel beyond Minster Street. Those words of Mr Wilmot's seemed to be working out their accomplishment; and she thought so the more, when in early spring one of Leonard's severe throat attacks led to his being sent after his recovery to assist the schoolmaster, instead of returning to the carpenter's shed; and he was found so valuable in the school that the master begged to retain his services.

That spring was a grievous one in Indiana. The war, which eighteen months previously was to have come to an immediate end, was still raging, and the successes that had once buoyed up the Northern States with hope had long since been chequered by terrible reverses. On, on, still fought either side, as though nothing could close the strife but exhaustion or extinction; and still ardent, still constant, through bereavement and privation, were either party to their blood-stained flag. Mordaunt Muller had fallen in one of the terrible battles on the Rappahannock; and Cora, while sobbing in Averil's arms, had still confessed herself thankful that it had been a glorious death for his country's cause! And even in her fresh grief, she had not endeavoured to withhold her other brother, when, at the urgent summons of Government, he too had gone forth to join the army.

Cora was advised to return to her friends at New York, but she declared her intention of remaining to keep house with Cousin Deborah. Unless Averil would come with her, nothing should induce her to leave Massissauga, certainly not while Ella and Averil were alternately laid low by the spring intermittent fever. Perhaps the fact was that, besides her strong affection for Averil, she felt that in her ignorance she had assisted her father in unscrupulously involving them in a hazardous and unsuccessful speculation, and that she was the more bound, in justice as well as in love and pity, to do her best for their assistance. At any rate, Rufus had no sooner left home, than she insisted on the three sisters coming to relieve her loneliness – in other words, in removing them from the thin ill-built frame house, gaping in every seam with the effects of weather, and with damp oozing up between every board of the floor, the pestiferous river-fog, the close air of the forest, and the view of the phantom trees, now decaying and falling one against another.

Cousin Deborah, who had learnt to love and pity the forlorn English girls, heartily concurred; and Averil consented, knowing that the dry house and pure air were the best hope of restoring Ella's health.

Averil and Ella quickly improved, grew stronger in the intervals, and suffered less during the attacks; but Minna, who in their own house had been less ill, had waited on both, and supplied the endless deficiencies of the kindly and faithful, but two-fisted Katty; Minna, whose wise and simple little head had never failed in sensible counsels, or tender comfort;

Minna, whom the rudest and most self-important far-wester never disobliged; Minna, the peace-maker, the comfort and blessing – was laid low by fever, and fever that, as the experienced eyes of Cousin Deborah at once perceived, 'meant mischief.' Then it was that the real kindliness of heart of the rough people of the West showed itself. The five wild young ladies, whose successive domestic services had been such trouble, and whose answer to a summons from the parlour had been, 'Did yer holler, Avy? I thort I heerd a scritch,' each, from Cleopatra Betsy to Hetta Mary, were constantly rushing in to inquire, or to present questionable dainties and nostrums from their respective ''Mas;' the charwomen, whom Minna had coaxed in her blandest manner to save trouble to Averil and disgust to Henry, were officious in volunteers of nursing and sitting up; the black cook at the hotel sent choice fabrics of jelly and fragrant ice; and even Henry's rival, who had been so strong against the insolence of a practitioner showing no testimonials, no sooner came under the influence of the yearning, entreating, but ever-patient eyes, than his attendance became assiduous, his interest in the case ardent.

Henry himself was in the camp, before Vicksburg, with his hands too full of piteous cases of wounds and fever to attempt the most hurried visit.

'Sister, dear,' said the soft slow voice, one day when Averil had been hoping her patient was asleep, 'are you writing to Henry?'

'Yes, my darling. Do you want to say anything?'

'Oh yes! so much;' and the eyes grew bright, and the breath gasping; 'please beg Henry – tell Henry – that I must – I can't bear it any longer if I don't——'

'You must what, dear child? Henry would let you do anything he could.'

'Oh, then, would he let me speak about dear Leonard?' and the child grew deadly white when the words were spoken; but her eyes still sought Averil's face, and grew terrified at the sight of the gush of tears. 'O Ave, Ave, tell me only – he is not dead!' and as Averil could only make a sign, 'I do have such dreadful fancies about him, and I think I could sleep if I only knew what was really true.'

'You shall, dear child, you shall, without waiting to hear from Henry; I know he would let you.'

And only then did Averil know the full misery that Henry's decision had inflicted on the gentle little heart, in childish ignorance, imagining fetters and dungeons, even in her sober waking moods, and a prey to untold horrors in every dream, exaggerated by feverishness and ailment – horrors that, for aught she knew, might be veritable, and made more awful by the treatment of his name as that of one dead.

To hear of him as enjoying the open air and light of day, going to church, singing their own favourite hymn tunes, and often visited by Dr May, was to her almost as great a joy as if she had heard of him at liberty. And Averil had a more than usually cheerful letter to read to her, one written in the infirmary during his recovery. His letters to her were always cheerful; but this one was particularly so, having been written while exhilarated by the relaxations permitted to convalescents, and by enjoying an unwanted amount of conversation with the chaplain and the doctor.

'So glad, so glad,' Minna was heard murmuring to herself again and again; her rest was calmer than it had been for weeks, and the doctor found her so much better that he trusted that a favourable change had begun.

But it was only a gleam of hope. The weary fever held its prey, and many as were the fluctuations, they always resulted in greater weakness; and the wandering mind was not always able to keep fast hold of the new comfort. Sometimes she would piteously clasp her sister's hand, and entreat, 'Tell me again;' and sometimes the haunting delirious fancies of chains and bars would drop forth from the tongue that had lost its self-control; yet even at the worst came the dear old recurring note, 'God will not let them hurt him, for he has not done it!' Sometimes, more trying to Averil than all, she would live over again the happy games with him, or sing their favourite hymns and chants, or she would be heard pleading, 'Oh Henry, don't be cross to Leonard.'

Cora could not fail to remark the new name that mingled in the unconscious talk; but she had learnt to respect Averil's reserve, and she forbore from all questioning, trying even to warn Cousin Deborah, who, with the experience of an elderly woman, remarked, 'That she had too much to do to mind what a sick child rambled about. When Cora had lived to her age, she would know how unaccountably they talked.'

But Averil felt the more impelled to an outpouring by this delicate forbearance, and the next time she and Cora were sent out together to breathe the air, while Cousin Deborah watched the patient, she told the history, and to a sympathizing listener, without a moment's doubt of Leonard's innocence, nor that American law would have managed matters better.

'And now, Cora, you know why I told you there were bitterer sorrows than yours.'

'Ah! Averil, I could have believed you once; but to know that he never can come again! Now you always have hope.'

'My hope has all but gone,' said Averil. 'There is only one thing left to look to. If I only can live till he is sent out to a colony, then nothing shall keep me back from him!'

'And what would I give for even such a hope?'

'We have a better hope, both of us,' murmured Averil. 'It won't seem so long when it is over.'

Well was it for Averil that this fresh link of sympathy was riveted, for day by day she saw the little patient wasting more hopelessly away, and the fever only turning lower for want of strength to feed on. Utterly exhausted and half torpid, there was not life or power enough left in the child for them to know whether she was aware of her condition. When they read Prayers, her lips always moved for the Lord's Prayer and Doxology; and when the clergyman came out from Winiamac, prayed by her and blessed her, she opened her eyes with a look of comprehension; and if, according to the custom from the beginning of her illness, the Psalms and Lessons were not read in her room, she was uneasy, though she could hardly listen. So came Easter Eve; and towards evening she was a little revived, and asked Averil what day it was, then answered, 'I thought it would have been nice to have died yesterday,' – it was the first time she mentioned death. Averil told her she was better, but half repented, as the child sank into torpor again; and Averil, no longer the bewildered girl who had been so easily led from the death scene, knew the fitful breath and fluttering pulse, and felt the blank dread stealing over her heart.

Again, however, the child looked up, and murmured, 'You have not read to-day.' Cora, who had the Bible on her knee, gently obeyed, and read on, where she was, the morning First Lesson, the same in the American Church as in our own. Averil, dull with watching and suffering, sat on dreamily, with the scent of primroses wafted to her, as it were, by the association of the words, though her power to attend to them was gone. Before the chapter was over, the doze had overshadowed the little girl again; and yet, more than once, as the night drew on, they heard her muttering what seemed like the echo of one of its verses, 'Turn you, turn you——'

At last, after hours of watching, and more than one vain endeavour of good Cousin Deborah to lead away the worn but absorbed nurses, the dread messenger came. Minna turned suddenly in her sister's arms, with more strength than Averil had thought was left in her, and eagerly stretched out her arms, while the words so long trembling on her lips found utterance. 'Turn you to the stronghold, ye prisoners of hope! O Leonard dear! it does not hurt!' But that last word was almost lost in the gasp – the last gasp. What 'did not hurt' was death without his sting.

'O Cora! Was he with her? Is he gone too?' was Averil's cry at the first moment, as she strained the form of her little comforter for the last time in her arms.

'And if he is, they are in joy together,' said Cousin Deborah, tenderly but firmly unloosing Averil's arms, though with the tears running down her cheeks. 'Take her away, Cora, and both of you sleep. This dear lamb is in better keeping than yours.'

Heavy, grievous, was the loss, crushing the grief; but it was such as to be at its softest and sweetest at Easter, amid the Resurrection joys, and the budding flowers, though Ella's bitterest fit of weeping was excited by there being no primroses – the primroses that Minna loved so much; and her first pleasurable thought was to sit down and write to her dear 'Mr Tom' to send her some primrose seed, for Minna's grave.

Minna's grave! Alas! Massissauga had but an untidy desolate-looking region, with a rude snake fence, all unconsecrated! Cora wanted to choose a shaded corner in her father's ground, where they might daily tend the child's earthly resting-place; but Averil shrank from this with horror; and finally, on one of the Easter holidays, the little wasted form in its coffin was reverently driven by Philetus to Winiamac, while the sisters and Cora slowly followed, thinking – the one of the nameless blood-stained graves of a battle-field; the other whether an equally-nameless grave-yard, but one looked on with a shudder unmixed with exultation, had opened for the other being she loved best. 'The Resurrection and the Life. – Yes, had not He made His grave with the wicked, and been numbered with the transgressors!'

Somehow, the present sorrow was more abundant in such comforts as these than all the pangs which her heart, grown old in sorrow, had yet endured.

Yet if her soul had bowed itself to meet sorrow more patiently and peacefully, it was at the expense of the bodily frame. Already weakened by the intermittent fever, the long strain of nursing had told on her; and that hysteric affection that had been so distressing at the time of her brother's trial recurred, and grew on her with every occasion for self-restraint. The suspense in which she lived – with one brother in the camp, in daily peril from battle and disease, the other in his convict prison – wore her down, and made every passing effect of climate or fatigue seize on her frame like a serious disorder; and the more she resigned her spirit, the more her body gave way. Yet she was infinitely happier. The repentance and submission were bearing fruit, and the ceasing to struggle had brought a strange calm and acceptance of all that might be sent; nay, her own decay was perhaps the sweetest solace and healing of the wearied spirit; and as to Ella, she would trust, and she did trust, that in some way or other all would be well.

She felt as if even Leonard's death could be accepted thankfully as the captive's release. But that sorrow was spared her.

The account of Leonard came from Mr Wilmot, who had carried him the tidings. The prisoner had calmly met him with the words, 'I know what you are come to tell me;' and he heard all in perfect calmness and resignation, saying little, but accepting all that the clergyman said, exactly as could most be desired.

From the chaplain, likewise, Mr Wilmot learnt that Leonard, though still only in the second stage of his penalty, stood morally in a very different position, and was relied on as a valuable assistant in all that was good, more effective among his fellow-prisoners than was possible to any one not in the same situation with themselves, and fully accepting that position when in contact either with convicts or officials. 'He has never referred to what brought him here,' said the chaplain, 'nor would I press him to do so; but his whole tone is of repentance, and acceptance of the penalty, without, like most of them, regarding it as expiation. It is this that renders his example so valuable among the men.'

After such a report as this, it was disappointing, on Dr May's next visit to Portland, at two months' end, to find Leonard drooping and downcast. The doctor was dismayed at his pale, dejected, stooping appearance, and the silence and indifference with which he met their ordinary topics of conversation, till the doctor began anxiously –

'You are not well?'

'Quite well, thank you.'

'You are looking out of condition. Do you sleep?'

'Some part of the night.'

'You want more exercise. You should apply to go back to the carpenter's shop – or shall I speak to the governor?'

'No, thank you. I believe they want me in school.'

'And you prefer school work?'

'I don't know, but it helps the master.'

'Do you think you make any progress with the men? We heard you were very effective with them.'

'I don't see that much can be done any way, certainly not by me.'

Then the doctor tried to talk of Henry and the sisters; but soon saw that Leonard had no power to dwell upon them. The brief answers were given with a stern compression and contraction of face; as if the manhood that had grown on him in these three years was no longer capable of the softening effusion of grief; and Dr May, with all his tenderness, felt that it must be respected, and turned the conversation.

'I have been calling at the Castle,' he said, 'with Ernescliffe, and the governor showed me a curious thing, a volume of Archbishop Usher, which had been the Duke of Lauderdale's study after he was taken at Worcester. He has made a note in the fly-leaf, "I began this book at Windsor, and finished it during my imprisonment here;" and below are mottoes in Hebrew, Greek, and Latin. I can't construe the Hebrew. The Greek is *οἴστεον καὶ ἐλπίστεον* (one must bear and hope), the Latin is *durate*. Will you accept your predecessor's legacy?'

'I think I read about him in an account of the island,' said Leonard, with a moment's awakened intelligence; 'was he not the L. of the Cabal, the persecutor in Old Mortality?'

'I am afraid you are right. Prosperity must have been worse for him than adversity.'

'Endure,' repeated Leonard, gravely. 'I will think of that, and what he would mean by hope *now*.'

The doctor came home much distressed; he had been unable to penetrate the dreary, resolute self-command that covered so much anguish; he had failed in probing or in healing, and feared that the apathy he had witnessed was a sign that the sustaining spring of vigour was failing in the monotonous life. The strong endurance had been a strain that the additional grief was rendering beyond his power; and the crushed resignation and air of extinguished hope, together with the indications of failing health, filled the doctor with misgivings.

'It will not last much longer,' he said. 'I do not mean that he is ill; but to hold up in this way takes it out of a man, especially at his age. The first thing that lays hold of him, he will have no strength nor will to resist, and then – Well, I did hope to live to see God show the right.'

CHAPTER XXIV

'We twa hae wandered o'er the braes,
  And pu'ed the gowans fine;
I've wandered many a weary foot
  Sin auld lang syne.'

These years had passed quietly at Stoneborough, with little change since Mary's marriage. She was the happy excellent wife that she was made to be; and perhaps it was better for Ethel that the first severance had been so decisive that Mary's attentions to her old home were received as favours, instead of as the mere scanty relics of her former attachment.

Mr Cheviot, as the family shook down together, became less afraid of Ethel, and did not think it so needful to snub her either by his dignity or jocularity; though she still knew that she was only on terms of sufferance, and had been, more than once, made to repent of unguarded observations. He was admirable; and the school was so rapidly improving that Norman had put his father into ecstasies by proposing to send home little Dickie to begin his education there. Moreover, the one element wanting, to accomplish the town improvements, had been supplied by a head-master on the side of progress, and Dr Spencer's victory had been won at last. There was a chance that Stoneborough might yet be clean, thanks to his reiteration of plans for purification, *à propos* to everything. Baths and wash-houses were adroitly carried as a monument to Prince Albert; and on the Prince of Wales's marriage, his perseverance actually induced the committee to finish up the drains with all the contributions that were neither eaten up nor fired away! Never had he been more happy and triumphant; and Dr May used to accuse him of perambulating the lower streets snuffing the deodorized air.

One autumn evening, contrary to his wont, he allowed himself to be drawn into the May drawing-room, and there fell into one of the bright bantering talks in which the two old friends delighted, quizzing each other, and bringing up stories of their life; while Ethel and Gertrude listened to and laughed at the traditions of a sunnier, gayer, and more reckless age than their own; and Ethel thought how insufficient are those pictures of life that close with the fever-dream of youthful passion, and leave untold those years of the real burthen of manhood, and still more the tranquil brightness when toil has been overlived, and the setting sun gilds the clouds that are drifting away.

Ethel's first knowledge of outer life the next morning was the sound of voices in her father's adjoining room, which made her call out,

'Are you sent for, papa?'

'Yes,' he answered, and in an agitated tone, 'Spencer; I'll send word.'

Should she mention what she had two years ago heard from Tom? There was no time, for the next moment she heard him hurrying down stairs, she saw him speeding up the garden. There was nothing for her to do but to dress as fast as possible, and as she was finishing she heard his tread slowly mounting, the very footfall warning her what to expect. She opened the door and met him. 'Thank God,' he said, as he took her hand into his own, 'it has been very merciful.'

'Is it——?'

'Yes. It must have been soon after he lay down at night. As calm as sleep. The heart. I am very thankful. I had thought he would have had much to suffer.'

And then it appeared that his own observations had made him sure of what Ethel had learnt from Tom; but as long as it was unavowed by his friend, he had thought himself bound to ignore it, and had so dreaded the protracted suffering, that the actual stroke was accepted as a loving dispensation.

Still, as the close of a life-long friendship, the end of a daily refreshing and sustaining intimacy, the loss was very great, and would be increasingly felt after the first stimulus was over. It would make Tom's defection a daily grievance, since much detail of hospital care, and, above all, town work, his chief fatigue, would now again fall upon him. But this was not his present thought. His first care was, that his friend's remains should rest with those with whom his lot in life had been cast, in the cloister of the old grammar-school; but here Mr Cheviot looked concerned, and with reluctance, but decision, declared it to be his duty not to consent, cited the funeral of one of his scholars at the cemetery, and referred to recent sanatory measures.

Dr May quickly exclaimed that he had looked into the matter, and that the cloister did not come under the Act.

'Not technically, sir,' said Mr Cheviot; 'but I am equally convinced of my duty, however much I may regret it.' And then, with a few words about Mary's presently coming up, he departed; while 'That is too bad,' was the general indignant outburst, even from Richard; from all but Dr May himself.

'He is quite right,' he said. 'Dear Spencer would be the first to say so. Richard, your church is his best monument, and you'll not shut him out of your churchyard nor me either.'

'Cheviot could not have meant——' began Richard.

'Yes, he did, I understood him, and I am glad you should have had it out now,' said Dr May, though not without a quivering lip. 'Your mother has *one* by her side, and we'll find each other out just as well as if we were in the cloister. I'll walk over to Cocksmoor with you, Ritchie, and mark the place.'

Thus sweetly did he put aside what might have been so severe a shock; and he took extra pains to show his son-in-law his complete acquiescence both for the present and the future. Charles Cheviot expressed to Richard his great satisfaction in finding sentiment thus surmounted by sense, not perceiving that it was faith and love surmounting both.

Dr Spencer's only surviving relation was a brother's son, who, on his arrival, proved to be an underbred, shrewd-looking man, evidently with strong prepossessions against the May family, whose hospitality he did not accept, consorting chiefly with 'Bramshaw and Anderson.' His disposition to reverse the arrangement for burying his uncle in 'an obscure village churchyard,' occasioned a reference to the will, drawn up two years previously. The executors were Thomas and Etheldred May, and it was marked on the outside that they were to have the sole direction of the funeral. Ethel, greatly astonished, but as much bewildered as touched, was infinitely relieved that this same day had brought a hurried note from Paris, announcing Tom's intention of coming to attend the funeral. *He* would be able to talk to the angry and suspicious nephew, without, like his father, betraying either indignation or disgust.

Another person was extremely anxious for Tom's arrival, namely, Sir Matthew Fleet, who, not a little to Dr May's gratification, came to show his respect to his old fellow-student; and arriving the evening before Tom, was urgent to know the probabilities of his appearance. An appointment in London was about to be vacant, so desirable in itself, and so valuable an introduction, that there was sure to be a great competition; but Sir Matthew was persuaded that with his own support, and an early canvass, Tom might be certain of success. Dr May could not help being grateful and gratified, declaring that the boy deserved it, and that dear Spencer would have been very much pleased; and then he told Ethel that it was wonderful to see the blessing upon Maggie's children; and went back, as usual, to his dear old Tate and Brady, with –

> 'His house the seat of wealth shall be,
> An inexhausted treasury;
> His justice, free from all decay,
> Shall blessings to his heirs convey.'

And Ethel, within herself, hoped it was no disrespect to smile at his having so unconsciously turned away the blessing from the father's to the mother's side.

It was his great pride and pleasure that so many of Maggie's children were round him to do honour to her old friend's burial – three sons, and four daughters, and three sons-in-law. They all stood round the grave, as near as might be to the stone that Gertrude, as a child, had laid under his care, when his silver hair had mingled with her golden locks; and with them was a concourse that evidently impressed the nephew with a new idea of the estimation in which his uncle had been held.

Tom had travelled all night, and had arrived only just in time. Nobody was able to say a word to him before setting off; and almost immediately after the return, Sir Matthew Fleet seized upon him to walk up to the station with him, and, to the infinite disgust of the nephew, the reading of the will was thus delayed until the executor came back, extremely grave and thoughtful.

After all, Mr Spencer had no available grievance. His uncle's property was very little altogether, amounting scarcely to a thousand pounds, but the bulk was bequeathed to the nephew; to Aubrey May was left his watch, and a piece of plate presented to him on his leaving India; to Dr May a few books; to Tom the chief of his library, his papers, notes, and instruments, and the manuscript of a work upon diseases connected with climate, on which he had been engaged for many years, but had never succeeded in polishing to his own fastidious satisfaction, or in coming to the end of new discoveries. To Etheldred, his only legacy was his writing-desk, with *all* its contents. And Mr Spencer looked so suspicious of those contents, that Tom made her open it before him, and show that they were nothing but letters.

It had been a morning of the mixture of feelings and restless bustle, so apt to take place where the affection is not explained by relationship; and when the strangers were gone, and the family were once again alone, there was a drawing of freer breath, and the doctor threw himself back in his chair, and indulged in a long, heavy sigh, with a weary sound in it.

'Can I go anywhere for you, father?' said Tom, turning to him with a kind and respectful manner.

'Oh no – no thank you,' he said, rousing himself, and laying his hand on the bell, 'I must go over to Overfield; but I shall be glad of the drive. Well, Dr Tom, what did you say to Fleet's proposal?'

'I said I would come up to town and settle about it when I had got through this executor business.'

'You always were a lucky fellow, Tom,' said Dr May, trying to be interested and sympathetic. 'You would not wish for anything better.'

'I don't know, I have not had time to think about it yet,' said Tom, pulling off his spectacles and pushing back his hair, with an action of sadness and fatigue.

'Ah! it was not the best of times to choose for the communication; but it was kindly meant. I never expected to see Fleet take so much trouble for any one. But you are done up, Tom, with your night journey.'

'Not at all,' he answered, briskly, 'if I can do anything for you. Could not I go down to the hospital?'

'Why, if I were not to be back till five,' began Dr May, considering, and calling him into the hall to receive directions, from which he came back, saying, 'There! now then, Ethel, we had better look over things, and get them in train.'

'You are so tired, Tom.'

'Not too much for that,' he said. But it was a vain boast; he was too much fatigued to turn his mind to business requiring thought, though capable of slow, languid reading and sorting of papers.

Aubrey's legacy was discovered with much difficulty. In fact, it had never been heard of, nor seen the light, since its presentation, and was at last found in a lumber closet, in a strong box, in Indian packing. It was a compromise between an epergne and a candelabrum, growing out of the howdah of an unfortunate elephant, pinning one tiger to the ground, and with another hanging on behind, in the midst of a jungle of palm-trees and cobras; and beneath was an elaborate inscription, so laudatory of Aubrey Spencer, M.D., that nobody wondered he had never unpacked it, and that it was yellow with tarnish – the only marvel was, that he had never disposed of it; but that it was likely to wait for the days when Aubrey might be a general and own a side-board.

The other bequests were far more appreciated. Tom had known of the book in hand, was certain of its value to the faculty, and was much gratified by the charge of it, both as a matter of feeling and of interest. But while he looked over and sorted the mass of curious notes, his attention was far more set on the desk, that reverently, almost timidly, Ethel examined, well knowing why she had been selected as the depositary of these relics. There they were, some embrowned by a burn in the corner, as though there had been an attempt to destroy them, in which there had been no heart to persevere. It was but little, after all; two formal notes in which Professor Norman Mackenzie asked the honour of Mr Spencer's company to dinner, but in handwriting that was none of the professor's – writing better known to Ethel than to Tom – and a series of their father's letters, from their first separation till the traveller's own silence had caused their correspondence to drop. Charming letters they were, such as people wrote before the penny-post had spoilt the epistolary art – long, minute, and overflowing with brilliant happiness. Several of them were urgent invitations to Stoneborough, and one of these was finished in that other hand – the delicate, well-rounded writing that *would* not be inherited – entreating Dr Spencer to give a few days to Stoneborough, 'it would be such a pleasure to Richard to show him the children.'

Ethel did not feel sure whether to see these would give pain or pleasure to her father. He would certainly be grieved to see how much suffering he must have inflicted in the innocence of his heart, and in the glory of his happiness; and Tom, with a sort of shudder, advised her to keep them to herself, he was sure they would give nothing but pain.

She had no choice just then, for it was a time of unusual occupation, and the difference made by their loss told immediately – the more, perhaps, because it was the beginning of November, and there was much municipal business to be attended to.

However it might be for the future, during the ensuing week Dr May never came in for a meal with the rest of the family; was too much fagged for anything but sleep when he came home at night; and on the Sunday morning, when they all had reckoned on going to Cocksmoor together, he was obliged to give it up, and only come into the minster at the end of the prayers. Every one knew that he was not a good manager of his time, and this made things worse; and he declared that he should make arrangements for being less taken up; but it was sad to see him overburthened, and Tom, as only a casual visitor, could do little to lessen his toil, though that little was done readily and attentively. There were no rubs between the two, and scarcely any conversation. Tom would not discuss his prospects; and it was not clear whether he meant to avail himself of Sir Matthew's patronage; he committed himself to nothing but his wish that it were possible to stay in Paris; and he avoided even talking to his sister.

Not till a week after he had left home for London came a letter.

'Dear Ethel,

'I have told Fleet that I am convinced of my only right course. I could never get the book finished properly if I got into his line, and I must have peaceable evenings for it at home. I suppose my father would not like to let Dr Spencer's house. If I might have it, and keep my own hours and habits, I think it would conduce to our working better together. I am afraid I kept you in needless distress about him, but I wanted to judge for myself of the necessity, and to think over the resignation of that quest. I must commit it to Brown. I hope it is not too great a risk; but it can't be helped. It is a matter of course that I should come home now the helper is gone; I always knew it would come to that. Manage it as quietly as you can. I must go to Paris for a fortnight, to bring home my things, and by that time my father had better get me appointed to the hospital.

'Yours ever,

'TH. MAY.'

Ethel was not so much surprised as her father, who thought she must have been working upon Tom's feelings; but this she disavowed, except that it had been impossible not to growl at patients' sending at unreasonable hours. Then he hoped that Fleet had not been disappointing the lad; but this notion was nullified by a remonstrance from the knight, on the impolicy of burying such talents for the sake of present help; and even proposing to send a promising young man in Tom's stead. 'Not too good for poor Stoneborough,' said Dr May, smiling. 'No, no, I'm not so decrepit as that, whatever he and Tom may have thought me; I fancy I could tire out both of them. I can't have the poor boy giving up all his prospects for my sake, Ethel. I never looked for it, and I shall write and tell him so! Mind, Ethel, I shall write, not you! I know you would only stroke him down, and bring him home to regret it. No, no, I won't always be treated like Karl, in *Debit and Credit*, who the old giant thought could neither write nor be written to, because his finger was off.'

And Dr May's letter was the first which this son had ever had from him.

'My dear Tom,

'I feel your kind intentions to the heart; it is like all the rest of your dear mother's children; but the young ought not to be sacrificed to the old, and I won't have it done. The whole tone of practice has altered since my time, and I do not want to bind you down to the routine. I had left off thinking of it since I knew of your distaste. I have some years of work in me yet, that will see out most of my old patients; and for the rest, Wright is a great advance on poor Ward, and I will leave more to him as I grow older. I mean to see you a great man yet, and I think you will be the greater and happier for the sacrifice you have been willing to make. His blessing on you.

'Your loving father,

'R.M.'

What was Tom's answer, but one of his cool 'good letters,' a demonstration that he was actuated by the calmest motives of convenience and self-interest, in preferring the certainties of Stoneborough to the contingencies of London, and that he only wanted time for study and the completion of Dr Spencer's book, enforcing his request for the house.

His resolution was, as usual, too evident to be combated, and it was also plain that he chose to keep on the mask of prudent selfishness, which he wore so naturally that it was hard to give him credit for any other features; but this time Dr May was not deceived. He fully estimated the sacrifice, and would have prevented it if he could; but he never questioned the sincerity of the motive, as it was not upon the surface; and the token of dutiful affection, as coming from the least likely quarter of his family, touched and comforted him. He dwelt on it with increasing satisfaction, and answered all hurries and worries with, 'I shall have time when Tom is come;' re-opened old schemes that had died away when he feared to have no successor, and now and then showed a certain comical dread of being drilled into conformity with Tom's orderly habits.

There was less danger of their clashing, as the son had outgrown the presumptions of early youth, and a change had passed over his nature which Ethel had felt, rather than seen, during his fleeting visits at home, more marked by negatives than positives, and untraced by confidences. The bitterness and self-assertion had ceased to tinge his words, the uncomfortable doubt that they were underlaid by satire had passed away, and methodical and self-possessed as he always was, the atmosphere of 'number one' was no longer apparent round all his doings. He could be out of spirits and reserved without being either ill-tempered or ironical; and Ethel, with this as the upshot of her week's observations, was reassured as to the hopes of the father and son working together without collisions. As soon as the die was cast, and there was no danger of undue persuasion in 'stroking him down,' she indulged herself by a warmly-grateful letter, and after she had sent it, was tormented by the fear that it would be a great offence. The answer was much longer than she had dared to expect, and alarmed her lest it should be one of his careful ways of making the worst of himself; but there was a large 'Private,' scored in almost menacing letters on the top of the first sheet, and so much blotted in the folding, that it was plain that he had taken alarm at the unreserve of his own letter.

'My dear Ethel,

'I have been to Portland. Really my father ought to make a stir and get Ward's health attended to; he looks very much altered, but will not own to anything being amiss. They say he has been depressed ever since he heard of Minna's death. I should say he ought to be doing out-of-doors work – perhaps at Gibraltar, but then he would be out of our reach. I could not get much from him, but that patient, contented look is almost more than one can bear. It laid hold of me when I saw him the first time, and has haunted me ever since. Verily I believe it is what is bringing me home! You need not thank me, for it is sober calculation that convinces me that no success on earth would compensate for the perpetual sense that my father was wearing himself out, and you pining over the sight. Except just at first, I always meant to come and see how the land lay before pledging myself to anything; and nothing can be clearer than that, in the state of things my father has allowed to spring up, he must have help. I am glad you have got me the old house, for I can be at peace there till I have learnt to stand his unmethodical ways. Don't let him expect too much of me, as I see he is going to do. It is not in me to be like Norman or Harry, and he must not look for it, least of all now. If you did not understand, and know when to hold your tongue, I do not think I could come home at all; as it is, you are all the comfort I look for. I cross to Paris to-morrow. That is a page I am very sorry to close. I had a confidence that I should have hunted down that fellow, and the sight of Portland and the accounts from Massissauga alike make one long to have one's hands on his throat; but that hope is ended now, and to loiter about Paris in search of him, when it is a plain duty to come away, would be one of the presumptuous acts that come to no good. Let them discuss what they will, there's nothing so hard to believe in as Divine Justice! And yet that uncomplaining face accepts it! You need say nothing about this letter. I will talk about Leonard with my father when I get home.

'Ever yours,

'THOMAS MAY.'

CHAPTER XXV

'But soon as once the genial plain
Has drunk the life-blood of the slain,
Indelible the spots remain;
And aye for vengeance call,
Till racking pangs of piercing pain
Upon the guilty fall.'

Æschylus. (*Translated by Professor Anstice.*)

If Tom May's arrival at home was eagerly anticipated there, it was with a heavy heart that he prepared for what he had never ceased to look on as a treadmill life. He had enjoyed Paris, both from the society and the abstract study, since he still retained that taste for theory rather than practice, which made him prefer diseases to sick people, and all sick people to those of Stoneborough. The student life, in the freedom of a foreign capital, was, even while devoid of licence and irregularity, much pleasanter than what he foresaw at home, even though he had obtained a separate establishment. His residence at Paris, with the vague hope it afforded, cost him more in the resignation than his prospects in London. It was the week when he would have been canvassing for the appointment, and he was glad to linger abroad out of reach of Sir Matthew's remonstrances, and his father's compunction, while he was engaged in arranging for a French translation of Dr Spencer's book, and likewise in watching an interesting case, esteemed a great medical curiosity, at the Hotel Dieu.

He was waiting in the lecture-room, when one of the house surgeons came in, saying, 'Ah! I am glad to see you here. A compatriot of yours has been brought in, mortally injured in a gambling fray. You may perhaps assist in getting him identified.'

Tom followed him to the accident ward, and beheld a senseless figure, with bloated and discoloured features, distorted by the effects of the injury, a blow upon the temple, which had caused a fall backwards on the sharp edge of a stove, occasioning fatal injury to the spine. Albeit well accustomed to gaze critically upon the tokens of mortal agony, Tom felt an unusual shudder of horror and repugnance as he glanced on the countenance, so disfigured and contorted that there was no chance of recognition, and turned his attention to the clothes, which lay in a heap on the floor. The contents of the pockets had been taken out, and consisted only of some pawnbroker's duplicates, a cigar case, and a memorandum-book, which last he took in his hand, and began to unfasten, without looking at it, while he took part in the conversation of the surgeons on the technical nature of the injuries. Thus he stood for some seconds, before, on the house surgeon asking if he had found any address, he cast his eyes on the pages which lay open in his hand.

'Ha! What have you found? – He does not hear! Is it the portrait of the beloved object? Is it a brother – an enemy – or a debt? But he is truly transfixed! It is an effect of the Gorgon's head!'

'July 15th, 1860. Received £120.

'L.A. WARD.'

There stood Tom May, like one petrified, deaf to the words around, his dazzled eyes fixed on the letters, his faculties concentrated in the endeavour to ascertain whether they were sight or imagination. Yes, there they were, the very words in the well-known writing, the schoolboy's forming into the clerk's, there was the blot in the top of the L! Tom's heart gave one wild bound, then all sensation, except the sight of the writing, ceased; the exclamations of those around him came surging gradually on his ear, as if from a distance, and he did not yet hear them distinctly when he replied alertly, almost lightly, 'Here is a name that surprises me. Let me look at the patient again.'

'No dear friend?' asked his chief intimate, in a tone ready to become gaiety or sympathy.

'No, indeed,' said Tom, shuddering as he stood over the insensible wretch, and perceived what it had been which had thrilled him with such unwonted horror; for, fixed by the paralysing convulsion of the fatal blow, he saw the scowl and grin of deadly malevolence that had been the terror of his childhood, and that had fascinated his eyes at the moment of Leonard's sentence. Changed by debauchery, defaced by violence, contorted by the injured brain, the features would scarcely have been recalled to him but for the frightful expression stamped on his memory by the miseries of his timid boyhood.

'Whoso sheddeth man's blood, by man shall his blood be shed.' The awful thought, answering his own struggle for faith in Divine Justice, crossed him, as he heard the injury on the head defined, in almost the same scientific terms that had so often rung on his ears as the causes of Francis Axworthy's death; but this was no society where he could give vent to his feelings, and mastering himself with difficulty he answered, 'I know him. He is from my own town.'

'Has he friends or relations?'

'Relations, yes,' said Tom, hardly able to restrain a trembling of the lip, half horror, half irony. 'None here, none near. They shall know.'

'And means?'

'Once he had. Probably none now.'

To Tom's great relief, a new case drew off general attention. There only remained the surgeon who had called him at first, and with whom he was particularly intimate.

'Gaspard,' he said, 'shall you have charge of this case?'

'Brief charge it will be, apparently! I will volunteer to watch it, if it is your desire! Is it friendship, or enmity, or simple humanity?'

'All!' said Tom, hastily. 'It is the clearing up of a horrible mystery – freedom for an innocent prisoner – I must tell you the rest at leisure. There is much to be done now in case of his reviving.'

This was remotely possible, but very doubtful; and Tom impressed on both Gaspard and the nursing sister the most stringent entreaties to summon him on the first symptom. He then gave the name of the unhappy man, and, though unwilling to separate himself from that invaluable pocket-book, perceived the necessity of leaving it as a deposit with the authorities of the hospital, after he had fully examined it, recognising Leonard's description in each particular, the cypher F.A. on the tarnished silver clasp, the shagreen cover, and the receipt on a page a little past the middle. On the other half of the leaf was the entry of some sums due to the house; and it contained other papers which the guilty wretch had been evidently eager to secure, yet afraid to employ, and that, no doubt, were the cause that, like so many other murderers on record, he had preserved that which was the most fatal proof against himself. Or could it be with some notion of future relenting, that he had refrained from its destruction?

With brain still seeming to reel at the discovery, and limbs actually trembling with the shock, Tom managed to preserve sufficient coolness and discretion to bring back to mind the measures he had so often planned for any such contingency. Calling a cabriolet, he repaired to the police-station nearest to the scene of the contest, and there learnt that Axworthy had long been watched as a dangerous subject, full of turbulence, and with no visible means of maintenance. The officials had taken charge of the few personal effects in his miserable lodgings, and were endeavouring to secure the person who had struck the fatal blow.

His next measure was to go to the British Embassy, where, through his sister Flora's introductions, and his own Eton connexions, he was already well known; and telling his story there, without any attempt to conceal his breathless agitation, he had no difficulty in bringing with him a companion who would authenticate the discovery of the receipt, and certify to any confession that might be obtained.

A confession! That was the one matter of the most intense interest. Tom considered whether to secure the presence of a clergyman, but suspected that this would put Axworthy on his guard rather than soften him, and therefore only wrote to the chaplain, begging him to hold himself in readiness for a summons to the Hotel Dieu, whither he drove rapidly back with his diplomatic friend, whom he wrought up well-nigh to his own pitch of expectation. He had already decided on his own first address – pitying, but manifesting that nothing, not even vengeance, could be gained by concealment; and then, according to the effect, would he try either softening or threatening to extort the truth.

Gaspard was eagerly awaiting them. 'I had already sent for you,' he said. 'The agony is commencing; he has spoken, but he has not his full consciousness.'

Tom hurried on, drawing after him the young diplomat, who would have hung back, questioning if there were any use in his witnessing the dying struggles of a delirious man.

'Come, come,' peremptorily repeated Tom, 'there must be some last words. Every moment is of importance.'

Yet his trust was shaken by the perception of the progress that death had made in the miserable frame during his absence. The fixed expression of malignity had been forced to yield to exhaustion and anguish; the lips moved, but the murmurs between the moans were scarcely articulate.

'He is almost past it,' said Tom, 'but there is the one chance that he may be roused by my voice.'

And having placed his friend conveniently, both for listening and making notes, he came close to the bed, and spoke in a tone of compassion. 'Axworthy, I say, Axworthy, is there anything I can do for you?'

There was a motion of the lid of the fast-glazing eye; but the terrible face of hatred came back, with the audible words, 'I tell you, you old fool, none of the Mays are to come prying about my place.'

Appalled by the deadly malice of the imprecation and the look that accompanied this partial recognition of his voice, Tom was nerving himself to speak again, when the dying man, as if roused by the echo of his own thought, burst out, 'Who? What is it? I say Dr May shall *not* be called in! He never attended the old man! Let him mind his own business! I was all night at the Three Goblets. Yes, I was! The new darling will catch it – going off with the money upon him–' and the laugh made their blood run cold. 'I've got the receipt;' and he made an attempt at thrusting his hand under the pillow, but failing, swore, shouted, howled with his last strength, that he had been robbed – the pocket-book – it would hang him! and with one of the most fearful shrieks of despair that had perhaps ever rung through that asylum of pain, woe, and death, the wretched spirit departed.

Tom May turned aside, made a few steps, and, to the infinite surprise of every one, fell helplessly down in a swoon. A nature of deep and real sensibility, though repressed by external reserve and prudence, could not with entire impunity undergo such a scene. The sudden discovery, the vehement excitement forced down, the intense strain of expectation, and finally, the closing horror of such a death, betraying the crime without repenting of it, passing to the other world with imprecations on the lips, and hatred in the glare of the eye, all the frightfulness enhanced by the familiarity of the allusions, and the ghastly association of the tones that had tempted and tyrannized over his childhood, altogether crushed and annihilated his faculties, mental and bodily.

Oh, when our very hearts burn for justice, how little do we know how intolerable would be the sight of it! Tom's caution and readiness returned as soon as – after a somewhat long interval – he began to distinguish the voices round him, and perceive the amazement he had created. Before he was able to sit up on the couch, where he had been laid out of sight of the scene which had affected him so strongly, he was urging his friend to set down all that had been spoken, and on Gaspard's writing a separate deposition. The pocket-book, and other effects, were readily ceded to the British authority, and were carried away with them.

How Tom got through the remaining hours of the day and the night he never recollected, though he knew it must have been in the bustle of preparation, and that he had imparted the tidings to Leonard's friend Brown; for when he and his friend had attended that which answered to an inquest on the body, and had obtained a report of the proceedings, he was ready to start by the night train, bearing with him the attestations of the death-bed scene at the Hotel Dieu, and the long-lost memorandum-book, and was assured that the next mail would carry an official letter to the Home Office, detailing the circumstances of Samuel Axworthy's decease. Brown came to bid him farewell, full of gladness and warm congratulation, which he longed to send to his friend, but which Tom only received with hasty, half-comprehending assents.

Late in the afternoon he reached Stoneborough, found no one come in, and sat down in the fire-light, where, for all his impatience, fatigue had made him drop asleep, when he was roused by Gertrude's voice, exclaiming, 'Here really is Tom come, as you said he would, without writing. Here are all his goods in the hall.'

'Is it you, Tom!' cried Ethel. 'Notice, or no notice, we are glad of you. But what is the matter!'

'Where's my father?'

'Coming. Charles Cheviot took him down to look at one of the boys. Is there anything the matter?' she added, after a pause.

'No, nothing.'

'You look very odd,' added Gertrude.

He gave a nervous laugh. 'You would look odd, if you had travelled all night.'

They commented, and began to tell home news; but Ethel noted that he neither spoke nor heard, only listened for his father. Gertrude grew tired of inattentive answers, and said she should go and dress. Ethel was turning to follow, when he caught hold of her cloak, and drew her close to him. 'Ethel,' he said, in a husky, stifled voice, 'do you know this?'

On her knees, by the red fire-light, she saw the 'L.A. Ward,' and looked up. 'Is it?' she said. He bowed his head.

And then Ethel put her arm round his neck, as he knelt down by her; and he found that her tears, her rare tears, were streaming down, silent but irrepressible. She had not spoken, had asked no question, made no remark, when Dr May's entrance was heard, and she loosed her hold on her brother, but without rising from the floor, looked up from under the shade of her hat, and said, 'Oh papa! it is found, and *he* has done it! Look there!'

Her choked voice, and tokens of emotion, startled the doctor; but Tom, in a matter-of-fact tone, took up the word: 'How are you, father! – Yes. I have only met with this little memorandum.'

Dr May recognised it with a burst of incoherent inquiry and exclamation, wringing Tom's hand, and giving no time for an answer; and indeed, his son attempted none – till, calming himself, the doctor subsided into his arm-chair, and with a deep sigh, exclaimed, 'Now then, Tom, let us hear. Where does this come from?'

'From the casualty ward at the Hotel Dieu.'

'And from——'

'He is dead,' said Tom, answering the unspoken question. 'You will find it all here. Ethel, do I sleep here to-night? My old room?' As he spoke, he bent to light a spill at the fire, and then the two candles on the side-table; but his hand shook nervously, and though he turned away his face, his father and sister saw the paleness of his cheek, and knew that he must have received a great shock. Neither spoke, while he put one candle conveniently for his father, took up the other, and went away with it. With one inquisitive glance at each other, they turned to the papers, and with eager eyes devoured the written narratives of Tom himself and of the attaché; then, with no less avidity, the French reports accompanying them. Hardly a word was spoken while Ethel leant against her father's knee, and he almost singed his hair in the candle, as they helped one another out in the difficulties of the crooked foreign writing.

'Will it be enough!' asked Ethel at last, holding her breath for the answer.

'If there is justice in England!' said Dr May. 'Heaven forgive me, Ethel, this business has tried my trust more than anything that ever befell me; but it will all be right now, and righter than right, if that boy comes out what I think him.'

'And oh, how soon?'

'Not a moment longer than can be helped. I'd go up by the mail train this very night if it would do any good.'

Tom, who reappeared as soon as he had spared himself the necessity of the narration, was willing and eager to set out; but Dr May, who by this time had gathered some idea of what he had gone through, and saw that he was restless, nervous, and unhinged, began to reconsider the expedience of another night journey, and was, for once in his life, the person cool enough to see that it would be wisest to call Bramshaw into their counsels, and only that night to send up a note mentioning that they would do themselves the honour of calling at the Home Office the next day, on matters connected with the intelligence received that morning from the British Embassy at Paris.

Tom was disappointed; he was in no mood for sitting still, and far less for talking. As a matter of business, he would elucidate any question, but conversation on what he had witnessed was impossible to him; and when Gertrude, with a girl's lightness, lamented over being baulked of a confession and explanation, he gravely answered, that she did not know what she was talking of; and his father led away from the subject. Indeed, Dr May was full of kindness and consideration, being evidently not only grateful for the discovery, but touched by his entire absence of exulting triumph, and his strong sense of awe in the retribution.

That changed and awe-struck manner impressed both the sisters, so that all the evening Ethel felt subdued as by a strange shock, and even through the night and morning could hardly realise that it was intense relief – joy, not sorrow – that made her feel so unlike herself, and that the burthen was taken away from her heart. Even then, there was a trembling of anxiety. The prisoner might be set free; but who could give back to him the sister who had pined away in exile, or the three years of his youthful brightness? There might be better things in store; but she knew she must not look again for the boy of ingenuous countenance, whose chivalrous devotion to herself had had such a charm, even while she tried to prize it at its lightest worth. It was foolish to recollect it with a pang, but there was no helping it. In the great tragedy, she had forgotten that the pretty comedy was over, but she regretted it, rather as she did the pleasant baby-days of Aubrey and Gertrude.

Indeed, during the day of suspense, while the two physicians were gone to London, taking with them the papers, and a minute detail of the evidence at the trial, Gertrude's high spirits, triumph over Charles Cheviot, and desire to trumpet forth the good news, were oppressive. How many times that day was Mab stroked, and assured that her master would come back! And how often did the two sisters endeavour to persuade themselves that she was not grown broader in the back! Mary was, of course, told early in the day; but Gertrude got less sympathy from her than answered to that damsel's extortionate expectations, for, according to her wicked account, Mary's little Charlie had sneezed three times, and his mamma must regret what sent all the medical science of Stoneborough away by the early train.

However, Tom came home at night. The interview had been satisfactory. The letters received in the morning had prepared the way, and revived the recollection of the unsatisfactory case of Leonard Axworthy Ward, and of the representations of the then Mayor of Market Stoneborough. After all the new lights upon the matter had been looked into, the father and son had been assured that, as soon as possible, a free pardon should be issued, so drawn up as to imply a declaration of innocence – the nearest possible approach to a reversal of the sentence; and they further were told of a mention of his exemplary conduct in a late report from Portland, containing a request that he might be promoted to a post of greater influence and trust before the ordinary time of probation had past. Dr May was eager to be at Portland at the same time as the pardon, so to give Leonard the first intelligence, and to bring him home; and he had warmly closed with Tom's offer to look after the work, while he himself waited till the necessary forms had been complied with. He had absolutely begged Tom's pardon for going in his stead. 'It is your right,' he said; 'but, somehow, I think, as I have been more with him, I might do better.' To which Tom had assented with all his heart, and had added that he would not go if he were paid for it. He had further taken care that the doctor should take with him a suit of clothes for Leonard to come home in, and had himself made the selection; then came back with the tidings that filled the house with the certainty of joy, and the uncertainty of expectation.

Nobody was, however, in such a fever as Tom himself. He was marvellously restless all the morning. Gertrude asserted it was because he was miserable at not venturing to set his father's study to rights; and to be sure he was seen looking round at the litter with a face of great disgust, and declaring that he was ashamed to see a patient in a room in such a mess. But this did not fully account for his being in and out, backwards and forwards, all the morning, looking wistfully at Ethel, and then asking some trivial question about messages left for his father, or matters respecting his own new abode, where he kept on Dr Spencer's old housekeeper, and was about to turn in paperers and painters. He had actually brought a drawing-room paper from Paris, a most delicate and graceful affair, much too lady-like for the old house, as Daisy told him, when she pursued him and her sister down to a consultation.

Late in the afternoon, as the sisters were coming up the High Street, they met him setting out in Hector's dog-cart. 'Oh, I say, Ethel,' he said, drawing up, 'do you like a drive out to Chilford? Here's a note come to ask my father to see the old lady there, and I want some one to give me courage to be looked at, like the curate in the pulpit instead of the crack preacher.'

It was an offer not to be despised, though Ethel knew what a waiting there would be, and what a dark drive home. Up she jumped, and Tom showed his usual thoughtfulness by ordering Gertrude to run home and fetch her muff and an additional cloak, tucking her up himself with the carriage rug. That affection of Tom's had been slow in coming, but always gave her a sense of gratitude and enjoyment.

They drove all the seven miles to Chilford without twenty words passing between them; and when there, she sat in the road, and watched one constellation after another fill up its complement of stars as well as the moon permitted, wondering whether Tom's near-sighted driving would be safe in the dark; but her heart was so light, so glad, that she could not be afraid, she did not care how long she waited, it was only sitting still to recollect that deliverance had come to the captive – Leonard was free – 'free as heart can think or eye can see,' as would keep ringing in her ears like a joy-bell; and some better things, too. 'Until the time came that his cause was known, the Word of the Lord tried him.'

Whether she were really too happy to note time, or that gossipry was deducted from the visit, Tom certainly returned sooner than her experience had led her to expect, made an exclamation of dismay at finding the machine was innocent of lamps, and remounted to his seat, prepared to be extremely careful.

'I could not get them to take me for my father in a new wig,' he said; 'but it was a very easy-going rheumatic case, and I think I satisfied her.'

Then on he drove for a mile, till he was out of the bad cross-country road, and at last he said, 'Ethel, I have made up my mind. There's no press of work just now, and I find it is advisable I should go to America before I get into harness here.'

'To America!'

'Yes, about this book of dear old Spencer's. It is a thing that must be complete, and I find he was in correspondence with some men of science there. I could satisfy my mind on a few points, which would make it infinitely more valuable, you see – and get it published there too. I know my father would wish every justice to be done to it.'

'I know he would; and,' continued Ethel, as innocently as she could, 'shall you see the Wards?'

'Why,' said Tom, in his deliberate voice, 'that is just one thing, I want particularly to see Henry. I had a talk with Wright this morning, and he tells me that young Baines, at Whitford, is going to the dogs, and the practice coming in to him. He thinks of having a partner, and I put out a feeler in case Henry Ward should choose to come back, and found it might do very well. But the proposal must come from him, and there's no time to be lost, so I thought of setting out as soon as I hear my father is on his way back.'

'Not waiting to see Leonard?'

'I did see him not a month ago. Besides——' and his voice came to a sudden end.

'Yes, the first news,' said Ethel. 'Indeed it is due to you, Tom.'

Ten minutes more of silence.

'Ethel, did she ever tell you?'

'Never,' said Ethel, her heart beating.

'Then how did you know all about it?'

'I didn't know. I only saw——'

'Saw what?'

'That you were very much distressed.'

'And very kind and rational you were about it,' said Tom warmly; 'I never thought any woman could have guessed so much, without making mischief. But you must not put any misconstruction on my present intention. All I mean to do as yet is to induce Henry to remove them out of that dismal swamp, and bring them home to comfort and civilization. Then it may be time to——'

He became silent; and Ethel longed ardently to ask further, but still she durst not, and he presently began again.

'Ethel, was I very intolerable that winter of the volunteers, when Harry was at home?'

'You are very much improved since,' she answered.

'That's just like Flora. Answer like yourself.'

'Well, you were! You were terribly rampant in Eton refinement, and very anxious to hinder all the others from making fools of themselves.'

'I remember! I thought you had all got into intimacies that were for nobody's good, and I still think it was foolish. I know it has done for me! Well,' hastily catching up this last admission, as if it had dropped out unawares, 'you think I made myself disagreeable?'

'On principle.'

'Ah! then you would not wonder at what she said – that she had never seen anything in me but contemptuous irony.'

'I think, sometimes feeling that you were satirical, she took *all* your courtesy for irony – whatever you meant. I have heard other people say the same. But when – was *this* on the day – the day you went to remonstrate?'

'Yes. I declare to you, Ethel, that I had no conception of what I was going to do! I never dreamt that I was in for it. I knew she was – was attractive – and that made me hate to see Harry with her, and I could not bear her being carried off to this horrible place – but as to myself, I never thought of it till I saw her – white and broken——' and then came that old action Ethel knew so well in her father, of clearing the dew from the glasses, and his voice was half sob, 'and with no creature but that selfish brother to take care of her. I couldn't help it, Ethel – no one could – and this – this was her answer. I don't wonder. I had been a supercilious prig, and I ought to have known better than to think I could comfort her.'

'I think the remembrance must have comforted her since.'

'What – what, has she said anything?'

'Oh no, she could not, you know. But I am sure, if it did anger her at the moment, there must have been comfort in recollecting that even such a terrible trouble had not alienated you. And now——'

'Now that's just what I don't want! I don't want to stalk in and say here's the hero of romance that has saved your brother! I want to get her home, and show her that I can be civil without being satirical, and then, perhaps, she would forgive me.'

'Forgive you——'

'I mean forgiveness won, not purchased. And after all, you know it was mere accident – Providence if you please – that brought me to that poor wretch; all my plans of tracking him had come to an end; any one else could have done what I did.'

'She will not feel that,' said Ethel; 'but indeed, Tom, I see what you mean, and like it. It is yourself, and not the conferrer of the benefit, that you want her to care for.'

'Exactly,' said Tom. 'And, Ethel, I must have seen her and judged of my chance before I can be good for anything. I tried to forget it – own it as a lucky escape – a mere passing matter, like Harry's affairs – but I could not do it. Perhaps I could if things had gone well; but that dear face of misery, that I only stung by my attempts to comfort, would stick fast with me, and to go and see Leonard only brought it more home. It is a horrid bad speculation, and Flora and Cheviot and Blanche will scout it; but, Ethel, you'll help me through, and my father will not mind, I know.'

'Papa will feel as I do, Tom – that it has been your great blessing, turn out as it may.'

'H'm! has it? A blessing on the wrong side of one's mouth – to go about with a barb one knew one was a fool for, and yet couldn't forget! Well, I know what you mean, and I believe it was. I would not have had it annihilated, when the first mood was over.'

'It was that which made it so hard to you to come home, was it not?'

'Yes; but it was old enough, however hard it was to think of coming, you always sent me away more at peace, Ethel. I can't think how you did it, knowing nothing.'

'I think you came at the right time.'

'You see, I did think that while Spencer lived, I might follow up the track, and see a little of the world – try if that would put out that face and voice. But it won't do. If this hadn't happened, I would have tied myself down, and done my best to get comfort out of you, and the hospital, and these "Diseases of Climate" – I suppose one might in time, if things went well with her; but, as it is, I can't rest till I have seen if they can be got home again. So, Ethel, don't mind if I go before my father comes home. I can't stand explanations with him, and I had rather you did not proclaim this. You see the book, and getting Henry home, are really the reasons, and I shan't molest her again – no – not till she has learnt to know what is irony.'

'I think if you did talk it over with papa, you would feel the comfort, and know him better.'

'Well, well, I dare say, but I can't do it, Ethel. Either he shuts me up at first, with some joke, or——' and Tom stopped; but Ethel knew what he meant. There was on her father's side an involuntary absence of perfect trust in this son, and on Tom's there was a character so sensitive that her father's playfulness grated, and so reserved that his demonstrative feelings were a still greater trial to one who could not endure outward emotion. 'Besides,' added Tom, 'there is really nothing – nothing to tell. I'm not going to commit myself. I don't know whether I ever shall. I was mad that day, and I want to satisfy my mind whether I think the same now I am sane, and if I do, I shall have enough to do to make her forget the winter when I made myself such an ass. When I have done that, it may be time to speak to my father. I really am going out about the book. When did you hear last?'

'That is what makes me anxious. I have not heard for two months, and that is longer than she ever was before without writing, except when Minna was ill.'

'We shall know if Leonard has heard.'

'No, she always writes under cover to us.'

The course that the conversation then took did not look much like Tom's doubt whether his own views would be the same. All the long-repressed discussion of Averil's merits, her beautiful eyes, her sweet voice, her refinement, her real worth, the wonder that she and Leonard should be so superior to the rest of the family, were freely indulged at last, and Ethel could give far heartier sympathy than if this had come to her three years ago. Averil had been for two years her correspondent, and the patient sweetness and cheerfulness of those letters had given a far higher estimate of her nature than the passing intercourse of the town life had left. The terrible discipline of these years of exile and sorrow had, Ethel could well believe, worked out something very different from the well-intentioned wilful girl, whose spirit of partizanship had been so fatal an element of discord. Distance had, in truth, made them acquainted, and won their love to one another.

Tom's last words, as he drew up under the lime-trees before the door, were, 'Mind, I am only going about "The Diseases of Climate."'

CHAPTER XXVI

'And Bishop Gawain as he rose,
Said, "Wilton, grieve not for thy woes,
Disgrace and trouble;
For He who honour best bestows,
Can give thee double."'

Marmion.

Dr May had written to Portland, entreating that no communication might be made to Leonard Ward before his arrival; and the good physician's affection for the prisoner had been so much observed, that no one would have felt it fair to anticipate him. Indeed, he presented himself at the prison gates only two hours after the arrival of the documents, when no one but the governor was aware of their contents.

Leonard was as usual at his business in the schoolmaster's department; and thither a summons was sent for him, while Dr May and the governor alone awaited his arrival. Tom's visit was still very recent; and Leonard entered with anxious eyes, brow drawn together, and compressed lips, as though braced to meet another blow; and the unusual room, the presence of the governor instead of the warder, and Dr May's irrepressible emotion, so confirmed the impression, that his face at once assumed a resolute look of painful expectation.

'My boy,' said Dr May, clasping both his hands in his own; 'you have borne much of ill. Can you bear to hear good news?'

'Am I to be sent out to Australia already?' said Leonard – for a shortening of the eight years before his ticket of leave was the sole hope that had presented itself.

'Sent out, yes; out to go wherever you please, Leonard. The right is come round. The truth is out. You are a free man! Do you know what that is? It is a pardon. Your pardon. All that can be done to right you, my boy – but it is as good as a reversal of the sentence.'

The doctor had spoken this with pauses; going on, as Leonard, instead of answering, stood like one in a dream, and at last said with difficulty, 'Who did it then?'

'It was as you always believed.'

'Has he told?' said Leonard, drawing his brows together with the effort to understand.

'No, Leonard. The vengeance he had brought on himself did not give space for repentance; but the pocket-book, with your receipt, was upon him, and your innocence is established.'

'And let me congratulate you,' added the governor, shaking hands with him; 'and add, that all I have known of you has been as complete an exculpation as any discovery can be.'

Leonard's hand was passive, his cheek had become white, his forehead still knit. 'Axworthy!' he said, still as in a trance.

'Yes. Hurt in a brawl at Paris. He was brought to the Hotel Dieu; and my son Tom was called to see him.'

'Sam Axworthy!' repeated Leonard, putting his hand over his eyes, as if one sensation overpowered everything else; and thus he stood for some seconds, to the perplexity of both.

They showed him the papers; he gazed, but without comprehension; and then putting the bag, provided by Tom, into his hand, they sent him, moving in a sort of mechanical obedience, into the room of one of the officials to change his dress.

Dr May poured out to the governor and chaplain, who by this time had joined them, the history of Leonard's generous behaviour at the time of the trial, and listened in return to their account of the growing impression he had created – a belief, almost reluctant, that instead of being their prime specimen, he could only be in their hands by mistake. He was too sincere not to have confessed had he been really guilty; and in the long-run, such behaviour as his would have been impossible in one unrepentant. He had been the more believed from the absence of complaint, demonstration, or assertion; and the constant endeavour to avoid notice, coupled with the quiet thorough execution of whatever was set before him with all his might.

This was a theme to occupy the doctor for a long time; but at last he grew eager for Leonard's return, and went to hasten him. He started up, still in the convict garb, the bag untouched.

'I beg your pardon,' he said, when his friend's exclamation had reminded him of what had been desired of him; and in a few minutes he re-appeared in the ordinary dress of a gentleman, but the change did not seem to have made him realize his freedom – there was the same submissive manner, the same conventional gesture of respect in reply to the chaplain's warm congratulation.

'Come, Leonard, I am always missing the boat, but I don't want to do so now. We must get home to-night. Have you anything to take with you?'

'My Bible and Prayer-book. They are my own, sir;' as he turned to the governor, 'May I go to my cell for them?'

Again they tarried long for him, and became afraid that he had fallen into another reverie; but going to fetch him, found that the delay was caused by the farewells of all who had come in his way. The tidings of his full justification had spread, and each official was eager to wish him good speed, and thank him for the aid of his example and support. The schoolmaster, who had of late treated him as a friend, kept close to him, rejoicing in his liberation, but expecting to miss him sorely; and such of the convicts as were within reach, were not without their share in the general exultation. He had never galled them by his superiority; and though Brown, the clerk, had been his only friend, he had done many an act of kindness; and when writing letters for the unlearned, had spoken many a wholesome simple word that had gone home to the heart. His hand was as ready for a parting grasp from a fellow-prisoner as from a warder; and his thought and voice were recalled to leave messages for men out of reach; his eyes moistened at the kindly felicitations; but when he was past the oft-trodden precincts of the inner court and long galleries, the passiveness returned, and he received the last good-byes of the governor and superior officers, as if only half alive to their import. And thus, silent, calm, and grave, his composure like that of a man walking in his sleep, did Leonard Ward pass the arched gateway, enter on the outer world, and end his three and a half years of penal servitude.

'I'm less like an angel than he is like St Peter,' thought Dr May, as he watched the fixed dreamy gaze; 'but this is like "yet wist he not that it was true, but thought he saw a vision." When will he realize liberty, and enjoy it? I shall do him a greater kindness by leaving him to himself.'

And in spite of his impatience, Dr May refrained from disturbing that open-eyed trance all the way down the long hill, trusting to the crowd in the steamer for rousing him to perceive that he was no longer among russet coats and blue shirts; but he stood motionless, gazing, or at least his face turned, towards the Dorset coast, uttering no word, making no movement, save when summoned by his guide – then obeying as implicitly as though it were his jailor.

So they came to the pier; and so they walked the length of Weymouth, paced the platform, and took their places in the train. Just as they had shot beyond the town, and come into the little wooded valleys beyond, Leonard turned round, and with the first sparkle in his eye, exclaimed, 'Trees! Oh, noble trees and hedges!' then turned again to look in enchantment at the passing groups – far from noble, though bright with autumn tints – that alternated with the chalk downs.

Dr May was pleased at this revival, and entertained at the start a glance of inquiring alarm from an old gentleman in the other corner. Presently, in the darkness of a cutting, again Leonard spoke; 'Where are you taking me, Dr May?'

'Home, of course.'

Whatever the word might imply to the poor lad, he was satisfied, and again became absorbed in the sight of fields, trees, and hedgerows; while Dr May watched the tokens of secret dismay in their fellow-traveller, who had no doubt understood (home) to mean his private asylum. Indeed, though the steady full dark eyes showed no aberration, there was a strange deep cave between the lid and the eyebrow, which gave a haggard look; the spare, worn, grave features had an expression – not indeed weak, nor wandering, but half bewildered, half absorbed; moreover, in spite of Tom's minute selection of apparel, it had been too hasty a toilette for the garments to look perfectly natural; and the cropped head was so suspicious, that it was no wonder that at the first station, the old gentleman gathered up his umbrella, with intense courtesy squeezed gingerly to the door, carefully avoiding any stumble over perilous toes, and made his escape – entering another carriage, whence he no doubt signed cautions against the lunatic and his keeper, since no one again invaded their privacy.

Perhaps this incident most fully revealed to the doctor, how unlike other people his charge was, how much changed from the handsome spirited lad on whom the trouble had fallen; and he looked again and again at the profile turned to the window, as fixed and set as though it had been carved.

'Ah, patience is an exhausting virtue!' said he to himself. 'Verily it is bearing – bearing up under the full weight; and the long bent spring is the slower in rebounding in proportion to its inherent strength. Poor lad, what protracted endurance it has been! There is health and force in his face; no line of sin, nor sickness, nor worldly care, such as it makes one's heart ache to see ageing young faces; yet how utterly unlike the face of one-and-twenty! I had rather see it sadder than so strangely settled and sedate! Shall I speak to him again? Not yet; those green hill-sides, those fields and cattle, must refresh him better than my clavers, after his grim stony mount of purgatory. I wish it were a brighter day to greet him, instead of this grey damp fog.'

The said fog prevented any semblance of sunset; but through the grey moonlit haze, Leonard kept his face to the window, pertinaciously clearing openings in the bedewed glass, as though the varying outline of the horizon had a fascination for him. At last, after ten minutes of glaring gas at a junction had by contrast rendered the mist impenetrable, and reduced the view to brightened clouds of steam, and to white telegraphic posts, erecting themselves every moment, with their wires changing their perspective in incessant monotony, he ceased his gaze, and sat upright in his place, with the same strange rigid somnambulist air.

Dr May resolved to rouse him.

'Well, Leonard,' he said, 'this has been a very long fever; but we are well through it at last – with the young doctor from Paris to our aid.'

Probably Leonard only heard the voice, not the words, for he passed his hand over his face, and looked up to the doctor, saying dreamily, 'Let me see! Is it all true?' and then, with a grave wistful look, 'It was not I who did that thing, then?'

'My dear!' exclaimed the doctor, starting forward, and catching hold of his hand, 'have they brought you to this?'

'I always meant to ask you, if I ever saw you alone again,' said Leonard.

'But you don't mean that you have imagined it!'

'Not constantly – not when any one was with me,' said Leonard, roused by Dr May's evident dismay; and drawn on by his face of anxious inquiry, 'At Milbank, I generally thought I remembered it just as they described it in court, and that it was some miserable ruinous delusion that hindered my confessing; but the odd thing was, that the moment any one opened my door, I forgot all about it – resolutions and all, and was myself again.'

'Then surely – surely you left that horror with the solitude?'

'Yes, till lately; but when it did come back, I could not be sure what was recollection of fact, and what of my own fancy;' and he drew his brows together in painful effort. 'Did I know who did it, or did I only guess?'

'You came to a right conclusion, and would not let me act on it.'

'And I really did write the receipt, and not dream it?'

'That receipt has been in my hand. It was what has brought you here.' And now to hearing ears, Dr May went over the narrative; and Leonard stood up under the little lamp in the roof of the carriage to read the papers.

'I recollect – I understand,' he said, presently, and sat down, grave and meditative – no longer dreamy, but going over events, which had at last acquired assurance to his memory from external circumstances. Presently his fingers were clasped together over his face, his head bent, and then he looked up, and said, 'Do they know it – my sister and brother?'

'No. We would not write till you were free. You must date the first letter from Stoneborough.'

The thought had brought a bitter pang. 'One half year sooner——' and he leant back in his seat, with fingers tightly pressed together, and trembling with emotion.

'Nay, Leonard; may not the dear child be the first to rejoice in the fulfilment of her own sweet note of comfort? They could not harm the innocent.'

'Not innocent,' he said; 'not innocent of causing all the discord that has ended in their exile, and the dear child's death.'

'Then this is what has preyed on you, and changed you so much more of late,' said Dr May.

'When I knew that I was indeed guilty of *her* death,' said Leonard, in a calm full conviction of too long standing to be accompanied with agitation, though permanently bowing him down.

'And you never spoke of this: not to the chaplain?'

'I never could. It would have implied all the rest that he could not believe. And it would not have changed the fact.'

'The aspect of it may change, Leonard. You know yourself how many immediate causes combined, of which you cannot accuse yourself – your brother's wrongheadedness, and all the rest. And,' added the doctor, recovering himself, 'you do see it in other aspects, I know. Think of the spirit set free to be near you – free from the world that has gone so hard with you!'

'I can't keep that thought long; I'm not worthy of it.'

Again he was silent; but presently said, as with a sudden thought, 'You would have told me if there were any news of Ave.'

'No, there has been no letter since her last inclosure for you;' and then Dr May gave the details from the papers on the doings of Henry's division of the army.

'Will Henry let me be with them?' said Leonard musingly.

'They will come home, depend upon it. You must wait till you hear.'

Leonard thought a little while, then said, 'Where did you say I was to go, Dr May?'

'Where, indeed? Home, Leonard – home. Ethel is waiting for us. To the High Street.'

Leonard looked up again with his bewildered face, then said, 'I know what you do with me will be right, but——'

'Had you rather not?' said the doctor, startled.

'Rather!' and the doctor, to his exceeding joy, saw the fingers over his eyes moist with the tears they tried to hide; 'I only meant——' he added, with an effort, 'you must think and judge – I can't think – whether I ought.'

'If you ask me that,' said Dr May, earnestly, 'all I have to say is, that I don't know what palace is worthy of you.'

There was not much said after that; and the doctor fell asleep, waking only at the halts at stations to ask where he was.

At last came 'Blewer!' and as the light shone on the clock, Leonard said, 'A quarter past twelve! It is the very train I went by! Is it a dream?'

Ten minutes more, and 'Stoneborough' was the cry.

Hastily springing out, shuffling the tickets into the porter's hand, and grappling Leonard's arm as if he feared an escape, Dr May hurried him into the empty streets, and strode on in silence.

The pull at the door-bell was answered instantly by Ethel herself. She held out her hand, and grasped that which Leonard had almost withheld, shrinking as from too sudden a vision; and then she ardently exchanged kisses with her father.

'Where's Tom? Gone to bed?' said Dr May, stepping into the bright drawing-room.

'No,' said Ethel, demurely; 'he is gone – he is gone to America.'

The doctor gave a prodigious start, and looked at her again.

'He went this afternoon,' she said. 'There is some matter about the "Diseases of Climate" that he must settle before the book is published; and he thought he could best be spared now. He has left messages that I will give you by-and-by; but you must both be famished.'

Her looks indicated that all was right; and both turned to welcome the guest, who stood where the first impulse had left him, in the hall, not moving forward, till he was invited in to the fire, and the meal already spread. He then obeyed, and took the place pointed out; while the doctor nervously expatiated on the cold, damp, and changes of train; and Ethel, in the active bashfulness of hidden agitation, made tea, cut bread, carved chicken, and waited on them with double assiduity, as Leonard, though eating as a man who had fasted since early morning, was passive as a little child, merely accepting what was offered to him, and not even passing his cup till she held out her hand for it.

She did not even dare to look at him; she could not bear that he should see her do so; it was enough to know that he was free – that he was there – that it was over. She did not want to see how it had changed him; and, half to set him at ease, half to work off her own excitement, she talked to her father, and told him of the little events of his absence till the meal was over; and, at half-past one, good nights were exchanged with Leonard, and the doctor saw him to his room, then returned to his daughter on her own threshold.

'That's a thing to have lived for,' he said.

Ethel locked her hands together, and looked up.

'And now, how about this other dénouement? I might have guessed that the wind sat in that quarter.'

'But you're not to guess it, papa. It is really and truly about the "Diseases of Climate."'

'Swamp fevers, eh! and agues!'

The 'if you can help it,' was a great comfort now; Ethel could venture on saying, 'Of course that has something to do with it; but he really does make the book his object; and please – please don't give any hint that you suspect anything else.'

'I suppose you are in his confidence; and I must ask no questions.'

'I hated not telling you, and letting you teaze him; but he trusted me just enough not to make me dare to say a word; though I never was sure there was a word to say. Now do just once own, papa, that Tom is the romantic one after all, to have done as he did in the height of the trouble.'

'Well in his place so should I,' said the doctor, with the perverseness of not satisfying expectations of amazement.

'*You* would,' said Ethel; 'but Tom! would you have thought it of Tom?'

'Tom has more in him than shows through his spectacles,' answered Dr May. 'So! that's the key to his restless fit. Poor fellow! How did it go with him? They have not been carrying it on all this time, surely!'

'Oh, no, no, papa! She cut him to the heart, poor boy! thought he was laughing at her – told him it had all been irony. He has no notion whether she will ever forgive him.'

'A very good lesson, Master Doctor Thomas,' said Dr May, with a twinkle in his eye; 'and turn out as it will, it has done him good – tided him over a dangerous time of life. Well, you must tell me all about it to-morrow; I'm too sleepy to know what I'm talking of.'

The sleepiness that always finished off the doctor's senses at the right moment, was a great preservative of his freshness and vigour; but Ethel was far from sharing it, and was very glad when the clock sounded a legitimate hour for getting up, and dressing by candle-light, briefly answering Gertrude's eager questions on the arrival. It was a pouring wet morning, and she forbade Daisy to go to church – indeed, it would have been too bad for herself on any morning but this – any but this, as she repeated, smiling at her own spring of thankfulness, as she fortified herself with a weight of waterproof, and came forth in the darkness of 7.45, on a grim November day.

A few steps before her, pacing on, umbrellaless, was a figure which made her hurry to overtake him.

'O Leonard! after your journey, and in this rain!'

He made a gesture of courtesy, but moved as if to follow, not join her. Did he not know whether he were within the pale of humanity?

'Here is half an umbrella. Won't you hold it for me?' she said; and as he followed his instinct of obedience, she put it into his hand, and took his arm, thinking that this familiarity would best restore him to a sense of his regained position; and, moreover, feeling glad and triumphant to be thus leaning, and to have that strong arm to contend with the driving blast that came howling round the corner of Minster Street, and fighting for their shelter. They were both out of breath when they paused to recover in the deep porch of the Minster.

'Is Dr May come home?'

'Yes – and——'

Ethel signed; and Mr Wilmot held out an earnest hand, with, 'This is well. I am glad to see you.'

'Thank you, sir,' said Leonard, heartily; 'and for all——'

'This is your new beginning of life, Leonard. God bless you in it.'

As Mr Wilmot passed on, Ethel for the first time ventured to look up into the eyes – and saw their hollow setting, their loss of sparkle, but their added steadfastness and resolution. She could not help repeating the long treasured lines: 'And, Leonard,

"– grieve not for thy woes,
Disgrace and trouble;
For He who honour best bestows,
Shall give thee double."'

'I've never ceased to be glad you read Marmion with me,' he hastily said, as they turned into church on hearing a clattering of choristers behind them.

Clara might have had such sensations when she bound the spurs on her knight's heels; yet even she could hardly have had so pure, unselfish, and exquisite a joy as Ethel's, in receiving the pupil who had been in a far different school from hers.

The grey dawn through the bloom, the depths of shadow in the twilight church, softening and rendering all more solemn and mysterious, were more in accordance than bright and beamy sunshine with her subdued grave thankfulness; and there was something suitable in the fewness of the congregation that had gathered in the Lady Chapel – so few, that there was no room for shyness, either in, or for, him who was again taking his place there, with steady composed demeanour, its stillness concealing so much.

Ethel had reckoned on the verse – 'That He might hear the mournings of such as are in captivity, and deliver the children appointed unto death.' But she had not reckoned on its falling on her ears in the deep full-toned melodious bass, that came in, giving body to the young notes of the choristers – a voice so altered and mellowed since she last had heard it, that it made her look across in doubt, and recognise in the uplifted face, that here indeed the freed captive was at home, and lifted above himself.

When the clause, in the Litany, for all prisoners and captives brought to her the thrill that she had only to look up to see the fulfilment of many and many a prayer for one captive, for once she did not hear the response, only saw the bent head, as though there were thoughts went too deep to find voice. And again, there was the special thanksgiving that Mr Wilmot could not refrain from introducing for one to whom a great mercy had been vouchsafed. If Ethel had had to swim home, she would not but have been there!

Charles Cheviot addressed them as they came out of church: 'Good morning – Mr Ward, I hope to do myself the honour of calling on you – I shall see you again, Ethel.'

And off he went over the glazy stones to his own house; Ethel knowing that this cordial salutation and intended call were meant to be honourable amends for his suspicions; but Leonard, unconscious of the import, and scarcely knowing indeed that he was addressed, made his mechanical gesture of respect, and looked up, down, and round, absorbed in the scene. 'How exactly the same it all looks,' he said; 'the cloister gate, and the Swan, and the postman in the very same waterproof cape.'

'Do you not feel like being just awake?'

'No; it is more like being a ghost, or somebody else.'

Then the wind drove them on too fast for speech, till as they crossed the High Street, Ethel pointed through the plane-trees to two round black eyes, and a shining black nose, at the dining-room window.

'My Mab, my poor little Mab! – You have kept her all this time! I was afraid to ask for her. I could not hope it.'

'I could not get my spoilt child, Gertrude, to bed without taking Mab, that she might see the meeting.'

Perhaps it served Daisy right that the meeting did not answer her expectations. Mab and her master had both grown older; she smelt round him long before she was sure of him, and then their content in one another was less shown by fervent rapture, than by the quiet hand smoothing her silken coat; and, in return, by her wistful eye, nestling gesture, gently waving tail.

And Leonard! How was it with him? It was not easy to tell in his absolute passiveness. He seemed to have neither will nor impulse to speak, move, or act, though whatever was desired of him, he did with the implicit obedience that no one could bear to see. They put books near him, but he did not voluntarily touch one: they asked if he would write to his sister, and he took the pen in his hand, but did not accomplish a commencement. Ethel asked him if he were tired, or had a head-ache.

'Thank you, no,' he said; 'I'll write,' and made a dip in the ink.

'I did not mean to teaze you,' she said; 'the mail is not going just yet, and there is no need for haste. I was only afraid something was wrong.'

'Thank you,' he said, submissively; 'I will – when I can think; but it is all too strange. I have not seen a lady, nor a room like this, since July three years.'

After that Ethel let him alone, satisfied that peace was the best means of recovering the exhaustion of his long-suffering.

The difficulty was that this was no house for quiet, especially the day after the master's return: the door-bell kept on ringing, and each time he looked startled and nervous, though assured that it was only patients. But at twelve o'clock in rushed Mr Cheviot's little brother, with a note from

Mary, lamenting that it was too wet for herself, but saying that Charles was coming in the afternoon, and that he intended to have a dinner-party of old Stoneborough scholars to welcome Leonard back.

Meanwhile, Martin Cheviot, wanting to see, and not to stare, and to unite cordiality and unconsciousness, made an awkward mixture of all, and did not know how to get away; and before he had accomplished it, Mr Edward Anderson was announced. He heartily shook hands with Leonard, eagerly welcomed him, and talked volubly; and his last communication was, 'If it clears, you will see Matilda this afternoon.'

'I did not know she was here.'

'Yes; she and Harvey are come to Mrs Ledwich's, to stay over Sunday;' and there was a laugh in the corner of his eye, that convinced Ethel that the torrents of rain would be no protection.

'Papa,' said she, darting out to meet her father in the hall, 'you must take Leonard out in your brougham this afternoon, if you don't want him driven distracted. If he is in the house, ropes won't hold Mrs Harvey Anderson from him!'

So Dr May invited his guest to share his drive; and the excitement began to seem unreal when the doctor returned alone.

'I dropped him at Cocksmoor,' he said. 'It was Richard's notion that he would be quieter there – able to get out, and go to church, without being stared at.'

'Did he like it?' asked Gertrude, disappointed.

'If one told him to chop off his finger, he would do it, and never show whether he liked it. Richard asked him, and he said, "Thank you." I never could get an opening to show him that we did not want to suppress him; I never saw spirit so quenched.'

Charles Cheviot thought it was a mistake to do what gave the appearance of suppression – he said that it was due to Leonard to welcome him as heartily as possible, and not to encourage false shame, where there was no disgrace; so he set his wife to fill up her cards for his dinner-party, and included in it Mr and Mrs Harvey Anderson, for the sake of their warm interest in the liberated prisoner.

'However, Leonard was out of the scrape,' as the doctor expressed it, for he had one of his severe sore throats, and was laid up at Cocksmoor. Richard was dismayed by his passive obedience – a novelty to the gentle eldest, who had all his life been submitting, and now was puzzled by his guest's unfailing acquiescence without a token of preference or independence: and comically amazed at the implicit fulfilment of his recommendation to keep the throat in bed – a wise suggestion, but one that the whole house of May, in their own persons, would have scouted. Nothing short of the highest authority ever kept them there.

The semblance of illness was perhaps a good starting-point for a return to the ways of the world; and on the day week of his going to Cocksmoor, Ethel found him by the fire, beginning his letters to his brother and sister, and looking brighter and more cheery, but so devoid of voice, that speech could not be expected of him.

She had just looked in again after some parish visiting, when a quick soldierly step was heard, and in walked Aubrey.

'No; I'm not come to you, Ethel; I'm only come to this fellow;' and he ardently grasped his hand. 'I've got leave till Monday, and I shall stay here and see nobody else. – What, a sore throat? Couldn't you get wrapped up enough between the two doctors?'

Leonard's eyes lighted as he muttered his hoarse 'Thank you;' and Ethel lingered for a little desultory talk to her brother, contrasting the changes that the three years had made in the two friends. Aubrey, drilled out of his home scholarly dreaminess by military and practical discipline, had exchanged his native languor for prompt upright alertness of bearing and speech; his eye had grown more steady, his mouth had lost its vague pensive expression, and was rendered sterner by the dark moustache; definite thought, purpose, and action, had moulded his whole countenance and person into hopeful manhood, instead of visionary boyhood. The other face, naturally the most full of fire and resolution, looked strangely different in its serious unsmiling gravity, the deeply worn stamp of patient endurance and utter isolation. There was much of rest and calm, and even of content – but withal a quenched look, as if the lustre of youth and hope had been extinguished, and the soul had been so driven in upon itself, that there was no opening to receive external sympathy – a settled expression, all the stranger on a face with the clear smoothness of early youth. One thing at least was unchanged – the firm friendship and affection – that kept the two constantly casting glances over one another, to assure themselves of the presence before them.

Ethel left them together; and her father, who made out that he should save time by going to Cocksmoor Church on Sunday morning, reported that the boys seemed very happy together in their own way; but that Richard reported himself to have been at the sole expense of conversation in the evening – the only time such an event could ever have occurred!

Aubrey returned home late on the Sunday evening; and Leonard set off to walk part of the way with him in the dusk, but ended by coming the whole distance, for the twilight opened their lips in this renewal of old habits.

'It is all right to be walking together again,' said Aubrey, warmly; 'though it is not like those spring days.'

'I've thought of them every Sunday.'

'And what are you going to do now, old fellow?'

'I don't know.'

'I hear Bramshaw is going to offer you to come into his office, Now, don't do that, Leonard, whatever you do!'

'I don't know.'

'You are to have all your property back, you know, and you could do much better for yourself than that.'

'I can't tell till I have heard from my brother.'

'But, Leonard, promise me now – you'll not go out and make a Yankee of yourself.'

'I can't tell; I shall do what he wishes.'

Aubrey presently found that Leonard seemed to have no capacity to think or speak of the future or the past. He set Aubrey off on his own concerns, and listened with interest, asking questions that showed him perfectly alive to what regarded his friend; but the passive inaction of will and spirits still continued, and made him almost a disappointment.

On Monday morning there was a squabble between the young engineer and the Daisy, who was a profound believer in the scientific object of Tom's journey, and greatly resented the far too obvious construction thereof.

'You must read lots of bad novels at Chatham, Aubrey; it is like the fag end of the most trumpery of them all!'

'You haven't gone far enough in your mathematics, you see, Daisy. You think one and one——'

'Make two. So I say.'

'I've gone into the higher branches.'

'I didn't think you were so simple and common-place. It would be so stupid to think he must – just because he could not help making this discovery.'

'All for want of the higher branches of mathematics! One plus one – equals one.'

'One minus common sense, plus folly, plus romance, minus anything to do. Your equation is worthy of Mrs Harvey Anderson. I gave *her* a good dose of the "Diseases of Climate!"'

Aubrey was looking at Ethel all the time Gertrude was triumphing; and finally he said, 'I've no absolute faith in disinterested philanthropy to a younger brother – whatever I had before I went to the Tyrol.'

'What has that to do with it?' asked Gertrude. 'Everybody was cut up, and wanted a change – and you more than all. I do believe the possibility of a love affair absolutely drives people mad: and now they must needs saddle it upon poor Tom – just the one of the family who is not so stupid, but has plenty of other things to think about.'

'So you think it a stupid pastime?'

'Of course it is. Why, just look. Hasn't everybody in the family turned stupid, and of no use, as soon as they went and fell in love? Only good old Ethel here has too much sense; and that's what makes her such a dear old gargoyle. And Harry – he is twice the fun after he comes home, before he gets his fit of love! And all the story books that begin pleasantly, the instant that love gets in, they are just alike – so stupid! And now, if you haven't done it yourself, you want to lug poor innocent Tom in for it.'

'When your time comes, may I be there to see!'

He retreated from her evident designs of clapper-clawing him; and she turned round to Ethel with, 'Now, isn't it stupid, Ethel?'

'Very stupid to think all the zest of life resides in one particular feeling,' said Ethel; 'but more stupid to talk of what you know nothing about.'

Aubrey put in his head for a hurried farewell, and, 'Telegraph to me when Mrs Thomas May comes home.'

'If Mrs Thomas May comes home, I'll——'

'Give her that chair cover,' said Ethel; and her idle needle-woman, having been eight months working one corner of it, went off into fits of laughter, regarding its completion as an equally monstrous feat with an act of cannibalism on the impossible Mrs Thomas May.

How different were these young things, with their rhodomontade and exuberant animation and spirits, from him in whom all the sparkle and aspiration of life seemed extinguished!

CHAPTER XXVII

'A cup was at my lips: it pass'd
As passes the wild desert blast!

* * *

I woke – around me was a gloom
And silence of the tomb;
But in that awful solitude
That little spirit by me stood –
But oh, how changed!'

Thoughts in Past Years.

Under Richard's kind let-alone system, Leonard was slowly recovering tone. First he took to ruling lines in the Cocksmoor account-books, then he helped in their audit; and with occupation came the sense of the power of voluntary exertion. He went and came freely, and began to take long rambles in the loneliest parts of the heath and plantations, while

Richard left him scrupulously to his own devices, and rejoiced to see them more defined and vigorous every day. The next step was to assist in the night-school where Richard had hitherto toiled single-handed among very rough subjects. The technical training and experience derived from Leonard's work under the schoolmaster at Portland were invaluable; and though taking the lead was the last thing he would have thought of, he no sooner entered the school than attention and authority were there, and Richard found that what had to him been a vain and patient struggle was becoming both effective and agreeable. Interest in his work was making Leonard cheerful and alert, though still grave, and shrinking from notice – avoiding the town by daylight, and only coming to Dr May's in the dark evenings.

On the last Sunday in Advent, Richard was engaged to preach at his original curacy, and that the days before and after it should likewise be spent away from home was insisted on after the manner of the friends of hard-working clergy. He had the less dislike to going that he could leave his schoolwork to Leonard, who was to be housed at his father's, and there was soon perceived to have become a much more ordinary member of society than on his first arrival.

One evening, there was a loud peal at the door-bell, and the maid – one of Ethel's experiments of training – came in.

'Please sir, a gentleman has brought a cockatoo and a letter and a little boy from the Archdeacon.'

'Archdeacon!' cried Dr May, catching sight of the handwriting on the letter and starting up. 'Archdeacon Norman——'

'One of Norman's stray missionaries and a Maori newly caught; oh what fun!' cried Daisy, in ecstasy.

At that moment, through the still open door, walking as if he had lived there all his life, there entered the prettiest little boy that ever was seen – a little knickerbocker boy, with floating rich dark ringlets, like a miniature cavalier coming forth from a picture, with a white cockatoo on his wrist. Not in the least confused, he went straight towards Dr May and said, 'Good morning, grandpapa.'

'Ha! And who may you be, my elfin prince?' said the doctor.

'I'm Dickie – Richard Rivers May – I'm not an elfin prince,' said the boy, with a moment's hurt feeling, 'Papa sent me.' By that time the boy was fast in his grandfather's embrace, and was only enough released to give him space to answer the eager question, 'Papa – papa here?'

'Oh no; I came with Mr Seaford.'

The doctor hastily turned Dickie over to the two aunts, and hastened forth to the stranger whose name he well knew as a colonist's son, a favourite and devoted clerical pupil of Norman's.

'Aunt Ethel,' said little Richard, with instant recognition; 'Mamma said you would be like her, but I don't think you will.'

'Nor I, Dickie, but we'll try. And who's that?'

'Yes, what am I to be like?' asked Gertrude.

'You're not Aunt Daisy – Aunt Daisy is a little girl.'

Gertrude made him the lowest of curtseys; for not to be taken for a little girl was the compliment she esteemed above all others. Dickie's next speech was, 'And is that Uncle Aubrey?'

'No, that's Leonard.'

Dickie shook hands with him very prettily; but then returning upon Ethel, observed, 'I thought it was Uncle Aubrey, because soldiers always cut their hair so close.'

The other guest was so thorough a colonist, and had so little idea of anything but primitive hospitality, that he had had no notion of writing beforehand to announce his coming, and accident had delayed the letters by which Norman and Meta had announced their decision of sending home their eldest boy under his care.

'Papa had no time to teach me alone,' said Dickie, who seemed to have been taken into the family councils; 'and mamma is always busy, and I wasn't getting any good with some of the boys that come to school to papa.'

'Indeed, Mr Dickie!' said the doctor, full of suppressed laughter.

'It is quite true,' said Mr Seaford; 'there are some boys that the Archdeacon feels bound to educate, but who are not desirable companions for his son.'

'It is a great sacrifice,' remarked the young gentleman.

'Oh Dickie, Dickie,' cried Gertrude in fits, 'don't you be a prig——'

'Mamma said it,' defiantly answered Dickie.

'Only a parrot,' said Ethel, behind her handkerchief; but Dickie, who heard whatever he was not meant to hear, answered –'

'It is not a parrot; it is a white cockatoo, that the chief of (something unutterable) brought down on his wrist like a hawk to the mission-ship; and that mamma sent as a present to Uncle George.'

'I prefer the parrot that has fallen to my share,' observed the doctor.

It was by this time perched beside him, looking perfectly at ease and thoroughly at home. There was something very amusing in the aspect of the little man; he so completely recalled his mother's humming-bird title by the perfect look of finished porcelain perfection that even a journey from the Antipodes with only gentleman nursemaids had not destroyed. The ringleted rich brown hair shone like glossy silk, the cheeks were like painting, the trim well-made legs and small hands and feet looked dainty and fairy-like, yet not at all effeminate; hands and face were a healthy brown, and contrasted with the little white collar, the set of which made Ethel exclaim, 'Just look, Daisy, that's what I always told you about Meta's doings. Only I can't understand it. – Dickie, have the fairies kept you in repair ever since mamma dressed you last?'

'We haven't any fairies in New Zealand,' he replied; 'and mamma never dressed me since I was a baby!'

'And what are you now?' said the doctor.

'I am eight years old,' said this piece of independence, perfectly well mannered, and *au fait* in all the customs of the tea-table; and when the meal was over, he confidentially said to his aunt, 'Shall I come and help you wash up? I never break anything.'

Ethel declined this kind offer; but he hung on her hand and asked if he might go and see the school-room, where papa and Uncle Harry used to blow soap bubbles. She lighted a candle, and the little gentleman showed himself minutely acquainted with the whole geography of the house, knew all the rooms and the pictures, and where everything had happened, even to adventures that Ethel had forgotten.

'It is of no use to say there are no fairies in New Zealand,' said Dr May, taking him on his knee, and looking into the blue depths of Norman's eyes. 'You have been head-waiter to Queen Mab, and perpetually here when she made you put a girdle round the earth in forty minutes.'

'Papa read that to the boys, and they said it was stupid and no use,' said Dickie; 'but papa said that the electric telegraph would do it.'

The little cavalier appeared not to know what it was to be at a loss for an answer, and the joint letter from his parents explained that his precocious quickness was one of their causes for sending him home. He was so deft and useful as to be important in the household, and necessarily always living with his father and mother, he took constant part in their conversation, and was far more learned in things than in books. In the place where they were settled, trustworthy boy society was unattainable, and they had felt their little son in danger of being spoilt and made forward from his very goodness and brightness – wrote Meta, 'If you find him a forward imp, recollect it is my fault for having depended so much on him.'

His escort was a specimen of the work Norman had done; not actual mission-work, but preparation and inspiriting of those who went forth on the actual task. He was a simple-minded single-hearted man, one of the first pupils in Norman's college, and the one who had most fully imbibed his spirit. He had been for some years a clergyman, and latterly had each winter joined the mission voyage among the Melanesian Isles, returning to their homes the lads brought for the summer for education to the mission college in New Zealand, and spending some time at a station upon one or other of the islands. He had come back from the last voyage much out of health, and had been for weeks nursed by Meta, until a long rest having been declared necessary, he had been sent to England as the only place where he would not be tempted to work, and was to visit his only remaining relation, a sister, who had married an officer and was in Ireland.

He was burning to go back again, and eagerly explained – sagely corroborated by the testimony of the tiny archdeacon – that his illness was to be laid to the blame of his own imprudence, not to the climate; and he dwelt upon the delights of the yearly voyage among the lovely islands, beautiful beyond imagination, fenced in by coral breakwaters, within which the limpid water displayed exquisite sea-flowers, shells, and fishes of magical gorgeousness of hue; of the brilliant white beach, fringing the glorious vegetation, cocoa-nut, bread-fruit, banana, and banyan, growing on the sloping sides of volcanic rocks; of mysterious red-glowing volcano lights seen far out at sea at night; of glades opening to show high-roofed huts covered with mats; of canoes decorated with the shining white shells resembling a poached egg; of natives clustering round, eager and excited, seldom otherwise than friendly; though in hitherto unvisited places, or in those where the wanton outrages of sandal-wood traders had excited distrust, caution was necessary, and there was peril enough to give the voyage a full character of heroism and adventure. Bows and poisoned arrows were sometimes brought down – and Dickie insisted that they had been used – but in general the mission was recognised, and an eager welcome given; presents of fish-hooks, or of braid and handkerchiefs, established a friendly feeling; and readiness – in which the Hand of the Maker must be recognised – was manifested to entrust lads to the mission for the summer's training at the college in New Zealand – wild lads, innocent of all clothing, except marvellous adornments of their woolly locks, wigged out sometimes into huge cauliflowers whitened with coral lime, or arranged quarterly red and white, and their noses decorated with rings, which were their nearest approach to a pocket, as they served for the suspension of fish-hooks, or any small article. A radiate arrangement of skewers from the nose, in unwitting imitation of a cat's whiskers, had even been known. A few days taught dressing and eating in a civilized fashion; and time, example, and the wonderful influence of the head of the mission, trained these naturally intelligent boys into much that was hopeful. Dickie, who had been often at the college, had much to tell of familiarity with the light canoes that some cut out and launched; of the teaching them English games; of their orderly ways in school and in hall; of the prayers in their many tongues, and of the Baptism of some, after full probation, and at least one winter's return to their own isles, as a test of their sincerity and constancy. Much as the May family had already heard of this wonderful work, it came all the closer and nearer now. The isle of Alan, Ernescliffe's burial-place, had now many Christians in it. Harry's friend, the young chief David, was dead; but his people were some of them already teachers and examples, and the whole region was full to overflowing of the harvest, calling out for labourers to gather it in.

Silent as usual, Leonard nevertheless was listening with all his heart, and with parted lips and kindling eyes that gave back somewhat of his former countenance. Suddenly his face struck Mr Seaford, and turning on him with a smile, he said, 'You should be with us yourself, you look cut out for mission work.'

Leonard murmured something, blushed up to the ears, and subsided; but the simple, single-hearted Mr Seaford, his soul all on one object, his experience only in one groove, by no means laid aside the thought, and the moment he was out of Leonard's presence, eagerly asked who that young man was.

'Leonard Ward? he is – he is the son of an old friend,' replied Dr May, a little perplexed to explain his connexion.

'What is he doing? I never saw any one looking more suited for our work.'

'Tell him so again,' said Dr May; 'I know no one that would be fitter.'

They were all taken up with the small grandson the next day. He was ready in his fairy-page trimness to go to the early service at the Minster; but he was full of the colonial *ni admirari* principle, and was quite above being struck by the grand old building, or allowing its superiority either to papa's own church or Auckland Cathedral. They took him to present to Mary on their way back from church, when he was the occasion of a great commotion by carrying the precious Master Charlie all across the hall to his mamma, and quietly observing in resentment at the outcry, that of course he always carried little Ethel about when mamma and nurse were busy. After breakfast, when he had finished his investigations of all Dr May's domains, and much entertained Gertrude by his knowledge of them, Ethel set him down to write a letter to his father, and her own to Meta being engrossing, she did not look much more after him till Dr May came in, and said, 'I want you to sketch off a portrait of her dicky bird for Meta;' and he put before her a natural history with a figure of that tiny humming-bird which is endowed with swansdown knickerbockers.

'By-the-bye, where is the sprite?'

He was not to be found; and when dinner-time, and much calling and searching failed to produce him, his grandfather declared that he was gone back to Elf-land; but Leonard recollected certain particular inquiries about the situation of the Grange and of Cocksmoor, and it was concluded that he had anticipated the doctor's intentions of taking him and Mr Seaford there in the afternoon. The notion was confirmed by the cockatoo having likewise disappeared; but there was no great anxiety, since the little New Zealander appeared as capable of taking care of himself as any gentleman in Her Majesty's dominions; and a note had already been sent to his aunt informing her of his arrival. Still, a summons to the doctor in an opposite direction was inopportune, the more so as the guest was to remain at Stoneborough only this one day, and had letters and messages for Mr and Mrs Rivers; while it was also desirable to see whether the boy had gone to Cocksmoor.

Leonard proposed to become Mr Seaford's guide to the Grange, learn whether Dickie were there, and meet the two ladies at Cocksmoor with the tidings, leaving Mr Seaford and the boy to be picked up by the doctor on his return. It was his first voluntary offer to go anywhere, though he had more than once been vainly invited to the Grange with Richard.

Much conversation on the mission took place during the walk, and resulted in Mr Seaford's asking Leonard if his profession were settled. 'No,' he said; and not at all aware that his companion did not know what every other person round him knew, he added, 'I have been thrown out of everything – I am waiting to hear from my brother.'

'Then you are not at a University?'

'Oh no; I was a clerk.'

'Then if nothing is decided, is it impossible that you should turn your eyes to our work?'

'Stay,' said Leonard, standing still; 'I must ask whether you know all about me. Would it be possible to admit to such work as yours one who, by a terrible mistake, has been under sentence of death and in confinement for three years?'

'I must think! Let us talk of this another time. Is that the Grange?' hastily exclaimed the missionary, rather breathlessly.

Leonard with perfect composure replied that it was, pointed out the different matters of interest, and, though a little more silent, showed no other change of manner. He was asking the servant at the door if Master May were there, when Mr Rivers came out and conducted both into the drawing-room, where little Dickie was, sure enough. It appeared that, cockatoo on wrist, he had put his pretty face up to the glass of Mrs Rivers's morning-room, and had asked her, 'Is this mamma's room, Aunt Flora? Where's Margaret?'

Uncle, aunt and cousin had all been captivated by him, and he was at present looking at the display of all Margaret's treasures, keenly appreciating the useful and ingenious, but condemning the merely ornamental as only fit for his baby sister. Margaret was wonderfully gracious and child-like; but perhaps she rather oppressed him; for when Leonard explained that he must go on to meet Miss May at Cocksmoor, the little fellow sprang up, declaring that he wanted to go thither; and though told that his grandfather was coming for him, and that the walk was long, he insisted that he was not tired; and Mr Seaford, finding him not to be dissuaded, broke off his conversation in the midst, and insisted on accompanying him, leaving Mr and Mrs Rivers rather amazed at colonial breeding.

The first time Mr Seaford could accomplish being alone with Dr May, he mysteriously shut the door, and began, 'I am afraid Mrs Rivers thought me very rude; but though no doubt he is quite harmless, I could not let the child or the ladies be alone with him.'

'With whom?'

'With your patient.'

'What patient of mine have you been seeing to-day?' asked Dr May, much puzzled.

'Oh, then you consider him as convalescent, and certainly he does seem rational on every other point; but is this one altogether an hallucination?'

'I have not made out either the hallucination or the convalescent. I beg your pardon,' said the courteous doctor; 'but I cannot understand whom you have seen.'

'Then is not that young Ward a patient of yours? He gave me to understand to-day that he has been under confinement for three years——'

'My poor Leonard!' exclaimed the doctor; 'I wish his hair would grow! This is the second time! And did you really never hear of the Blewer murder, and of Leonard Ward?'

Mr Seaford had some compound edifice of various murders in his mind, and required full enlightenment. Having heard the whole, he was ardent to repair his mistake, both for Leonard's own sake, and that of his cause. The young man was indeed looking ill and haggard; but there was something in the steady eyes, hollow though they still were, and in the determined cast of features, that strangely impressed the missionary with a sense of his being moulded for the work; and on the first opportunity a simple straightforward explanation of the error was laid before Leonard, with an entreaty that if he had no duties to bind him at home, he would consider the need of labourers in the great harvest of the Southern Seas.

Leonard made no answer save 'Thank you,' and that he would think. The grave set features did not light up as they had done unconsciously when listening without personal thought; he only looked considering, and accepted Mr Seaford's address in Ireland, promising to write after hearing from his brother.

Next morning, Dr May gave notice that an old patient was coming to see him, and must be asked to luncheon. Leonard soon after told Ethel that he should not be at home till the evening, and she thought he was going to Cocksmoor, by way of avoiding the stranger. In the twilight, however, Dr May, going up to the station to see his patient off, was astonished to see Leonard emerge from a second-class carriage.

'You here! the last person I expected.'

'I have only been to W—— about my teeth.'

'What, have you been having tooth-ache?'

'At times, but I have had two out, so I hope there is an end of it.'

'And you never mentioned it, you Stoic?'

'It was only at night.'

'And how long has this been?'

'Since I had that cold; but it was no matter.'

'No matter, except that it kept you looking like Count Ugolino, and me always wondering what was the matter with you. And' – detaining him for a moment under the lights of the station – 'this extraction must have been a pretty business, to judge by your looks! What did the dentist do to you?'

'It is not so much that,' said Leonard, low and sadly; 'but I began to have a hope, and I see it won't do.'

'What do you mean, my dear boy? what have you been doing?'

'I have been into my old cell again,' said he, under his breath; and Dr May, leaning on his arm, felt his nervous tremor.

'Prisoner of the Bastille, eh Leonard?'

'I had long been thinking that I ought to go and call on Mr Reeve and thank him.'

'But he does not receive calls there.'

'No,' said Leonard, as if the old impulse to confidence had returned; 'but I have never been so happy since, as I was in that cell, and I wanted to see it again. Not only for that reason,' he added, 'but something that Mr Seaford said brought back a remembrance of what Mr Wilmot told me when my life was granted – something about the whole being preparation for future work – something that made me feel ready for anything. It had all gone from me – all but the remembrance of the sense of a blessed Presence and support in that condemned cell, and I thought perhaps ten minutes in the same place would bring it back to me.'

'And did they?'

'No, indeed. As soon as the door was locked, it all went back to July 1860, and worse. Things that were mercifully kept from me then, mere abject terror of death, and of that kind of death – the disgrace – the crowds – all came on me; and with them, the misery all in one of those nine months; the loathing of those eternal narrow waved white walls, the sense of their closing in, the sickening of their sameness, the longing for a voice, the other horror of thinking myself guilty. The warder said it was ten minutes – I thought it hours! I was quite done for, and could hardly get downstairs. I knew the spirit was being crushed out of me by the solitary period, and it is plain that I must think of nothing that needs nerve or presence of mind!' he added, in a tone of quiet dejection.

'You are hardly in a state to judge of your nerve, after sleepless nights and the loss of your teeth. Besides, there is a difference between the real and imaginary, as you have found; you who, in the terrible time of real anticipation, were a marvel in that very point of physical resolution.'

'I could keep thoughts out *then*,' he said; 'I was master of myself.'

'You mean that the solitude unhinged you? Yet I always found you brave and cheerful.'

'The sight of you made me so. Nay, the very sight or sound of any human being made a difference! And now you all treat me as if I had borne it well; but I did not. It was all that was left me to do, but indeed I did not.'

'What do you mean by bearing it well?' said the doctor, in the tone in which he would have questioned a patient.

'Living – as – as I thought I should when I made up my mind to life instead of death,' said Leonard; 'but all that went away. I let it slip, and instead came everything possible of cowardice, and hatred, and bitterness. I lost my hold of certainty what I had done or what I had not; and the horror, the malice, the rebellion that used to come on me in that frightful light white silent place, were unutterable! I wish you would not have me among you all, when I know there can hardly be a wicked thought that did not surge over me.'

'To be conquered.'

'To conquer me,' he said, in utter lassitude.

'Stay. Did they ever make you offend wilfully?'

'There was nothing I could offend in.'

'Your tasks of work, for instance.'

'I often had a savage frantic abhorrence of it; but I always brought myself to do it, and it did me good; it would have done more if it had been less mechanical. But it often was only the instinct of not degrading myself like the lowest prisoners.'

'Well, there was your conduct to the officials.'

'Oh! one could not help being amenable to them, they were so kind. Besides, these demons never came over me except when I was alone.'

'And one thing more, Leonard; did these demons, as you well call them, invade your devotions?'

'Never,' he answered readily; then recalling himself – 'not at the set times I mean, though they often made me think the comfort I had there mere hypocrisy and delusion, and be nearly ready to give over what depended on myself. Chapel was always joy; it brought change and the presence of others, if nothing else; and that would in itself have been enough to banish the hauntings.'

'And they did not interfere with your own readings?' said the doctor, preferring this to the word that he meant.

'I could not let them,' said Leonard. 'There was always refreshment; it was only before and after that all would seem mockery, profanation, or worse still, delusion and superstition – as if my very condition proved that there was none to hear.'

'The hobgoblin had all but struck the book out of Christian's hand,' said Dr May, pressing his grasp on Leonard's shuddering arm. 'You are only telling me that you have been in the valley of the shadow of death; you have not told me that you lost the rod and staff.'

'No, I must have been helped, or I should not have my senses now.'

And perhaps it was the repressed tremor of voice and frame rather than the actual words that induced the doctor to reply – 'That is the very point, Leonard. It is the temptation to us doctors to ascribe too much to the physical and too little to the moral; and perhaps you would be more convinced by Mr Wilmot than by me; but I do verily believe that all the anguish you describe could and would have been insanity, if grace had not been given you to conquer it. It was a tottering of the mind upon its balance; and, humanly speaking, it was the self-control that enabled you to force yourself to your duties, and find relief in them, which saved you. I should just as soon call David conquered because the "deep waters had come in over his soul."'

'You can never know how true those verses are,' said Leonard, with another shiver.

'At least I know to what kind of verses they all lead,' said the doctor; 'and I am sure they led you, and that you had more and brighter hours than you now remember.'

'Yes, it was not all darkness. I believe there were more spaces than I can think of now, when I was very fairly happy, even at Pentonville; and at Portland all did well with me, till last spring, and then the news from Massissauga brought back all the sense of blood-guiltiness, and it was worse than ever.'

'And that sense was just as morbid as your other horrible doubt, about which you asked me when we were coming home.'

'I see it was now, but that was the worst time of all – the monotony of school, and the sense of hypocrisy and delusion in teaching – the craving to confess, if only for the sake of the excitement, and the absolute inability to certify myself whether there was any crime to confess – I can't talk about it. And even chapel was not the same refreshment, when one was always teaching a class in it, as coming in fresh only for the service. Even that was failing me, or I thought it was! No, I do not know how I could have borne it much longer.'

'No, Leonard, you could not; Tom and I both saw that in your looks, and quite expected to hear of your being ill; but you see, we are never tried above what we can bear!'

'No,' said Leonard, very low, as if he had been much struck; and then he added, after an interval, 'It is over now, and there's no need to recollect it except in the way of thanks. The question is what it has left me fit for. You know, Dr May;' and his voice trembled; 'my first and best design in the happy time of Coombe, the very crown of my life, was this very thing – to be a missionary. But for myself, I might be in training now. If I had only conquered my temper, and accepted that kind offer of Mr Cheviot's, all this would never have been, and I should have had my youth, my strength, and spirit, my best, to devote. I turned aside because of my obstinacy, against warning; and now how can I offer? – one who has stood at the bar, lived among felons, thought such thoughts – the released convict with a disgraced name! It would just be an insult to the ministry! No, I know how prisoners feel. I can deal with them. Let me go back to what I am trained for. My nerve and spirit have been crushed out; I am fit for nothing else. The worst thing that has remained with me is this nervousness – cowardice is its right name – starting at the sound of a door, or at a fresh face – a pretty notion that I should land among savages!'

Dr May had begun an answer about the remains of the terrible ordeal that might in itself have been part of Leonard's training, when they reached the house door.

These nerves, or whatever they were, did indeed seem disposed to have no mercy on their owner; for no sooner had he sat down in the warm drawing-room, than such severe pain attacked his face as surpassed even his powers of concealment. Dr May declared it was all retribution for his unfriendliness in never seeking sympathy or advice, which might have proved the evil to be neuralgia and saved the teeth, instead of aggravating the evil by their extraction.

'I suspect he has been living on nothing,' said Dr May, when, in a lull of the pain, Leonard had gone to bed.

'Papa!' exclaimed Gertrude, 'don't you know what Richard's housekeeping is? Don't you recollect his taking that widow for a cook because she was such a good woman?'

'I don't think it was greatly Richard's fault,' said Ethel. 'I can hardly get Leonard to make a sparrow's meal here, and most likely his mouth has been too uncomfortable.'

'Ay, that never seeking sympathy is to me one of the saddest parts of all. He has been so long shut within himself, that he can hardly feel that any one cares for him.'

'He does so more than at first,' said Ethel.

'Much more. I have heard things from him to-night that are a revelation to me. Well, he has come through, and I believe he is recovering it; but the three threads of our being have all had a terrible wrench, and if body and mind come out unscathed, it is the soundness of the spirit that has brought them through.'

A sleepless night and morning of violent pain ensued; but at least thus much had been gained – that there was no refusal of sympathy, but a grateful acceptance of kindness, so that it almost seemed a recurrence to the Coombe days; and as the pain lessened, the enjoyment of Ethel's attendance seemed to grow upon Leonard in the gentle languor of relief; and when, as she was going out for the afternoon, she came back to see if he was comfortable in his easy chair by the drawing-room fire, and put a screen before his face, he looked up and thanked her with a smile – the first she had seen.

When she returned, the winter twilight had closed in, and he was leaning back in the same attitude, but started up, so that she asked if he had been asleep.

'I don't know – I have seen her again.'

'Seen whom?'

'Minna, my dear little Minna!'

'Dreamt of her?'

'I cannot tell,' he said; 'I only know she was there;' and then rising and standing beside Ethel, he continued – 'Miss May, you remember the night of her death?'

'Easter Eve?'

'Well,' continued he, 'that night I saw her.'

'I remember,' said Ethel, 'that Mr Wilmot told us you knew at once what he was come to tell you.'

'It was soon after I was in bed, the lights were out, and I do not think I was asleep, when she was by me – not the plump rosy thing she used to be, but tall and white, her hair short and waving back, her eyes – oh! so sad and wistful, but glad too – and her hands held out – and she said, 'Turn you to the stronghold, ye prisoners of hope. O Leonard, dear, it does not hurt."'

'It was the last thing she did say.'

'Yes, so Ave's letter said. And observe, one o'clock in Indiana is half-past nine with us. Then her hair – I wrote to ask, for you know it used to be in long curls, but it had been cut short, like what I saw. Surely, surely, it was the dear loving spirit allowed to show itself to me before going quite away to her home!'

'And you have seen her again?'

'Just now' – his voice was even lower than before – 'since it grew dark, as I sat there. I had left off reading, and had been thinking, when there she was, all white but not wistful now; "Leonard, dear," she said, "it *has* not hurt;" and then, "He brought me forth, He brought me forth even to a place of liberty, because He had a favour unto me."'

'Oh Leonard, it must have made you very happy.'

'I am very thankful for it,' he said. Then after a pause, 'You will not speak of it – you will not tell me to think it the action of my own mind upon itself.'

'I can only believe it a great blessing come to comfort you and cheer you,' said Ethel: 'cheer you as with the robin-note, as papa called it, that sung all through the worst of times! Leonard, I am afraid you will think it unkind of me to have withheld it so long, but papa told me you could not yet bear to hear of Minna. I have her last present for you in charge – the slippers she was working for that eighteenth birth-day of yours. She would go on, and we never knew whether she fully understood your danger; it was always "they could not hurt you," and at last, when they were finished, and I had to make her understand that you could not have them, she only looked up to me and said, "Please keep them, and give them to him when he comes home." She never doubted, first or last.'

Ethel, who had daily been watching for the moment, took out the parcel from the drawer, with the address in the childish writing, the date in her own.

Large tears came dropping from Leonard's eyes, as he undid the paper, and looked at the work, then said, 'Last time I saw that pattern, my mother was working it! Dear child! Yes, Miss May, I am glad you did not give them to me before. I always felt as if my blow had glanced aside and fallen on Minna; but somehow I feel more fully how happy she is!'

'She was the messenger of comfort throughout to Ave and to Ella,' said Ethel, 'and well she may be to you still.'

'I have dreaded to ask,' said Leonard; 'but there was a line in one letter I was shown that made me believe that climate was not the whole cause.'

'No,' said Ethel; 'at least the force to resist it had been lost, as far as we can see. It was a grievous error of your brother's to think her a child who could forget. She pined to hear of you, and that one constant effort of faith and love was too much, and wasted away the little tender body. But oh, Leonard, how truly she can say that her captivity is over, and that it has not hurt!'

'It has not hurt,' musingly repeated Leonard. 'No, she is beyond the reach of distracting temptations and sorrows; it has only made her brighter to have suffered what it breaks one's heart to think of. It has not hurt.'

'Nothing from without does hurt!' said Ethel, 'unless one lets it.'

'Hurt what?' he asked.

'The soul,' returned Ethel. 'Mind and body may be hurt, and it is not possible to know one's mind from one's soul while one is alive; but as long as the will and faith are right, to think the soul can be hurt seems to me like doubting our Protector.'

'But if the will has been astray?'

'Then while we repent, we must not doubt our Redeemer.'

Dickie ran in at the moment, calling for Aunt Ethel. She had dropped her muff. Leonard picked it up, and as she took it, he wrung her hand with an earnestness that showed his gratitude.

CHAPTER XXVIII

'Tender as woman; manliness and meekness
In him were so allied,
That those who judged him by his strength or weakness,
Knew but a single side.'

J. Whittler.

It promised to be a brilliant Christmas at Stoneborough, though little Dickie regarded the feast coming in winter as a perverse English innovation, and was grand on the superiority of supple jack above holly. Decorations had been gradually making their way into the Minster, and had advanced from being just tolerated to being absolutely delighted in; but Dr Spencer, with his knack of doing everything, was sorely missed as a head, and Mr Wilmot insisted that the May forces should come down and work the Minster, on the 23rd, leaving the Eve for the adornment of Cocksmoor, after the return of its incumbent. Mary, always highly efficient in that line, joined them; and Leonard's handiness and dexterity in the arts relating to carpentry were as quietly useful as little Dickie's bright readiness in always handing whatever was wanting.

The work was pretty well over, when Aubrey, who had just arrived with leave for a week, came down, and made it desultory. Dickie, whose imagination had been a good deal occupied by his soldier uncle, wanted to study him, and Gertrude was never steady when Aubrey was near. Presently it was discovered that the door to the tower stair was open. The ascent of the tower was a feat performed two or three times in a lifetime at Stoneborough. Harry had once beguiled Ethel and Mary up, but Gertrude had never gone, and was crazy to go, as was likewise Dickie. Moreover, Aubrey and Gertrude insisted that it was only proper that Ethel should pay her respects to her prototype the gurgoyle, they wanted to compare her with him, and ordered her up; in fact their spirits were too high for them to be at ease within the church, and Ethel, maugre her thirty years, partook of the exhilaration enough to delight in an extraordinary enterprise, and as nothing remained but a little sweeping up, they left this to the superintendence of Mary and Mr Wilmot, and embarked upon the narrow crumbling steps of the spiral stair, that led up within an unnatural thickening of one of the great piers that supported the tower, at the intersection of nave and transepts. After a long period of dust and darkness, and the monotony of always going with the same leg foremost, came a narrow door, leading to the ringers' region, with all their ropes hanging down. Ethel was thankful when she had got her youngsters past without an essay on them; she doubted if she should have succeeded, but for Leonard's being an element of soberness. Other little doors ensued, leading out to the various elevations of roof, which were at all sorts of different heights, the chancel lower than the nave, and one transept than the other; besides that the nave had both triforium and clerestory. It was a sort of labyrinth, and they wondered whether any one, except perhaps the plumber's foreman, knew his way among all the doors. Then there was one leading inwards to the eight bells – from whose fascinations Ethel thought Dickie never would be taken away – and still more charming, to the clock, which clanged a tremendous three, as they were in the act of looking at it, causing Leonard to make a great start, and then colour painfully. It was hard to believe, as Daisy said, that the old tower, that looked so short and squat below, could be so very high when you came to go up it; but the glimpses of the country, through the little loop-hole windows, were most inviting. At last, Aubrey, who was foremost, pushed up the trap-door, and emerged; but, as Dickie followed him, exclaimed, 'Here we are; but you ladies in crinolines will never follow! You'll stick fast for ever, and Leonard can't pass, so there you'll all have to stay.'

'Aunt Daisy will sail away like a balloon,' added Dickie, roguishly, looking back at her, and holding on his cap.

But Gertrude vigorously compressed her hoop, and squeezed through, followed by Ethel and Leonard. There was a considerable space, square, leaded and protected by the battle-mented parapet, with a deep moulding round, and a gutter resulting in the pipe smoked by Ethel's likeness, the gurgoyle. Of course the first thing Dickie and Aubrey did was to look for the letters that commemorated the ascent of H.M., E.M., M.M., in 1852; and it was equally needful that R.R.M., if nobody else, should likewise leave a record on the leads. There was an R.M. of 1820, that made it impossible to gainsay him. The view was not grand in itself, but there was a considerable charm in looking down on the rooks in their leafless trees, cawing over their old nests, and in seeing the roofs of the town; far away, too, the grey Welsh hills, and between, the country lying like a map, with rivers traced in light instead of black. Leonard stood still, his face turned towards the greenest of the meadows, and the river where it dashed over the wheel of a mill.

'Have you seen it again?' asked Ethel, as she stood by him, and watched his eye.

'No. I am rather glad to see it first from so far off,' he answered, 'I mean to walk over some day.'

'Ethel,' called Gertrude, 'is this your gurgoyle? His profile, as seen from above, isn't flattering.'

'Oh Daisy, don't lean over so far.'

'Quite safe;' but at that instant a gust of wind caught her hat, she grasped at it, but only saved it from whirling away, and made it fall short. 'There, Ethel, your image has put on my hat; and henceforth will appear to the wondering city in a black hat and feather!'

'I'll get it,' exclaimed the ever ready Dickie; and in another moment he had mounted the parapet and was reaching for it. Whether it were Gertrude's shriek, or the natural recoil away from the grasping hand, or that his hold on the side of the adjoining pinnacle was insecure, he lost his balance, and with a sudden cry, vanished from their eyes.

The frightful consternation of that moment none of those four could ever bear to recall; the next, they remembered that he *could* only fall as far as the roof, but it was Ethel and Leonard alone who durst press to the parapet, and at the same moment a cry came up –

'Oh, come! I'm holding on, but it cuts! Oh, come!'

Ethel saw, some five-and-twenty feet below, the little boy upon the transept roof, a smooth slope of lead, only broken by a skylight, a bit of churchwarden's architecture still remaining. The child had gone crashing against the window, and now lay back clinging to its iron frame. Behind him was the entire height within to the church floor, before him a rapid slope, ended by a course of stone, wide enough indeed to walk on, but too narrow to check the impetus from slipping down the inclination above. Ethel's brain swam; she just perceived that both Aubrey and Leonard had disappeared, and then had barely power to support Gertrude, who reeled against her, giddy with horror. 'Oh look, look Ethel,' she cried; 'I can't. Where is he?'

'There! Yes, hold on, Dickie, they are coming. Look up – not down – hold on!'

A door opened, and out dashed Aubrey! Alas! it was on the nave clerestory, he might as well have been a hundred miles off. Another door, and Leonard appeared, and on the right level, but with a giddy unguarded ridge on which to pass round the angle of the tower. She saw his head pass safely round; but, even then, the horror was not over. Could he steady himself sufficiently to reach the child, or might not Dickie lose hold too soon? It was too close below for sight, the moulding and gurgoyle impeded her agonized view, but she saw the child's look of joyful relief, she heard the steady voice, 'Wait, don't let go yet. There,' and after a few more sounds, came up a shout, 'all right!' Infinitely relieved, she had to give her whole attention to poor Gertrude, who, overset by the accident, giddy with the attempt to look over, horrified by the danger, confused and distressed by the hair that came wildly flapping about her head and face, and by the puffs of wind at her hoop, had sunk down in the centre of the little leaden square, clinging with all her might to the staff of the weathercock, and feeling as if the whole tower were rocking with her, absolutely seeing the battlements dance. How was she ever to be safely got down the rickety ladder leading to the crumbling stone stair? Ethel knelt by her, twisted up the fluttering hair, bade her shut her eyes and compose her thoughts; and then called over the battlements to Aubrey, who, confused by the shock, continued to emerge at wrong doors and lose himself on the roofs, and was like one in a bad dream, nearly as much dizzied as his sister, to whose help he came the more readily, as the way up was the only one plain before him.

The detention would have been more dreadful to Ethel had she known all that was passing below, and that when the little boy, at Leonard's sign, lowered himself towards the outreaching arms of the young man, who was steadying himself against the wall of the tower, it was with a look of great pain, and leaving a trail of blood behind him. When, at length, he stood at the angle, Leonard calmly said, 'Now go before me, round that corner, in at the door. Hold by the wall, I'll hold your shoulder.' The boy implicitly obeyed, the notion of giddiness never seemed to occur to him, and both safely came to the little door, on the threshold of which Leonard sat down, and lifting him on his knee, asked where he was hurt? 'My leg,' said Dickie, 'the glass was running in all the time, and I could not move; but it does not hurt so much now.'

Perhaps not; but a large piece of glass had broken into the slender little calf, and Leonard steadied himself to withdraw it, as, happily, the fragment was large enough to give a hold for his hand. The sensible little fellow, without a word, held up the limb across Leonard's knee, and threw an arm round his neck to hold himself still, just saying, 'Thank you;' when it was over.

'Did it hurt much, Dickie?'

'Not very much,' he answered; 'but how it bleeds! Where's Aunt Ethel?'

'On the tower. She will come in a moment,' said Leonard, startled by the exceeding flow of blood, and binding the gash round with his handkerchief. 'Now, I'll carry you down.'

The boy did not speak all the weary winding way down the dark stairs; but Leonard heard gasps of oppression, and felt the head lean on his shoulder; moreover, a touch convinced him that the handkerchief was soaking, nay dripping, and when he issued at length into the freer air of the church, the face was deadly white. No one was near, and Leonard laid him on a bench. He was still conscious, and looked up with languid eyes. 'Mayn't I go home?' he said, faintly, 'Aunt Ethel!'

'Let me try to stop this bleeding first,' said Leonard. 'My dear little man, if you will only be quiet, I think I can.'

Leonard took the handkerchief from his throat, and wound it to its tightest just above the hurt, Dickie remonstrating for a moment with, 'That's not the place. It is too tight.'

'It will cut off the blood from coming,' said Leonard; and in the same understanding way, the child submitted, feebly asking, 'Shall I bleed to death? Mamma will be so sorry!'

'I trust – I hope not,' said Leonard; he durst utter no encouragement, for the life-blood continued to pour forth unchecked, and the next murmur was, 'I'm so sick. I can't say my prayers. Papa! Mamma!' Already, however, Leonard had torn down a holly bough, and twisted off (he would have given worlds for a knife) a short stout stick, which he thrust into one of the folds of the ligature, and pulled it much tighter, so that his answer was, 'Thank God, Dickie, that will do! the bleeding has stopped. You must not mind if it hurts for a little while.'

An ejaculation of 'Poor little dear,' here made him aware of the presence of the sexton's wife; but in reply to her offer to carry him in to Mrs Cheviot's, Dickie faintly answered, 'Please let me go home;' and Leonard, 'Yes, I will take him home. Tell Miss May it is a cut from the glass, I am taking him to have it dressed, and will bring him home. Now my dear little patient fellow, can you put your arms round my neck?'

Sensible, according to both meanings of the word, Dickie clasped his friend's neck, and laid his head on his shoulder, not speaking again till he found Leonard was not turning towards the High Street, when he said, 'That is not the way home.'

'No, Dickie, but we must get your leg bound up directly, and the hospital is the only place where we can be sure of finding any one to do it. I will take you home directly afterwards.'

'Thank you,' said the courteous little gentleman; and in a few minutes more Leonard had rung the bell, and begged the house surgeon would come at once to Dr May's grandson. A few drops of stimulant much revived Dickie, and he showed perfect trust and composure, only holding Leonard's hands, and now and then begging to know what they were doing, while he was turned over on his face for the dressing of the wound, bearing all without a sound, except an occasional sobbing gasp, accompanied by a squeeze of Leonard's finger. Just as this business had been completed, the surgeon exclaimed, 'There's Dr May's step,' and Dickie at once sat up, as his grandfather hurried in, nearly as pale as the boy himself. 'Oh grandpapa, never mind, it is almost well now; and has Aunt Daisy got her hat?'

'What is it, my dear? what have you been doing?' said the doctor; looking in amazement from the boy to Leonard, who was covered with blood. 'They told me you had fallen off the Minster tower!'

'Yes, I did,' said Dickie, 'I reached after Aunt Daisy's hat, but I fell on the roof, and I was sliding, sliding down to the wall; but there was a window, and the glass broke and cut me, but I got my feet against the bottom of it, and held on by the iron bar, till Leonard came and took me down;' and he lay back on the pillow, quiet and exhausted, but bright-eyed and attentive as ever, listening to Leonard's equally brief version of the adventure.

'Didn't he save my life, grandpapa?' said the boy, at the close.

'Twice over, you may say,' added the surgeon; and his words as to the nature of the injury manifested that all had depended on the immediate stoppage of the haemorrhage. With so young a child, delay from indecision or want of resource would probably have been fatal.

'There would have been no doing anything, if this little man had not been so good and sensible,' said Leonard, leaning over him.

'And I did not cry. You will tell papa I did not cry,' said Dickie eagerly, but only half gratified by such girlish treatment as that agitated kiss of his grandfather, after being a little bit of a hero; but then Dickie's wondering eyes really beheld such another kiss bestowed over his head upon Leonard, and quite thought there were tears on grandpapa's cheeks. Perhaps old gentlemen could do what was childish in little boys.

Dickie was to be transported home. He wished to be carried by Leonard, but the brougham was at the door, and he had to content himself with being laid on the seat, with his friend to watch over him, the doctor pointing out that Leonard was a savage spectacle for the eyes of Stoneborough, and hurrying home by the short cut. Ethel met him in extreme alarm. Gertrude's half-restored senses had been totally scattered by the sight of the crimson traces on the spot of Leonard's operations, and she had been left to Mary's care; while Ethel and Aubrey had hastened home, and not finding any one there, the latter had dashed off to Bankside, whilst Ethel waited, arranging the little fellow's bed, and trying to trust to Leonard's message, and not let her mind go back to that fearful day of like waiting, sixteen years ago, nor on to what she might have to write to Norman and Meta of the charge they had sent to her. Her father's cheerful face at first was a pang, and then came the rebound of gladness at the words, 'He is coming. No fear for him, gallant little man – thanks for God's mercy, and to that noble fellow, Leonard.'

At the same moment Aubrey burst in – 'No one at Wright's – won't be in no one knows how long! What is to become of us?' And he sank down on a chair.

'Ay, what would become of any of us, if no one had a better pate than yours, sir?' said Dr May. 'You have one single perfection, and you had better make the most of it – that of knowing how to choose your friends. There's the carriage.'

After a moment's delay, the cushion was lifted out with the little wounded cavalier, still like a picture; for, true to his humming-bird nature, a few scarcely-conscious movements of his hands had done away with looks of disarray – the rich glossy curls were scarcely disordered, and no stains of blood had adhered to the upper part of his small person, whereas Leonard was a ghastly spectacle from head to foot.

'So, Master Dicky-bird,' said Dr May, as they rested him a moment on the hall-table, 'give me that claw of yours. Yes, you'll do very well, only you must go to bed now; and, mind, whatever you did when you were in Fairy-land, we don't fly here in Stoneborough – and it does not answer.'

'I am not to go to bed for being naughty, am I?' said Dickie, his brave white lip for the first time quivering; 'indeed, I did not know it was wrong.'

The poor little man's spirits were so exhausted, that the re-assurance on this head absolutely brought the much-dreaded tears into his eyes; and he could only be carried up gently to his bed, and left to be undressed by his aunt, so great an aggravation to the troubles of this small fragment of independence, that it had almost overset his courtesy and self-command. There was no contenting him till he had had all traces of the disaster washed from face and hands, and the other foot; and then, over his tea, though his little clear chirrup was weak, he must needs give a lucid description of Leonard's bandaging, in the midst of which came a knock at the door, and a gasping voice – 'I'll be quite quiet – indeed I will! Only just let me come in and kiss him, and see that he is safe.'

'Oh Auntie Daisy, have you got your hat?'

Wan, tear-stained, dishevelled, Gertrude bit her lip to save an outburst, gave the stipulated kiss, and retreated to Mary, who stood in the doorway like a dragon.

'Auntie Daisy has been crying,' said Dickie, turning his eyes back to Ethel. 'Please tell her I shall be well very soon, and then I'll go up again and try to get her hat, if I may have a hook and line – I'll tell you how.'

'My dear Dickie, you had better lie down, and settle it as you go to sleep,' said Ethel, her flesh creeping at the notion of his going up again.

'But if I go to sleep now, I shall not know when to say my prayers.'

'Had you not better do so now, Dickie?'

Next came the child's scruple about not kneeling; but at last he was satisfied, if Aunt Ethel would give him his little book out of the drawer – that little delicately-illuminated book with the pointed writing and the twisted cypher, Meta's hand in every touch. Presently he looked up, and said: 'Aunt Ethel, isn't there a verse somewhere about giving the angels charge? I want you to find it for me, for I think they helped me to hold on, and helped Leonard upon the narrow place. You know they are sure to be flying about the church.'

Ethel read the ninety-first Psalm to him. He listened all through, and thanked her; but in a few minutes more he was fast asleep.

As she left the room she met Leonard coming down, and held out her hands to him with a mute intensity of thanks, telling him, in a low voice, what Dickie had said of the angels' care.

'I am sure it was true,' said Leonard. 'What else could have saved the brave child from dizziness?'

Downstairs Leonard's reception from Dr May was, 'Pretty well for a nervous man!'

'Anybody can do what comes to hand.'

'I beg your pardon. Some bodies lose their wits, like your friend Aubrey, who tells me, if he had stood still, he would have fainted away. As long as nerves can do what comes to hand, they need not be blamed, even if they play troublesome tricks at other times, as I suspect they are doing now.'

'Yes; my face is aching a little.'

'Not to say a great deal,' said the doctor. 'Well, I am not going to pity you; for I think you can feel to-day that most of us would be glad to be in your place!'

'I am very glad,' said Leonard.

'You remember that child's parents? No, you have grown so old, that I am always forgetting what a boy you ought to be; but if you had ever seen the tenderness of his father, and that sunbeam of a Meta, you would know all the more how we bless you for what you have spared them. Leonard, if anything had been needed to do so, you have won to yourself such a brother in Norman as you have in Aubrey!'

Meantime Ethel was soothing Gertrude, to whom the shock had been in proportion to the triumphal heights of her careless gaiety. Charles Cheviot had come in while his wife was restoring her; and he had plainly said what no one else would have intimated to the spoilt darling – that the whole accident had been owing to her recklessness, and that he had always expected some fatal consequences to give her a lesson!

Gertrude had been fairly cowed by such unwonted treatment; and when he would only take her home on condition of composure and self-command, her trembling limbs obliged her to accept his arm, and he subdued her into meek silence, and repression of all agitation, till she was safe in her room, when she took a little bit of revenge upon Mary by crying her heart out, and declaring it was very cruel of Charles, when she did not mean it.

And Mary, on her side, varied between assurances that Charles did not mean it, and that he was quite right – the sister now predominating in her, and now the wife.

'Mean what?' said Ethel, sitting down among them before they were aware.

'That – that it was all my fault!' burst out Gertrude. 'If it was, I don't see what concern it is of his!'

'But, Daisy dear, he is your brother!'

'I've got plenty of brothers of my own! I don't count those people-in-law——'

'She's past reasoning with, Mary,' said Ethel. 'Leave her to me; she will come to her senses by-and-by!'

'But indeed, Ethel, you won't be hard on her? I am sure dear Charles never thought what he said would have been taken in this way.'

'Why did he say it then?' cried Gertrude, firing up.

'My dear Mary, do please go down, before we get into the pitiable last-word condition!'

That condition was reached already; but in Ethel's own bedroom Mary's implicit obedience revived, and away she went, carrying off with her most of what was naughtiness in Gertrude.

'Ethel – Ethel dear!' cried she at once, 'I know you are coming down on me. I deserve it all, only Charles had no business to say it. And wasn't it very cruel and unkind when he saw the state I was in?'

'I suppose Charles thought it was the only chance of giving a lesson, and therefore true kindness. Come, Daisy, is this terrible fit of pride a proper return for such a mercy as we have had to-day?'

'If I didn't say so to myself a dozen times on the way home! – only Mary came and made me so intolerably angry, by expecting me to take it as if it had come from you or papa.'

'Ah, Daisy, that is the evil! If I had done my duty by you all, this would not have been!'

'Now, Ethel, when you want to be worse, and more cutting than anything, you go and tell me my faults are yours! For pity's sake, don't come to that!'

'But I must, Daisy, for it is true. Oh, if you had only been a naughty little girl!'

'What – and had it out then?' said Daisy, who was lying across the bed, and put her golden head caressingly on Ethel's knee. 'If I had plagued you then, you would have broken me in out of self-defence.'

'Something like it,' said Ethel. 'But you know, Daisy, the little last treasure that mamma left did always seem something we could not make enough of, and it didn't make you fractious or tiresome – at least not to us – till we thought you could not be spoilt. And then I didn't see the little faults so soon as I ought; and I'm only an elder sister, after all, without any authority.'

'No, you're not to say that, Ethel; I mind your authority, and always will. You are never a bother.'

'Ah, that's it, Daisy! If I had only been a bother, you might never have got ahead of yourself.'

'Then you really think, like Charles Cheviot, that it was my doing, Ethel?'

'What do you think yourself?'

Great tears gathered in the corners of the blue eyes. Was it weak in Ethel not to bear the sight?

'My poor Daisy,' she said, 'yours is not all the burden! I ought not to have taken up such a giddy company, or else I should have kept the boy under my hand. But he is so discreet and independent, that it is more like having a gentleman staying in the house, than a child under one's charge; and one forgets how little he is; and I was as much off my balance with spirits as you. It was the flightiness of us all; and we have only to be thankful, and to be sobered for another time. I am afraid the pride about being reproved is really the worse fault.'

'And what do you want me to do? – to go and tell papa all about it? I mean to do that, of course; it is the only way to get comforted.'

'Of course it is; but——'

'You horrid creature, Ethel! I'll never say you aren't a bother again. You really do want me to go and tell Charles Cheviot that he was quite right, and Mary that I'm ready to be trampled on by all my brothers-in-law in a row! Well, there won't be any more. You'll never give me one – that's one comfort!' said Gertrude, wriggling herself up, and flinging an arm round Ethel's neck. 'As long as you don't do that, I'll do anything for you.'

'Not for me.'

'Well, you know that, you old thing! only you might take it as a personal compliment. I really will do it; for, of course, one could not keep one's Christmas otherwise!' It was rather too business-like; but elders are often surprised to find what was a hard achievement in their time a matter of course to their pupils – almost lightly passed over.

Dickie slept till morning, when he was found very pale, but lively and good-humoured as ever. Mr Wright, coming up to see him, found the hurt going on well, and told Ethel, that if she could keep him in bed and undisturbed for the day, it would be better and safer; but that if he became restless and fretful, there would be no great risk in taking him to a sofa. Restless and fretful! Mr Wright little knew the discretion, or the happy power of accommodation to circumstances, that had descended to Meta's firstborn.

He was quite resigned as soon as the explanation had been made – perhaps, indeed, there was an instinctive sense, that to be dressed and moved would be fatiguing; but he had plenty of smiles and animation for his visitors, and, when propped up in bed, was full of devices for occupation. Moreover he acquired a slave; he made a regular appropriation of Leonard, whom he quickly perceived to be the most likely person to assist in his great design of constructing a model of the clock in the Minster tower, for the edification of his little brother Harry. Leonard worked away at the table by the bedside with interest nearly equal to the child's; and when wire and cardboard were wanting, he put aside all his dislike to facing the Stoneborough streets and tradesmen in open day, and, at Dickie's request, sallied forth in quest of the materials. And when the bookseller made inquiries after the boy, Leonard, in the fullness of his heart, replied freely and in detail – nay, he was so happy in the little man's well-doing, that he was by no means disconcerted even by a full encounter of Mrs Harvey Anderson in the street, but answered all her inquiries, in entire oblivion of all but the general rejoicing in little Dickie's wonderful escape.

'Well,' said Aubrey to his sisters, after a visit to his nephew's room, 'Dickie has the best right to him, certainly, to-day. It is an absolute appropriation! They were talking away with all their might when I came up, but came to a stop when I went in, and Master Dick sent me to the right-about.'

The truth was, that Dickie, who with eyes and ears all alive, had gathered up some fragments of Leonard's history, had taken this opportunity of catechizing him upon it in a manner that it was impossible to elude, and which the child's pretty tact carried off, as it did many things which would not have been tolerated if done rudely and abruptly. Step by step, in the way of question and remark, he led Leonard to tell him all that had happened; and when once fairly embarked in the reminiscence, there was in it a kind of peace and pleasure. The fresh, loving, wondering sympathy of the little boy was unspeakably comforting; and besides, the bringing the facts in their simple form to the grasp of the childish mind, restored their proportion, which their terrible consequences had a good deal disturbed. They seemed to pass from the present to the historical, and to assume the balance that they took in the child's mind, coming newly upon them. It was like bathing in a clear limpid stream, that washed away the remains of morbid oppression.

'I wish mamma was here,' said the little friend, at last.

'Do you want her? Are you missing her, my dear?'

'I miss her always,' said Dickie. 'But it was not that – only mamma always makes everybody so happy; and she would be so fond of you, because you have had so much trouble.'

'But, Dickie, don't you think I am happy to be with your grandfather and aunt, and hoping to see my own sisters very soon – your aunt, who taught me what bore me through it all?'

'Aunt Ethel?' sad Dickie, considering. 'I like Aunt Ethel very much; but then she is *not* like mamma!'

There could be no doubt that Leonard was much better and happier after this adventure. Reluctantly, Dickie let him go back to Cocksmoor, where his services in church-decking and in singing had been too much depended on to be dispensed with; but he was to come back with Richard for the family assembly on Christmas evening.

Moreover, Gertrude, who was quite herself again, having made her peace with the Cheviots, and endured the reception of her apologies, seized on him to lay plots for a Christmas tree, for the delectation of Dickie on his sofa, and likewise of Margaret Rivers, and of the *élite* of the Cocksmoor schools. He gave into it heartily, and on the appointed day worked with great spirits at the arrangements in the dining-room, where Gertrude, favoured by the captive state of the little boy, conducted her preparations, relegating the family meals to the schoolroom.

This tree was made the occasion for furnishing Leonard with all the little appliances of personal property that had been swept away from him; and, after all, he was the most delighted of the party. The small Charlie Cheviot had to be carried off shrieking; Margaret Rivers was critical; even Cocksmoor was experienced in Christmas trees; and Dickie, when placed in the best situation, and asked if such trees grew in New Zealand, made answer that he helped mamma to make one every year for the Maori children. It was very kind of Aunt Daisy, he added, with unfailing courtesy; but he was too zealous for his colony to be dazzled – too utilitarian to be much gratified by any of his gifts, excepting a knife of perilous excellence, which Aubrey, in contempt of Stoneborough productions, had sacrificed from his own pocket at the last moment.

Leonard and Dickie together were in a state of great delight at the little packets handed to the former; studs, purse, pencil-case, writing materials; from Hector Ernescliffe, a watch, with the entreaty that his gifts might not be regarded as unlucky; from Ethel, a photographic book, with the cartes of his own family, whose old negatives had been hunted up for the purpose; also a recent one of Dr May with his grandson on his knee, the duplicate of which was gone to New Zealand, with the doctor's inscription, 'The modern Cyropaedia, Astyages confounded.' There was Richard, very good, young and pretty; there was Ethel, exactly like the doctor, 'only more so;' there was Gertrude, like nobody, not even herself, and her brothers much in the same predicament; there was the latest of Mr Rivers's many likenesses, with the cockatoo on his wrist, and there was the least truculent and witchlike of the numerous attempts on Flora; there was Mrs Cheviot, broad-faced and smiling over her son, and Mr and Mrs Ernescliffe, pinioning the limbs of their offspring, as in preparation for a family holocaust; there was Dickie's mamma, unspoilable in her loveliness even by photography, and his papa grown very bald and archidiaconal; there was Ethel's great achievement of influence, Dr Spencer, beautiful in his white hair; there were the vicar and the late and present head-masters. The pleasure excited by all these gifts far exceeded the anticipations of their donors; it seemed as if they had fallen on the very moment when they would convey a sense of home, welcome, and restoration. He did not say much, but looked up with liquid lustrous eyes, and earnest 'thank you's,' and caressingly handled and examined the treasures over and over again, as they lay round him on Dickie's couch. 'I suppose,' said the child to him, 'it is like Job, when all his friends came to see him, and every one gave him a piece of money.'

'He could hardly have enjoyed it more,' murmured Leonard, feeling the restful capacity of happiness in the new possession of the child's ardent love, and of the kind looks of all around, above all, of the one presence that still gave him his chief sense of sunshine. The boyish and romantic touch of passion had, as Ethel had long seen, been burnt and seared away, and yet there was something left, something that, as on this evening she felt, made his voice softer, his eye more deferential, to her than to any one else. Perhaps she had once been his guiding star; and if in the wild tempests of the night he had learnt instead to direct his course by the

'Brightest and best of the sons of the morning,'

still the star would be prized and distinguished, as the first and most honoured among inferior constellations.

CHAPTER XXIX

'Till now the dark was worn, and overhead
The lights of sunset and of sunrise mixed.'

Tennyson.

At New York, Tom wrote a short letter to announce his safe arrival, and then pushed on by railway into Indiana. Winter had completely set in; and when he at length arrived at Winiamac, he found that a sleigh was a far readier mode of conveyance to Massissauga than the wagons used in summer. His drive, through the white cathedral-like arcades of forest, hung with transparent icicles, and with the deep blue sky above, becoming orange towards the west, was enjoyable; and even Massissauga itself, when its skeleton trees were like their neighbours, embellished by the pure snowy covering, looked less forlorn than when their death contrasted with the exuberant life around. He stopped at the hotel, left his baggage there, and after undergoing a catechism on his personal affairs, was directed to Mr Muller's house, and made his way up its hard-trodden path of snow, towards the green door, at which he knocked two or three times before it was opened by a woman, whose hair and freckled skin were tinted nowhere but in Ireland.

He made a step forward out of the cutting blast into the narrow entry, and began to ask, 'Is Miss Ward here? I mean, can I see Miss Warden?' when, as if at the sound of his voice, there rang from within the door close by a shriek – one of the hoarse hysterical cries he had heard upon the day of the Inquest. Without a moment's hesitation, he pushed open the door, and beheld a young lady in speechless terror hanging over the stiffened figure on the couch – the eyes wide open, the limbs straight and rigid. He sprang forward, and lifted her into a more favourable posture, hastily asking for simple remedies likely to be at hand, and producing a certain amount of revival for a few moments, though the stiffness was not passing – nor was there evidence of consciousness.

'Are you Leonard?' said Cora Muller under her breath, in this brief interval gazing into his face with frightened puzzled eyes.

'No; but I am come to tell her that he is free!' But the words were cut short by another terrible access, of that most distressing kind that stimulates convulsion; and again the terrified women instinctively rendered obedience to the stranger in the measures he rapidly took, and his words, 'hysteria – a form of hysteria,' were forced from him by the necessity of lessening Cora's intense alarm, so as to enable her to be effective. 'We must send for Dr Laidlaw,' she began in the first breathing moment, and again he looked up and said 'I am a physician!'

'Mr Tom?' she asked with the faintest shadow of a smile; he bent his head, and that was their introduction, broken again by another frightful attack; and when quiescence, if not consciousness, was regained, Tom knelt by the sofa, gazing with a sense of heart-rending despair at the wasted features and thin hands, the waxen whiteness of the cheek, and the tokens in which he clearly read long and consuming illness as well as the overthrow of the sudden shock.

'What is this?' he asked, looking up to Cora's beautiful anxious face.

'Oh, she has been very sick, very sick,' she answered; 'it was an attack of pleurisy; but she is getting better at last, though she will not think so, and this news will make all well. Does she hear? Say it again!'

Tom shook his head, afraid of the sound of the name as yet, and scarcely durst even utter the word 'Ella' above his breath.

'She is gone out with Cousin Deborah to an apple bee,' was the re-assuring answer. 'She wanted change, poor child! Is she getting better?'

Averil was roused by a cough, the sound which tore Tom's heart by its import, but he drew back out of her sight, and let Cora raise her, and give her drink, in a soothing tender manner, that was evident restoration. 'Cora dear, is it you?' she said, faintly; 'didn't I hear some one else's voice? Didn't they say——?' and the shiver that crept over her was almost a return of the hysteric fit.

'We said he was free,' said Cora, holding her in her arms.

'Free – yes, I know what that means – free among the dead,' said Averil, calmly, smoothing Cora's hair, and looking in her face. 'Don't be afraid to let me hear. I shall be there with him and Minna soon. Didn't somebody come to tell me? Please let him in, I'll be quiet now.'

And as she made gestures of arranging her hair and dress, Tom guardedly presented himself, saying in a voice that trembled with his endeavour to render it calm, 'Did you think I should have come if I had nothing better to tell you?' and as she put out her hand in greeting, he took it in both his own, and met her eyes looking at him wide open, in the first dawning of the hope of an impossible gladness. 'Yes,' he said, 'the truth is come out – he is cleared – he is at home – at Stoneborough!'

The hot fingers closed convulsively on his own, then she raised herself, pressed her hands together, and gasped and struggled fearfully for breath. The joy and effort for self-command were more than the enfeebled frame could support, and there was a terrible and prolonged renewal of those agonizing paroxysms, driving away every thought from the other two except of the immediate needs. At last, when the violence of the attack had subsided, and left what was either fainting or stupor, they judged it best to carry her to her bed, and trust that, reviving without the associations of the other room, the agitation would be less likely to return, and that she might sleep under the influence of an anodyne. Poor Tom! it was not the reception he had figured to himself; and after he had laid her down, and left her to Cora and to Katty to be undressed, he returned to the parlour, and stood over the sinking wood-fire in dejection and dreariness of heart – wrung by the sufferings he had witnessed, with the bitter words (too late) echoing in his brain, and with the still more cruel thought – had it been his father or one of his brothers – any one to whose kindness she could trust, the shock had not been so great, and there would have been more sense of soothing and comfort! And then he tried to collect his impressions of her condition, and judge what would serve for her relief, but all his senses seemed to be scattered; dismay, compassion, and sympathy, had driven away all power of forming a conclusion – he was no longer the doctor – he was only the anxious listener for the faintest sound from the room above, but none reached him save the creaking of the floor under Katty's heavy tread.

The gay tinkle of sleigh-bells was the next noise he heard, and presently the door was opened, and two muffled hooded figures looked into the room, now only lighted by the red embers of the fire.

'Where's Cora? where's Ave?' said the bright tone of the lesser. 'It is all dark!' and she was raising her voice to call, when Tom instinctively uttered a 'Hush,' and moved forward; 'hush, Ella, your sister has been ill.'

The little muffled figure started at the first sound of his voice, but as he stepped nearer recoiled for a second, then with a low cry, almost a sob of recognition, exclaimed, 'Mr Tom! Oh, Mr Tom! I knew you would come! Cousin Deborah, it's Mr Tom!' and she flew into his arms, and clung with an ecstasy of joy, unknowing the why or how, but with a sense that light had shone, and that her troubles were over. She asked no questions, she only leant against him with, 'Mr Tom! Mr Tom!' under her breath.

'But what is it, stranger? Do tell! Where are the girls? What's this about Avy's being sick? Do you know the stranger, Ella!'

'It's Mr Tom,' she cried, holding his arm round her neck, looking up in a rapturous restfulness.

'I brought Miss Ward – en some good news that I fear has been too much for her,' said he; 'I am – only waiting to – hear how she is.'

By way of answer, Deborah opened another door which threw more light on the scene from the cooking stove in the kitchen, and at the same moment Cora with a candle came down the stairs.

'Oh Dr May,' she said, 'you have been too long left alone in the dark. I think she is asleep now. You will stay. We will have tea directly.'

Tom faltered something about the hotel, and began to look at Cousin Deborah, and to consider the proprieties of life; but Cousin Deborah, Cora, and Ella, began declaring with one voice that he must remain for the evening meal, and a bustle of cheerful preparation commenced, while Ella still hung on his hand.

'But, Ella, you've never asked my good news.'

'Oh dear! I was too glad! Are we going home then?'

'Yes, I trust so, I hope so, my dear; for Leonard's innocence has come to light, and he is free.'

'Then Henry won't mind – and we may be called by our proper name again – and Ave will be well,' cried the child, as the ideas came more fully on her comprehension. 'Oh Cora! Oh Cousin Deborah, do you hear? Does Ave know? May I run up and tell Ave?'

This of course was checked, but next Ella impetuously tore off her wraps for the convenience of spinning up and down wildly about the kitchen and parlour. Leonard himself did not seem to have great part in her joy; Henry's policy had really nearly rooted out the thought of him personally, and there was a veil of confusion over the painful period of his trial, which at the time she had only partially comprehended. But she did understand that his liberation would be the term of exile; and though his name was to her connected with a mysterious shudder that made her shrink from uttering or hearing details, she had a security that Mr Tom would set all right, and she loved him so heartily, that his presence was sunshine enough for her.

A little discomfited at the trouble he was causing, Tom was obliged to wait while not only Cousin Deborah, but Cora busied herself in the kitchen, and Ella in her restless joy came backwards and forwards to report their preparations, and at times to tarry a short space by his side, and tell of the recent troubles. Ave had been very ill, she said, very ill indeed about a month ago, and Henry had come home to see her, but had been obliged to go away to the siege of Charleston when she was better. They had all been ill ever since they came there; but now Mr Tom was come, should not they all go home to dear Stoneborough, away from this miserable place? If they could only take Cora with them!

It was still a childish tongue; but Ella had outgrown all her plump roundness, and was so tall and pale that Tom would hardly have known her. Her welcome was relief and comfort, and she almost inspired her own belief that now all would be well. His English ideas were rather set at rest by finding that Mrs Deborah was to preside at the tea-table, and that he was not to be almost *tête-à-tête* with Miss Muller. Deborah having concluded her hospitable cares, catechized him to her full content, and satisfied herself on the mystery of the Wardens' life.

And now what brought himself out? She guessed he could not find an opening in the old country. Tom smiled, explained his opening at home, and mentioned his charge of his late friend's book.

'So you are come out about the book, and just come a few hundred miles out of the way to bring this bit of news, that you could have telegraphed,' said the Yankee dame, looking at him with her keen eyes. 'Well, if you were coming, it was a pity you were not sooner. She has pined away every since she came here; and to such a worn-down condition as hers, poor child, I doubt joy's kinder more upsetting than trouble, when one is used to it. There; I'll fix the things, and go up and sit with Avy. She'll be less likely to work herself into a flight again if she sees me than one of you.'

So Tom – less embarrassed now – found himself sitting by the fire, with Ella roasting her favourite nuts for him, and Miss Muller opposite. He was taken by surprise by her beautiful face, elegant figure, and lady-like manner, and far more by her evidently earnest affection for Averil.

She told him that ever since the fatal turn of little Minna's illness, Averil had been subject to distressing attacks of gasping and rigidity, often passing into faintness; and though at the moment of emotion she often showed composure and self-command, yet that nature always thus revenged herself. Suspense – letters from home or from Henry – even verses, or times connected with the past, would almost certainly bring on the affection; and the heat of the summer had relaxed her frame, so as to render it even more unable to resist. There had been hope in the bracing of winter, but the first frosts had brought a chill, and a terrible attack of pleurisy, so dangerous that her brother had been summoned; she had struggled through, however, and recovered to a certain point, but there had stopped short, often suffering pain in the side, and never without panting breath and recurring cough. This had been a slightly better day, and she had been lying on the sofa, counting the days to Leonard's next letter, when the well-known voice fell on her ears, and the one strong effort to control herself had resulted in the frightful spasms, which had been worse than any Cora had yet witnessed.

'But she will get well, and we shall go home,' said Ella, looking up wistfully into Tom's mournful face.

'And I shall lose you,' said Cora; 'but indeed I have long seen it was the only thing. If I had only known, she never should have come here.'

'No, indeed, I feel that you would have led her to nothing that was not for her good and comfort.'

'Ah! but I did *not* know,' said Cora; 'I had not been here – and I only thought of my own pleasure in having her. But if there is any way of freeing her from this unfortunate speculation without a dead loss, I will make father tell me.'

This – from Cora's pretty mouth – though only honest and prudent, rather jarred upon Tom in the midst of his present fears; and he began to prepare for his departure to the inn, after having sent up Ella to ask for her sister, and hearing that she still slept soundly under the influence of the opiate.

When Averil awoke it was already morning, and Cora was standing by her bed, with her eyes smiling with congratulation, like veronicas on a sunny day.

'Cora, is it true?' she said, looking up.

Cora bent down and kissed her, and whispered, 'I wish you joy, my dear.'

'Then it is,' she said; 'it is not all a dream?'

'No dream, dearest.'

'Who said it?' she asked. 'Oh Cora, *that* could not be true!' and the colour rose in her cheek.

'That! yes, Averil, if you mean that we had a visitor last evening. I took him for Leonard, do you know? Only I thought his eyes and hair did not quite answer the description.'

'He is a very gentlemanlike person. Did you not think so?' said Averil.

'Ah! Ave, I've heard a great deal. Don't you think you had better tell me some more?'

'No, no!' exclaimed Averil; 'you are not to think of folly,' as coughing cut her short.

'I'll not think of any more than I can help, except what you tell me.'

'Never think at all, Cora. Oh! what has brought him here! I don't know how I can dare to see him again; and yet he is not gone, is he?'

'Oh no, he is only at the inn. He is coming back again.'

'I must be up. Let me get up,' said Averil, raising herself, but pausing from weakness and breathlessness.

And when they had forced some food upon her, she carried out her resolution, though twice absolutely fainting in the course of dressing; and at length crept softly, leaning on Cora's arm, into the parlour. Though Tom was waiting there, he neither spoke nor came forward till she was safely placed upon the sofa, and then gathering breath, she sought him with her eager eyes, shining, large, lustrous, and wistful, as they looked out of the white thin face, where the once glowing colour had dwindled to two burning carnation spots. It was so piteous a change that as he took her hand he was silent, from sheer inability to speak calmly.

'You have come to tell me,' she said. 'I am afraid I could not thank you last night.' How different that soft pleading languid voice from the old half defiant tone!

'I did not know you had been so unwell,' he forced himself to say, 'or I would not have come so suddenly.'

'I am grown so silly,' she said, trying to smile. 'I hardly even understood last night;' and the voice died away in the intense desire to hear.

'I – I was coming on business, and I thought you would not turn from the good tidings, though I was the bearer,' he said, in a broken, agitated, apologetic way.

'Only let me hear it again,' she said. 'Did you say he was free?'

'Yes, free as you are, or I. At home. My father was gone to fetch him.'

She put her hands over her face, and looked up with the sweetest smile he had ever seen, and whispered, 'Now I can sing my *nunc dimittis*.'

He could not at once speak; and before he had done more than make one deprecatory gesture, she asked, 'You have seen him?'

'Not since this – not since September.'

'I know. You have been very good; and he is at home – ah! not home – but Dr May's. Was he well? Was he very glad?'

'I have not seen him; I have not heard; you will hear soon. I came at once with the tidings.'

'Thank you;' and she clasped her hands together. 'Have you seen Henry? does he know?'

'Could I? Had not you the first right?'

'Leonard! Oh, dear Leonard!' She lay back for a few moments, panting under the gust of exceeding joy; while he was silent, and tried not to seem to observe her with his anxious eyes. Then she recovered a little and said, 'The truth come out! Did you say so? What was the truth?'

He paused a moment, afraid of the shock, and remembering that the suspicion had been all unknown to her. She recalled probabilities, and said,

'Was it from a confession? Is it known who – who was the real unhappy person?'

'Yes. Had you no suspicion?'

'No – none,' said Averil, shuddering, 'unless it was some robber. Who was it?'

'You had never thought of the other nephew?'

'You don't mean Samuel Axworthy? Oh! no. Why, the last thing Leonard bade me, was always to pray for him.'

'Ah!' said Tom, with bent head, and colouring cheeks; 'but who are those for whom such as Leonard would feel bound to pray?'

There was a moment's silence, and then she said, 'His enemy! Is that what you mean? But then he would have known it was he.'

'He was entirely convinced that so it must have been, but there was no proof, and an unsupported accusation would only have made his own case worse.'

'And has he confessed? has he been touched, and cleared Leonard at last?'

'No; he had no space granted him. It was the receipt in your brother's writing that was found upon him.'

'The receipt? Yes, Leonard always said the receipt would clear him! But oh, how dreadful! He must have had it all the time. How could he be so cruel! Oh! I never felt before that such wickedness could be;' and she lay, looking appalled and overpowered.

'Think of your brother knowing it all, and bidding – and giving you that injunction – ' said Tom, feeling the necessity of overcoming evil with good.

'Oh! if I had known it, I could not – I could not have been like Leonard! And where – what has become of him?' she asked, breathlessly. 'You speak as if he was dead.'

'Yes. He was killed in a fray at a gaming-house!'

There was a long silence, first of awe, then of thankfulness plainly beaming in her upraised eyes and transparent countenance, which Tom watched, filled with sensations, mournful but not wholly wretched. Shattered as she was, sinking away from her new-found happiness, it was a precious privilege to be holding to her the longed-for draught of joy.

'Tell me about it, please,' she presently said. 'Where – how did the receipt come to light? Were the police told to watch for it? I want to know whom I have to thank.'

His heart beat high, but there was a spirit within him that could not brook any attempt to recall the promise he had pursued her with, the promise that he would not rest till he had proved her brother's innocence. He dreaded her even guessing any allusion to it, or fancying he had brought the proffered price in his hand; and when he began with, 'Can you bear to hear of the most shocking scene I ever witnessed?' he gave no hint of his true motive in residing at Paris, of the clue that Bilson's draft had given him in thither pursuing Axworthy, nor of his severe struggle in relinquishing the quest. He threw over all the completest accidental air, and scarcely made it evident that it was he who had recognised the writing, and all that turned on it. Averil listened to the narration, was silent for some space, then having gone over it in her own mind, looked up and said –

'Then all this came of your being at that hospital;' and a burning blush spread over the pale cheek, and made Tom shrink, start, and feel guilty of having touched the chord of obligation, connected with that obtrusive pledge of his. Above all, however, to repress emotion was his prime object; and he calmly answered, 'It was a good Providence that brought any one there who knew the circumstances.'

She was silent; and he was about to rise and relieve her from the sense of his presuming on her gratitude, when a cough, accompanied with a pressure of her hand on her side, betrayed an excess of suffering, that drew him on to his other purpose of endeavouring to learn her condition, and to do what he could for her relief. His manner, curiously like his father's, and all the home associations connected with it, easily drew from her what he wanted to ascertain, and she perfectly understood its purport, and was calm and even bright.

'I was glad to be better when Henry went away,' she said; 'he had so much to do, and we thought I was getting well then. You must not frighten him and hurry him here, if you please,' she said, earnestly, 'for he must not be wasting his time here, and you think it will last a month or two, don't you?'

'I want to persuade Henry to bring you all home, and enter into partnership with Mr Wright,' said Tom. 'The voyage would – might – it would be the best thing for you.'

'Could I ever be well enough again? Oh, don't tell me to think about it! The one thing I asked for before I die has been given me, and now I know he is free, I will – will not set my mind on anything else.'

There was a look so near heaven on her face, as she spoke, that Tom durst not say any more of home, or earthly schemes; but, quiet, grave, and awe-stricken, left her to the repose she needed, and betook himself to the other room, where Ella, of course, flew on him, having been hardly detained by Cora from breaking in before. His object was to go to see the medical man who had been attending Averil; and Cora assuring him the horse had nothing to do in the frost, and telling him the times of the day when he would be most likely to find Dr Laidlaw, he set forth.

Averil meantime lay on her sofa calmly happy, and thankful, the worn and wearied spirit full of rest and gladness unspeakable, in the fullness of gratitude for the answered prayer that she might know her brother free before her death. If she had ever doubted of her own state, she had read full confirmation in her physician's saddened eyes, and the absence of all hopeful auguries, except the single hint that she might survive a voyage to England; and that she wished unsaid. Life, for the last five years, had been mournful work; there had been one year of blind self-will, discord, and bitterness, then a crushing stroke, and the rest exhausted submission and hopeless bending to sorrow after sorrow, with self-reproach running through all. Wearied out, she was glad to lay down the burthen, and accept the evening gleam as sunset radiance, without energy to believe it as the dawn of a brighter day. She shrank from being made even to wish to see Leonard. If once she began to think it possible, it would be a hard sacrifice to give it up; and on one point her resolution was fixed, that she would not be made a cause for bringing him to share their wretchedness in America. Life and things of life were over with her, and she would only be thankful for the softening blessings that came at its close, without stirring up vain longings for more. That kindness of Tom May, for instance, how soothing it was after her long self-reproach for her petulant and cutting unjust reply to his generous affection – generous above all at such a moment!

And after all, it was he – it was he and no other who had cleared Leonard – he had fulfilled the pledge he had given when he did not know what he was talking of. How she hated the blush that the sudden remembrance had called up on her face! It was quite plain that he had been disgusted by her unkind, undignified, improper tone of rejection; and though out of humanity he had brought her the tidings, he would not let her approach to thanking him, she was ashamed that he should have traced an allusion, the most distant, to the scene he had, doubtless, loathed in remembrance. He would, no doubt, go away to-day or to-morrow, and then these foolish thoughts would subside, and she should be left alone with Cora and her thankfulness, to think again of the great change before her!

But Tom was not gone. Indeed Averil was much more ill before the next morning, partly from hysteria, the reaction of the morning's excitement, and partly from an aggravation of the more serious pulmonary affection. It was a temporary matter, and one that made his remaining the merest act of common humanity, since he had found Dr Laidlaw a very third-rate specimen, and her brother was too far off to have arrived in time to be of use. The fresh science and skill of the young physician were indeed of the highest value, and under his care Averil rallied after a few days of prostration and suffering, during which she had watched and observed a good deal, and especially the good understanding between her doctor and Cora Muller. When Cousin Deborah was sitting with her, they always seemed to be talking in the drawing-room; nay, there were reports of his joining in the fabrication of some of the delicacies that were triumphantly brought to her room; and Ella was in a state of impatient pique at being slighted by 'Mr Tom,' who, she complained, was always fighting with Cora about their politics; and Cora herself used to bring what Dr May had said, as the choicest entertainment to her sick friend; while to herself he was merely the physician, kind and gentle to the utmost degree; but keeping his distance so scrupulously, that the pang awoke that he absolutely disliked her, and only attended her from common compassion; and, it might be, found consolation in being thus brought in contact with Cora. Oh, if it were only possible to own her wrongs, and ask his pardon without a compromise of maidenliness! Perhaps – perhaps she might, when she was still nearer death, and when she was supposed to know how it was between him and Cora. Dear Cora, it would be a beautiful reward for them both, and they would take care of Ella. Cora would be happier than ever yet among the Mays – and – Oh! why, why was there so much unkind selfish jealousy left, that instead of being glad, the notion left her so very miserable? Why did the prospect of such happiness for her self-devoted friend and nurse make her feel full of bitterness, and hardly able to bear it patiently, when she heard her speak the name of Dr May?

Averil had again left her bed, and resumed her place on the sofa before letters arrived. There was Leonard's from Cocksmoor Parsonage, the first real letter she had had from him since his term of servitude had begun. It was a grave and thankful letter, very short, doing little more than mention every one's kindness, and express a hope of soon meeting her and Ella, however and wherever Henry should think best. Brief as it was, it made her more thoroughly realize his liberty, and feel that the yearning towards him in her heart was growing more and more ardent, in spite of her strivings not to let it awaken.

The same post brought Henry's answer to Tom May's representation. It was decisive. He had broken off his whole connexion with England, and did not wish to return to a neighbourhood so full of painful recollections. He was making his way rapidly upwards in his present position, and it would be folly to give up the advantages it offered; moreover, he had no fears of the future well-doing of the Massissauga Company. As soon as the weather permitted it, he hoped to remove his sister to a healthier locality for change of air, but she could not be fit for a journey in the winter. There were plenty of acknowledgments to the Mays for their kindness to Leonard, from whom Henry said he had heard, as well as from Dr May, and others at

Stoneborough. He should advise Leonard by all means to close with Mr Bramshaw's offer, for he saw no opening for him in the United States at present, although the ultimate triumph over rebellion, &c. &c. &c. – in the most inflated style of Henry's truly adopted country. No one who had not known the whole affair would ever enter into Leonard's entire innocence, the stigma of conviction would cleave to him, and create an impression against him and his family among strangers, and it was highly desirable that he should remain among friends. In fact, it was plain that Henry was still ashamed of him, and wished to be free of a dangerous appendage.

Tom was so savagely angry at this letter that he could only work off his wrath by a wild expedition in the snow, in the course of which he lost his way, wandered till the adventure began to grow perilous, came at last upon a squatter, with great difficulty induced him to indicate the track sufficiently for his English density, and arrived at Massissauga at nine o'clock at night. Averil was still on her sofa, quite calm and quiet, all but her two red spots; but afterwards, in her own room, she had one of her worst fits of spasms.

However, she was up and dressed by the middle of the next day, and, contrary to her wont since the first time, she sent Ella out of the room when her doctor came to see her.

'I wanted to speak to you,' she said, 'I have a great favour to ask of you. You will soon be going home? Would you, could you take Ella with you? I know it is a great, a too great thing to ask. But I would not have her in any one's way. I am going to write to Mrs Wills, at the school where I was, and Ella's means are quite enough to keep her there, holidays and all, till Leonard can give her a home. It will be much better for her, and a relief to Henry; and it will be giving back one – one to Leonard! It will be one thing more that I shall be happy about.'

Tom had let her go on with her short gentle sentences, because he knew not how to answer; but at last she said, 'Forgive me, and do not think of it, if I have asked what I ought not, or would be troublesome.'

'Troublesome! no, indeed! I was only thinking – if it might not be better managed,' he answered, rather by way of giving himself time to debate whether the utterance of the one thought in his heart would lead to his being driven away.

'Pray do not propose Leonard's coming for her! He must come to this feverish place in spring. And if he came, and I were not here, and Henry not wanting him! Oh no, no; do not let me think of his coming!'

'Averil,' he said, kneeling on one knee so as to be nearer, and to be able to speak lower, 'you are so unearthly in your unselfishness, that I dare the less to put before you the one way in which I could take Ella home to him. It is if you would overlook the past, and give me a brother's right in them both.'

She turned in amazement to see if she had heard aright. He had removed his glasses, and the deep blue expressive eyes so seldom plainly visible were wistfully, pleadingly, fixed on her, brimming over with the dew of earnestness. Her face of inquiry gave him courage to go on, 'If you would only let me, I think I could bring you home to see him; and if you would believe it and try, I believe I could make you happier,' and with an uncontrollable shake in his voice he ceased – and only looked.

She sat upright, her hands clasped in her lap, her eyes shut, trying to collect her thoughts; and the silence lasted for several seconds. At last she said, opening her eyes, but gazing straight before her, not at him, 'I do not think I ought. Do you really know what you are saying? You know I cannot get well.'

'I know,' he said. 'All I ask is, to tend and watch over you while I may, to bring you home to Leonard, and to be Ella's brother.'

His voice was still and low, and he laid his hand on her folded ones with reverent solemnity; but though it did not tremble, its touch was cold as marble, and conveyed to Averil an instant sense of the force of his repressed emotion. She started under it, and exclaimed with the first agitation she had shown, 'No, no; it would cost you too much. You, young, beginning life – you must not take a sorrow upon you.'

'Is it not there already?' he said, almost inaudibly. 'Would it lessen it to be kept away from you?'

'Oh, do not go on, do not tempt me,' she cried. 'Think of your father.'

'Nay, think what he is yourself. Or rather look here,' and he took out a part of a letter from Ethel, and laid it before her.

'As to papa not guessing your object,' she said, 'that was a vain delusion if you ever entertained it, so you must not mind my having explained. He said if he had been you, it was just what he should have done himself, and he is quite ready to throw his heart into it if you will only trust to his kindness. I do so want you really to try what that is.'

'And you came for this,' faltered Averil, leaning back, almost overcome.

'I did not come meaning to hurry the subject on you. I hoped to have induced Henry to have brought you all home, and then, when I had done my best to efface the recollection of that unpardonable behaviour, to have tried whether you could look on me differently.'

'I don't like you to say that,' said Averil, simply but earnestly; 'I have felt over and over again how wrong I was – how ungrateful – to have utterly missed all the nobleness and generosity of your behaviour, and answered in that unjust, ill-tempered way.'

'Nothing was ever more deserved,' he answered; 'I have hated myself ever since, and I hope I am not as obnoxious now.'

'It was I!' she said; 'I have lived every bit of the winter over again, and seen that I was always ready to be offended, and somehow I could not help caring so much for what you said, that lesser things from you hurt and cut as other people's did not.'

'Do you know what that proves?' said Tom, with an arch subsmile lighting on his eyes and mouth; and as a glow awoke on her pale cheek, he added, 'and won't you believe, too, that my propensity to "contemptuous irony," was all from my instinctive fear of what you could do to me?'

'Oh, don't repeat that! I have been so bitterly ashamed of it!'

'I am sure I have.'

'And I have longed so to ask your pardon. I thought I would leave a letter or message with Ella that you would understand.'

'You can do better than that now. You can forgive me.'

'Oh!' said Averil, her hands suddenly joined over her face, 'this is one joy more! I cannot think why it is all growing so bright just at last – at last. It is all come now! How good it is!'

He saw that she could bear no more. He pressed no more for a decisive answer; he did not return to the subject; but from that time he treated her as what belonged to him, as if it was his business to think, act, and judge for her, and to watch over her; and her acquiescence was absolute.

There was not much speaking between them; there were chiefly skirmishes between him and Cora, to which she listened in smiling passive amusement; and even when alone together they said little – actually nothing at all about the future. He had written to Ethel on his first arrival, and on the reply, as well as on Averil's state, all must depend. Meanwhile such a look of satisfied repose and peace shone upon Averil's face as was most sweet to look upon; and though extremely feeble, and not essentially better, she was less suffering, and could in great languor, but in calm enjoyment, pass through day by day of the precious present that had come to crown her long trial.

CHAPTER XXX

'Oh, when its flower seems fain to die,
The full heart grudges smile or sigh
To aught beside, though fair and dear;
Like a bruised leaf, at touch of fear,
Its hidden fragrance love gives out.'

Lyra Innocentium.

'The letters at last! One to Ethel, and three to Leonard! Now for it, Ethel!'

Ethel opened – read – ran out of the room without a word, and sought her father in his study, where she laid before him Tom's letter, written from Massissauga the day after his arrival.

'Dear Ethel,

'I have found my darling, but too late to arrest the disease – the work of her brother's perverseness and wrong-headedness. I have no hope of saving her; though it will probably be a matter of several months – that is, with care, and removal from this vile spot.

'I am writing to Henry, but I imagine that he is too much charmed with his present prospects to give them up; and in her angelic self-sacrifice she insists on Leonard's not coming out. Indeed, there would be no use in his doing so unless she leaves this place; but should no unforeseen complication supervene, it is my full persuasion that she could be removed, safely make the voyage, and even be spared for this summer among us. Surely my father will not object! It will be but a short time; and she has suffered so much, so piteously needs love and cherishing, that it is not in him to refuse. He, who consented to Margaret's engagement, cannot but feel for us. I would work for him all my life! I would never cast a thought beyond home, if only once hallowed by this dear presence for ever so short a time. Only let the answers be so cordial as to remove all doubts or scruples; and when they are sent prepare for her. I would bring her as quickly as her health permits. No time must be lost in taking her from hence; and I wait only for the letters to obtain her consent to an immediate marriage. Furnish the house at once; I will repay you on my return. There is 200*l.* for the first floor, sitting, and bed-rooms; for the rest the old will do. Only regard the making these perfect; colouring pink – all as cheerful and pleasant as money can accomplish. If Flora will bear with me, get her to help you; or else Mary, if Cheviot forgives me. Only don't spare cost. I will make it up some way, if you find more wanted. I saw an invalid sofa, an improvement on Margaret's, which I will write to Gaspard to send from Paris. If you could only see the desolateness of the house where she has wasted away these three years, you would long to make a bower of bliss for her. I trust to you. I find I must trust everything to you. I cannot write to my father; I have made nine beginnings, and must leave it to you. He has comforted her, he knows her sorrows; he could not see her and bid me leave her. Only there must be no hesitation. *That*, or even remonstrance, would prevent her from consenting; and as to the objections, I cannot know them better than I do. Indeed, all this may be in vain; she is so near Heaven, that I dare not talk to her of this; but I have written to Leonard, dwelling chiefly on the chance of bringing her to him. Her desire to keep him from attempting to come out will I trust be an inducement; but if you could only see her, you would know how irreverent it seems to persecute one so nearly an angel with such matters. If I may only tend her to the last! I trust to you. This is for my father.

'Ever yours,

'THOMAS MAY.'

The last sentence referred to a brief medical summary of her symptoms, on a separate paper.

'Can this be Tom?' was the doctor's exclamation. 'Poor boy! it is going very hard with him!'

'This would soften it more than anything else could,' said Ethel.

'Oh yes! You write. Yes, and I'll write, and tell him he is free to take his own way. Poor child! she would have been a good girl if she had known how. Well, of all my eleven children that Tom should be the one to go on in this way!'

'Poor dear Tom! What do you think of his statement of her case? Is she so very ill?'

Dr May screwed up his face. 'A sad variety of mischief,' he said; 'if all be as he thinks, I doubt his getting her home; but he is young, and has his heart in it. I have seen her mother in A state like this – only without the diseased lungs. You can't remember it; but poor Ward never thought he could be grateful enough after she was pulled through. However, this is an aggravated case, and looks bad – very bad! It is mournful ending for that poor boy's patience – it will sink very deep, and he will be a sadder man all his days; but I would not hinder his laying up a treasure that will brighten as he grows older.'

'Thank you, papa. I shall tell him what you say.'

'I shall write – to her I think. I owe him something for not proving that it is all as a study of pneumonia. I say, Ethel, what is become of the Diseases of Climate?' he added, with a twinkle in his eye.

'In the nine beginnings.'

'And how about the Massissanga Company?'

'You heartless old worldly-minded father!' said Ethel. 'When you take to prudence for Tom, what is the world coming to?'

'Into order,' said the doctor, shaking himself into the coat she held for him. 'Tom surrendered to a pet patient of mine. Now for poor Leonard! Good-bye, young people! I am off to Cocksmoor!'

'Please take me, grandpapa,' cried Dickie, hopping into the hall.

'You, you one-legged manikin! I'm going over all the world; and how are you to get home?'

'On Leonard's back,' said the undaunted Dickie.

'Not so, master: poor Leonard has news here that will take the taste of nonsense out of his mouth.'

'I am his friend,' said Dickie, with dignity.

'Then your friendship must not disturb him over his letters. And can you sit in the carriage and twirl your thumbs while I am at Fordham?'

'I shall not twirl my thumbs. I shall make out a problem on my ship chess-board.'

'That's the boy who was sent from the Antipodes, that he might not be spoilt!' quoth Aubrey, as the doctor followed the child into the carriage.

'Granting reasonable wishes is not spoiling,' said Ethel.

'May the system succeed as well with Dickie as with——' and Aubrey in one flourish indicated Gertrude and himself.

'Ay, we shall judge by the reception of Ethel's tidings!' cried Gertrude. 'Now for it, Ethel. Read us Tom's letter, confute the engineer, hoist with his own *petard*.'

'Now, Ethel, confute the Daisy, the green field daisy – the simple innocent daisy, deluded by Diseases of Climate.'

'Ethel looks as concerned as if it were fatal truth,' added Gertrude.

'What is it?' asked Aubrey. 'If Henry Ward has gone down in a Monitor at Charleston, I'll forgive him.'

'Not that,' said Ethel; 'but we little thought how ill poor Ave is.'

'Dangerously?' said Aubrey, gravely.

'Not perhaps immediately so; but Tom means to marry at once, that he may have a chance of bringing her home to see Leonard.'

'Another shock for Leonard,' said Aubrey, quite subdued; 'why can't he have a little respite?'

'May they at least meet once more!' said Ethel; 'there will be some comfort in looking to that!'

'And what a fellow Tom is to have thought of it,' added Aubrey. 'Nobody will ever dare to say again that he is not the best of the kit of us! I must be off now to the meet: but if you are writing, Ethel, I wish you would give her my love, or whatever he would like, and tell him he is a credit to the family. I say, may I tell George Rivers?'

'Oh yes; it will soon be in the air; and Charles Cheviot will be down on us!'

Away went Aubrey to mount the hunter that George Rivers placed at his service.

Gertrude, who had been struck dumb, looked up to ask, 'Then it is really so?'

'Indeed it is.'

'Then,' cried Gertrude, vehemently, 'you and he have been deceiving us all this time!'

'No, Gertrude; there was nothing to tell. I did not really know, and I could not gossip about him.'

'You might have hinted.'

'I tried, but I was clumsy.'

'I hate hints!' exclaimed the impetuous young lady; 'one can't understand them, and gets the credit of neglecting them. If people have a secret attachment, they ought to let all their family know!'

'Perhaps they do in Ireland.'

'You don't feel one grain for me, Ethel,' said Gertrude, with tears in her eyes. 'Only think how Tom led me on to say horrid things about the Wards; and now to recollect them, when she is so ill too – and he——' She burst into sobs.

'My poor Daisy! I dare say it was half my fault.'

Gertrude gave an impatient leap. 'There you go again! calling it your fault is worse than Charles's improving the circumstance. It was my fault, and it shall be my fault, and nobody else's fault, except Tom's, and he will hate me, and never let me come near her to show that I am not a nasty spiteful thing!'

'I think that if you are quiet and kind, and not flighty, he will forget all that, and be glad to let you be a sister to her.'

'A sister to Ave Ward! Pretty preferment!' muttered Gertrude.

'Poor Ave! After the way she has borne her troubles, we shall feel it an honour to be sisters to her.'

'And that chair!' broke out Gertrude. 'O Ethel, you did out of malice prepense make me vow it should be for Mrs Thomas May.'

'Well, Daisy, if you won't suspect me of improving the circumstance, I should say that finishing it for her would be capital discipline.'

'Horrid mockery, I should say,' returned Gertrude, sadly; 'a gaudy rose-coloured chair, all over white fox-gloves, for a person in that state——'

'Poor Tom's great wish is to have her drawing-room made as charming as possible; and it would be a real welcome to her.'

'Luckily,' said Gertrude, breaking into laughter again, 'they don't know when it began; how in a weak moment I admired the pattern, and Blanche inflicted it and all its appurtenances on me, hoping to convert me to a fancy-work-woman! Dear me, pride has a fall! I loved to answer "Three stitches," when Mrs Blanche asked after my progress."

'Ah Daisy, if you did but respect any one!'

'If they would not all be tiresome! Seriously, I know I must finish the thing, because of my word.'

'Yes, and I believe keeping a light word that has turned out heavy, is the best help in bridling the tongue.'

'And, Ethel, I will really try to be seen and not heard while I am about the work,' said Gertrude, with an earnestness which proved that she was more sorry than her manner conveyed.

Her resolution stood the trying test of a visit from the elder married sisters; for, as Ethel said, the scent of the tidings attracted both Flora and the Cheviots; and the head master endeavoured to institute a kind of family committee, to represent to the doctor how undesirable the match would be, entailing inconveniences that would not end with the poor bride's life, and bringing at once upon Tom a crushing anxiety and sorrow. Ethel's opinion was of course set aside by Mr Cheviot, but he did expect concurrence from Mrs Rivers and from Richard; and Flora assented to all his objections, but she was not to be induced to say she would remonstrate with her father or with Tom; and she intimated the uselessness thereof so plainly, that she almost hoped that Charles Cheviot would be less eager to assail the doctor with his arguments.

'No hope of that,' said Ethel, when he had taken leave. 'He will disburthen his conscience; but then papa is well able to take care of himself! Flora, I am so thankful you don't object.'

'No indeed,' said Flora. 'We all know it is a pity; but it would be a far greater pity to break if off now – and do Tom an infinity of harm. Now tell me all.'

And she threw herself into the subject in the homelike manner that had grown on her, almost in proportion to Mary's guest-like ways and absorption in her own affairs.

Six weeks from that time, another hasty note announced that Dr and Mrs Thomas May and Ella were at Liverpool; adding that Averil had been exceedingly ill throughout the voyage, though on being carried ashore, she had so far revived, that Tom hoped to bring her home the next day; but emotion was so dangerous, that he begged not to be met at the station, and above all, that Leonard would not show himself till summoned.

Dr May being unavoidably absent, Ethel alone repaired to the newly-furnished house for this strange sad bridal welcome.

The first person to appear when the carriage door was opened was a young girl, pale, tall, thin, only to be recognised by her black eyes. With a rapid kiss and greeting, Ethel handed her on to the further door, where she might satisfy the eager embrace of the brother who there awaited her; while Tom almost lifted out the veiled muffled figure of his bride, and led her upstairs to the sitting-room, where divesting her of hat, cloak, muff, and respirator, he laid her on the sofa, and looked anxiously for her re-assuring smile before he even seemed to perceive his sister or left room for her greeting.

The squarely made, high complexioned, handsome Averil Ward was entirely gone. In Averil May, Ethel saw delicately refined and sharpened features, dark beautiful eyes, enlarged, softened, and beaming with perilous lustre, a transparently white blue-veined skin, with a lovely roseate tint, deepening or fading with every word, look, or movement, and a smile painfully sweet and touching, as first of the three, the invalid found voice for thanks and inquiries for all.

'Quite well,' said Ethel. 'But papa has been most unluckily sent for to Whitford, and can't get home till the last train.'

'It may be as well,' said Tom: 'we must have perfect quiet till after the night's rest.'

'May I see no-one else to-night?' she wistfully asked.

'Let us see how you are when you have had some coffee and are rested.'

'Very well,' she said, with a gentle submission, that was as new a sight as Tom's tenderness; 'but indeed I am not tired; and it is so pretty and pleasant. Is this really Dr Spencer's old house? Can there be such a charming room in it?'

'I did not think so,' said Tom, looking in amazement at the effect produced by the bright modern grate with its cheerful fire, the warm delicate tints of the furniture, the appliances for comfort and ornament already giving a home look. 'I know this is in the main your doing, Ethel; but who was the hand?'

'All of us were hands,' said Ethel; 'but Flora was the moving spring. She went to London for a week about it.'

'Mrs Rivers! Oh, how good!' said Averil, flushing with surprise; then raising herself, as her coffee was brought in a dainty little service, she exclaimed, 'And oh, if it were possible, I should say that was my dear old piano!'

'Yes,' said Ethel, 'we thought you would like it; and Hector Ernescliffe gave Mrs Wright a new one for it.'

This was almost too much. Averil's lip trembled, but she looked up into her husband's face and made an answer, which would have been odd had she not been speaking to his thought.

'Never mind! It is only happiness and the kindness.' And she drank the coffee with an effort, and smiled at him again, as she asked, 'Where is Ella?'

'At our house,' said Ethel; 'we mean her to be there for the present.'

Knowing with whom Ella must be, and fearing to show discontent with the mandate of patience, Averil again began to admire. 'What a beautiful chair! Look, Tom! is it not exquisite? Whose work is it?'

'Gertrude's.'

'That is the most fabulous thing of all,' said Tom, walking round it. 'Daisy! Her present, not her work?'

'Her work, every stitch. It has been a race with time.'

The gratification of Averil's flush and smile was laid up by Ethel for Gertrude's reward; but it was plain that Tom wanted complete rest for his wife, and Ethel only waited to install her in the adjoining bed-room, which was as delightfully fitted up as the first apartment. Averil clung to her for the instant they were alone together, and whispered, 'Oh, it is all so sweet! Don't think I don't feel it! But you see it is all I can do for him to be as quiet as I can! Say so, please!'

Ethel felt the throb of the heart, and knew to whom she was to say so; but Tom's restless approaching step made Averil detach herself, and sink into an arm-chair. Ethel left her, feeling that the short clasp of their arms had sealed their sisterhood here and for ever.

'It is too sad, too beautiful to be talked about,' she said to Gertrude, who was anxiously on the watch for tidings.

Obedient as Averil was, she had not understood her husband's desire that she should seek her pillow at once. She was feeling brisk and fresh, and by no means ready for captivity, and she presently came forth again with her soft, feeble, noiseless step; but she had nearly retreated again, feeling herself mistaken and bewildered, for in the drawing-room stood neither Tom nor his sisters, but a stranger – a dark, grave, thoughtful man of a singularly resolute and settled cast of countenance. The rustle of her dress made him look up as she turned. 'Ave!' he exclaimed; and as their eyes met, the light in those brown depths restored the whole past. She durst not trust herself to speak, as her head rested on his shoulder, his arms were round her; only as her husband came on the scene with a gesture of surprise, she said, 'Indeed, I did not mean it! I did not know he was here.'

'I might have known you could not be kept apart if I once let Leonard in,' he said, as he arranged her on the sofa, and satisfied himself that there were no tokens of the repressed agitation that left such dangerous effects. 'Will you both be very good if I leave you to be happy together?' he presently added, after a few indifferent words had passed.

Averil looked wistfully after him, as if he were wanted to complete full felicity even in Leonard's presence. How little would they once have thought that her first words to her brother would be, 'Oh, was there ever any one like him?'

'We owe it all to him,' said Leonard.

'So kind,' added Averil, 'not to be vexed, though he dreaded our meeting so much; and you see I could not grieve him by making a fuss. But this is nice!' she added, with a sigh going far beyond the effect of the homely word.

'You are better. Ella said so.'

'I am feeling well to-night. Come, let me look at you, and learn your face.'

He knelt down beside her, and she stroked back the hair, which had fulfilled his wish that she should find it as long, though much darker than of old. Posture and action recalled that meeting, when her couch had been his prison bed, and the cold white prison walls had frowned on them; yet even in the rosy light of the cheerful room there was on them the solemnity of an approaching doom.

'Where is the old face?' Averil said. 'You look as you did in the fever. Your smile brings back something of yourself. But, oh, those hollow eyes!'

'Count Ugolino is Dr May's name for me; but, indeed, Ave, I have tried to fatten for your inspection.'

'It is not thinness,' she said; 'but I had carried about with me the bright daring open face of my own boy. I shall learn to like this better now.'

'Nay, it is you and Ella that are changed. Oh Ave, you never let me know what a place you were in.'

'There were many things better than you fancy,' she answered; 'and it is over – it is all gladness now.'

'I see that in your face,' he said, gazing his fill. 'You do look ill indeed; but, Ave, I never saw you so content.'

'I can't help it,' she said, smiling. 'Every moment comes some fresh kindness from him. The more trouble I give him the kinder he is. Is it not as if the tempest was over, and we had been driven into the smoothest little sun-shiny bay?'

'To rest and refit,' he said, thoughtfully.

'For me, "the last long wave;" and a most gentle smooth one it is,' said Averil, 'for you to refit for a fresh voyage. Dear Leonard, I have often guessed what you would do.'

'What have you guessed?'

'Only what we used to plan, in the old times after you had been at Coombe, Leonard.'

'Dear sister! And you would let me go!'

'Our parting is near, any way,' she said, her eye turning to the print from Ary Scheffer's St Augustine and Monica. 'Whoever gave us that, divined how we ought to feel in these last days together.'

'It was Richard May's gift,' said Leonard. 'Ave, there was nothing wanting but your liking this.'

'Then so it is?' she asked.

'Unless the past disqualifies me,' he said. 'I have spoken to no one yet, except little Dickie. When I thought I ought to find some present employment, and wanted to take a clerkship at Bramshaw's, Dr May made me promise to wait till I had seen you before I fixed on anything; but my mind is made up, and I shall speak now – with your blessing on it Ave.'

'I knew it!' she said.

He saw it was safer to quit this subject, and asked of Henry.

'He sent his love. He met us at New York. He is grown so soldierly, with such a black beard, that he is more grown out of knowledge than any of us; but I scarcely saw him, for he was quite overset at my appearance, and Tom thought it did me harm. I wish our new sister would have come to see me.'

'Sister!'

'Oh, did you not know? I thought Tom had written! She is a Virginian lady, whose first husband was a doctor, who died of camp-fever early in the war. A Federal, of course. And they are to be married as soon as Charleston has fallen.'

Leonard smiled. And Averil expressed her certainty that it had fallen by that time.

'And he is quite Americanized?' asked Leonard. 'Does he return to our own name? No! Then I do not wonder he did not wish for me. Perhaps he may yet bear to meet me, some day when we are grown old.'

'At least we can pray to be altogether, where one is gone already,' said Averil. 'That was the one comfort in parting with the dear Cora – my blessing through all the worst! Leonard, she would not go to live in the fine house her father has taken at New York, but she is gone to be one of the nurses in the midst of all the hospital miseries. And, oh, what comfort she will carry with her!'

Here Tom returned, but made no objection to her brother's stay, perceiving that his aspect and voice were like fulness to the hungry heart that had pined so long – but keeping all the others away; and they meanwhile were much entertained by Ella, who was in joyous spirits; a little subdued, indeed, by the unknown brother, but in his absence very communicative. Gertrude was greatly amused with her account of the marriage, in the sitting-room at Massissauga, and of Tom's being so unprepared for the brevity of the American form, that he never knew where he was in the Service, and completed it with a puzzled 'Is that all?'

Averil had, according to Ella, been infinitely more calm and composed. 'She does nothing but watch his eyes,' said Ella; 'and ever since we parted from Cora, I have had no one to speak to! In the cabin he never stirred from sitting by her; and if she could speak at all, it was so low that I could not hear. School will be quite lively.'

'Are you going to school?'

'Oh yes! where Ave was. That is quite fixed; and I have had enough of playing third person,' said Ella, with her precocious Western manner. 'You know I have all my own property, so I shall be on no one's hands! Oh, and Cora made her father buy all Ave's Massissauga shares – at a dead loss to us of course.'

'Well,' said Gertrude, 'I am sorry Tom is not an American shareholder. It was such fun!'

'He wanted to have made them all over to Henry; but Cora was determined; and her father is making heaps of money as a commissary, so I am sure he could afford it. Some day, when the rebellion is subdued, I mean to go and see Cora and Henry and his wife,' added Ella, whose tinge of Americanism formed an amusing contrast with Dickie's colonial ease – especially when she began to detail the discomforts of Massissauga, and he made practical suggestions for the remedies of each – describing how mamma and he himself managed.

The younger ones had all gone to bed, Richard had returned home, and Ethel was waiting to let her father in, when Leonard came back from the new arrivals.

'I did not think you would be allowed to stay so late,' said Ethel.

'We did not talk much. I was playing chants most of the time; and after she went to bed, I stayed with Tom.'

'What do you think of her?'

'I cannot think. I can only feel a sort of awe. End as it may, it will have been a blessed thing to have had her among us like this.'

'Yes, it ought to do us all good. And I think she is full of enjoyment.'

'Perfect enjoyment!' repeated Leonard. 'Thank God for that!'

After some pause, during which he turned over his pocket-book, as if seeking for something, he came to her, and said, 'Miss May, Averil has assented to a purpose that has long been growing up within me – and that I had rather consult you about than any one, because you first inspired it.'

'I think I know the purpose you mean,' said Ethel, her heart beating high.

'The first best purpose of my boyhood,' he said. 'If only it may be given back to me! Will you be kind enough to look over this rough copy?'

It was the draught of a letter to the Missionary Bishop, Mr Seaford's diocesan, briefly setting forth Leonard's early history, his conviction, and his pardon, referring to Archdeacon May as a witness to the truth of his narrative.

'After this statement,' he proceeded, 'it appears to me little short of effrontery to offer myself for any share of the sacred labour in which your Lordship is engaged; and though it had been the wish of the best days of my youth, I should not have ventured on the thought but for the encouragement I received from Mr Seaford, your Lordship's chaplain. I have a small income of my own, so that I should not be a burthen on the mission, and understanding that mechanical arts are found useful, I will mention that I learnt shoe-making at Milbank, and carpentry at Portland, and I would gladly undertake any manual occupation needed in a mission. Latterly I was employed in the schoolmaster's department; and I have some knowledge of music. My education is, of course, imperfect, but I am endeavouring to improve myself. My age is twenty-one; I have good health, and I believe I can bring power of endurance and willingness to be employed in any manner that may be serviceable, whether as artisan or catechist.'

'I don't think they will make a shoemaker of you,' said Ethel, with her heart full.

'Will they have me at all? There will always be a sort of ticket-of-leave flavour about me,' said Leonard, speaking simply, straightforwardly, but without dejection; 'and I might be doubtful material for a mission.'

'Your brother put that in your head.'

'He implied that my case half known would be a discredit to him, and I am prepared for others thinking so. If so, I can get a situation at Portland, and I know I can be useful there; but when such a hope as this was opened to me again, I could not help making an attempt. Do you think I may show that letter to Dr May?'

'O Leonard, this is one of the best days of one's life!'

'But what?' he asked, as she looked over the letter, 'what shall I alter?'

'I do not know only you are so business-like; you do not seem to care enough.'

'If I let myself out, it would look like unbecoming pressing of myself, considering what I am; but if you think I ought, I will say more. I have become so much used to writing letters under constraint, that I know I am very dry.'

'Let papa see it first,' said Ethel. 'After all, earnestness is best out of sight.'

'Mr Wilmot and he shall decide whether I may send it,' he said; 'and in the meantime I would go to St. Augustine's, if they will have me.'

'I see you have thought it all over.'

'Yes. I only waited to have spoken with my sister, and she – dear, dear Ave – had separately thought of such a destination for me. It was more than acquiescence, more than I dared to hope!'

'Her spirit will be with you, wherever she is! And,' with a sudden smile, 'Leonard, was not this the secret between you and Dickie?'

'Yes,' said Leonard, smiling too; 'the dear little fellow is so fresh and loving, as well as so wise and discreet, that he draws out all that is in one's heart. It has been a new life to me ever since he took to me! Do you know, I believe he has been writing a letter of recommendation of me on his own account to the Bishop; I told him he must enclose it to his father if he presumed to send it, though he claims the Bishop as his intimate friend.'

'Ah,' said Ethel, 'papa is always telling him that they can't get on in New Zealand for want of the small archdeacon, and that, I really think, abashes him more than anything else.'

'He is not forward, he is only sensible,' said Leonard, on whose heart Dickie had far too fast a hold for even this slight disparagement not to be rebutted. 'I had forgotten what a child could be till I was with him; I felt like a stock or a stone among you all.'

Ethel smiled. 'I was nearly giving you Marmion, in remembrance of old times, on the night of the Christmas-tree,' she said; 'but I did not then feel as if the "giving double" for all your care and trouble had begun.'

'The heart to feel it so was not come,' said Leonard; 'now since I have grasped this hope of making known to others the way to that Grace that held me up,' – he paused with excess of feeling – 'all has been joy, even in the recollection of the darkest days. Mr Wilmot's words come back now, that it may all have been training for my Master's work. Even the manual labour may have been my preparation!' His eyes brightened, and he was indeed more like eager, hopeful youth she remembered than she had ever hoped to see him; but this brightness was the flash of steel, tried, strengthened, and refined in the fire – a brightness that might well be trusted.

'One knew it must be so,' was all she could say.

'Yes, yes,' he said, eagerly. 'You sent me words of greeting that held up my faith; and, above all, when we read those books at Coombe, you put the key of comfort in my hand, and I never quite lost it. Miss May,' he added, as Dr May's latch-key was heard in the front door, 'if ever I come to any good, I owe it to you!'

And that was the result of the boy's romance.

The first tidings of the travellers next morning were brought near the end of breakfast by Tom, who came in looking thin, worn, and anxious, saying that Averil had called herself too happy to sleep till morning, when a short doze had only rendered her feeble, exhausted, and depressed:

'I shall go and see her,' said Dr May; 'I like my patients best in that mood.'

Nor would the doctor let his restless, anxious son do more than make the introduction, but despatched him to the Hospital; whence returning to find himself still excluded, he could endure nothing but pacing up and down the lawn in sight of his father's head in the window, and seeking as usual Ethel's sympathy.

There was some truth in what Charles Cheviot had said. Wedlock did enhance the grief and loss, and Tom found the privilege of these months of tendance more heart-wringing that he had anticipated, though of course more precious and inestimable. Moreoever, Averil's depression had been a phase of her illness which had not before revealed itself in such a degree.

'Generally,' he said, 'she has talked as if what she looks to were all such pure hope and joy, that though it broke one's heart to hear it, one saw it made her happy, and could stand it. Fancy, Ethel, not an hour after we were married, I found her trying the ring on this finger, and saying I should be able to wear it like my father! It seemed as if she would regret nothing but my sorrow, and that my keeping it out of sight was all that was needful to her happiness. But to-day she has been blaming herself for – for grieving to leave all so soon, just as her happiness might have been beginning! Think, Ethel! Reproaching herself for unthankfulness even to tears! It might have been more for her peace to have remained with her where she had no revival of these associations, if they are only pain to her.'

'Oh, no, no, Tom. It only proves the pleasure they do give her. You know it with my understanding, Ethel, but as to reasoning about her as if she was anybody else, the thing is mere mockery. What can my father be about?' he added, for the twentieth time. 'Talking to her in the morning always knocks her up. If he had only let me warn him; but he hurried me off in his inconsiderate way.'

At last, however, the head disappeared, and Tom rushed in-doors.

'So, Tom, you have made shorter work of twenty-five patients than I of one.'

'I'll go again,' said poor Tom, in the desperation of resolute meekness; 'only let me see how she is.'

'Let Ethel go up now. She is very cheery except for a little head-ache.'

While Ethel obeyed, Dr May began a minute interrogation of his son, so lengthened that Tom could hardly restrain sharp impatient replies to such apparent trifling with his agony to learn how long his father thought he could keep his treasure, and how much suffering might be spared to her.

At last Dr May said, 'I may be wrong. Your science is fresher than mine; but to me there seem indications that the organic disease is in the way of being arrested. Good health of course she cannot have; but if she weathers another winter, I think you may look for as many years of happiness with her as in an ordinary case.'

It was the first accent of hope since the hysteric scream that had been his greeting, and all his reserve and dread of emotion could not prevent his covering his face with his hands, and sobbing aloud. 'Father, father,' he said, 'you cannot tell what this is to me!'

'I can in part, my boy,' said the doctor, sadly.

'And,' he started up and walked about the room, 'you shall have the whole treatment. I will only follow your measures. No one at New York saw the slightest hope of checking it.'

'They had your account, and you hardly allowed enough for the hysterical affection. I do not say it it certainly – far less health.'

'Any way, any way, If I may only have her to lie and look at me, it is happiness unlooked for! You don't think I could have treated her otherwise?'

'No. Under His blessing you saved her yourself. You would have preceived the change is she had been an indifferent person.'

Tom made another turn to the door, and came back still half wild, and laid his face on his arms upon the table. 'You tell her,' he said, 'I shall never be able–'

Knocking at Averil's door, Dr May was answered by a call of 'Tom.'

'Not this time, my dear. He is coming, but we have been talking you over. Ave, you have a very young doctor, and rather too much interested.'

'Indeed!' she said, indignantly; 'he has made me much better.'

'Exactly so, my dear; so much better that he agrees with me that he expressed a strong opinion prematurely.'

'They thought the same at New York,' she said, still resolved on his defence.

'My dear, unless you are bent on growing worse in order to justify his first opinion, I think you will prove that which he now holds. And, Ave, it was, under Providence, skill that we may be proud of by which he has subdued the really fatal disorder. You may have much to undergo, and must submit to a sofa life and much nursing; but I think you will not leave him so soon.'

There was a long pause; at last she said, 'Oh Dr May, I beg your pardon. If I had known, I would never——'

'Never what, my dear?'

'Never have consented! It is such a grievous thing for a professional man to have a sick wife.'

'It is exactly what he wanted, my dear, if you will not fly at me for saying so. Nothing else could teach him that patients are not cases but persons; and here he comes to tell you what he thinks of the trouble of a sick wife.'

'Well,' said Dr May, as he and Ethel walked away together, 'poor young things, they have a chequered time before them. Pretty well for the doctor who hated sick people, Wards, and Stoneborough; but, after all, I have liked none of our weddings better. I like people to rub one another brighter.'

'And I am proud when the least unselfish nature has from first to last done the most unselfish things. No one of us has ever given up so much as Tom, and I am sure he will be happy in it.'

More can hardly be said without straying into the realms of prediction; yet such of our readers as are bent on carrying on their knowledge of the Daisies beyond the last sentence, may be told that, to the best of our belief, Leonard's shoemaking is not his foremost office in the mission, where he finds that fulness of hopeful gladness which experience shows is literally often vouchsafed to those who have given up home, land, and friends, for the Gospel's sake. His letters are the delight of more than one at Stoneborough; and his sister, upon her sofa, is that home member of a mission without whom nothing can be done – the copier of letters, the depôt of gifts, the purveyor of commissions, the maker of clothes, the collector of books, the keeper of accounts – so that the house still merits the name of the S.P.G. office, as it used to be called in the Spenserian era. But Mrs Thomas May is a good deal more than this. Her sofa is almost a renewal of the family centre that once Margaret's was; the region where all tidings are brought fresh for discussion, all joys and sorrows poured out, the external influence that above all has tended to soften Gertrude into the bright grace of womanhood. Mary Cheviot and Blanche Ernescliffe cannot be cured of a pitying 'poor Tom' – as they speak of 'the Professor' – in which title the awkward sound of Dr Tom has been merged since an appointment subsequent to the appearance of the Diseases of Climate. But every one else holds that not his honours as a scientific physician, his discoveries, and ably-written papers – not even his father's full and loving confidence and gratitude, give Professor May as much happiness as that bright-eyed delicate wife, with whom all his thoughts seem to begin and end.